Himawari House

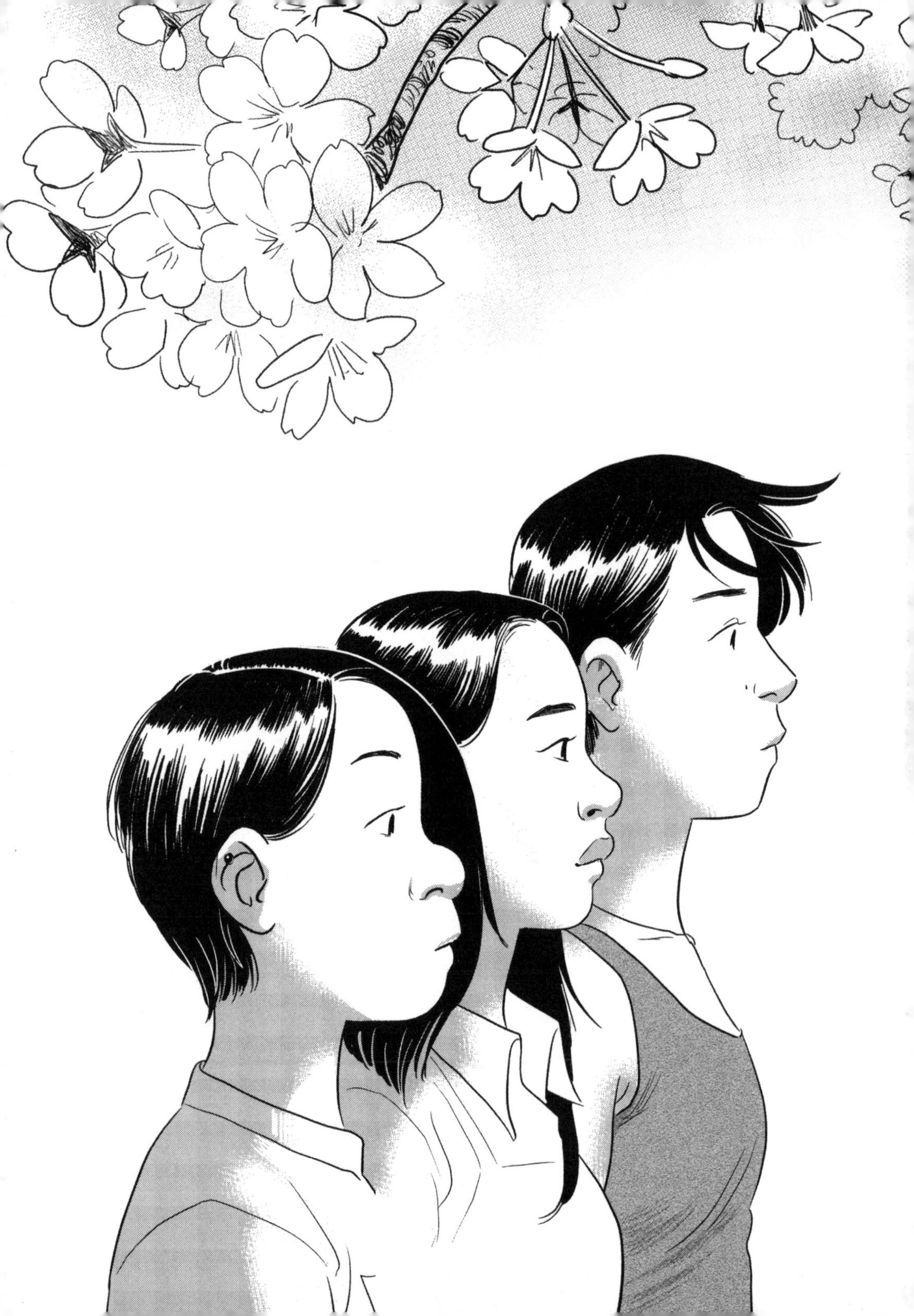

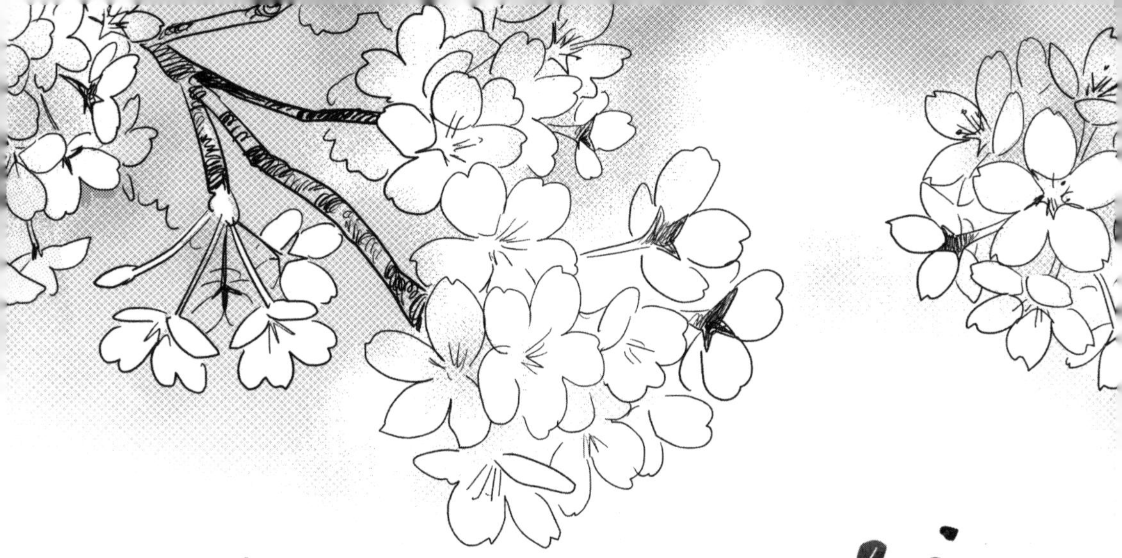

Himawari House

Harmony Becker

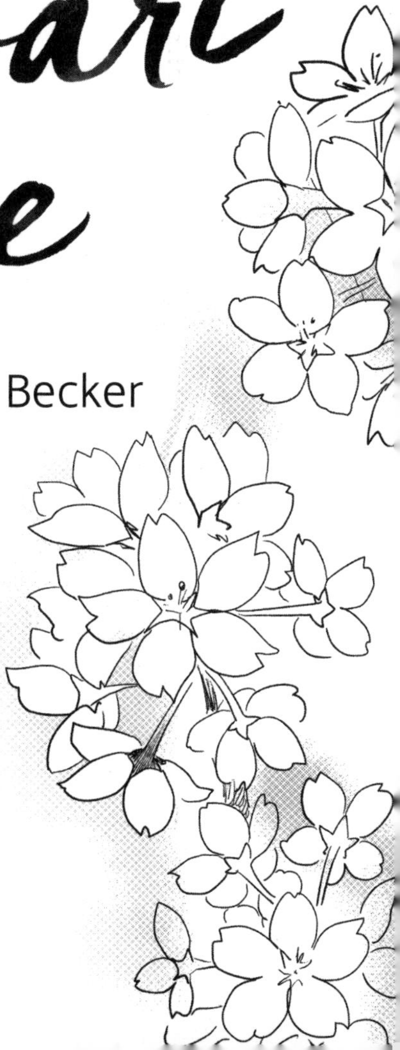

First Second

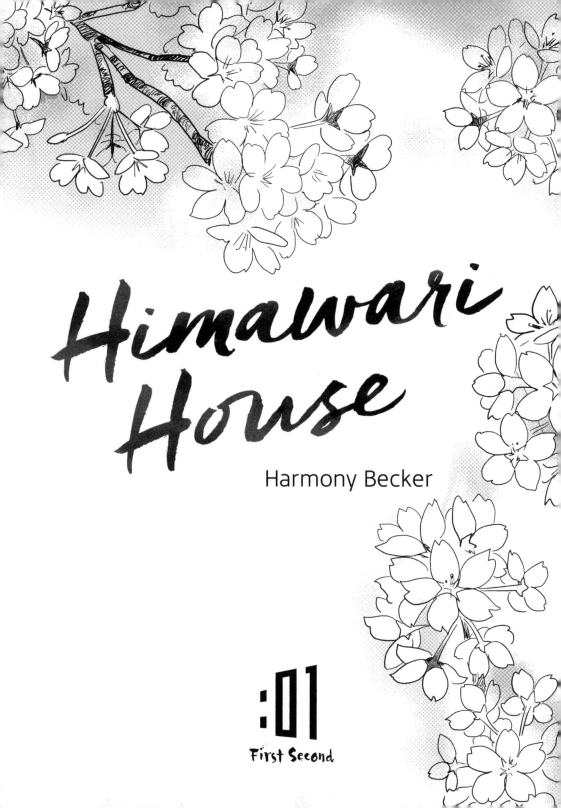

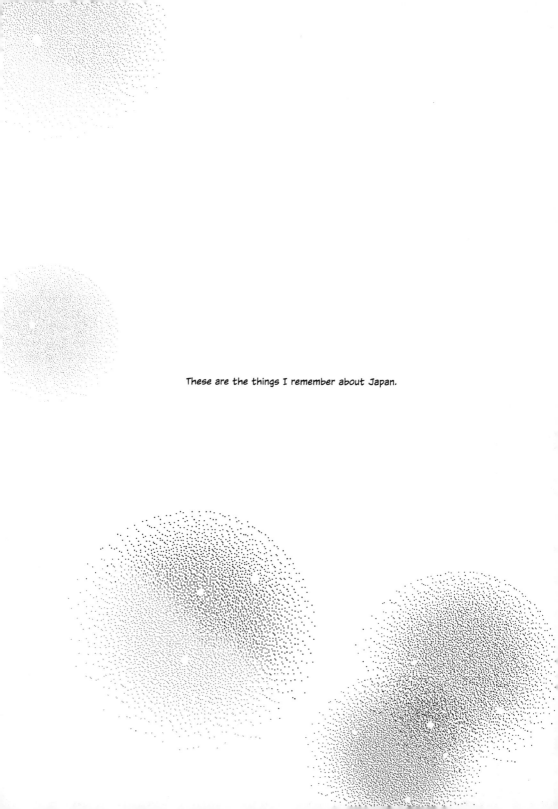

These are the things I remember about Japan.

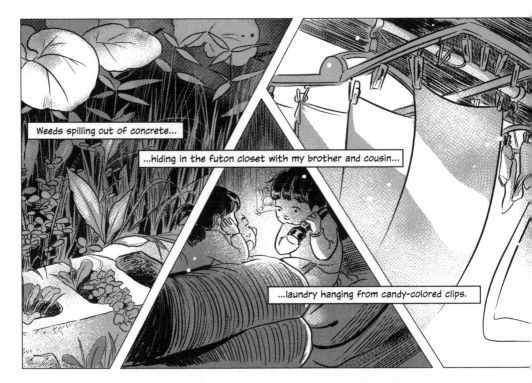

Weeds spilling out of concrete...

...hiding in the futon closet with my brother and cousin...

...laundry hanging from candy-colored clips.

My treasure box, and the scent it contained.

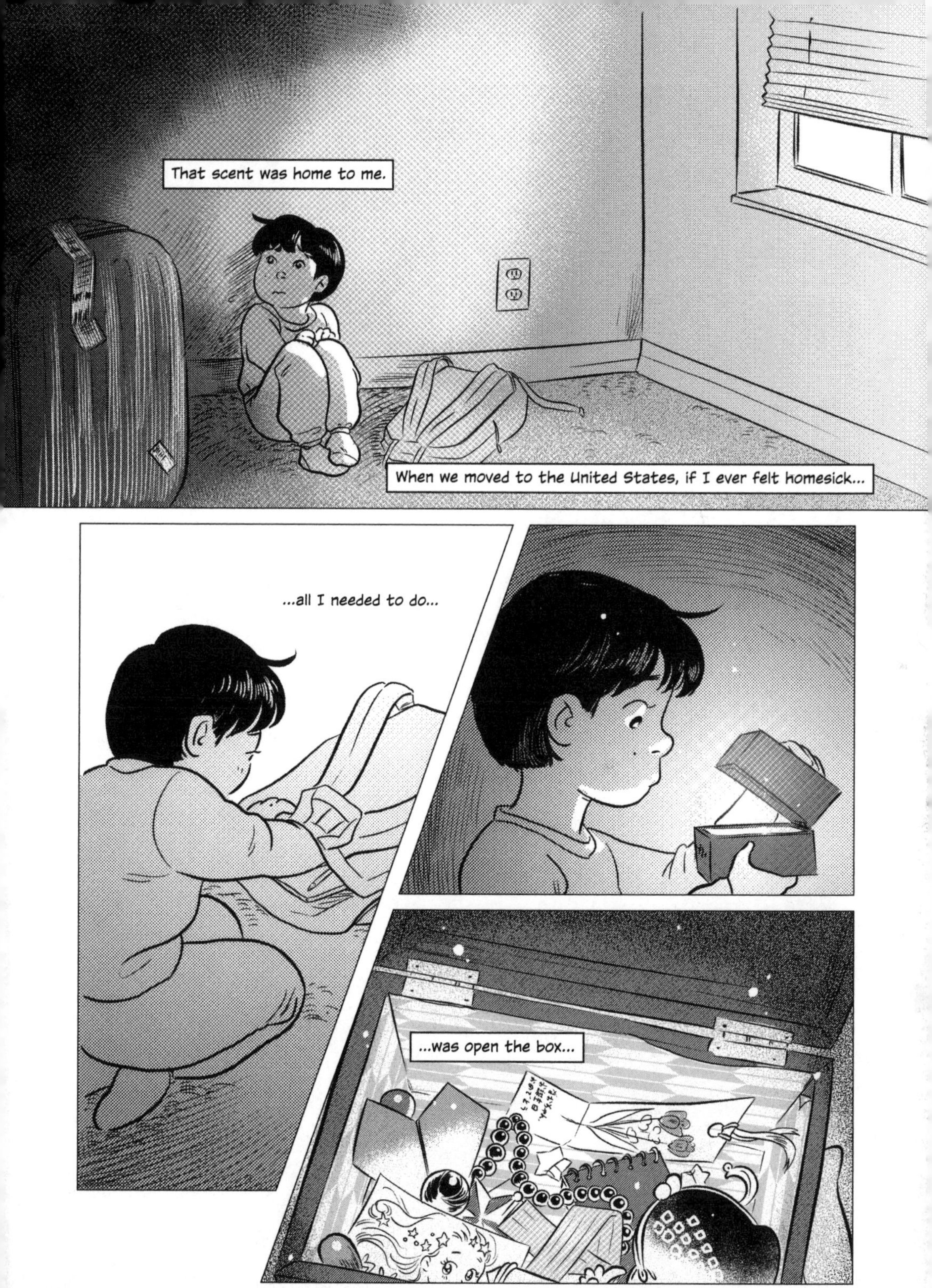
That scent was home to me.
When we moved to the United States, if I ever felt homesick...
...all I needed to do...
...was open the box...

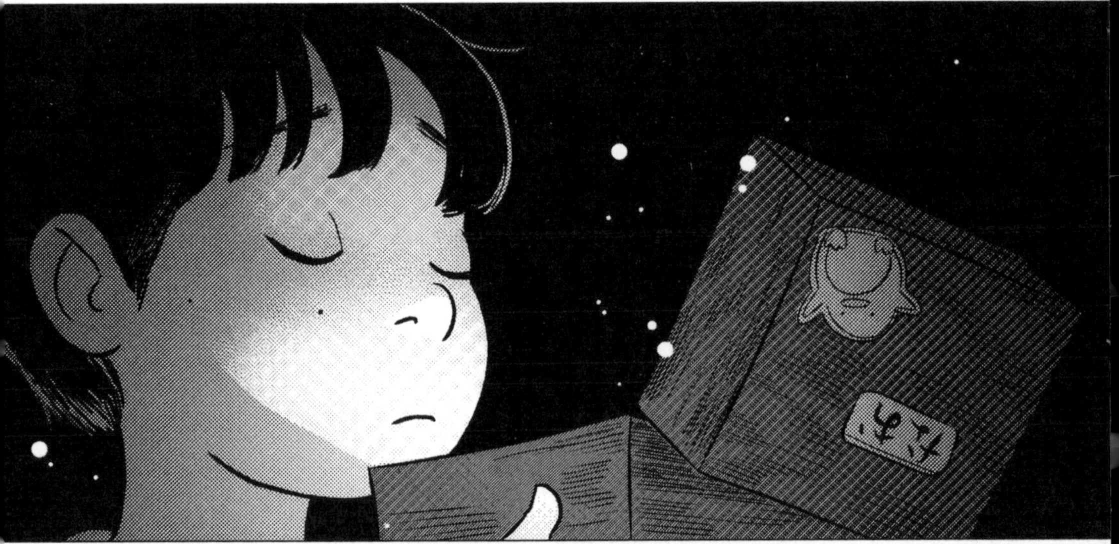

...and breathe in deep.

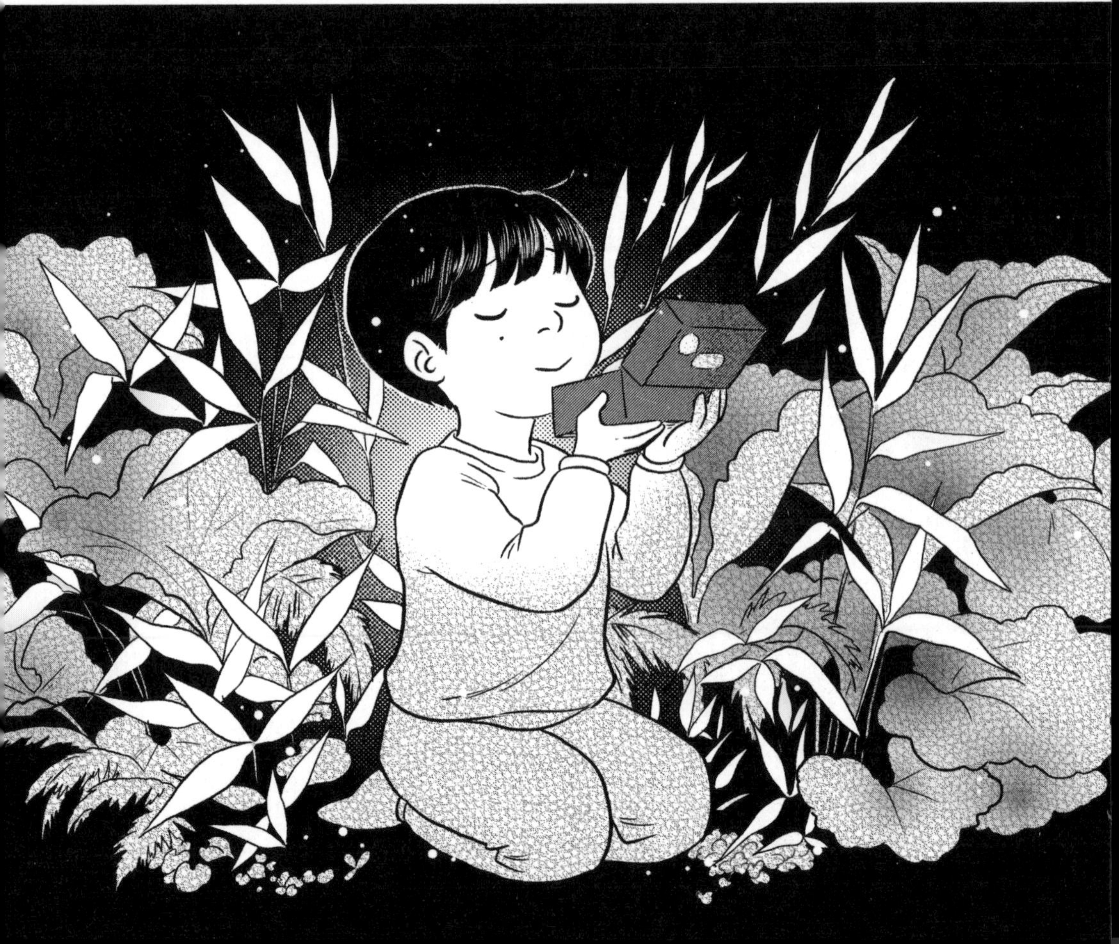

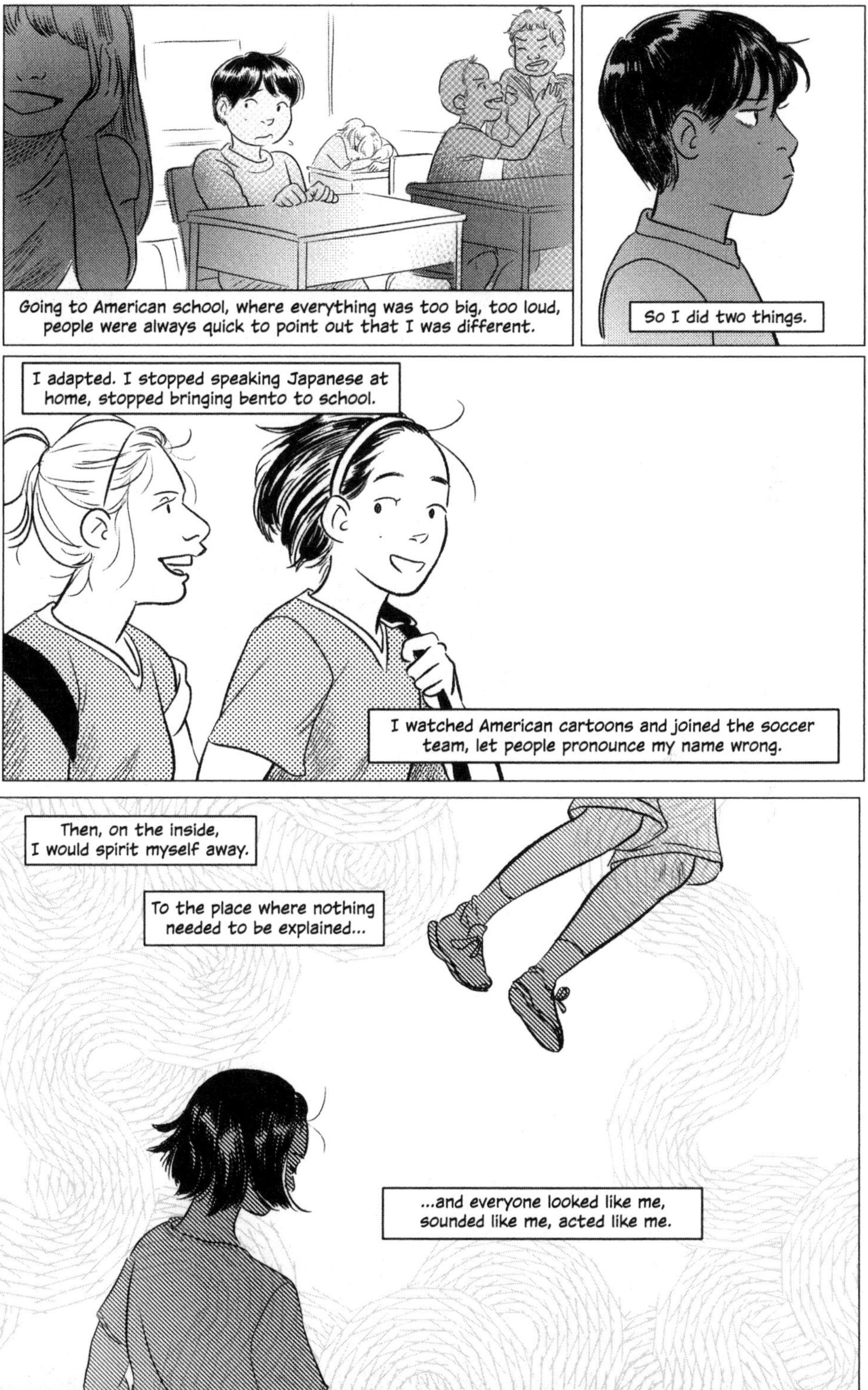
Going to American school, where everything was too big, too loud, people were always quick to point out that I was different.
So I did two things.
I adapted. I stopped speaking Japanese at home, stopped bringing bento to school.
I watched American cartoons and joined the soccer team, let people pronounce my name wrong.
Then, on the inside, I would spirit myself away.
To the place where nothing needed to be explained...
...and everyone looked like me, sounded like me, acted like me.

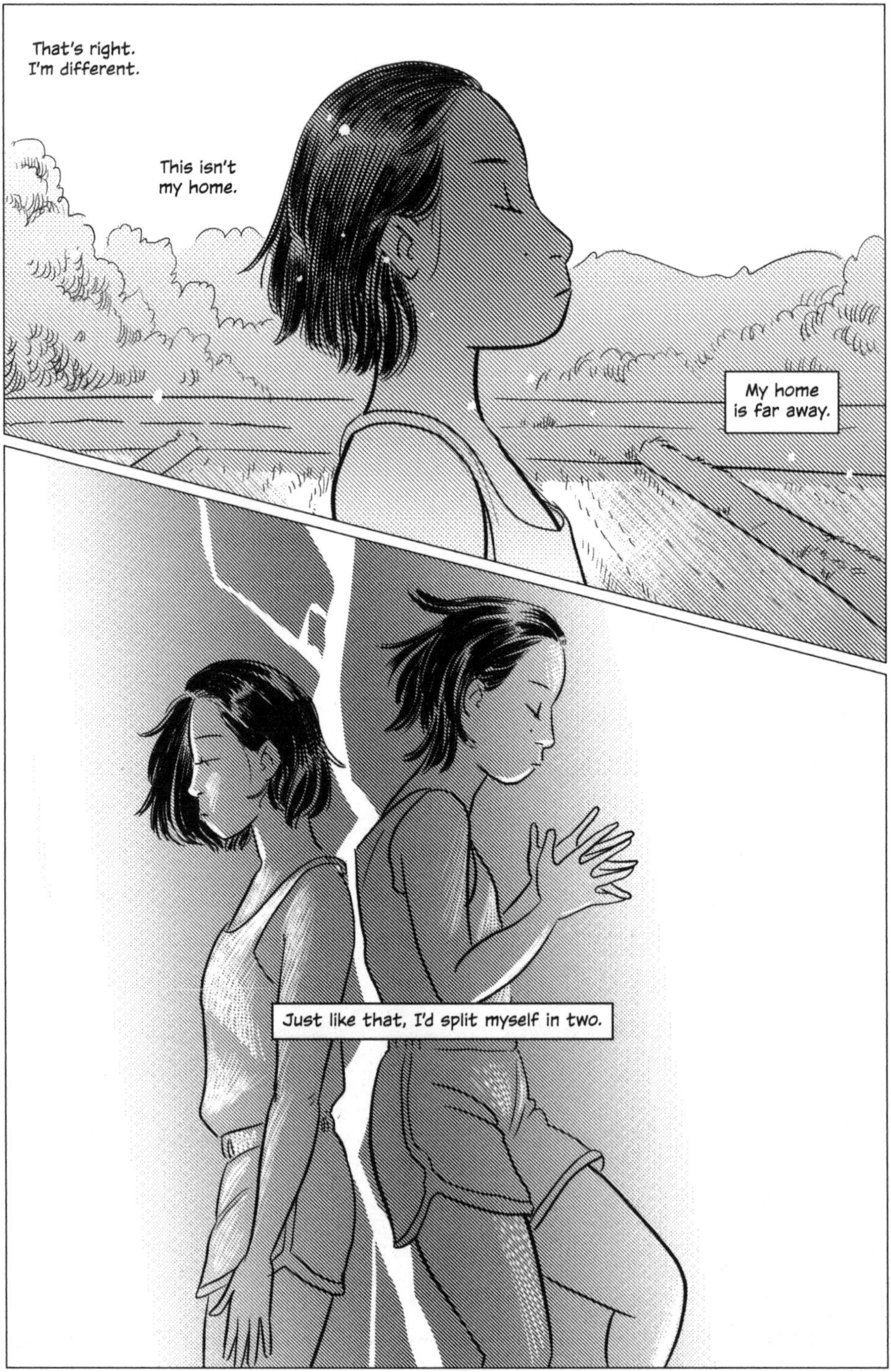
That's right.
I'm different.
This isn't
my home.
My home
is far away.
Just like that, I'd split myself in two.

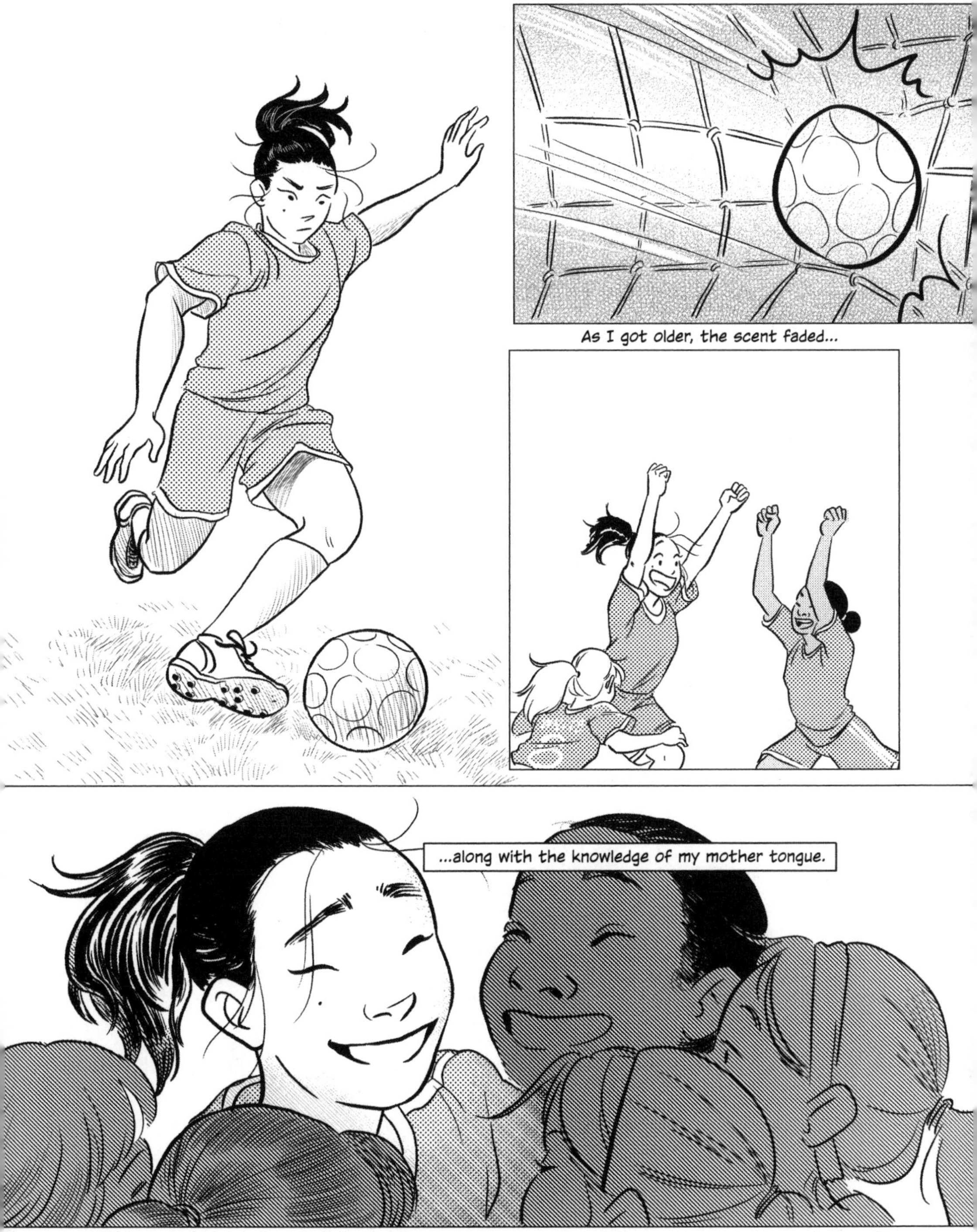
As I got older, the scent faded...
...along with the knowledge of my mother tongue.

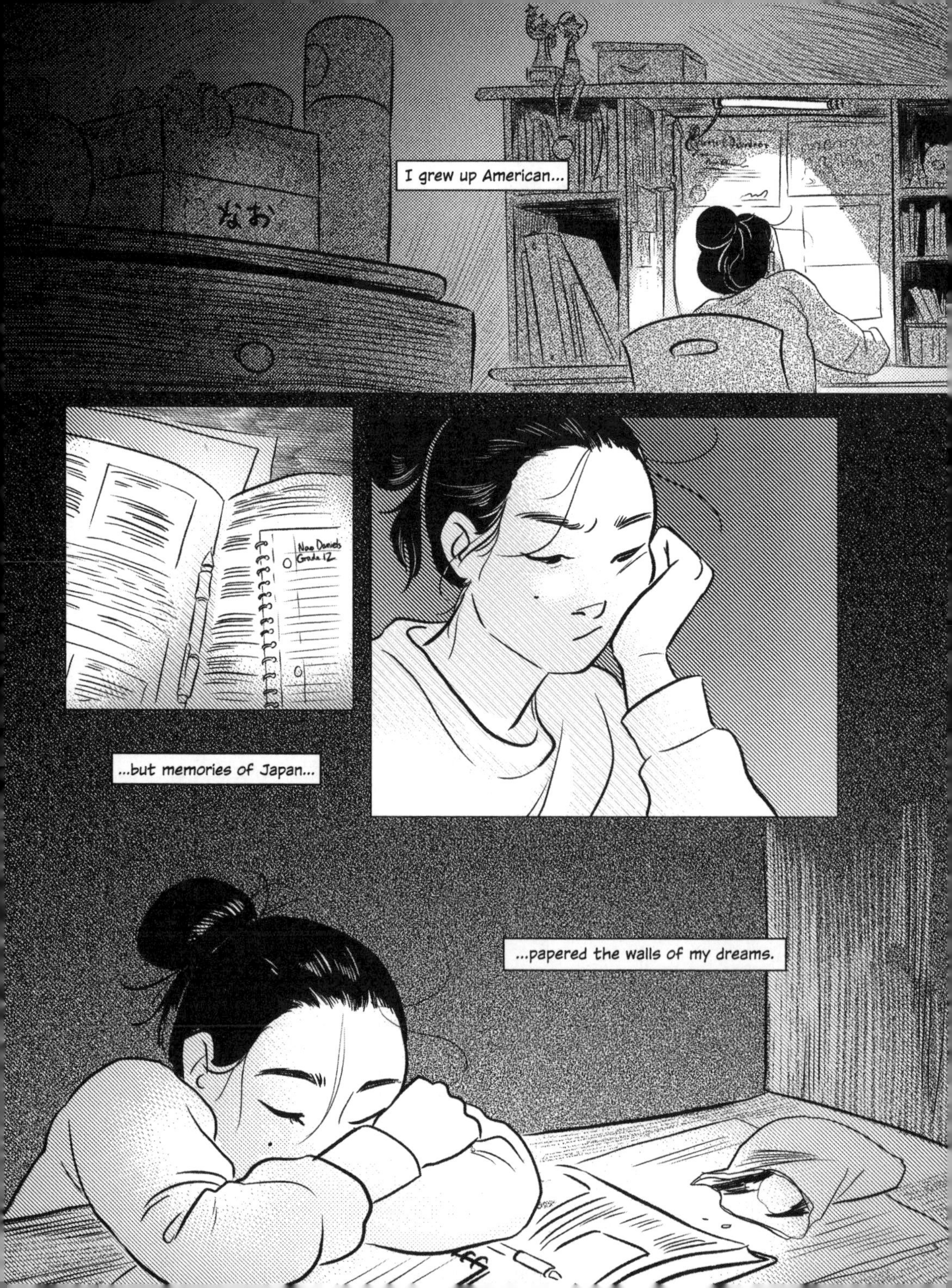
I grew up American...
なお
Nao Daniels
Grade 12
...but memories of Japan...
...papered the walls of my dreams.

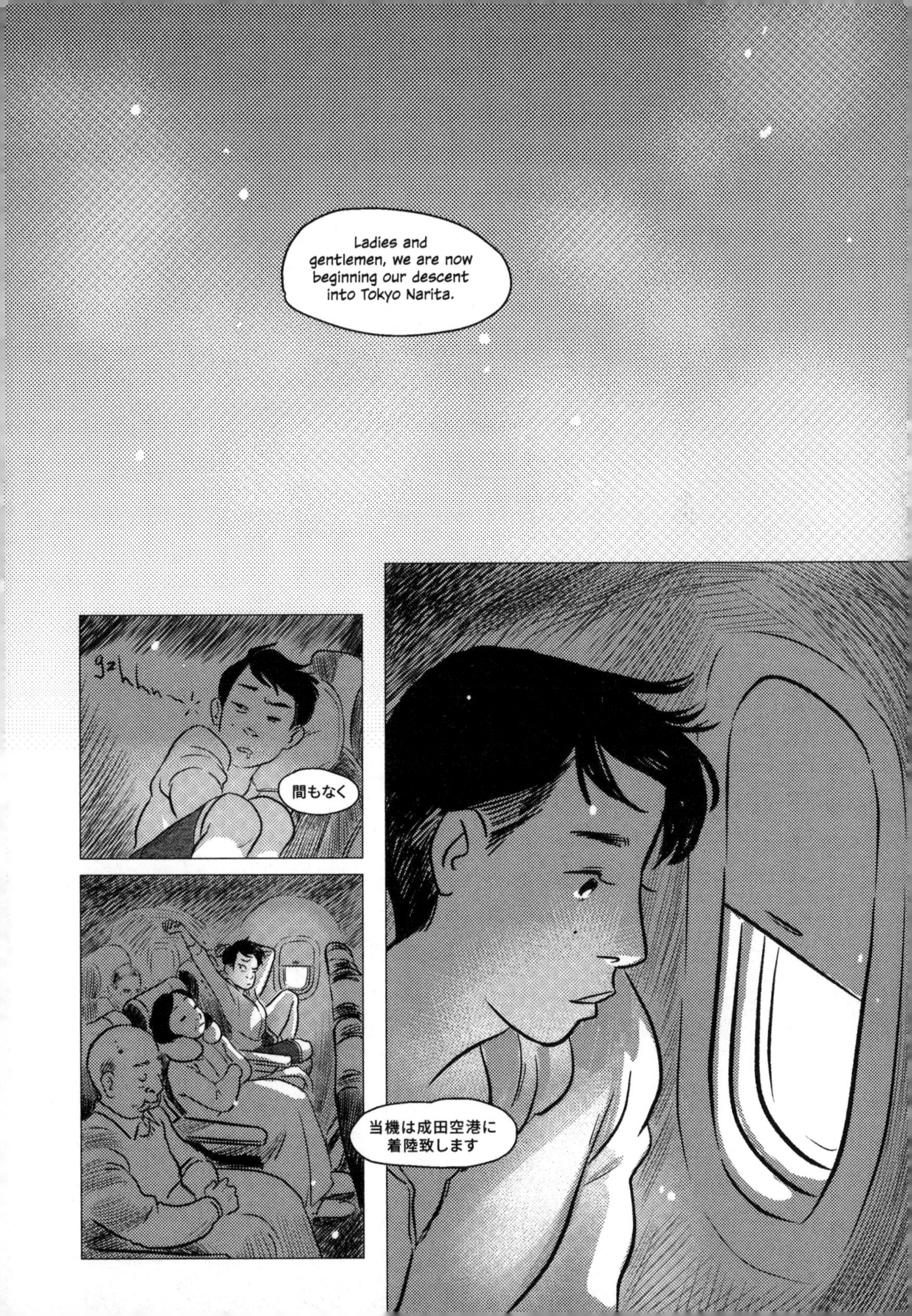
Ladies and gentlemen, we are now beginning our descent into Tokyo Narita.
間もなく
当機は成田空港に
着陸致します

Chapter 1

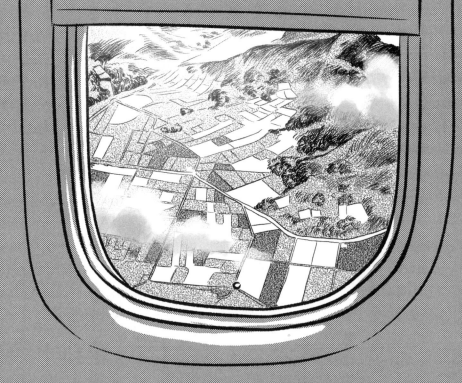

I don't know where Singapore is

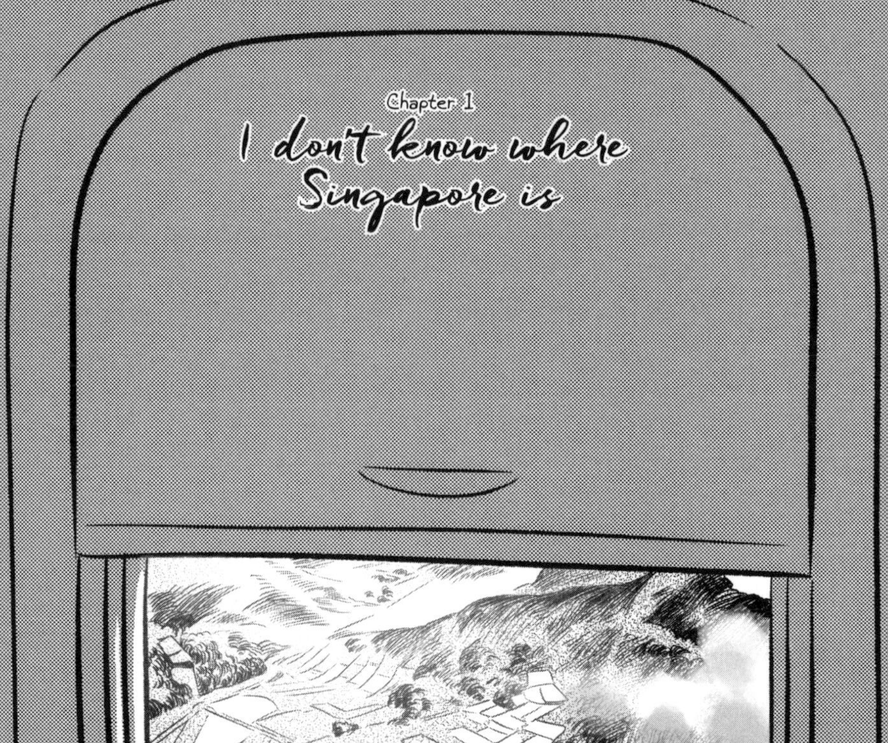

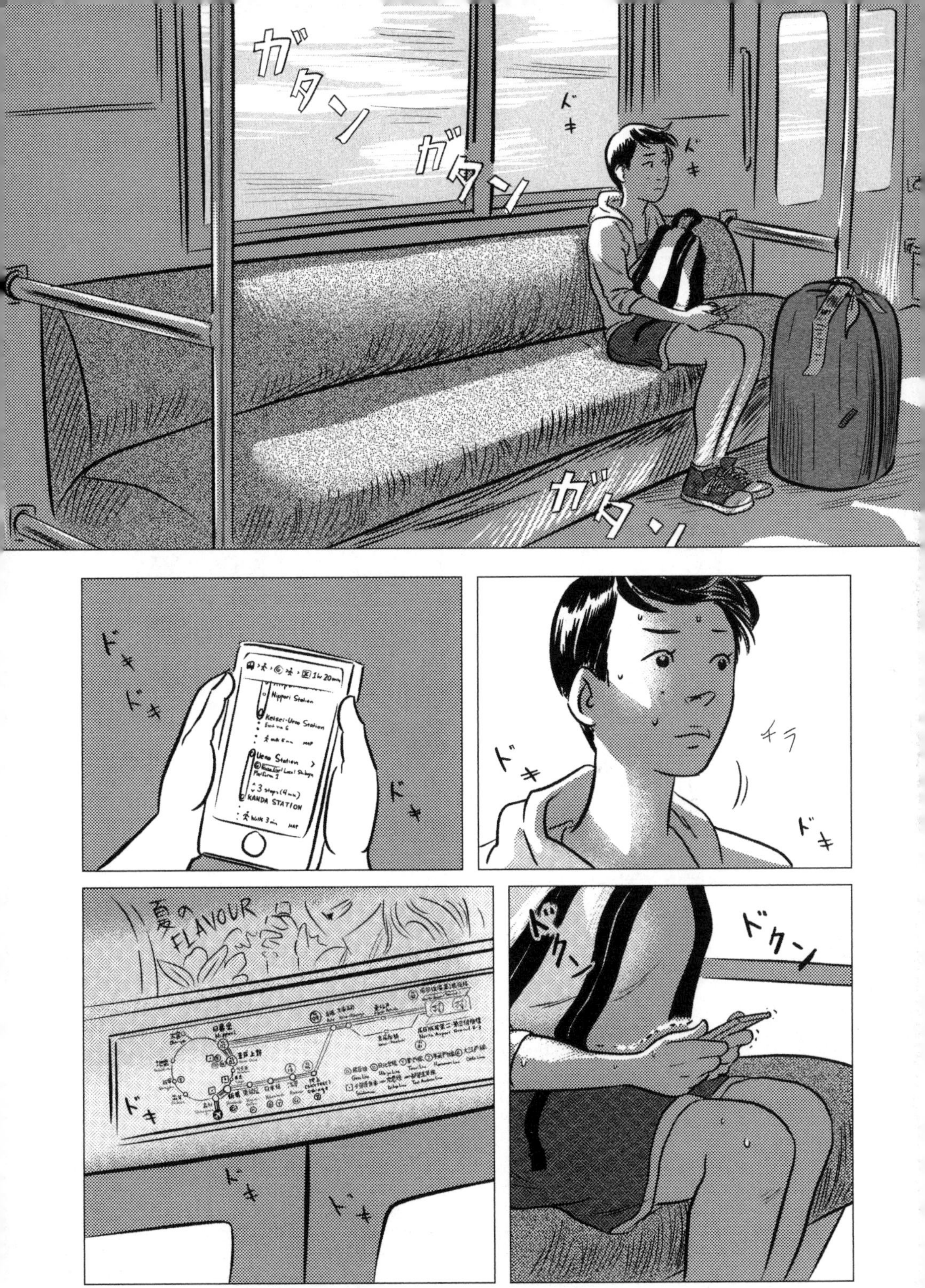
ガタン
ドキ
ガタン
ドキ
ガタン
ドキ
ドキ
Nippori Station
Keisei-Ueno Station
Ueno Station
KANDA STATION
ドキ
ドキ
チラ
ドキ
夏のFLAVOUR
ドキ
ドキ
ドキ
ドクン
ドクン

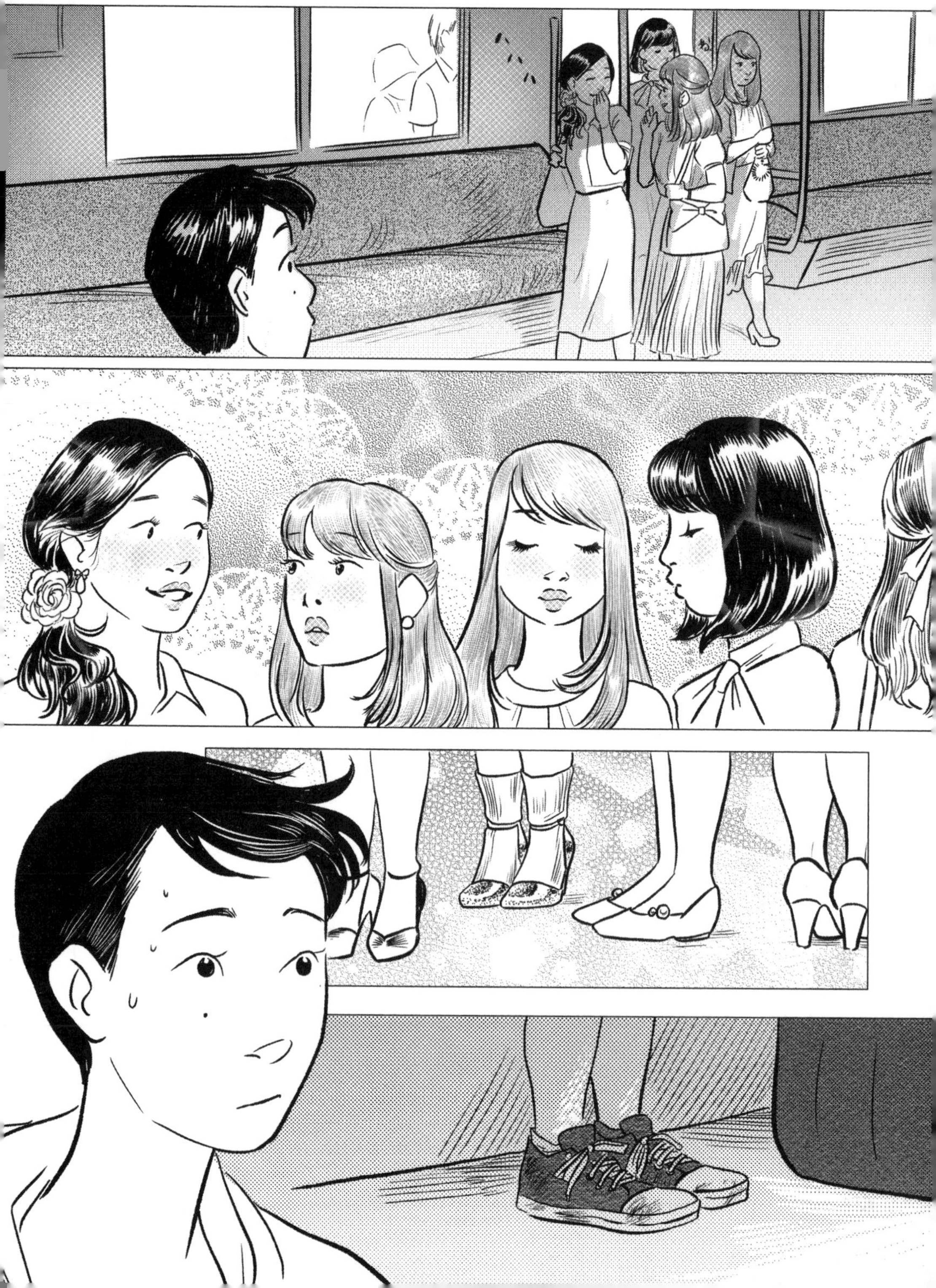

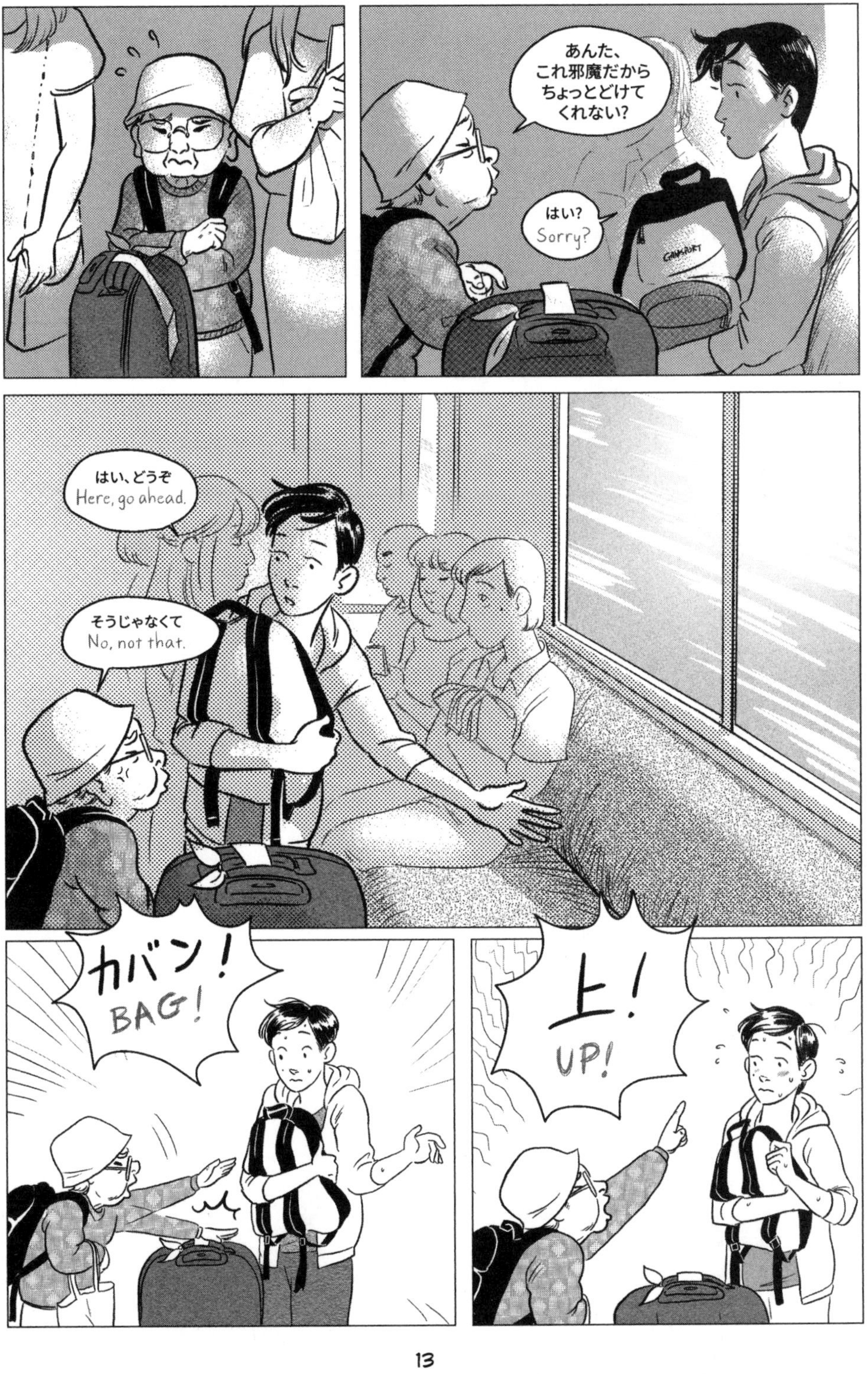
あんた、
これ邪魔だから
ちょっとどけて
くれない?
はい?
Sorry?
はい、どうぞ
Here, go ahead.
そうじゃなくて
No, not that.
カバン!
BAG!
上!
UP!

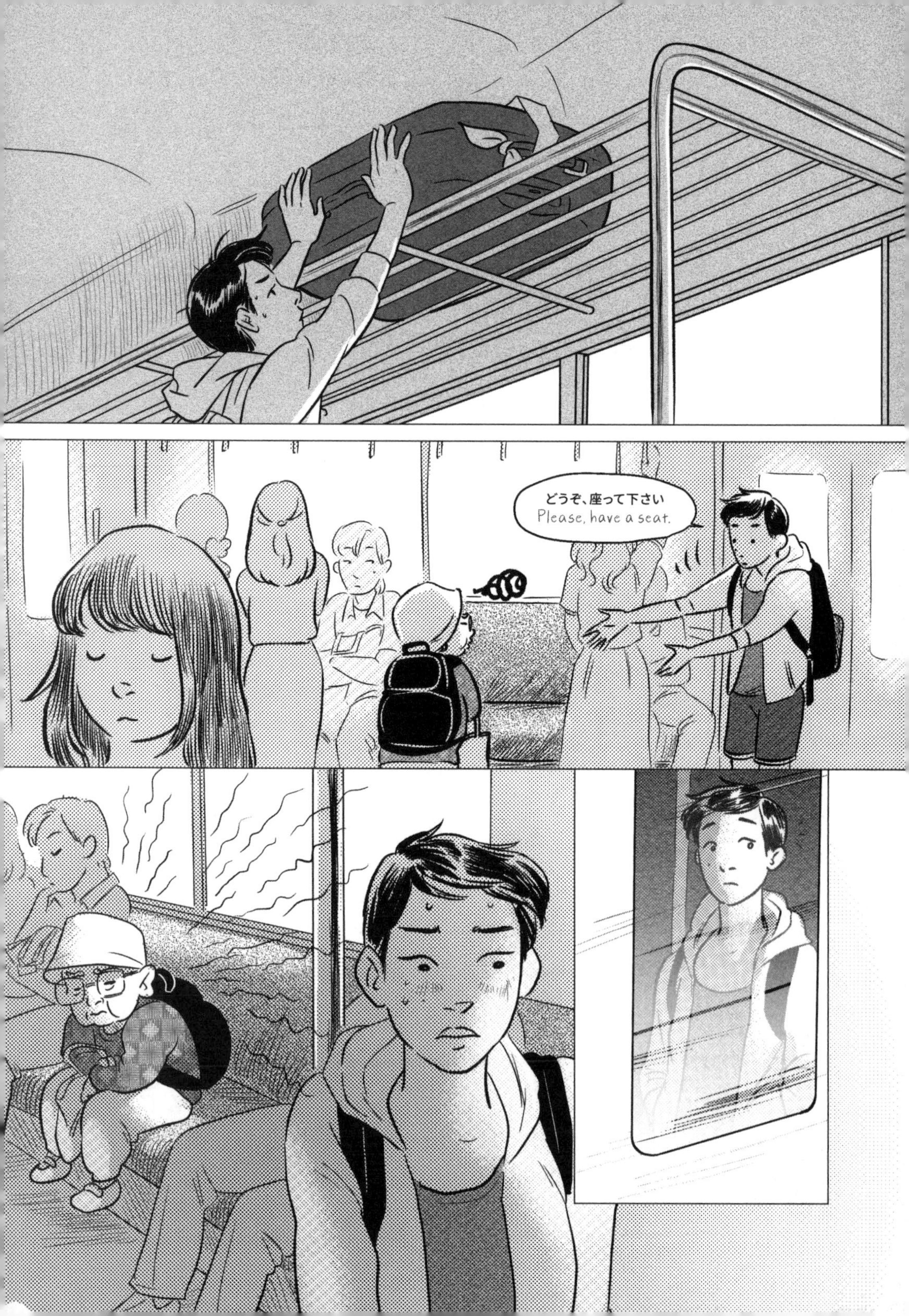
どうぞ、座って下さい
Please, have a seat.

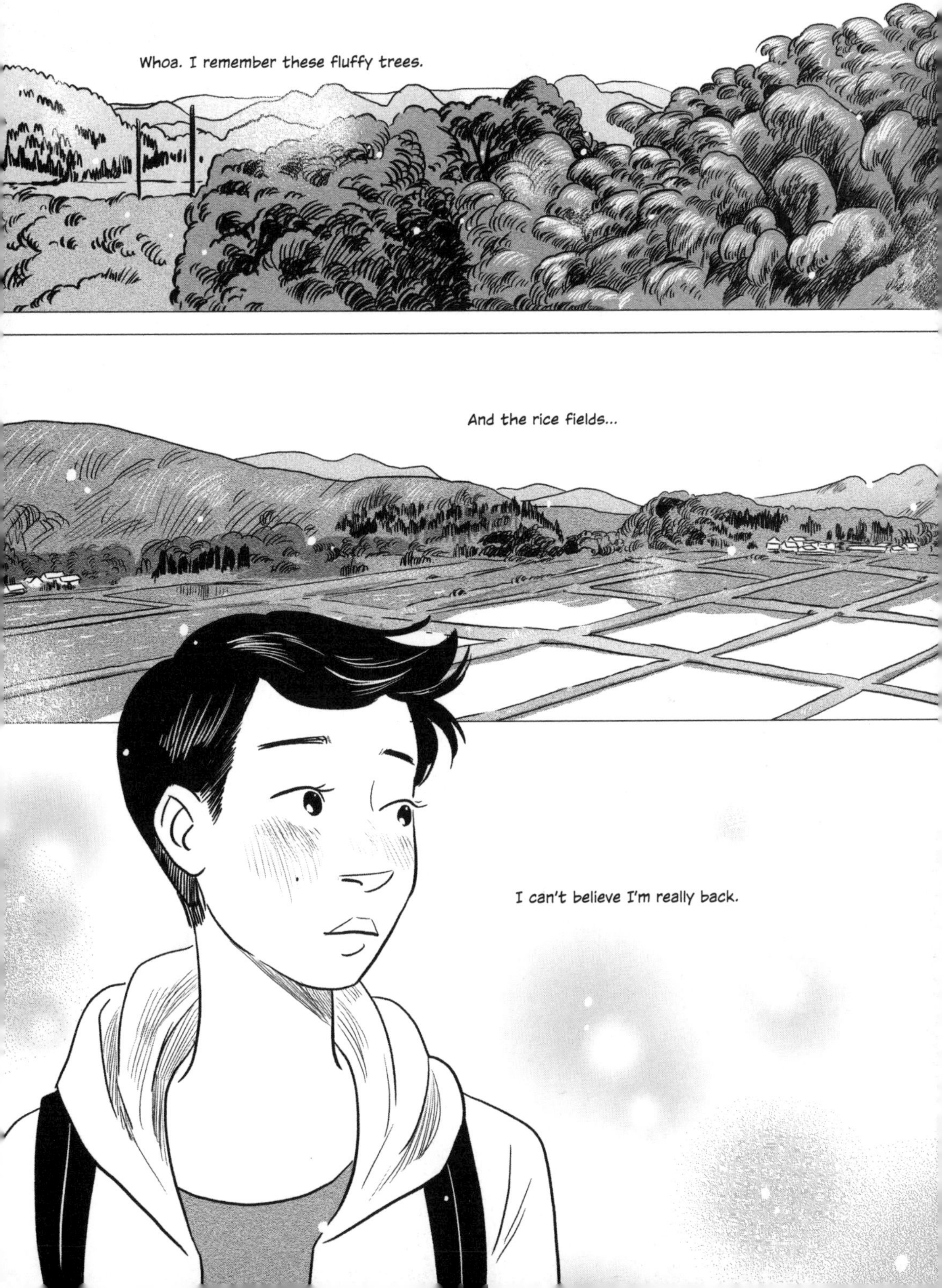
Whoa. I remember these fluffy trees.
And the rice fields...
I can't believe I'm really back.

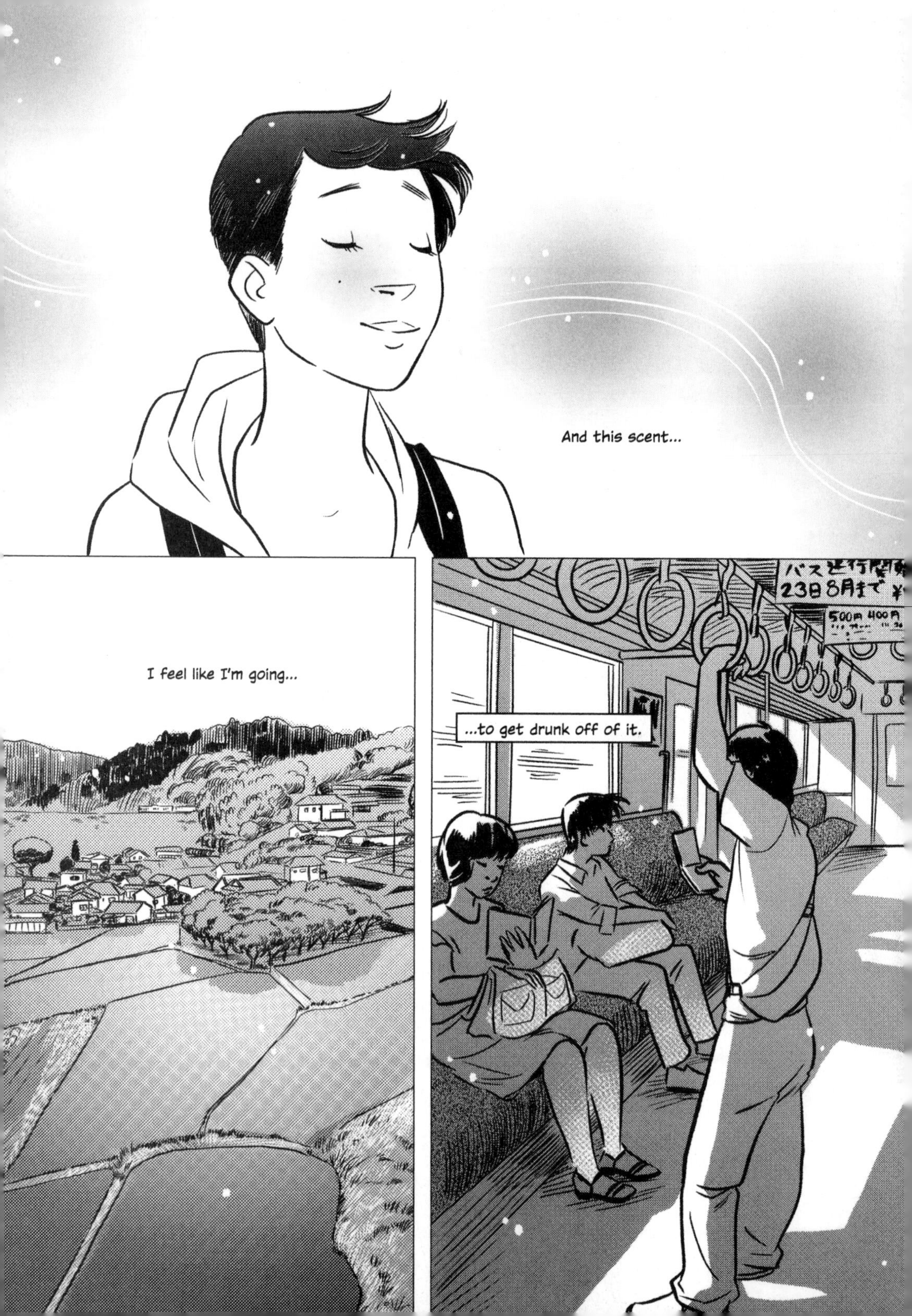
And this scent...
I feel like I'm going...
...to get drunk off of it.

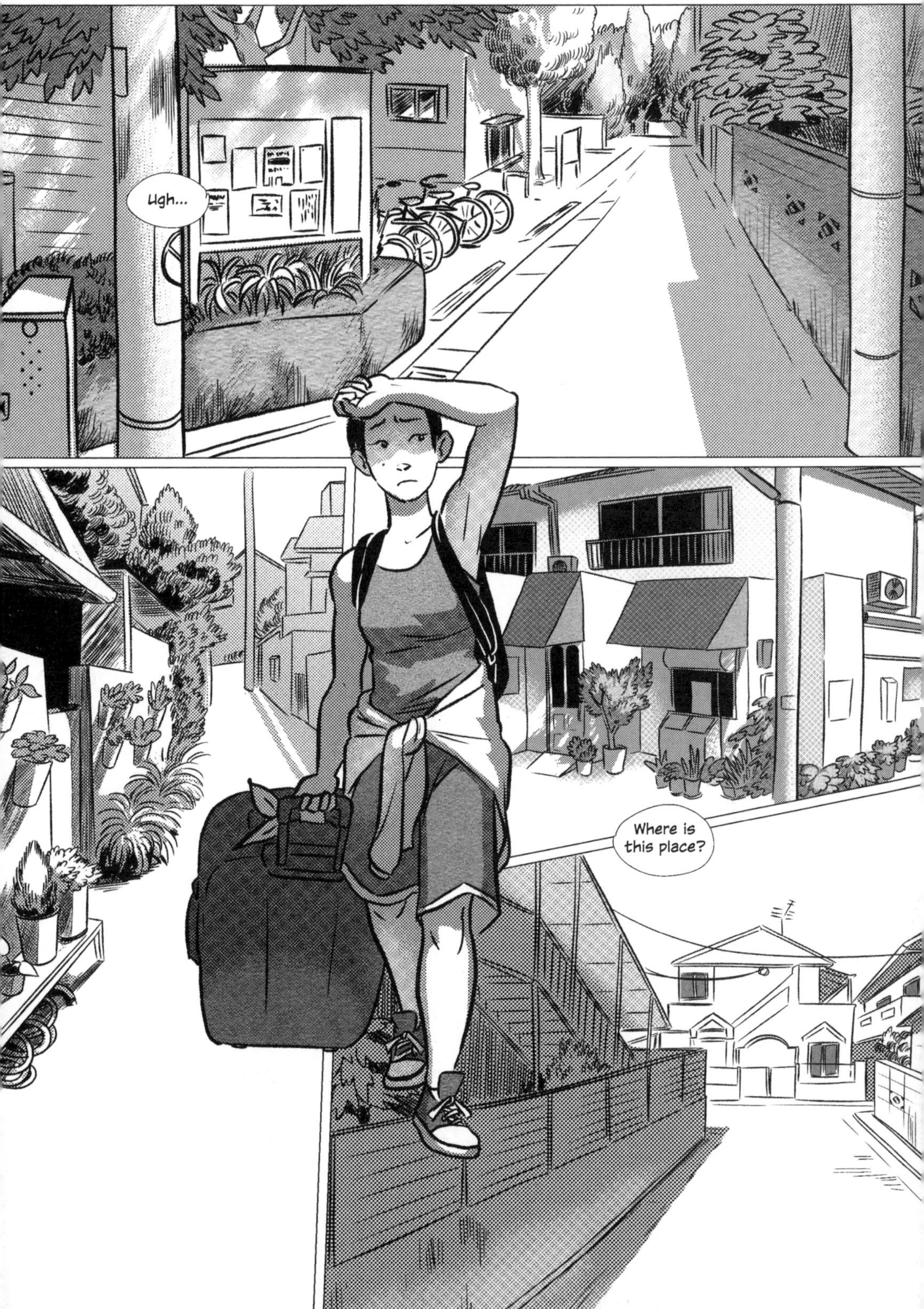
Ugh...
Where is this place?

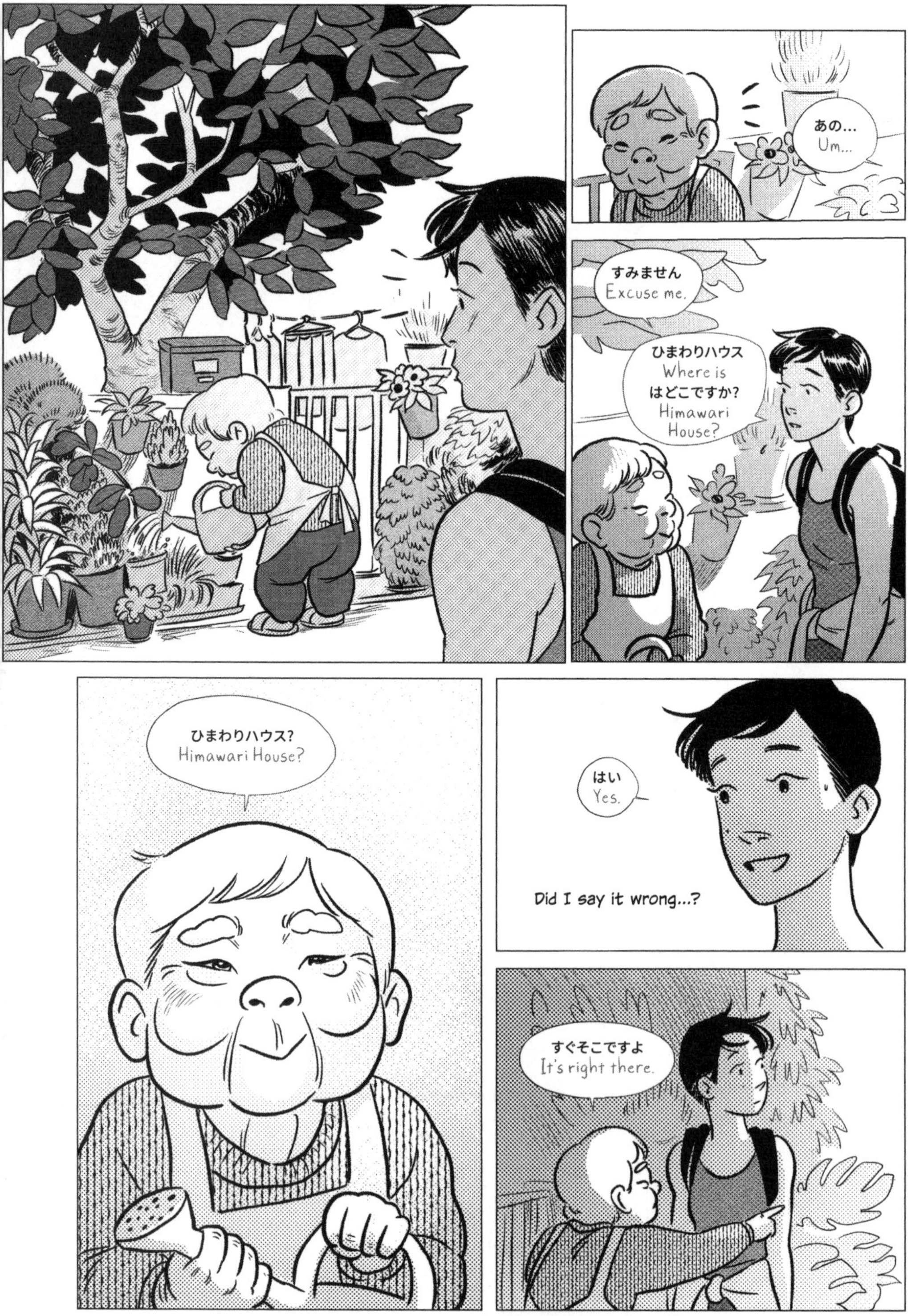
あの…
Um...
すみません
Excuse me.
ひまわりハウス
Where is
はどこですか?
Himawari House?
ひまわりハウス?
Himawari House?
はい
Yes.
Did I say it wrong...?
すぐそこですよ
It's right there.

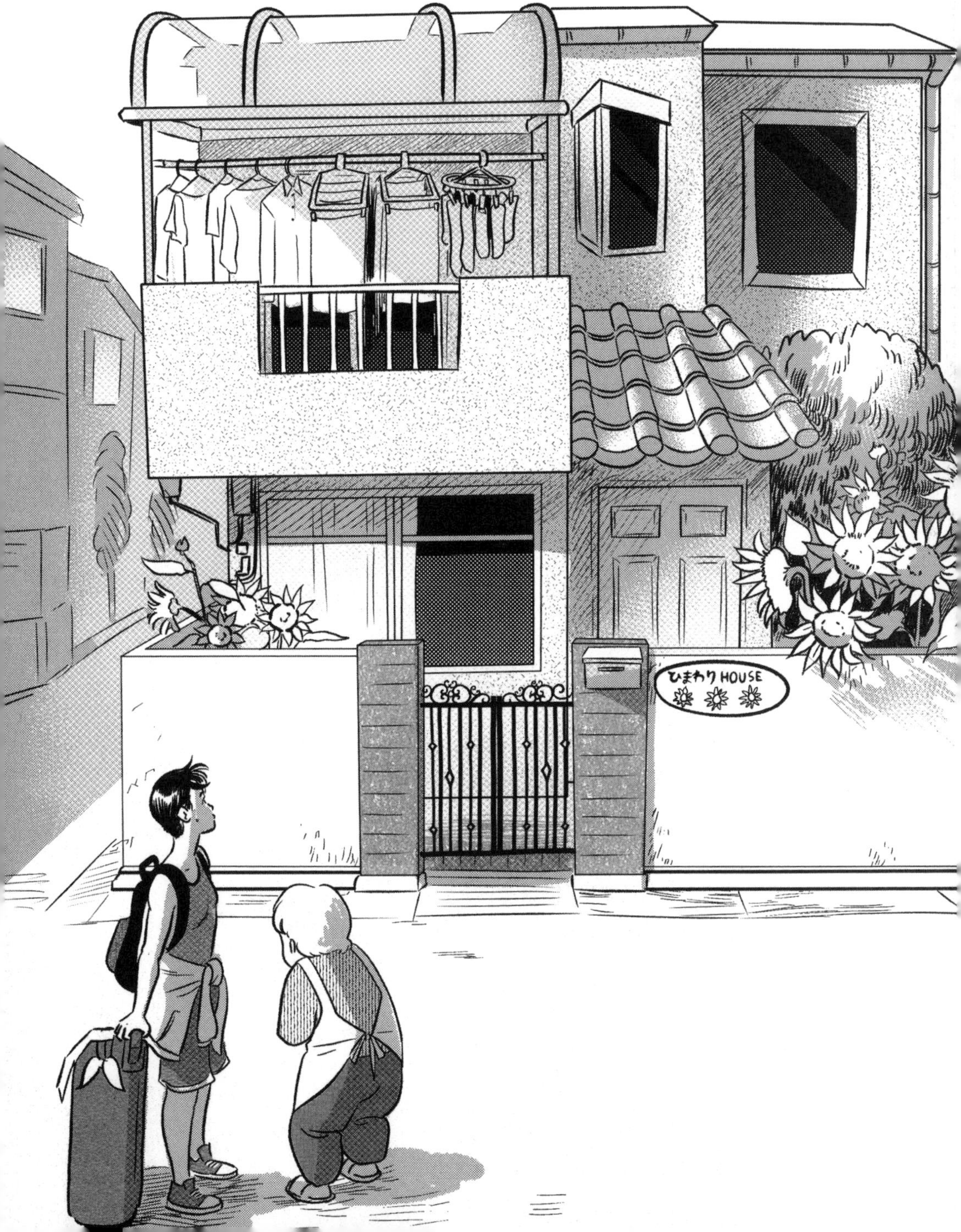
ひまわりHOUSE

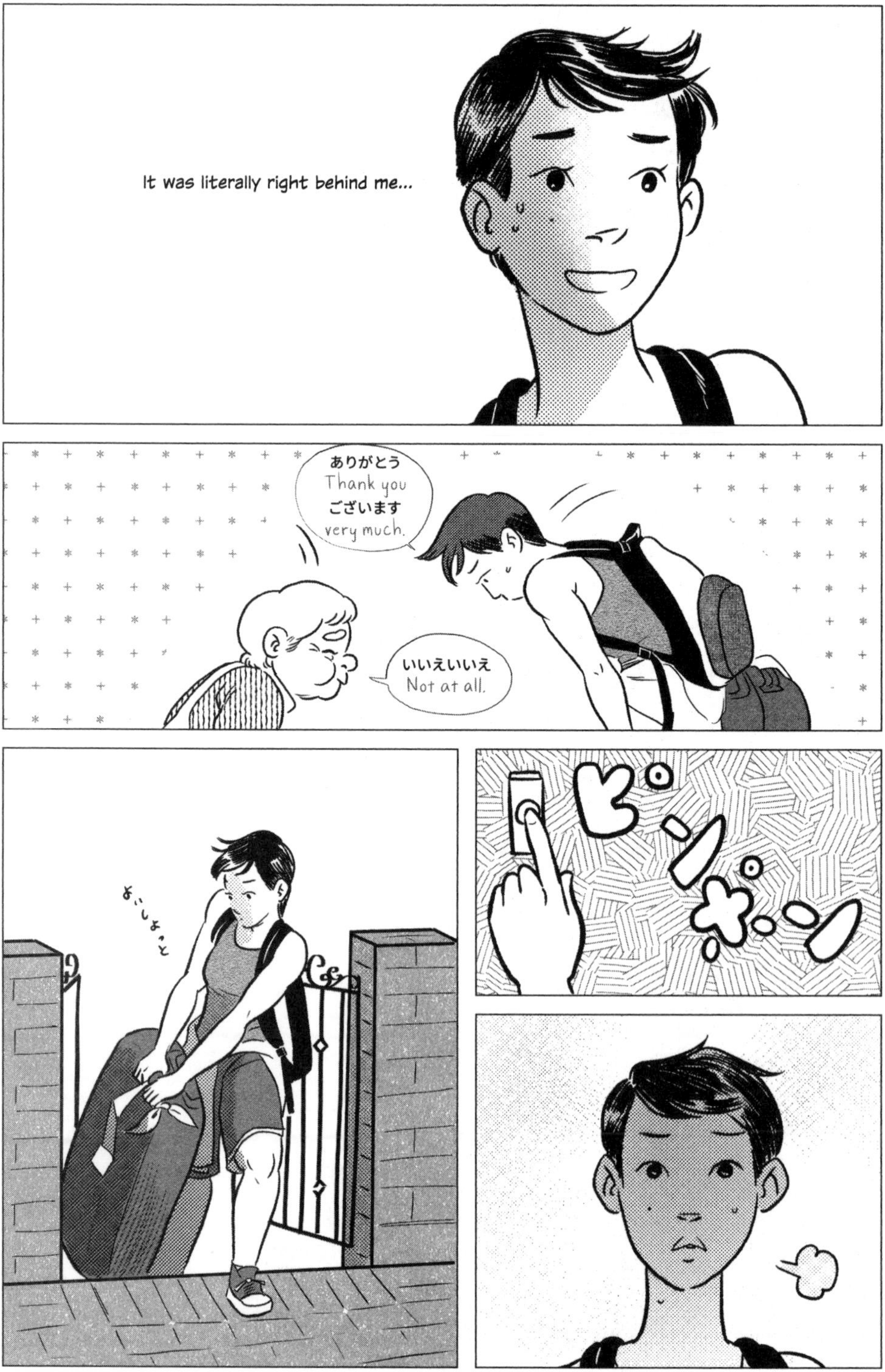
It was literally right behind me...
ありがとう
Thank you
ございます
very much.
いいえいいえ
Not at all.
よいしょっと
ピンポーン

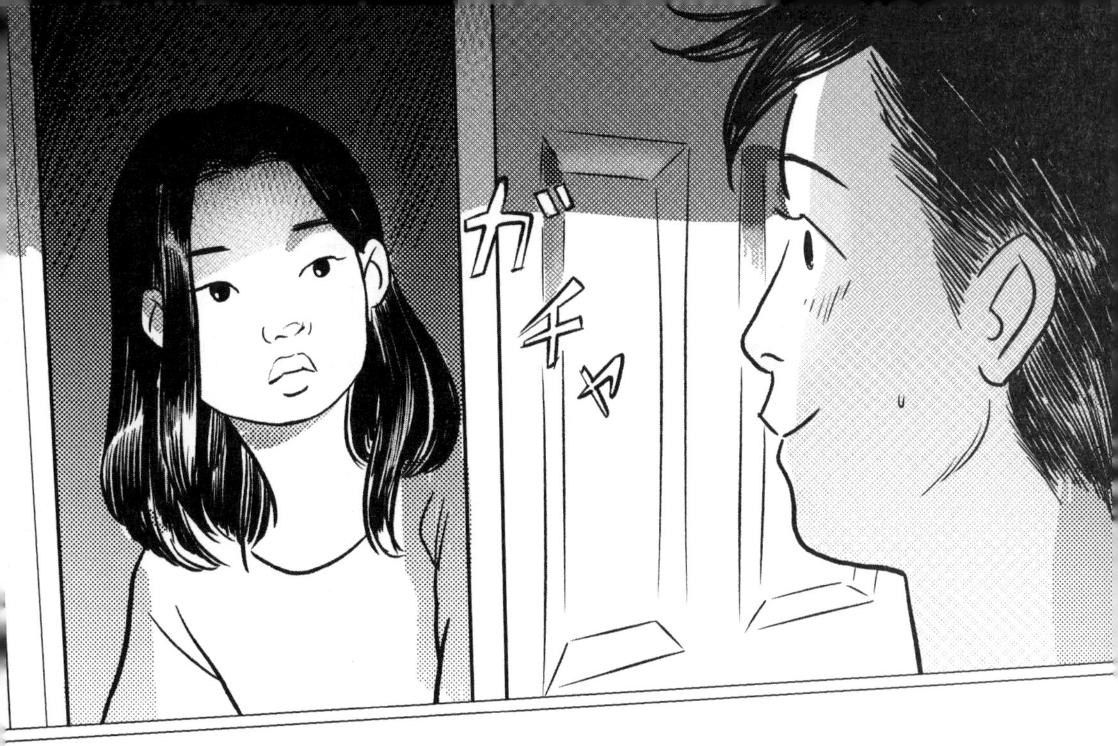
ガチャ

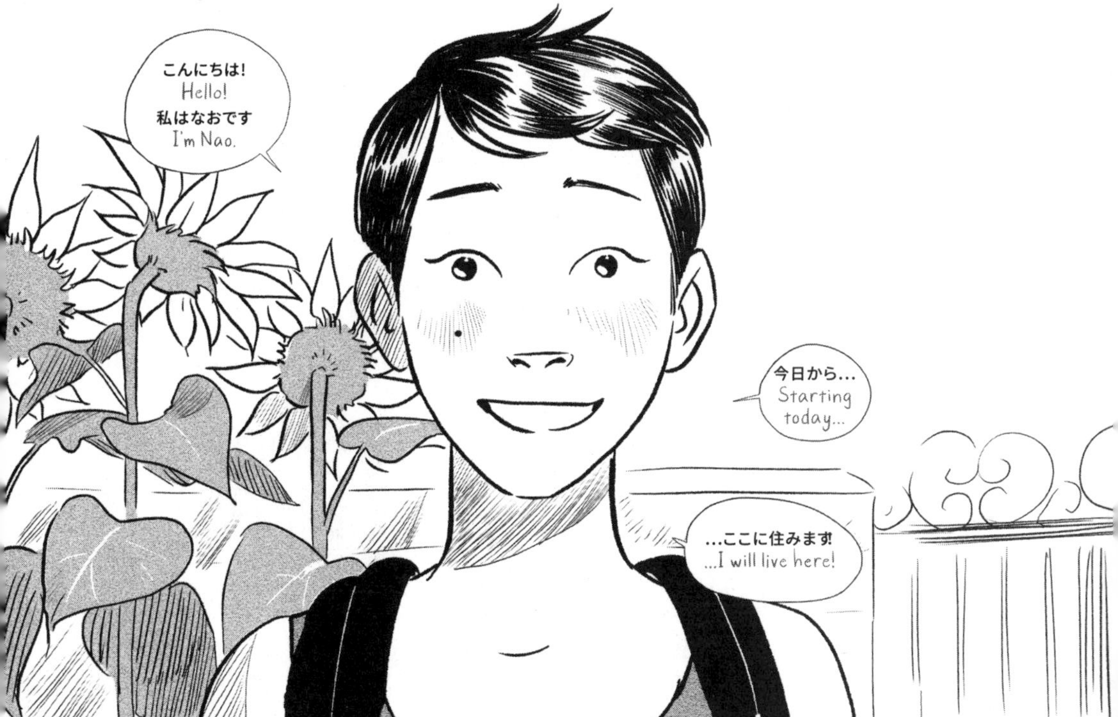
こんにちは! Hello! 私はなおです I'm Nao.
今日から... Starting today...
...ここに住みます! ...I will live here!

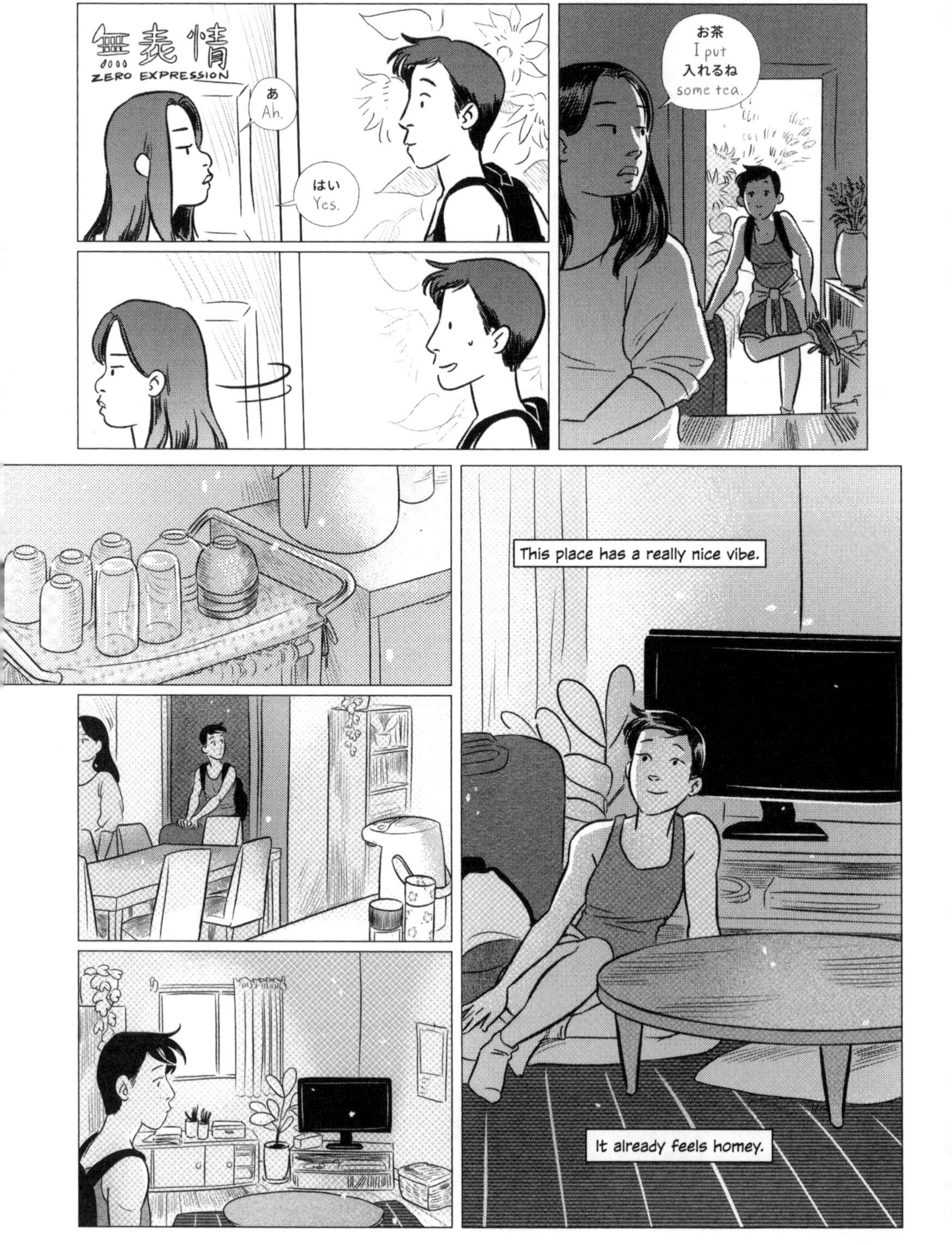
無表情
ZERO EXPRESSION
あ
Ah.
はい
Yes.
お茶
I put
入れるね
some tea.
This place has a really nice vibe.
It already feels homey.

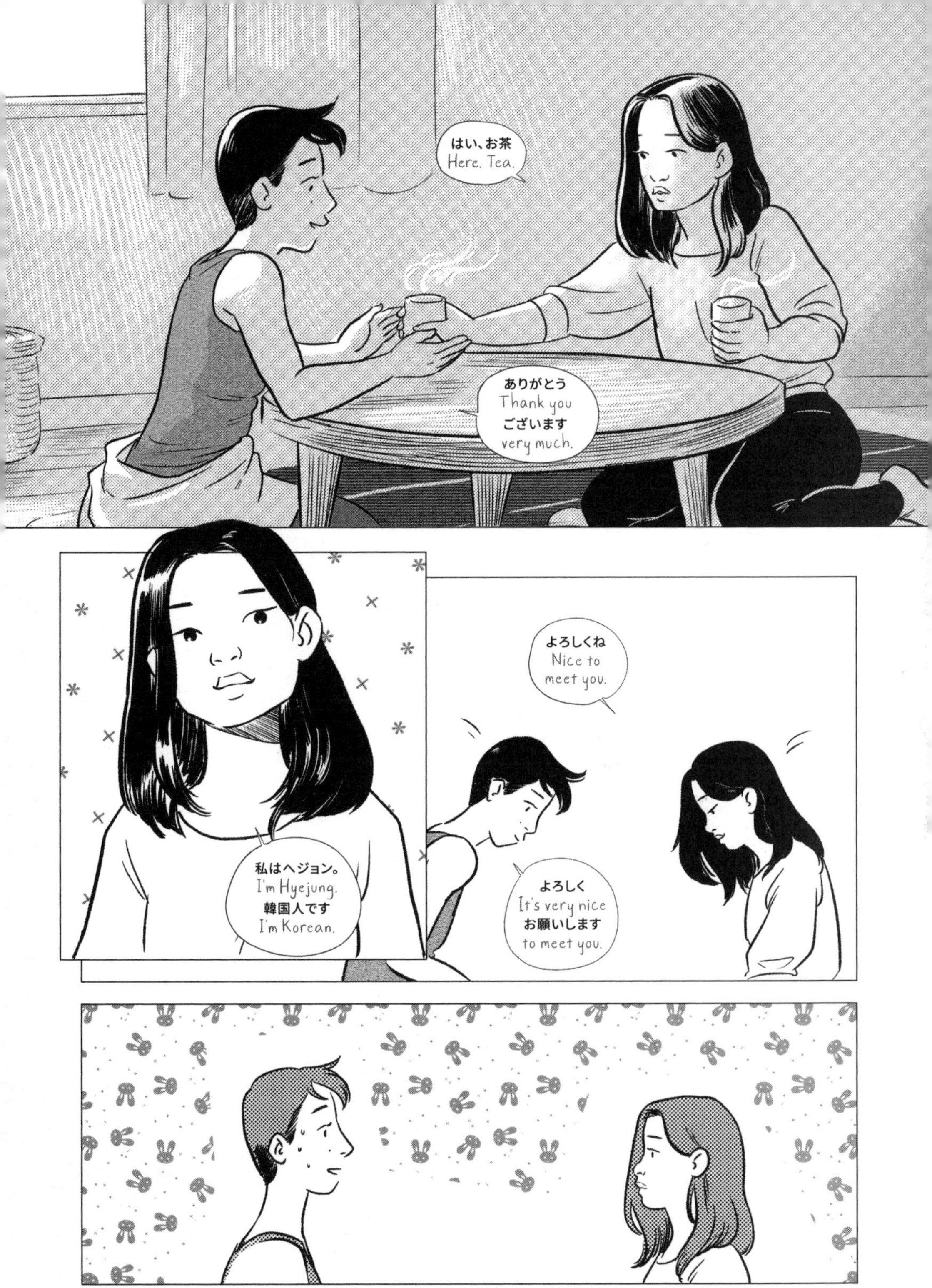
はい、お茶
Here. Tea.
ありがとう
Thank you
ございます
very much.
私はヘジョン。
I'm Hyejung.
韓国人です
I'm Korean.
よろしくね
Nice to meet you.
よろしく
It's very nice
お願いします
to meet you.

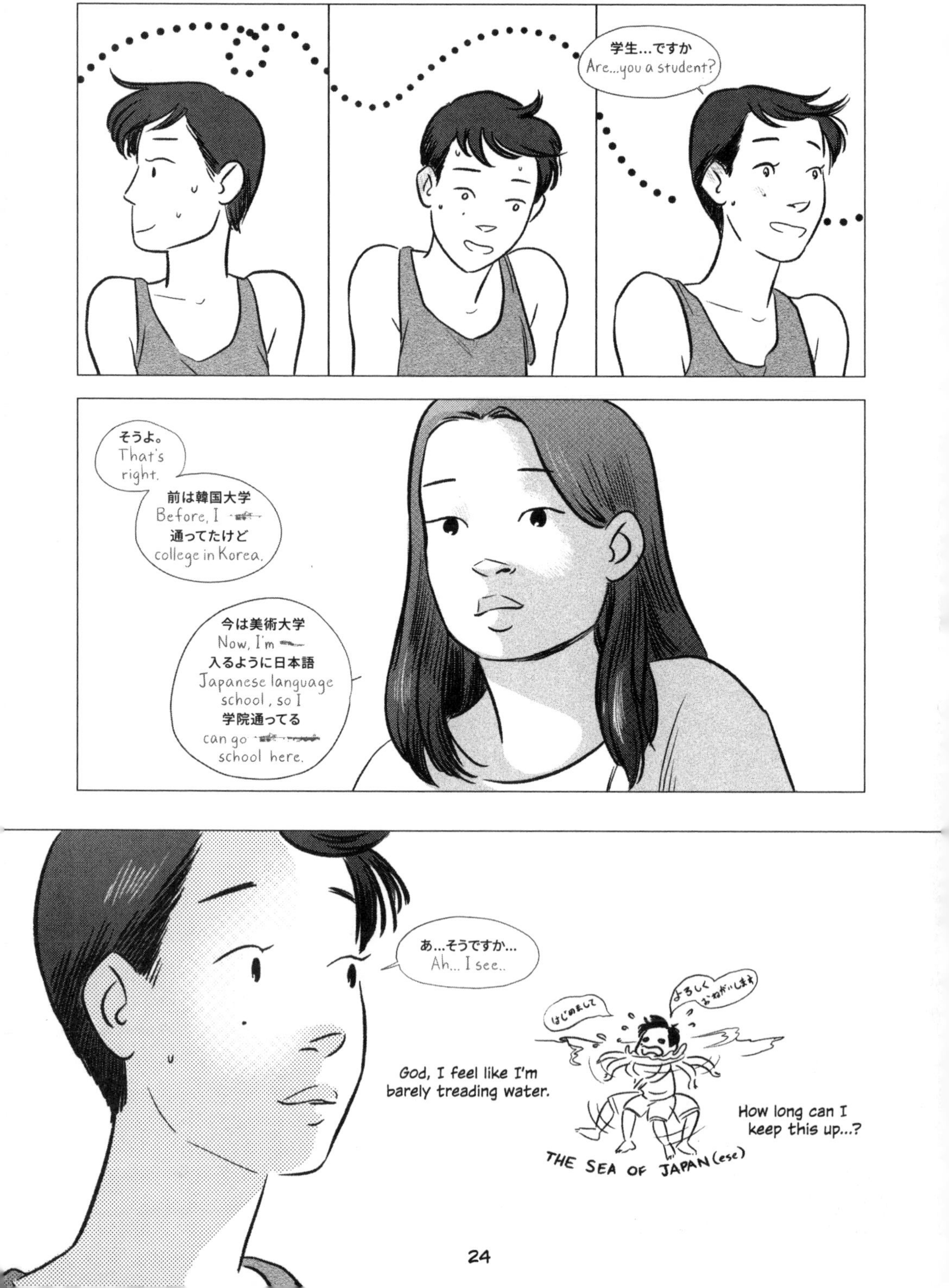

学生…ですか
Are…you a student?
そうよ。
That's right.
前は韓国大学
Before, I
通ってたけど
college in Korea.
今は美術大学
Now, I'm
入るように日本語
Japanese language school, so I
学院通ってる
can go
school here.
あ…そうですか…
Ah… I see..
はじめまして
よろしくおねがいします
God, I feel like I'm barely treading water.
THE SEA OF JAPAN(ese)
How long can I keep this up...?

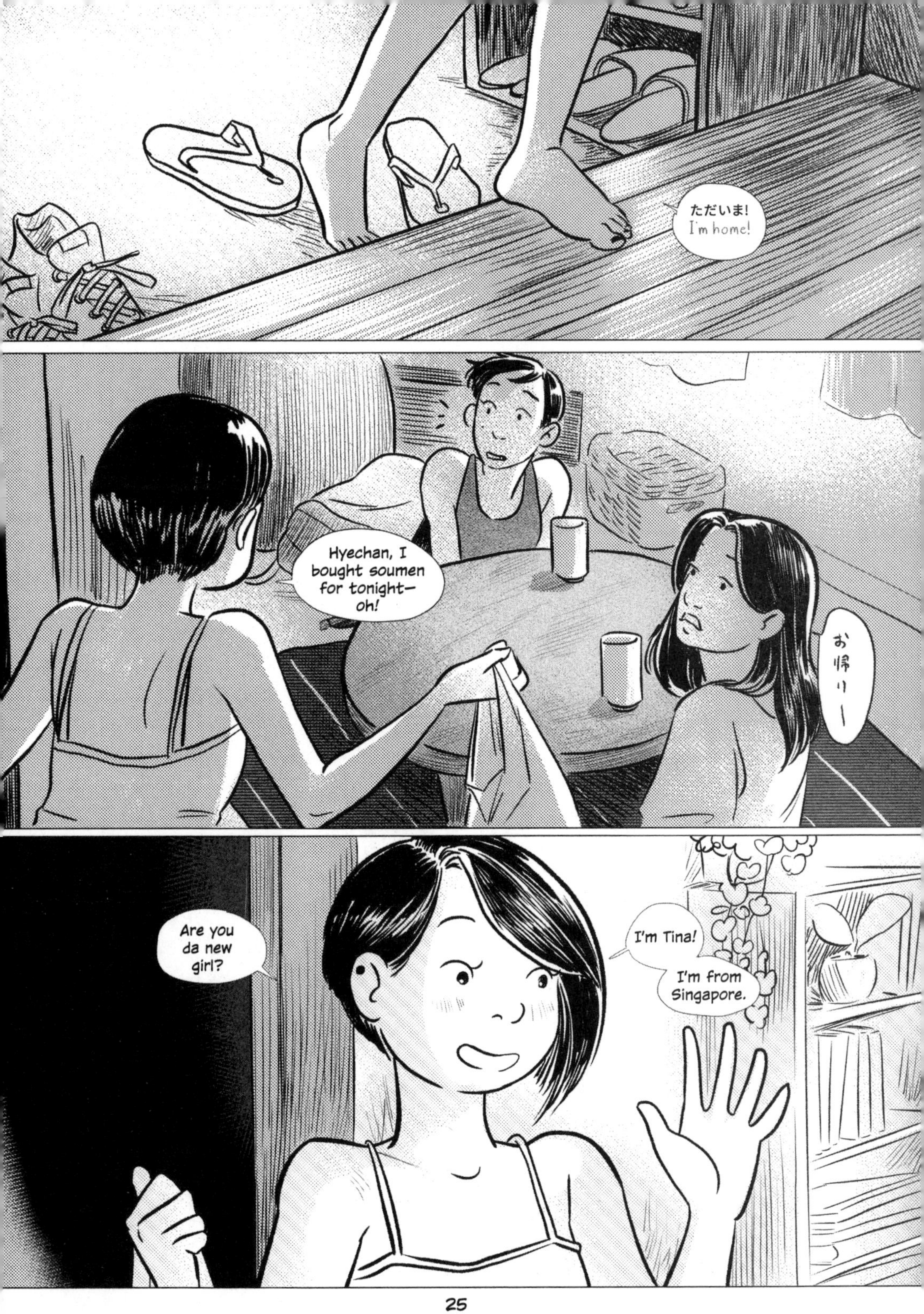
ただいま!
I'm home!
Hyechan, I bought soumen for tonight— oh!
お帰りー
Are you da new girl?
I'm Tina!
I'm from Singapore.

LAND! I see land!!!
Hi, I'm Nao.
뭐야—
You speak Engulishi?
Eh?
Wait, YOU speak English?
Beddah den Japanese!
AAAAH~
Nao reaches the shores of English
Thank god!
:gasp:
Hahaha! You were so polite to me bepo'!
Sou sou!
English more relax mah!

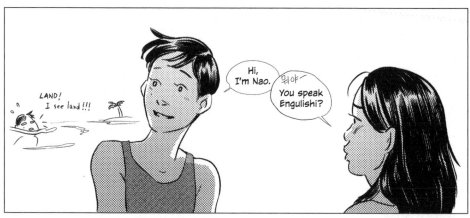

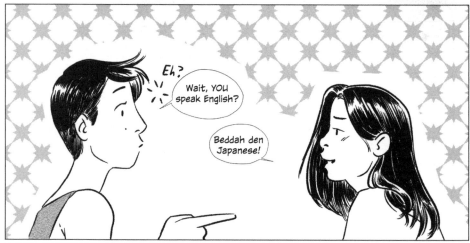

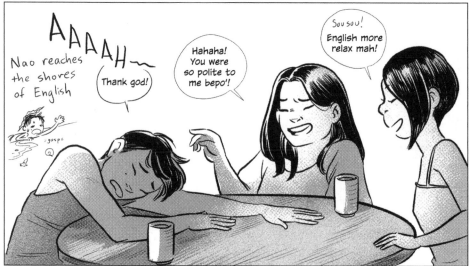

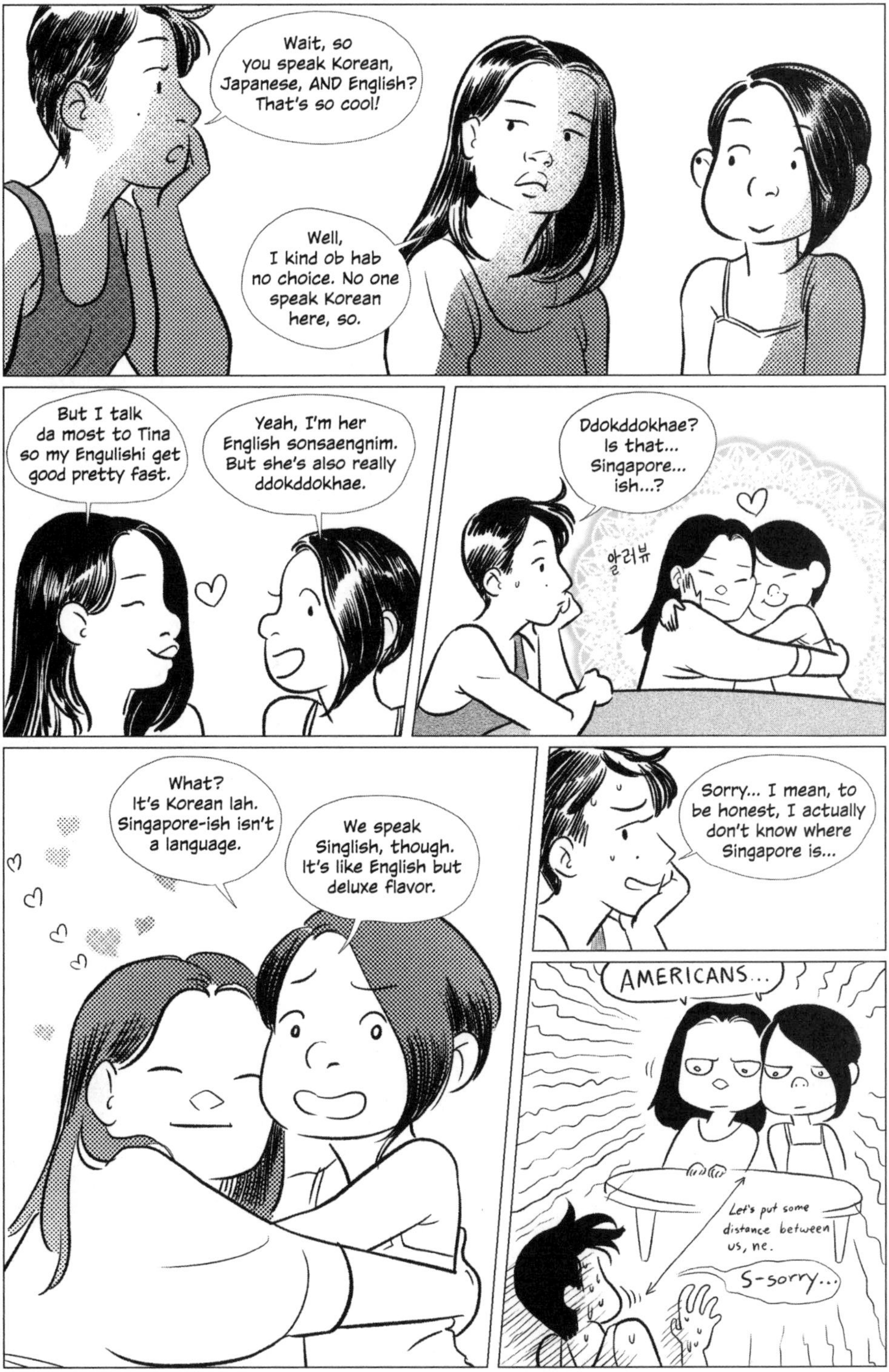
Wait, so you speak Korean, Japanese, AND English? That's so cool!
Well, I kind ob hab no choice. No one speak Korean here, so.
But I talk da most to Tina so my Engulishi get good pretty fast.
Yeah, I'm her English sonsaengnim. But she's also really ddokddokhae.
Ddokddokhae? Is that... Singapore... ish...?
알러뷰
What? It's Korean lah. Singapore-ish isn't a language.
We speak Singlish, though. It's like English but deluxe flavor.
Sorry... I mean, to be honest, I actually don't know where Singapore is...
AMERICANS...
Let's put some distance between us, ne.
S-sorry...

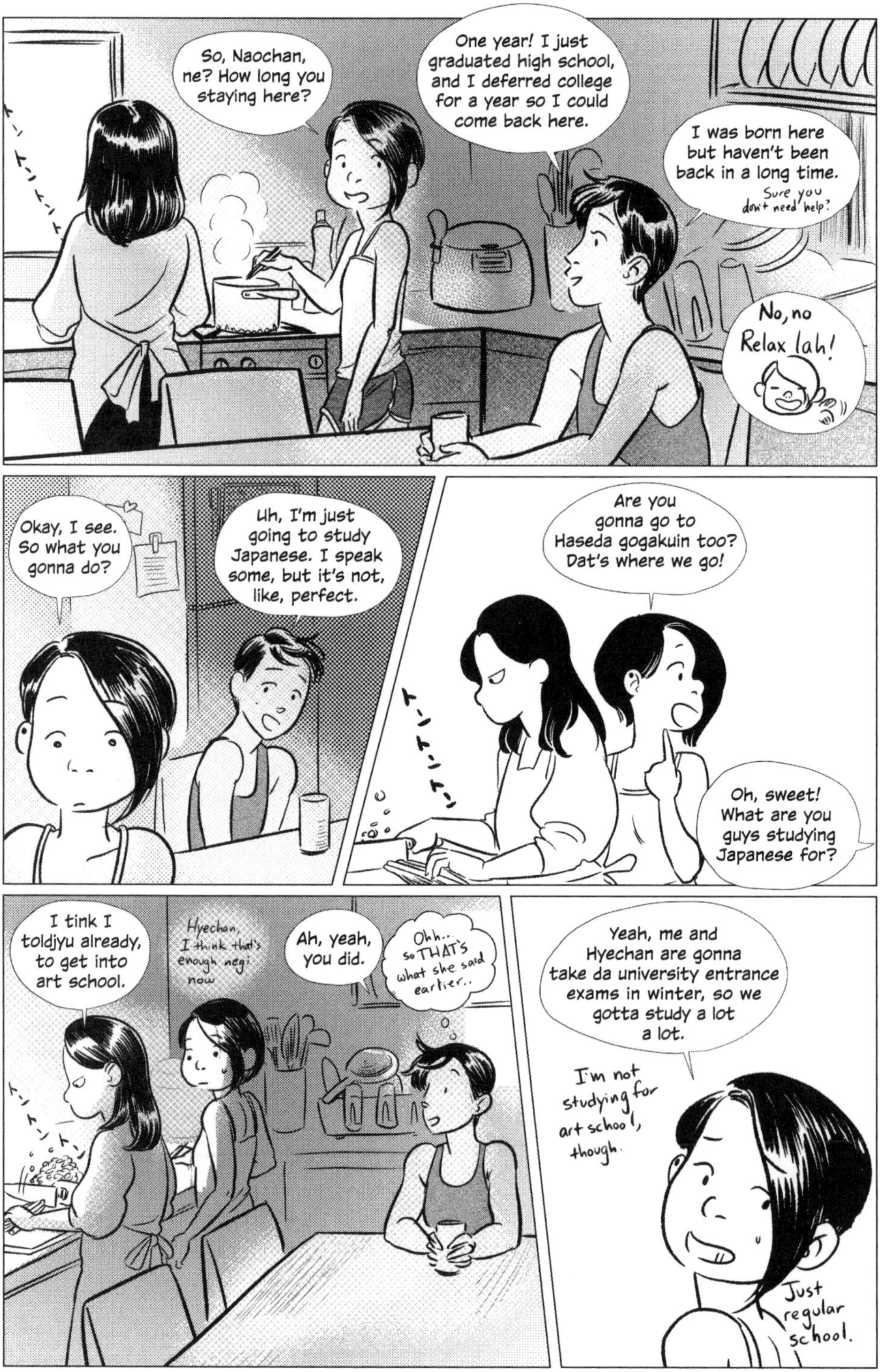

So, Naochan, ne? How long you staying here?
One year! I just graduated high school, and I deferred college for a year so I could come back here.
I was born here but haven't been back in a long time.
Sure you don't need help?
No, no Relax lah!
Okay, I see. So what you gonna do?
Uh, I'm just going to study Japanese. I speak some, but it's not, like, perfect.
Are you gonna go to Haseda gogakuin too? Dat's where we go!
Oh, sweet! What are you guys studying Japanese for?
I tink I toldjyu already, to get into art school.
Hyechan, I think that's enough negi now
Ah, yeah, you did.
Ohh... so THAT'S what she said earlier..
Yeah, me and Hyechan are gonna take da university entrance exams in winter, so we gotta study a lot a lot.
I'm not studying for art school, though.
Just regular school.

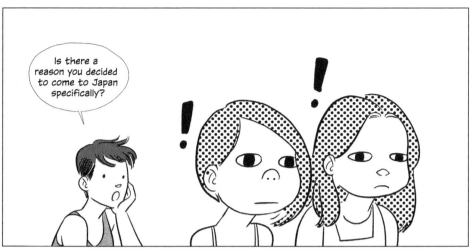

Is there a reason you decided to come to Japan specifically?
!
!
Hmmmmmmmmmm
What was the reason why
Why
Why Japan
NNNNNNNNNNNNNNNN
Why... why Japan...
Because is close to Korea but far at same time?
Actually, yeah. Wit' Singapore, I felt da same.
I think we both just wanna try living in another country, you know?
Unnnn. Souka.

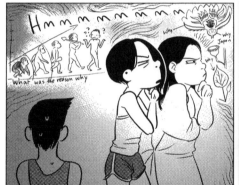

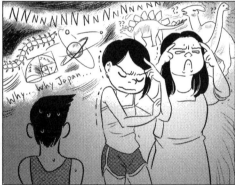

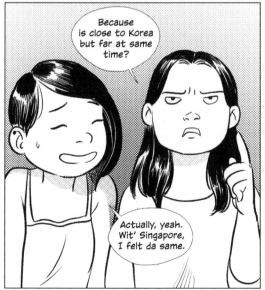

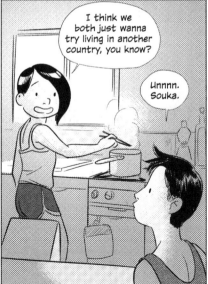

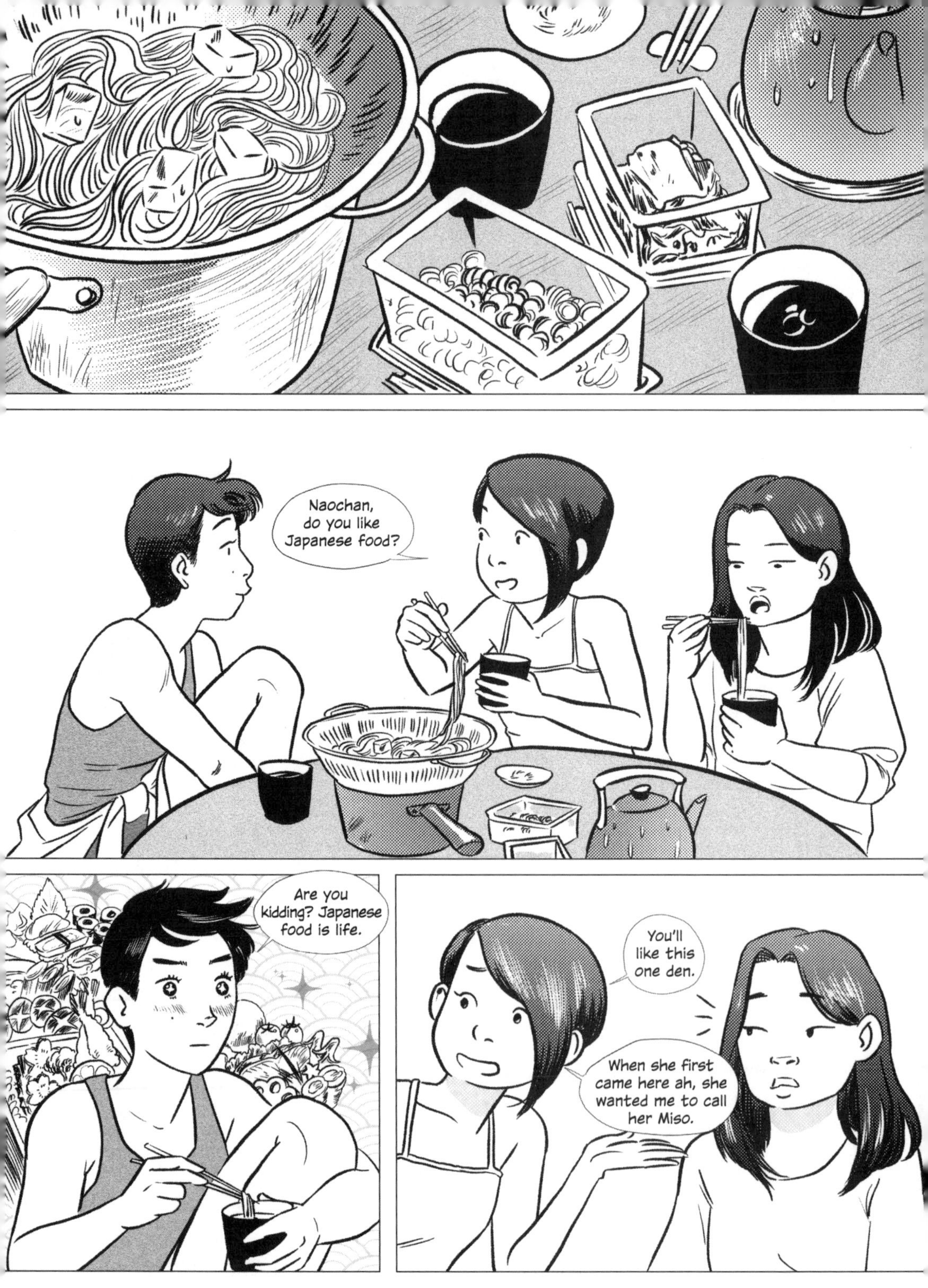

Naochan, do you like Japanese food?
Are you kidding? Japanese food is life.
You'll like this one den.
When she first came here ah, she wanted me to call her Miso.

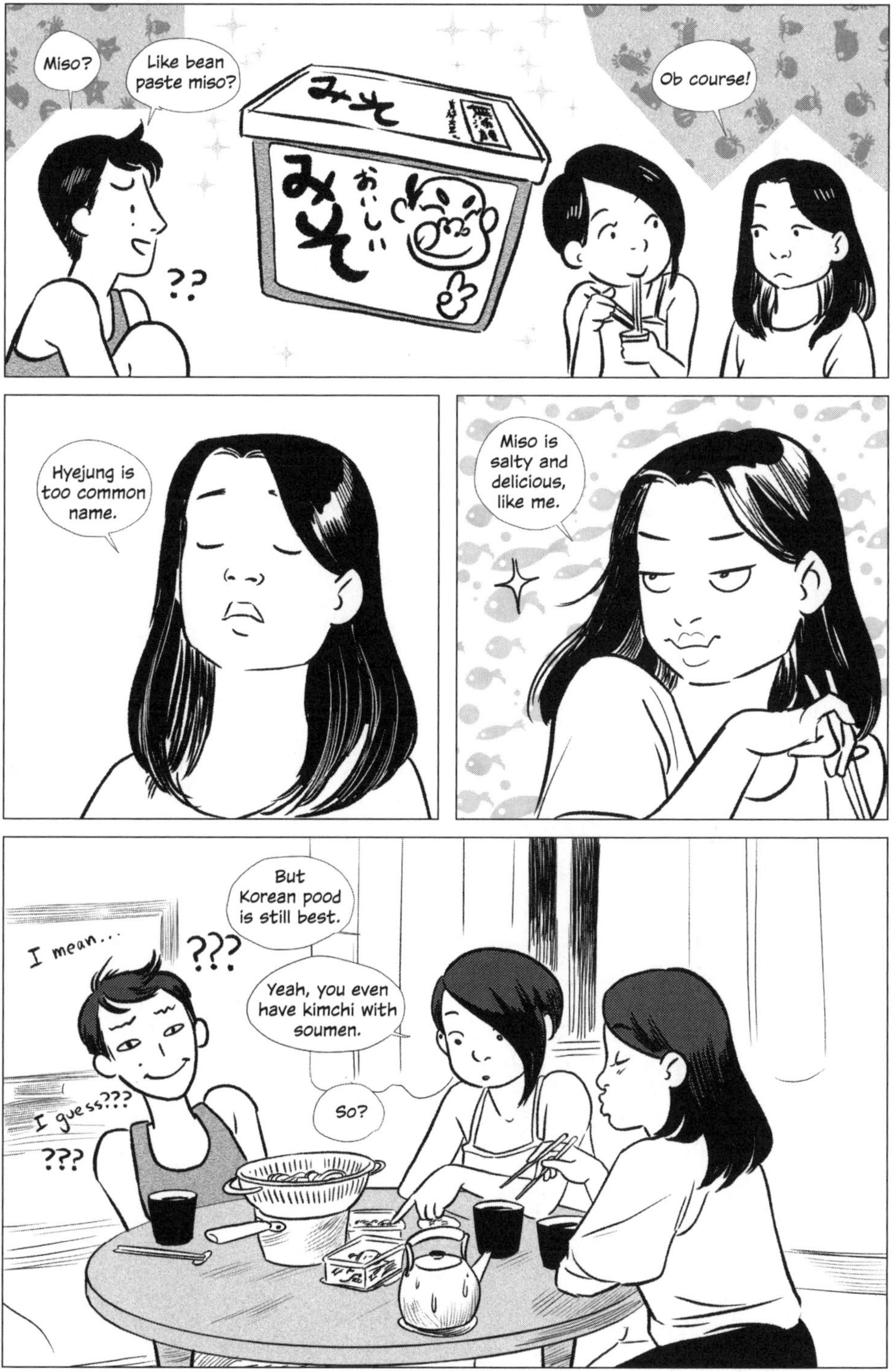

Miso?
Like bean paste miso?
??
みそ
みそ
おいしい
Ob course!
Hyejung is too common name.
Miso is salty and delicious, like me.
But Korean pood is still best.
I mean...
???
Yeah, you even have kimchi with soumen.
So?
I guess???
???

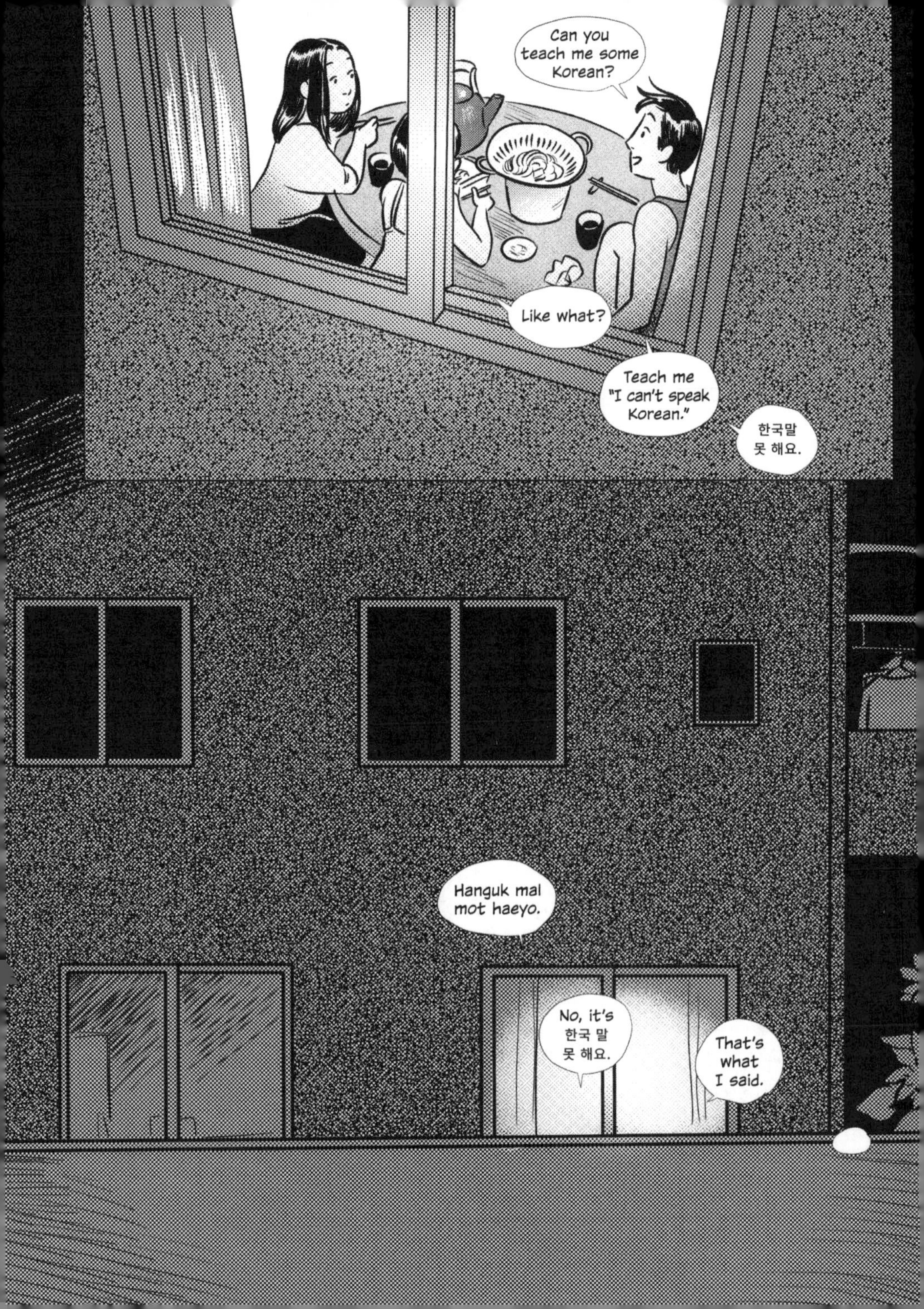
Can you teach me some Korean?
Like what?
Teach me "I can't speak Korean."
한국말 못 해요.
Hanguk mal mot haeyo.
No, it's 한국 말 못 해요.
That's what I said.

Chapter 2

The Road Home

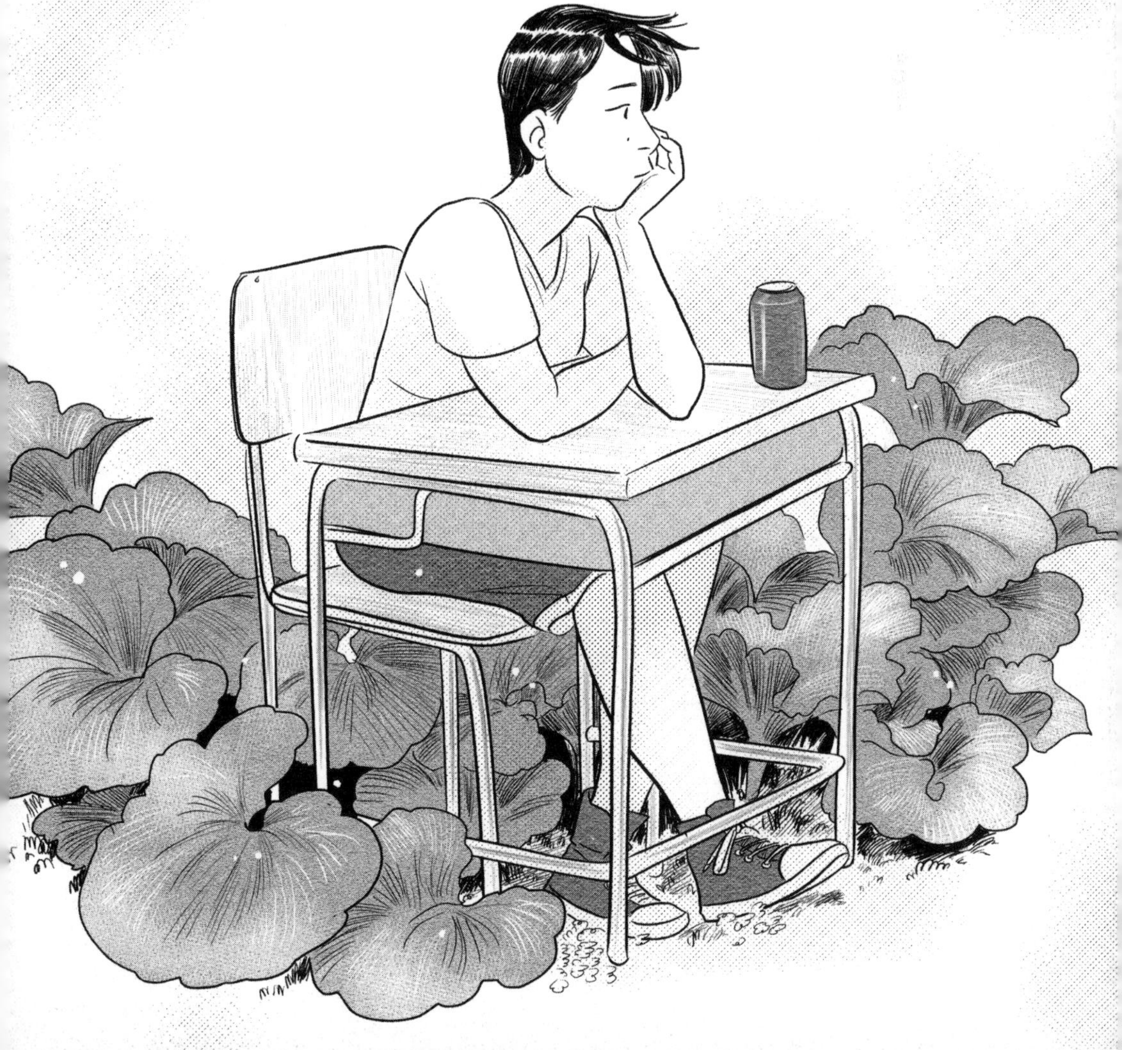

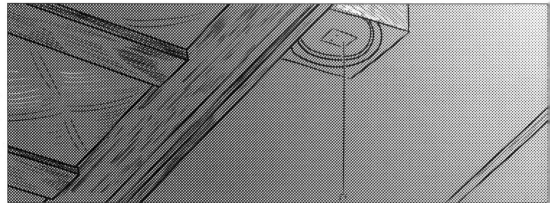

Wait...where am I again...?

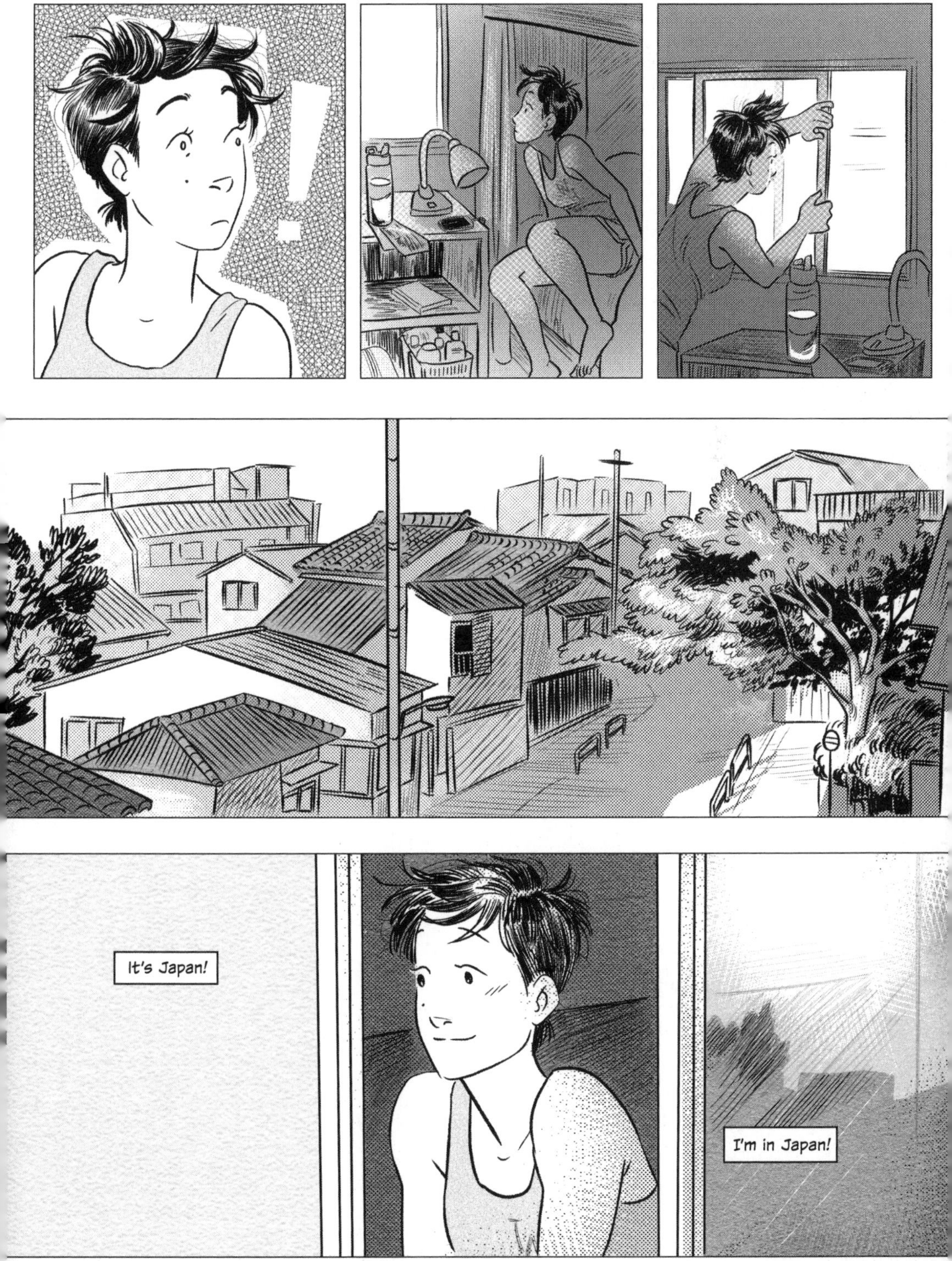
It's Japan!
I'm in Japan!

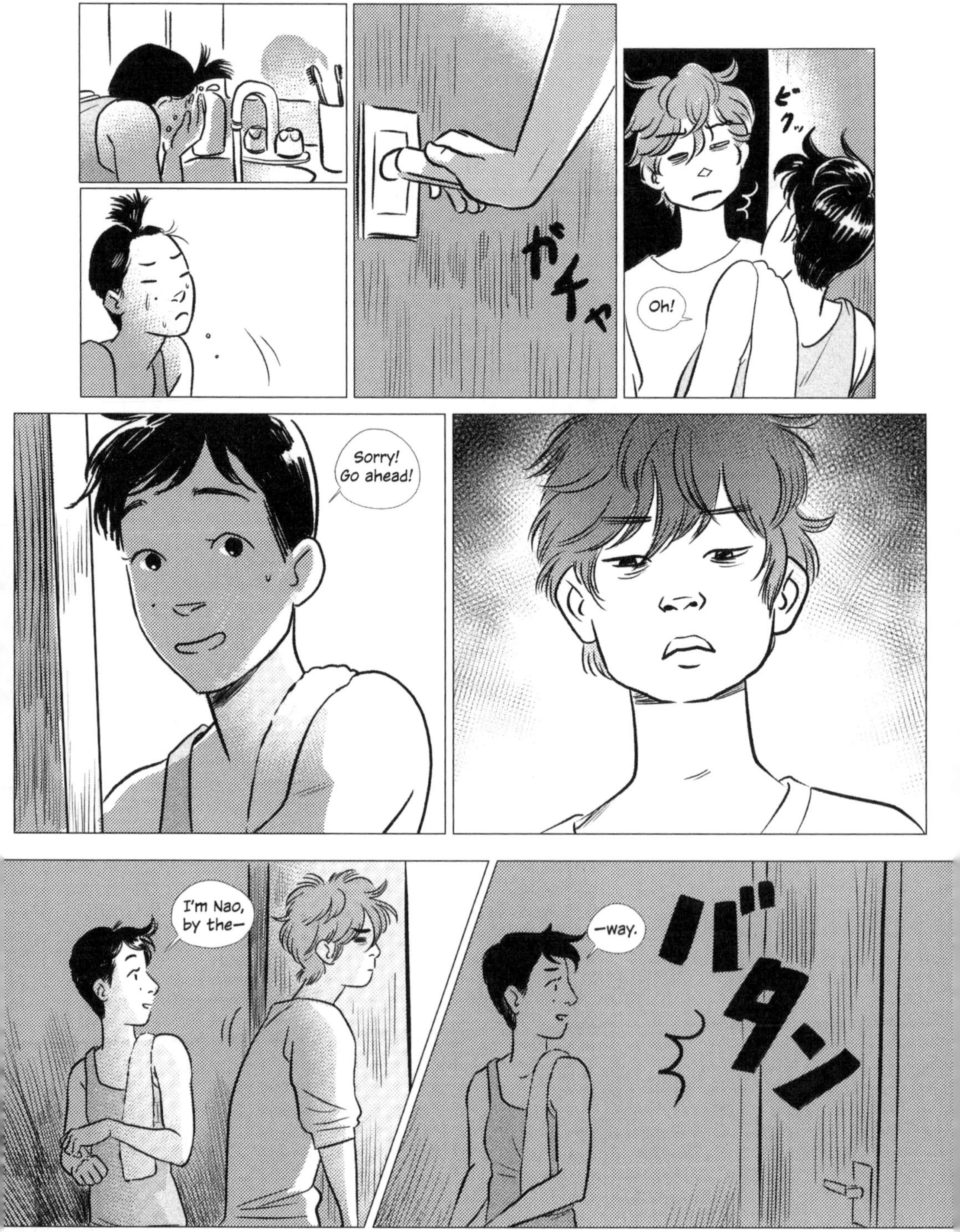
ガチャ
ビクッ
Oh!
Sorry! Go ahead!
I'm Nao, by the—
—way.
バタン

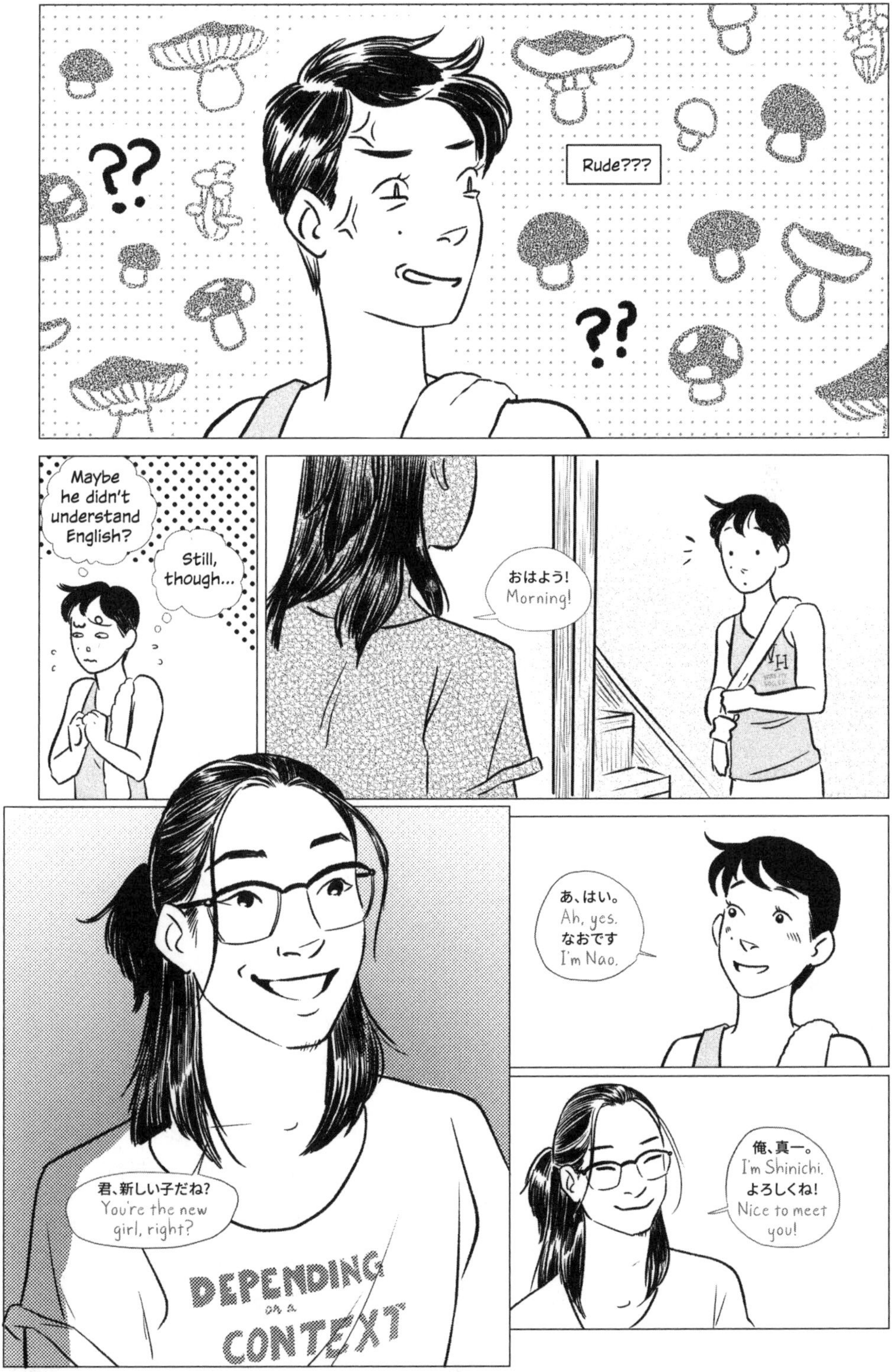
Rude???
Maybe he didn't understand English?
Still, though...
おはよう! Morning!
君、新しい子だね? You're the new girl, right?
あ、はい。Ah, yes. なおです I'm Nao.
俺、真一。I'm Shinichi. よろしくね! Nice to meet you!
DEPENDING on a CONTEXT

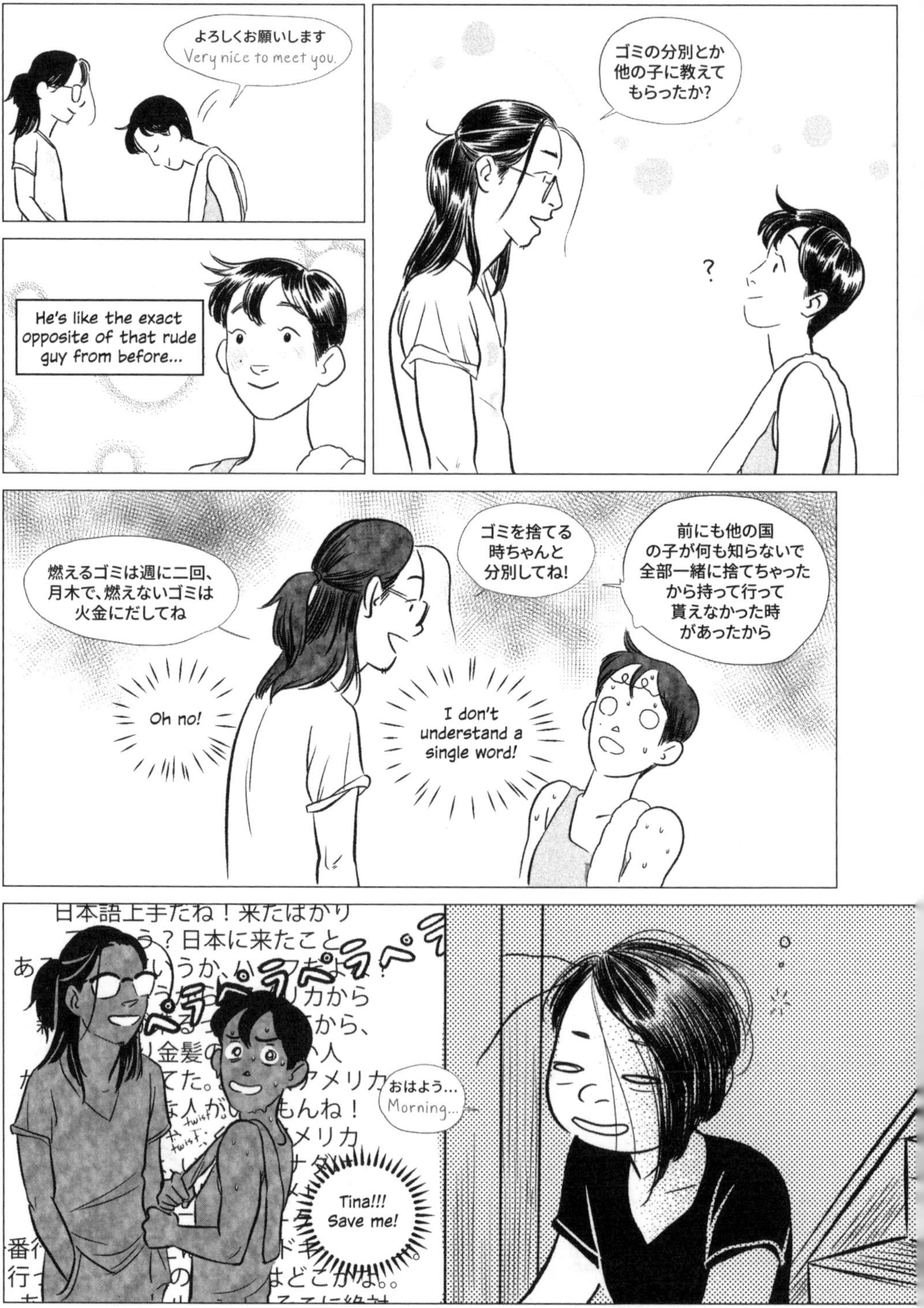
よろしくお願いします
Very nice to meet you.
He's like the exact opposite of that rude guy from before...
ゴミの分別とか
他の子に教えて
もらったか?
?
燃えるゴミは週に二回、
月木で、燃えないゴミは
火金にだしてね
ゴミを捨てる
時ちゃんと
分別してね!
前にも他の国
の子が何も知らないで
全部一緒に捨てちゃった
から持って行って
貰えなかった時
があったから
Oh no!
I don't understand a single word!
twist twist
Tina!!! Save me!
おはよう…
Morning…

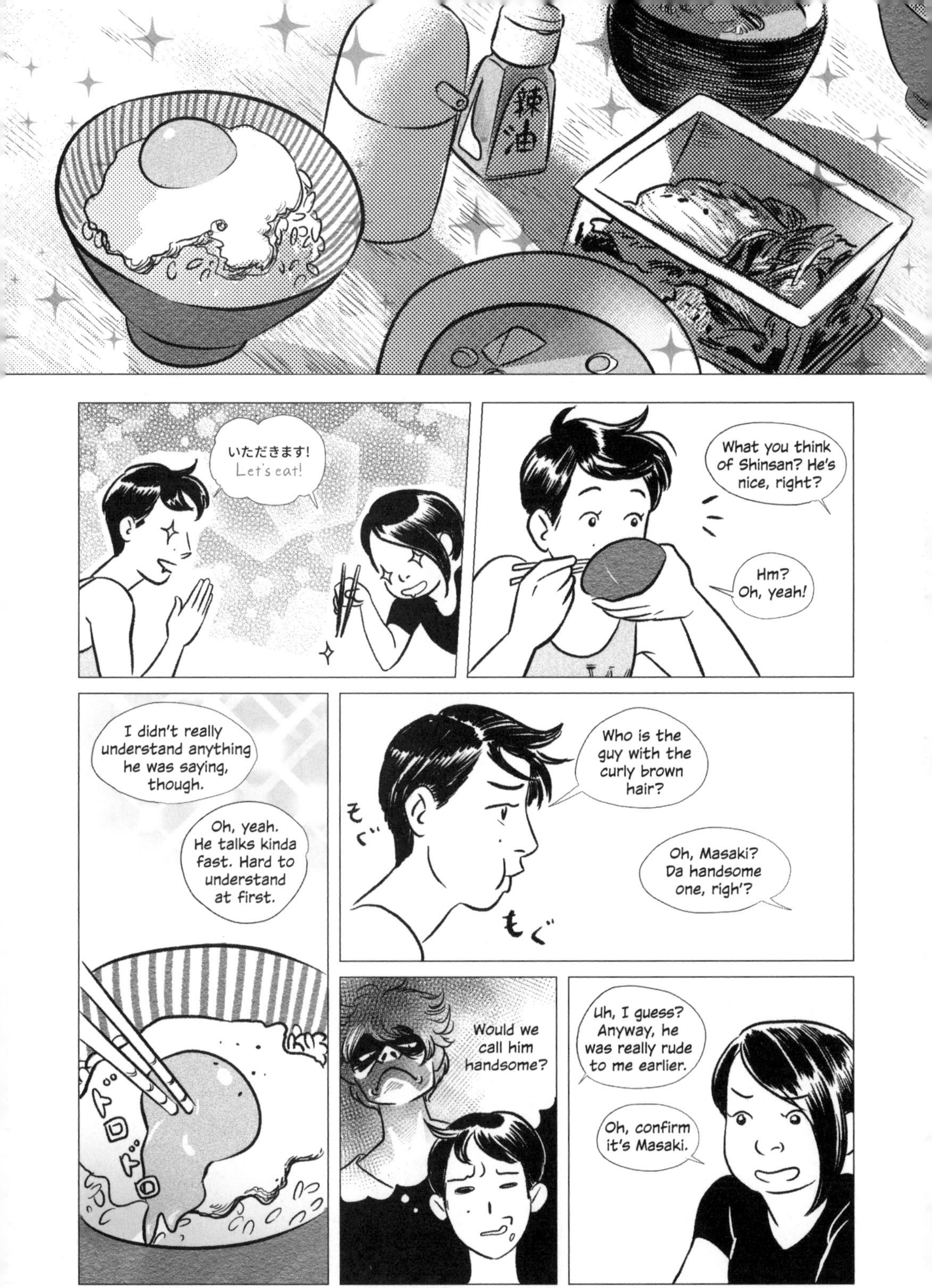

辣油
いただきます!
Let's eat!
What you think of Shinsan? He's nice, right?
Hm? Oh, yeah!
I didn't really understand anything he was saying, though.
Oh, yeah. He talks kinda fast. Hard to understand at first.
Who is the guy with the curly brown hair?
もぐ
もぐ
Oh, Masaki? Da handsome one, righ'?
Would we call him handsome?
Uh, I guess? Anyway, he was really rude to me earlier.
Oh, confirm it's Masaki.

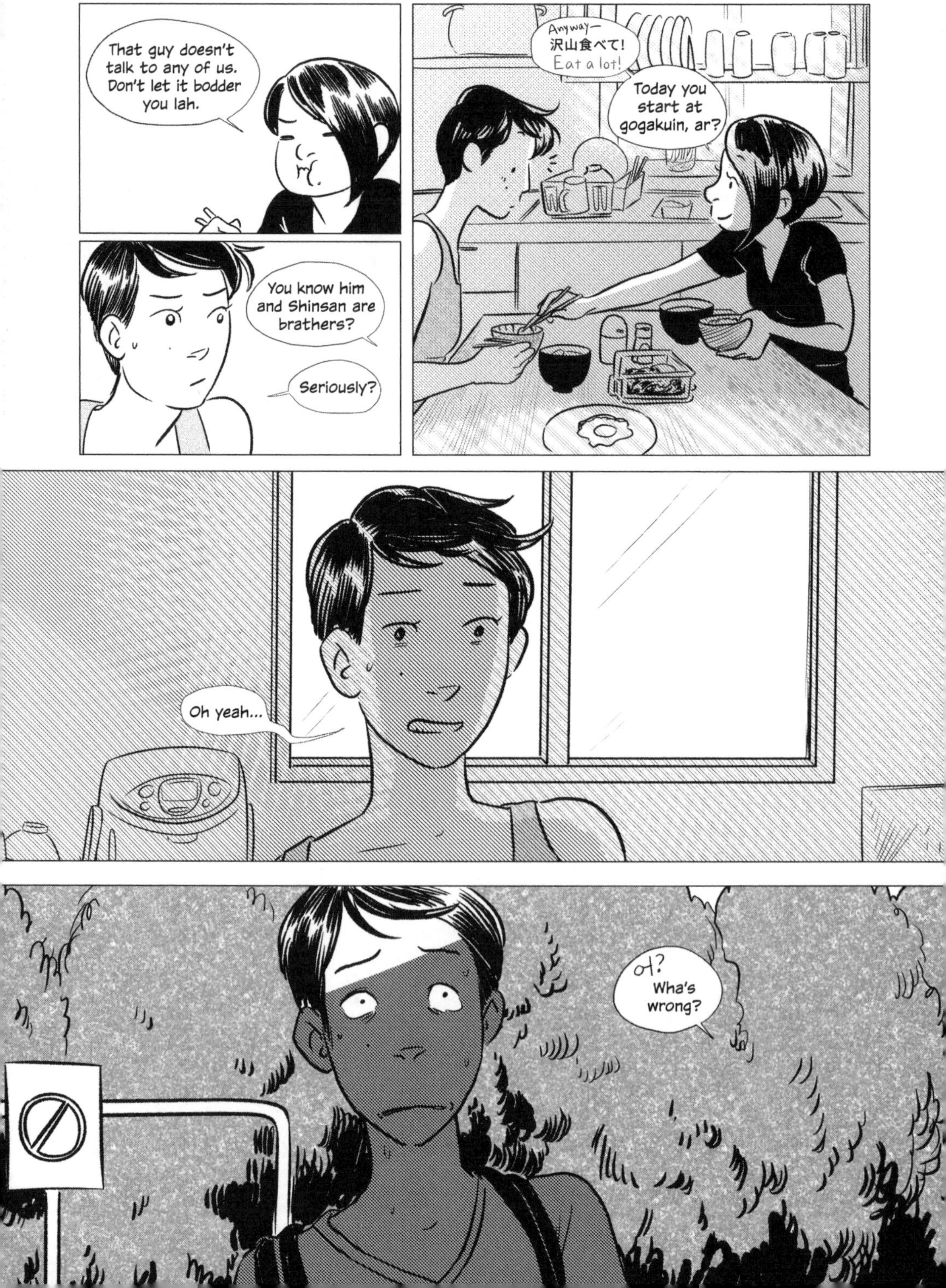
That guy doesn't talk to any of us. Don't let it bodder you lah.
You know him and Shinsan are brathers?
Seriously?
Anyway— 沢山食べて! Eat a lot!
Today you start at gogakuin, ar?
Oh yeah...
어? Wha's wrong?

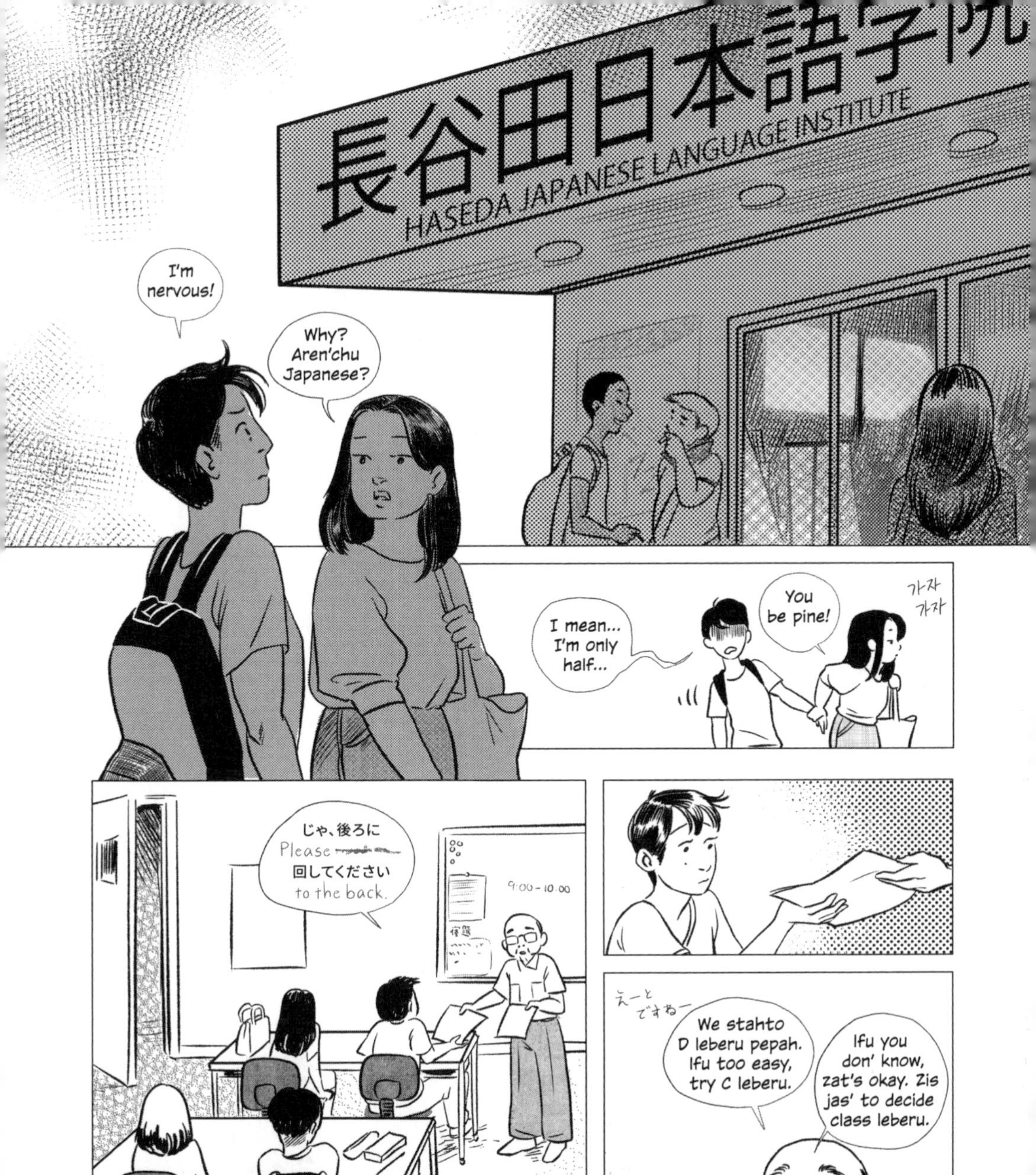

長谷田日本語学院
HASEDA JAPANESE LANGUAGE INSTITUTE
I'm nervous!
Why? Aren'chu Japanese?
I mean... I'm only half...
You be pine!
가자 가자
じゃ、後ろに
Please
回してください
to the back.
9:00 - 10:00
えーとですねー
We stahto D leberu pepah. Ifu too easy, try C leberu.
Ifu you don' know, zat's okay. Zis jas' to decide class leberu.

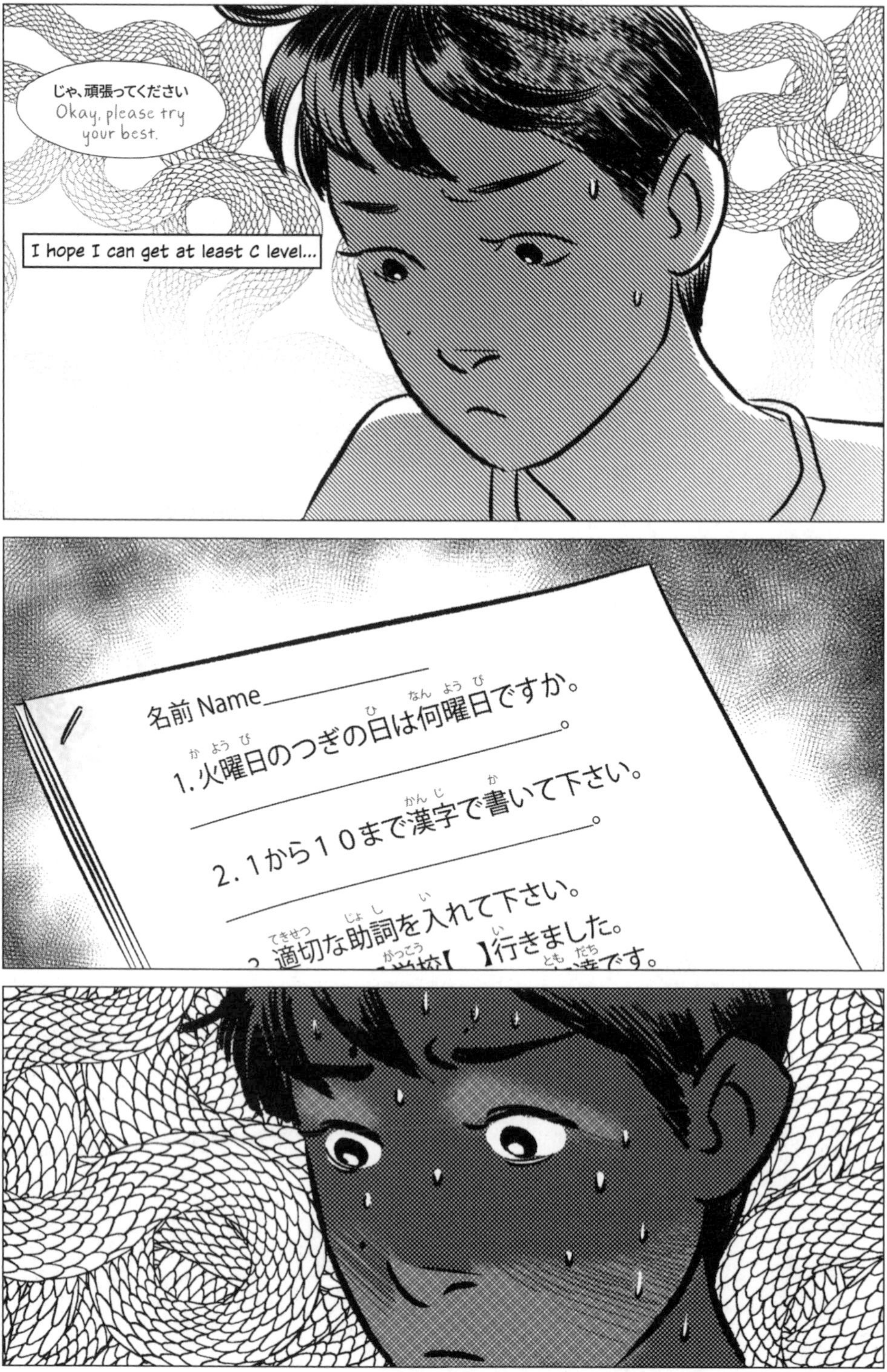

じゃ、頑張ってください
Okay, please try your best.
I hope I can get at least C level...
名前 Name
1. 火曜日のつぎの日は何曜日ですか。
2. 1から10まで漢字で書いて下さい。
適切な助詞を入れて下さい。
】行きました。

Hai—
Letter at top ofu pe-ji izu your new class leberu and room namba.

Purizu find your new class by 11:00.

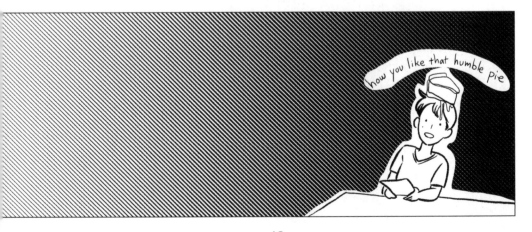

how you like that humble pie

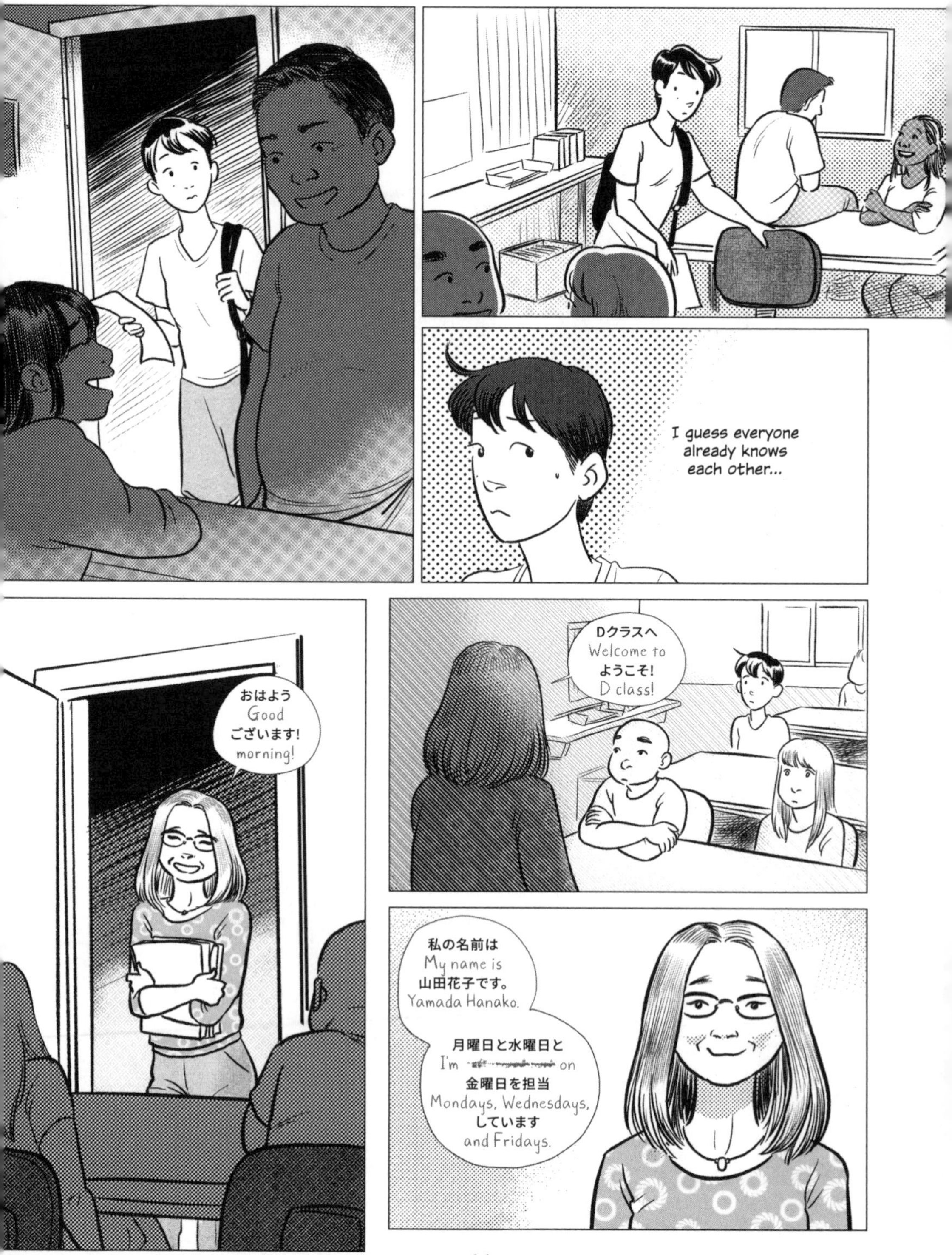
I guess everyone already knows each other...
おはよう Good ございます! morning!
Dクラスへ Welcome to ようこそ! D class!
私の名前は My name is 山田花子です。 Yamada Hanako.
月曜日と水曜日と I'm on 金曜日を担当 Mondays, Wednesdays, しています and Fridays.

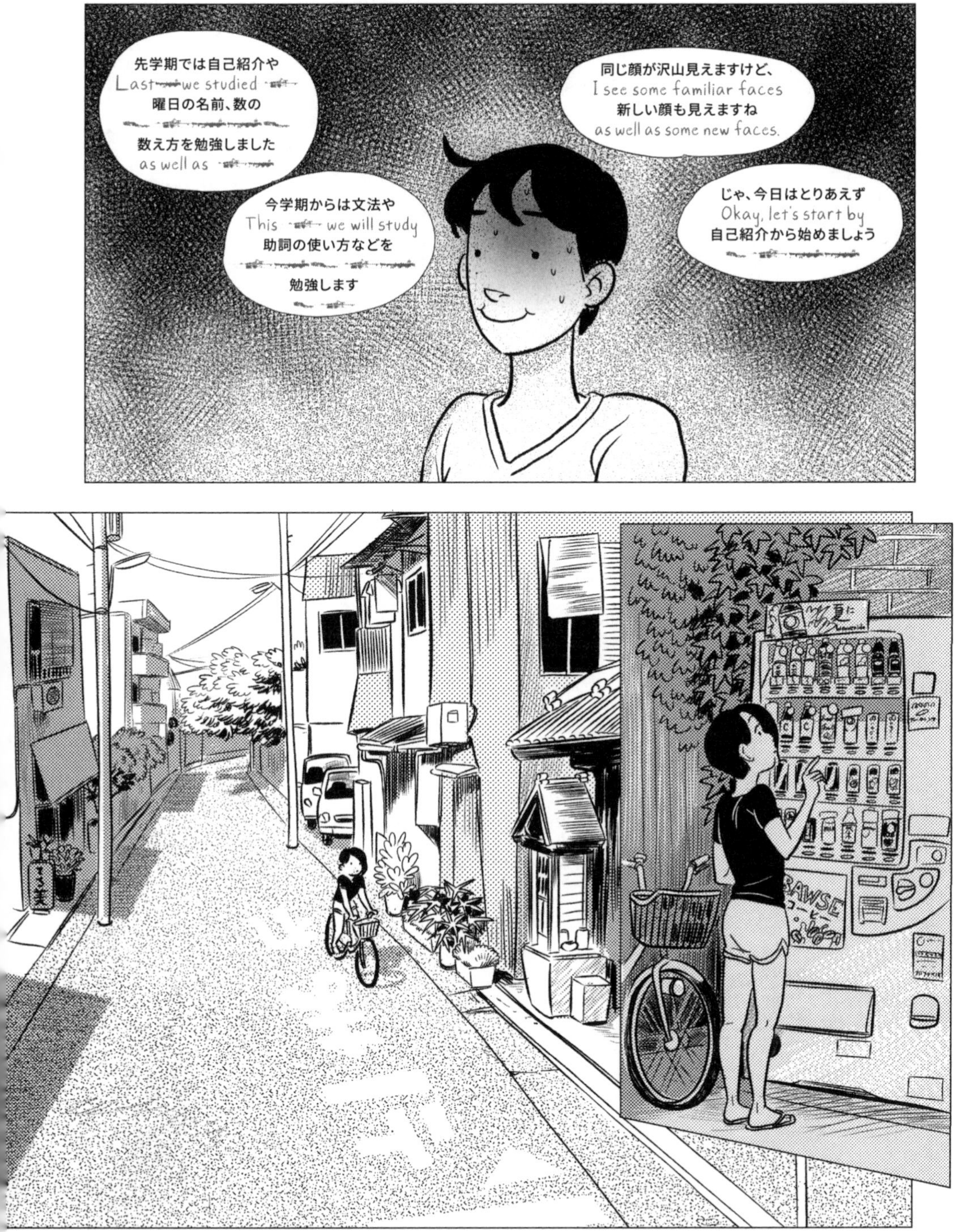
先学期では自己紹介や
Last we studied
曜日の名前、数の
数え方を勉強しました
as well as
今学期からは文法や
This we will study
助詞の使い方などを
勉強します
同じ顔が沢山見えますけど、
I see some familiar faces
新しい顔も見えますね
as well as some new faces.
じゃ、今日はとりあえず
Okay, let's start by
自己紹介から始めましょう

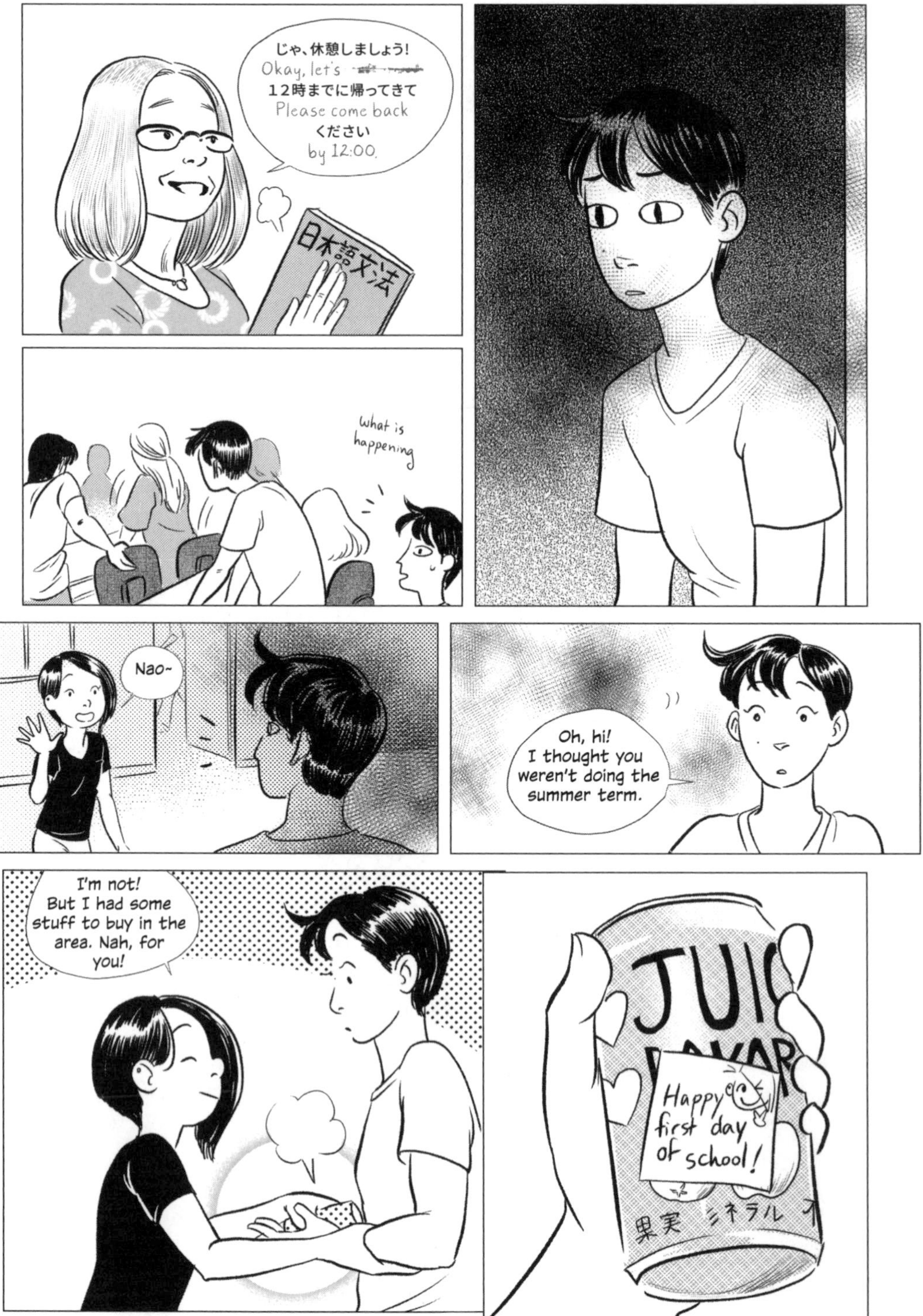
じゃ、休憩しましょう!
Okay, let's
12時までに帰ってきて
Please come back
ください
by 12:00.
日本語文法
what is happening
Nao~
Oh, hi! I thought you weren't doing the summer term.
I'm not! But I had some stuff to buy in the area. Nah, for you!
JUIC
Happy first day of school!
果実

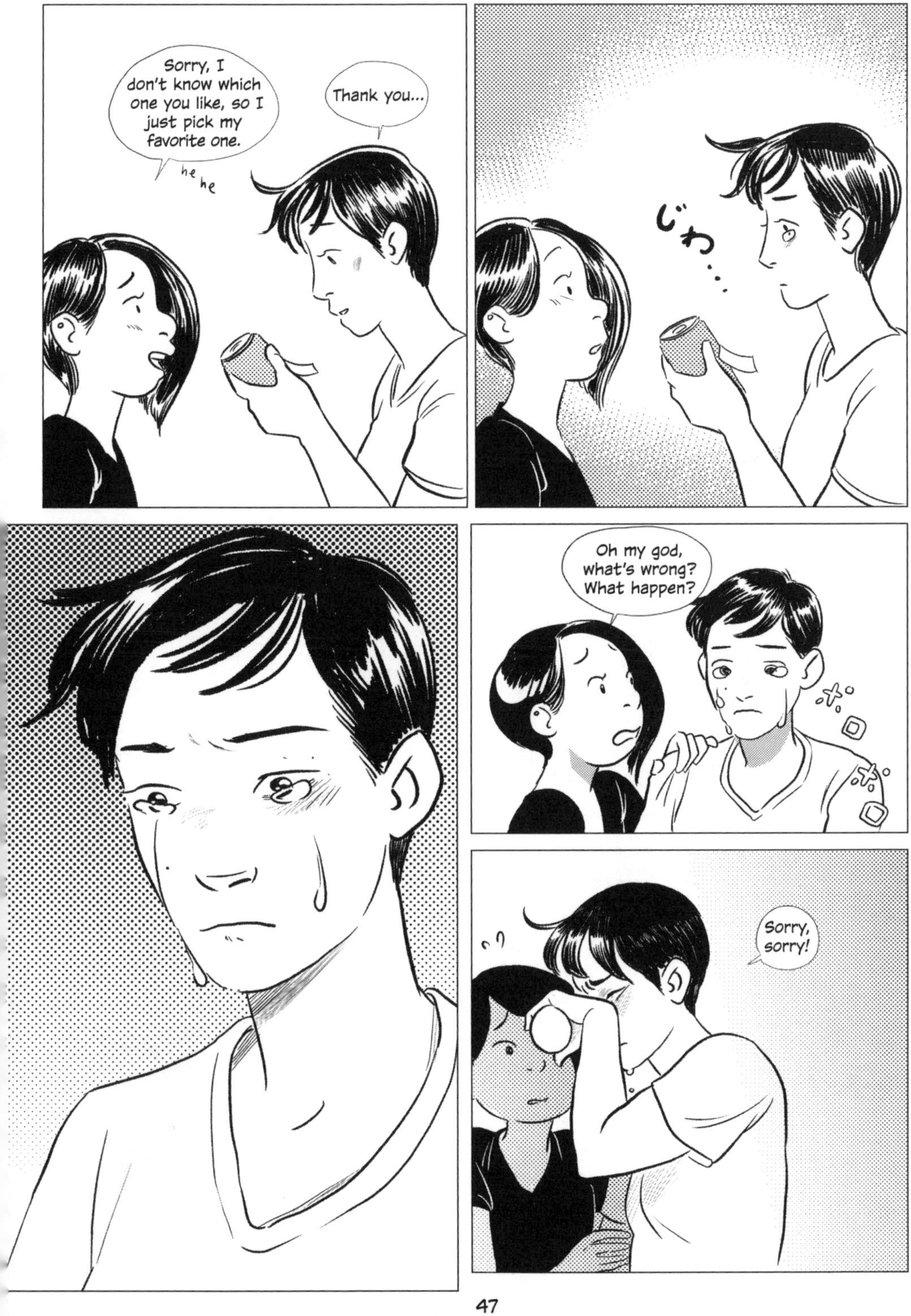
Sorry, I don't know which one you like, so I just pick my favorite one.
he he
Thank you...
じわ…
Oh my god, what's wrong? What happen?
Sorry, sorry!

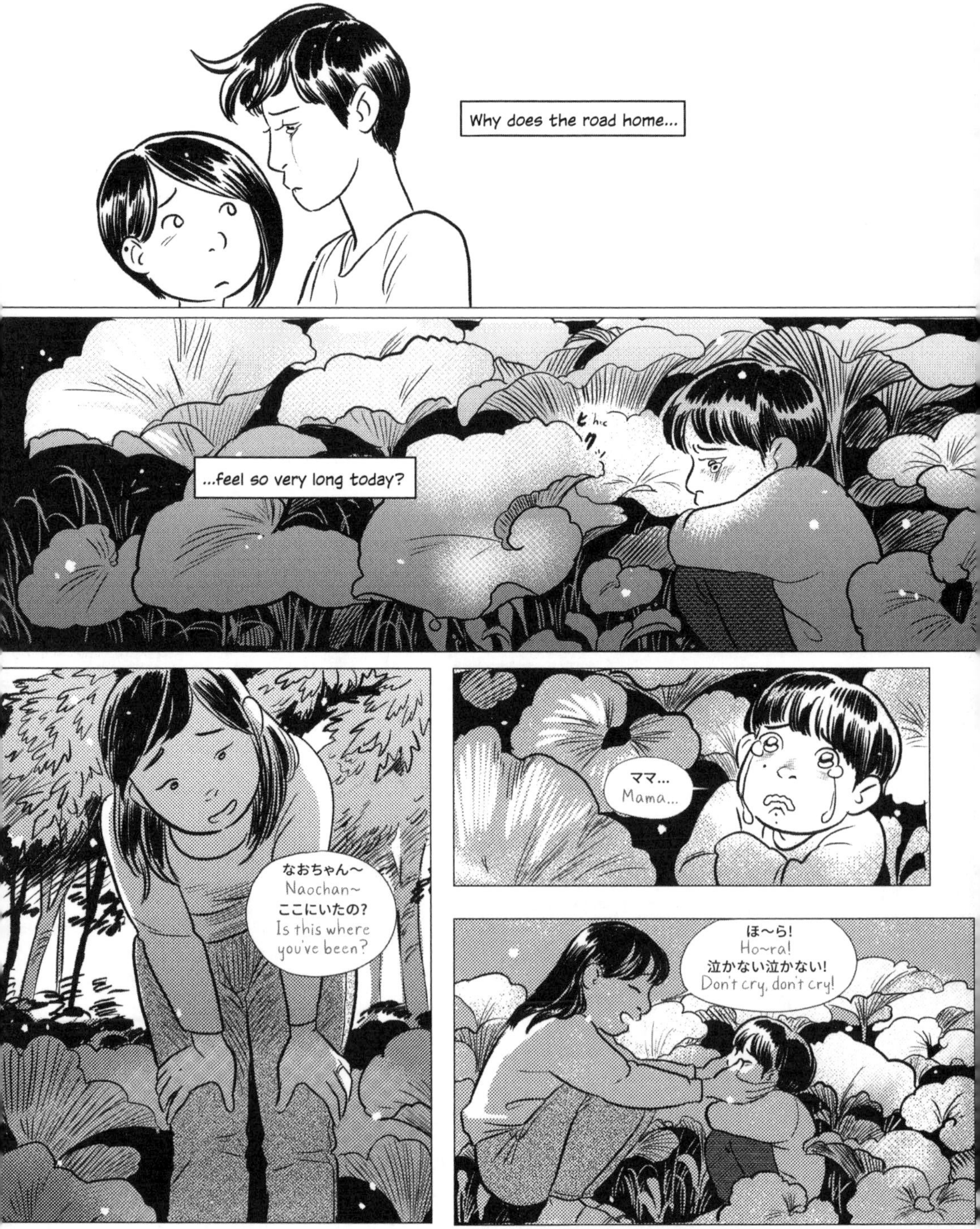

Why does the road home...
ヒクッ
hic
...feel so very long today?
なおちゃん~
Naochan~
ここにいたの?
Is this where you've been?
ママ...
Mama...
ほ~ら!
Ho~ra!
泣かない泣かない!
Don't cry, don't cry!

よしよし〜
Yoshi yoshi〜
もう大丈夫
It's okay now.

帰ろう?
Shall we
go home?

うん
Yeah.

あのね、なおね
You know, Nao—
迷子になっちゃった
Nao got lost.

そうね
That's right,
you did.

怖かったでしょう。
もう一人で行っちゃ
いけな

いつまで?
大きくなったら
ママ見たいに
一人で行っ
い

When did all the words that flowed so freely between my mother and I...

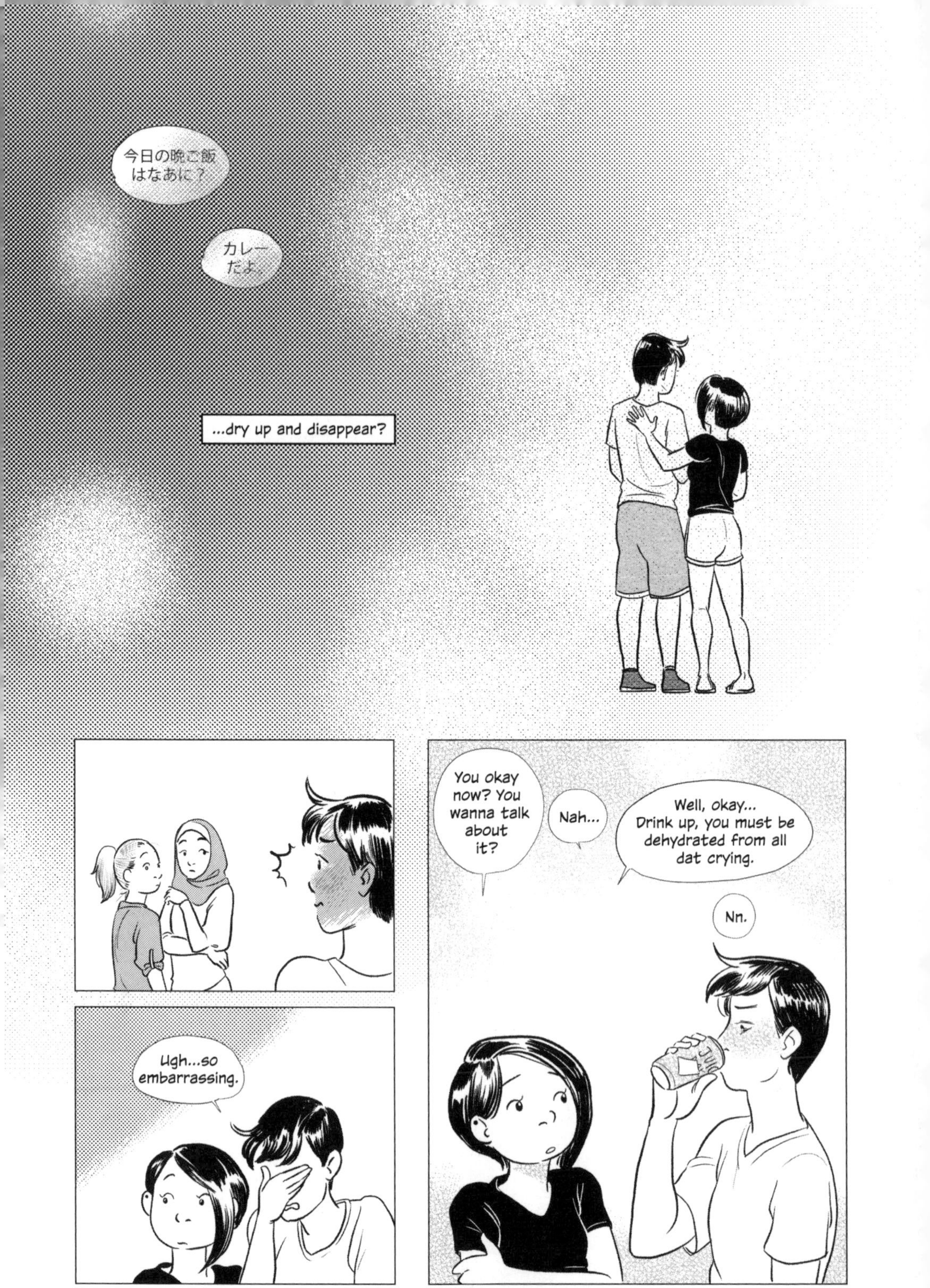
今日の晩ご飯はなあに？
カレーだよ。
...dry up and disappear?
Ugh...so embarrassing.
You okay now? You wanna talk about it?
Nah...
Well, okay... Drink up, you must be dehydrated from all dat crying.
Nn.

Chapter 3

Awa Odori

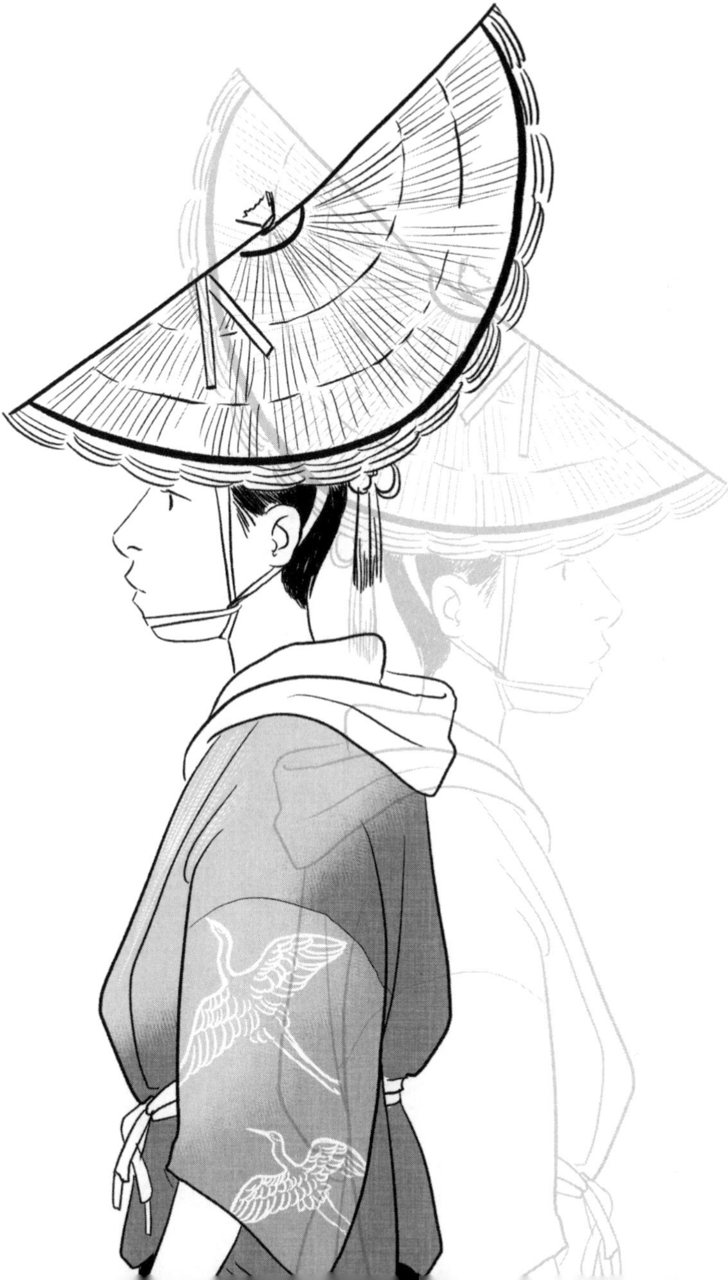

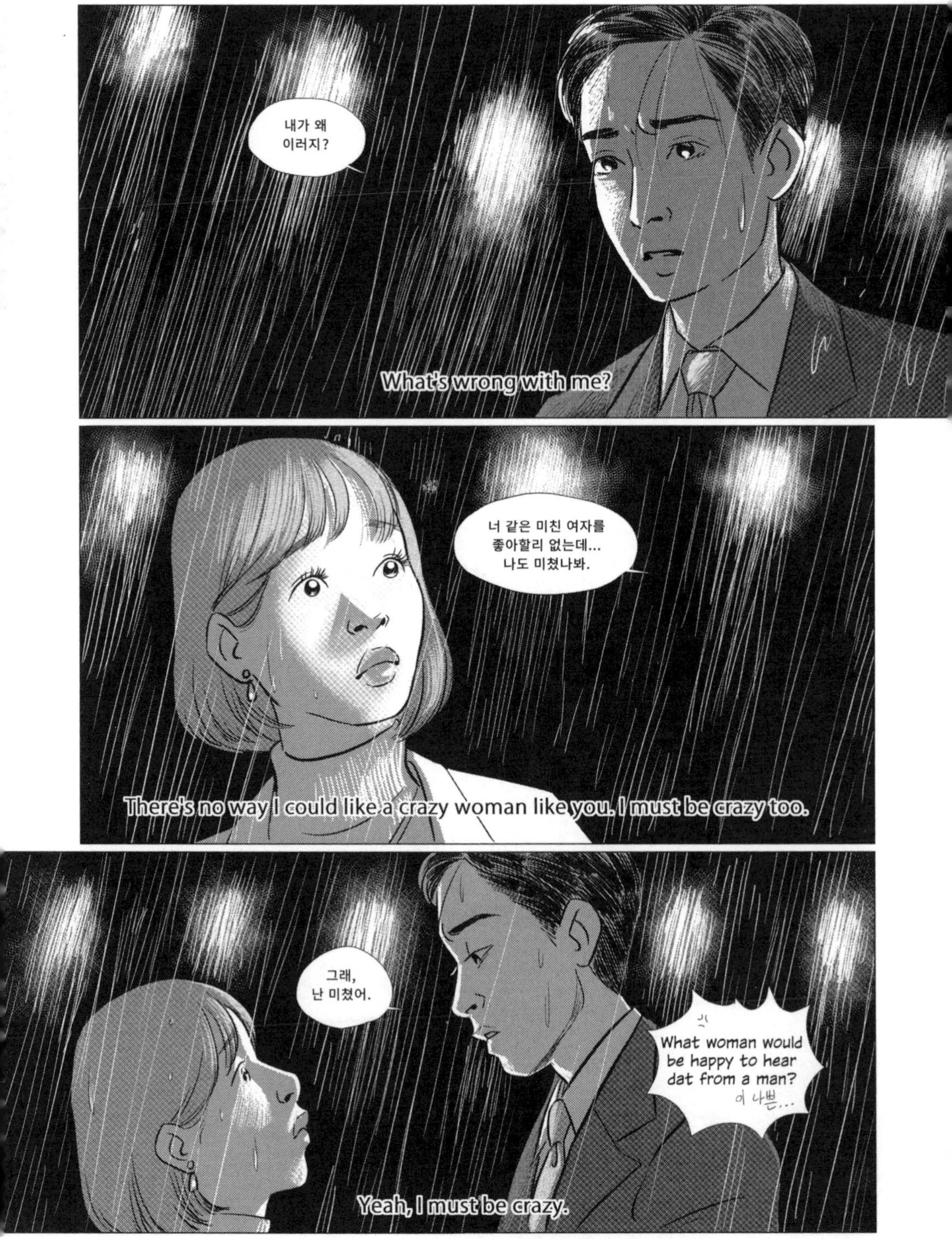
내가 왜 이러지?
What's wrong with me?
너 같은 미친 여자를 좋아할리 없는데... 나도 미쳤나봐.
There's no way I could like a crazy woman like you. I must be crazy too.
그래, 난 미쳤어.
What woman would be happy to hear dat from a man?
이 나쁜...
Yeah, I must be crazy.

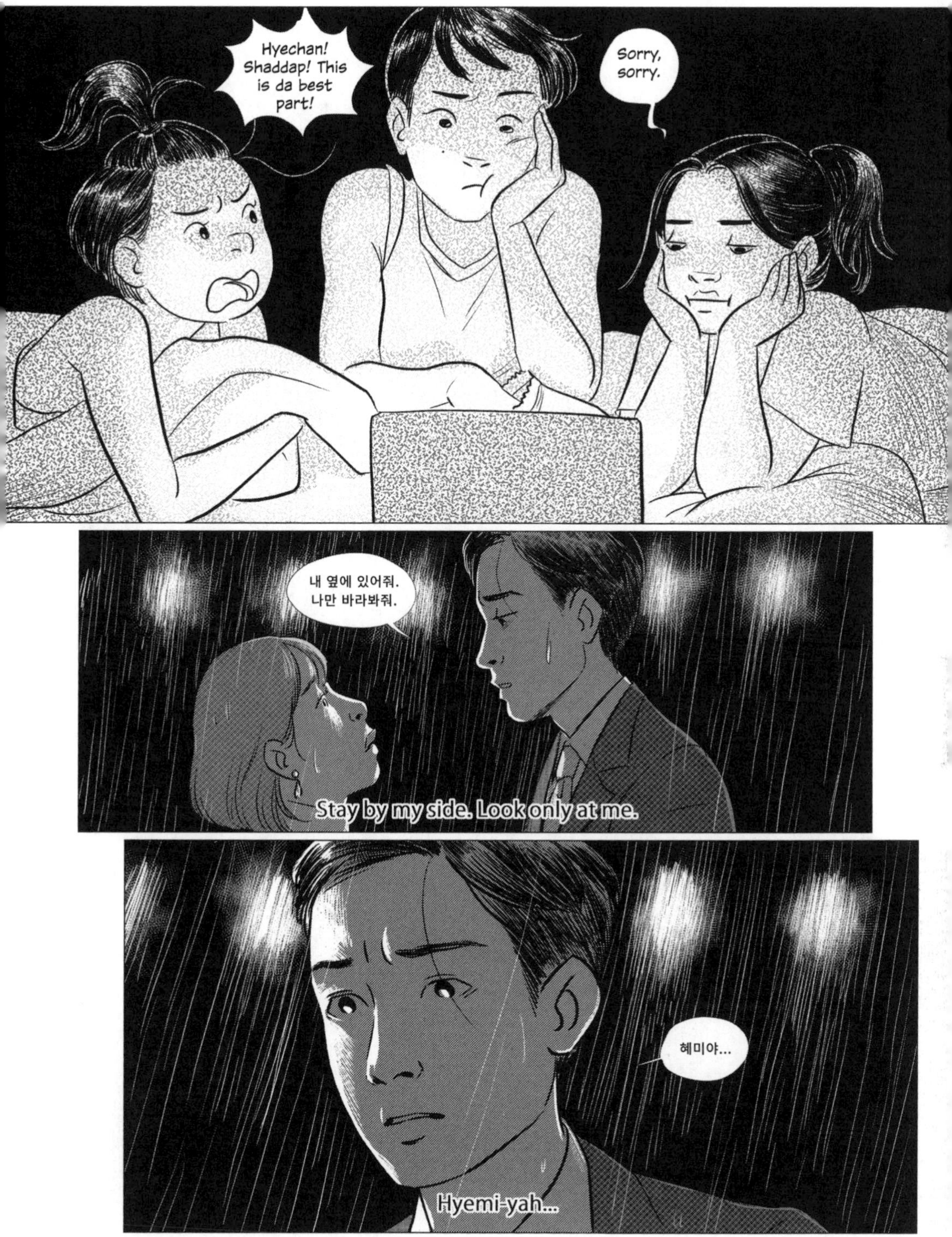
Hyechan! Shaddap! This is da best part!
Sorry, sorry.
내 옆에 있어줘.
나만 바라봐줘.
Stay by my side. Look only at me.
혜미야...
Hyemi-yah...

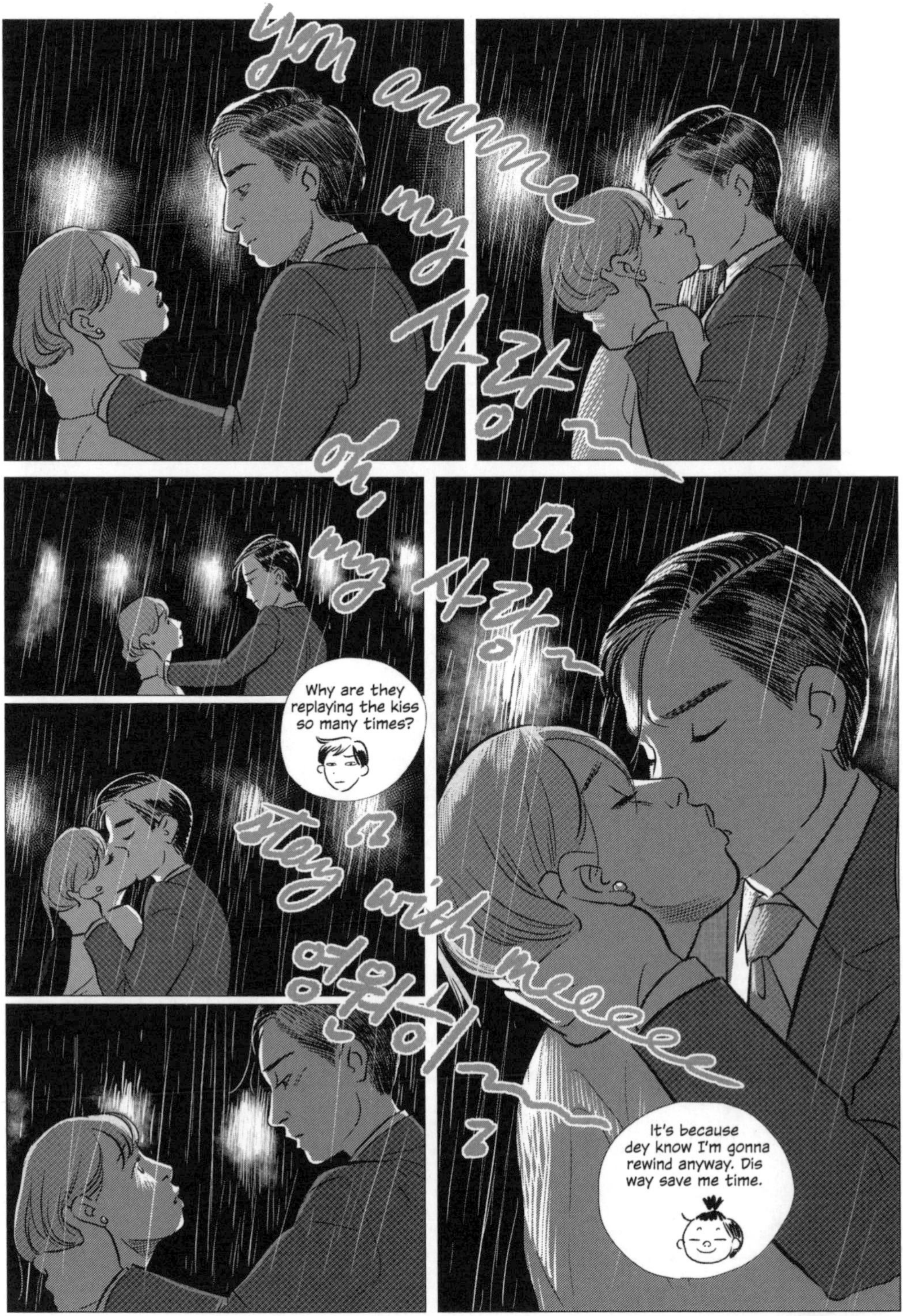

you arrrre my 사랑~
oh, my 사랑~
Why are they replaying the kiss so many times?
stay with meeeee
영원히~~
It's because dey know I'm gonna rewind anyway. Dis way save me time.

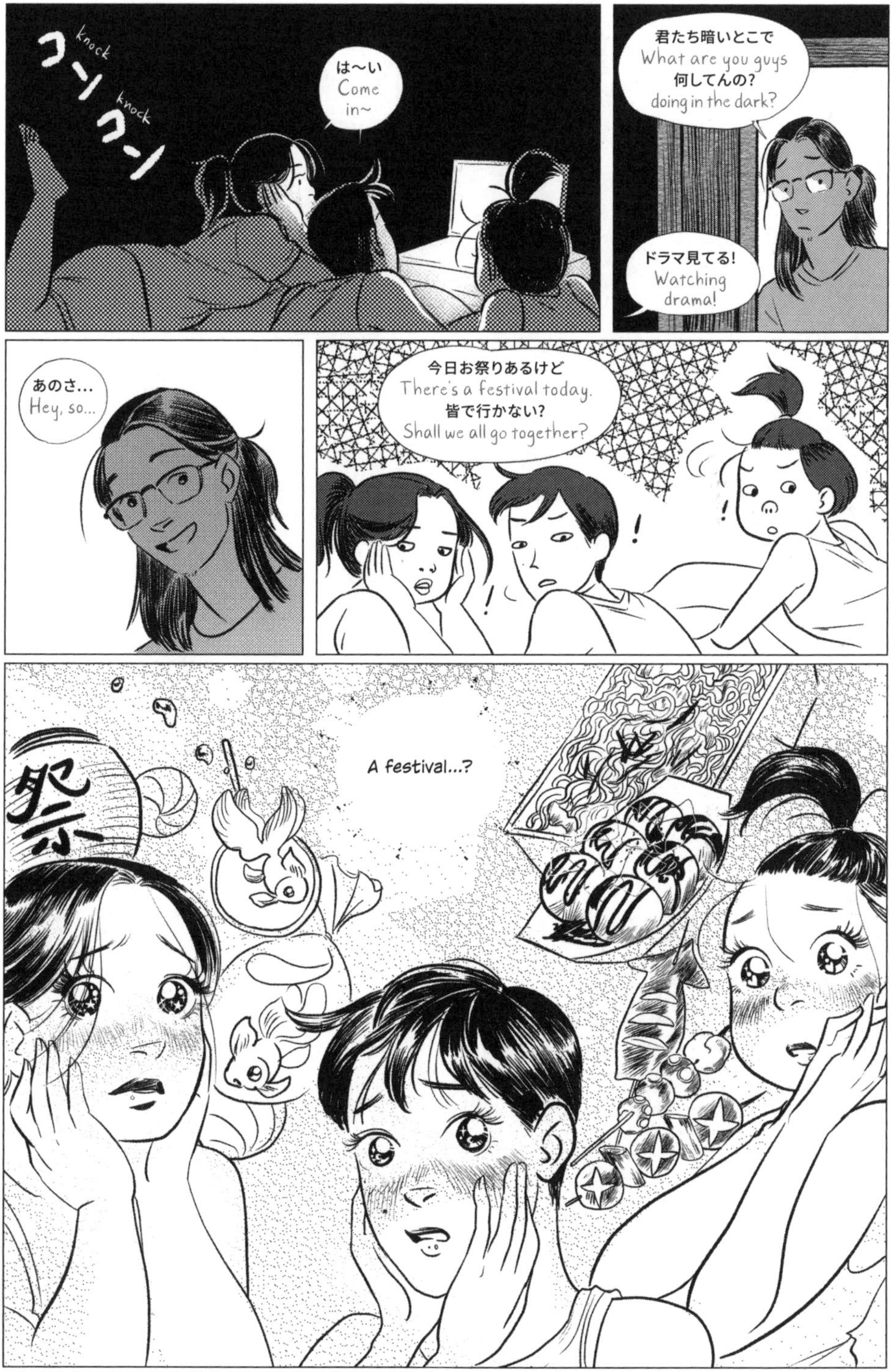

コンコン
knock knock
は～い
Come in~
君たち暗いとこで
What are you guys
何してんの?
doing in the dark?
ドラマ見てる!
Watching drama!
あのさ…
Hey, so…
今日お祭りあるけど
There's a festival today.
皆で行かない?
Shall we all go together?
祭
A festival…?

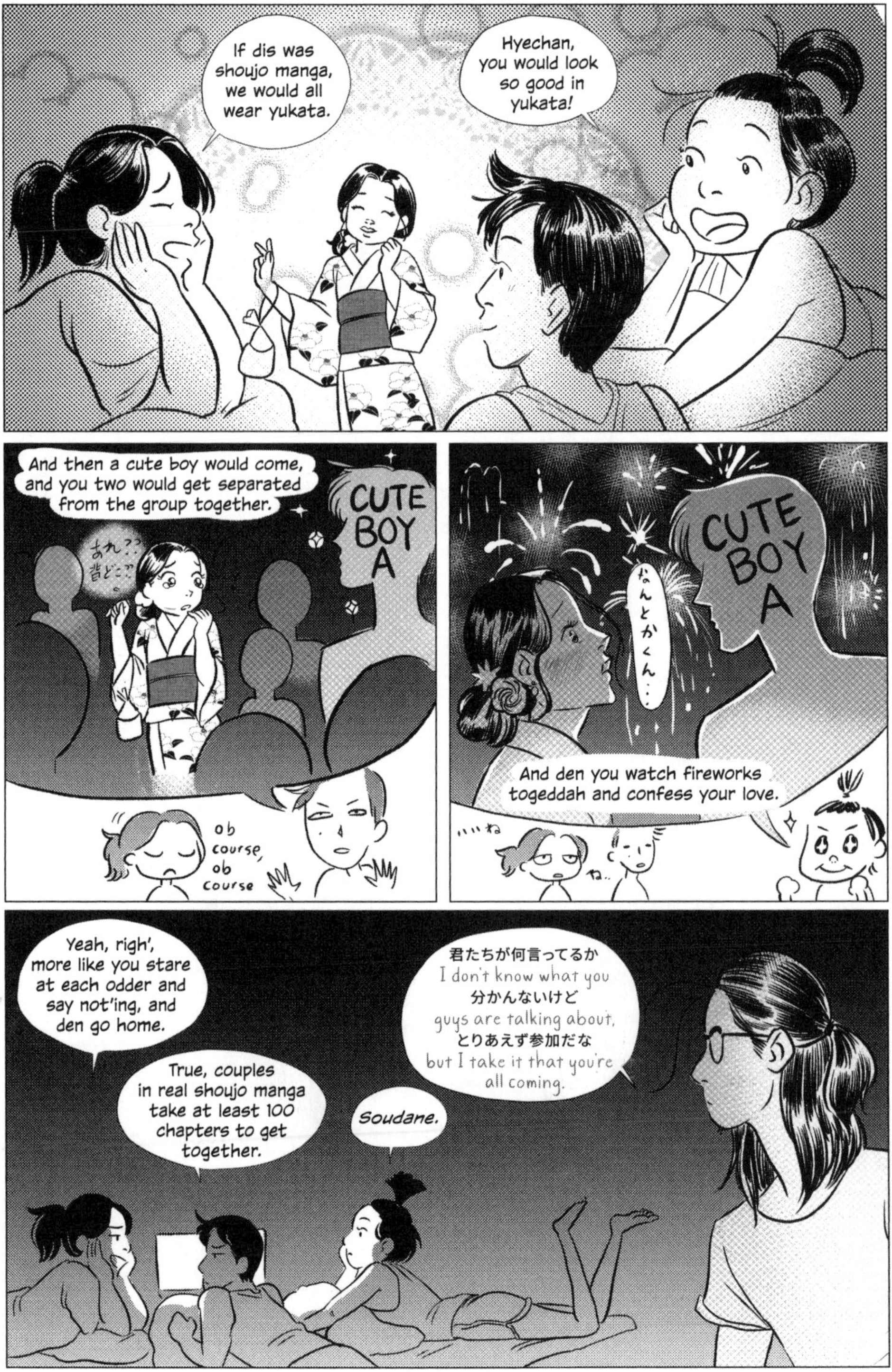
If dis was shoujo manga, we would all wear yukata.
Hyechan, you would look so good in yukata!
And then a cute boy would come, and you two would get separated from the group together.
CUTE BOY A
あれ??
皆どこ??
ob course, ob course
CUTE BOY A
なんとかくん…
And den you watch fireworks togeddah and confess your love.
いいね
ね..
Yeah, righ', more like you stare at each odder and say not'ing, and den go home.
True, couples in real shoujo manga take at least 100 chapters to get together.
Soudane.
君たちが何言ってるか
I don't know what you
分かんないけど
guys are talking about,
とりあえず参加だな
but I take it that you're all coming.

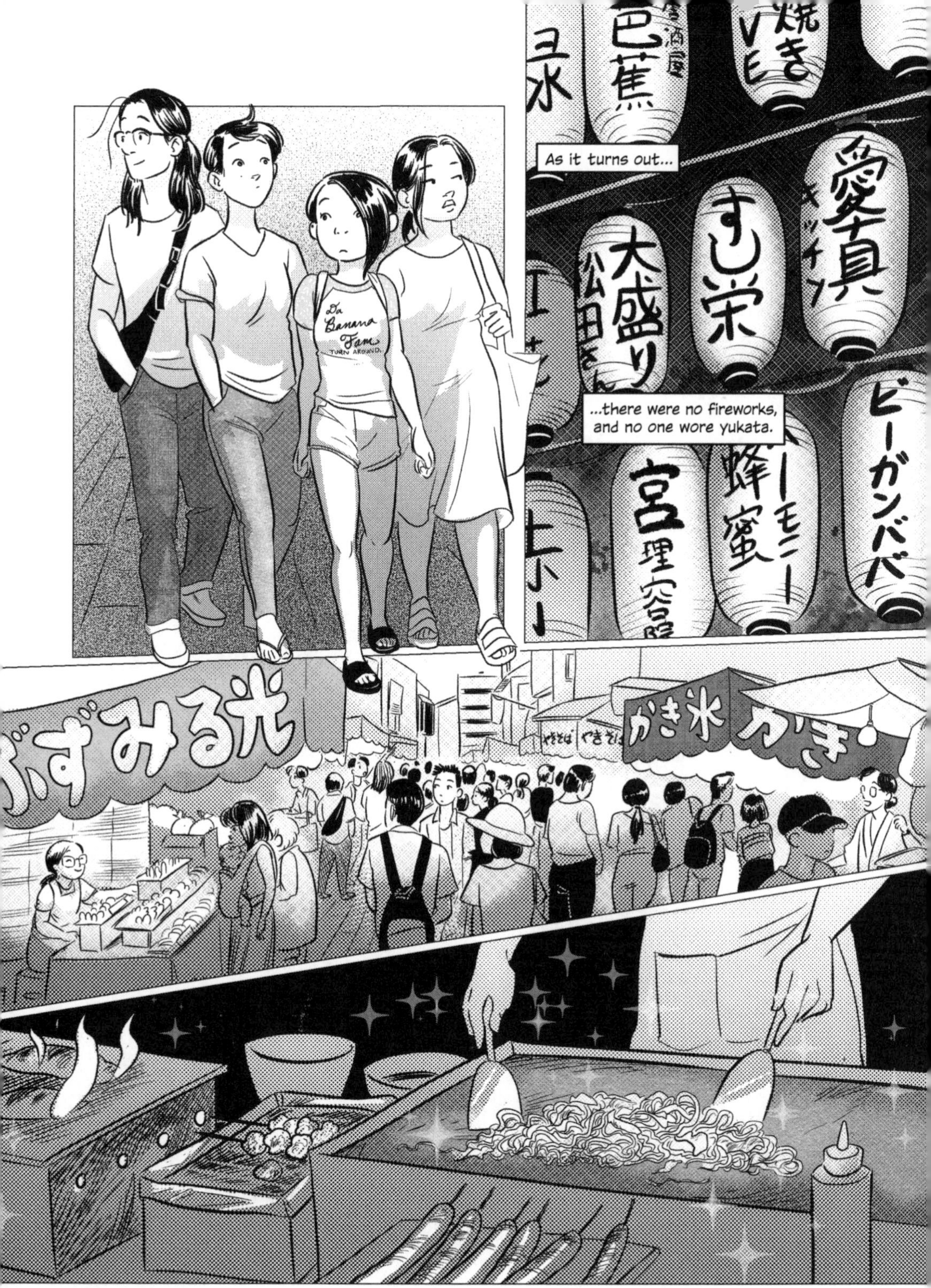

Da Banana Fam
TURN AROUND.
As it turns out...
...there were no fireworks, and no one wore yukata.
すし栄
大盛り
ビーガンババ
蜂蜜
かき氷

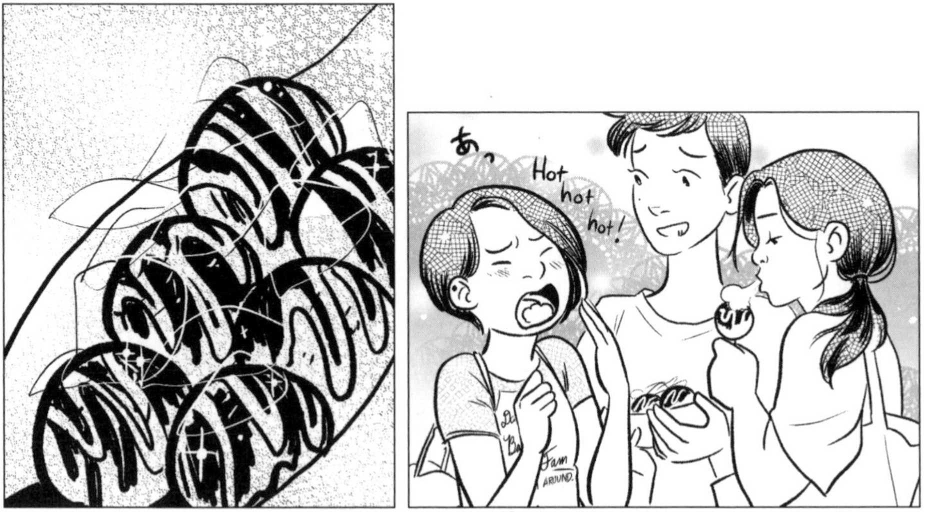

あっ
Hot hot hot!

Instead, we just stuffed our faces.

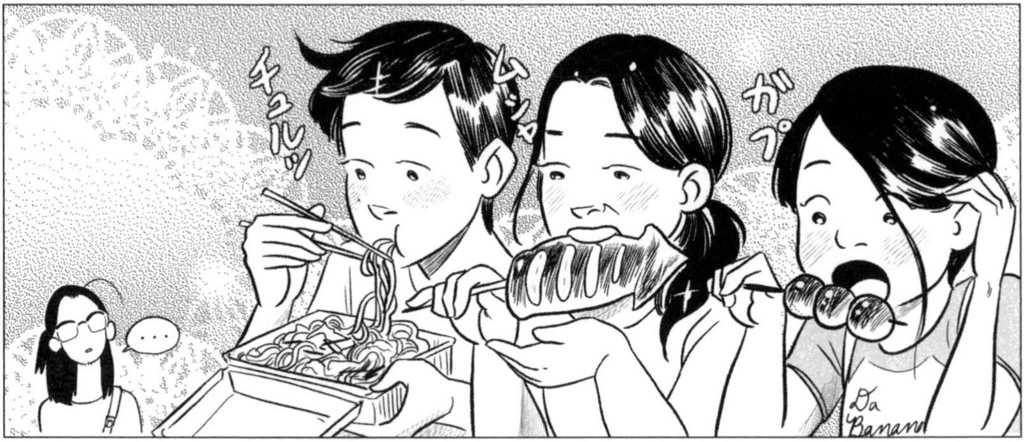

チュルッ
ムシャ
ガブ
...
Da Banana

Which was just as good, if not better, than fireworks with a cute boy.

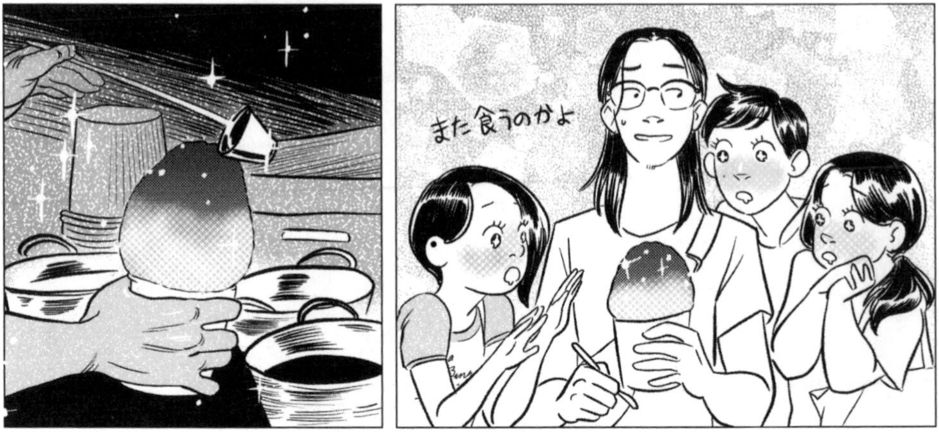

また食うのかよ

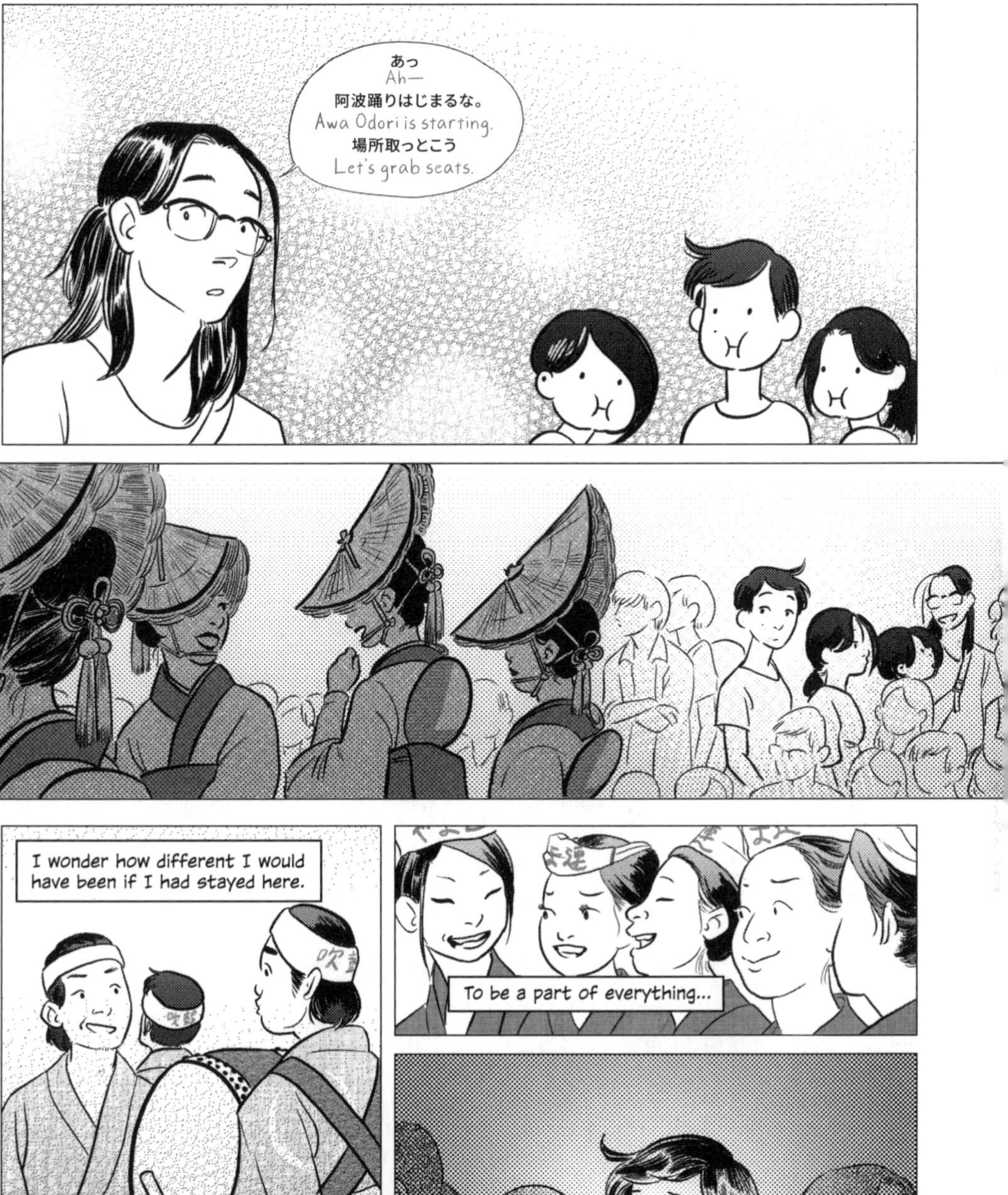
あっ
Ah—
阿波踊りはじまるな。
Awa Odori is starting.
場所取っとこう
Let's grab seats.
I wonder how different I would have been if I had stayed here.
To be a part of everything...
...not just a bystander.

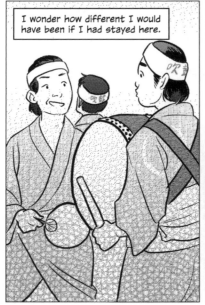

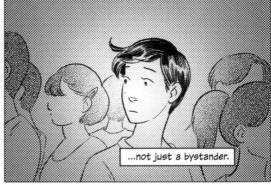

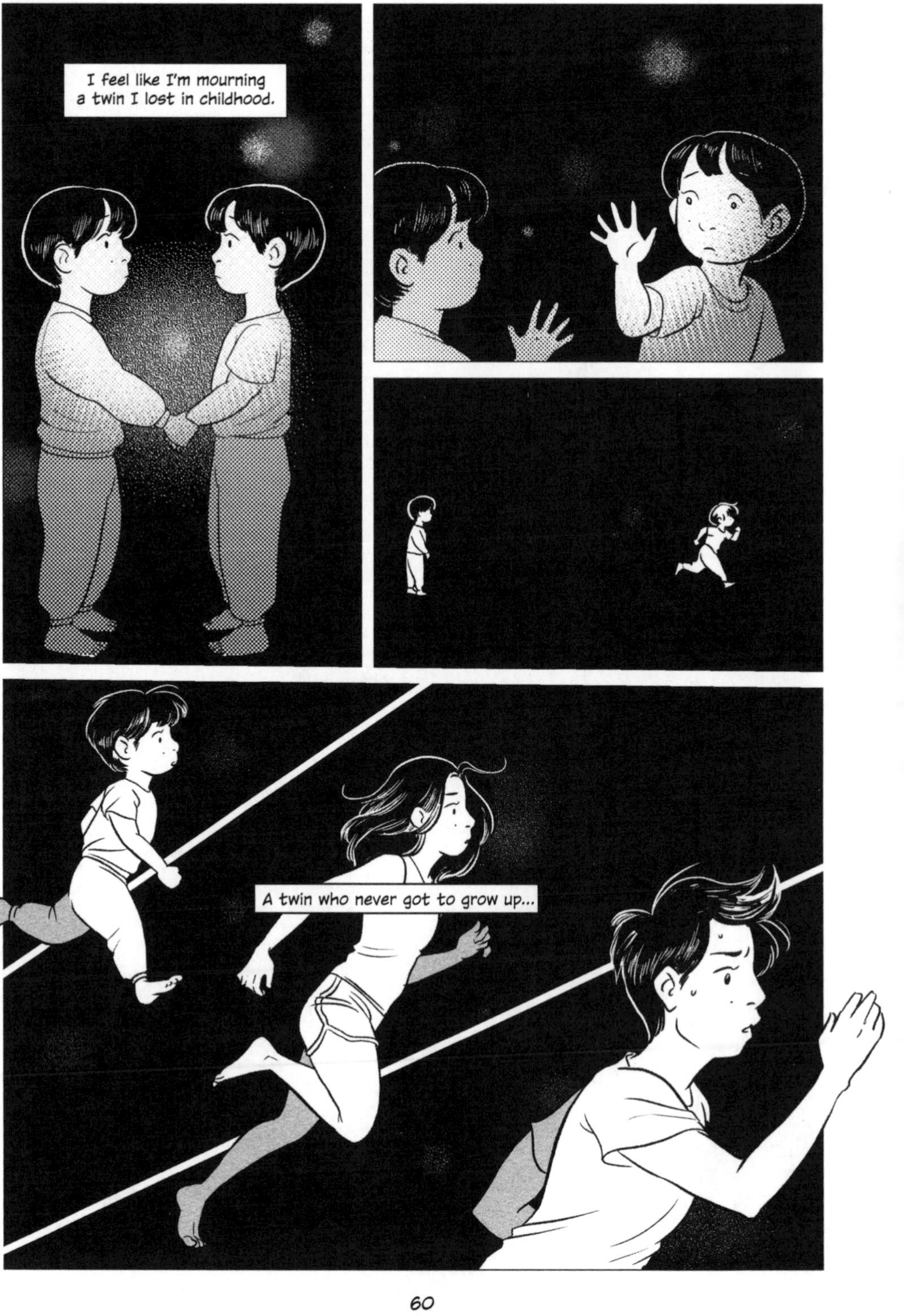
I feel like I'm mourning a twin I lost in childhood.
A twin who never got to grow up...

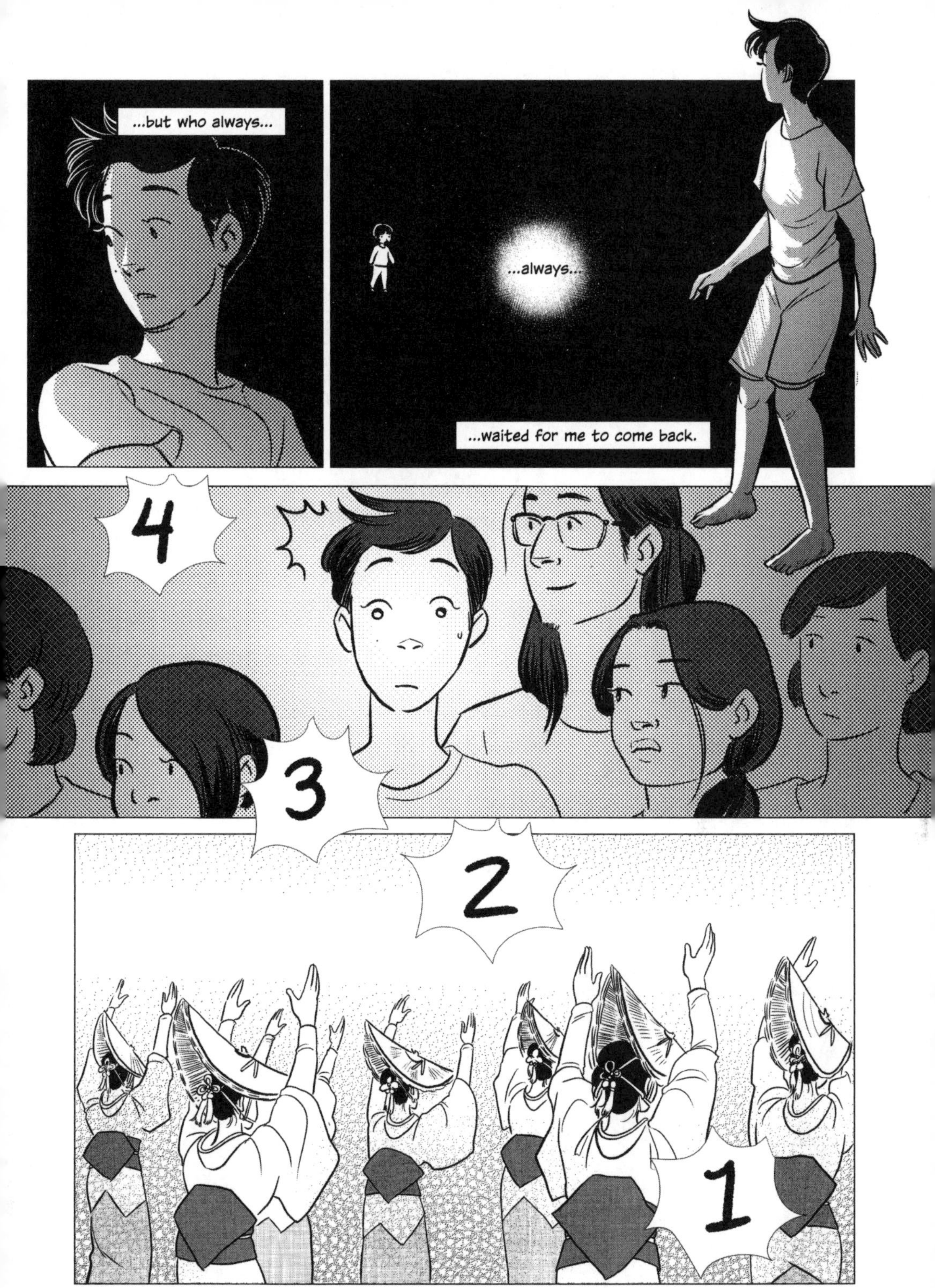
...but who always...
...always...
...waited for me to come back.
4
3
2
1

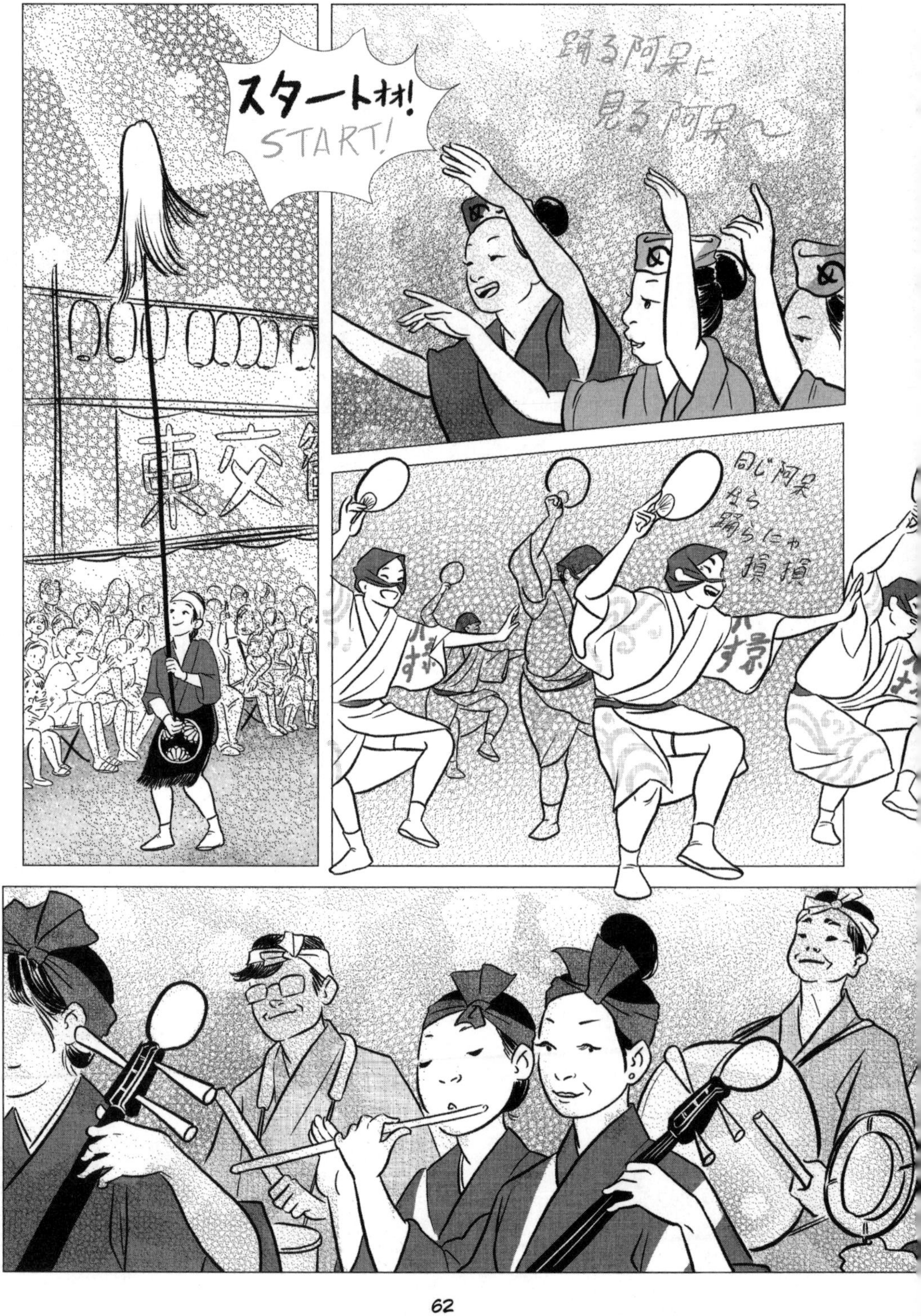
スタートォォ!
START!
踊る阿呆に
見る阿呆〜
同じ阿呆なら踊らにゃ損損

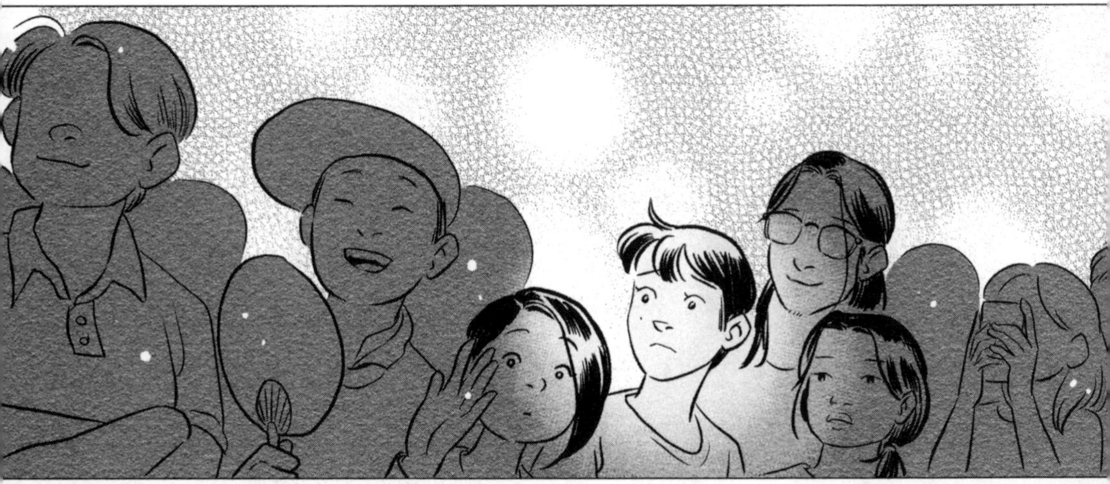

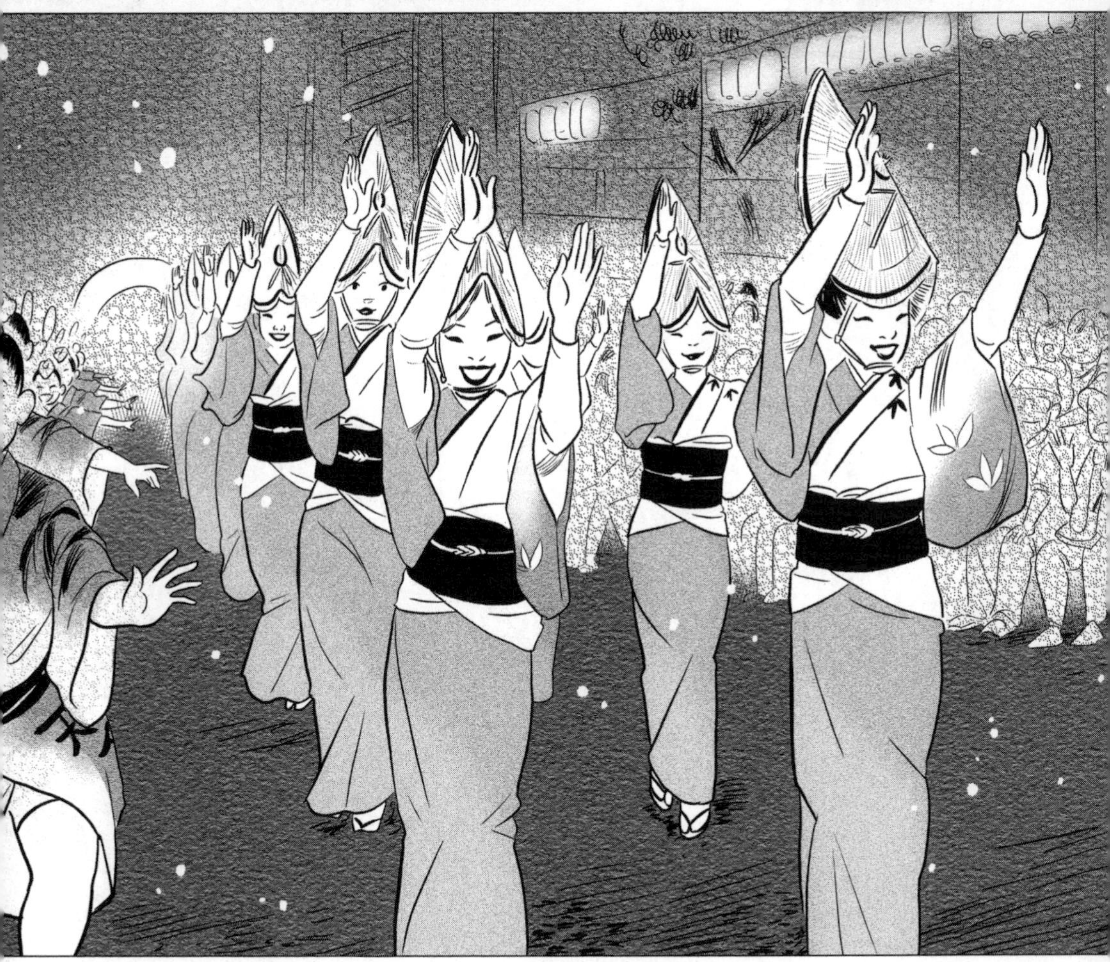

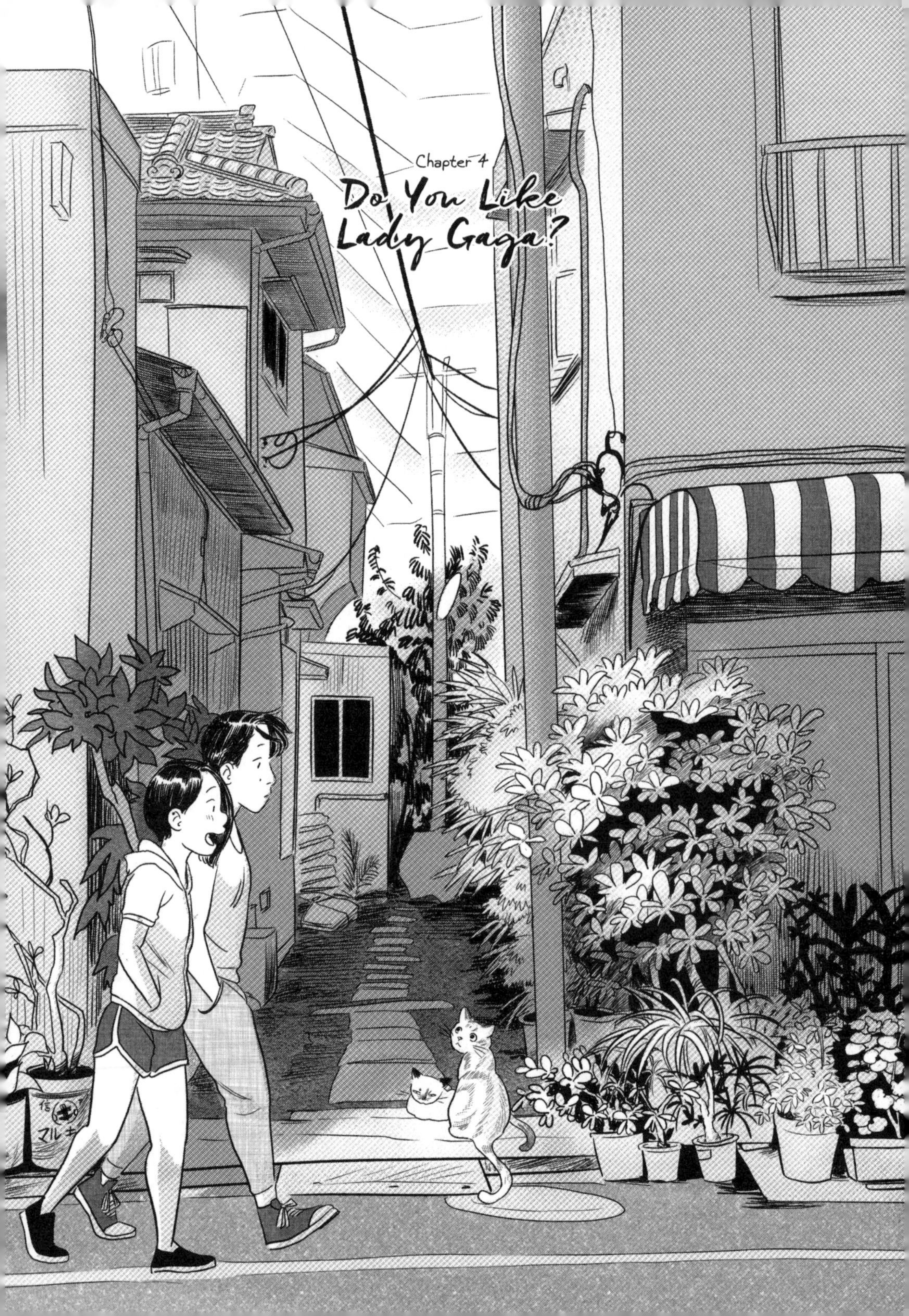
Chapter 4
Do You Like Lady Gaga?

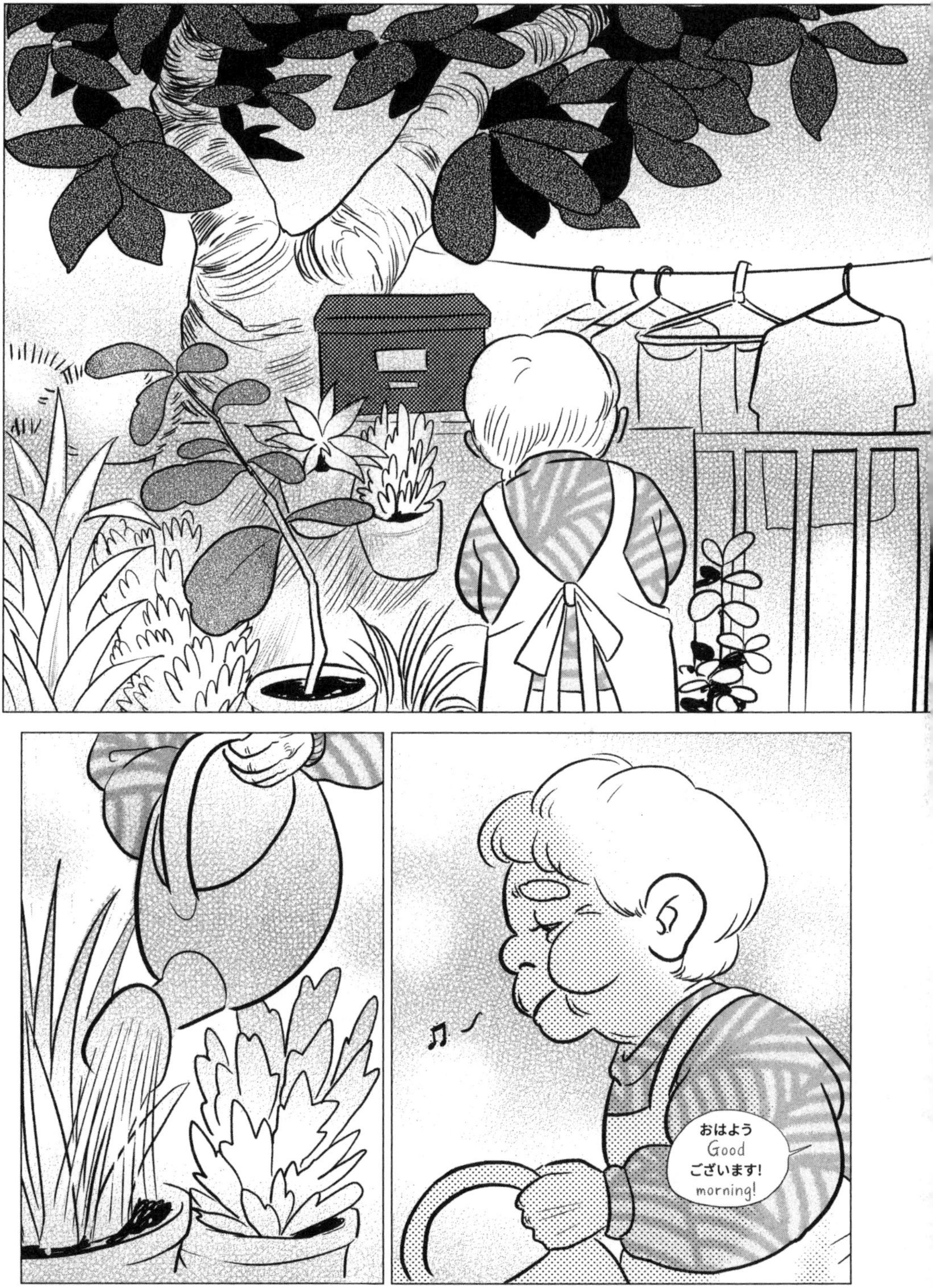
♫ ~
おはよう Good ございます! morning!

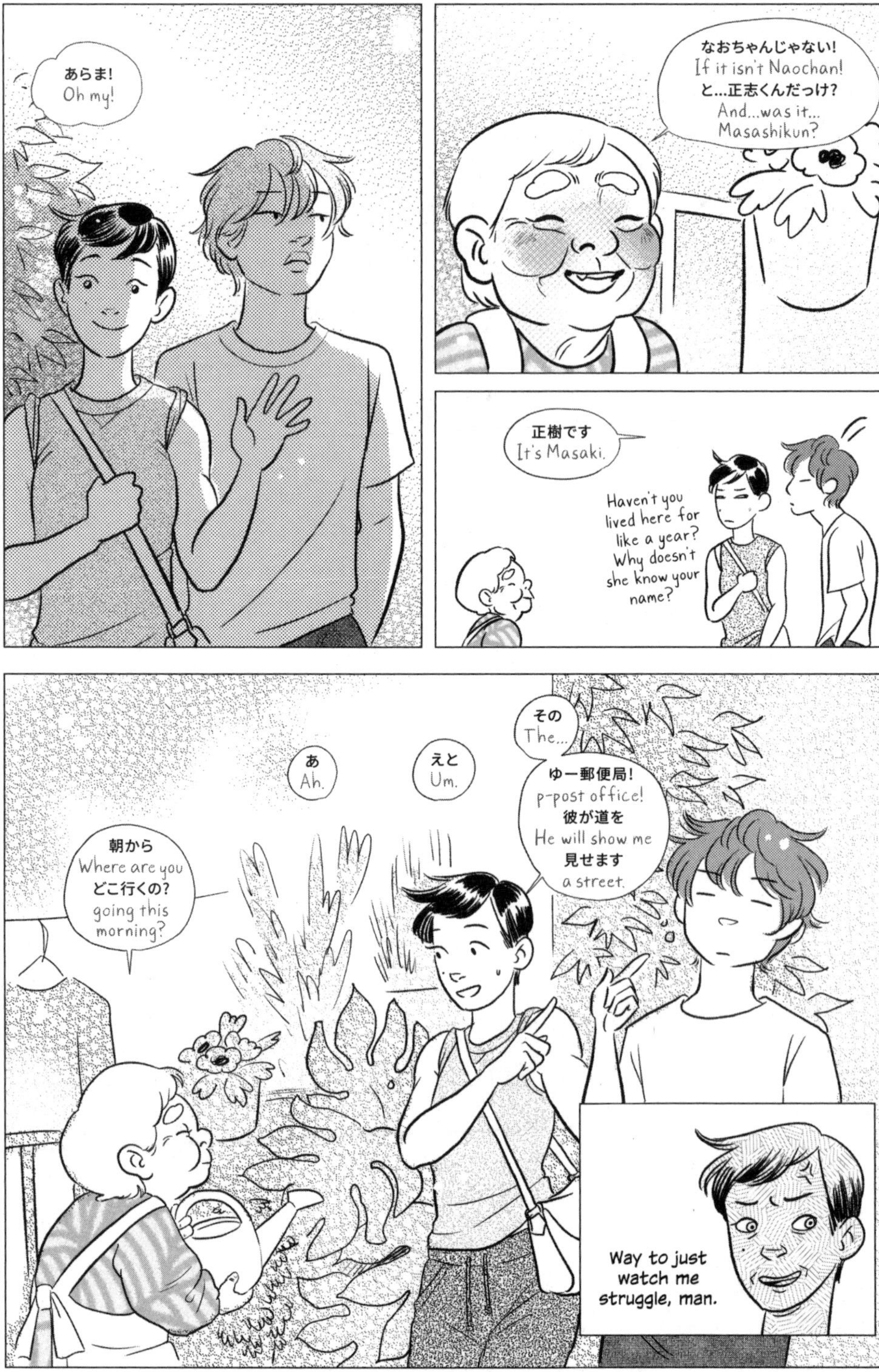
あらま!
Oh my!
なおちゃんじゃない!
If it isn't Naochan!
と...正志くんだっけ?
And...was it... Masashikun?
正樹です
It's Masaki.
Haven't you lived here for like a year? Why doesn't she know your name?
朝から
Where are you
どこ行くの?
going this morning?
あ
Ah.
えと
Um.
その
The...
ゆー郵便局!
p-post office!
彼が道を
He will show me
見せます
a street.
Way to just watch me struggle, man.

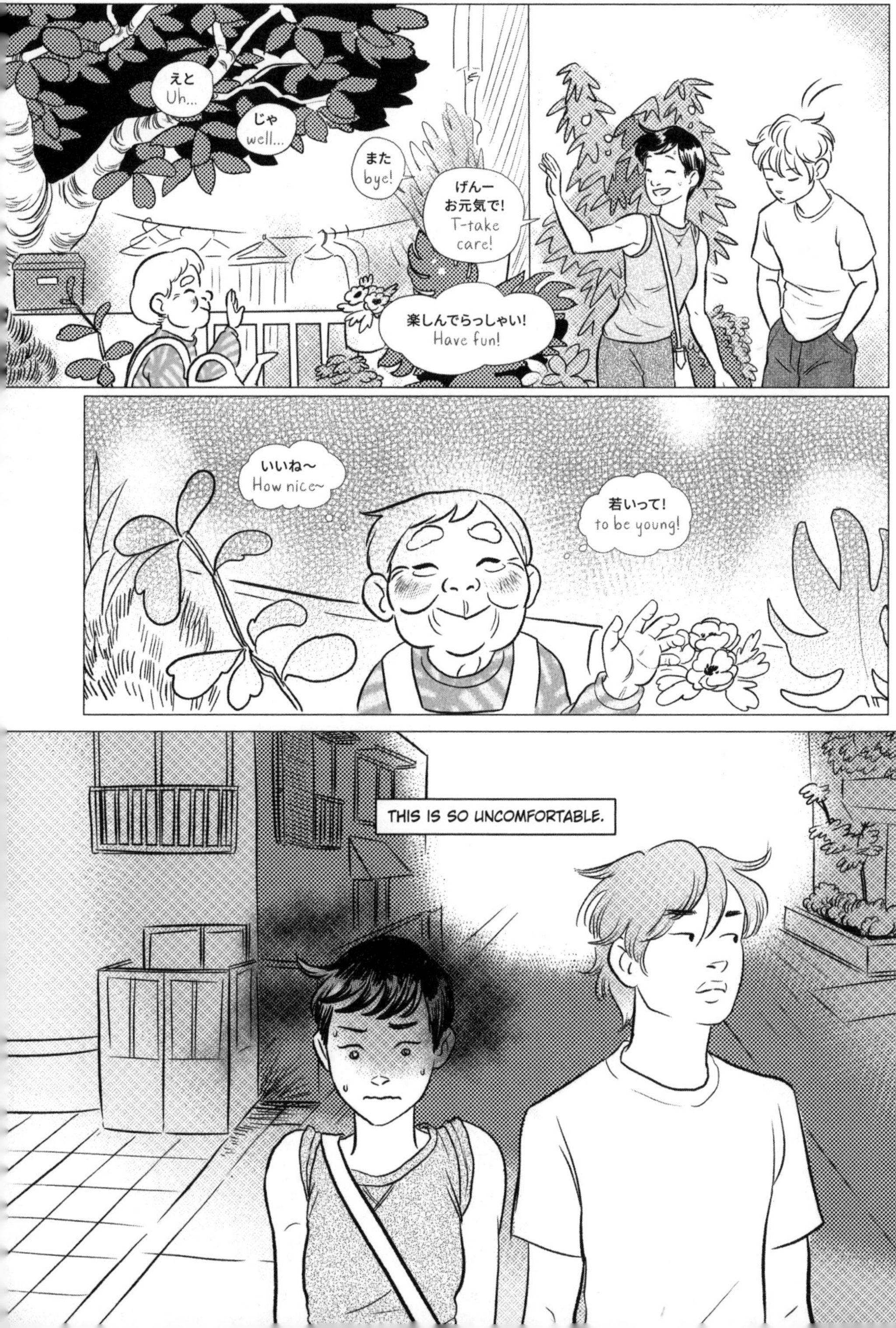

えと
Uh...
じゃ
well...
また
bye!
げんー
お元気で!
T-take
care!
楽しんでらっしゃい!
Have fun!
いいね~
How nice~
若いって!
to be young!
THIS IS SO UNCOMFORTABLE.

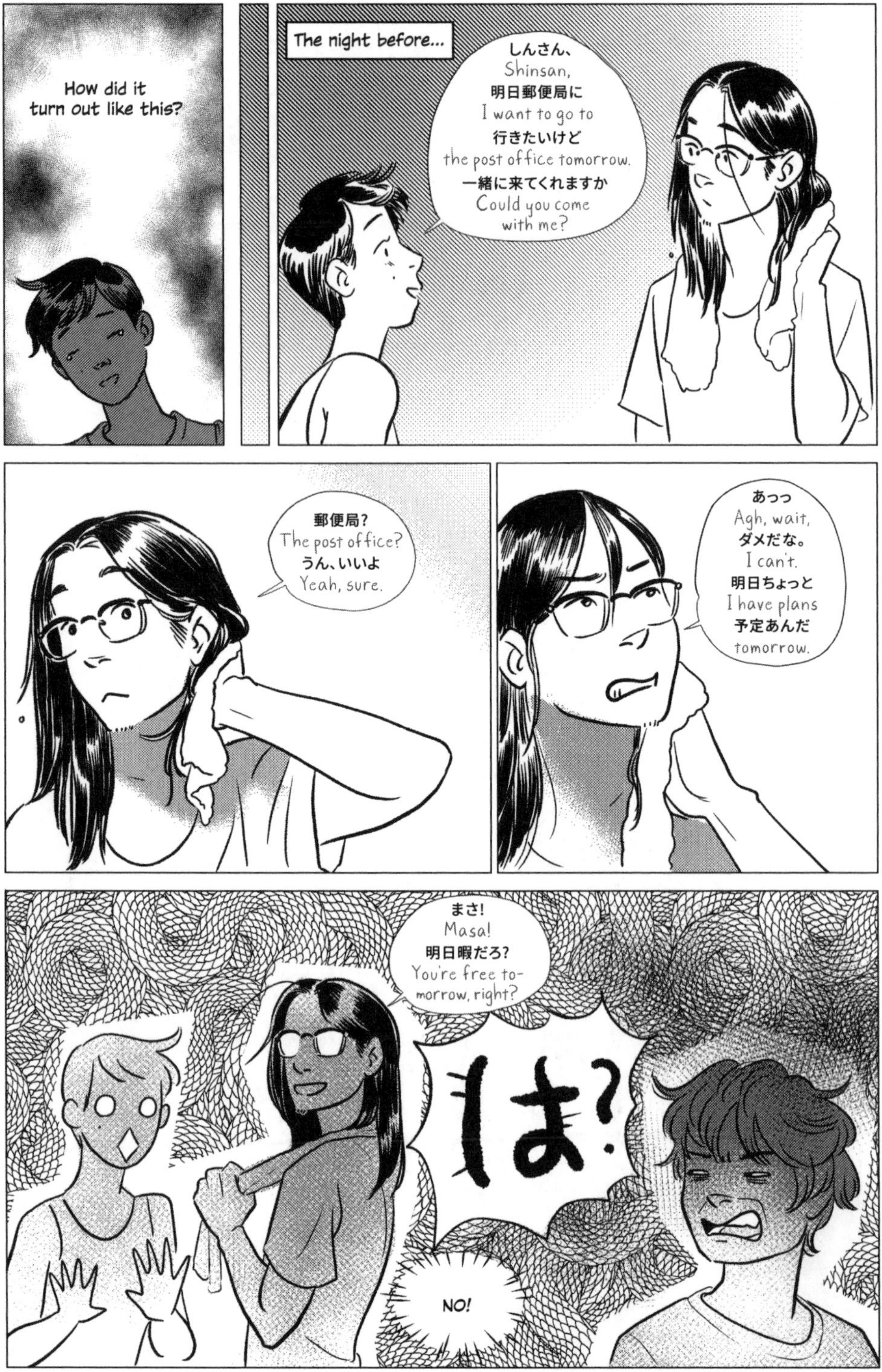
How did it turn out like this?
The night before...
しんさん、 Shinsan, 明日郵便局に I want to go to 行きたいけど the post office tomorrow. 一緒に来てくれますか Could you come with me?
郵便局? The post office? うん、いいよ Yeah, sure.
あっっ Agh, wait, ダメだな。 I can't. 明日ちょっと I have plans 予定あんだ tomorrow.
まさ! Masa! 明日暇だろ? You're free to-morrow, right?
は?
NO!

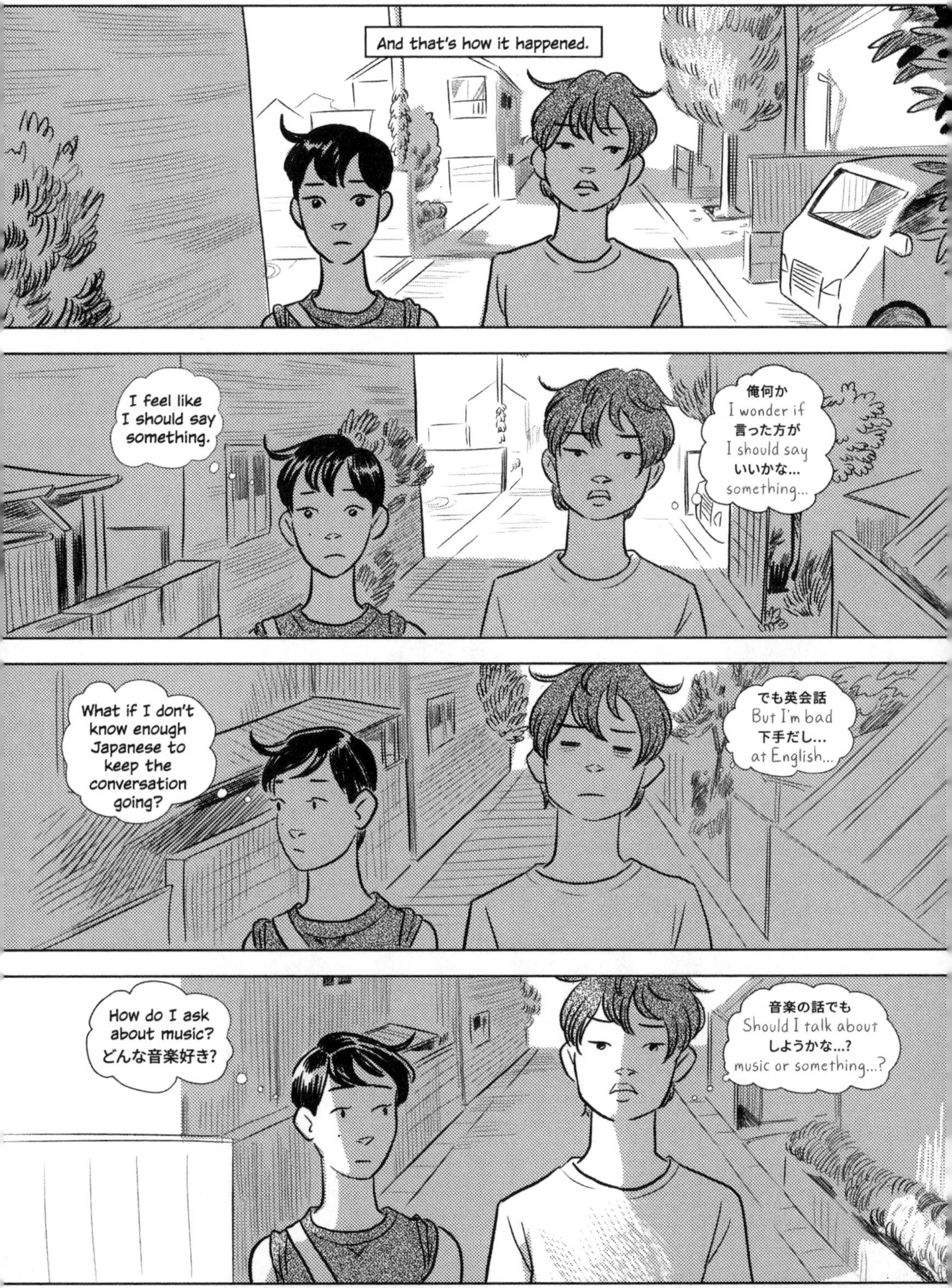
And that's how it happened.
I feel like I should say something.
俺何か I wonder if 言った方が I should say いいかな... something...
What if I don't know enough Japanese to keep the conversation going?
でも英会話 But I'm bad 下手だし... at English...
How do I ask about music? どんな音楽好き?
音楽の話でも Should I talk about しようかな...? music or something...?

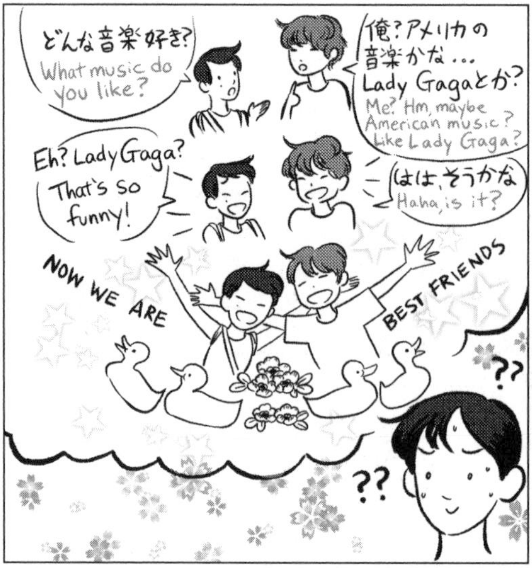
どんな音楽好き?
What music do you like?
俺?アメリカの音楽かな…
Lady Gagaとか?
Me? Hm, maybe American music? Like Lady Gaga?
Eh? Lady Gaga? That's so funny!
ははそうかな
Haha, is it?
NOW WE ARE BEST FRIENDS
??
??

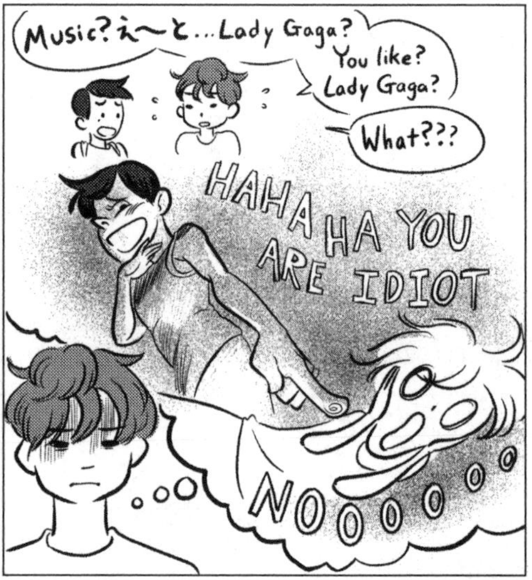
Music?え〜と…Lady Gaga?
You like? Lady Gaga?
What???
HAHA HA YOU ARE IDIOT
NOOOOOOO

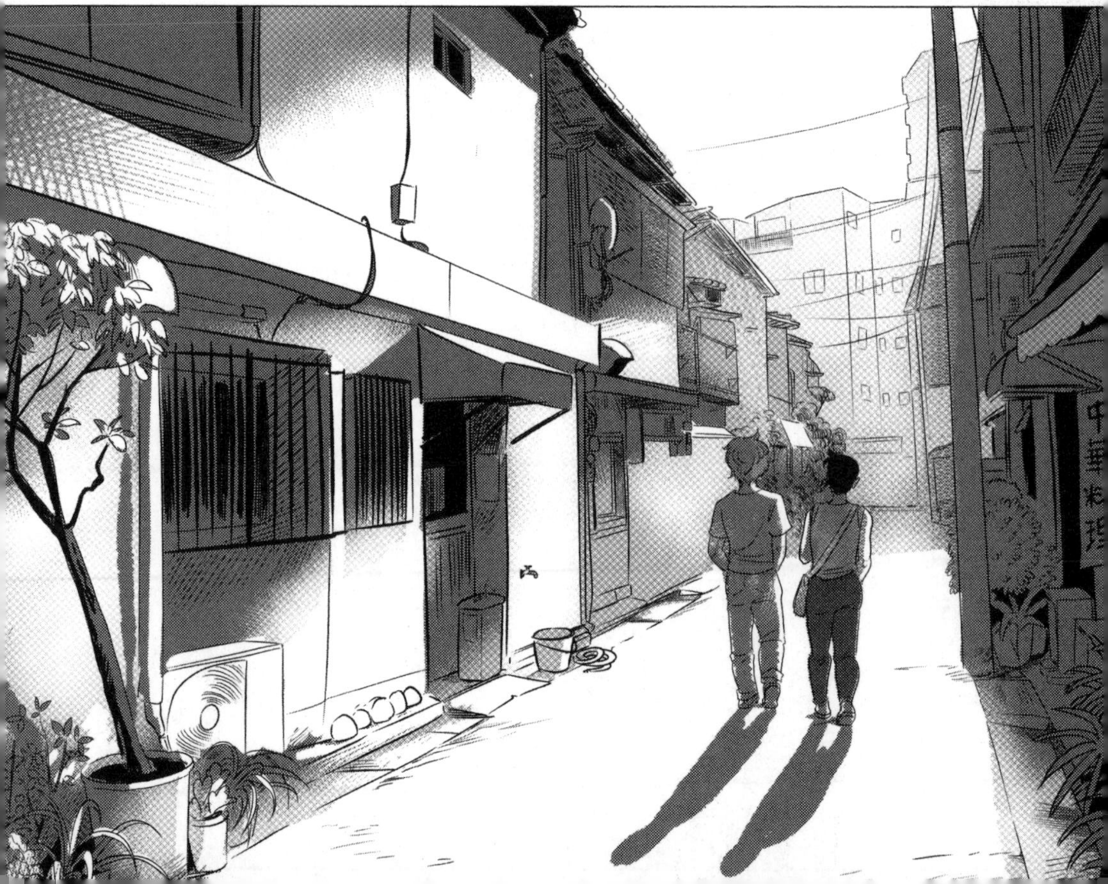

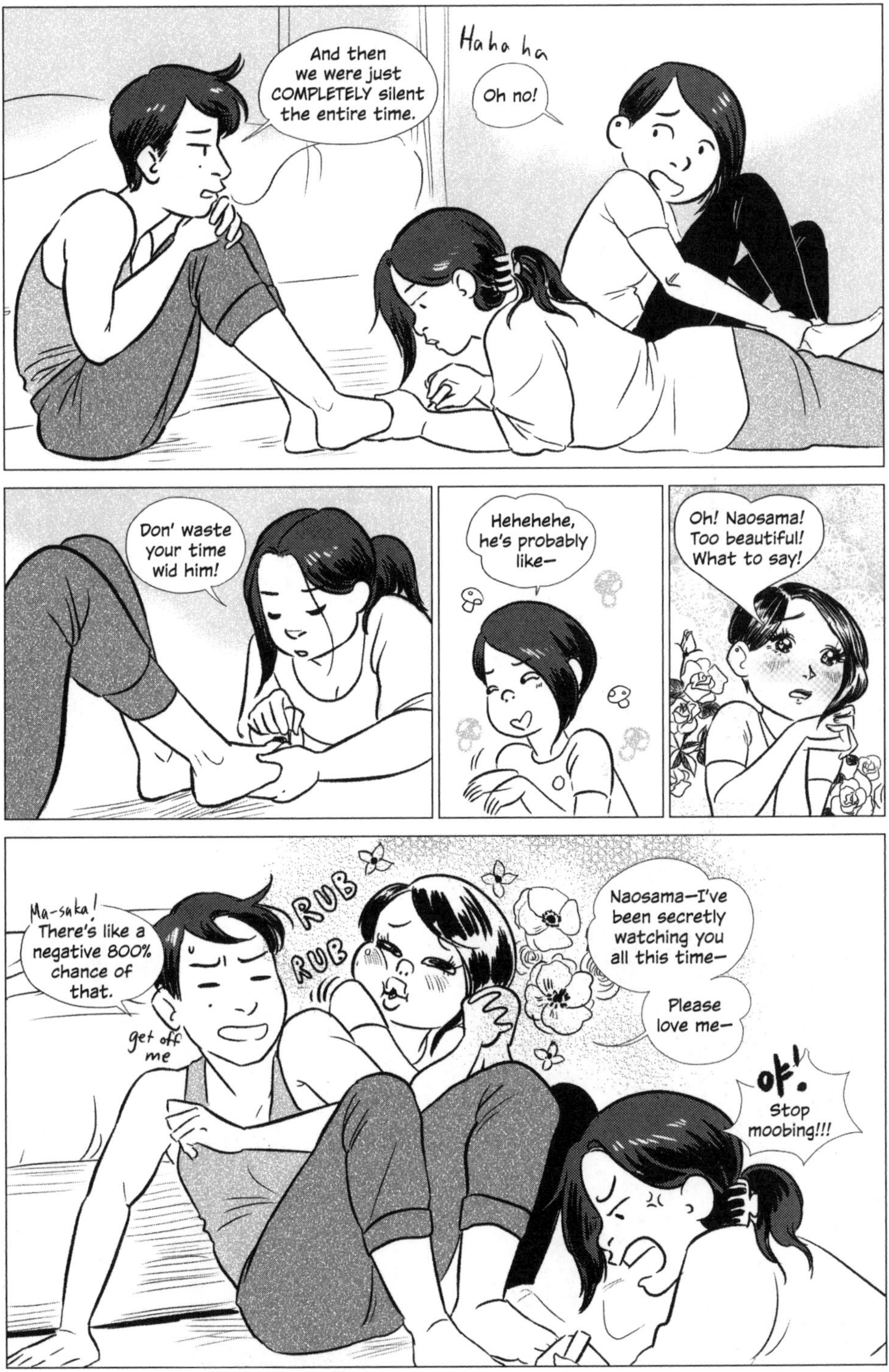
And then we were just COMPLETELY silent the entire time.
Hahaha
Oh no!
Don' waste your time wid him!
Hehehehe, he's probably like—
Oh! Naosama! Too beautiful! What to say!
Ma-saka! There's like a negative 800% chance of that.
get off me
RUB RUB
Naosama—I've been secretly watching you all this time—
Please love me—
야!
Stop moobing!!!

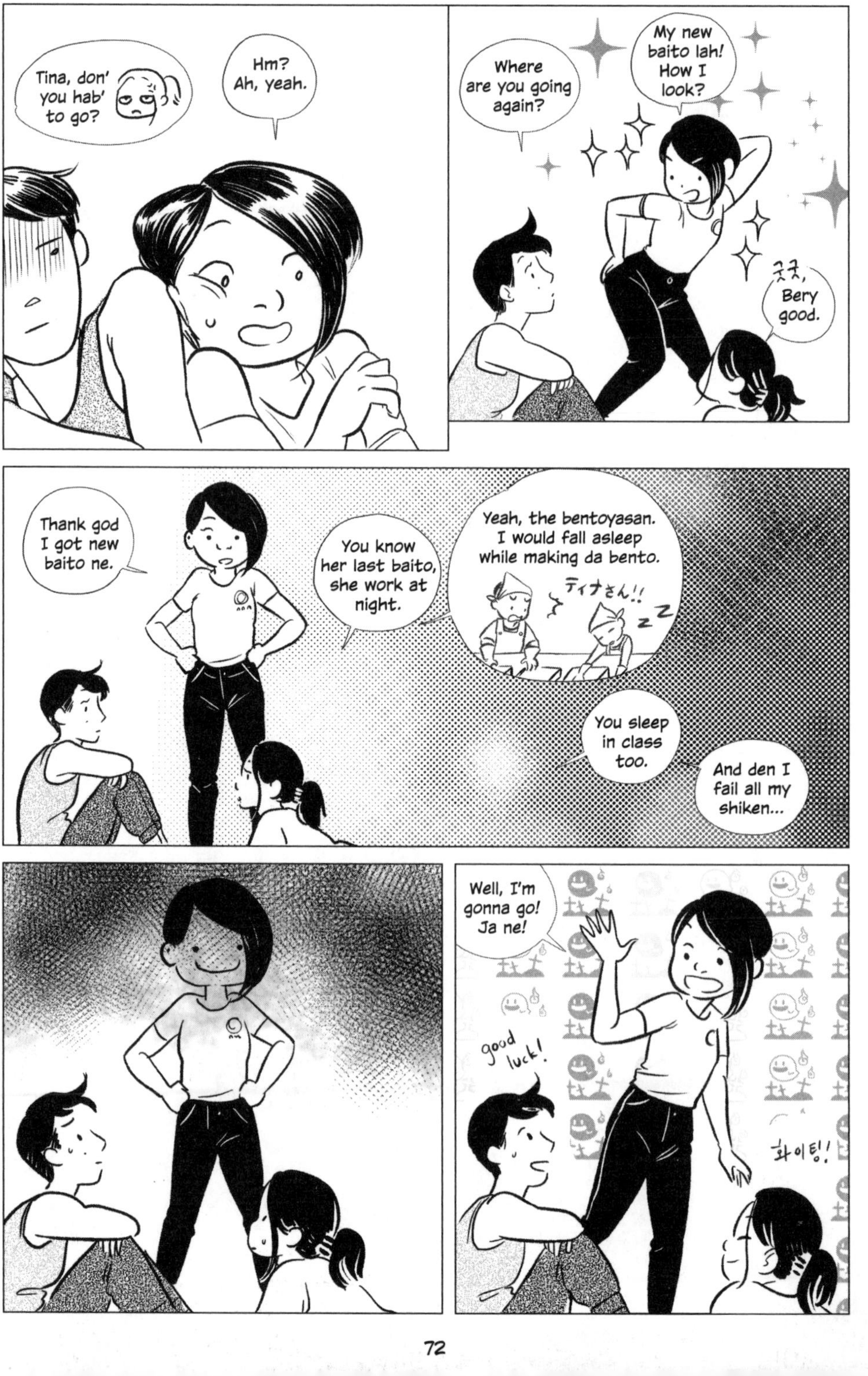

Tina, don' you hab' to go?
Hm? Ah, yeah.
Where are you going again?
My new baito lah! How I look?
굿굿, Bery good.
Thank god I got new baito ne.
You know her last baito, she work at night.
Yeah, the bentoyasan. I would fall asleep while making da bento.
ティナさん!!
Z Z
You sleep in class too.
And den I fail all my shiken...
Well, I'm gonna go! Ja ne!
good luck!
화이팅!!

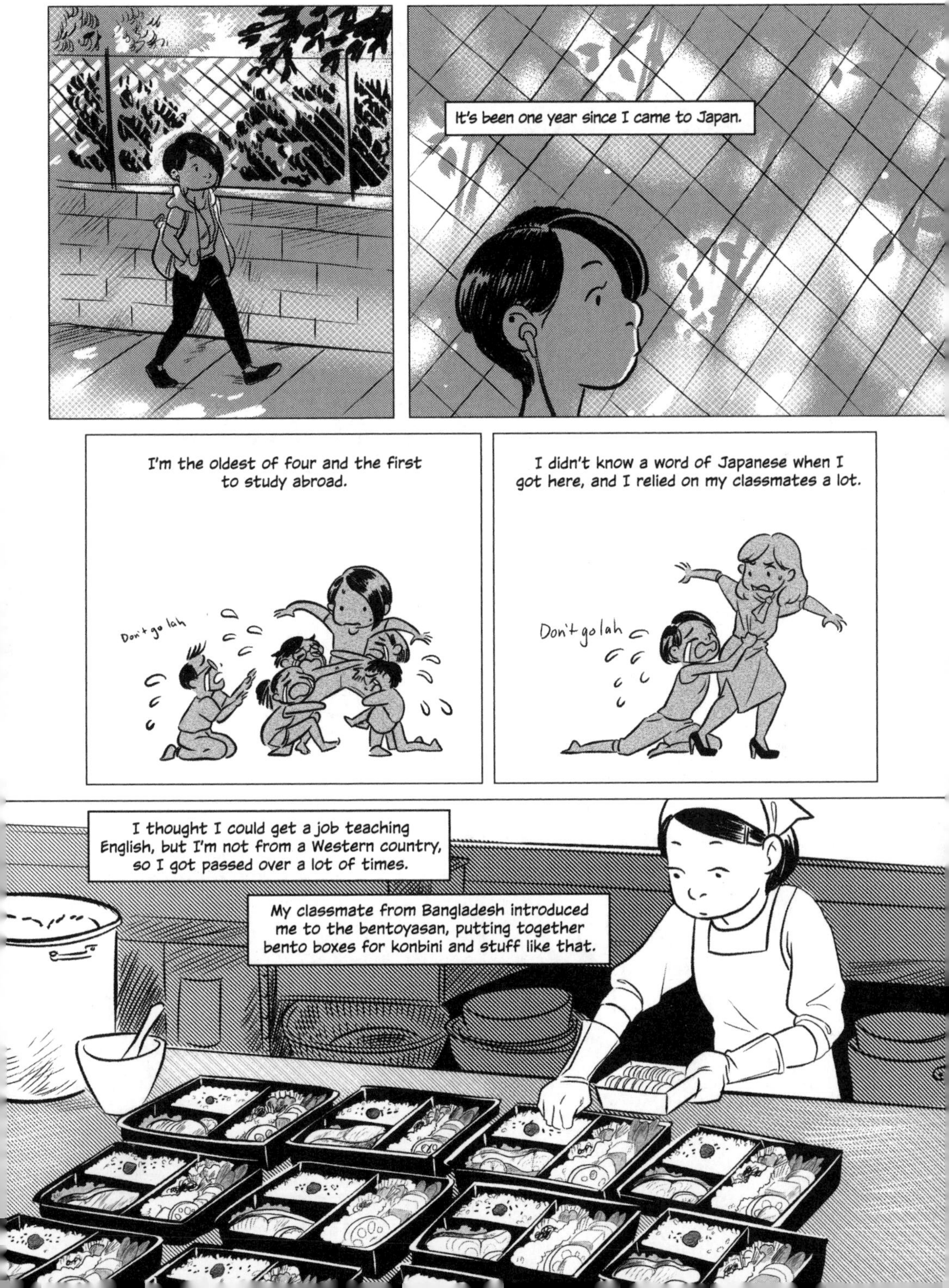
It's been one year since I came to Japan.
I'm the oldest of four and the first to study abroad.
Don't go lah
I didn't know a word of Japanese when I got here, and I relied on my classmates a lot.
Don't go lah
I thought I could get a job teaching English, but I'm not from a Western country, so I got passed over a lot of times.
My classmate from Bangladesh introduced me to the bentoyasan, putting together bento boxes for konbini and stuff like that.

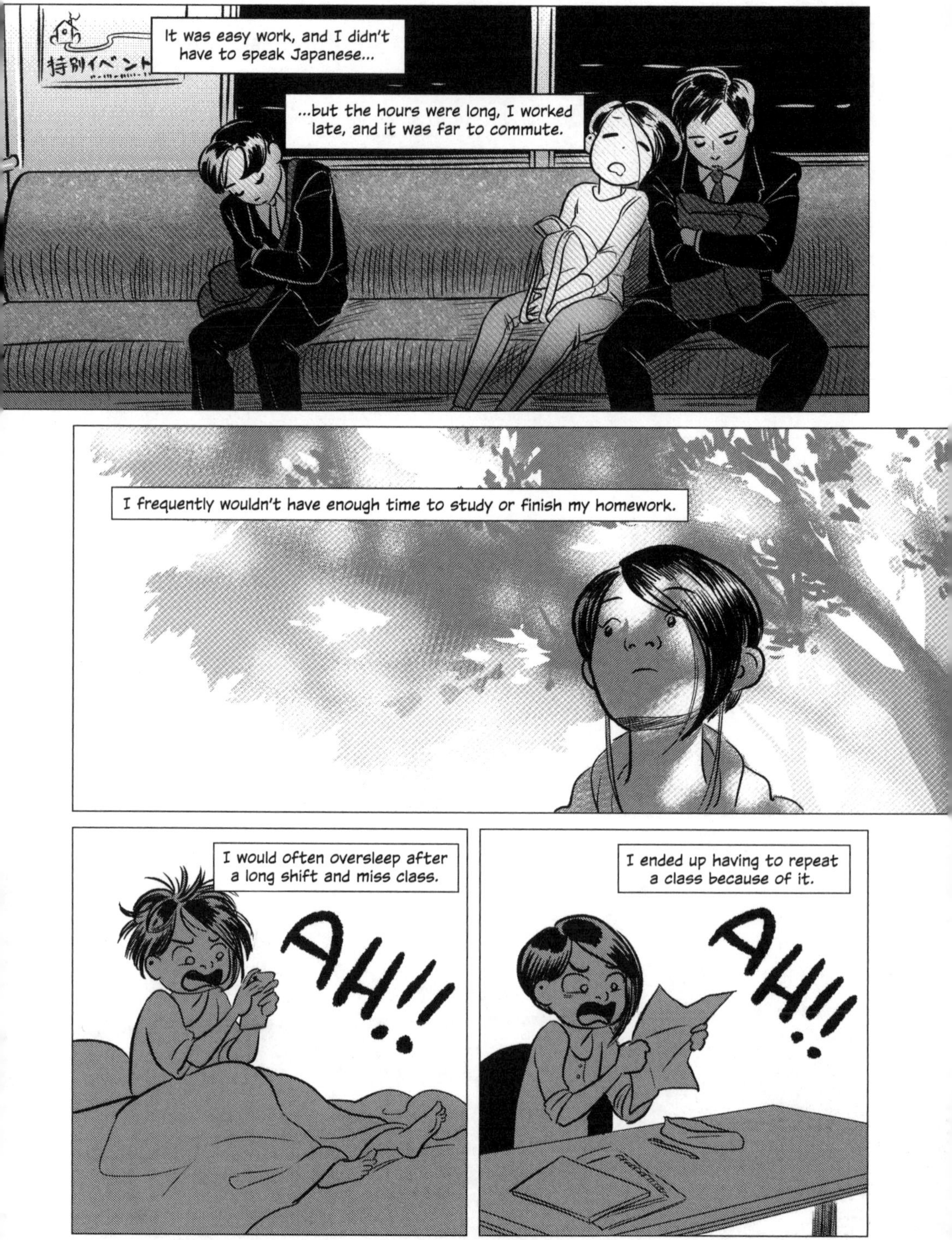

It was easy work, and I didn't have to speak Japanese...
...but the hours were long, I worked late, and it was far to commute.
I frequently wouldn't have enough time to study or finish my homework.
I would often oversleep after a long shift and miss class.
AH!!
I ended up having to repeat a class because of it.
AH!!

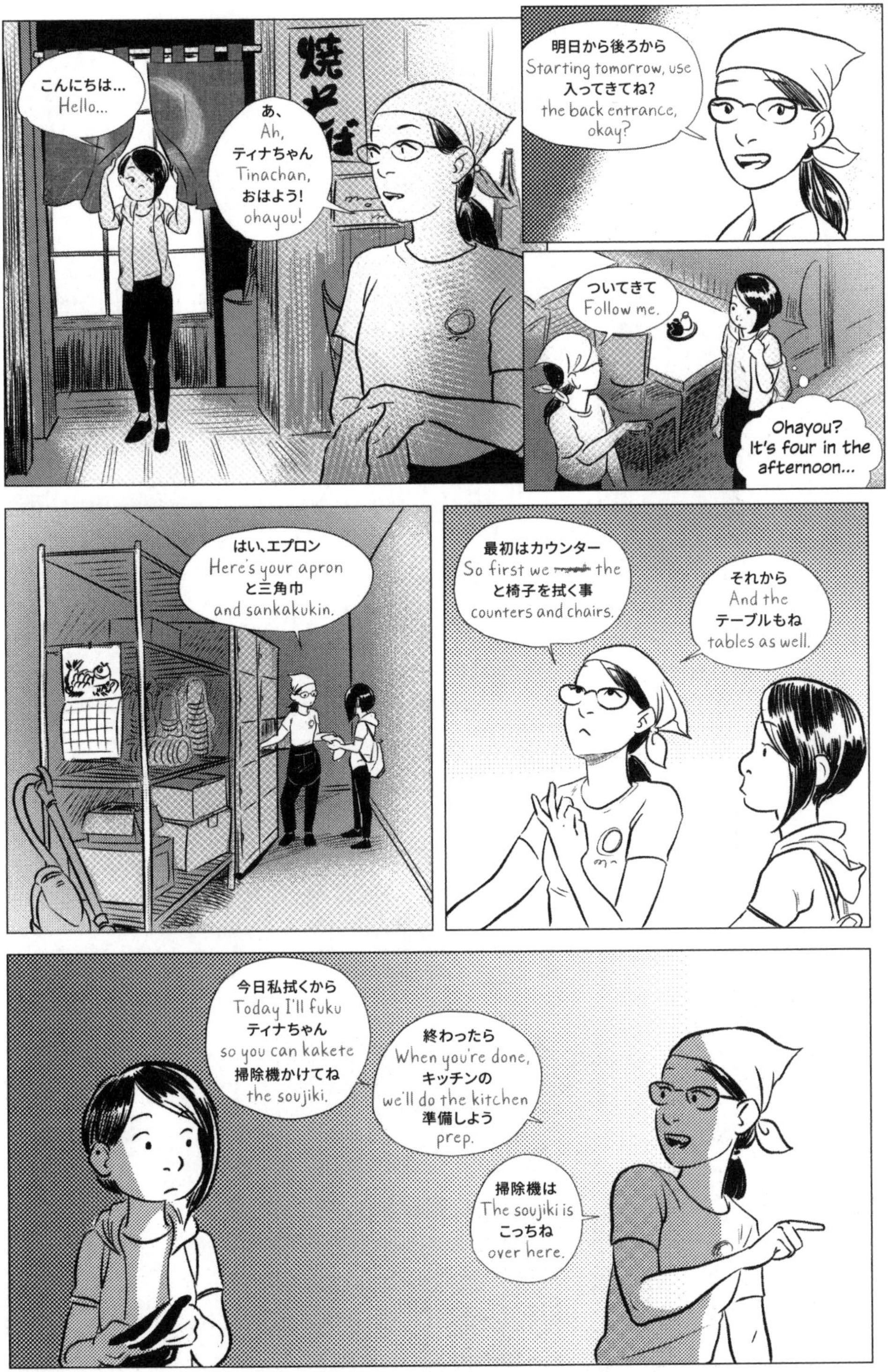

こんにちは...
Hello...
あ、
Ah,
ティナちゃん
Tinachan,
おはよう!
ohayou!
明日から後ろから
Starting tomorrow, use
入ってきてね?
the back entrance,
okay?
ついてきて
Follow me.
Ohayou? It's four in the afternoon...
はい、エプロン
Here's your apron
と三角巾
and sankakukin.
最初はカウンター
So first we the
と椅子を拭く事
counters and chairs.
それから
And the
テーブルもね
tables as well.
今日私拭くから
Today I'll fuku
ティナちゃん
so you can kakete
掃除機かけてね
the soujiki.
終わったら
When you're done,
キッチンの
we'll do the kitchen
準備しよう
prep.
掃除機は
The soujiki is
こっちね
over here.

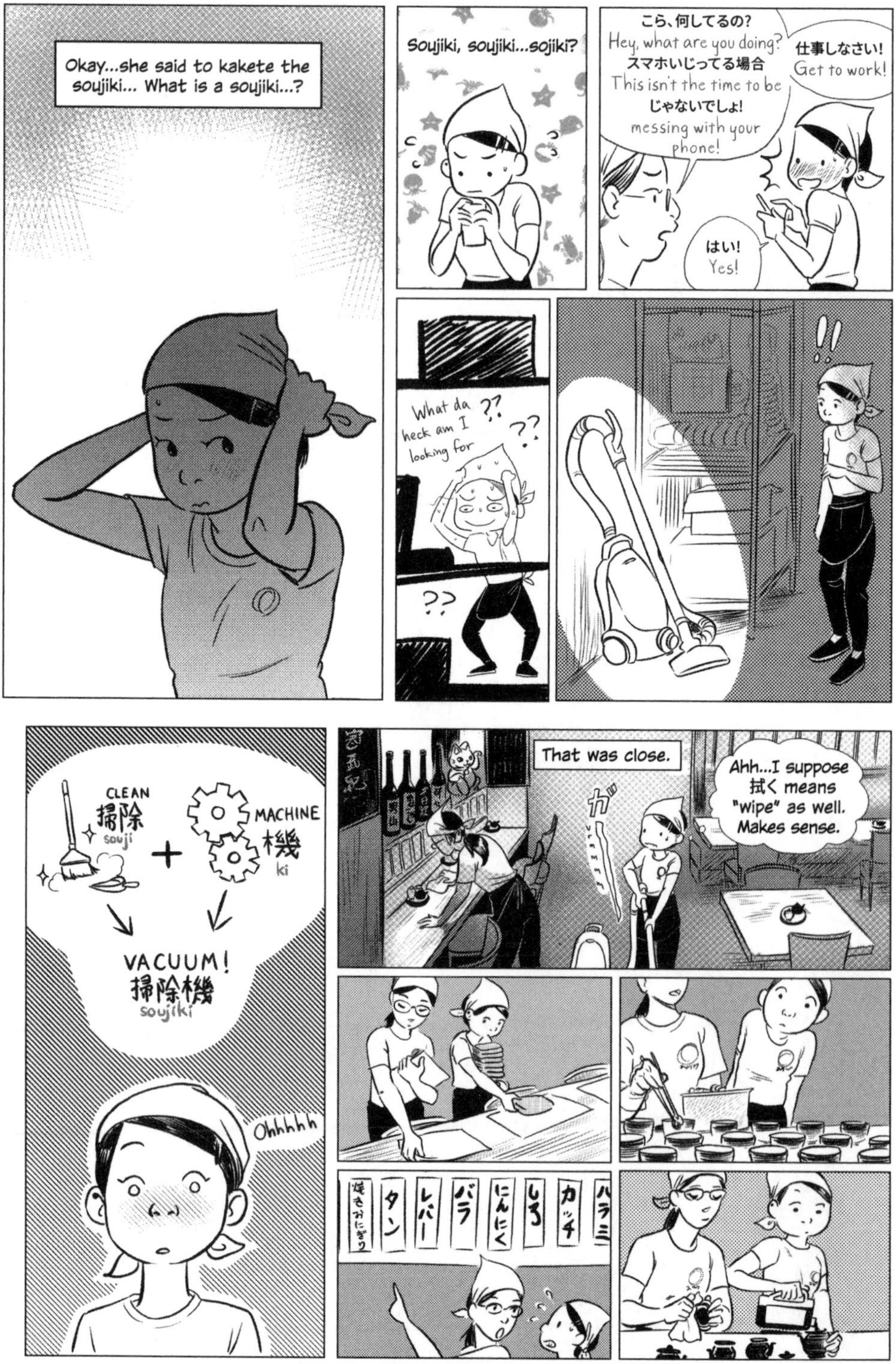
Okay...she said to kakete the soujiki... What is a soujiki...?
Soujiki, soujiki...sojiki?
こら、何してるの?
Hey, what are you doing?
スマホいじってる場合じゃないでしょ!
This isn't the time to be messing with your phone!
仕事しなさい!
Get to work!
はい!
Yes!
What da heck am I looking for
!!
CLEAN
掃除
souji
MACHINE
機
ki
VACUUM!
掃除機
soujiki
Ohhhhh
That was close.
ガー
Ahh...I suppose 拭く means "wipe" as well. Makes sense.
ハラミ
カッチ
しろ
にんにく
バラ
レバー
タン
焼きおにぎり

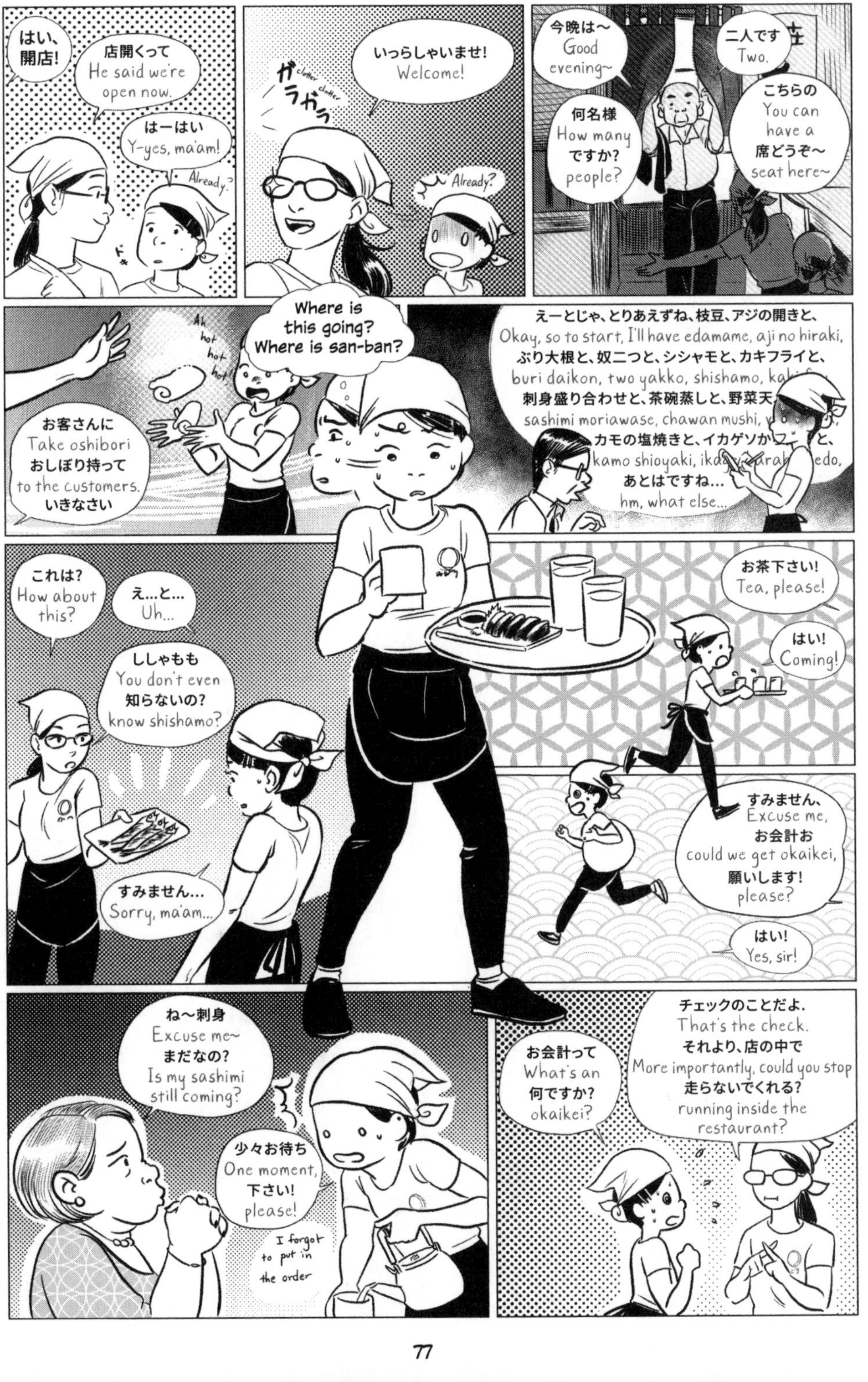
はい、開店!
店開くって
He said we're open now.
はーはい
Y-yes, ma'am!
Already?
ドキ
ガラガラ clatter clatter
いっらしゃいませ!
Welcome!
Already?
今晩は〜
Good evening~
何名様
How many
ですか?
people?
二人です
Two.
こちらの
You can have a
席どうぞ〜
seat here~
Ah hot hot hot
お客さんに
Take oshibori
おしぼり持って
to the customers.
いきなさい
Where is this going? Where is san-ban?
えーとじゃ、とりあえずね、枝豆、アジの開きと、
Okay, so to start, I'll have edamame, aji no hiraki,
ぶり大根と、奴二つと、シシャモと、カキフライと、
buri daikon, two yakko, shishamo,
刺身盛り合わせと、茶碗蒸しと、野菜天
sashimi moriawase, chawan mushi,
カモの塩焼きと、イカゲソか
kamo shioyaki,
あとはですね…
hm, what else…
これは?
How about this?
え…と…
Uh…
ししゃもも
You don't even
知らないの?
know shishamo?
すみません…
Sorry, ma'am…
お茶下さい!
Tea, please!
はい!
Coming!
すみません、
Excuse me,
お会計お
could we get okaikei,
願いします!
please?
はい!
Yes, sir!
ね〜刺身
Excuse me~
まだなの?
Is my sashimi still coming?
少々お待ち
One moment,
下さい!
please!
I forgot to put in the order
お会計って
What's an
何ですか?
okaikei?
チェックのことだよ.
That's the check.
それより、店の中で
More importantly, could you stop
走らないでくれる?
running inside the restaurant?

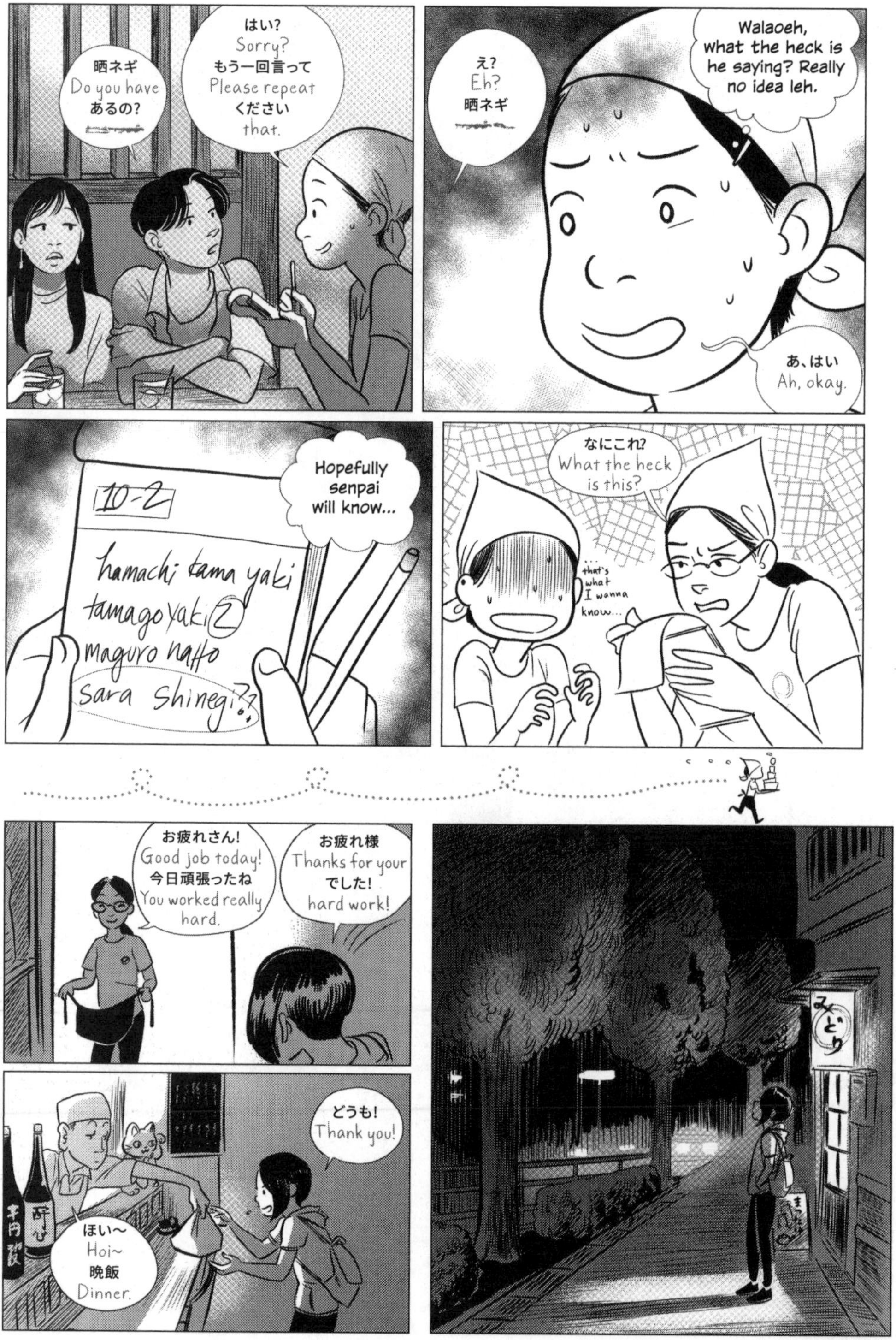

晒ネギ
Do you have
あるの?
はい?
Sorry?
もう一回言って
Please repeat
ください
that.
え?
Eh?
晒ネギ
Walaoeh, what the heck is he saying? Really no idea leh.
あ、はい
Ah, okay.
10-2
hamachi tama yaki
tamago yaki 2
maguro natto
sara shinegi???
Hopefully senpai will know...
なにこれ?
What the heck is this?
... that's what I wanna know...
お疲れさん!
Good job today!
今日頑張ったね
You worked really hard.
お疲れ様
Thanks for your
でした!
hard work!
どうも!
Thank you!
ほい~
Hoi~
晩飯
Dinner.

Tachibana Tetsuya
Tired Night

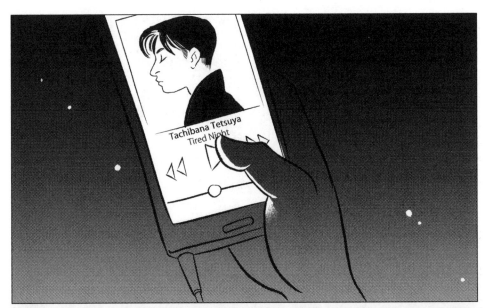

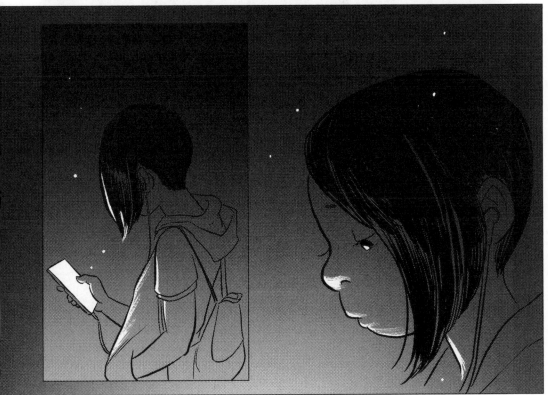

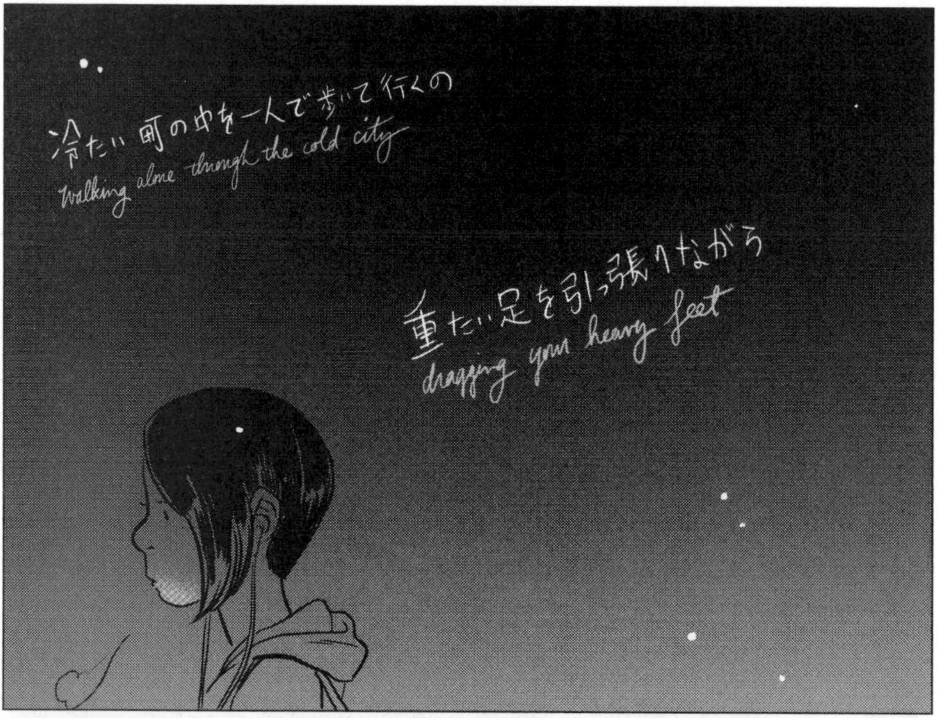
冷たい町の中を一人で歩いて行くの
Walking alone through the cold city
重たい足を引っ張りながら
dragging your heavy feet

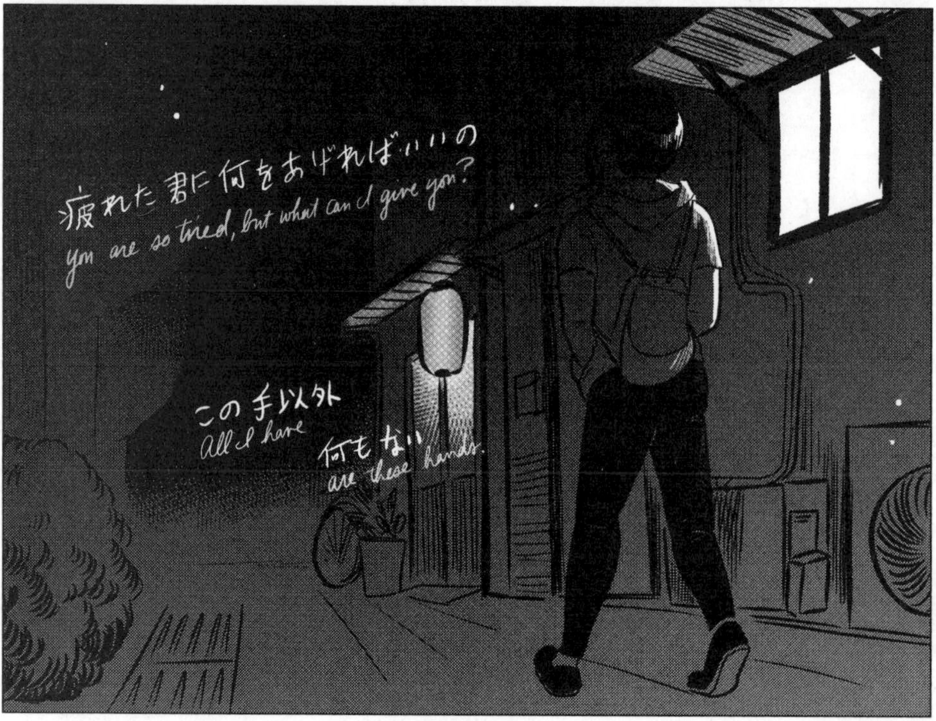
疲れた君に何をあげればいいの
You are so tired, but what can I give you?
この手以外
All I have
何もない
are these hands.

Chapter 5
Appa

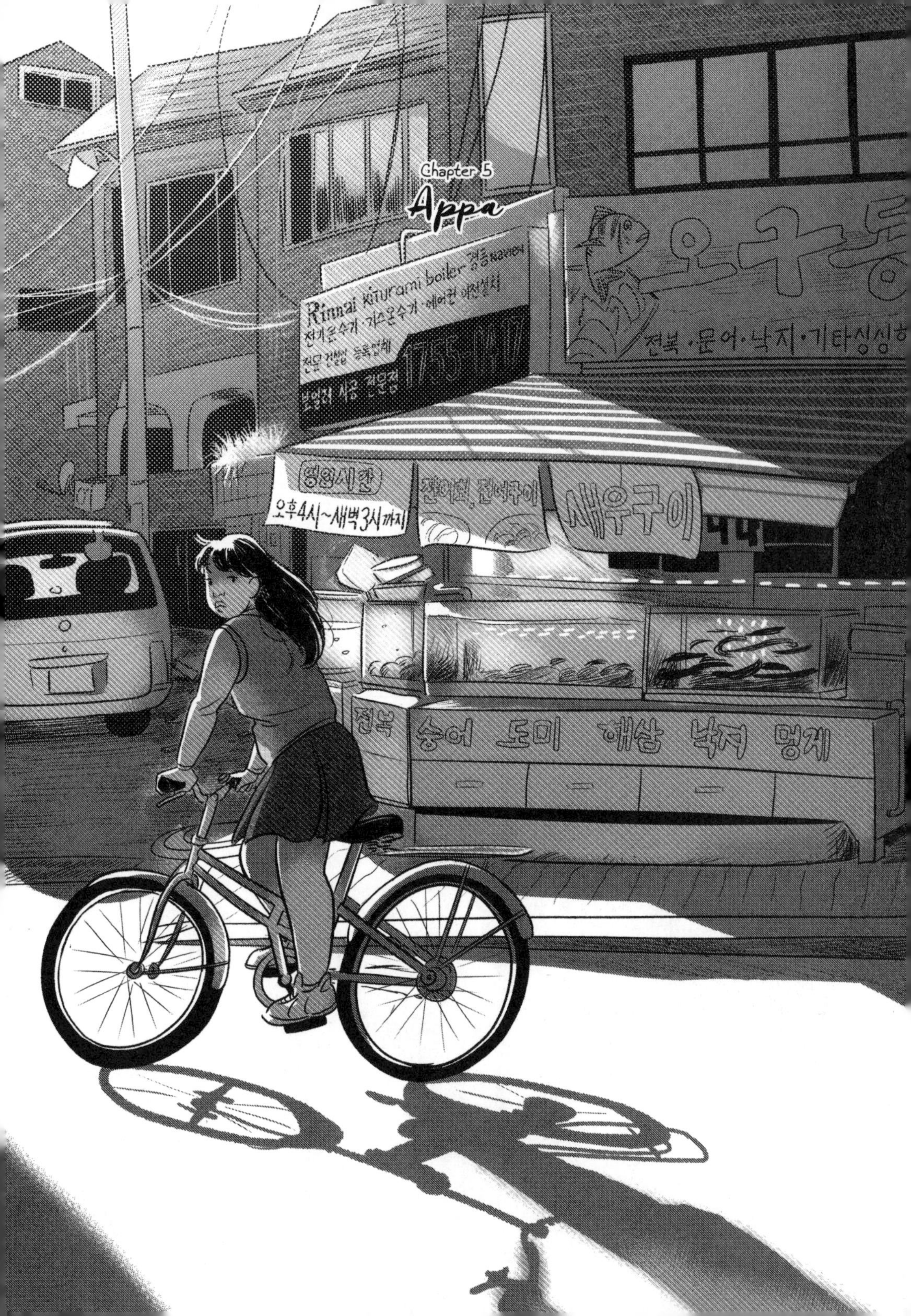
Rinnai kiturami boiler
영업시간
오후4시~새벽3시까지
새우구이
전복 숭어 도미 해삼 낙지 멍게

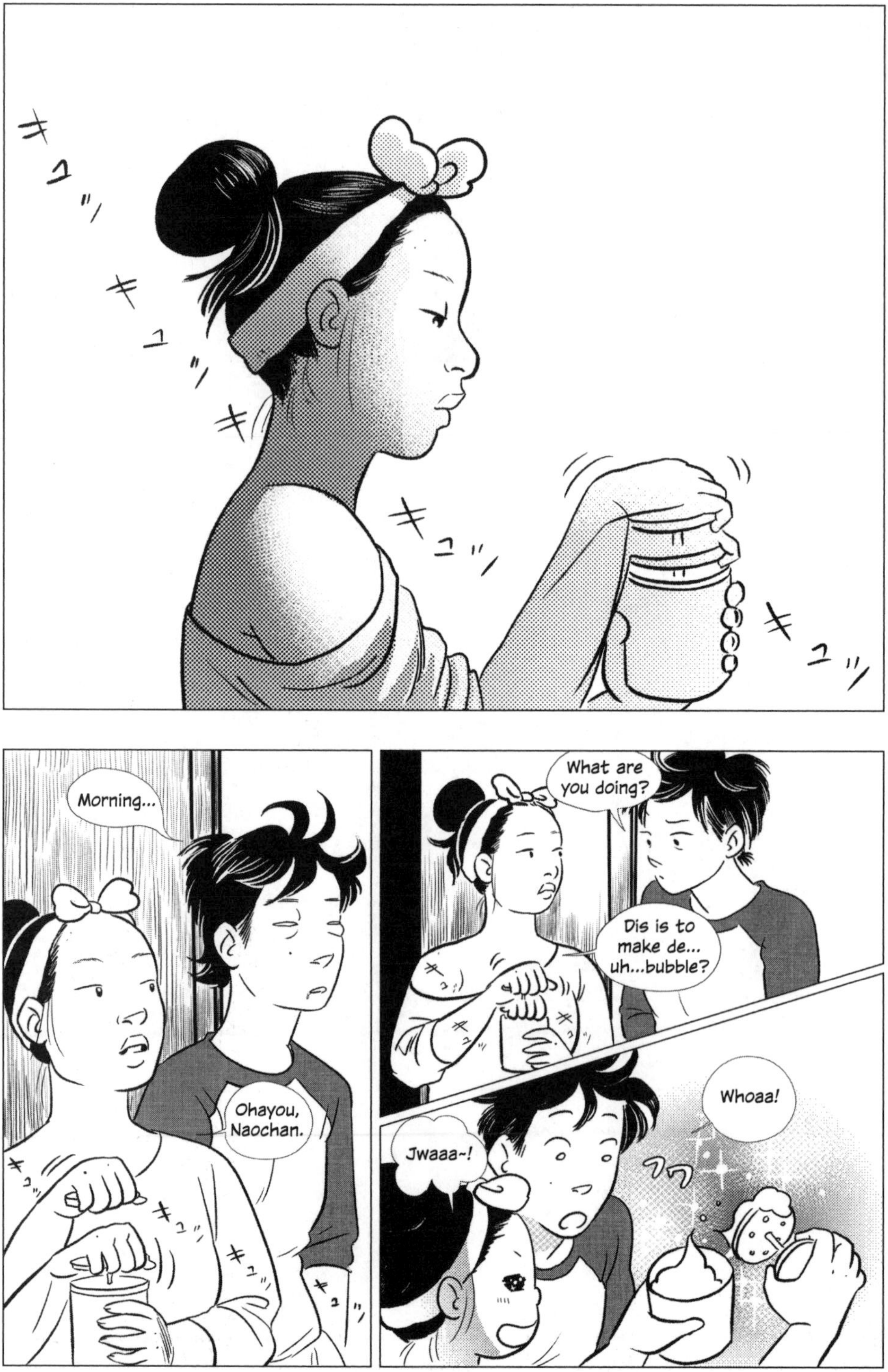

キュッ
キュッ
キ
キュッ
キュッ
Morning...
Ohayou, Naochan.
キュッ
キュッ
キュッ
キュッ
What are you doing?
Dis is to make de... uh...bubble?
Jwaaa~!
Whoa!
フワ

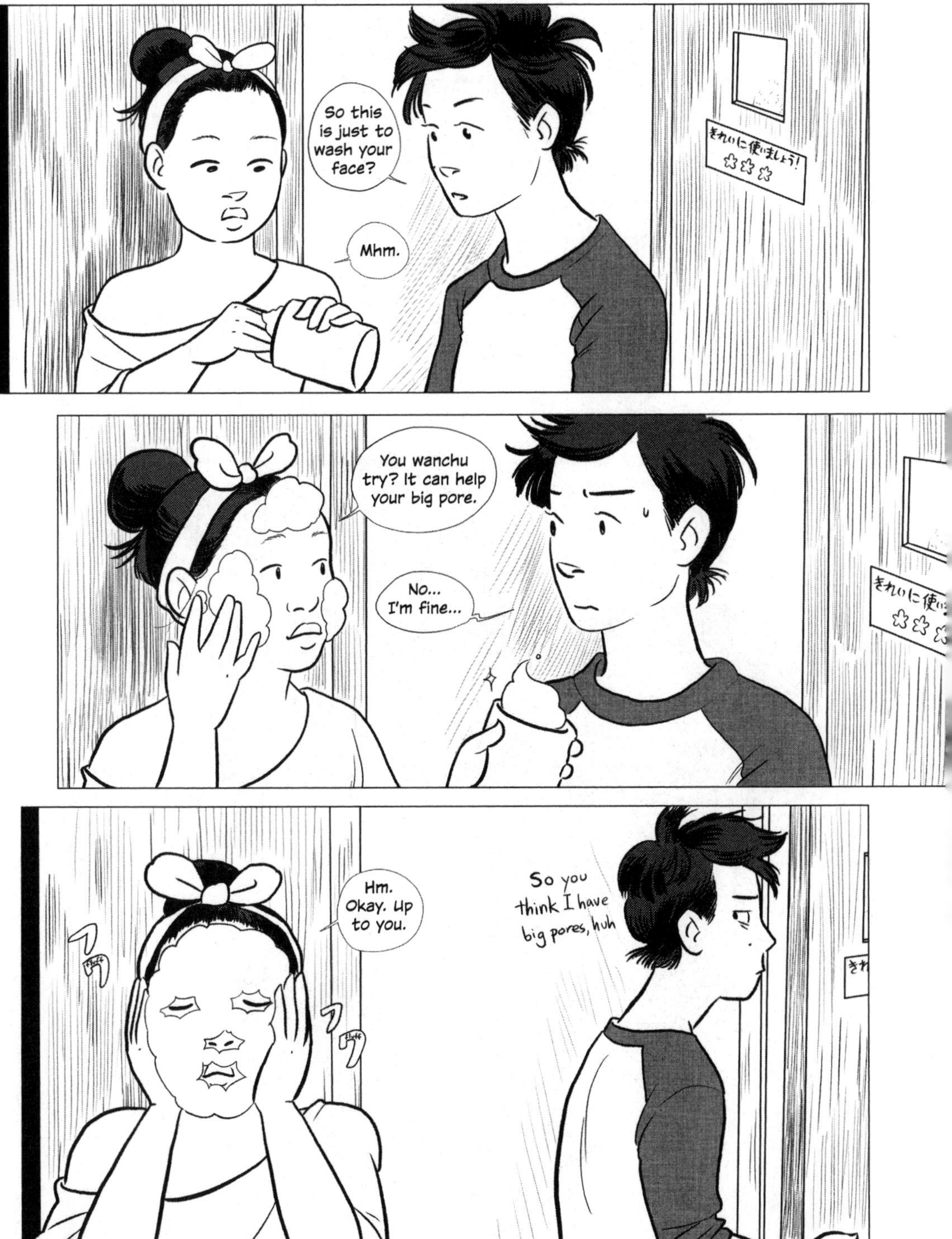

So this is just to wash your face?
Mhm.
きれいに使いましょう!
You wanchu try? It can help your big pore.
No... I'm fine...
Hm. Okay. Up to you.
So you think I have big pores, huh

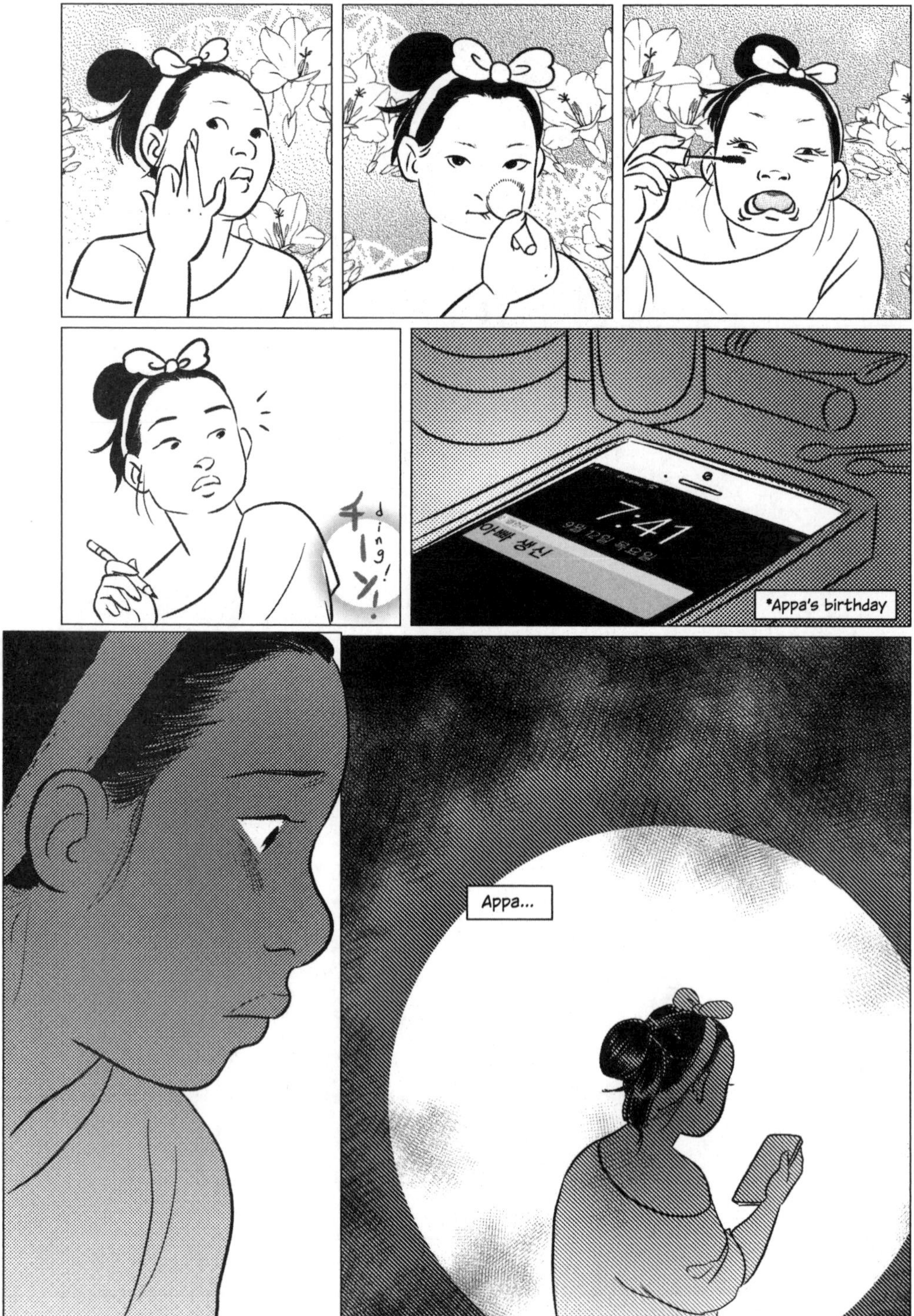
チーン!
ding!
7:41
6월 12일 토요일
아빠 생신
*Appa's birthday
Appa...

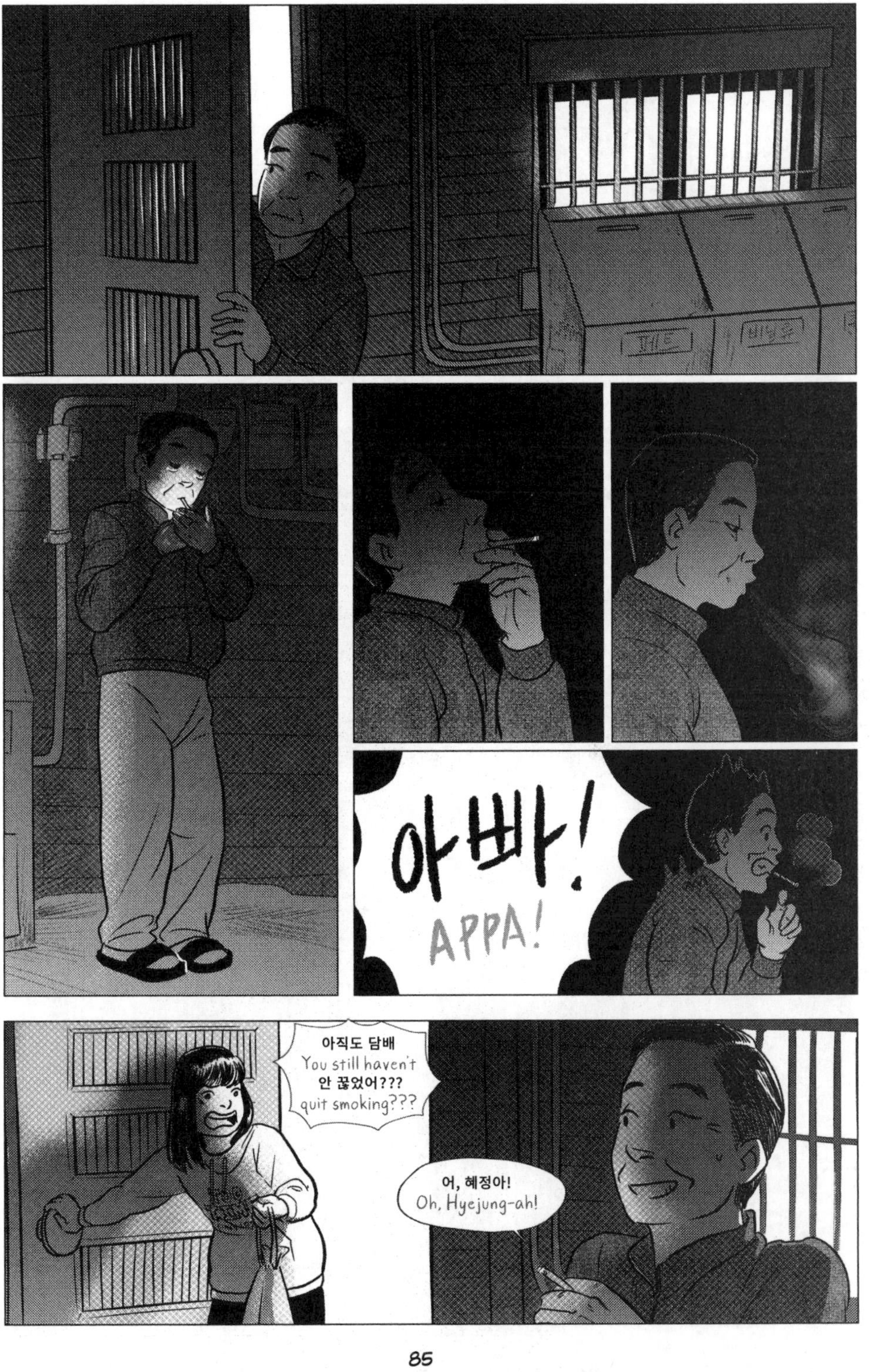

아빠!
APPA!
아직도 담배
You still haven't
안 끊었어???
quit smoking???
어, 혜정아!
Oh, Hyejung-ah!

아빠가 요즘,
Appa's been pretty
스트레스가
stressed out these
많아 가지고...
days, you know...

아무리 그래도...
Still...you know
건강에 안 좋잖아.
it's not good for you.
선생님이 말씀 하셨잖아...
The doctor said...

어, 그래,
I know,
그래,
I know.

?

Ah...when did Appa get so old?

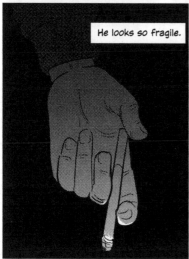

He looks so fragile.

아빠 너무
Appa, you
일만 하는 것 같아.
work too much.
무리
Don't
하지마.
overdo it.

갑자기
What's
왜그래?
gotten into
you all of a
sudden?

Like he could just disappear.

86

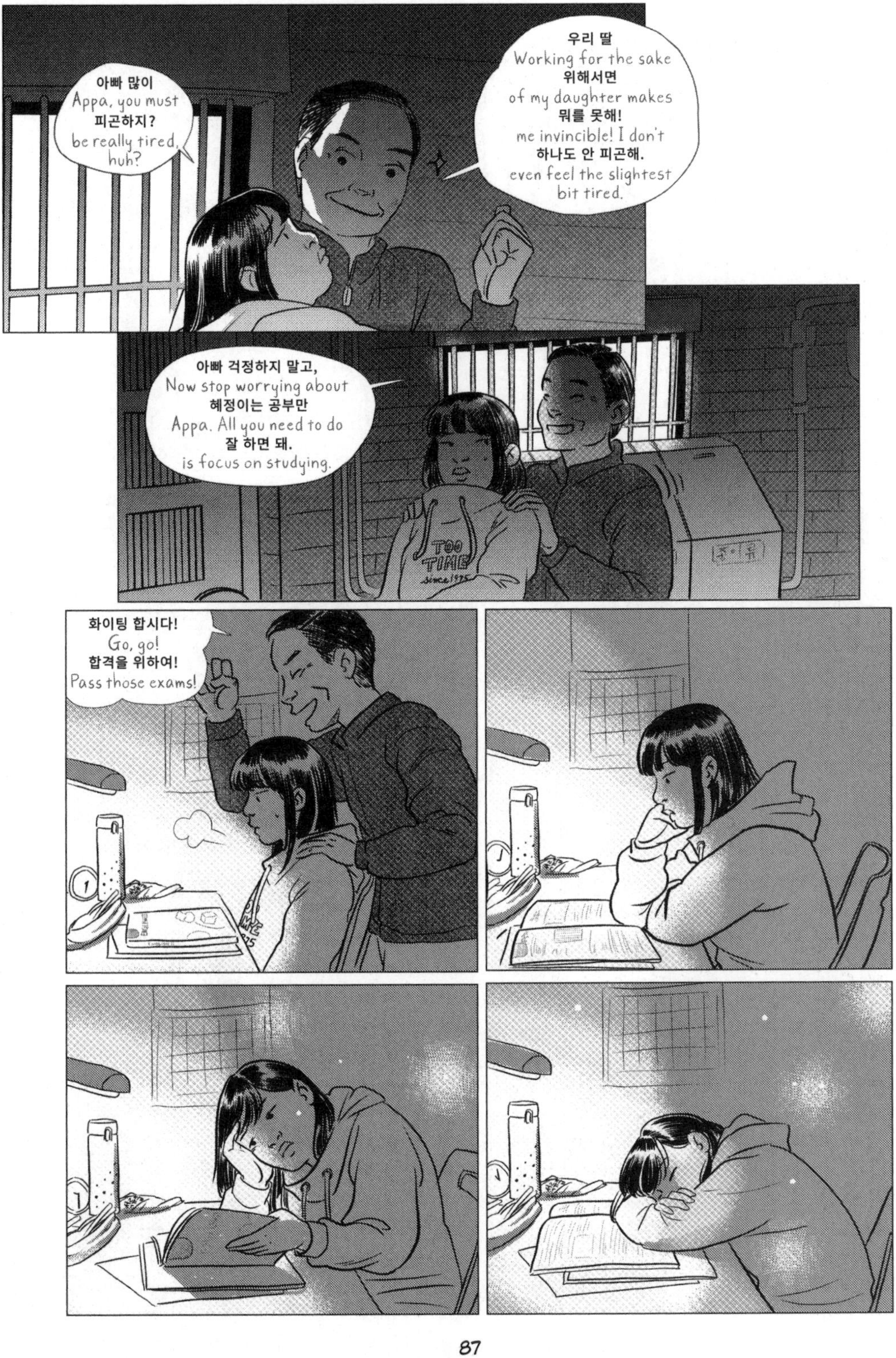
아빠 많이 Appa, you must 피곤하지? be really tired, huh?
우리 딸 Working for the sake 위해서면 of my daughter makes 뭐를 못해! me invincible! I don't 하나도 안 피곤해. even feel the slightest bit tired.
아빠 걱정하지 말고, Now stop worrying about 혜정이는 공부만 Appa. All you need to do 잘 하면 돼. is focus on studying.
TOO TIME since 1975
화이팅 합시다! Go, go! 합격을 위하여! Pass those exams!

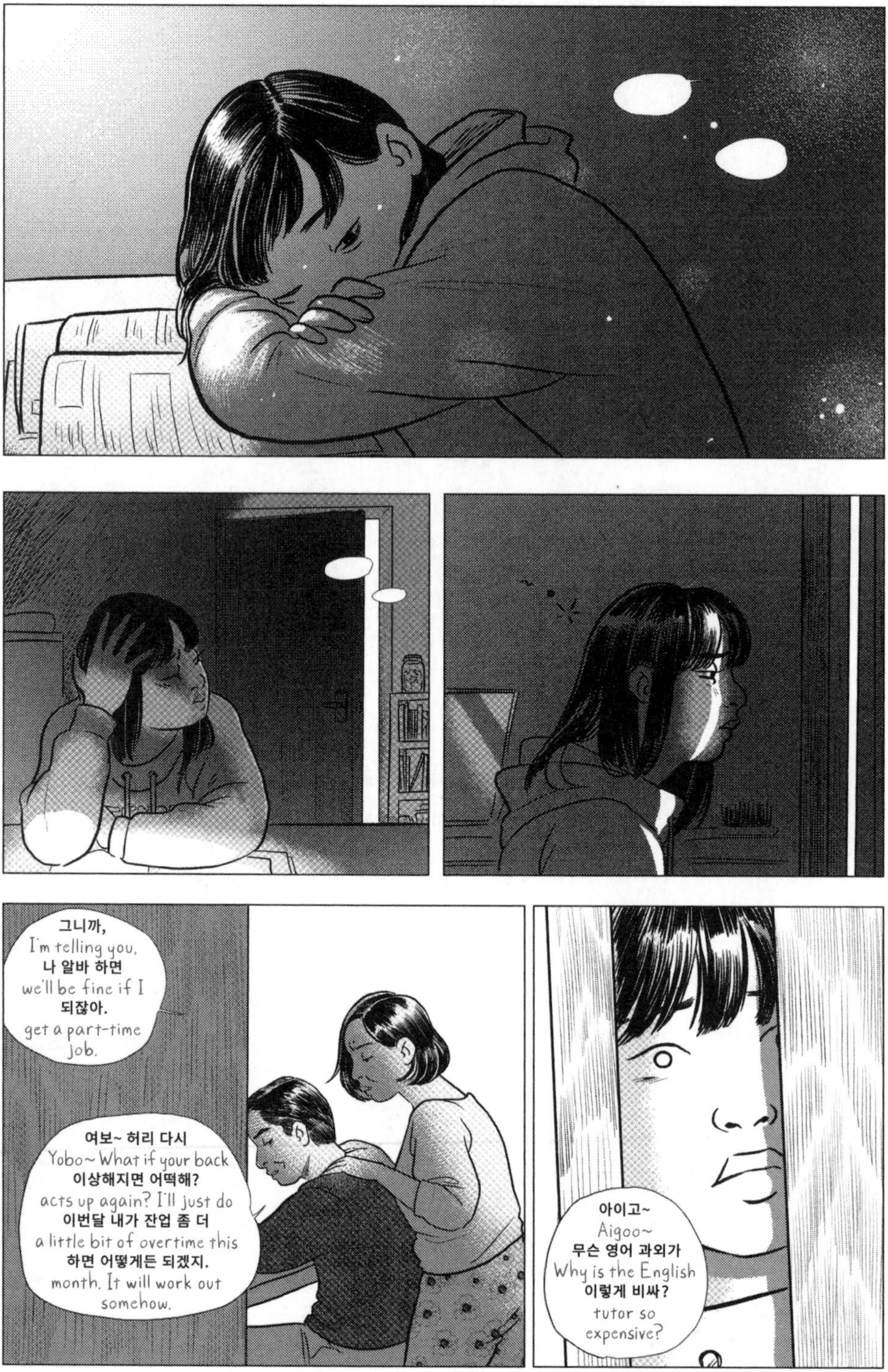
그니까, I'm telling you, 나 알바 하면 we'll be fine if I 되잖아. get a part-time job.
여보~ 허리 다시 Yobo~ What if your back 이상해지면 어떡해? acts up again? I'll just do 이번달 내가 잔업 좀 더 a little bit of overtime this 하면 어떻게든 되겠지. month. It will work out somehow.
아이고~ Aigoo~ 무슨 영어 과외가 Why is the English 이렇게 비싸? tutor so expensive?

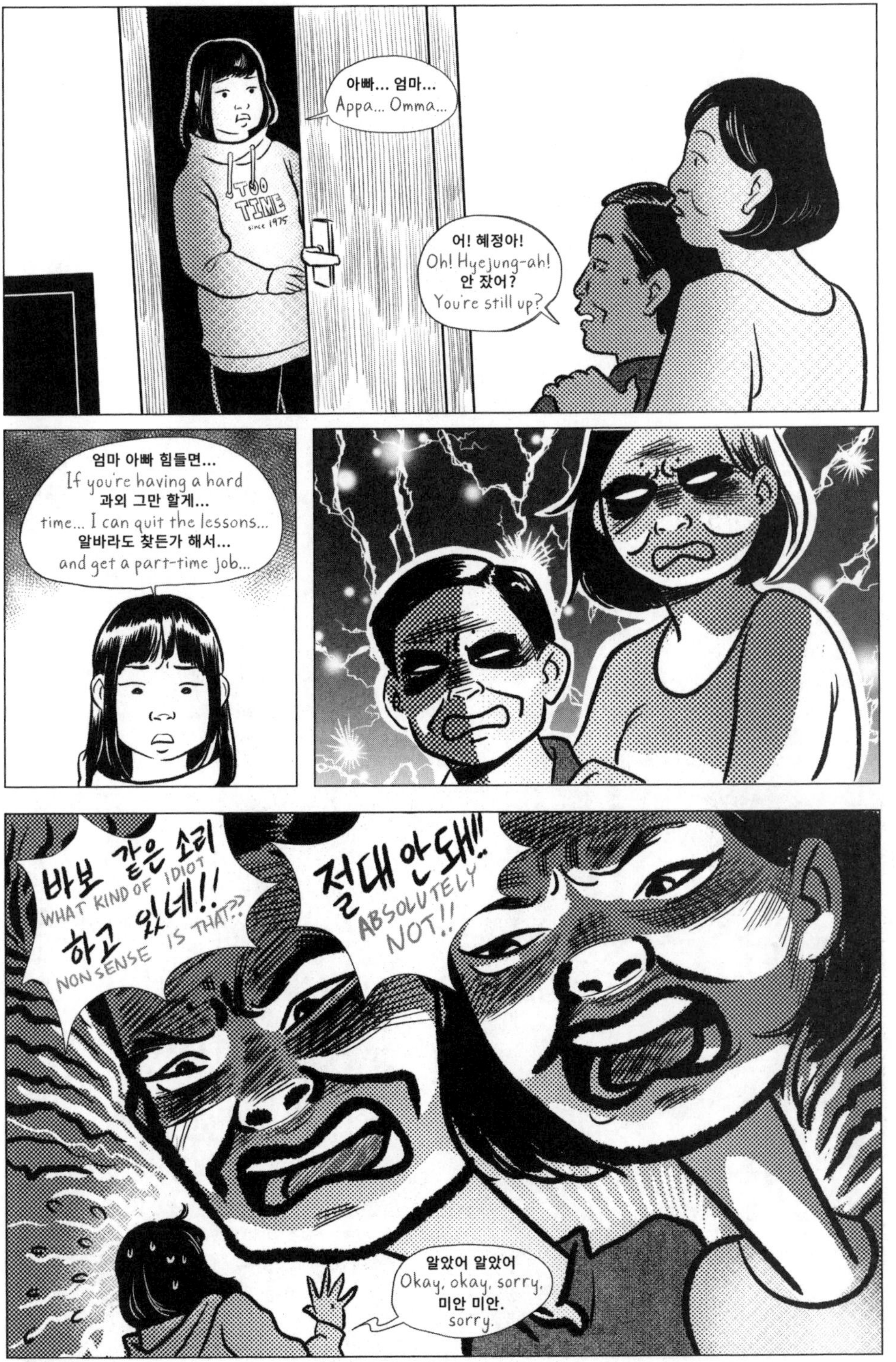
아빠... 엄마...
Appa... Omma...
어! 혜정아!
Oh! Hyejung-ah!
안 잤어?
You're still up?
엄마 아빠 힘들면...
If you're having a hard
과외 그만 할게...
time... I can quit the lessons...
알바라도 찾든가 해서...
and get a part-time job...
바보 같은 소리 하고 있네!!
WHAT KIND OF IDIOT NONSENSE IS THAT??
절대 안돼!!
ABSOLUTELY NOT!!
알았어 알았어
Okay, okay, sorry,
미안 미안.
sorry.

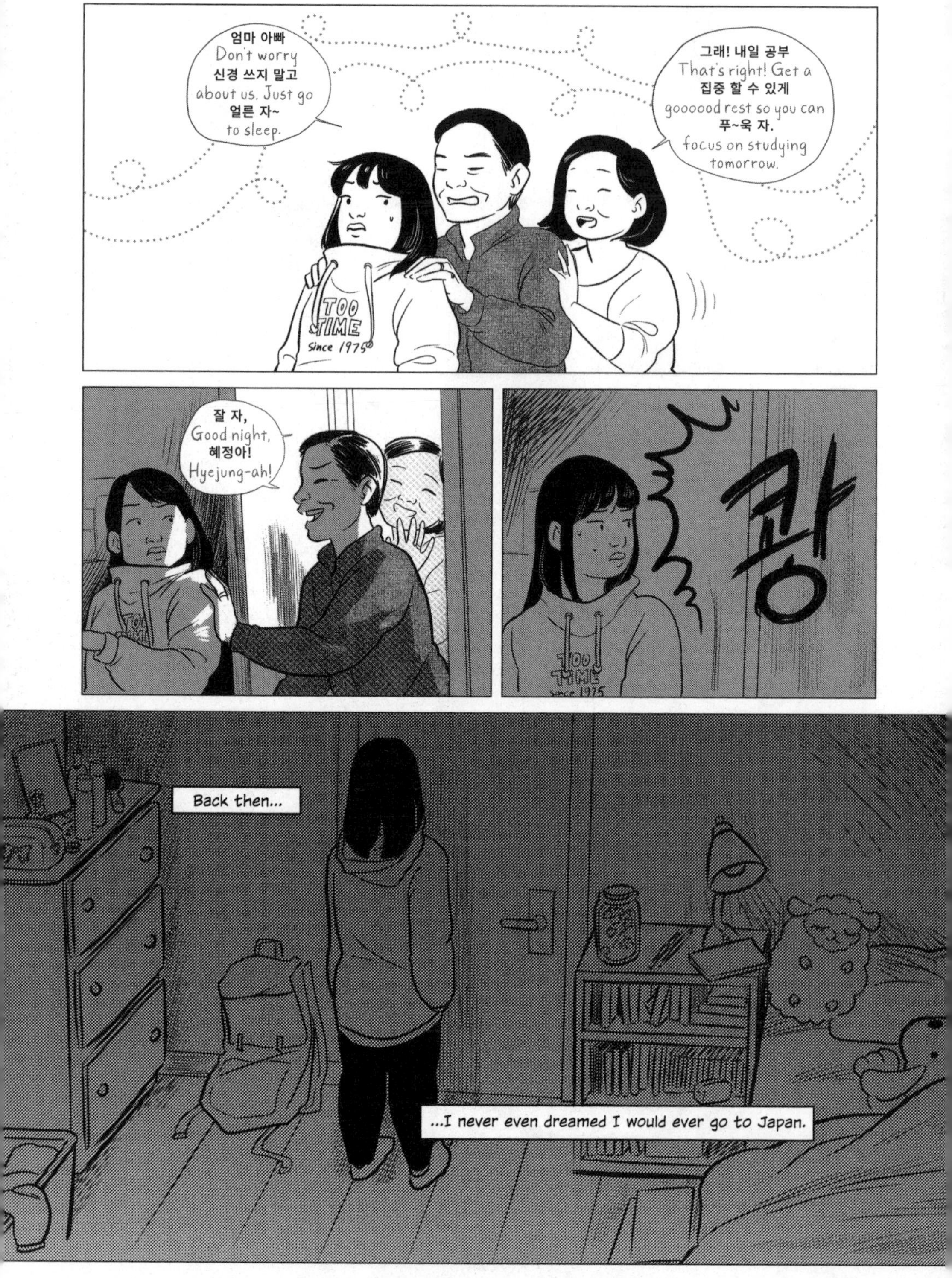
엄마 아빠
Don't worry
신경 쓰지 말고
about us. Just go
얼른 자~
to sleep.
그래! 내일 공부
That's right! Get a
집중 할 수 있게
goooood rest so you can
푸~욱 자.
focus on studying
tomorrow.
TOO TIME
Since 1975
잘 자,
Good night,
혜정아!
Hyejung-ah!
쾅
Back then...
...I never even dreamed I would ever go to Japan.

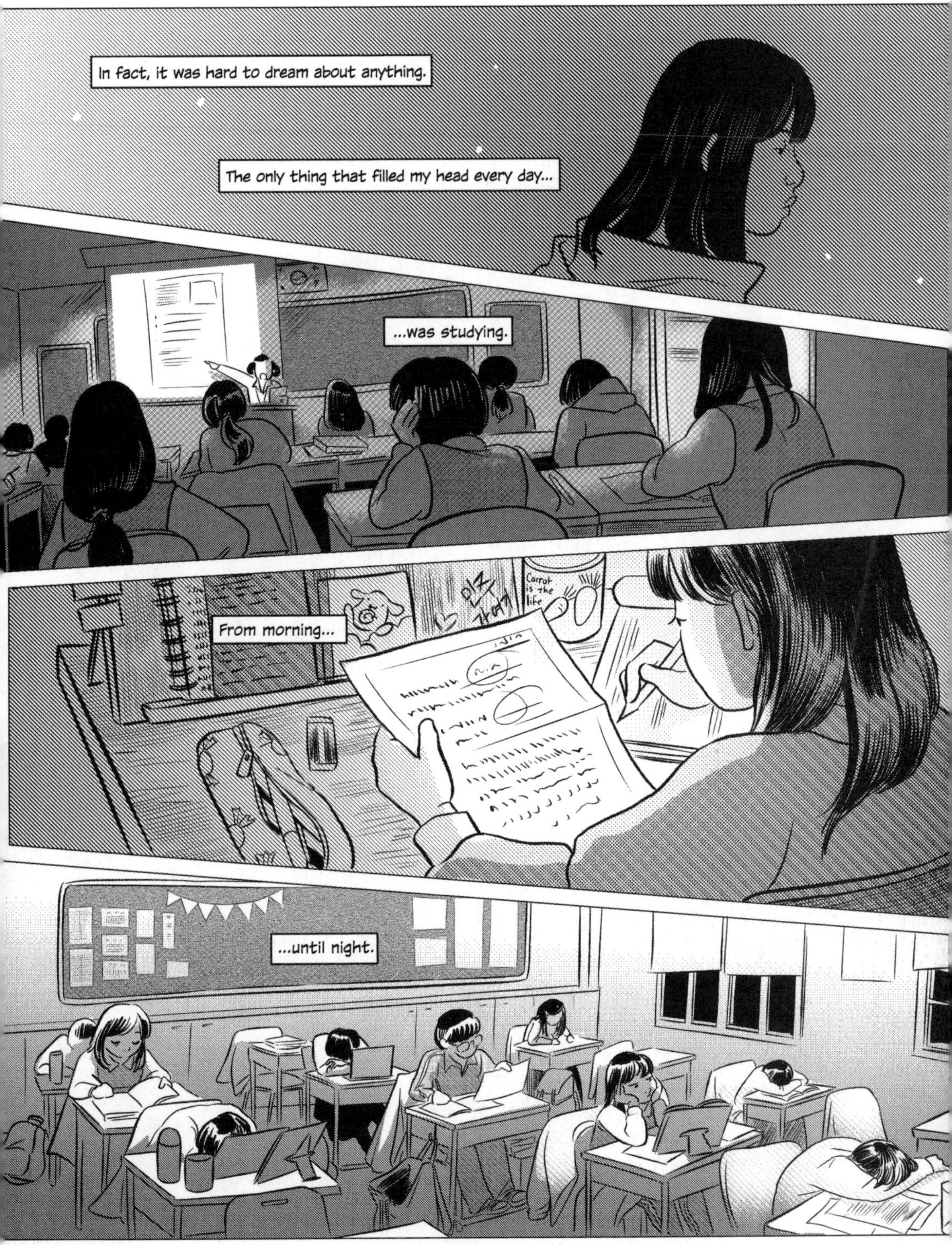
In fact, it was hard to dream about anything.
The only thing that filled my head every day...
...was studying.
From morning...
Carrot is the life
...until night.

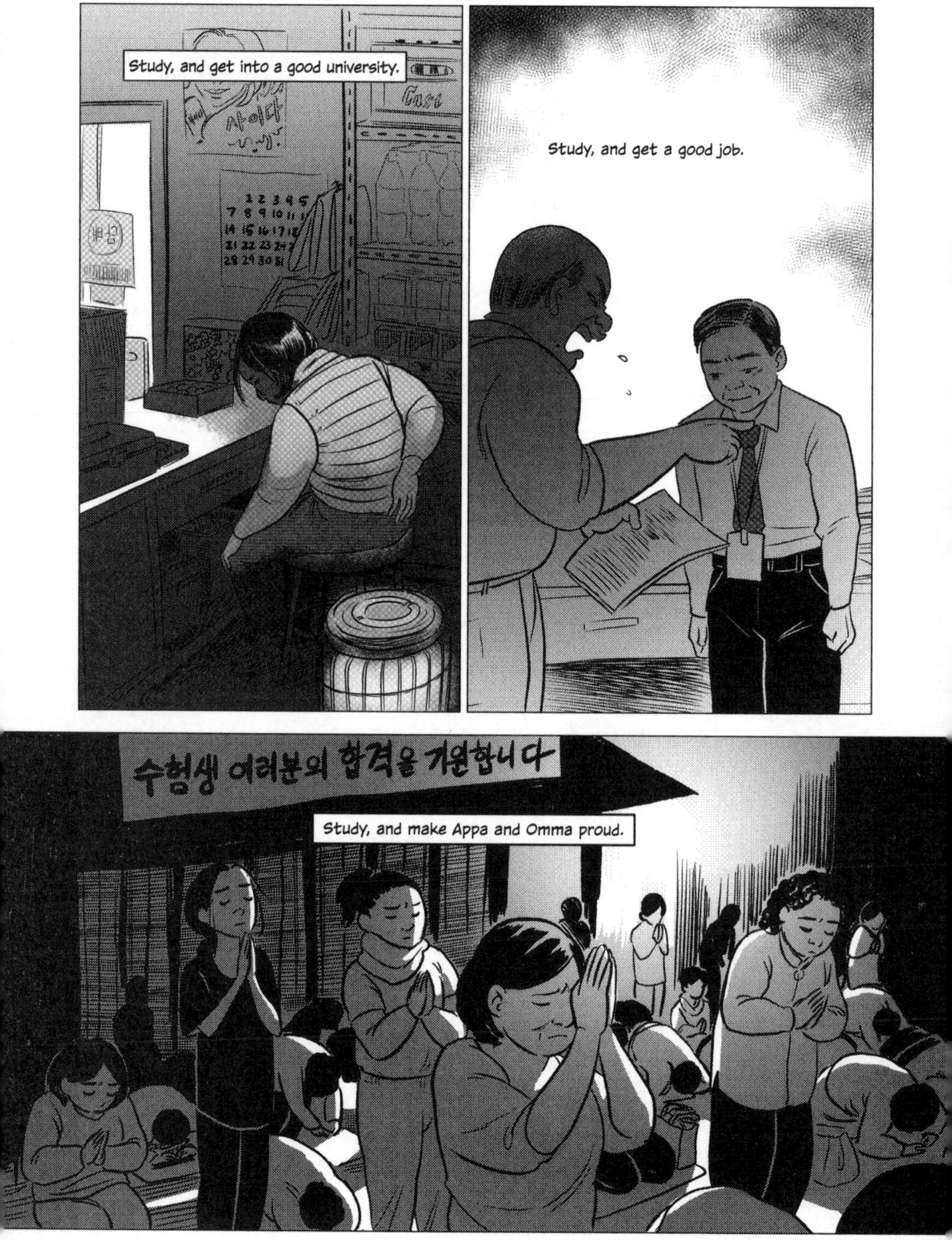
Study, and get into a good university.
사이다
Study, and get a good job.
수험생 여러분의 합격을 기원합니다
Study, and make Appa and Omma proud.

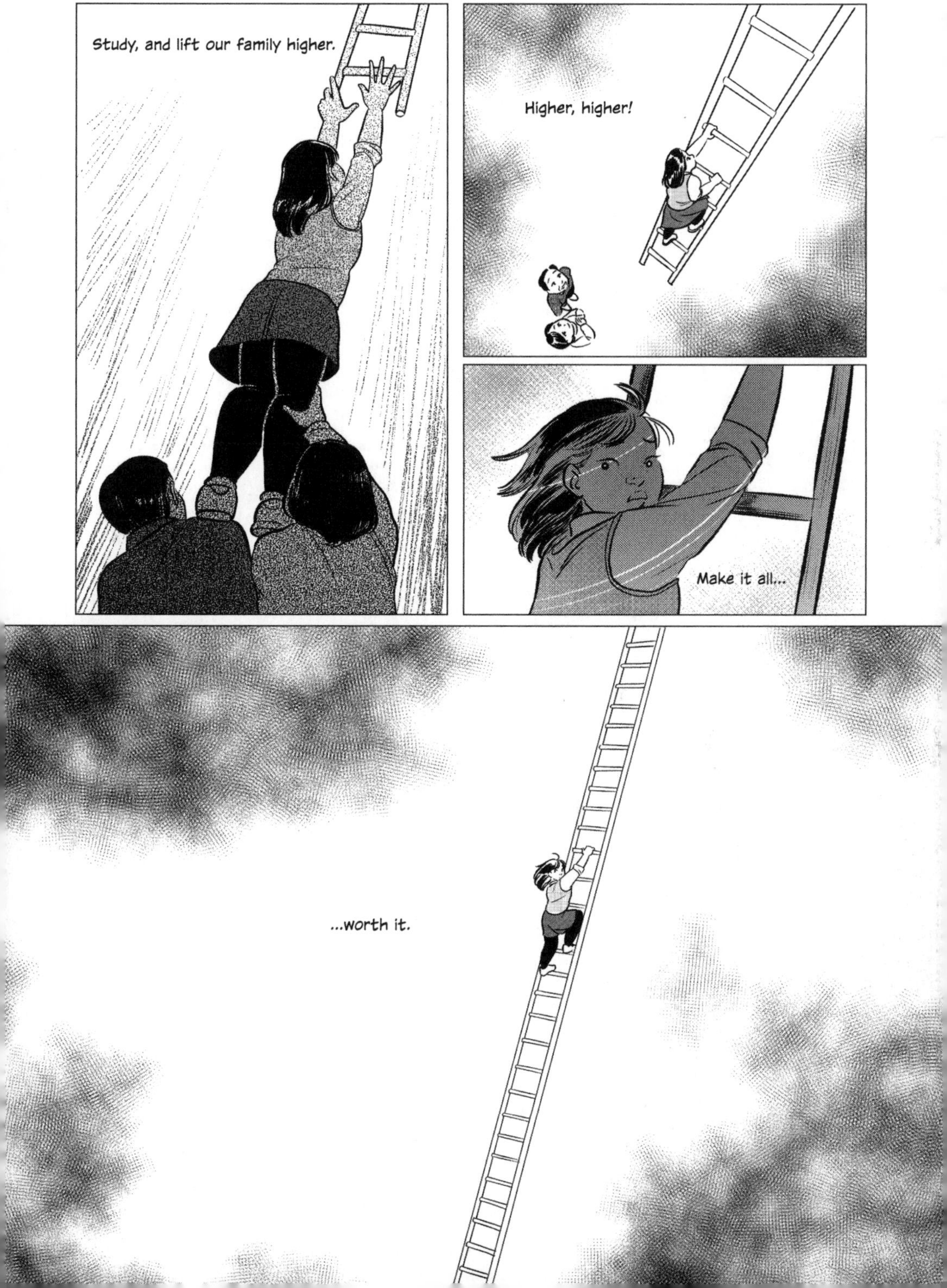
Study, and lift our family higher.
Higher, higher!
Make it all...
...worth it.

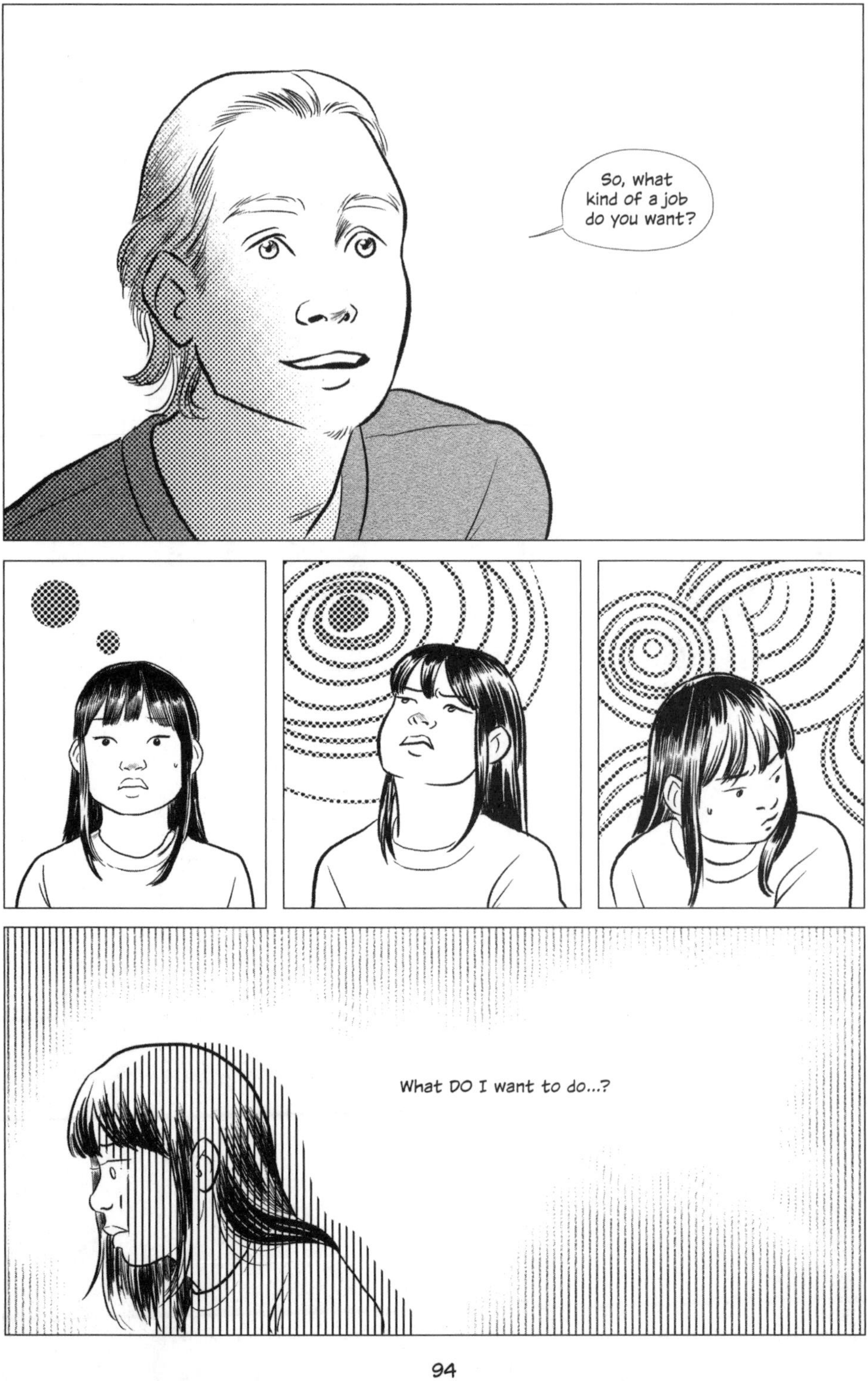
So, what kind of a job do you want?
What DO I want to do...?

Did you not understand the question?

No, I unduhstand. But...I don' know.

English Gram...

Well, what do you like to do? What are you interested in?

...

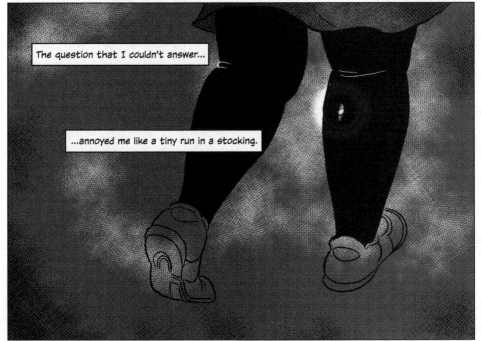

The question that I couldn't answer...

...annoyed me like a tiny run in a stocking.

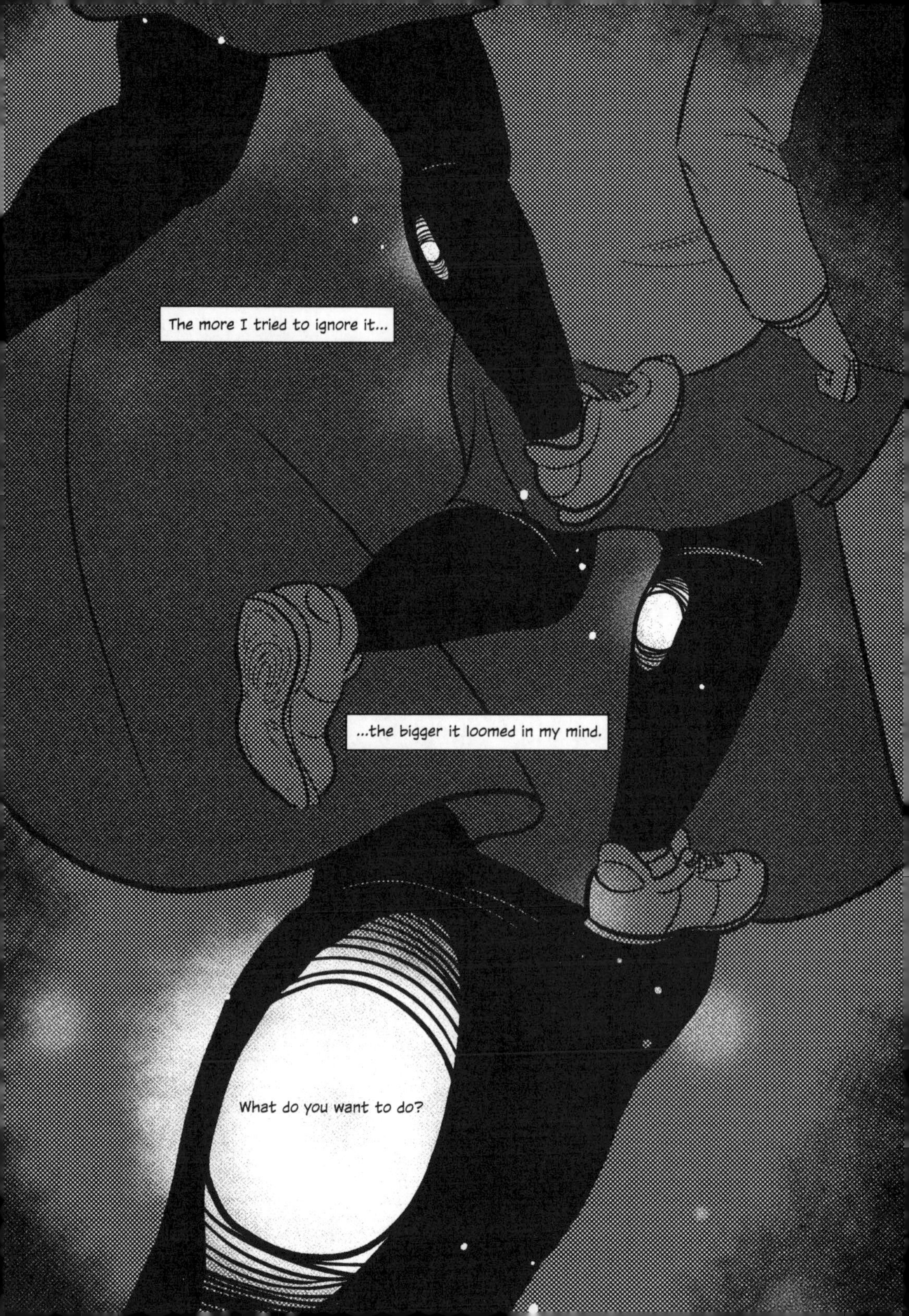
The more I tried to ignore it...
...the bigger it loomed in my mind.
What do you want to do?

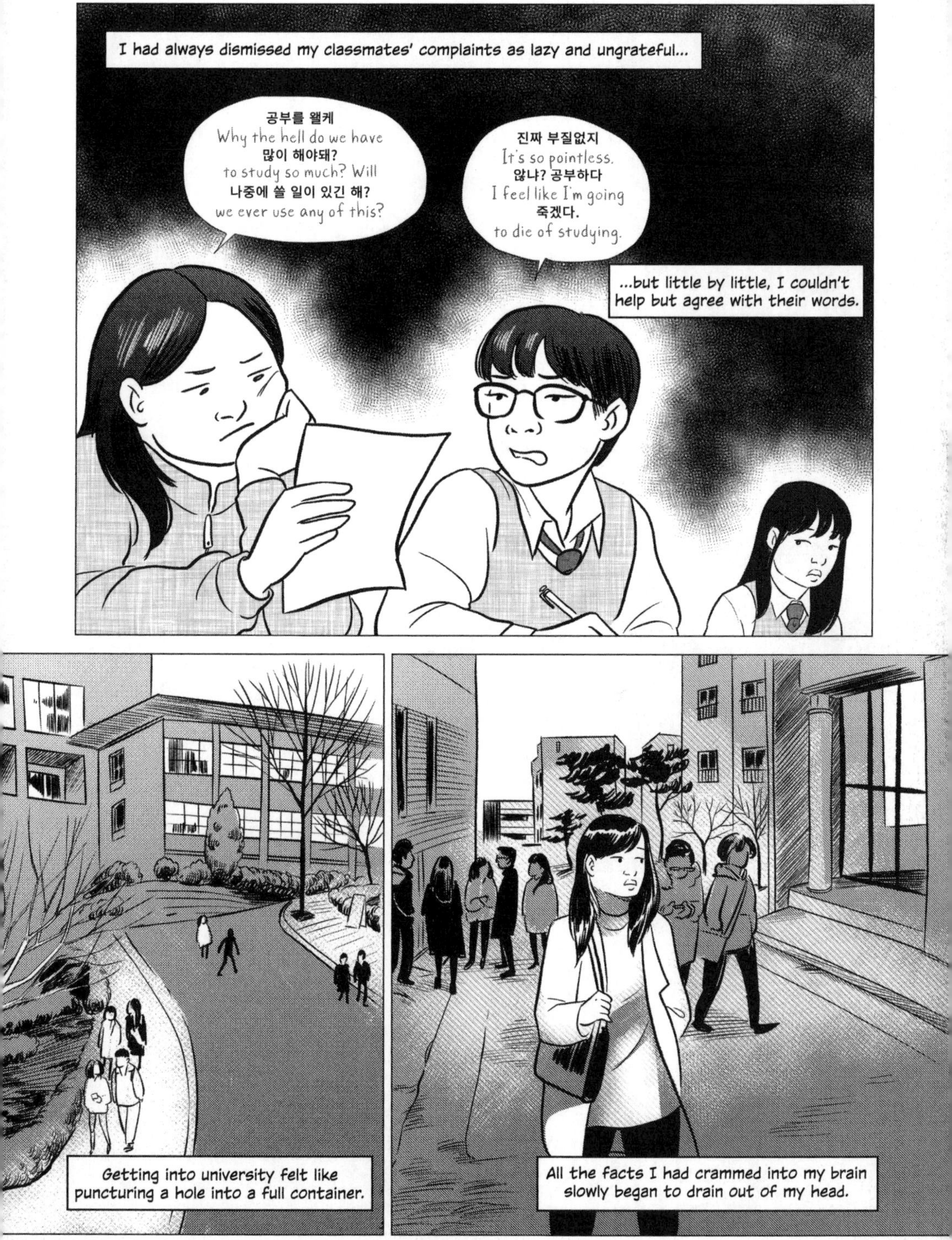
I had always dismissed my classmates' complaints as lazy and ungrateful...
공부를 왤케 Why the hell do we have 많이 해야돼? to study so much? Will 나중에 쓸 일이 있긴 해? we ever use any of this?
진짜 부질없지 It's so pointless. 않냐? 공부하다 I feel like I'm going 죽겠다. to die of studying.
...but little by little, I couldn't help but agree with their words.
Getting into university felt like puncturing a hole into a full container.
All the facts I had crammed into my brain slowly began to drain out of my head.

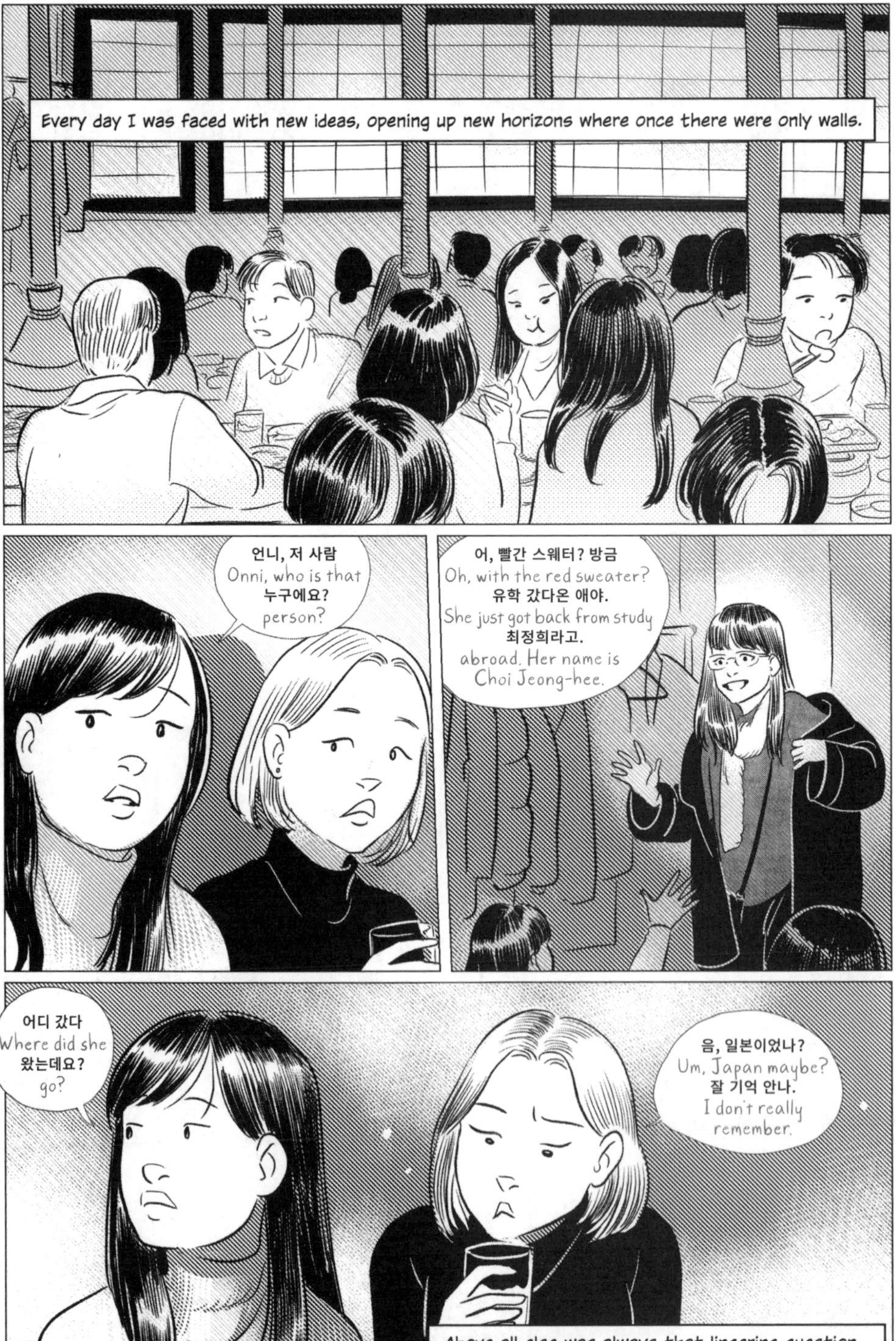
Every day I was faced with new ideas, opening up new horizons where once there were only walls.
언니, 저 사람 누구에요?
Onni, who is that person?
어, 빨간 스웨터? 방금 유학 갔다온 애야. 최정희라고.
Oh, with the red sweater? She just got back from study abroad. Her name is Choi Jeong-hee.
어디 갔다 왔는데요?
Where did she go?
음, 일본이었나? 잘 기억 안나.
Um, Japan maybe? I don't really remember.
Above all else was always that lingering question...

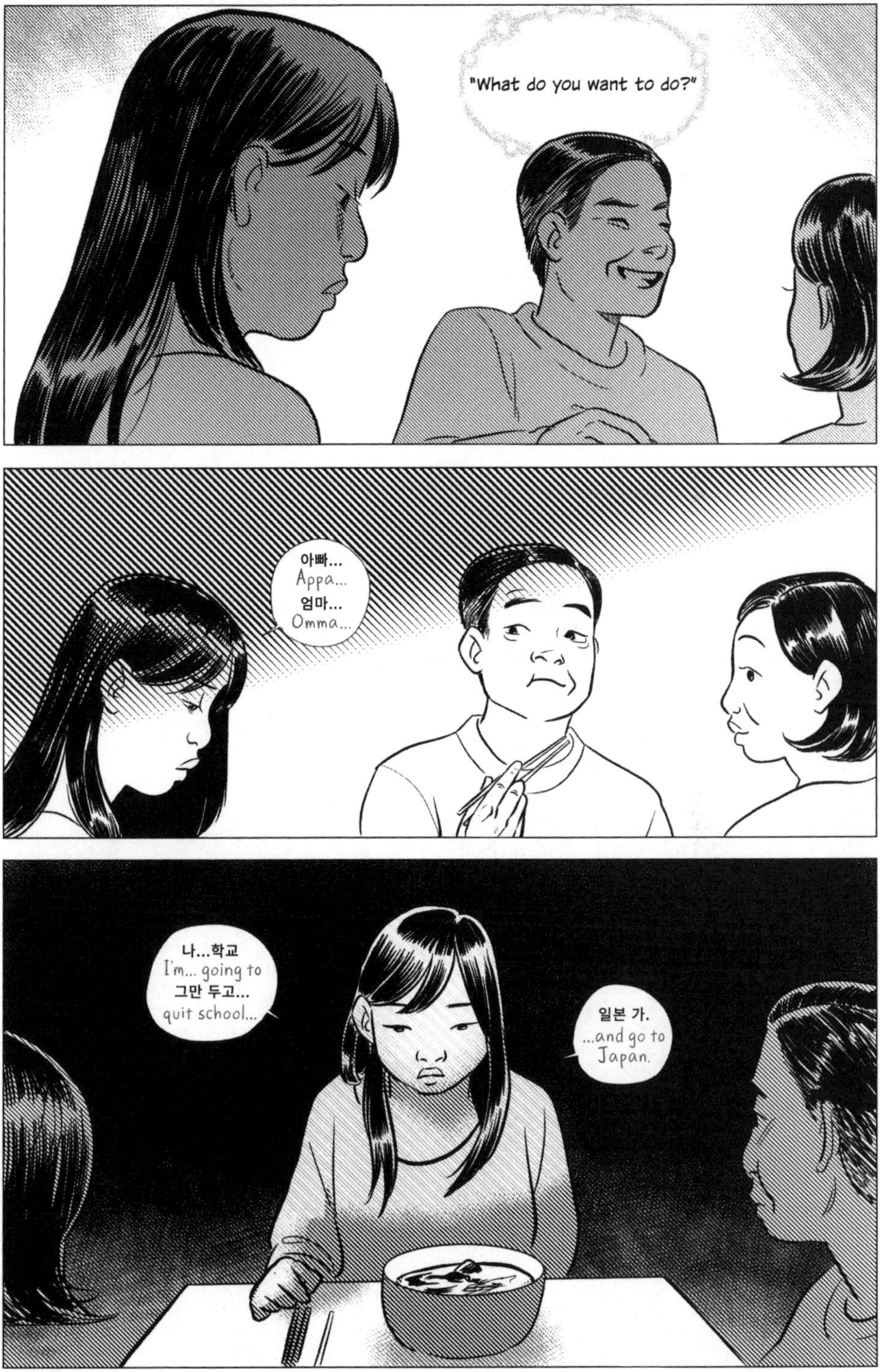
"What do you want to do?"
아빠... Appa... 엄마... Omma...
나...학교 I'm... going to 그만 두고... quit school...
일본 가. ...and go to Japan.

Chapter 6
Chuseok

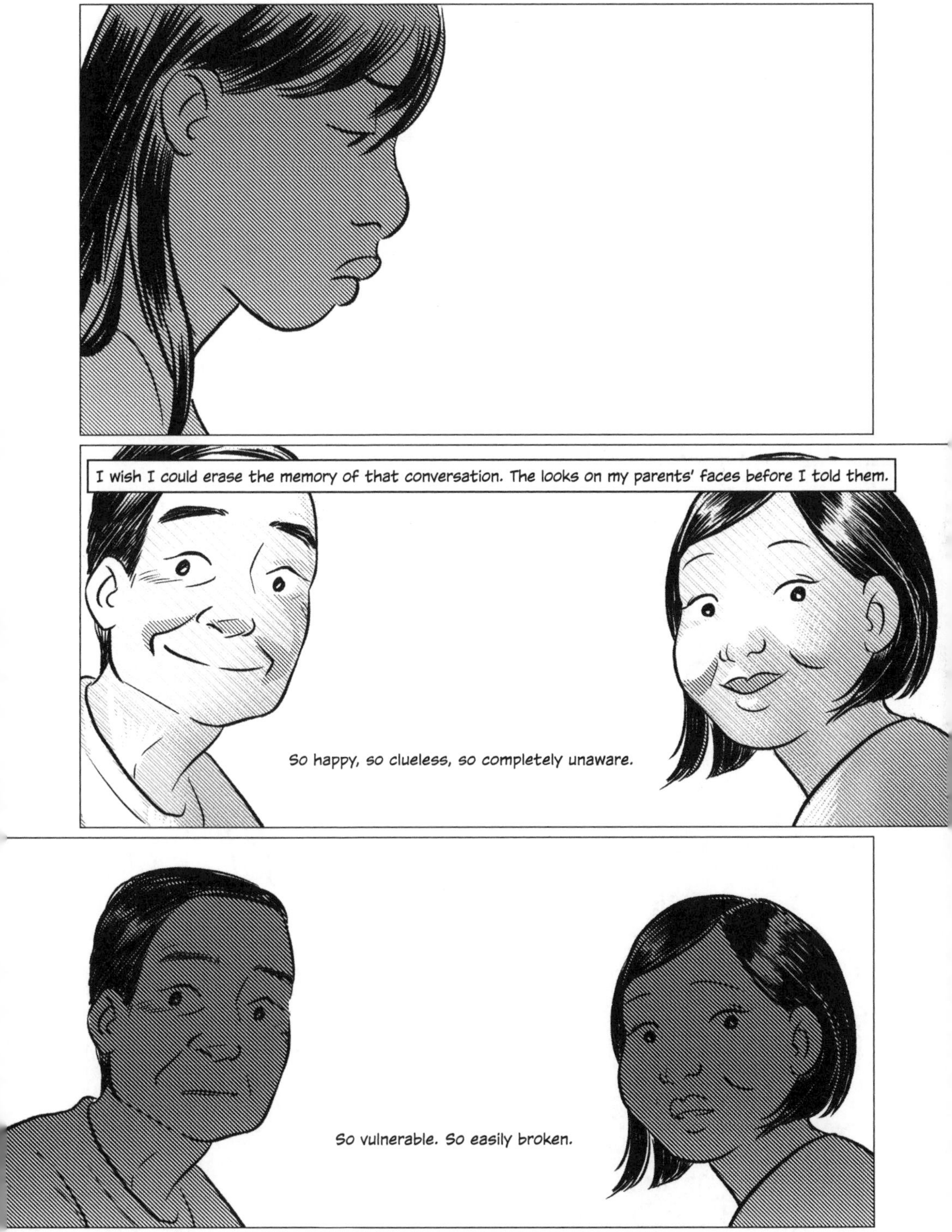
I wish I could erase the memory of that conversation. The looks on my parents' faces before I told them.
So happy, so clueless, so completely unaware.
So vulnerable. So easily broken.

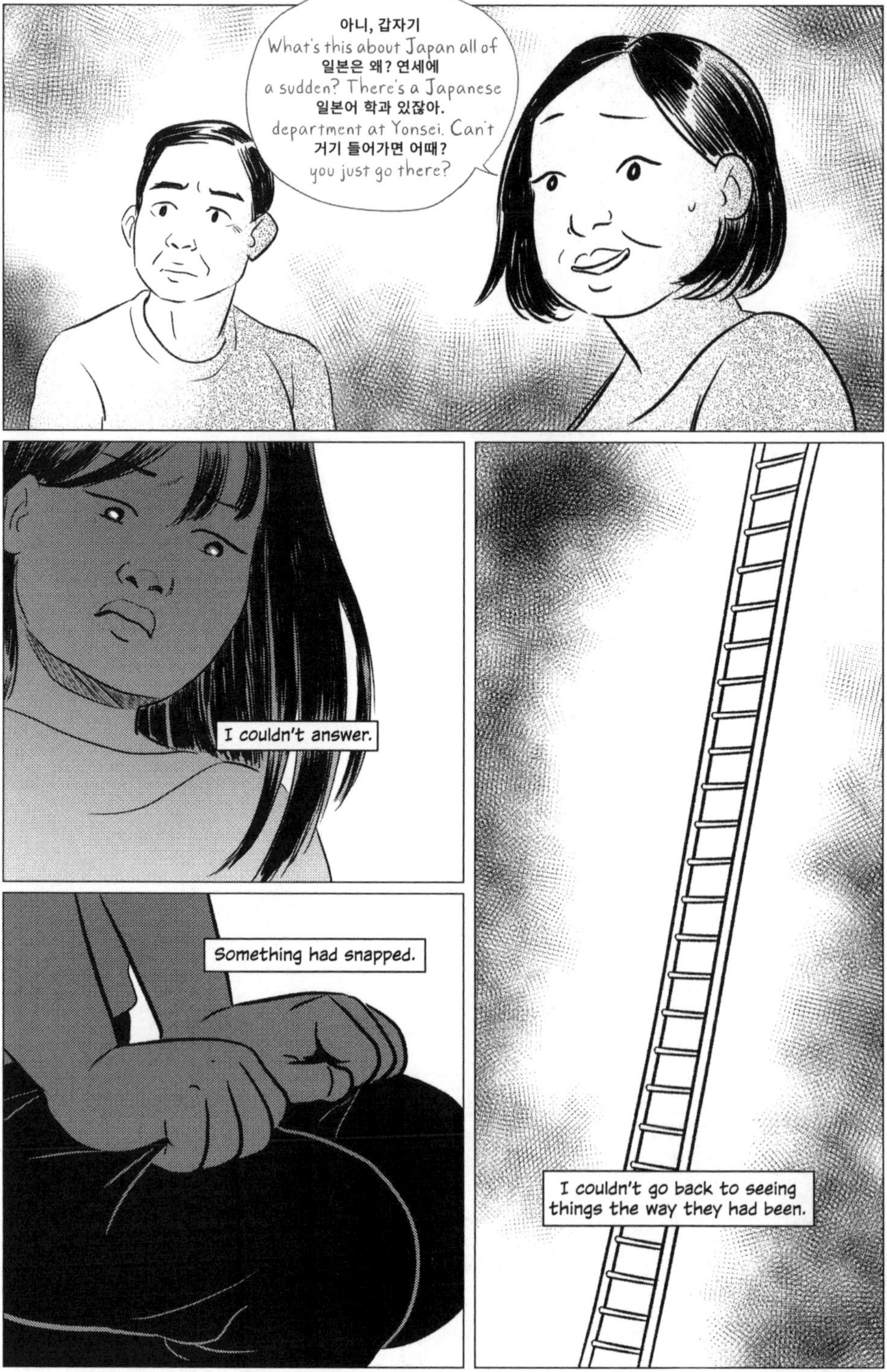
아니, 갑자기
What's this about Japan all of
일본은 왜? 연세에
a sudden? There's a Japanese
일본어 학과 있잖아.
department at Yonsei. Can't
거기 들어가면 어때?
you just go there?
I couldn't answer.
Something had snapped.
I couldn't go back to seeing things the way they had been.

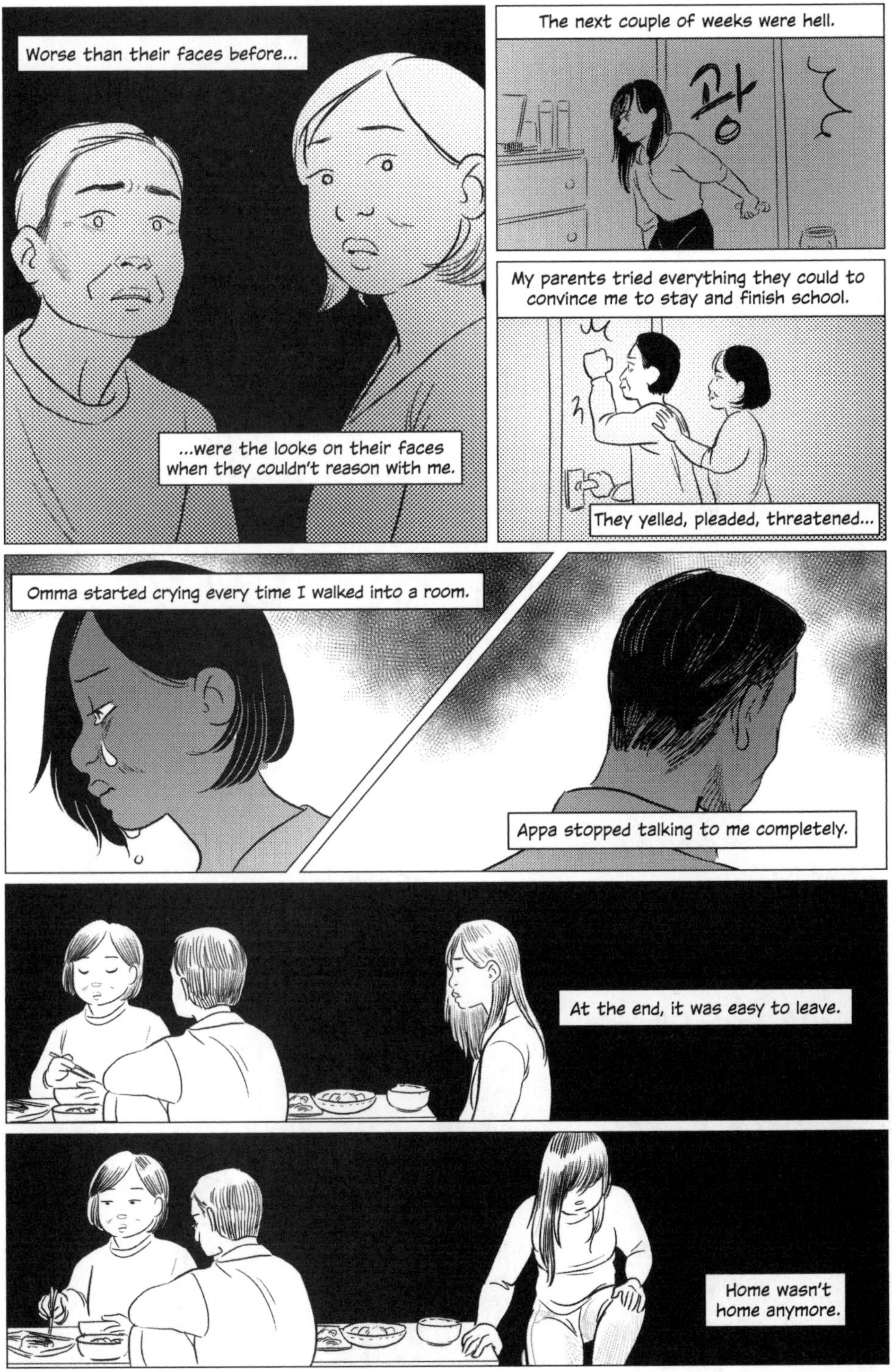
Worse than their faces before...
...were the looks on their faces when they couldn't reason with me.
The next couple of weeks were hell.
광
My parents tried everything they could to convince me to stay and finish school.
They yelled, pleaded, threatened...
Omma started crying every time I walked into a room.
Appa stopped talking to me completely.
At the end, it was easy to leave.
Home wasn't home anymore.

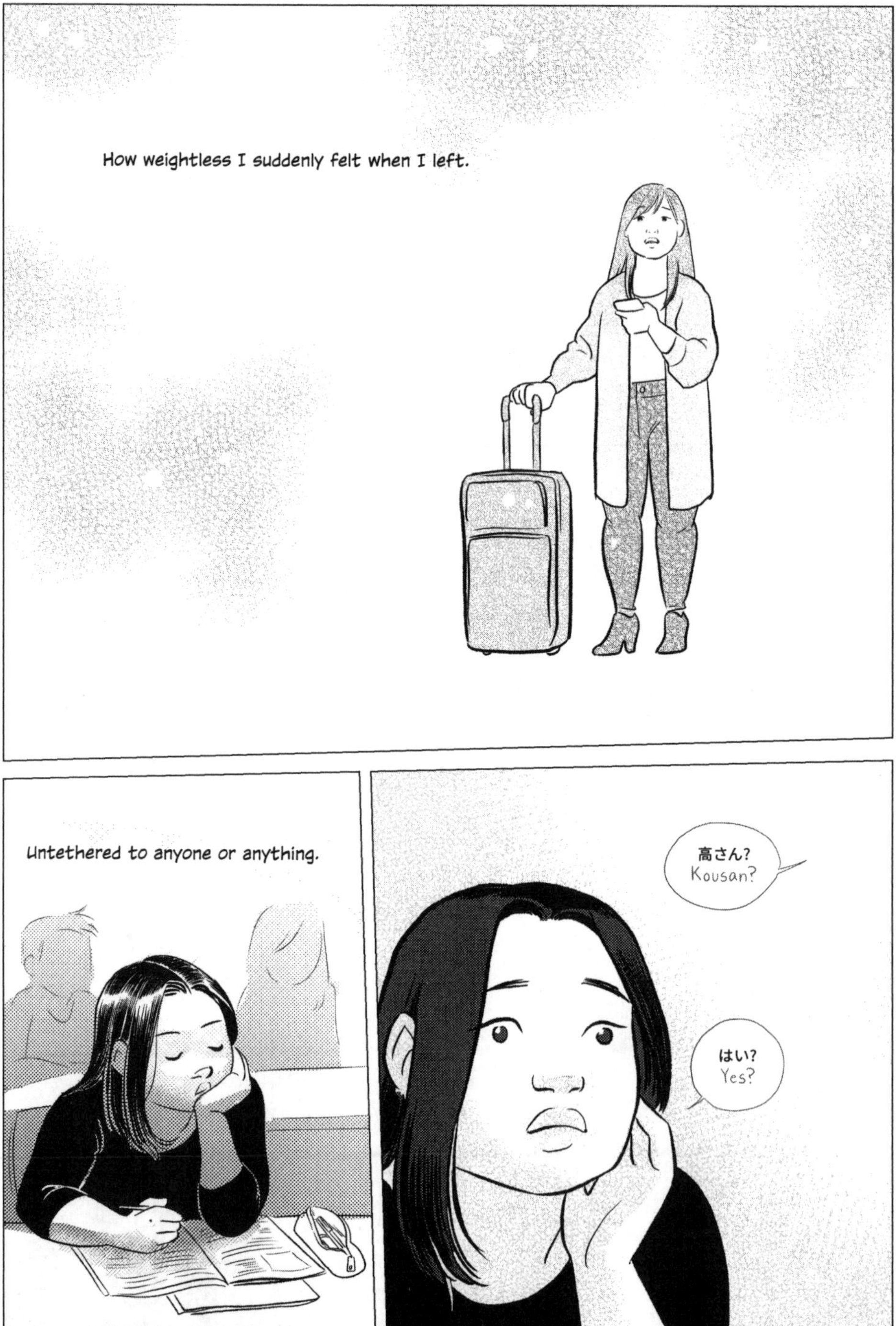
How weightless I suddenly felt when I left.
Untethered to anyone or anything.
高さん?
Kousan?
はい?
Yes?

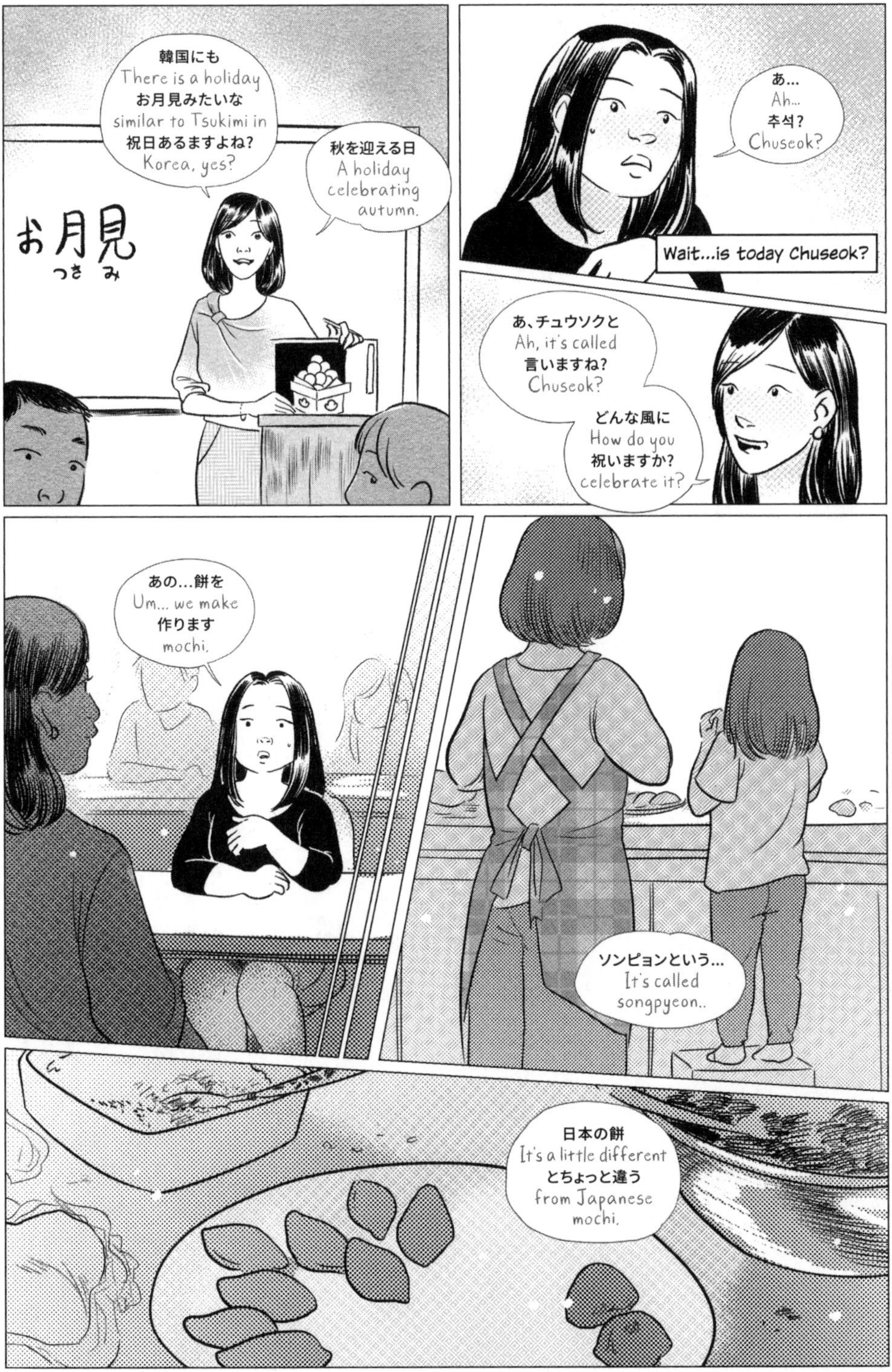

韓国にも
There is a holiday
お月見みたいな
similar to Tsukimi in
祝日あるますよね?
Korea, yes?
秋を迎える日
A holiday celebrating autumn.
お月見
つきみ
あ...
Ah...
추석?
Chuseok?
Wait...is today Chuseok?
あ、チュウソクと
Ah, it's called
言いますね?
Chuseok?
どんな風に
How do you
祝いますか?
celebrate it?
あの...餅を
Um... we make
作ります
mochi.
ソンピョンという...
It's called songpyeon..
日本の餅
It's a little different
とちょっと違う
from Japanese mochi.

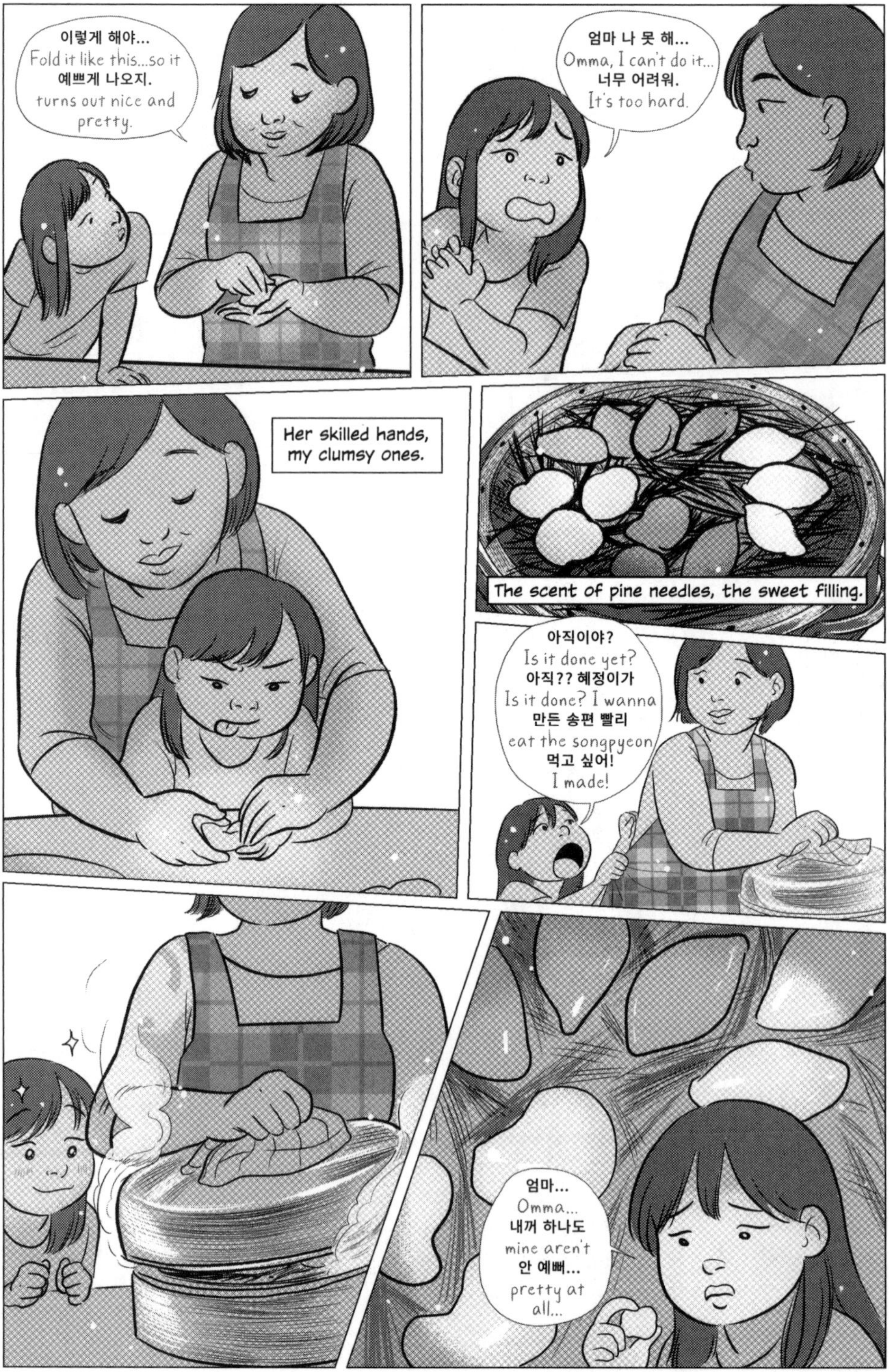
이렇게 해야... Fold it like this...so it 예쁘게 나오지. turns out nice and pretty.
엄마 나 못 해... Omma, I can't do it... 너무 어려워. It's too hard.
Her skilled hands, my clumsy ones.
The scent of pine needles, the sweet filling.
아직이야? Is it done yet? 아직?? 혜정이가 Is it done? I wanna 만든 송편 빨리 eat the songpyeon 먹고 싶어! I made!
엄마... Omma... 내꺼 하나도 mine aren't 안 예뻐... pretty at all...

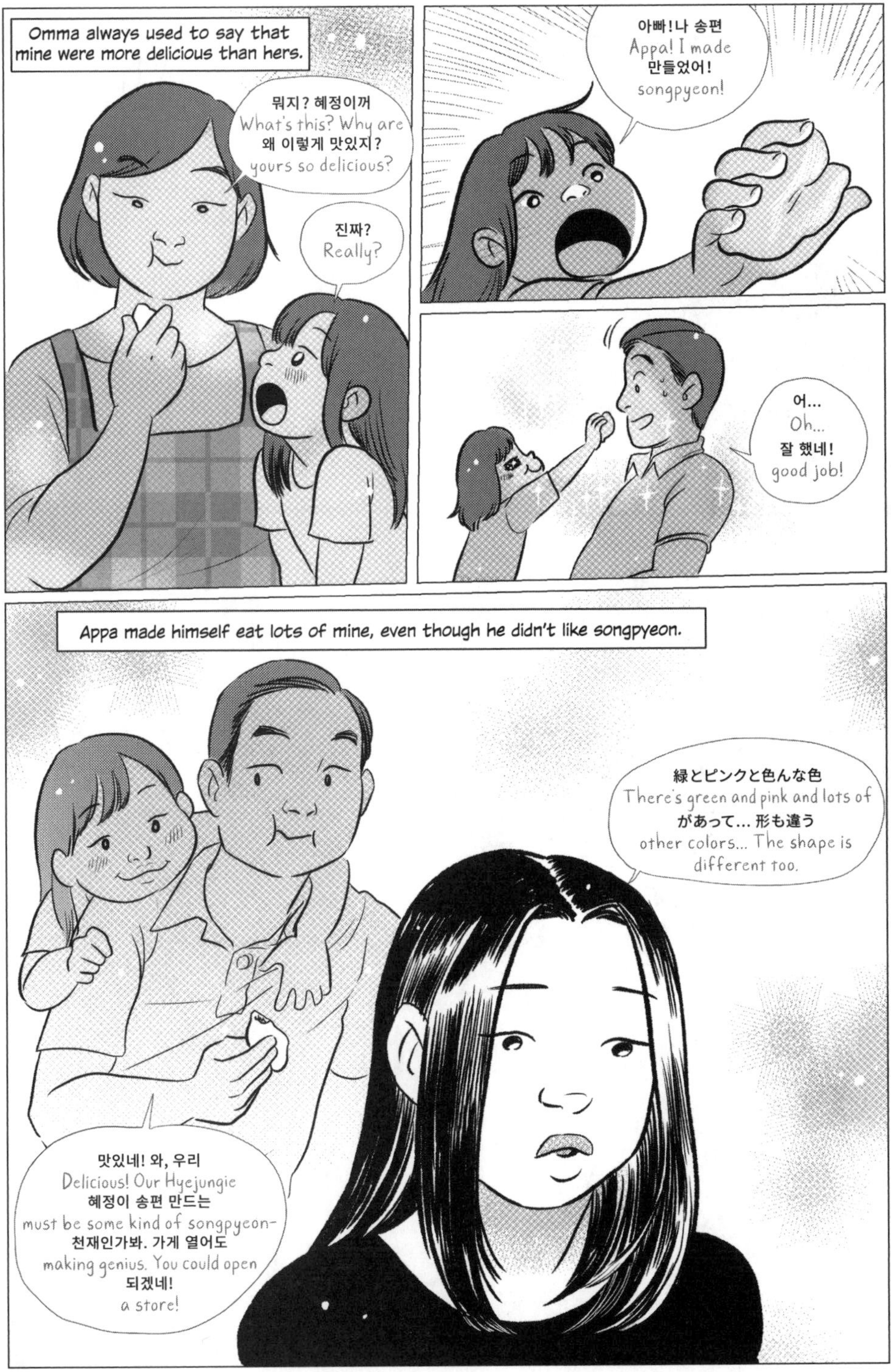

Omma always used to say that mine were more delicious than hers.
뭐지? 혜정이꺼 What's this? Why are 왜 이렇게 맛있지? yours so delicious?
진짜? Really?
아빠! 나 송편 Appa! I made 만들었어! songpyeon!
어... Oh... 잘 했네! good job!
Appa made himself eat lots of mine, even though he didn't like songpyeon.
緑とピンクと色んな色 There's green and pink and lots of があって… 形も違う other colors... The shape is different too.
맛있네! 와, 우리 Delicious! Our Hyejungie 혜정이 송편 만드는 must be some kind of songpyeon- 천재인가봐. 가게 열어도 making genius. You could open 되겠네! a store!

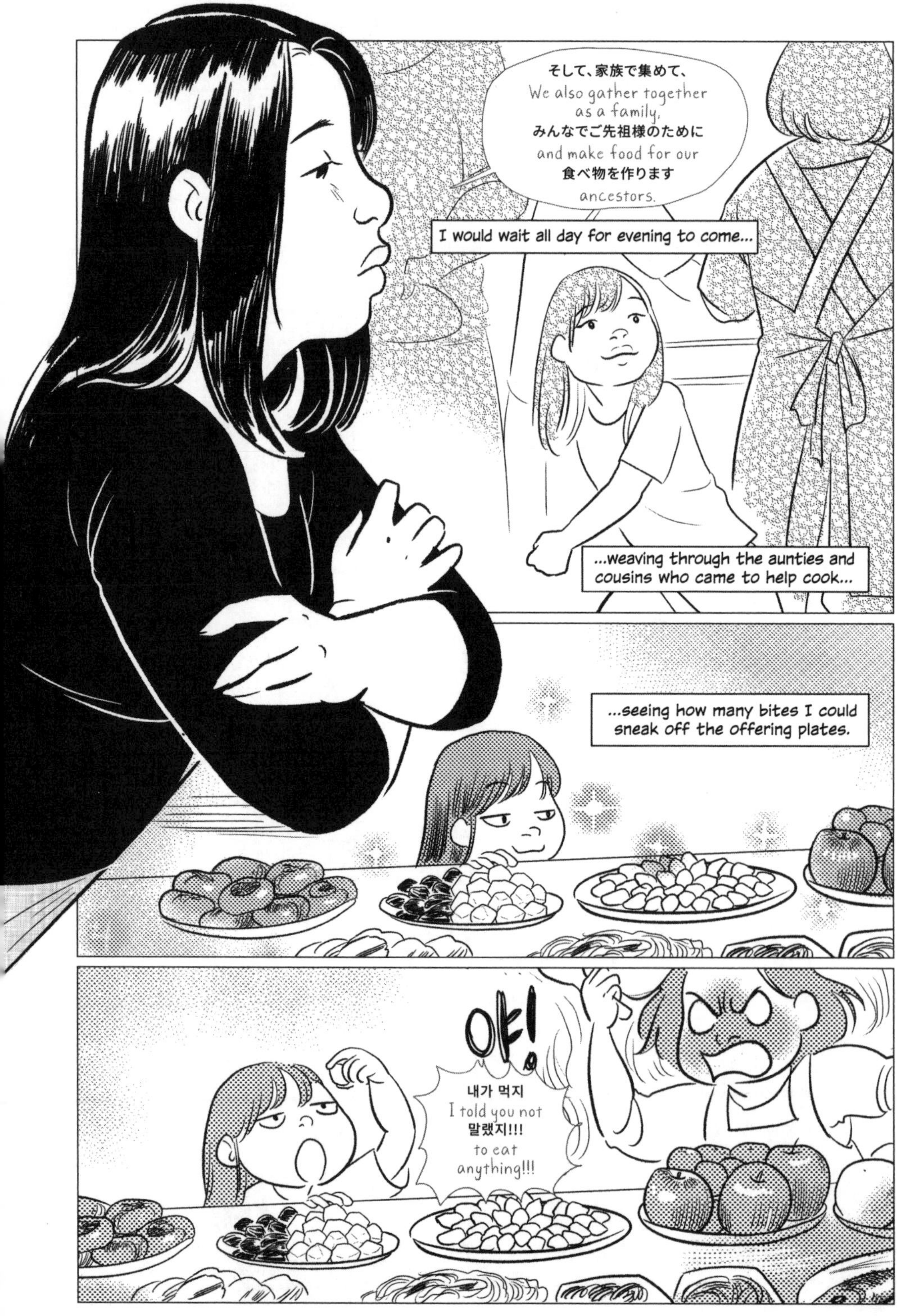

そして、家族で集めて、
We also gather together as a family,
みんなでご先祖様のために
and make food for our
食べ物を作ります
ancestors.
I would wait all day for evening to come...
...weaving through the aunties and cousins who came to help cook...
...seeing how many bites I could sneak off the offering plates.
야!
내가 먹지
I told you not
말랬지!!!
to eat anything!!!

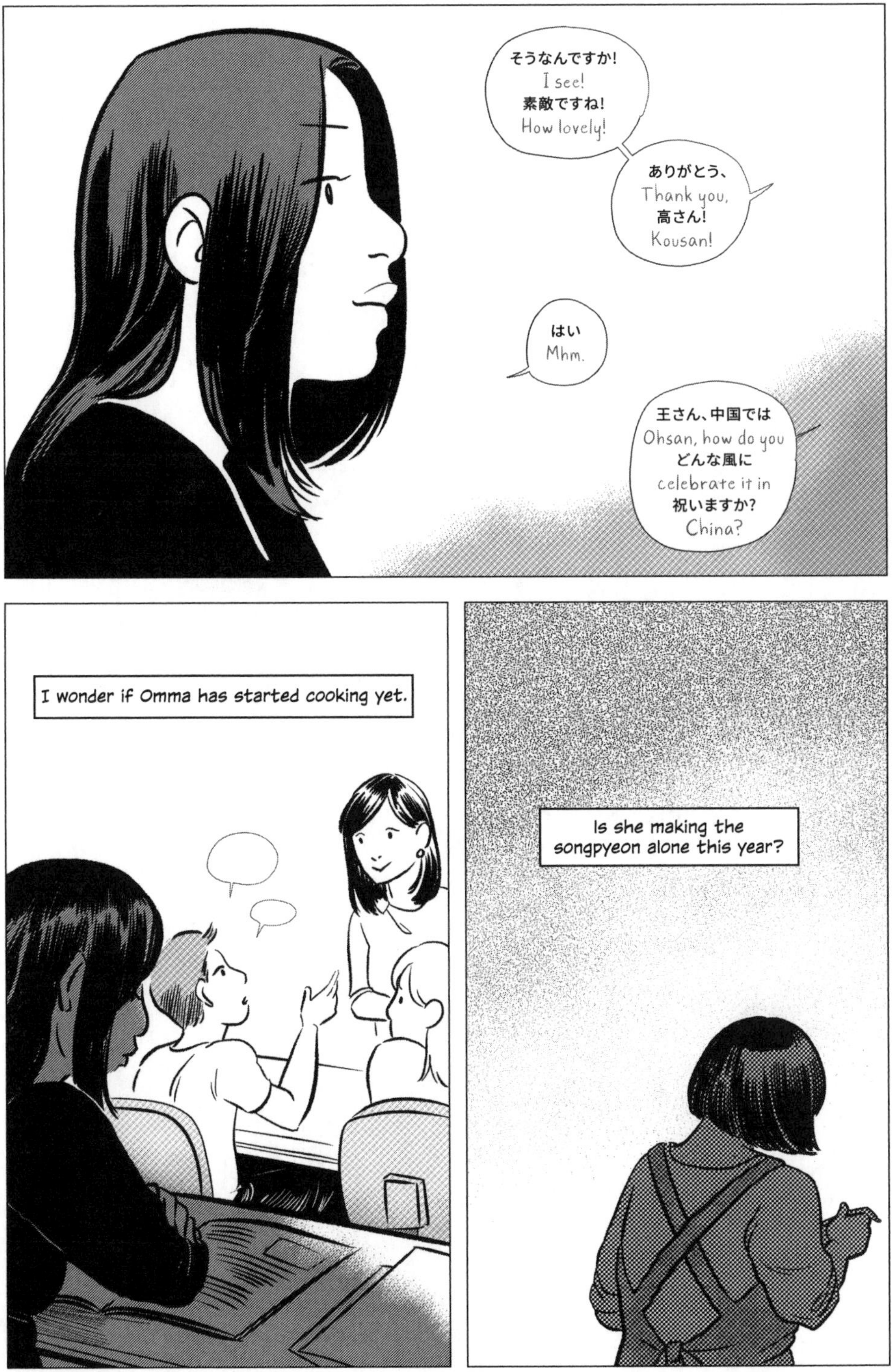
そうなんですか！
I see!
素敵ですね！
How lovely!
ありがとう、
Thank you,
高さん！
Kousan!
はい
Mhm.
王さん、中国では
Ohsan, how do you
どんな風に
celebrate it in
祝いますか？
China?
I wonder if Omma has started cooking yet.
Is she making the songpyeon alone this year?

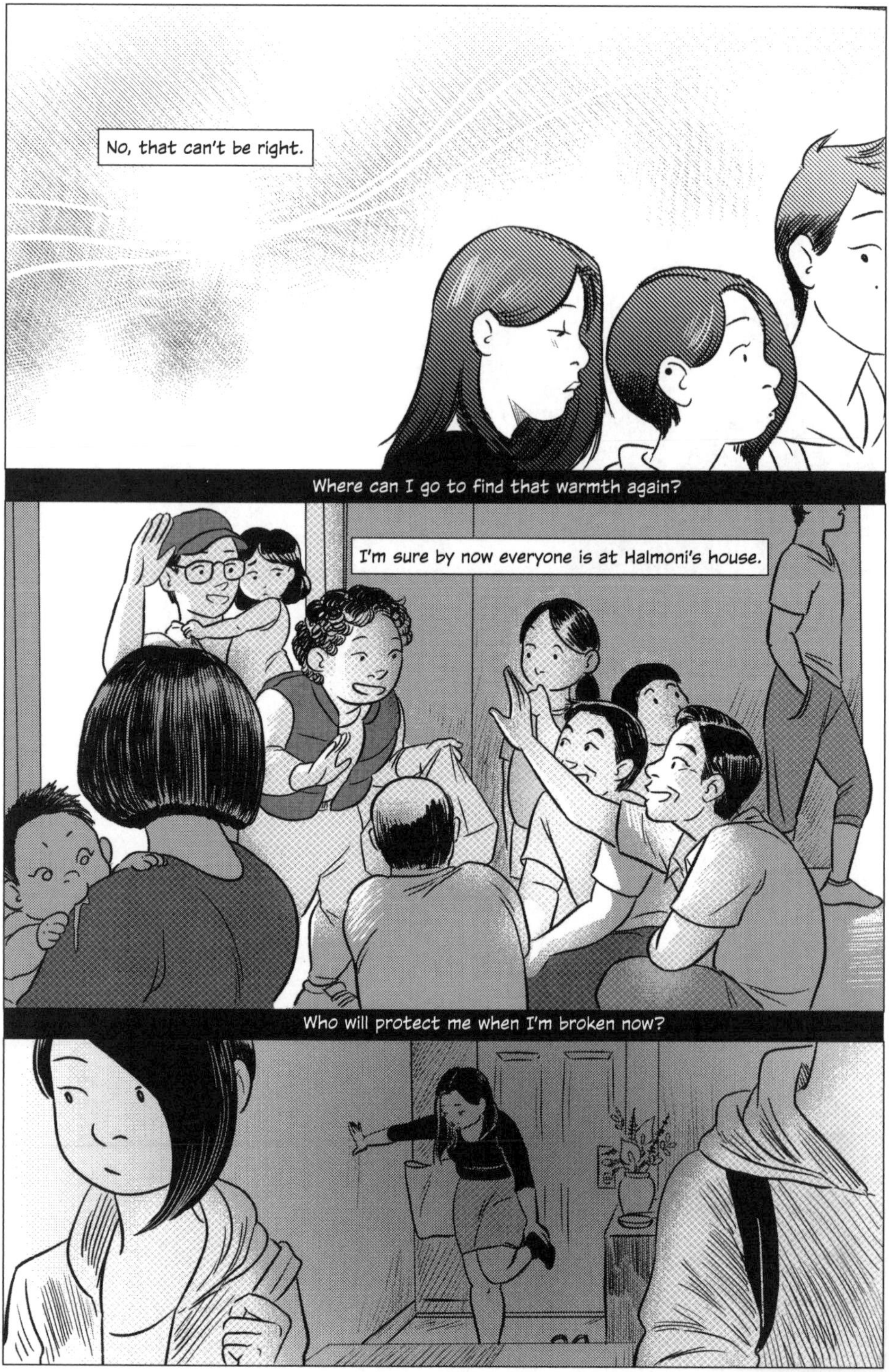
No, that can't be right.
Where can I go to find that warmth again?
I'm sure by now everyone is at Halmoni's house.
Who will protect me when I'm broken now?

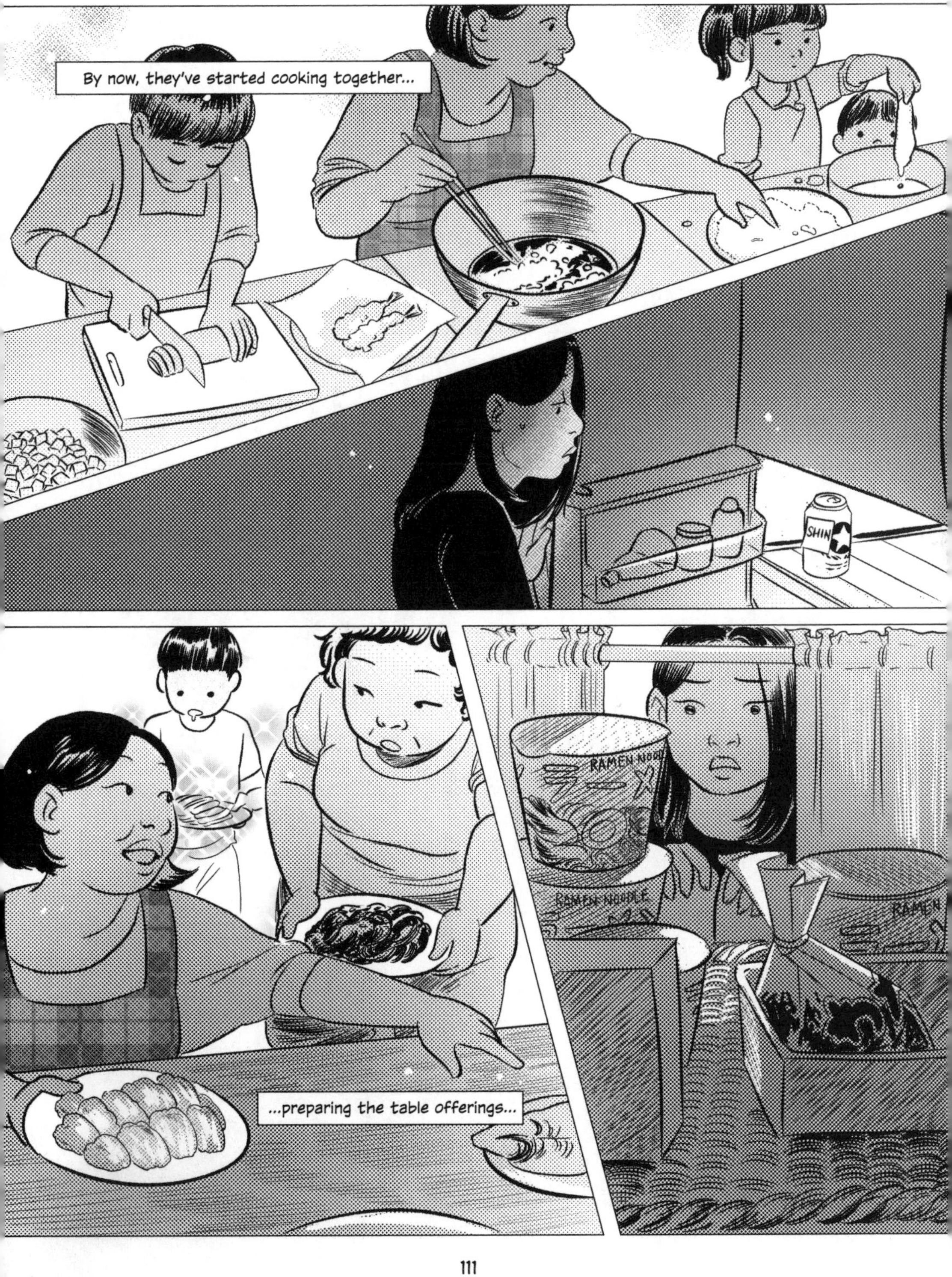
By now, they've started cooking together...
SHIN
RAMEN NOODLE
RAMEN
...preparing the table offerings...

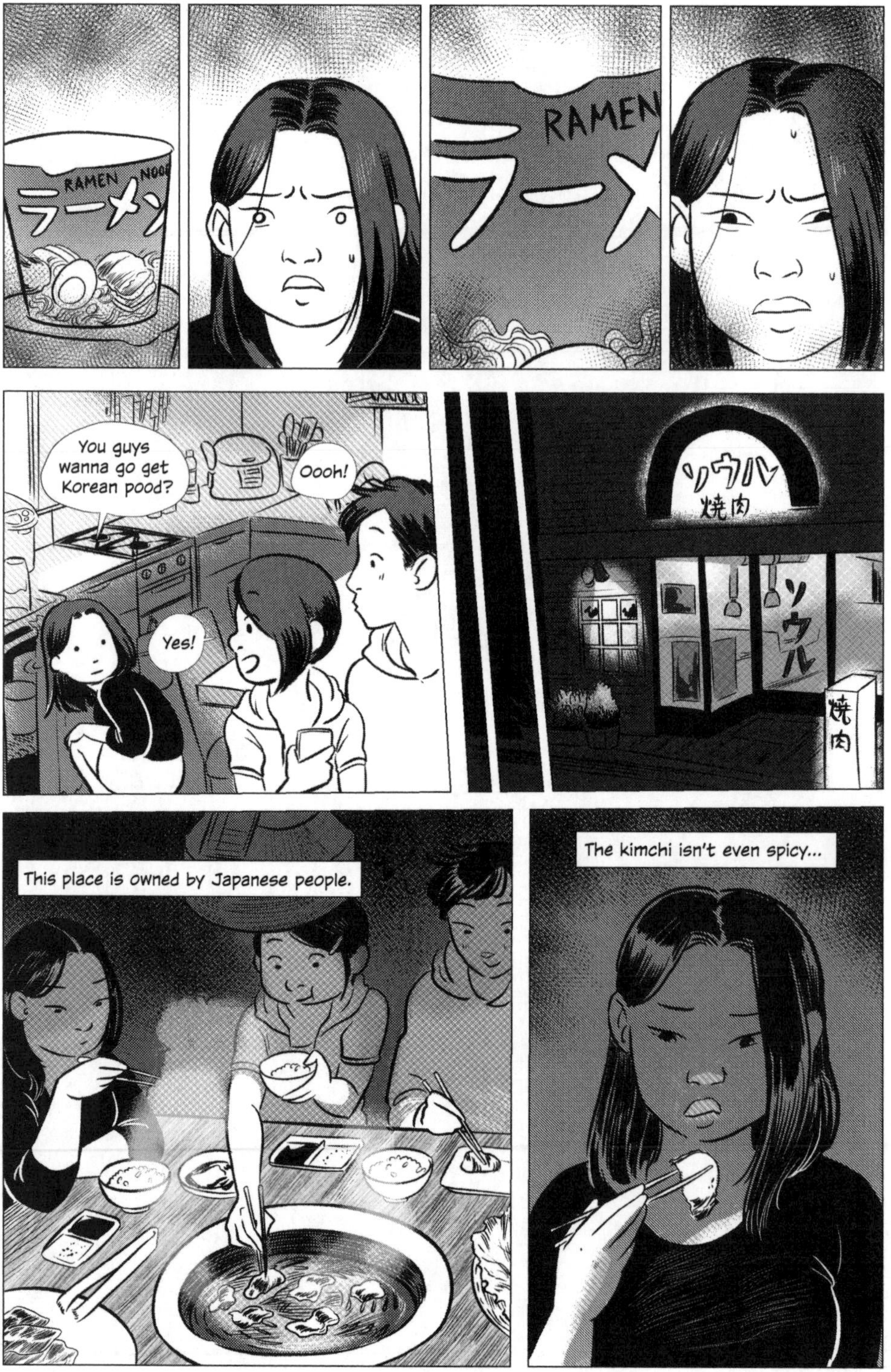
RAMEN NOO
ラーメン
RAMEN
ラーメ
You guys wanna go get Korean pood?
Oooh!
Yes!
ソウル
焼肉
ソウル
焼肉
This place is owned by Japanese people.
The kimchi isn't even spicy...

すみません! ソジュ
Excuse me! One more
もう一本下さい!
bottle of soju, please!

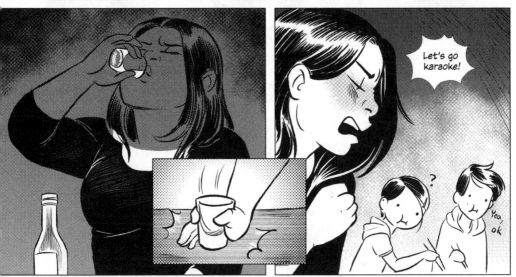

Let's go karaoke!

Yea, ok

Ugh.

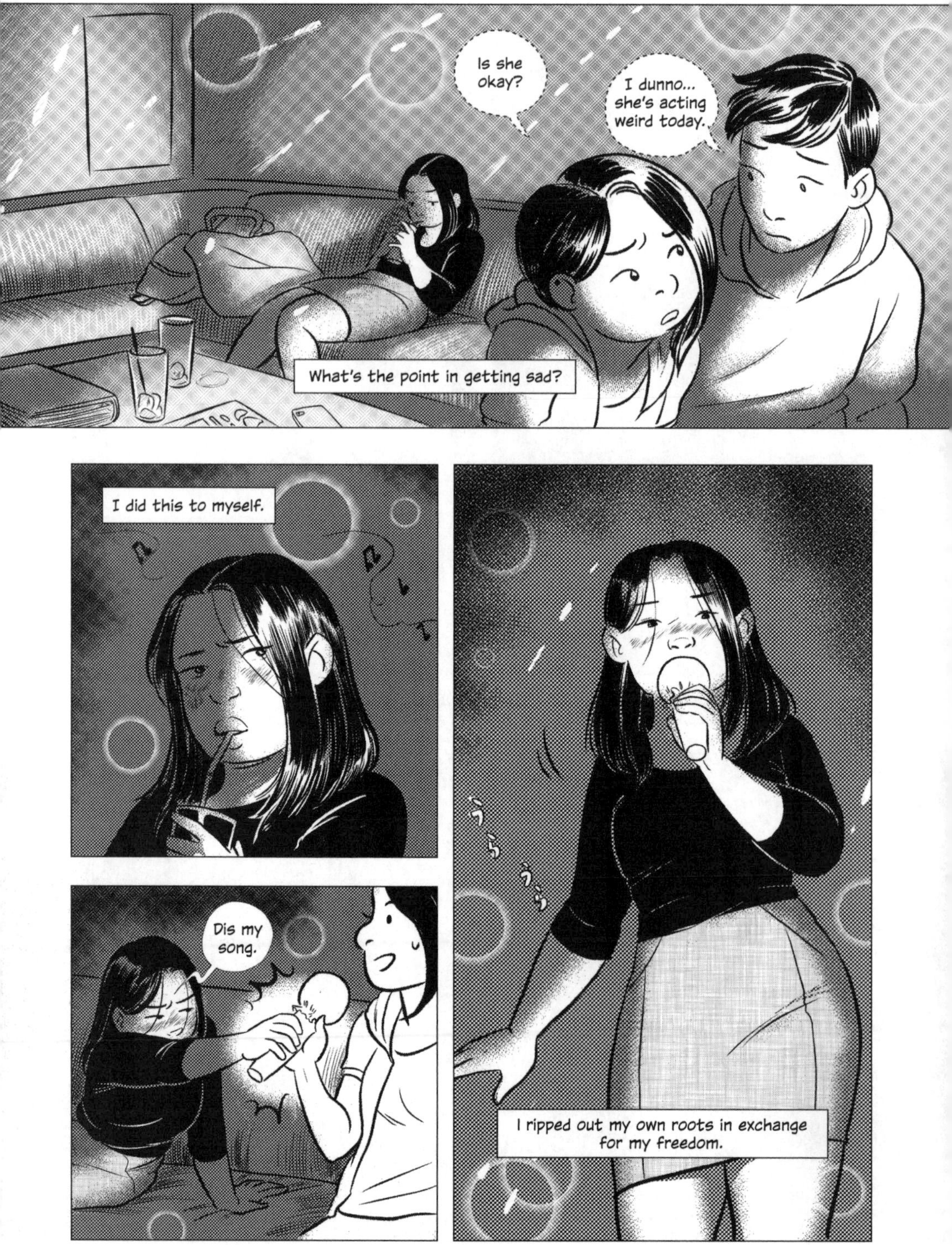
Is she okay?
I dunno... she's acting weird today.
What's the point in getting sad?
I did this to myself.
Dis my song.
I ripped out my own roots in exchange for my freedom.

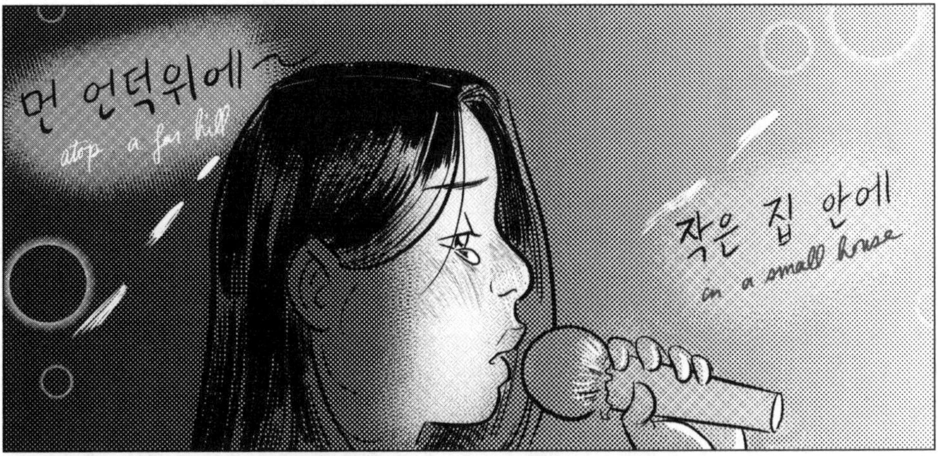
먼 언덕위에~
atop a far hill
작은 집 안에
in a small house

What right do I have to miss my parents?

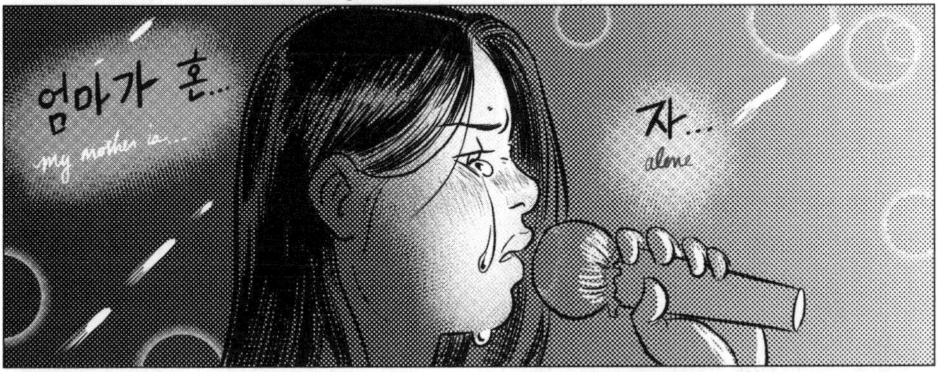
엄마가 혼...
my mother is...
자...
alone

I crushed their dreams with my own two hands.

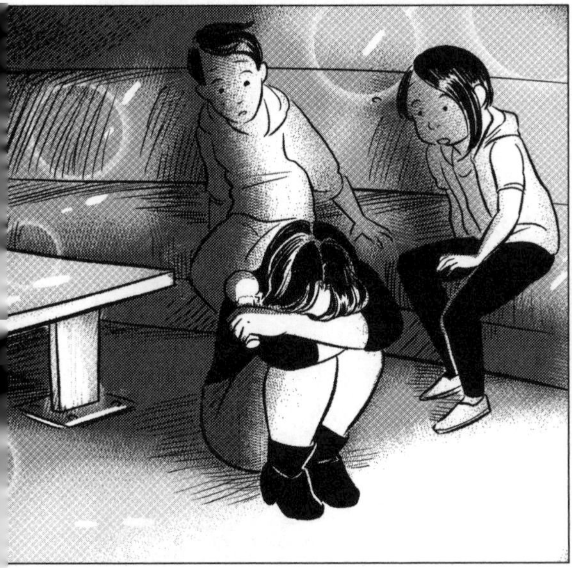

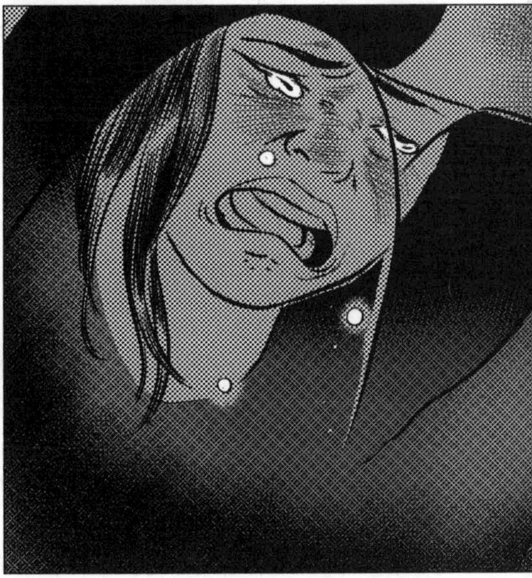

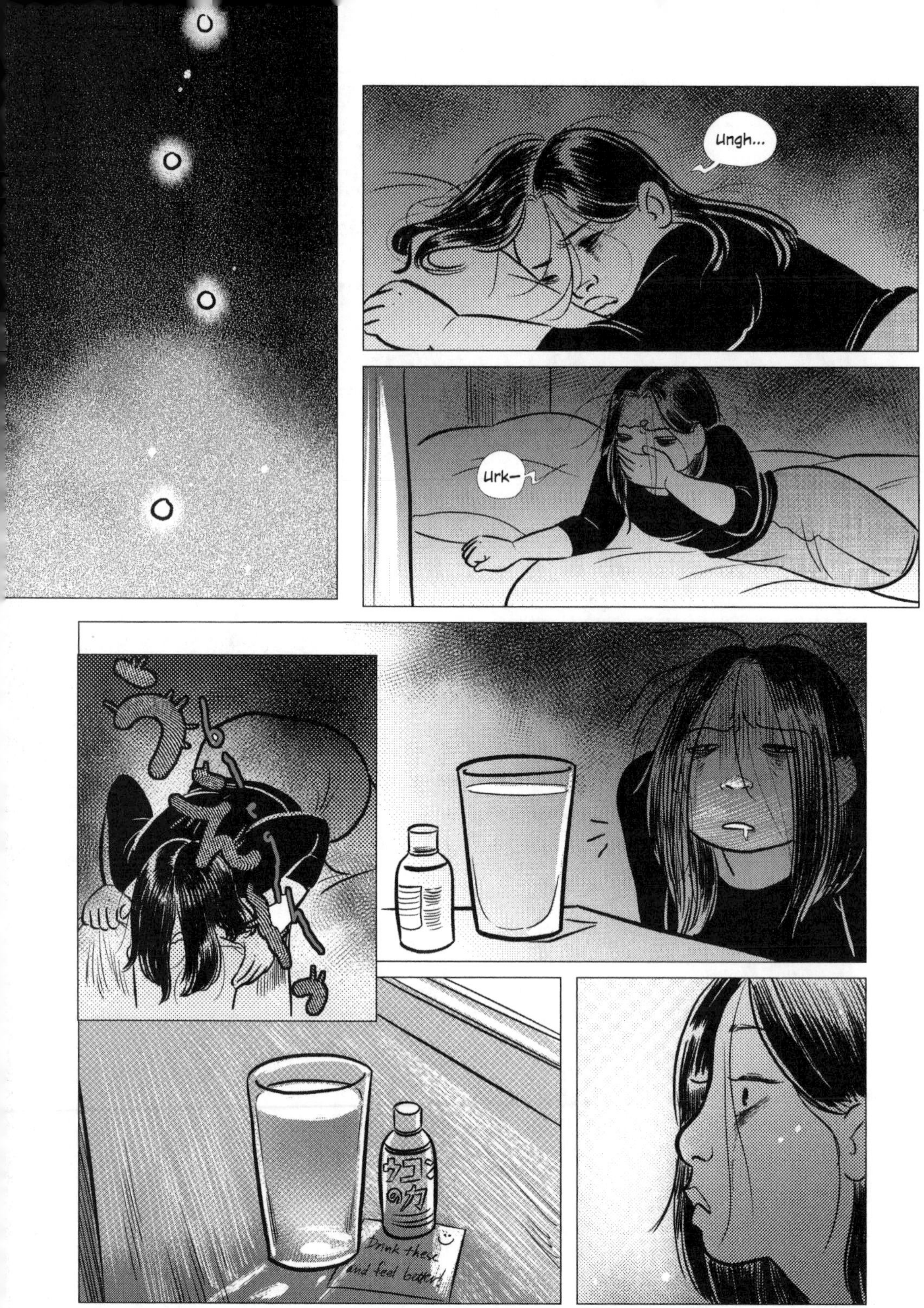
Ungh...
Urk—
ウコンの力
Drink these and feel better!

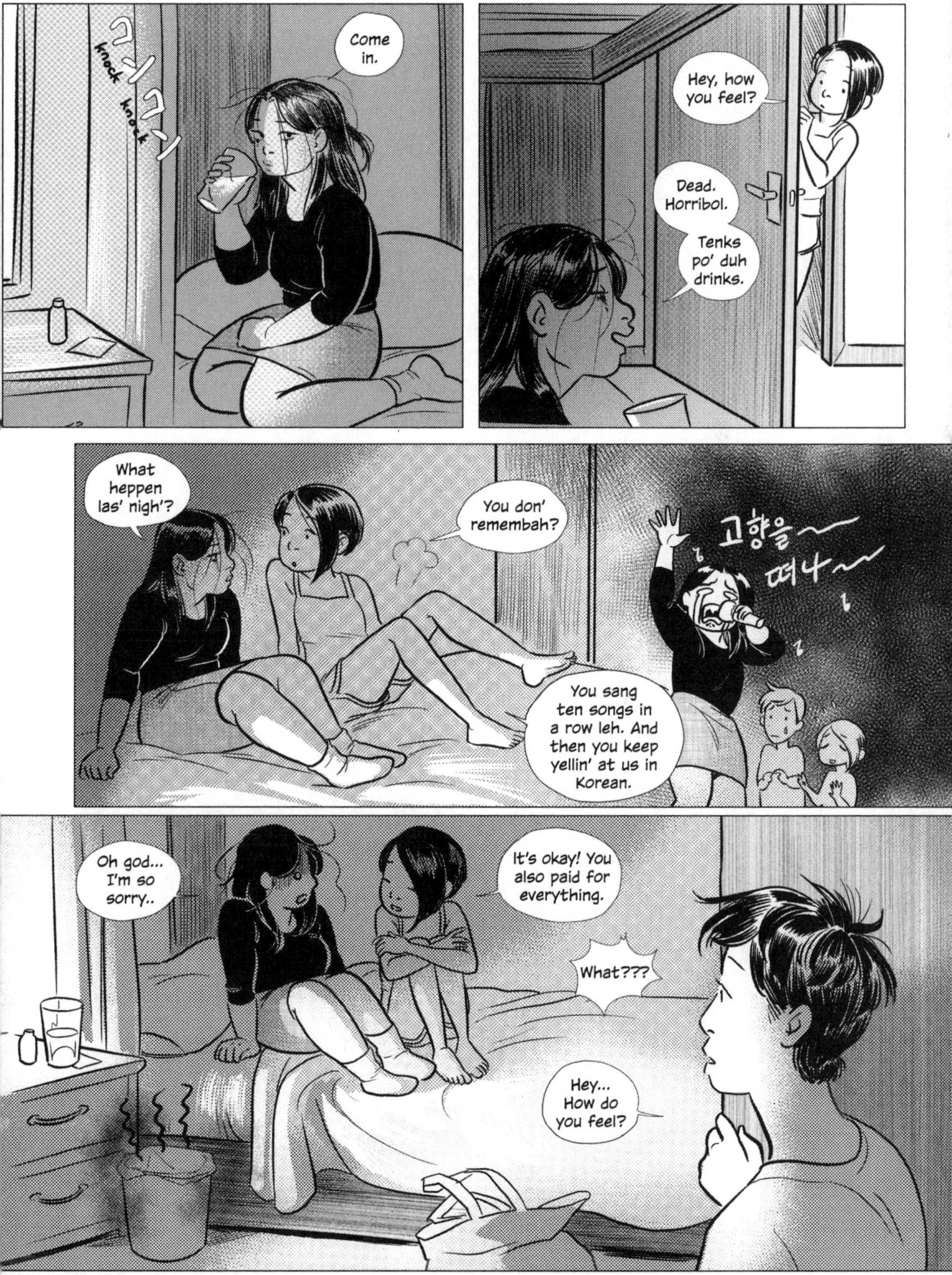

コンコン
knock knock
Come in.
Hey, how you feel?
Dead. Horribol.
Tenks po' duh drinks.
What heppen las' nigh'?
You don' remembah?
고향을~
떠나~
You sang ten songs in a row leh. And then you keep yellin' at us in Korean.
Oh god... I'm so sorry..
It's okay! You also paid for everything.
What???
Hey... How do you feel?

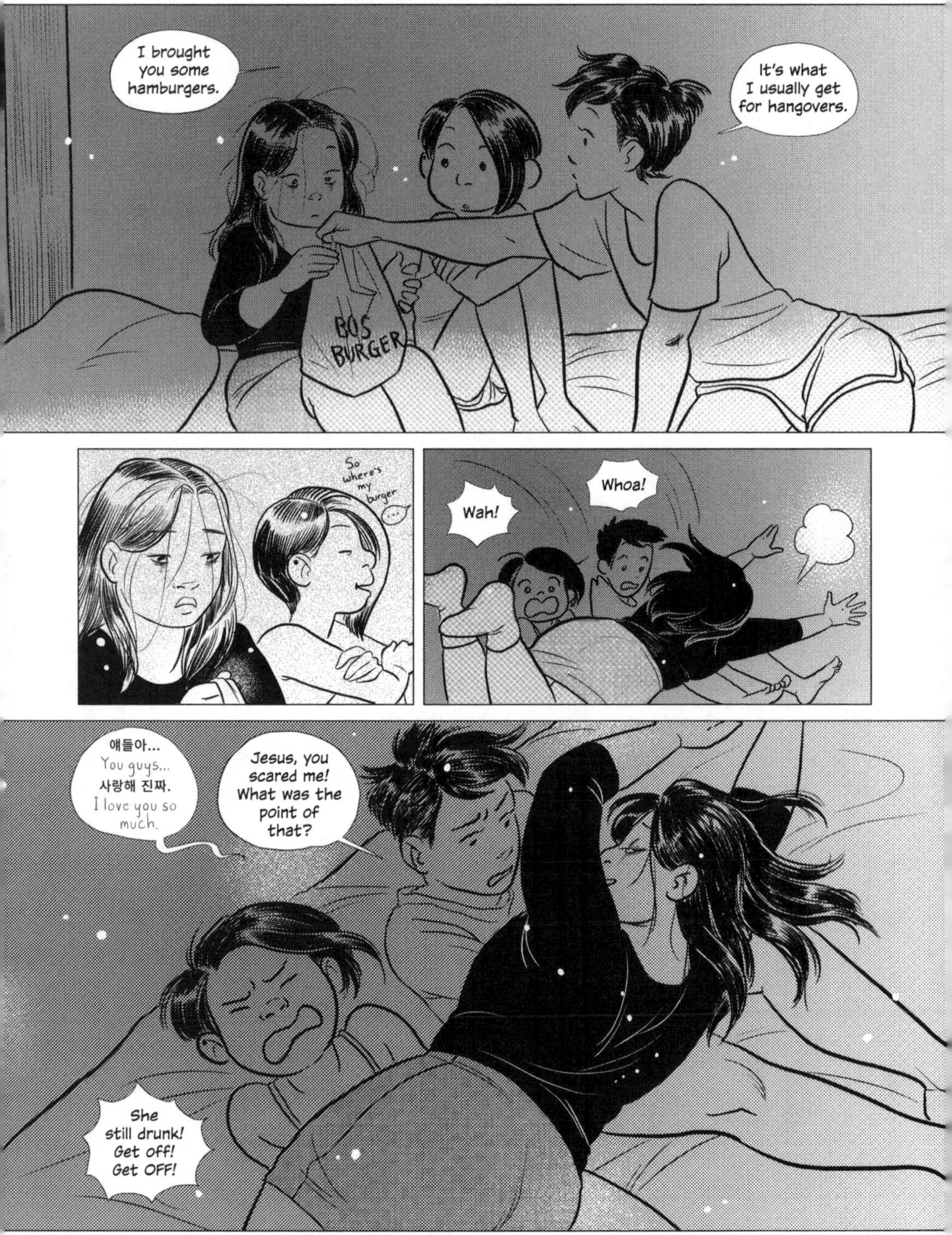
I brought you some hamburgers.
It's what I usually get for hangovers.
BOS BURGER
So where's my burger
...
Wah!
Whoa!
애들아... You guys... 사랑해 진짜. I love you so much.
Jesus, you scared me! What was the point of that?
She still drunk! Get off! Get OFF!

Chapter 7

Kaitenzushi

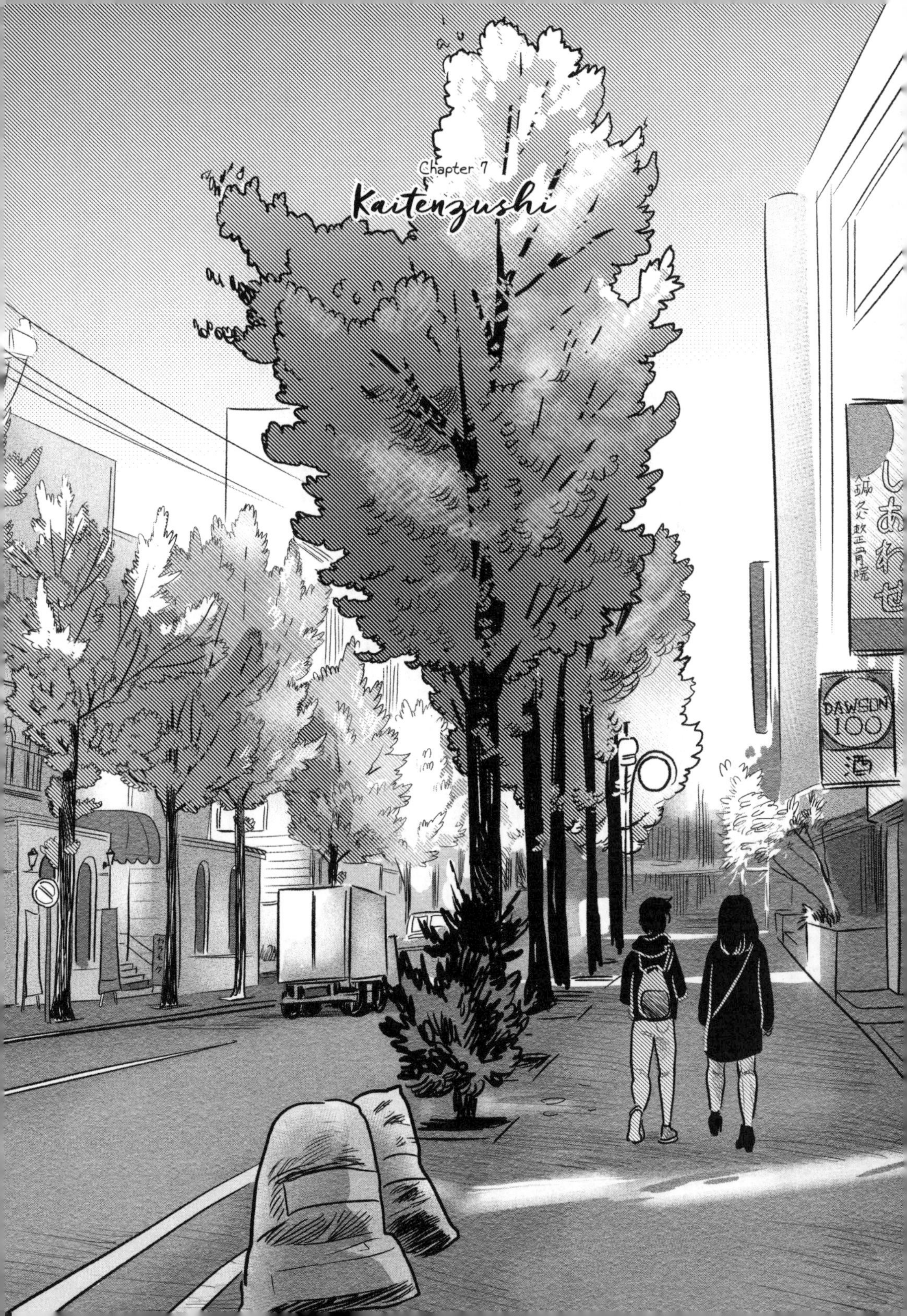
鍼灸整骨院
DAWSON 100
酒

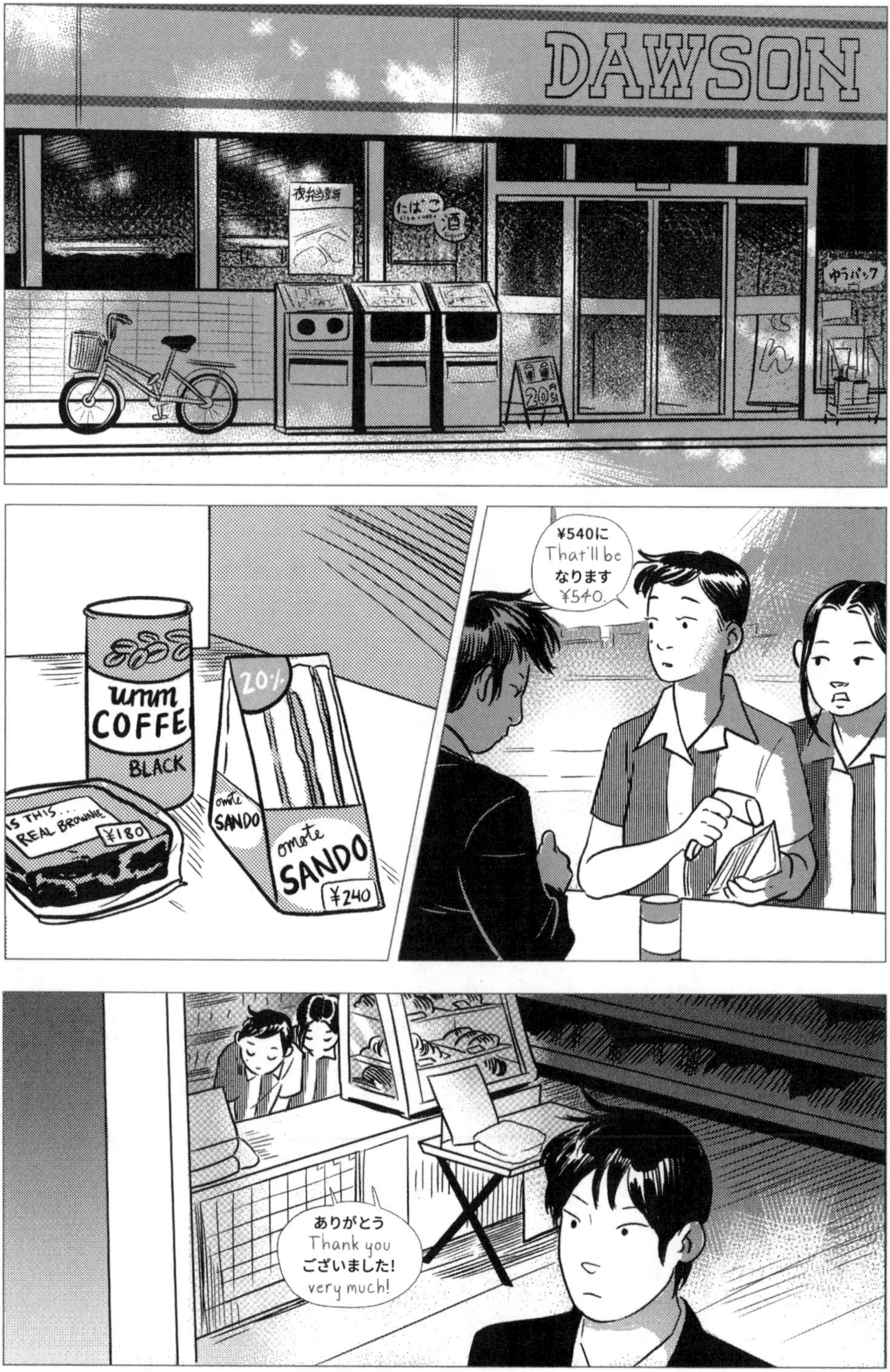
DAWSON
たばこ 酒
ゆうパック
umm COFFE BLACK
IS THIS... REAL BROWNIE ¥180
20%
omote SANDO
omote SANDO ¥240
¥540になります
That'll be ¥540.
ありがとうございました!
Thank you very much!

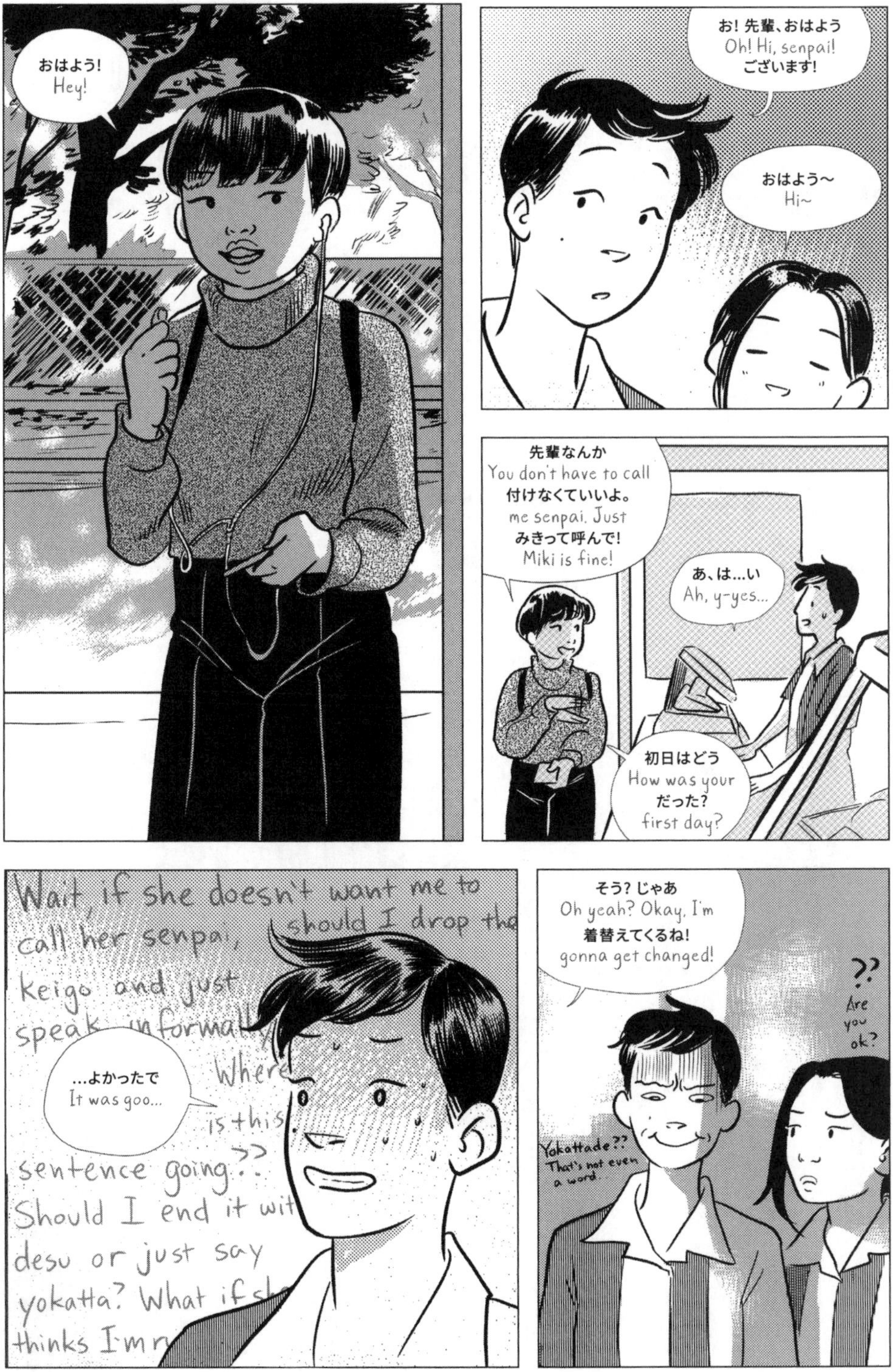
おはよう! Hey!
お! 先輩、おはよう Oh! Hi, senpai! ございます!
おはよう〜 Hi~
先輩なんか You don't have to call 付けなくていいよ。 me senpai. Just みきって呼んで! Miki is fine!
あ、は…い Ah, y-yes...
初日はどう How was your だった? first day?
Wait, if she doesn't want me to call her senpai, should I drop the keigo and just speak informal
…よかったで It was goo...
Where is this sentence going??
Should I end it wit desu or just say yokatta? What if sh thinks I'm r
そう? じゃあ Oh yeah? Okay, I'm 着替えてくるね! gonna get changed!
?? Are you ok?
Yokattade?? That's not even a word...

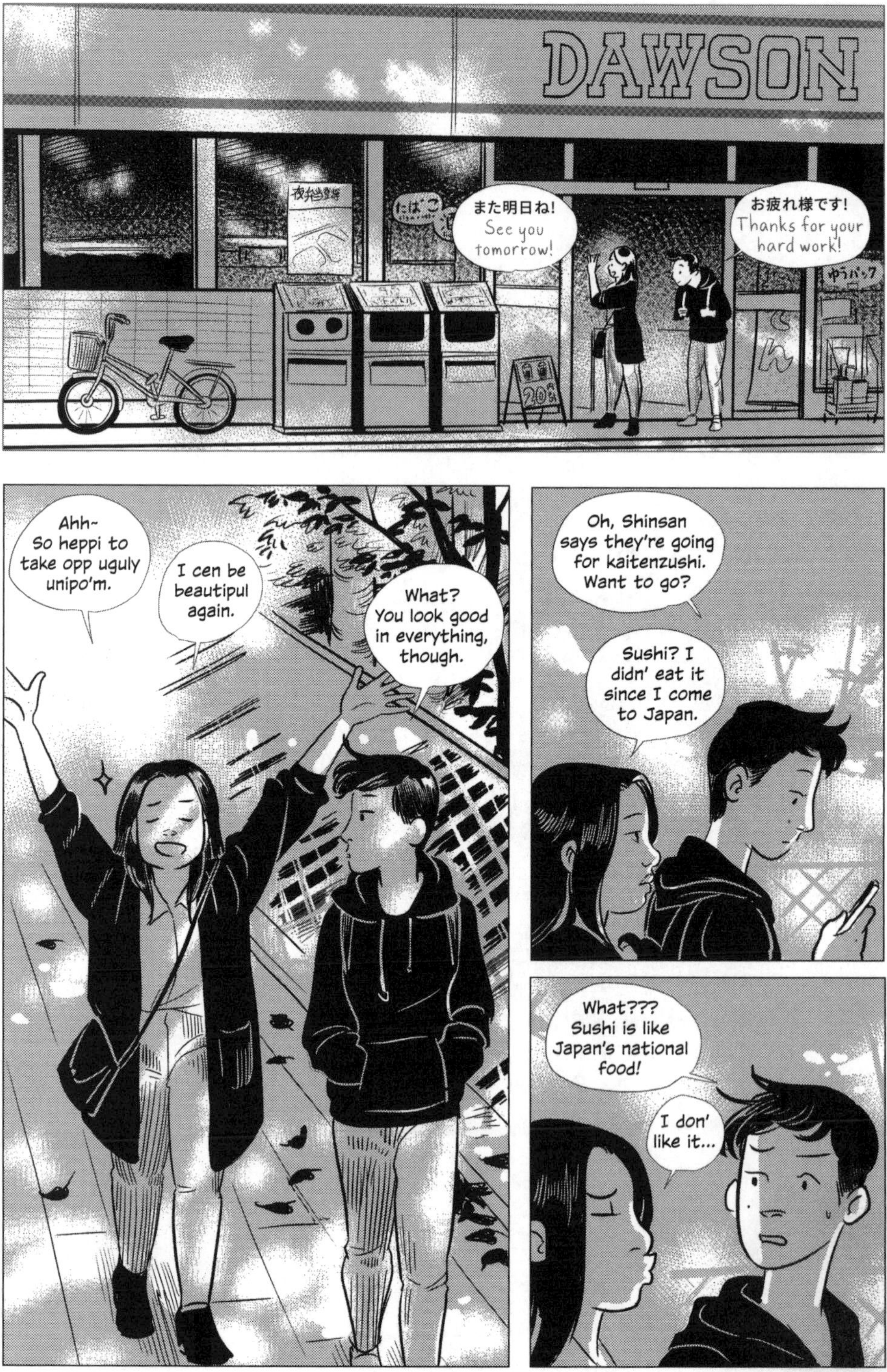
DAWSON
また明日ね! See you tomorrow!
お疲れ様です! Thanks for your hard work!
Ahh~ So heppi to take opp uguly unipo'm.
I cen be beautipul again.
What? You look good in everything, though.
Oh, Shinsan says they're going for kaitenzushi. Want to go?
Sushi? I didn' eat it since I come to Japan.
What??? Sushi is like Japan's national food!
I don' like it...

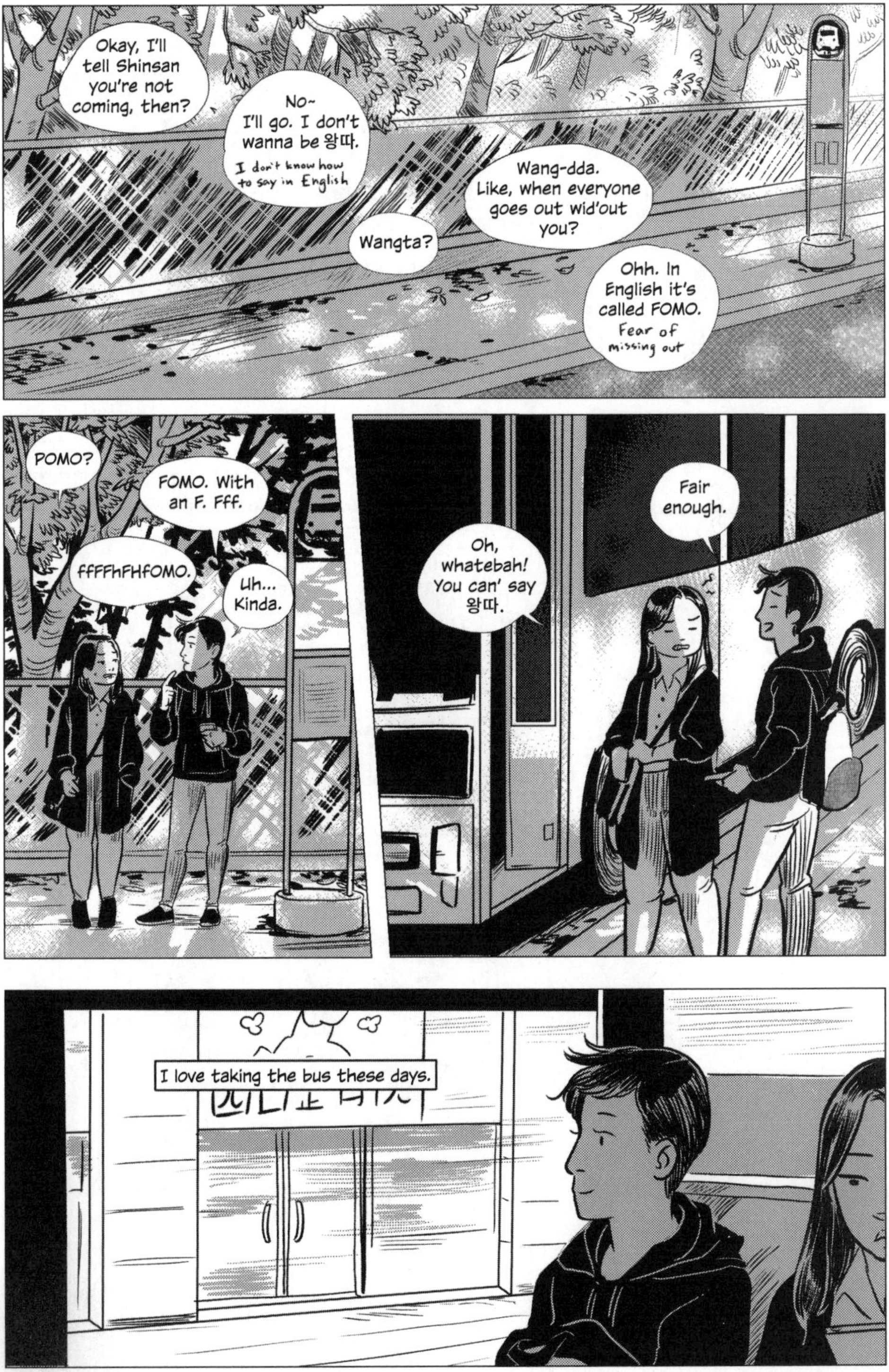
Okay, I'll tell Shinsan you're not coming, then?
No~ I'll go. I don't wanna be 왕따.
I don't know how to say in English
Wangta?
Wang-dda. Like, when everyone goes out wid'out you?
Ohh. In English it's called FOMO.
Fear of missing out
POMO?
FOMO. With an F. Fff.
ffffhFHfOMO.
Uh... Kinda.
Oh, whatebah! You can' say 왕따.
Fair enough.
I love taking the bus these days.

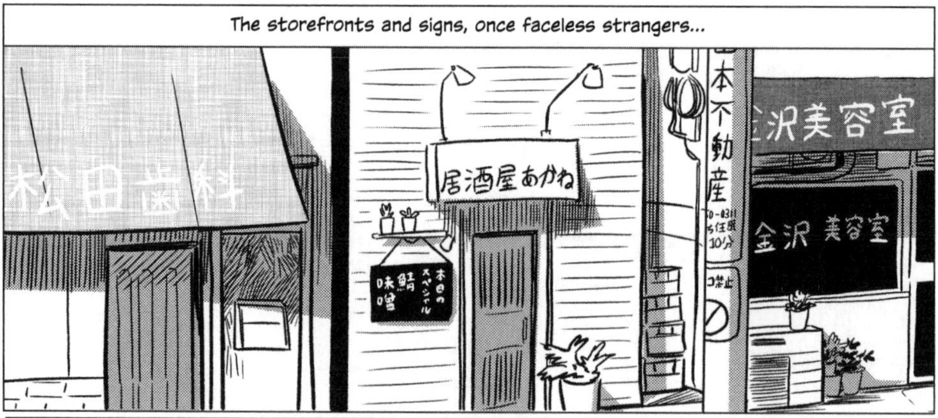
The storefronts and signs, once faceless strangers...
松田歯科
居酒屋あかね
本日のスペシャル 鯖味噌
金沢美容室
金沢 美容室

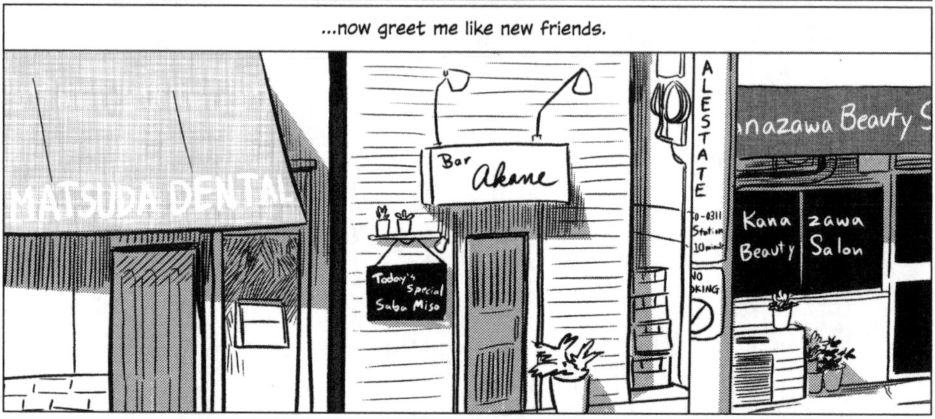
...now greet me like new friends.
MATSUDA DENTAL
Bar Akane
Today's Special Saba Miso
ALESTATE
Kana zawa Beauty Salon

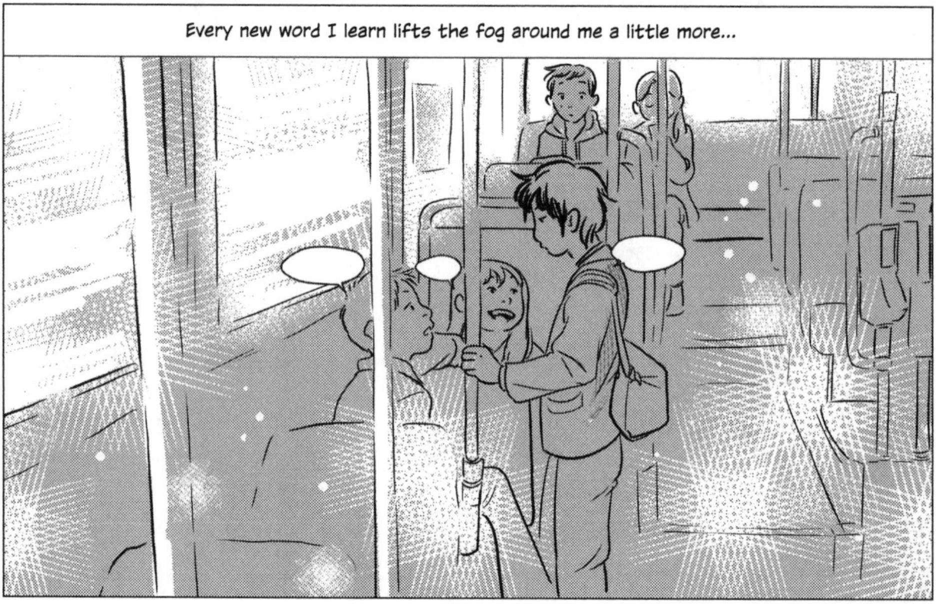
Every new word I learn lifts the fog around me a little more...

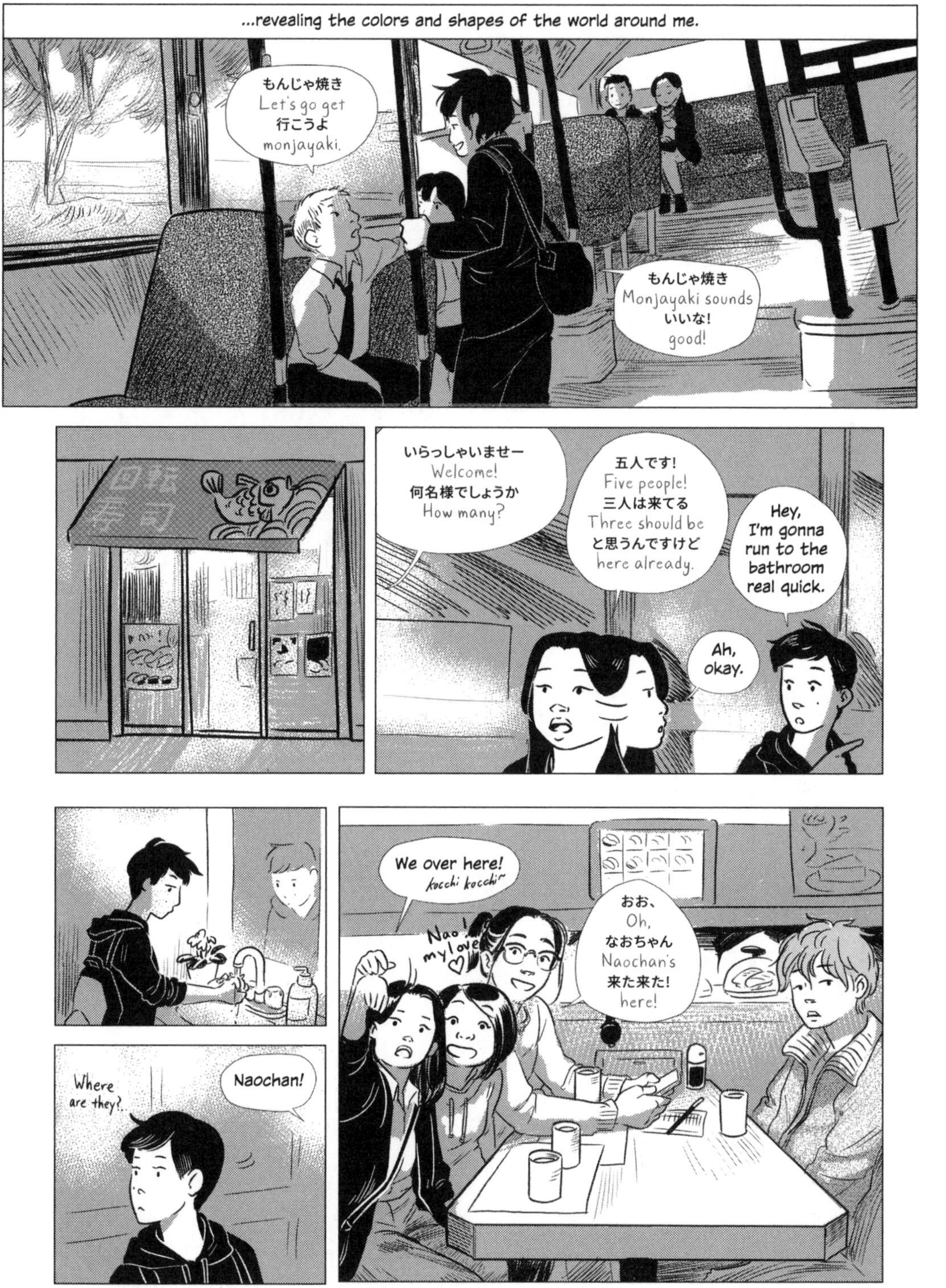

...revealing the colors and shapes of the world around me.
もんじゃ焼き Let's go get 行こうよ monjayaki.
もんじゃ焼き Monjayaki sounds いいな! good!
いらっしゃいませー Welcome! 何名様でしょうか How many?
五人です! Five people! 三人は来てる Three should be と思うんですけど here already.
Hey, I'm gonna run to the bathroom real quick.
Ah, okay.
We over here! kocchi kocchi~
Nao! my love ♡
おお、Oh, なおちゃん Naochan's 来た来た! here!
Where are they?
Naochan!

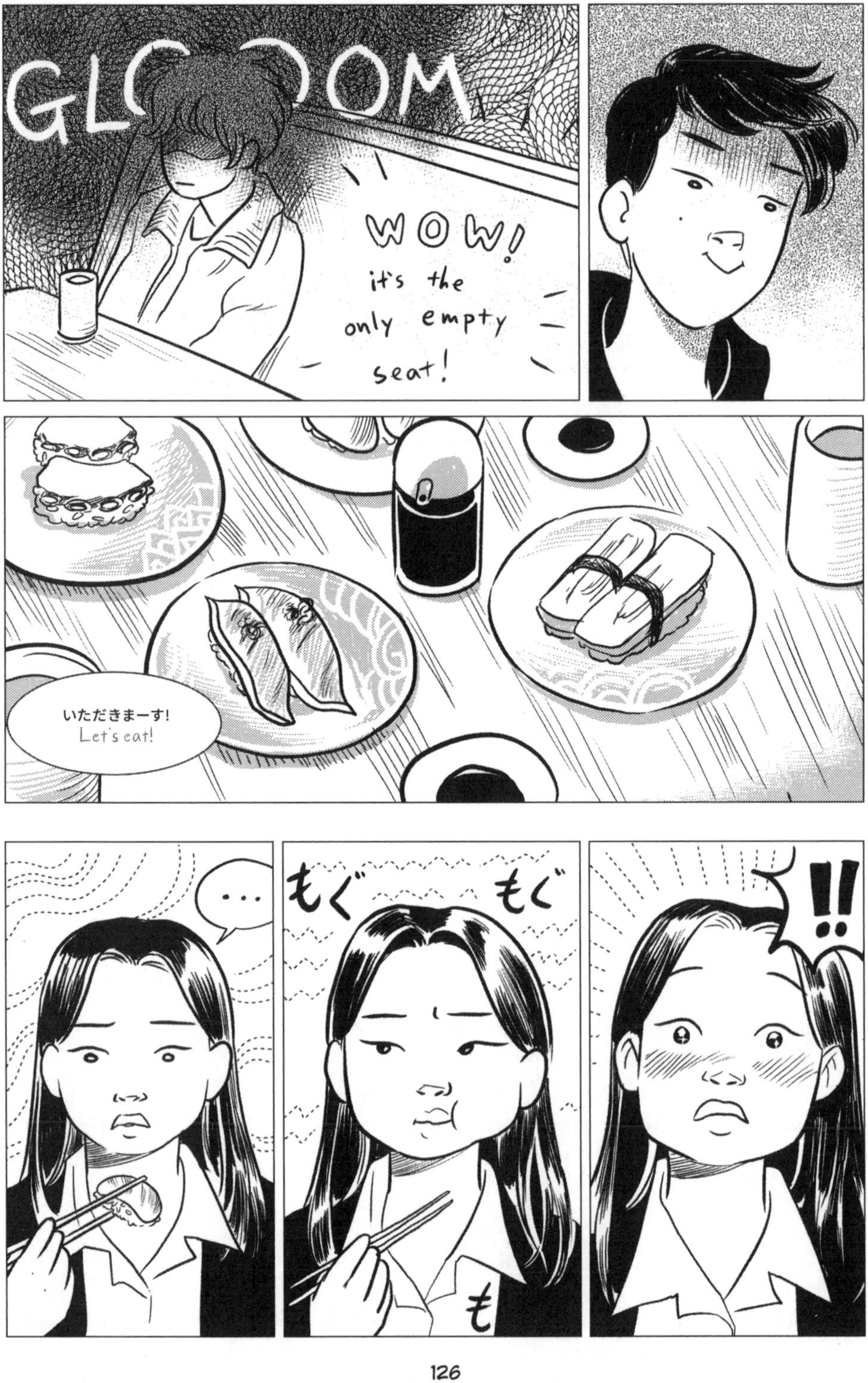
GLOOOM
WOW!
it's the only empty seat!
いただきまーす!
Let's eat!
...
もぐ もぐ
も
!!

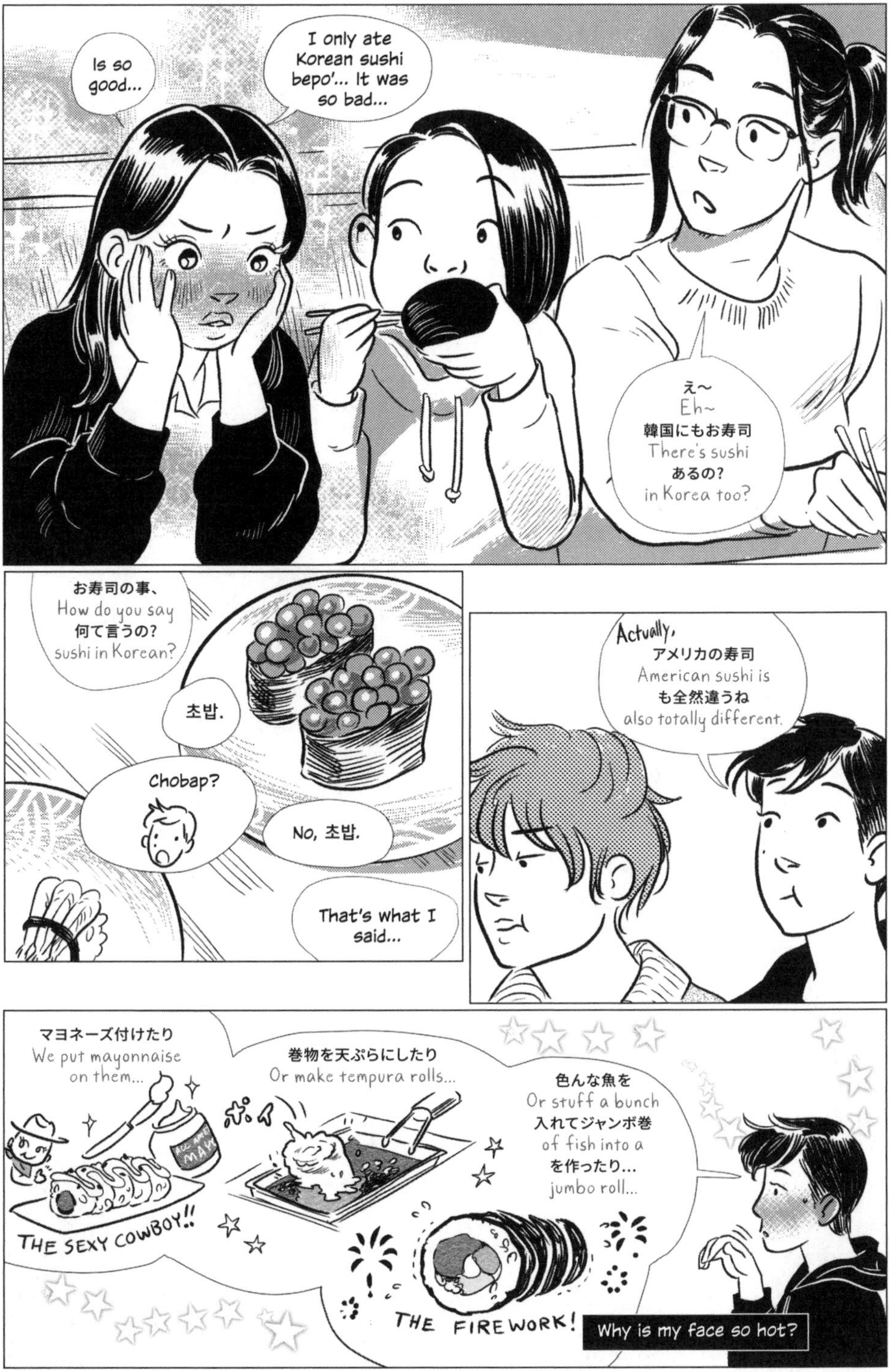
Is so good...
I only ate Korean sushi bepo'... It was so bad...
え~
Eh~
韓国にもお寿司
There's sushi
あるの?
in Korea too?
お寿司の事、
How do you say
何て言うの?
sushi in Korean?
초밥.
Chobap?
No, 초밥.
That's what I said...
Actually,
アメリカの寿司
American sushi is
も全然違うね
also totally different.
マヨネーズ付けたり
We put mayonnaise on them...
巻物を天ぷらにしたり
Or make tempura rolls...
ポイ
色んな魚を
Or stuff a bunch
入れてジャンボ巻
of fish into a
を作ったり...
jumbo roll...
THE SEXY COWBOY!!
THE FIREWORK!
Why is my face so hot?

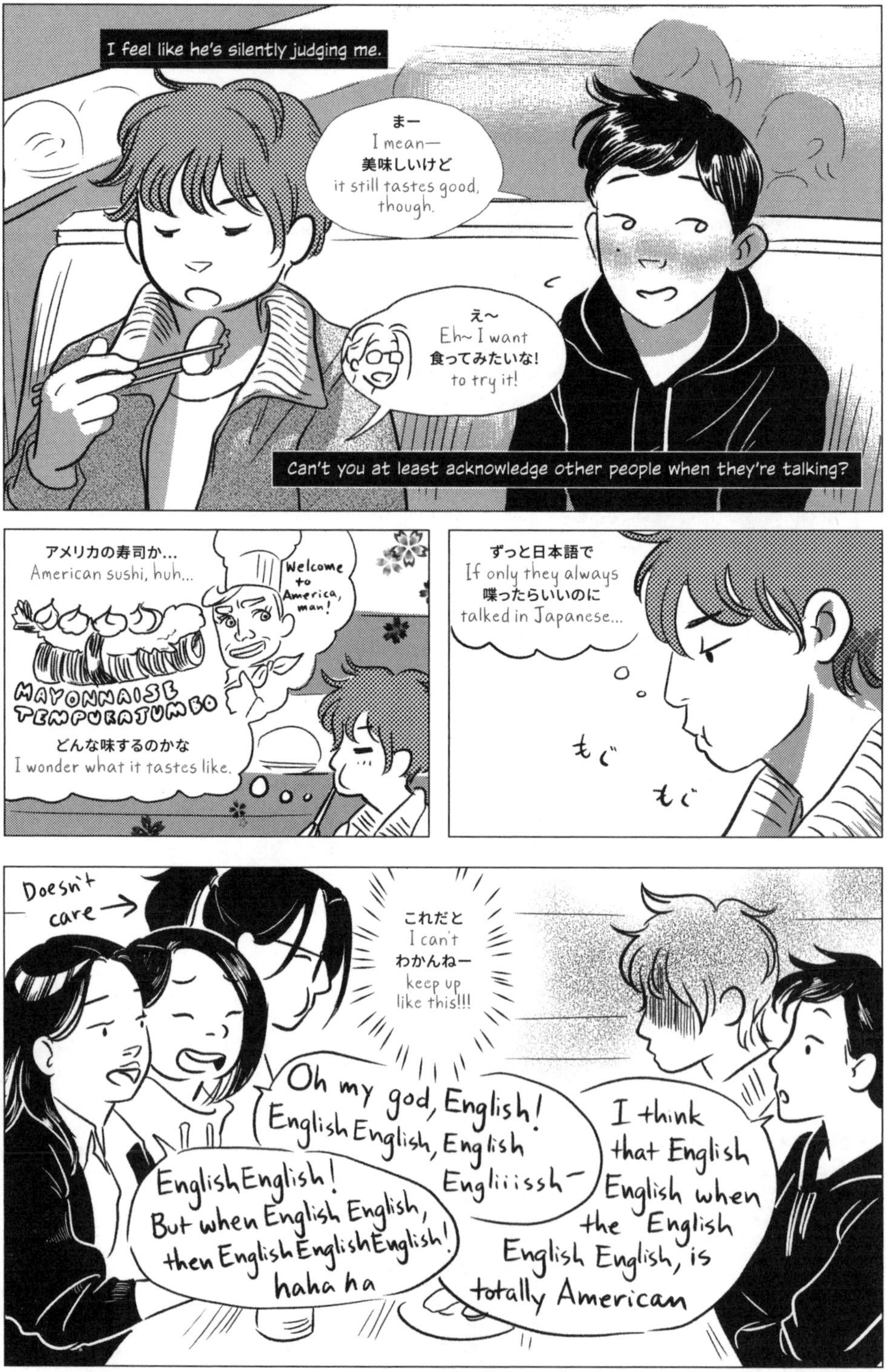

I feel like he's silently judging me.
まー
I mean—
美味しいけど
it still tastes good, though.
え~
Eh~ I want
食ってみたいな!
to try it!
Can't you at least acknowledge other people when they're talking?
アメリカの寿司か…
American sushi, huh…
Welcome to America, man!
MAYONNAISE TEMPURAJUMBO
どんな味するのかな
I wonder what it tastes like.
ずっと日本語で
If only they always
喋ったらいいのに
talked in Japanese…
もぐ
もぐ
Doesn't care
これだと
I can't
わかんねー
keep up like this!!!
Oh my god, English! English English, English Engliiissh—
English English! But when English English, then English English English! haha ha
I think that English English when the English English English, is totally American

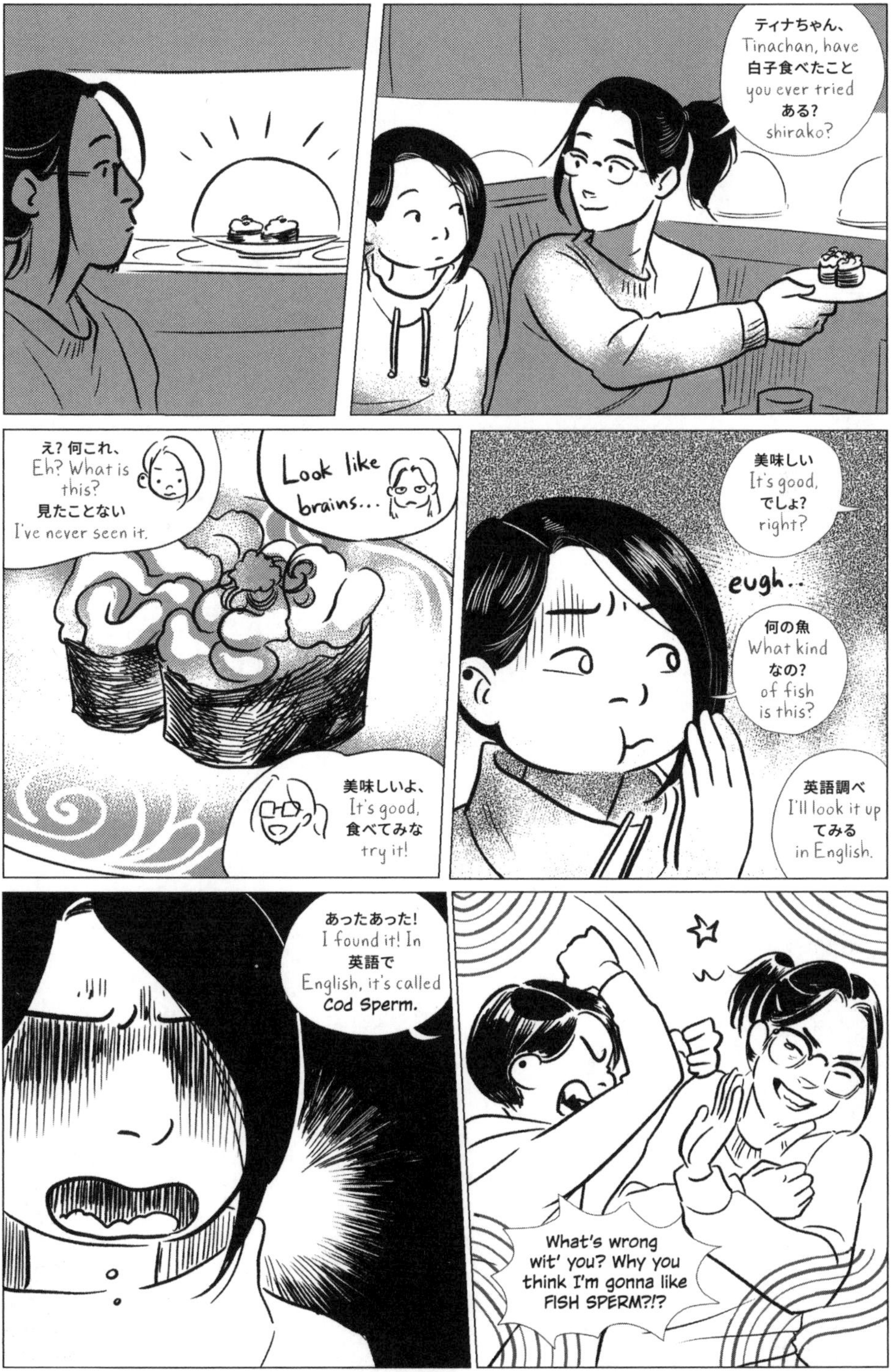

ティナちゃん、 Tinachan, have 白子食べたこと you ever tried ある? shirako?
え? 何これ、 Eh? What is this? 見たことない I've never seen it.
Look like brains...
美味しいよ、 It's good, 食べてみな try it!
美味しい It's good, でしょ? right?
eugh..
何の魚 What kind なの? of fish is this?
英語調べ I'll look it up てみる in English.
あったあった! I found it! In 英語で English, it's called Cod Sperm.
What's wrong wit' you? Why you think I'm gonna like FISH SPERM?!?

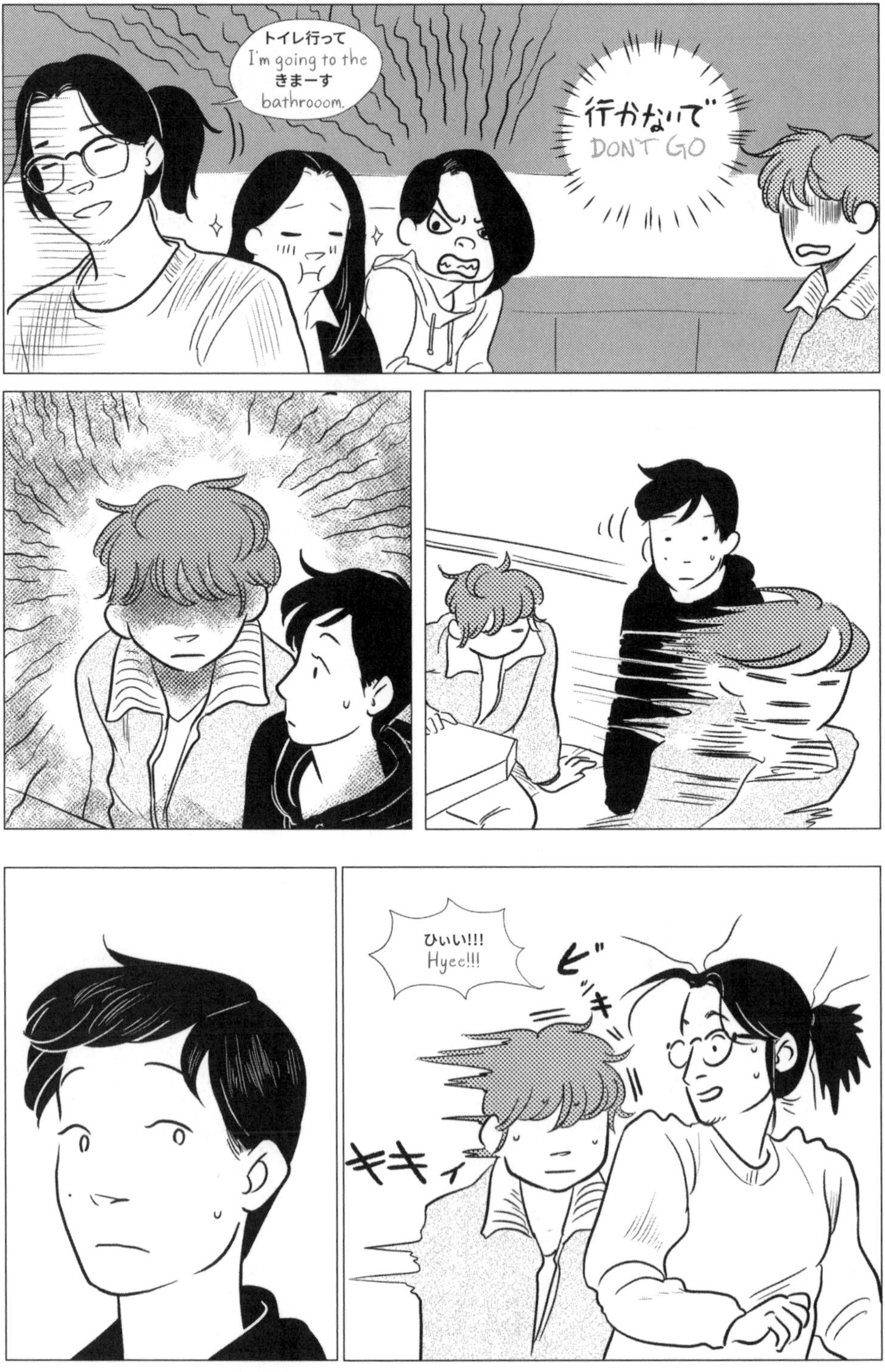
トイレ行って
I'm going to the
きまーす
bathrooom.
行かないで
DON'T GO
ひいい!!!
Hyee!!!
ビッキ
キキィ

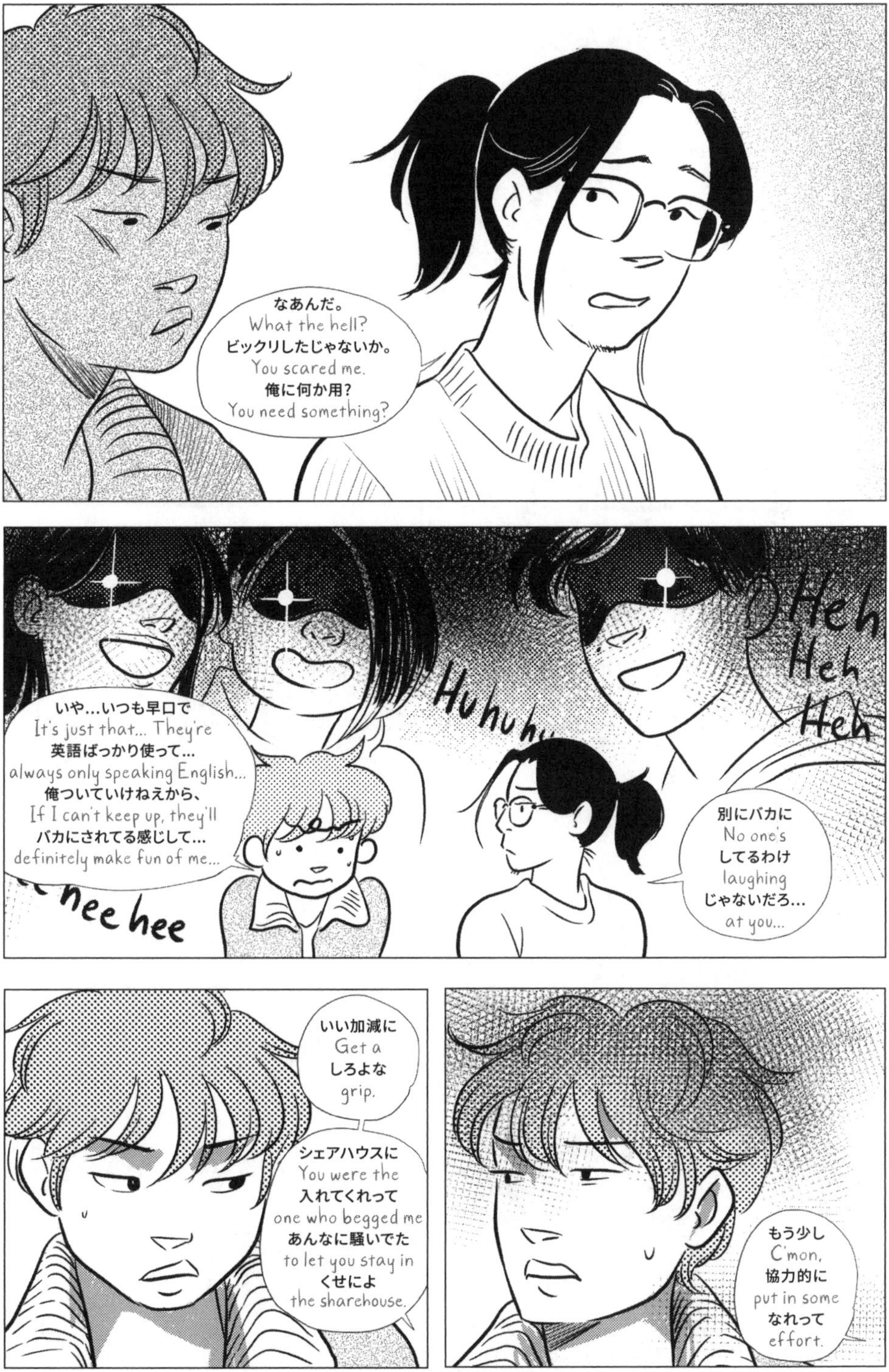
なあんだ。
What the hell?
ビックリしたじゃないか。
You scared me.
俺に何か用?
You need something?
いや…いつも早口で
It's just that... They're
英語ばっかり使って…
always only speaking English...
俺ついていけねえから、
If I can't keep up, they'll
バカにされてる感じして…
definitely make fun of me...
hee hee
Huhuhu
Heh
Heh
Heh
別にバカに
No one's
してるわけ
laughing
じゃないだろ…
at you...
いい加減に
Get a
しろよな
grip.
シェアハウスに
You were the
入れてくれって
one who begged me
あんなに騒いでた
to let you stay in
くせによ
the sharehouse.
もう少し
C'mon,
協力的に
put in some
なれって
effort.

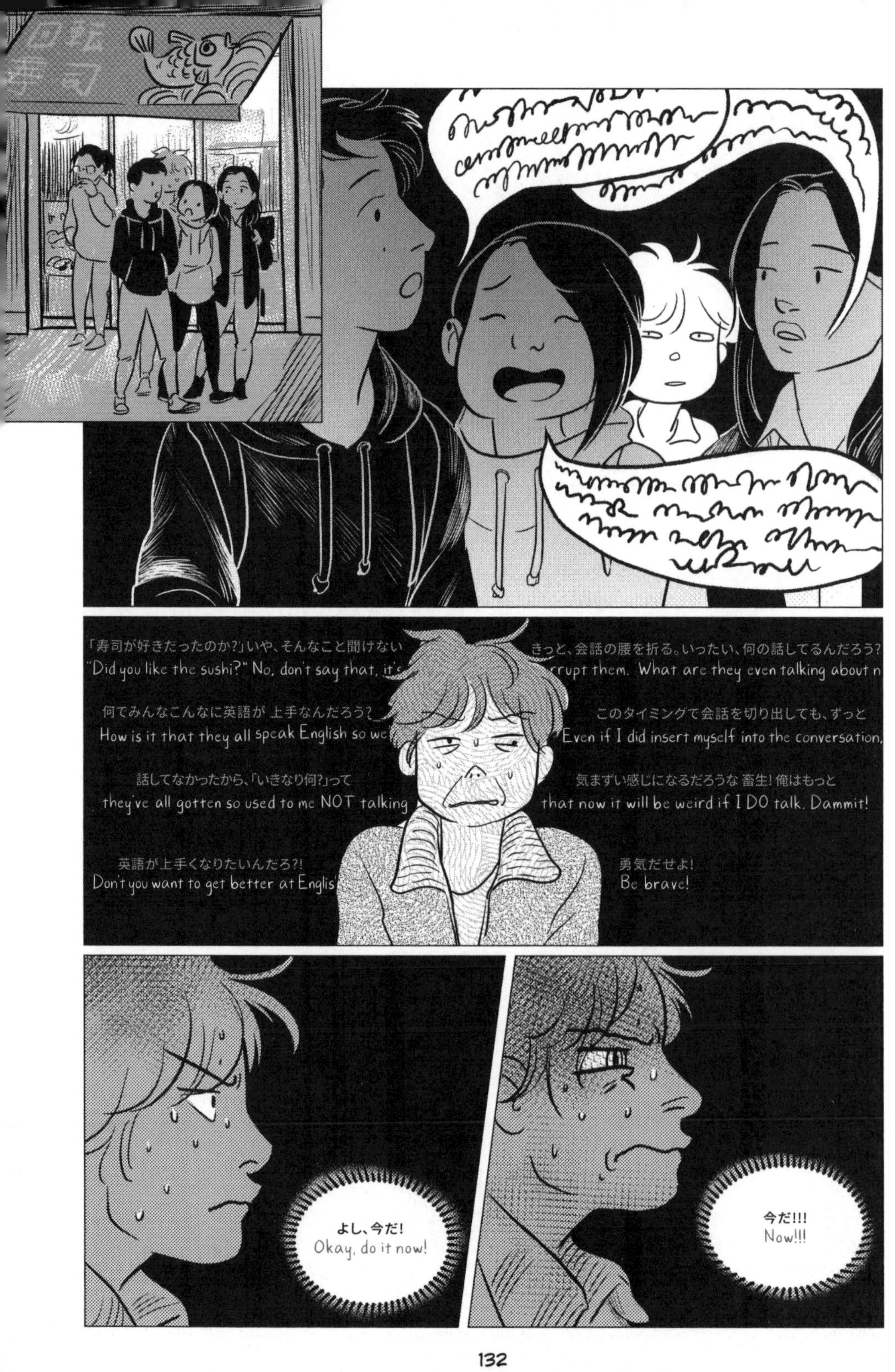
「寿司が好きだったのか?」いや、そんなこと聞けない
"Did you like the sushi?" No, don't say that, it's
きっと、会話の腰を折る。いったい、何の話してるんだろう?
rrupt them. What are they even talking about
何でみんなこんなに英語が 上手なんだろう?
How is it that they all speak English so we
このタイミングで会話を切り出しても、ずっと
Even if I did insert myself into the conversation,
話してなかったから、「いきなり何?」って
they've all gotten so used to me NOT talking
気まずい感じになるだろうな 畜生! 俺はもっと
that now it will be weird if I DO talk. Dammit!
英語が上手くなりたいんだろ?!
Don't you want to get better at Englis
勇気だせよ!
Be brave!
よし、今だ!
Okay, do it now!
今だ!!!
Now!!!

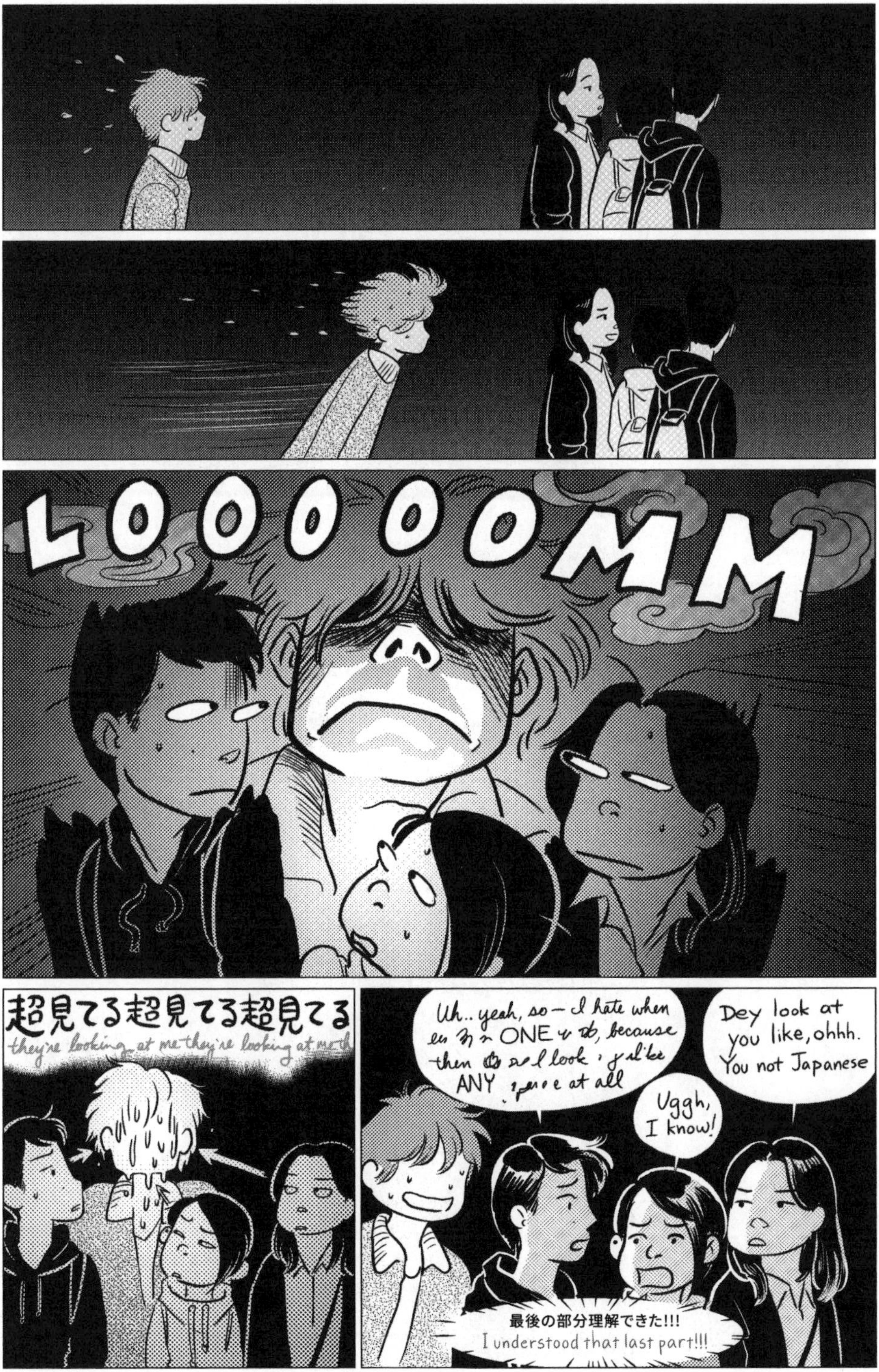
LOOOOOMM
超見てる超見てる超見てる
they're looking at me they're looking at me
Uh.. yeah, so— I hate when ONE, because then look ANY at all
Dey look at you like, ohhh. You not Japanese
Uggh, I know!
最後の部分理解できた!!!
I understood that last part!!!

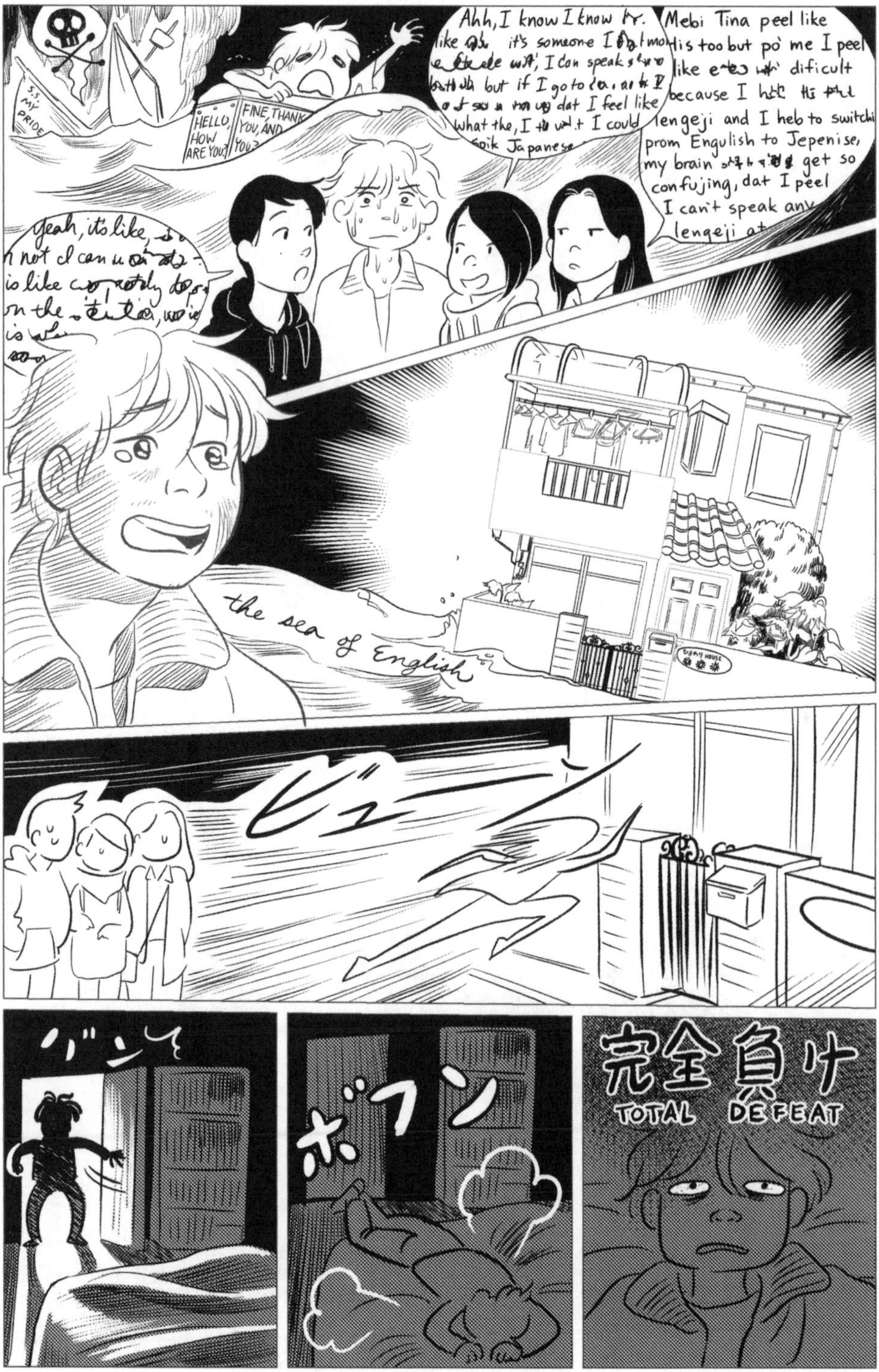
S.S. MY PRIDE
HELLO, HOW ARE YOU?
FINE, THANK YOU, AND YOU?
Ahh, I know I know it's someone I I can speak but if I go dat I feel like what the, I I could spik Japanese
Mebi Tina peel like dis too but po' me I peel like dificult because I lengeji and I heb to switchi prom Engulish to Jepenise, my brain get so confujing, dat I peel I can't speak any lengeji at
yeah, it's like, is like on the
the sea of English
ビューン
バン
ボフン
完全負け
TOTAL DEFEAT

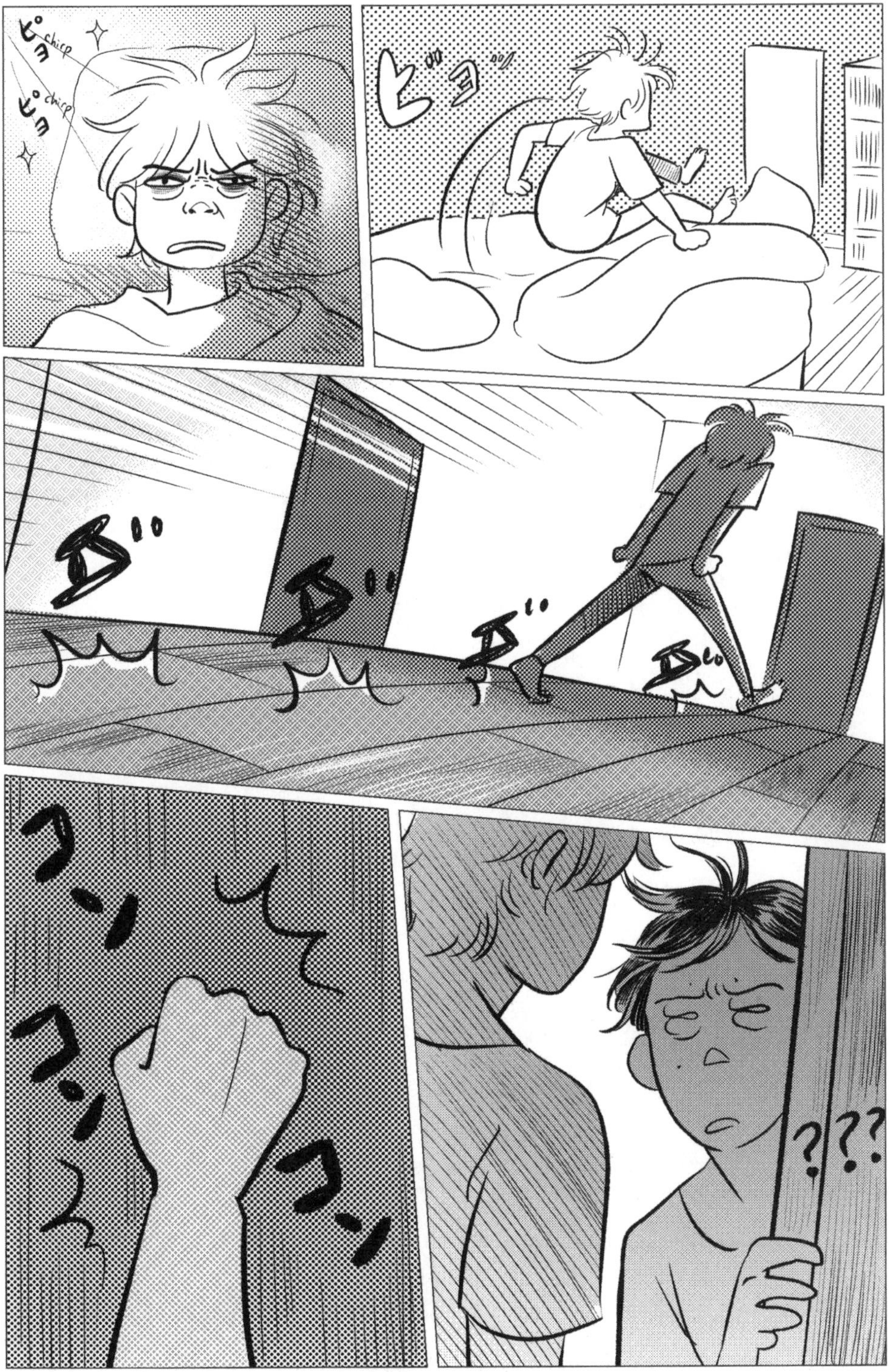
ピヨ
chirp
ピヨ
chirp
ピヨ
コン
コン
コン
???

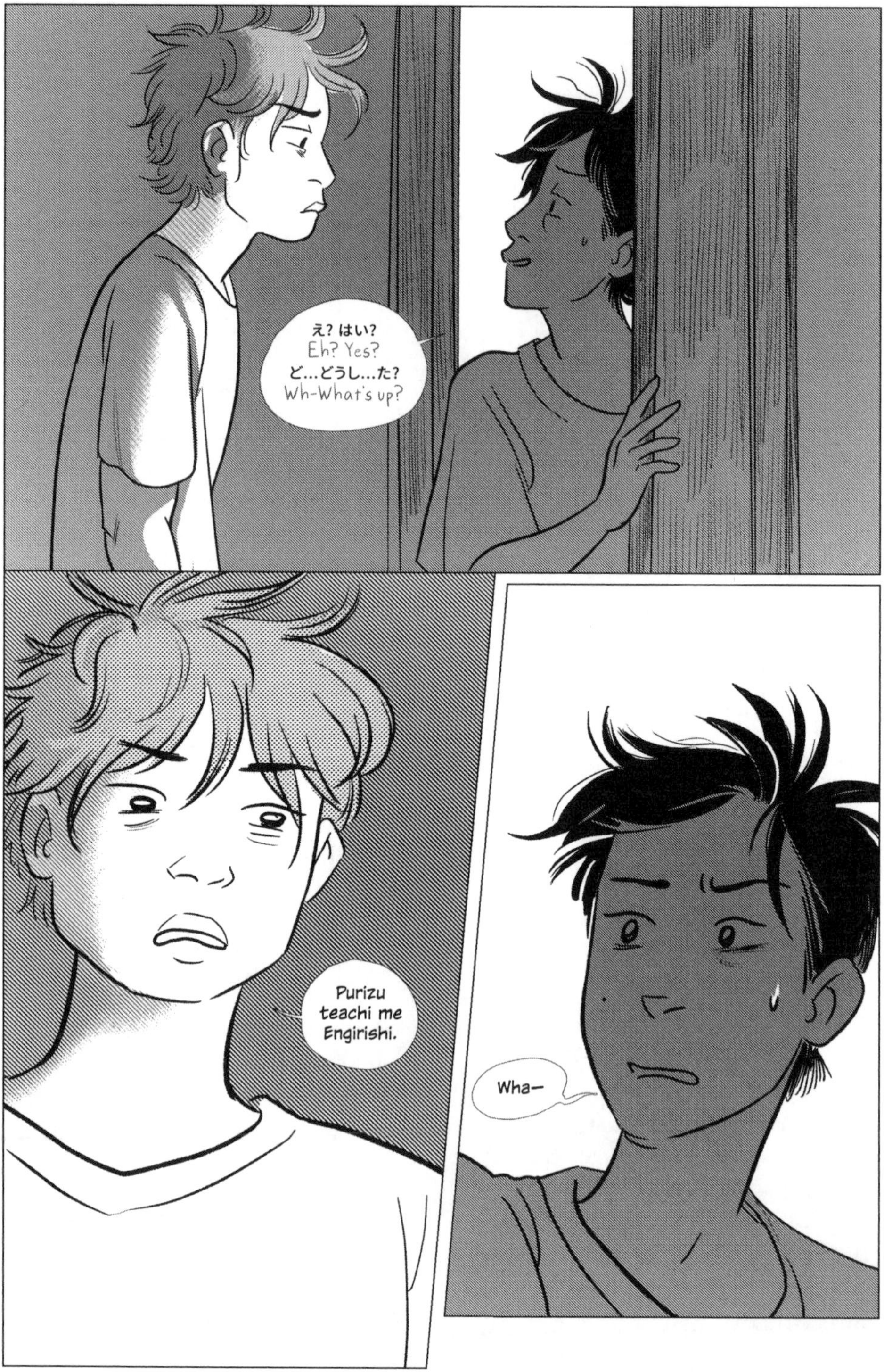
え? はい?
Eh? Yes?
ど…どうし…た?
Wh-What's up?
Purizu teachi me Engirishi.
Wha—

Chapter 8
Harajuku

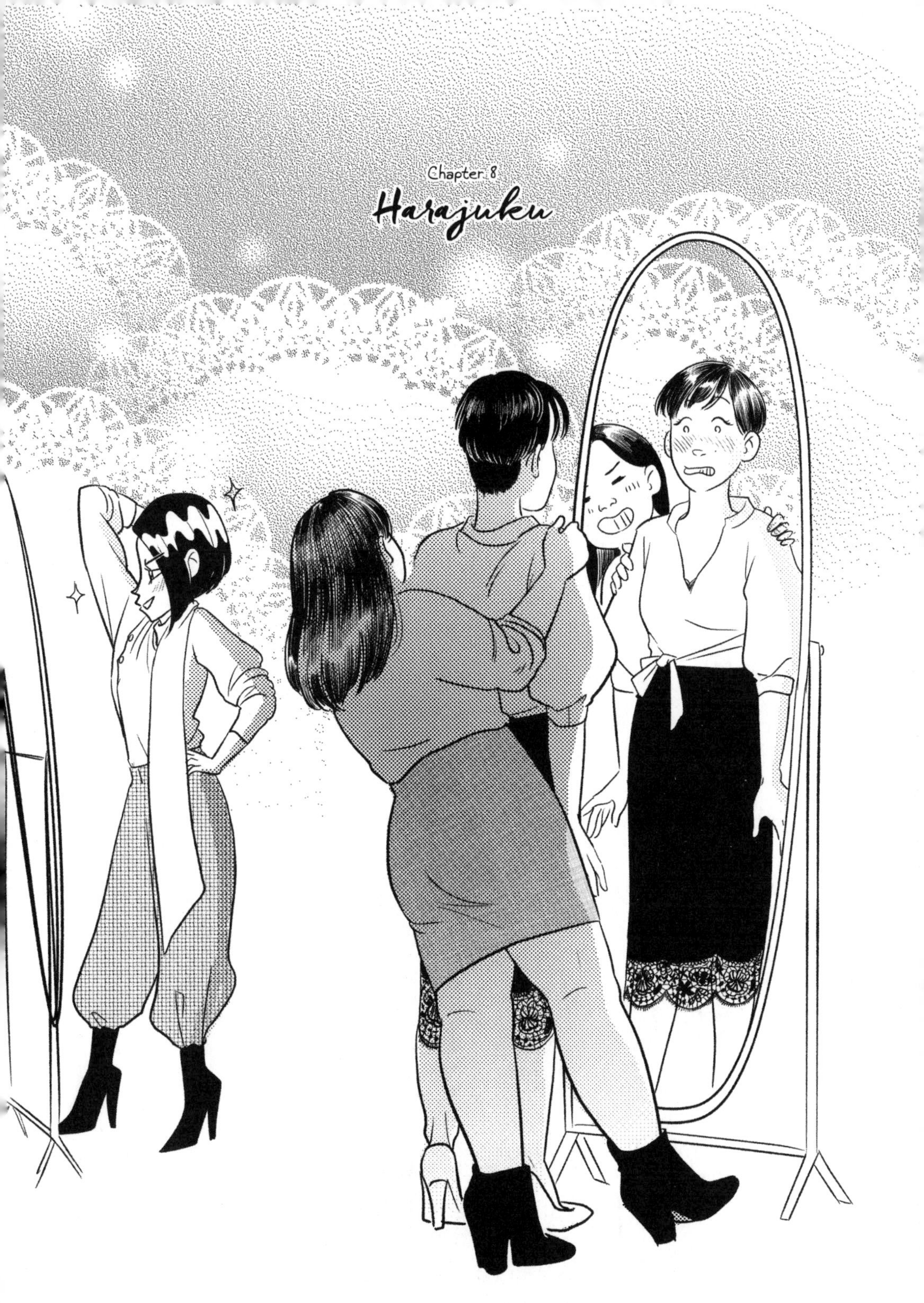

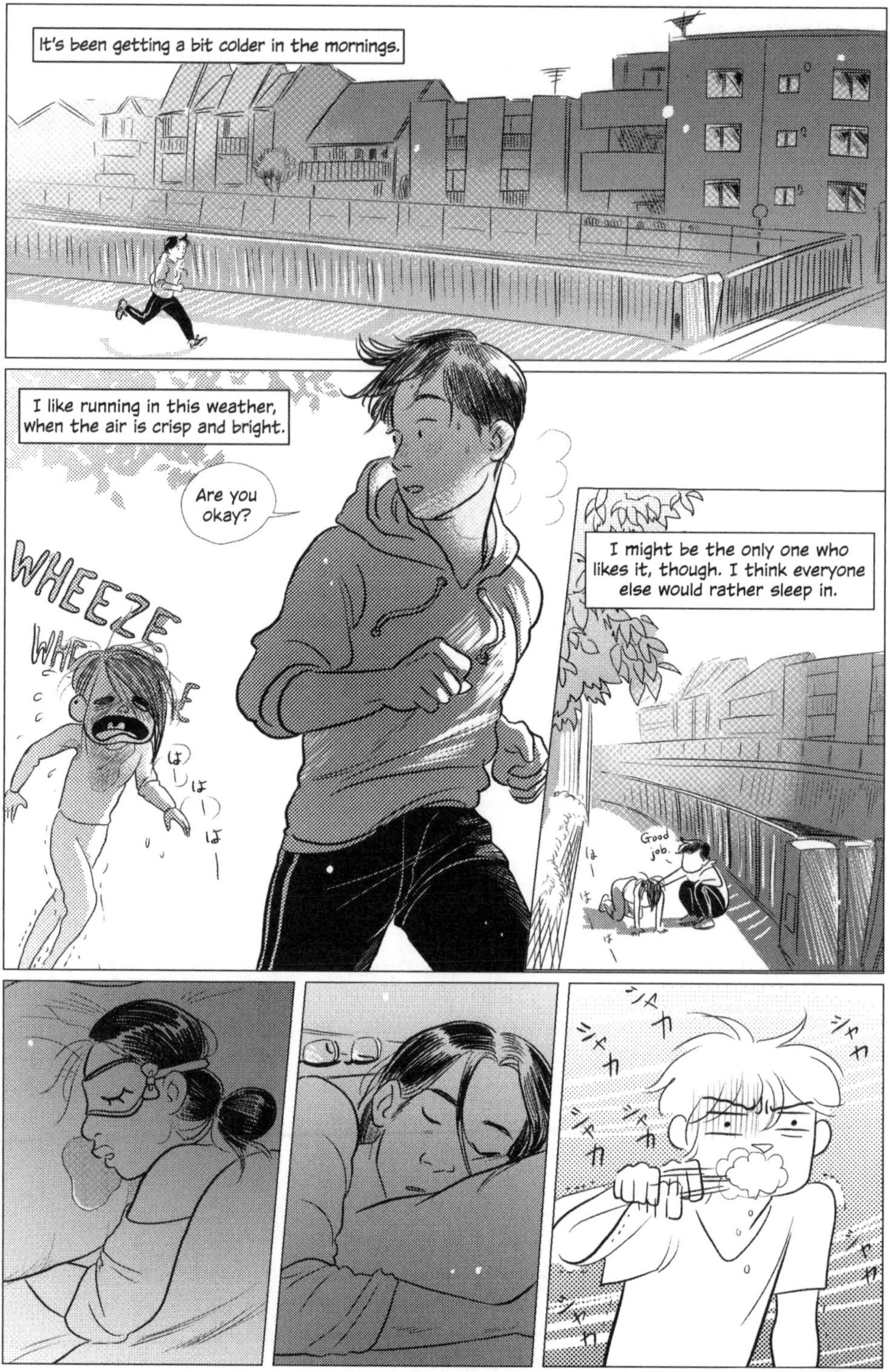

It's been getting a bit colder in the mornings.
I like running in this weather, when the air is crisp and bright.
Are you okay?
WHEEZE
I might be the only one who likes it, though. I think everyone else would rather sleep in.
Good job.

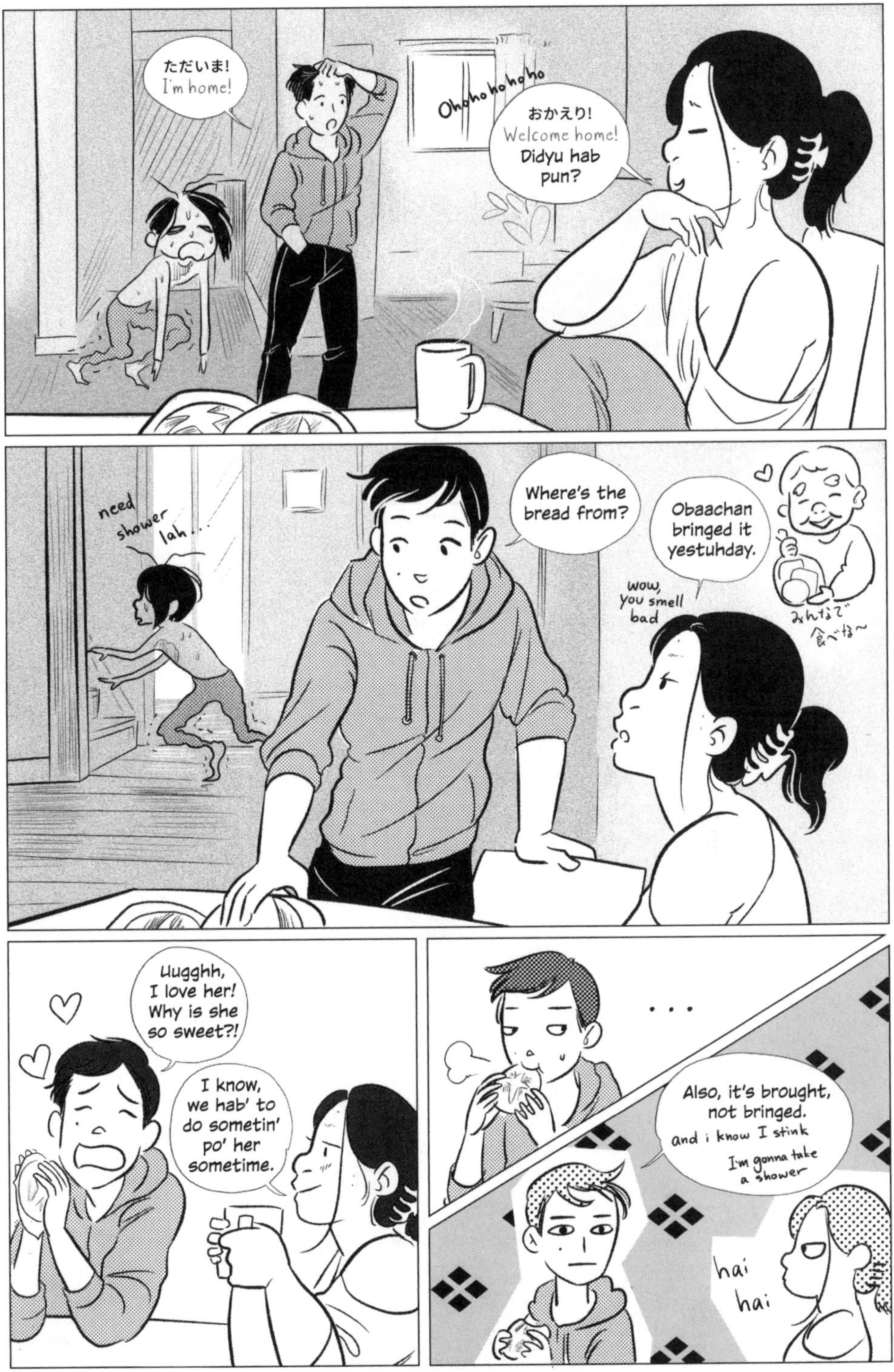
ただいま!
I'm home!
Ohohohohoho
おかえり!
Welcome home!
Didyu hab pun?
need shower lah...
Where's the bread from?
Obaachan bringed it yestuhday.
wow, you smell bad
みんなで食べな～
Uugghh, I love her! Why is she so sweet?!
I know, we hab' to do sometin' po' her sometime.
. . .
Also, it's brought, not bringed.
and i know I stink
I'm gonna take a shower
hai hai

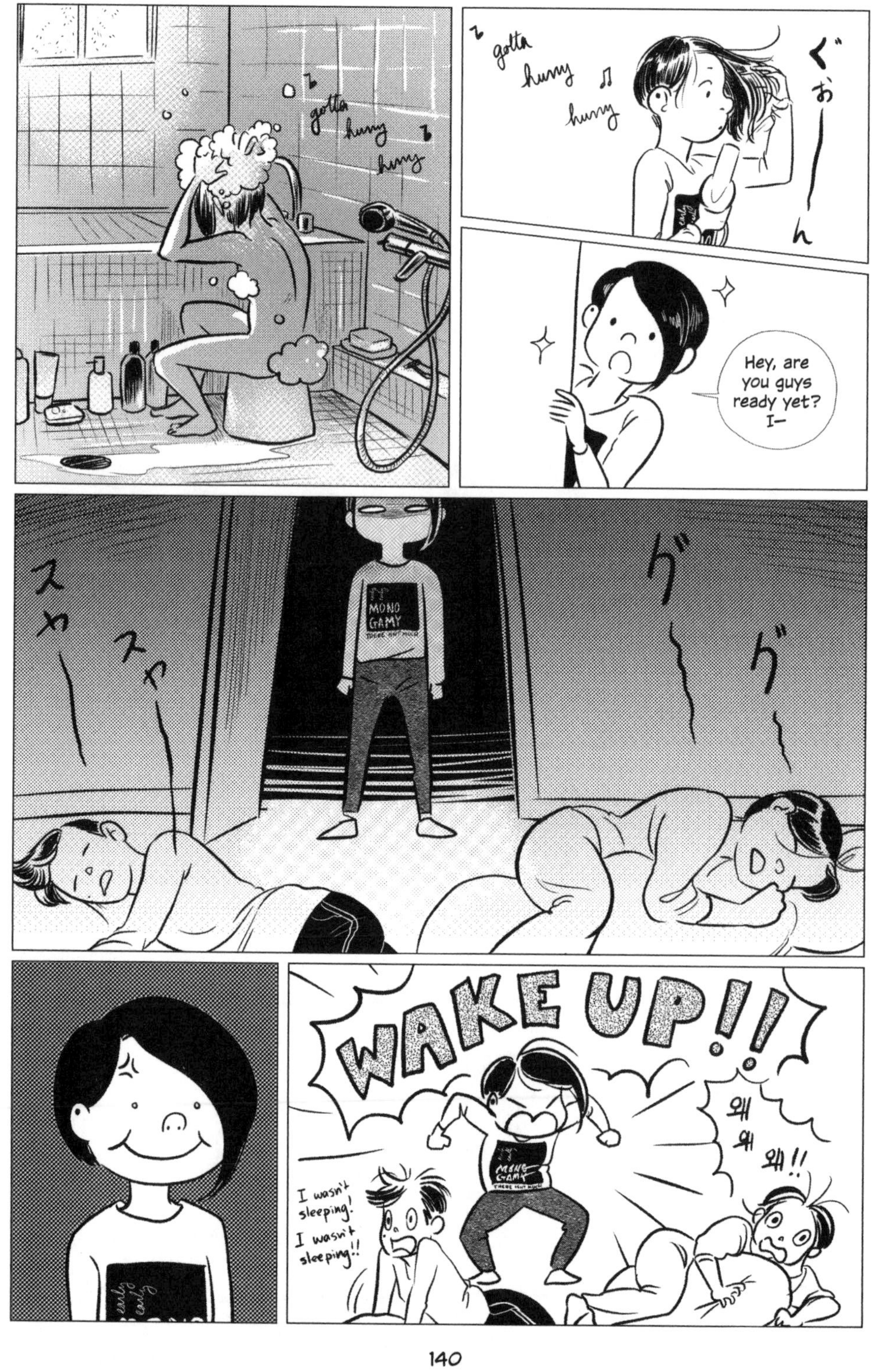
gotta hurry hurry
gotta hurry hurry
ぐおーん
Hey, are you guys ready yet? I—
スヤスヤ
グーグー
WAKE UP!!
I wasn't sleeping! I wasn't sleeping!!
왜왜왜!!

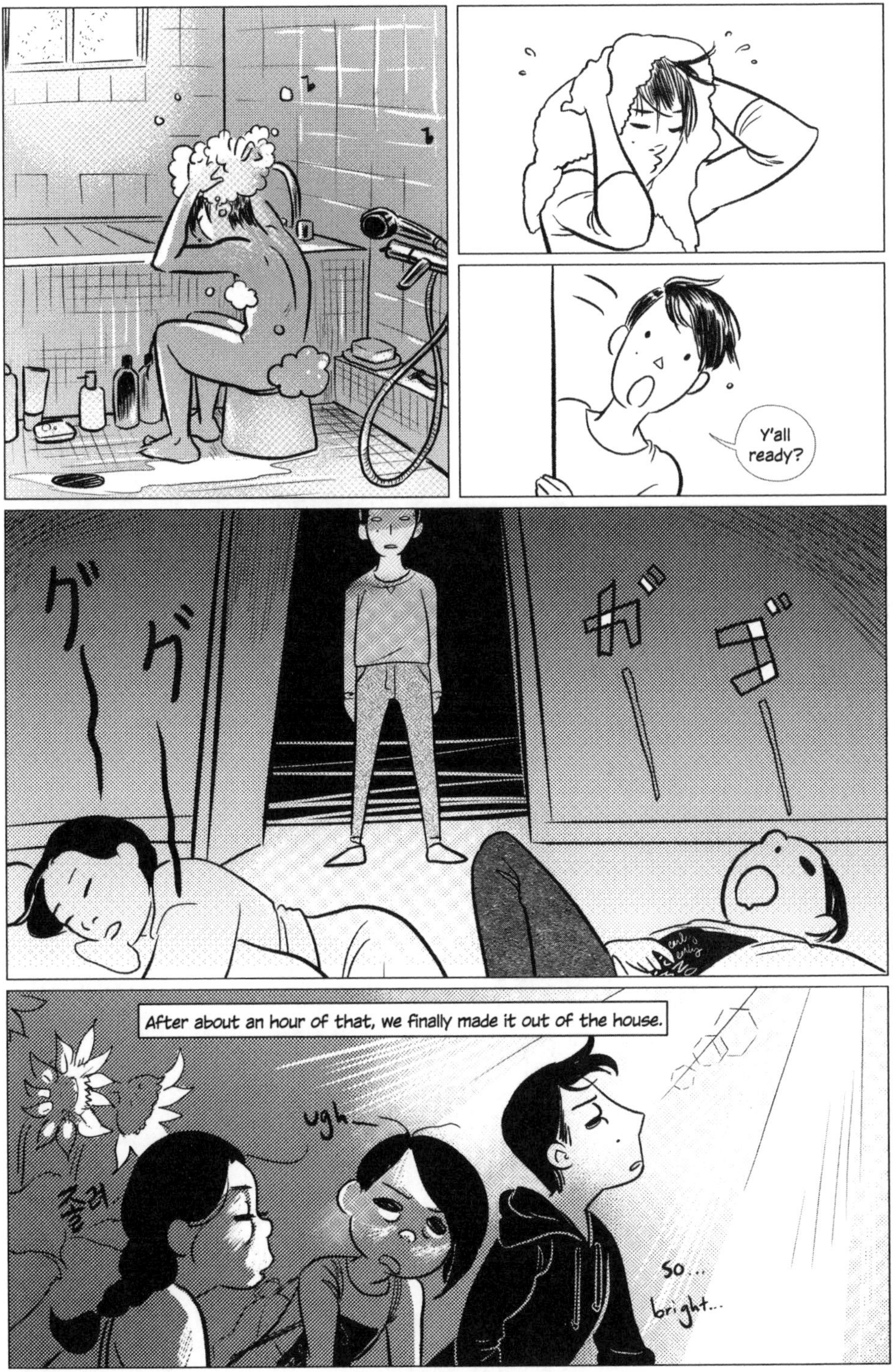
Y'all ready?
グー グー
ガー ゴー
After about an hour of that, we finally made it out of the house.
졸려...
ugh...
so... bright...

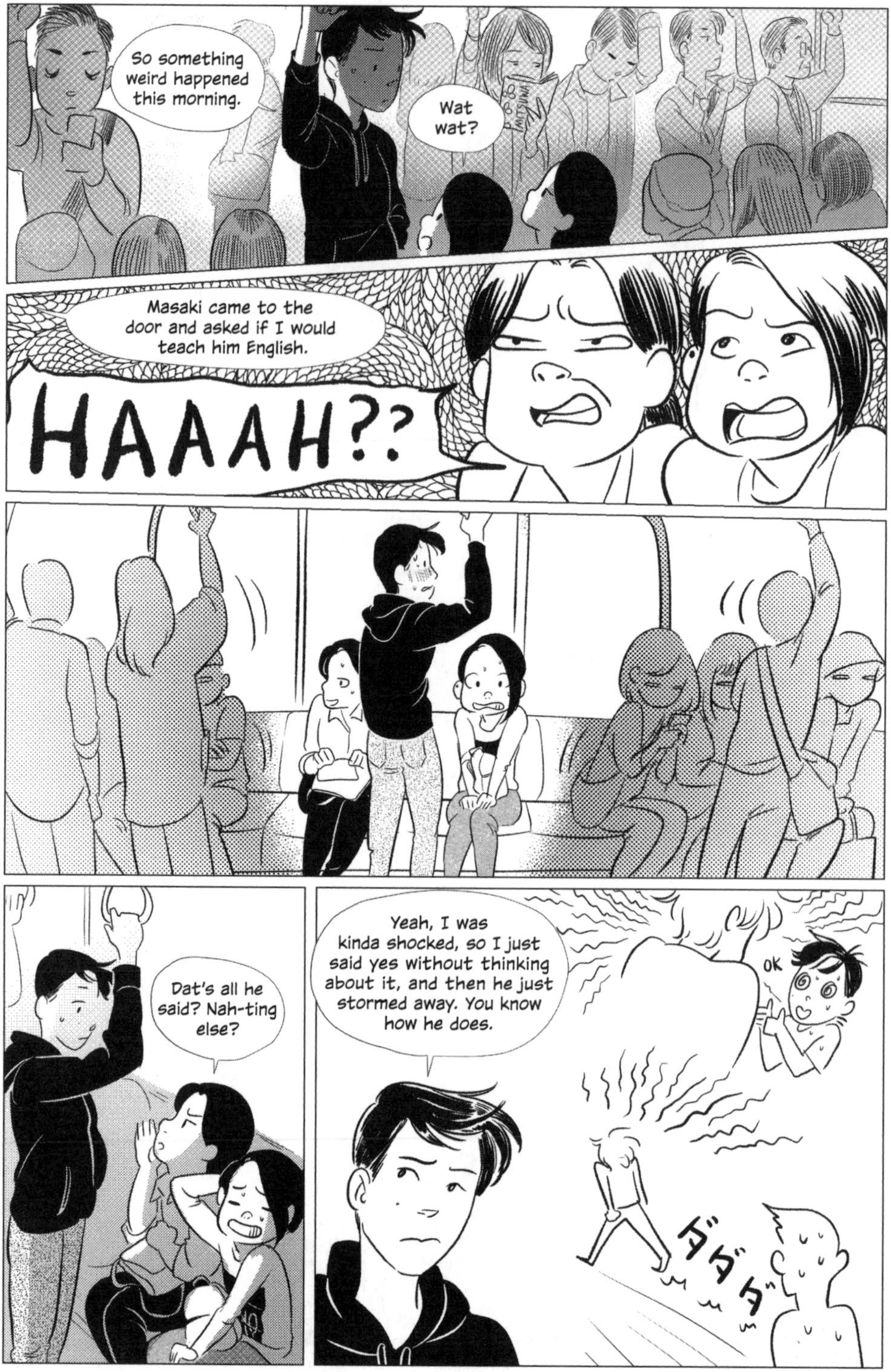
So something weird happened this morning.
Wat wat?
Masaki came to the door and asked if I would teach him English.
HAAAH??
Dat's all he said? Nah-ting else?
Yeah, I was kinda shocked, so I just said yes without thinking about it, and then he just stormed away. You know how he does.
OK
ダダダ

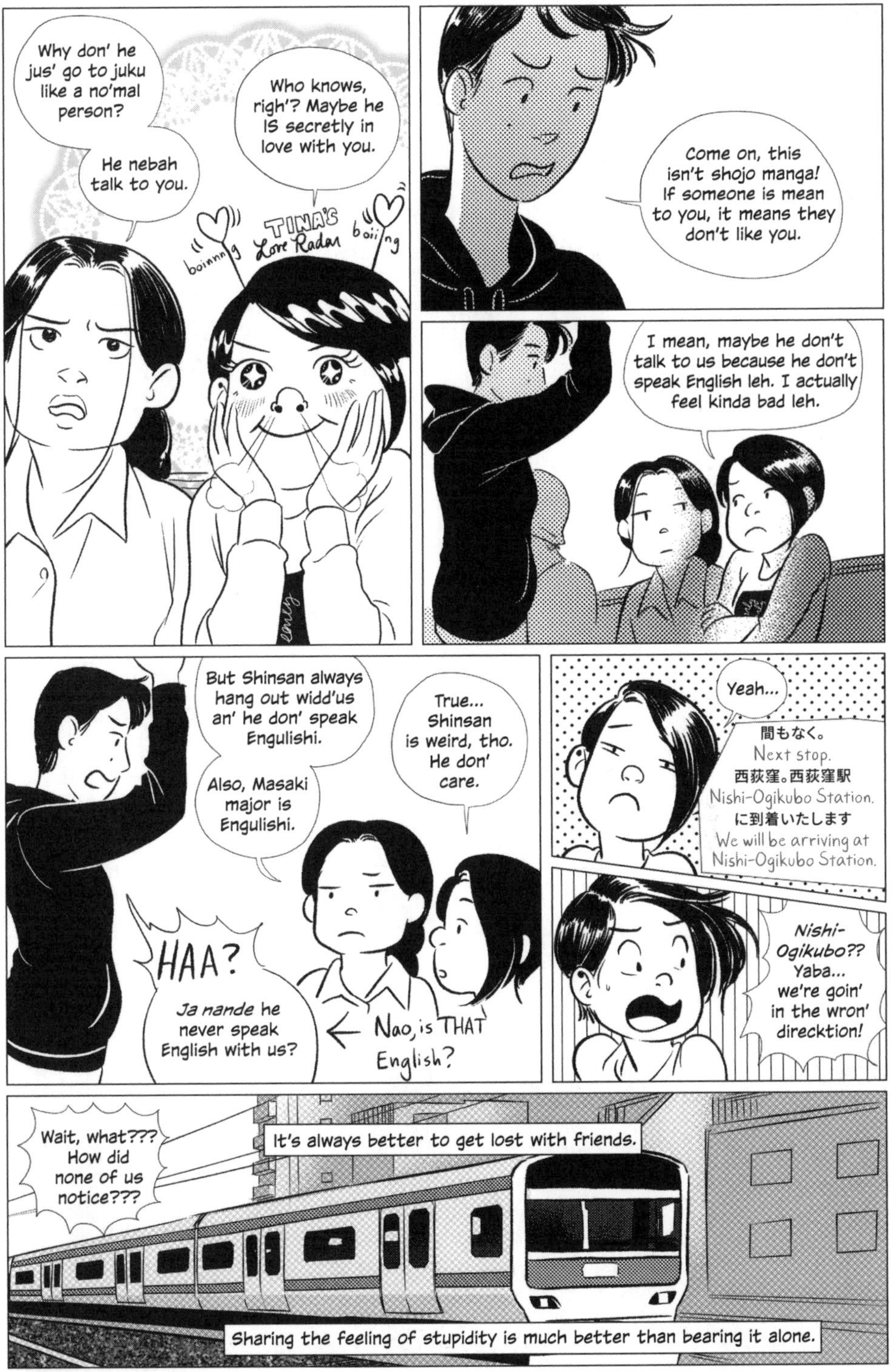
Why don' he jus' go to juku like a no'mal person?
He nebah talk to you.
Who knows, righ'? Maybe he IS secretly in love with you.
boinnng
TINA'S Love Radar
boiing
Come on, this isn't shojo manga! If someone is mean to you, it means they don't like you.
I mean, maybe he don't talk to us because he don't speak English leh. I actually feel kinda bad leh.
But Shinsan always hang out widd'us an' he don' speak Engulishi.
Also, Masaki major is Engulishi.
True... Shinsan is weird, tho. He don' care.
HAA?
Ja nande he never speak English with us?
Nao, is THAT English?
Yeah...
間もなく。
Next stop.
西荻窪。西荻窪駅
Nishi-Ogikubo Station.
に到着いたします
We will be arriving at Nishi-Ogikubo Station.
Nishi-Ogikubo?? Yaba... we're goin' in the wron' direcktion!
Wait, what??? How did none of us notice???
It's always better to get lost with friends.
Sharing the feeling of stupidity is much better than bearing it alone.

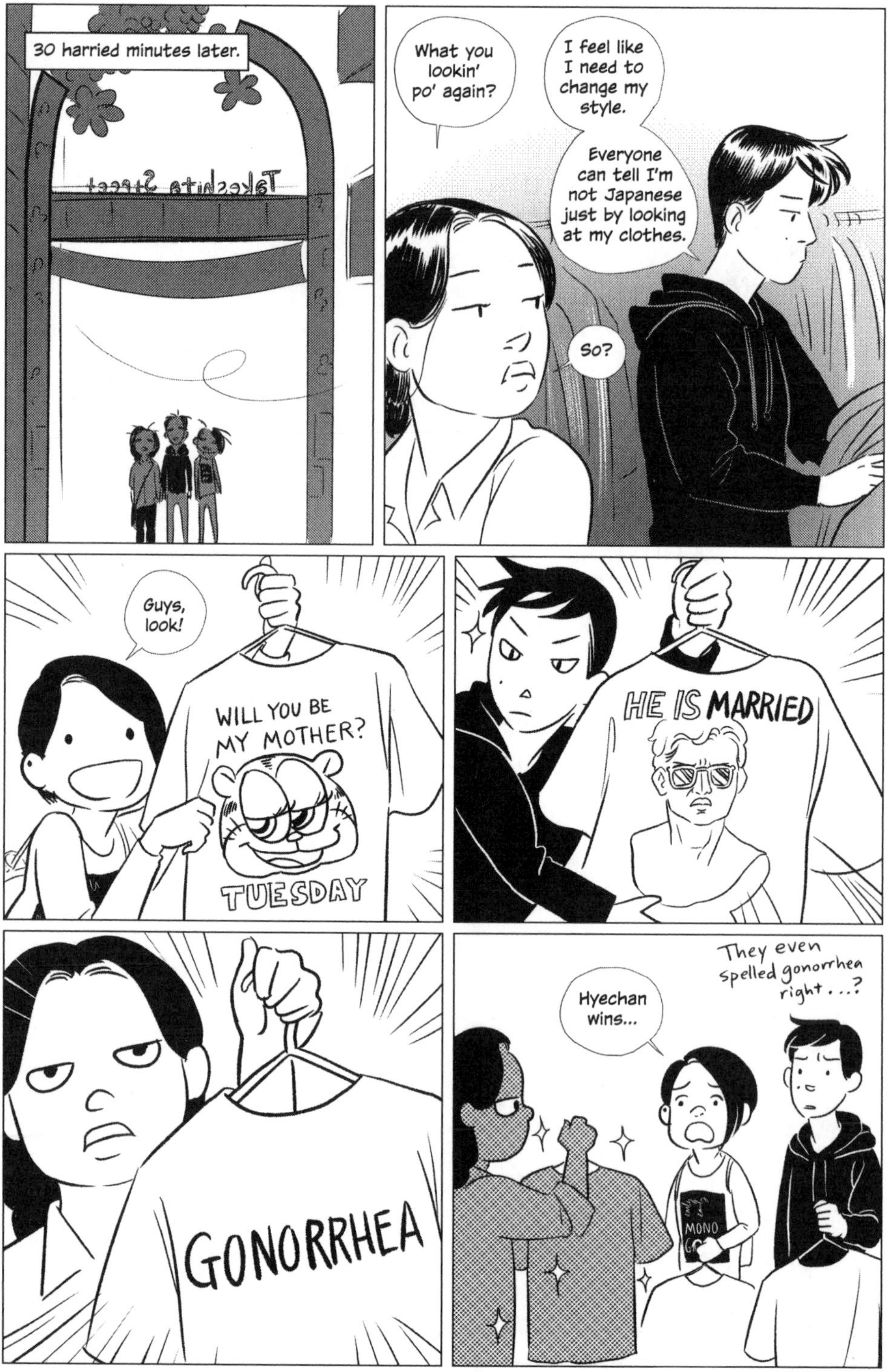
30 harried minutes later.
Takeshita Street
What you lookin' po' again?
I feel like I need to change my style.
Everyone can tell I'm not Japanese just by looking at my clothes.
So?
Guys, look!
WILL YOU BE MY MOTHER?
TUESDAY
HE IS MARRIED
GONORRHEA
They even spelled gonorrhea right . . .?
Hyechan wins...
MONO

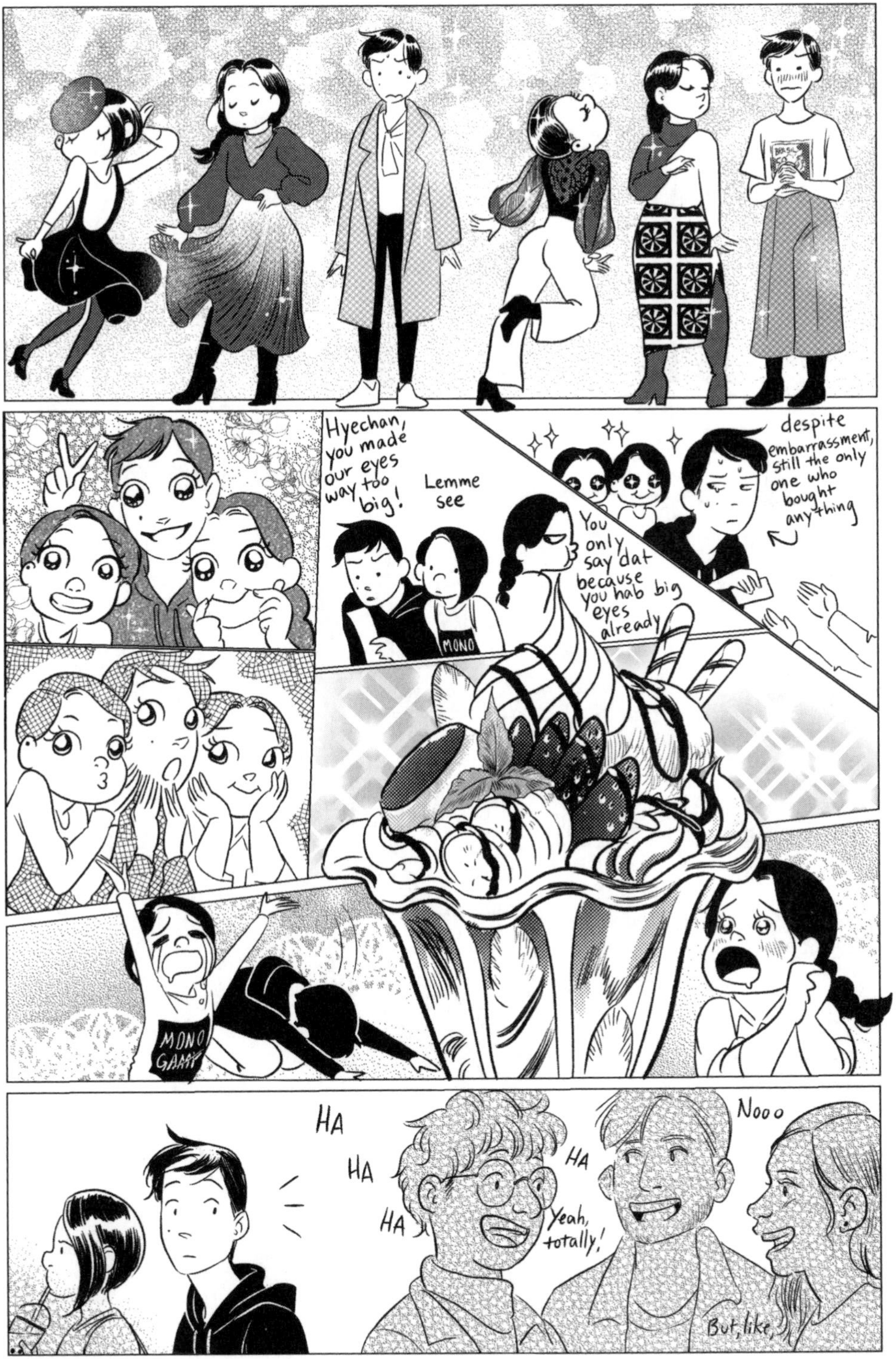
Hyechan, you made our eyes way too big!
Lemme see
You only say dat because you hab big eyes already
despite embarrassment, still the only one who bought anything
MONO
MONO GAMY
HA
HA
HA
HA
Yeah, totally!
Nooo
But, like,

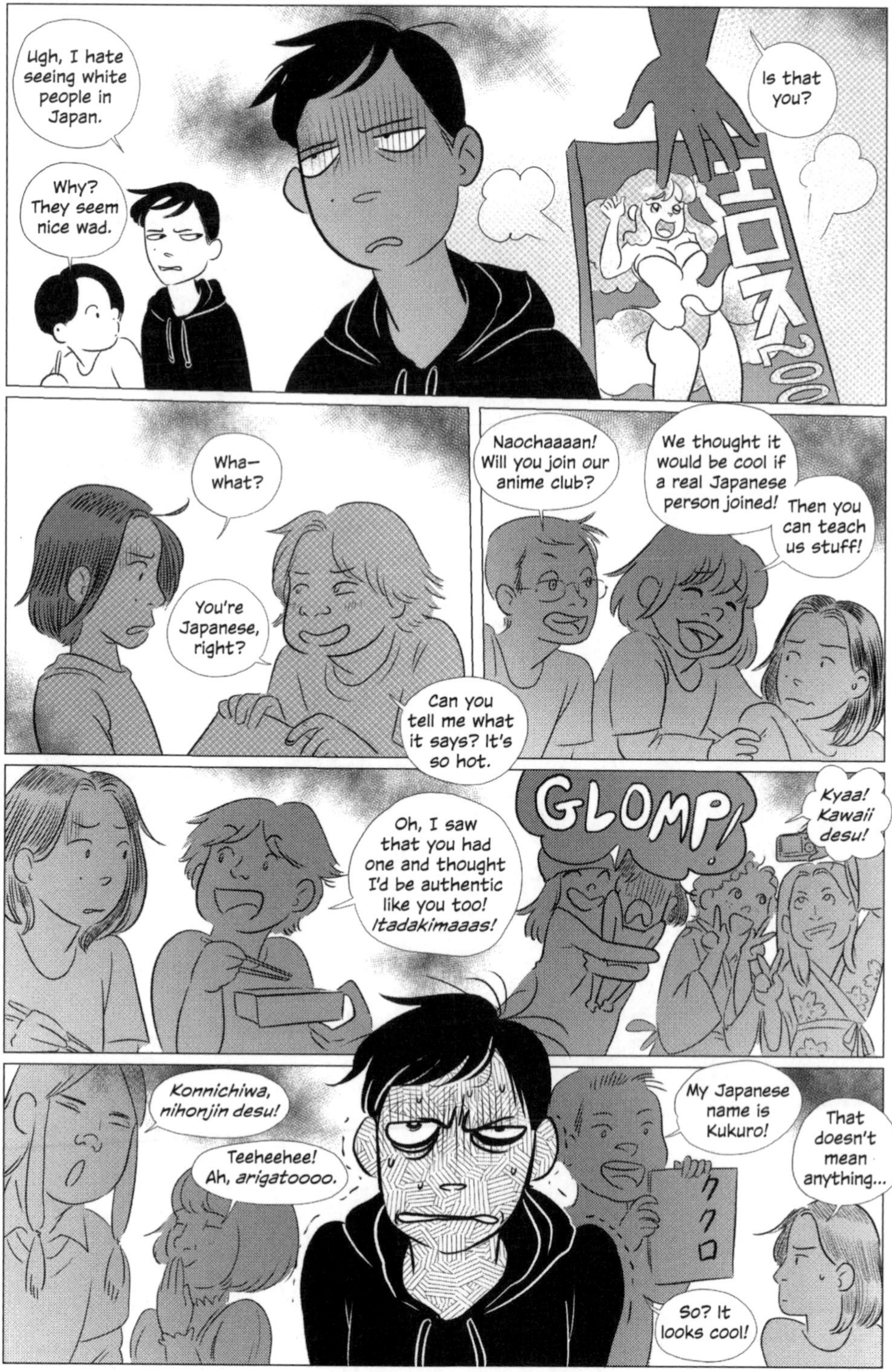
Ugh, I hate seeing white people in Japan.
Why? They seem nice wad.
Is that you?
エロス2000
Wha— what?
You're Japanese, right?
Can you tell me what it says? It's so hot.
Naochaaaan! Will you join our anime club?
We thought it would be cool if a real Japanese person joined!
Then you can teach us stuff!
Oh, I saw that you had one and thought I'd be authentic like you too! *Itadakimaaas!*
GLOMP!
Kyaa! Kawaii desu!
Konnichiwa, nihonjin desu!
Teeheehee! Ah, *arigatoooo.*
My Japanese name is Kukuro!
クク口
That doesn't mean anything...
So? It looks cool!

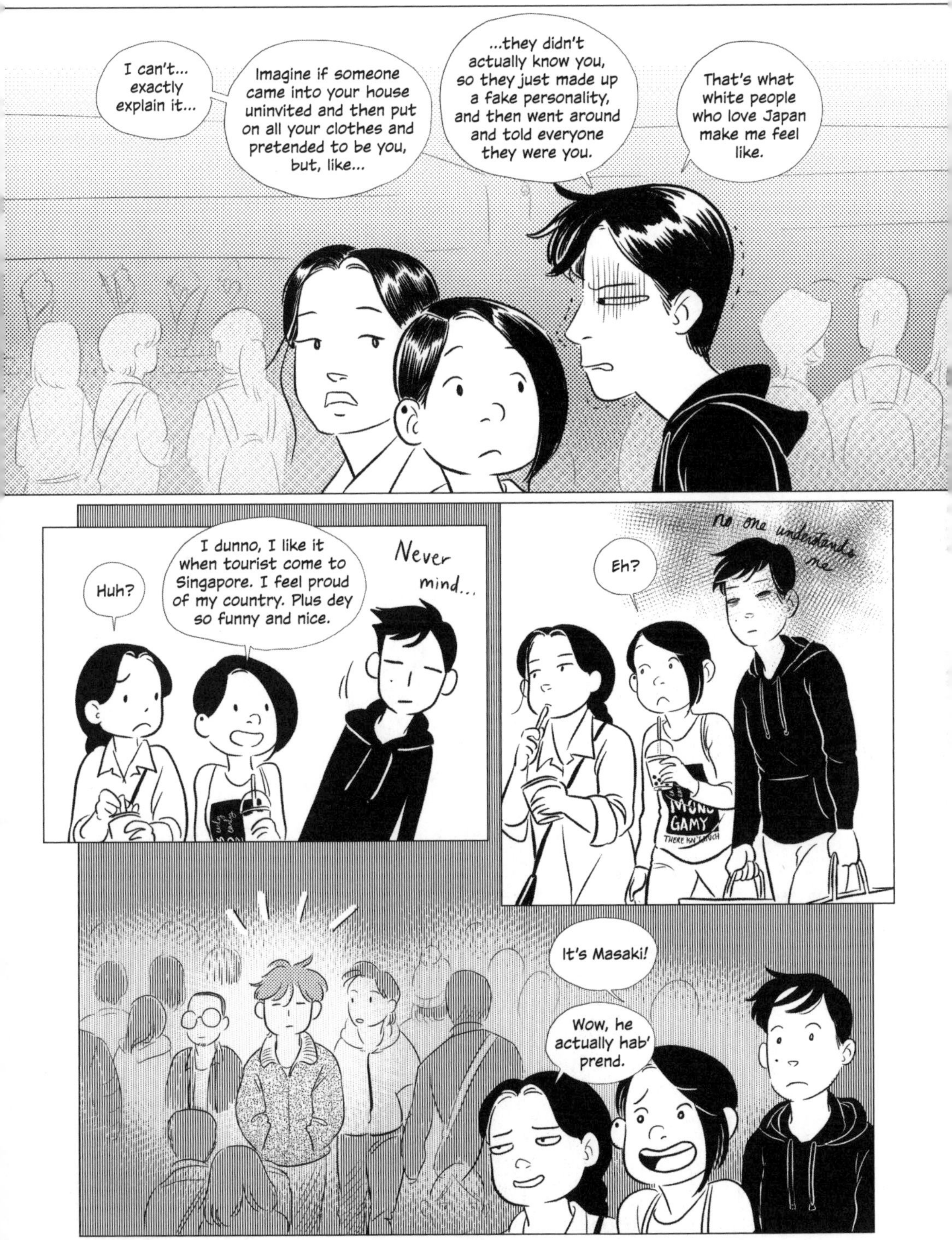
I can't... exactly explain it...
Imagine if someone came into your house uninvited and then put on all your clothes and pretended to be you, but, like...
...they didn't actually know you, so they just made up a fake personality, and then went around and told everyone they were you.
That's what white people who love Japan make me feel like.
Huh?
I dunno, I like it when tourist come to Singapore. I feel proud of my country. Plus dey so funny and nice.
Never mind...
Eh?
no one understands me
It's Masaki!
Wow, he actually hab' prend.

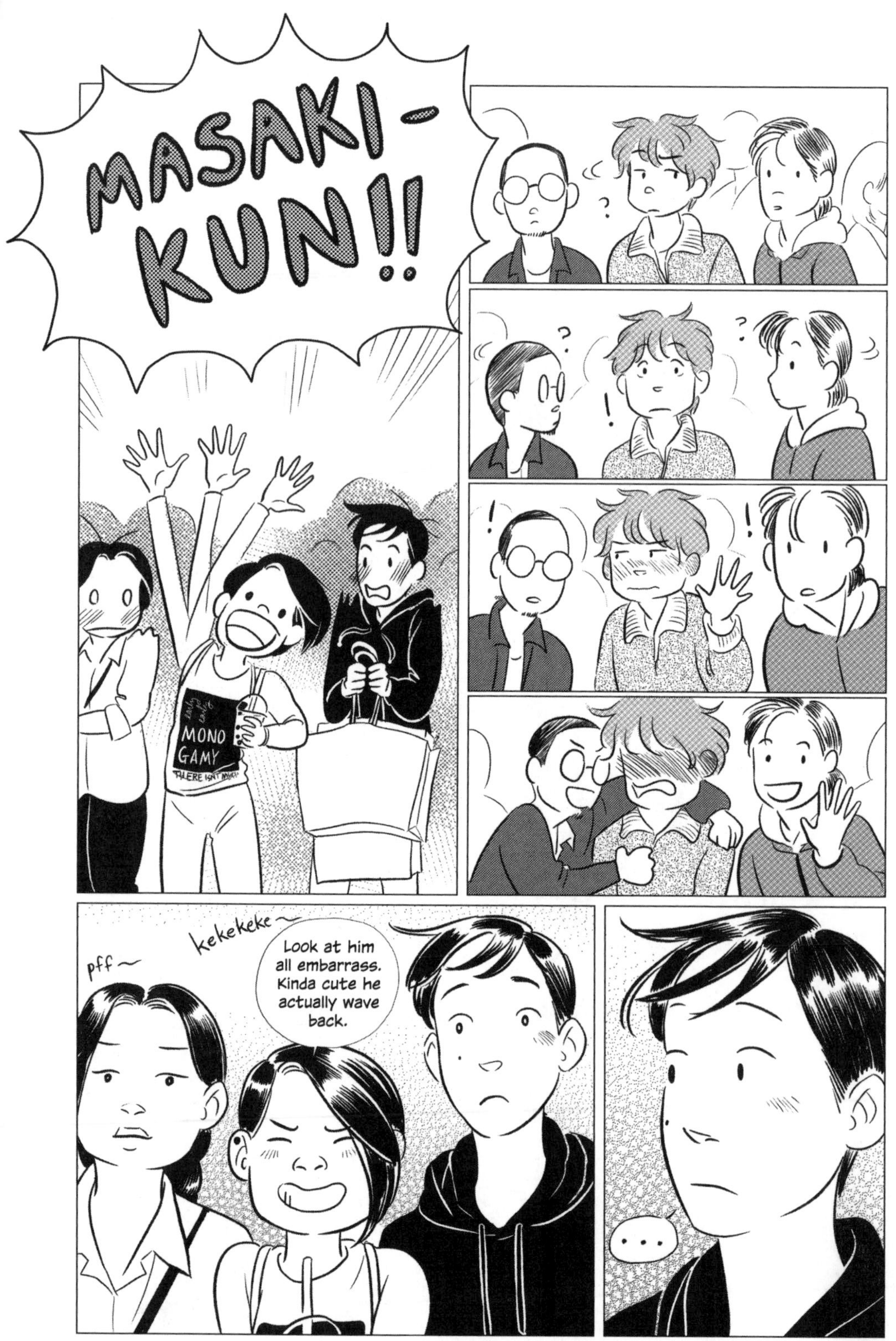
MASAKI-KUN!!
?
? !
? ?
! !
MONOGAMY
pff~
kekekeke~
Look at him all embarrass. Kinda cute he actually wave back.
...

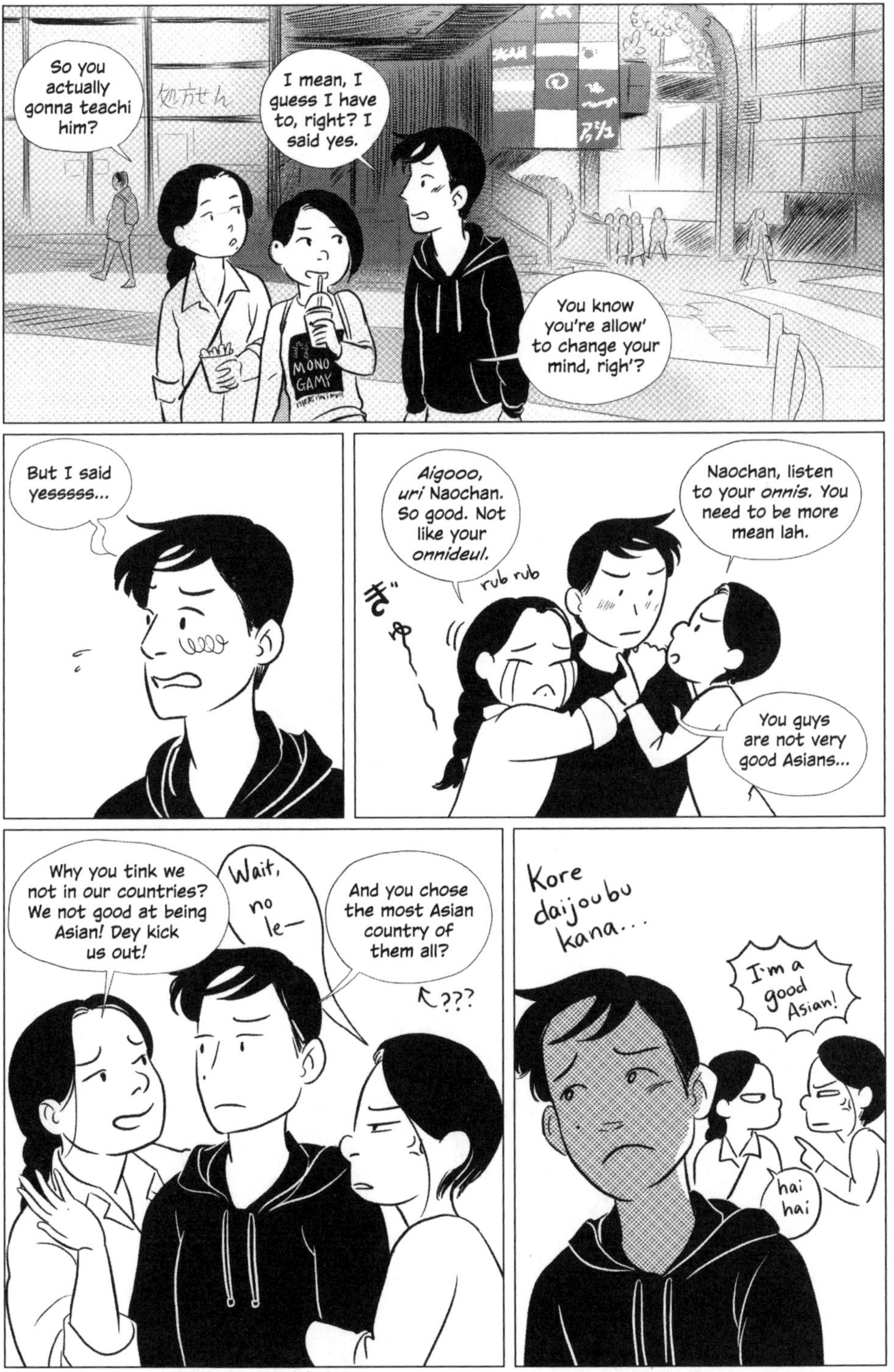
So you actually gonna teachi him?
I mean, I guess I have to, right? I said yes.
You know you're allow' to change your mind, righ'?
But I said yesssss...
Aigooo, uri Naochan. So good. Not like your onnideul.
rub rub
Naochan, listen to your onnis. You need to be more mean lah.
You guys are not very good Asians...
Why you tink we not in our countries? We not good at being Asian! Dey kick us out!
Wait, no le—
And you chose the most Asian country of them all?
???
Kore daijoubu kana...
I'm a good Asian!
hai hai

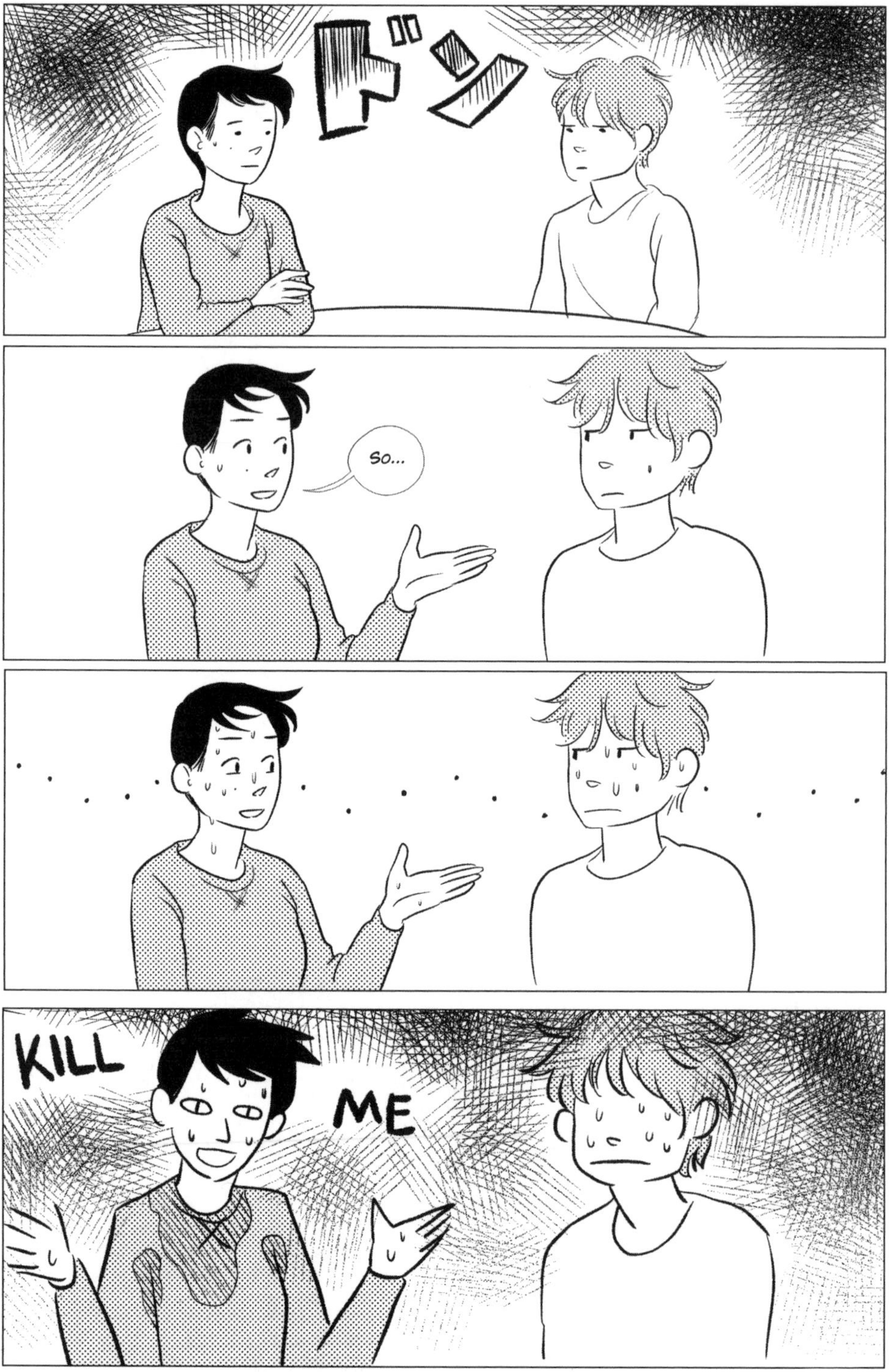
ドン
so...
KILL
ME

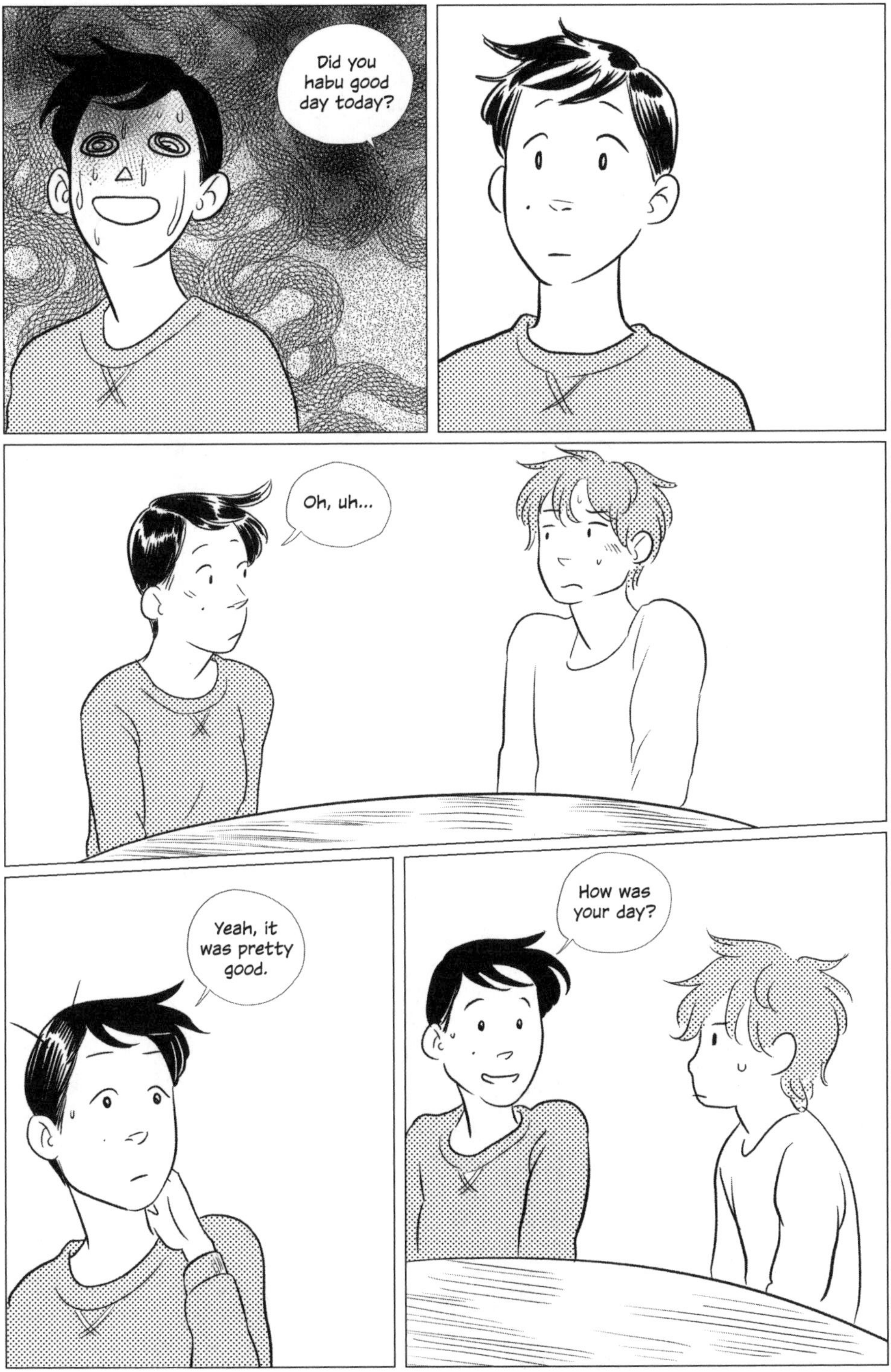
Did you habu good day today?
Oh, uh...
Yeah, it was pretty good.
How was your day?

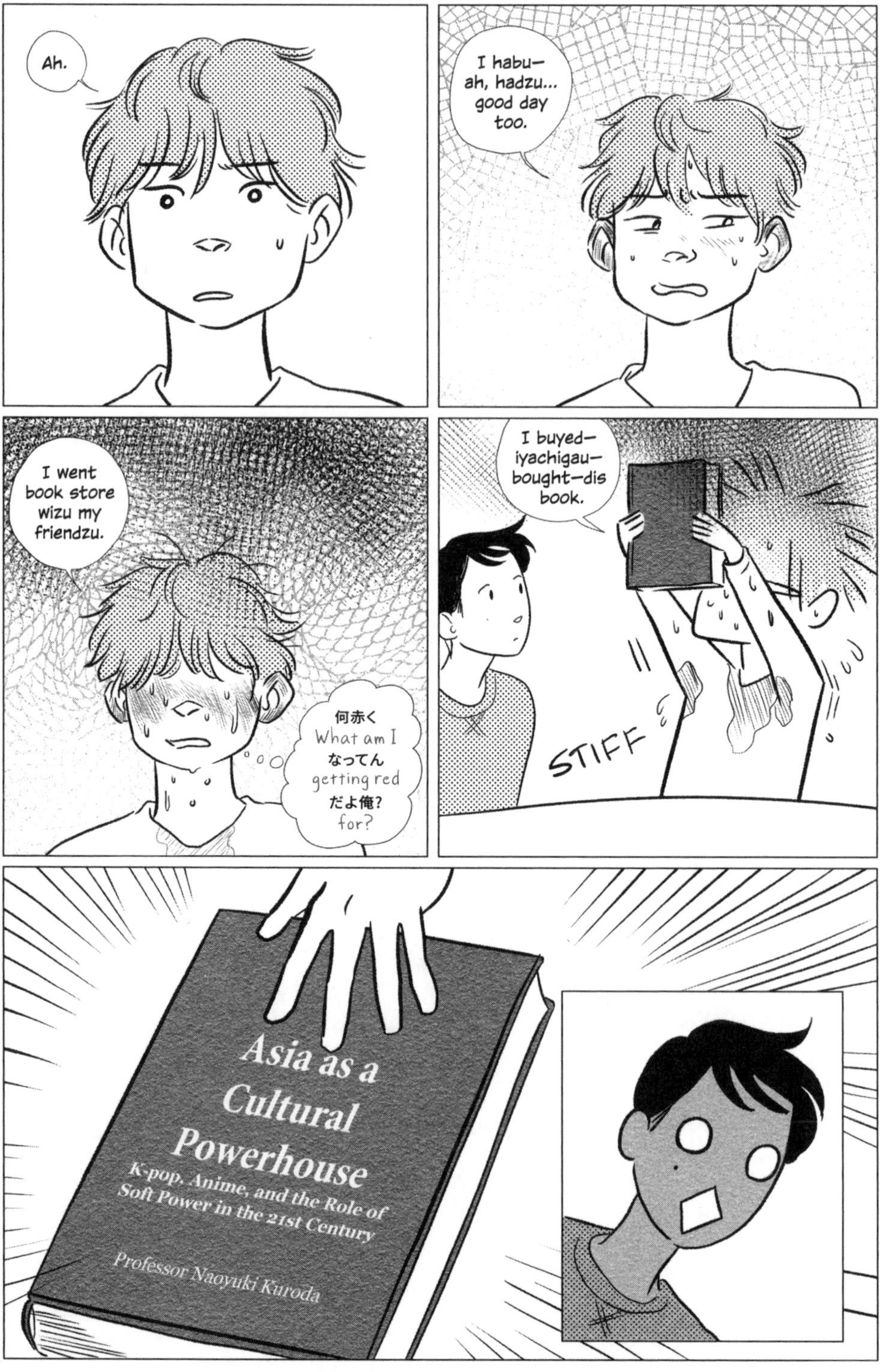
Ah.
I habu— ah, hadzu... good day too.
I went book store wizu my friendzu.
何赤く What am I なってん getting red だよ俺? for?
I buyed— iyachigau— bought—dis book.
STIFF
Asia as a Cultural Powerhouse
K-pop, Anime, and the Role of Soft Power in the 21st Century
Professor Naoyuki Kuroda

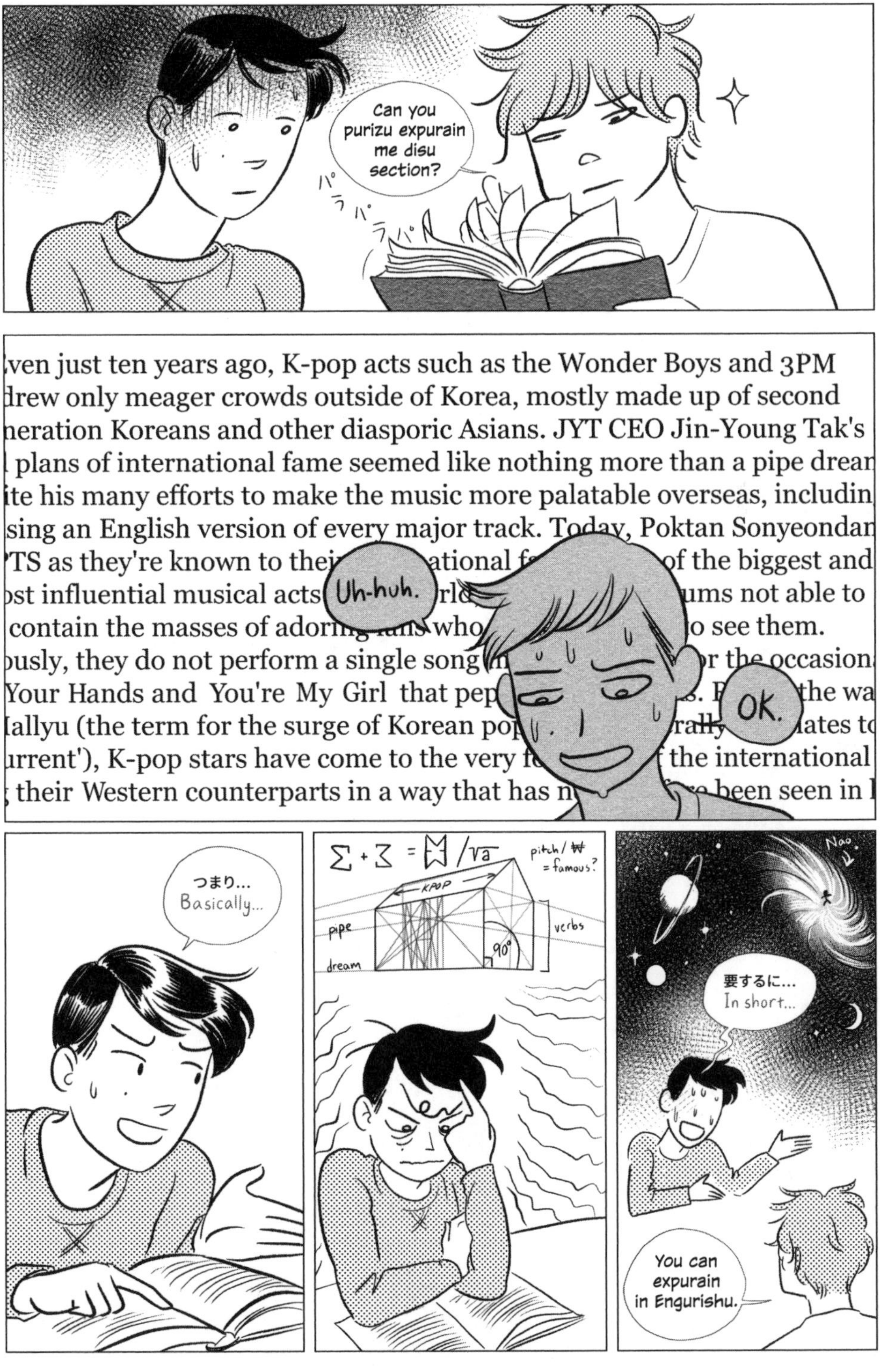
Can you purizu expurain me disu section?
パラパラパラパ
ven just ten years ago, K-pop acts such as the Wonder Boys and 3PM
drew only meager crowds outside of Korea, mostly made up of second
neration Koreans and other diasporic Asians. JYT CEO Jin-Young Tak's
plans of international fame seemed like nothing more than a pipe drear
ite his many efforts to make the music more palatable overseas, includin
sing an English version of every major track. Today, Poktan Sonyeondan
TS as they're known to thei ational f of the biggest and
ost influential musical acts rld ums not able to
contain the masses of adori who o see them.
ously, they do not perform a single song r the occasion
Your Hands and You're My Girl that pep s. the wa
allyu (the term for the surge of Korean pop rally lates to
urrent'), K-pop stars have come to the very f the international
their Western counterparts in a way that has n een seen in
Uh-huh.
OK.
つまり…
Basically…
Σ + Ʒ = ⋈ / √a
pitch / ₩ = famous?
KPOP
pipe
dream
90°
verbs
Nao
要するに…
In short…
You can expurain in Engurishu.

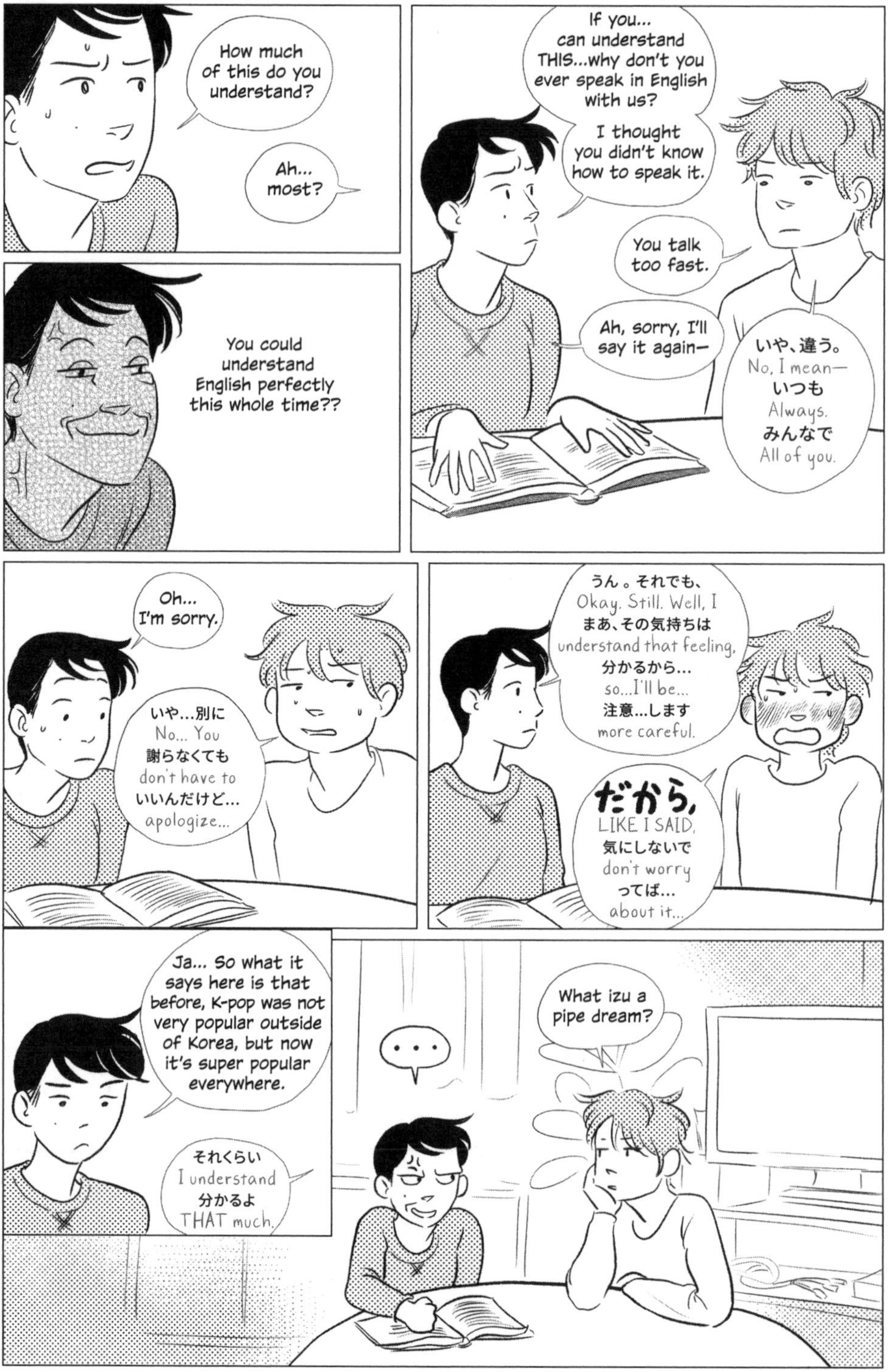
How much of this do you understand?
Ah... most?
If you... can understand THIS...why don't you ever speak in English with us?
I thought you didn't know how to speak it.
You talk too fast.
Ah, sorry, I'll say it again—
いや、違う。
No, I mean—
いつも
Always.
みんなで
All of you.
You could understand English perfectly this whole time??
Oh... I'm sorry.
いや…別に
No... You
謝らなくても
don't have to
いいんだけど…
apologize...
うん 。それでも、
Okay. Still. Well, I
まあ、その気持ちは
understand that feeling,
分かるから…
so...I'll be...
注意…します
more careful.
だから,
LIKE I SAID,
気にしないで
don't worry
ってば…
about it...
Ja... So what it says here is that before, K-pop was not very popular outside of Korea, but now it's super popular everywhere.
それくらい
I understand
分かるよ
THAT much.
...
What izu a pipe dream?

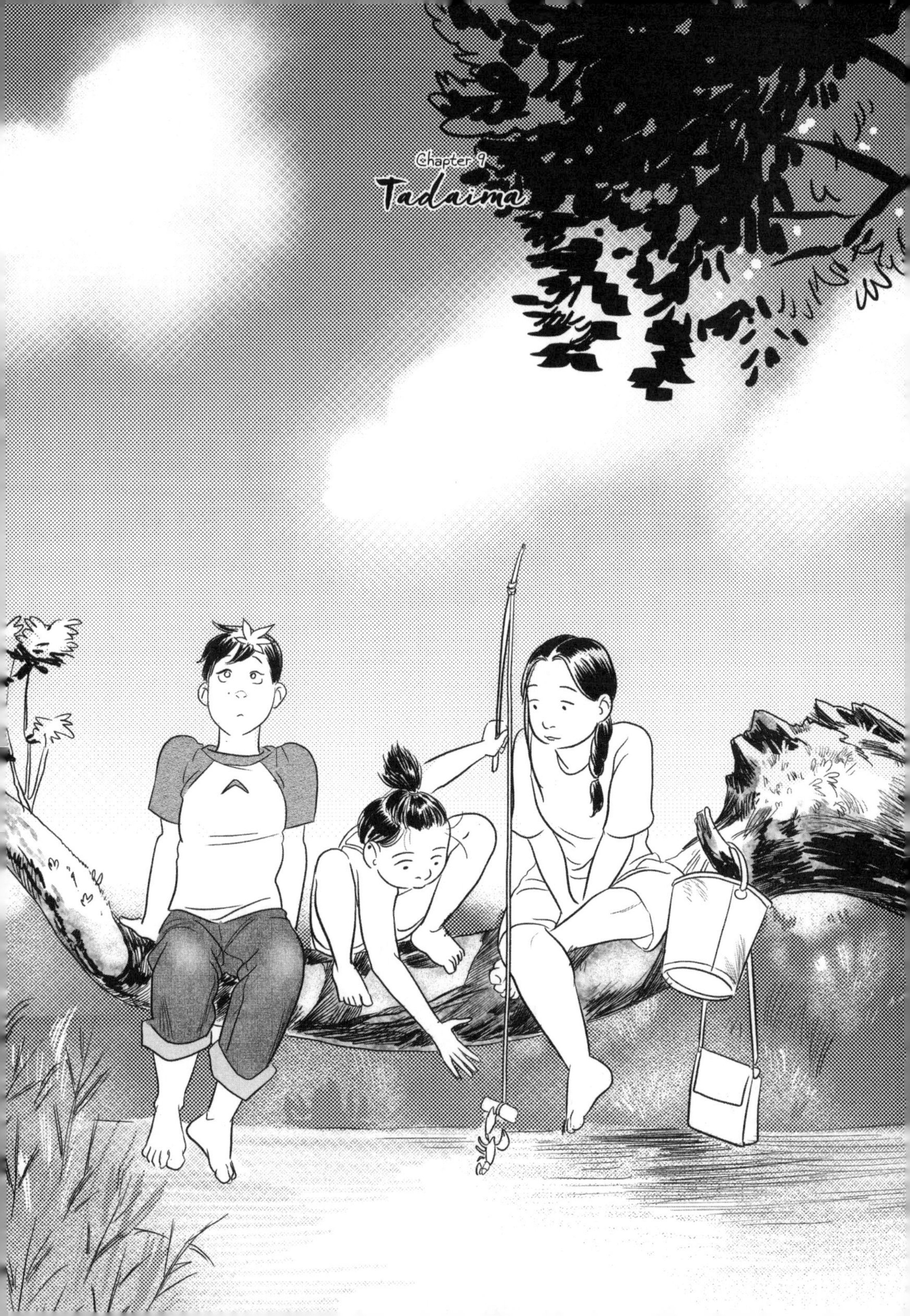
Chapter 9
Tadaima

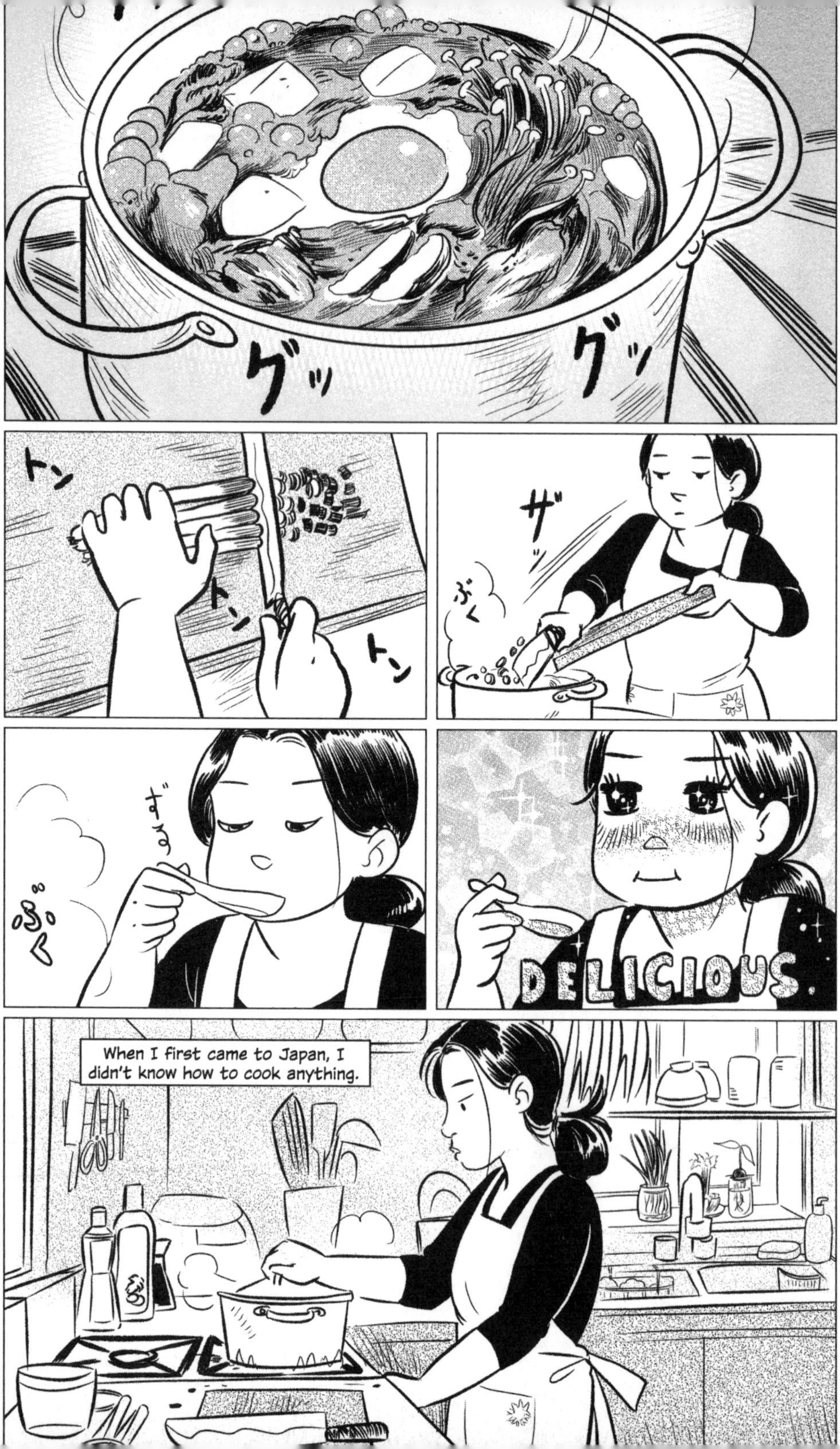
グッ
グッ
トン
トン
トン
ザッ
ぷく
ずず
ふぅ
DELICIOUS.
When I first came to Japan, I didn't know how to cook anything.

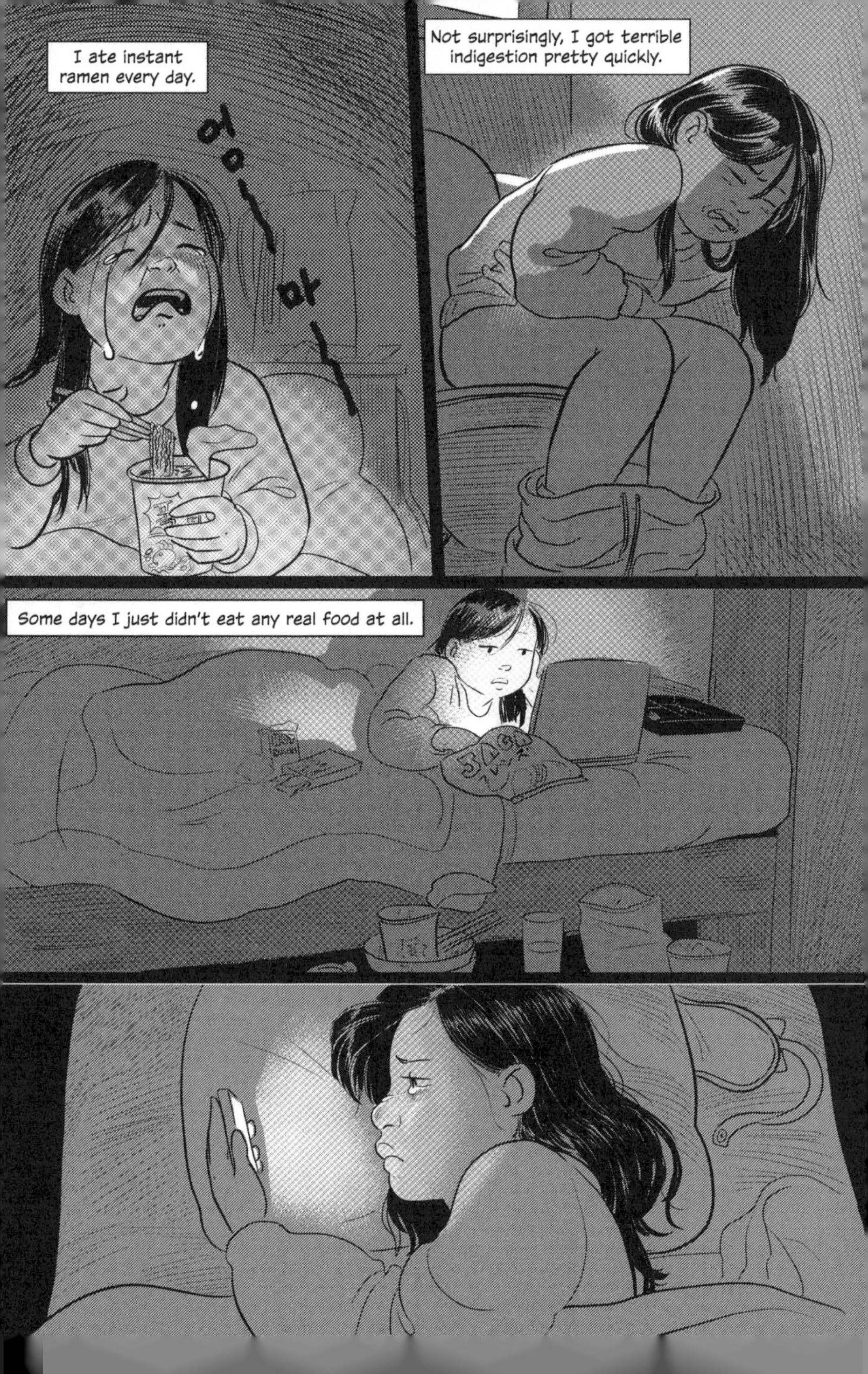
I ate instant ramen every day.
엉— 아—
Not surprisingly, I got terrible indigestion pretty quickly.
Some days I just didn't eat any real food at all.

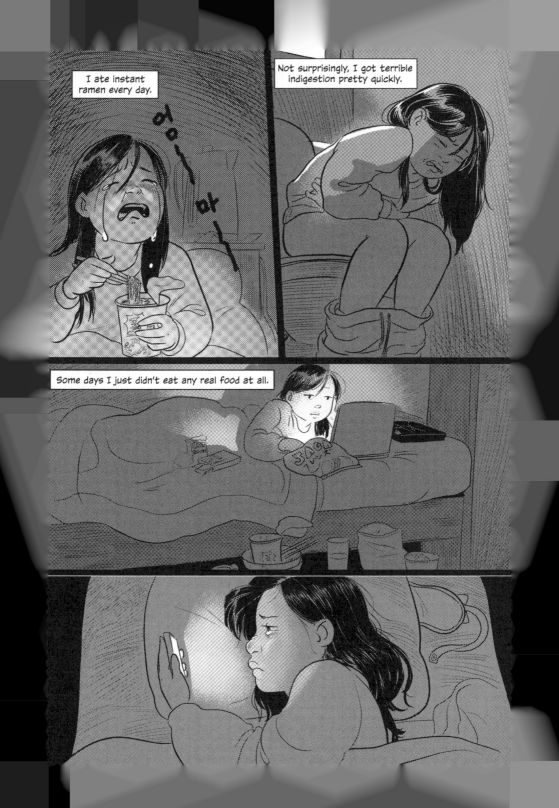

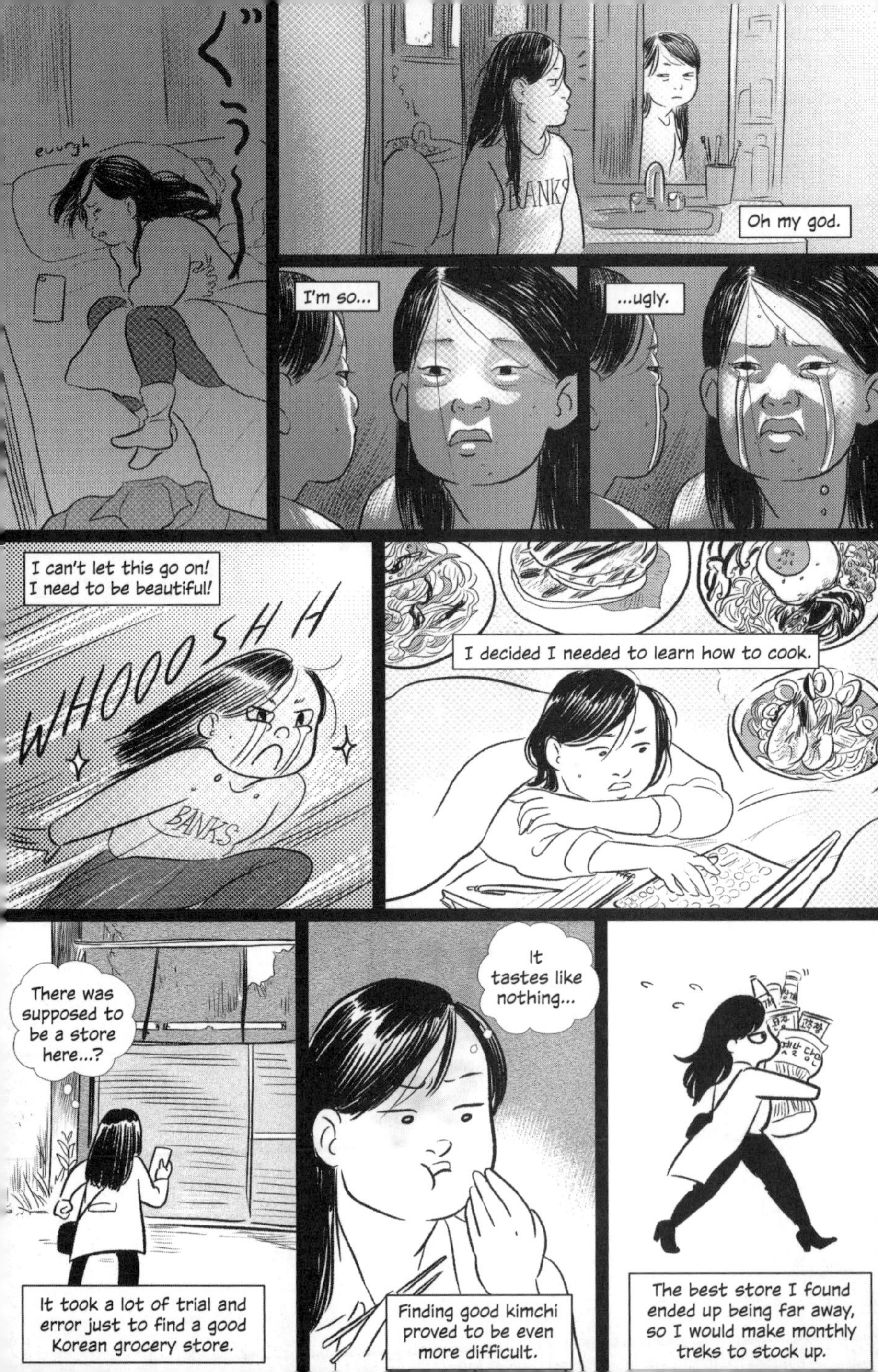

euurgh
ぐう〜
Oh my god.
I'm so...
...ugly.
I can't let this go on! I need to be beautiful!
WHOOOSHH
BANKS
I decided I needed to learn how to cook.
There was supposed to be a store here...?
It took a lot of trial and error just to find a good Korean grocery store.
It tastes like nothing...
Finding good kimchi proved to be even more difficult.
The best store I found ended up being far away, so I would make monthly treks to stock up.

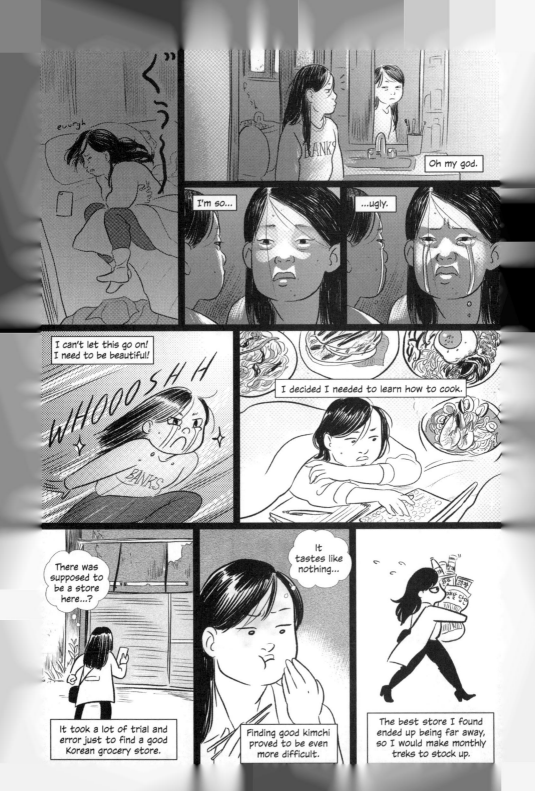

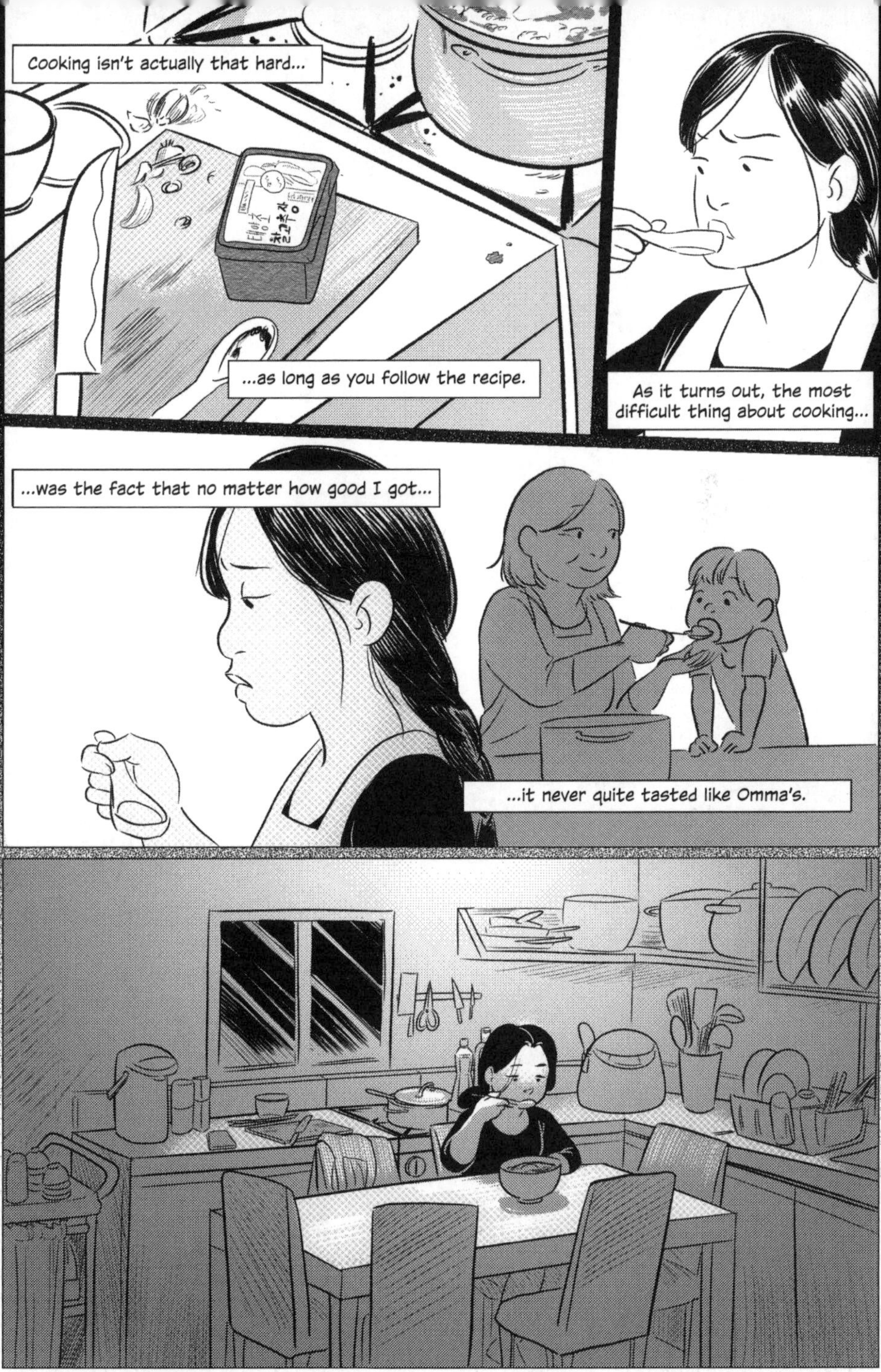
Cooking isn't actually that hard...
...as long as you follow the recipe.
As it turns out, the most difficult thing about cooking...
...was the fact that no matter how good I got...
...it never quite tasted like Omma's.

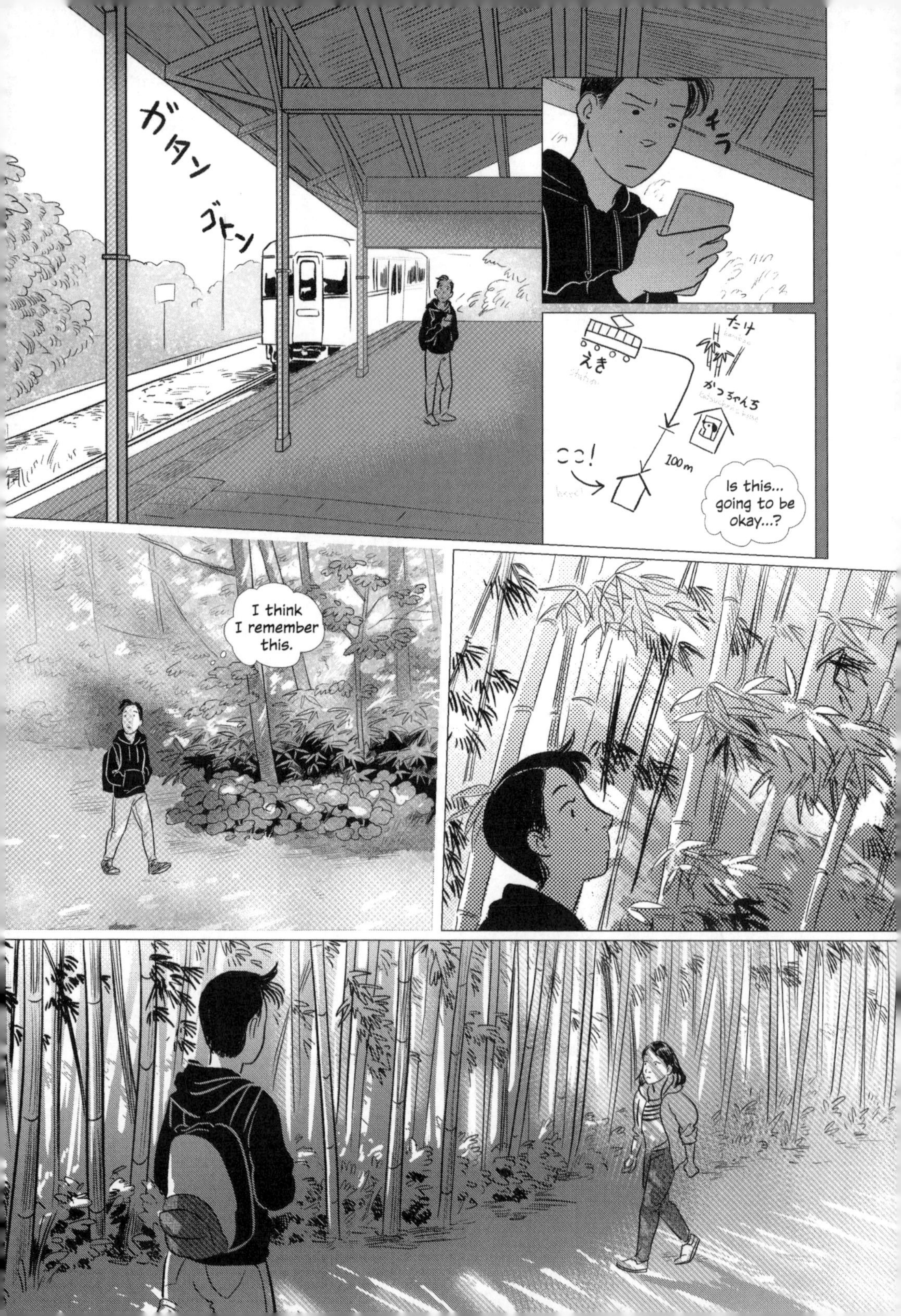
ガタン
ゴトン
キラ
えき
たけ
かつちゃんち
100m
ここ!
Is this... going to be okay...?
I think I remember this.

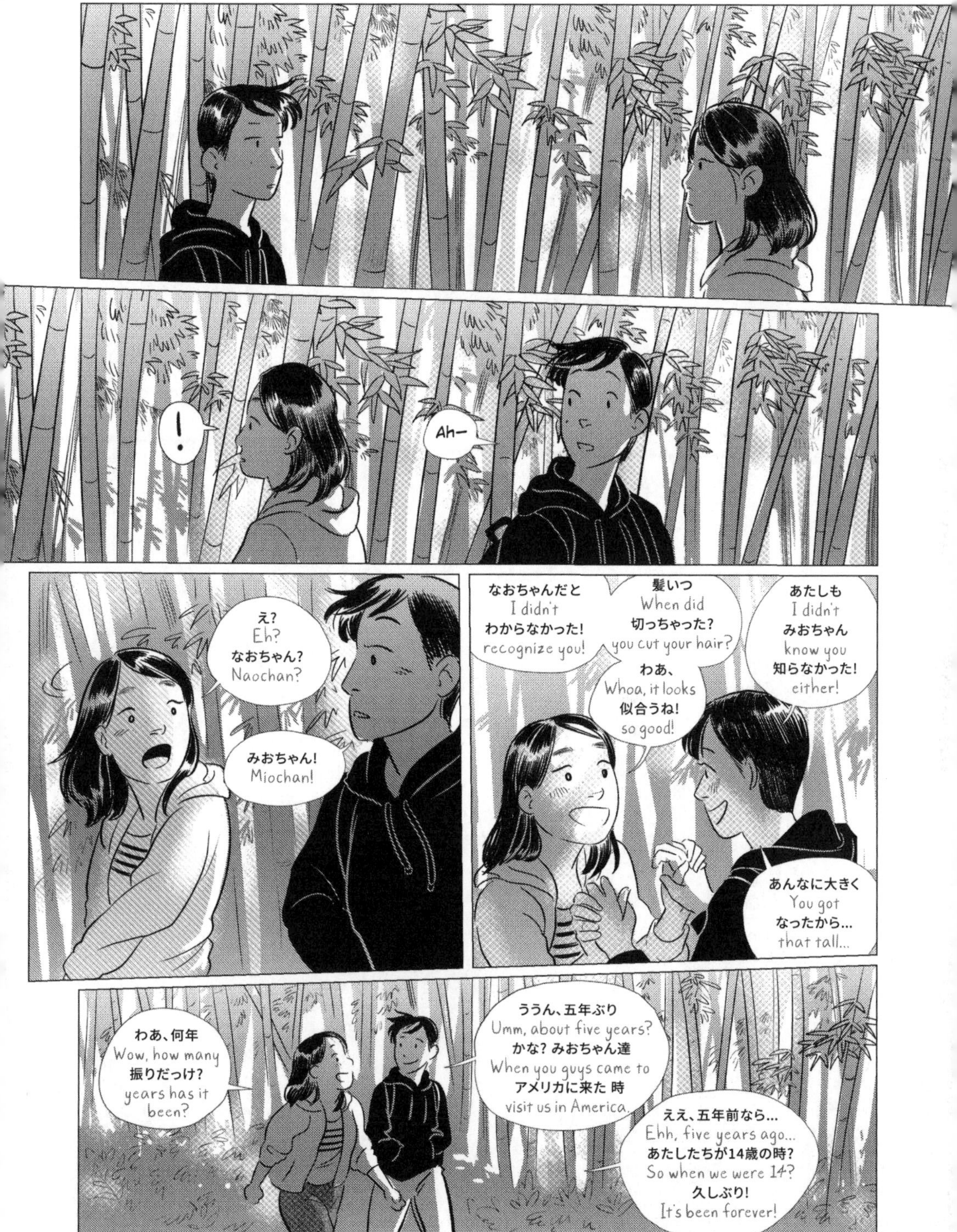
!
Ah—
え? Eh? なおちゃん? Naochan?
みおちゃん! Miochan!
なおちゃんだと I didn't わからなかった! recognize you!
髪いつ When did 切っちゃった? you cut your hair?
わあ、Whoa, it looks 似合うね! so good!
あたしも I didn't みおちゃん know you 知らなかった! either!
あんなに大きく You got なったから... that tall...
わあ、何年 Wow, how many 振りだっけ? years has it been?
ううん、五年ぶり Umm, about five years? かな? みおちゃん達 When you guys came to アメリカに来た 時 visit us in America.
ええ、五年前なら... Ehh, five years ago... あたしたちが14歳の時? So when we were 14? 久しぶり! It's been forever!

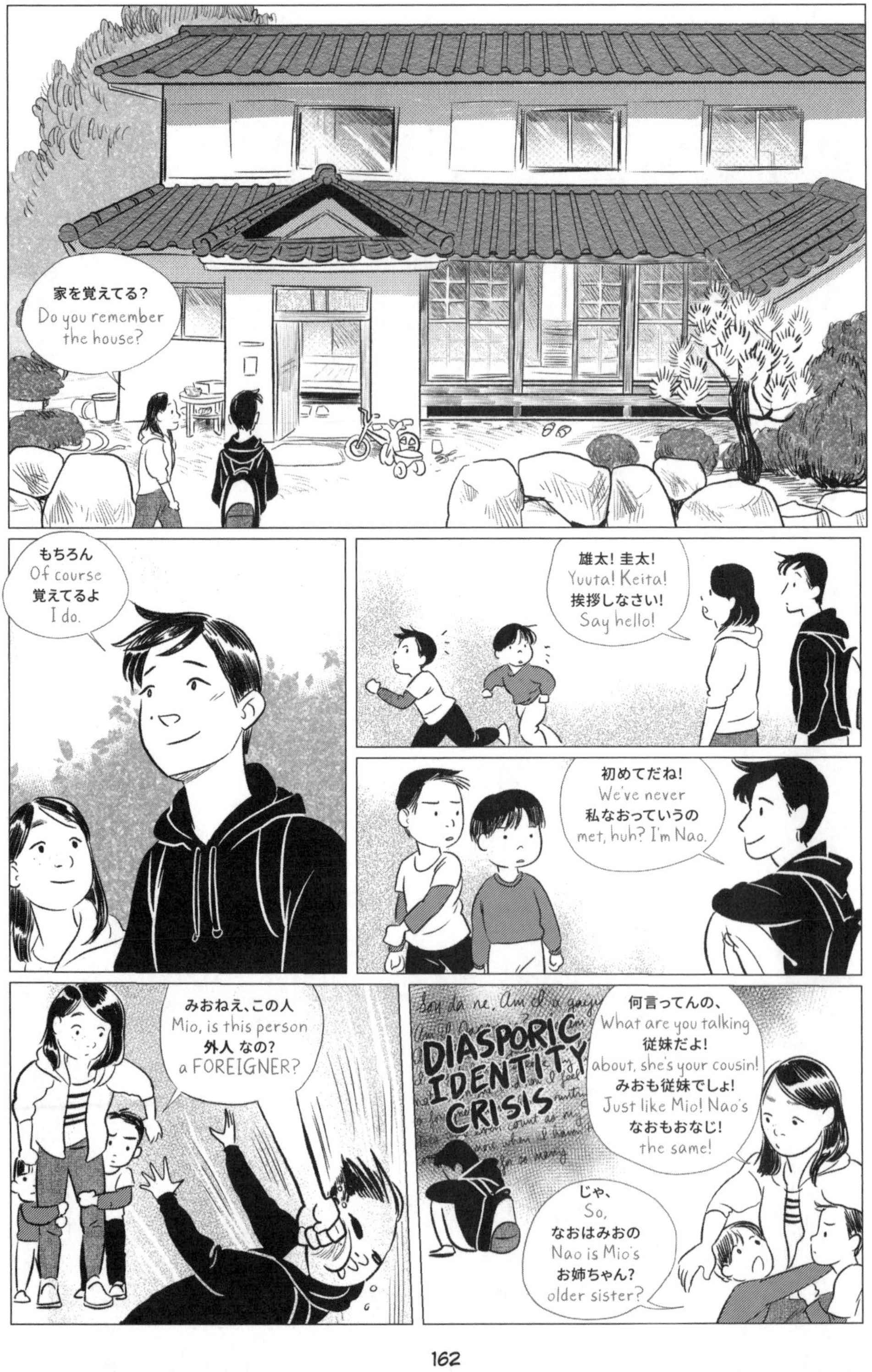
家を覚えてる?
Do you remember the house?
もちろん
Of course
覚えてるよ
I do.
雄太! 圭太!
Yuuta! Keita!
挨拶しなさい!
Say hello!
初めてだね!
We've never
私なおっていうの
met, huh? I'm Nao.
みおねえ、この人
Mio, is this person
外人 なの?
a FOREIGNER?
DIASPORIC IDENTITY CRISIS
何言ってんの、
What are you talking
従妹だよ!
about, she's your cousin!
みおも従妹でしょ!
Just like Mio! Nao's
なおもおなじ!
the same!
じゃ、
So,
なおはみおの
Nao is Mio's
お姉ちゃん?
older sister?

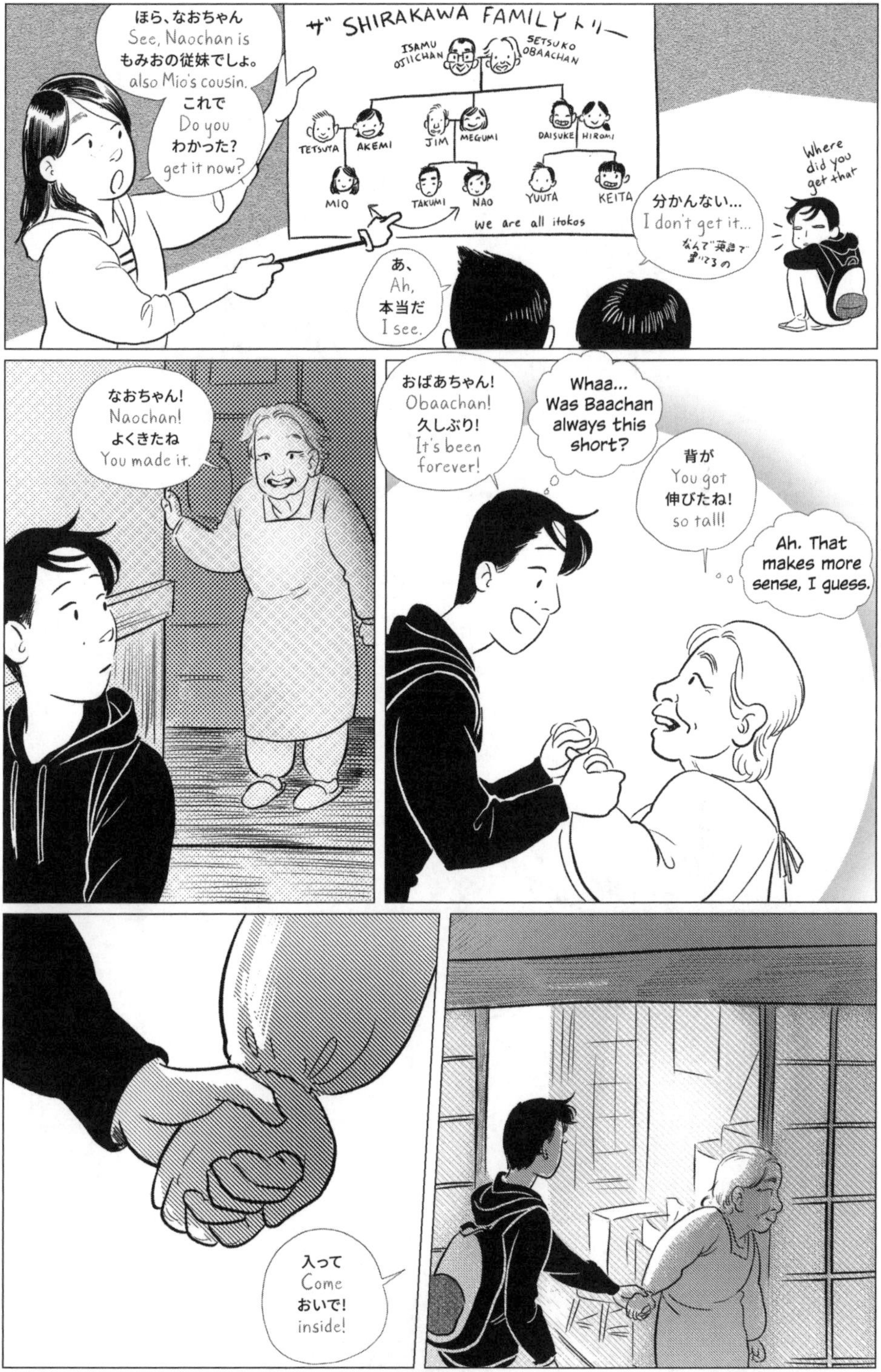
ほら、なおちゃん
See, Naochan is
もみおの従妹でしょ。
also Mio's cousin.
これで
Do you
わかった?
get it now?
ザ SHIRAKAWA FAMILYトリー
ISAMU OJIICHAN
SETSUKO OBAACHAN
TETSUYA
AKEMI
JIM
MEGUMI
DAISUKE
HIROMI
MIO
TAKUMI
NAO
YUUTA
KEITA
we are all itokos
分かんない…
I don't get it…
なんで英語で書いてるの
Where did you get that
あ、
Ah,
本当だ
I see.
なおちゃん!
Naochan!
よくきたね
You made it.
おばあちゃん!
Obaachan!
久しぶり!
It's been forever!
Whaa… Was Baachan always this short?
背が
You got
伸びたね!
so tall!
Ah. That makes more sense, I guess.
入って
Come
おいで!
inside!

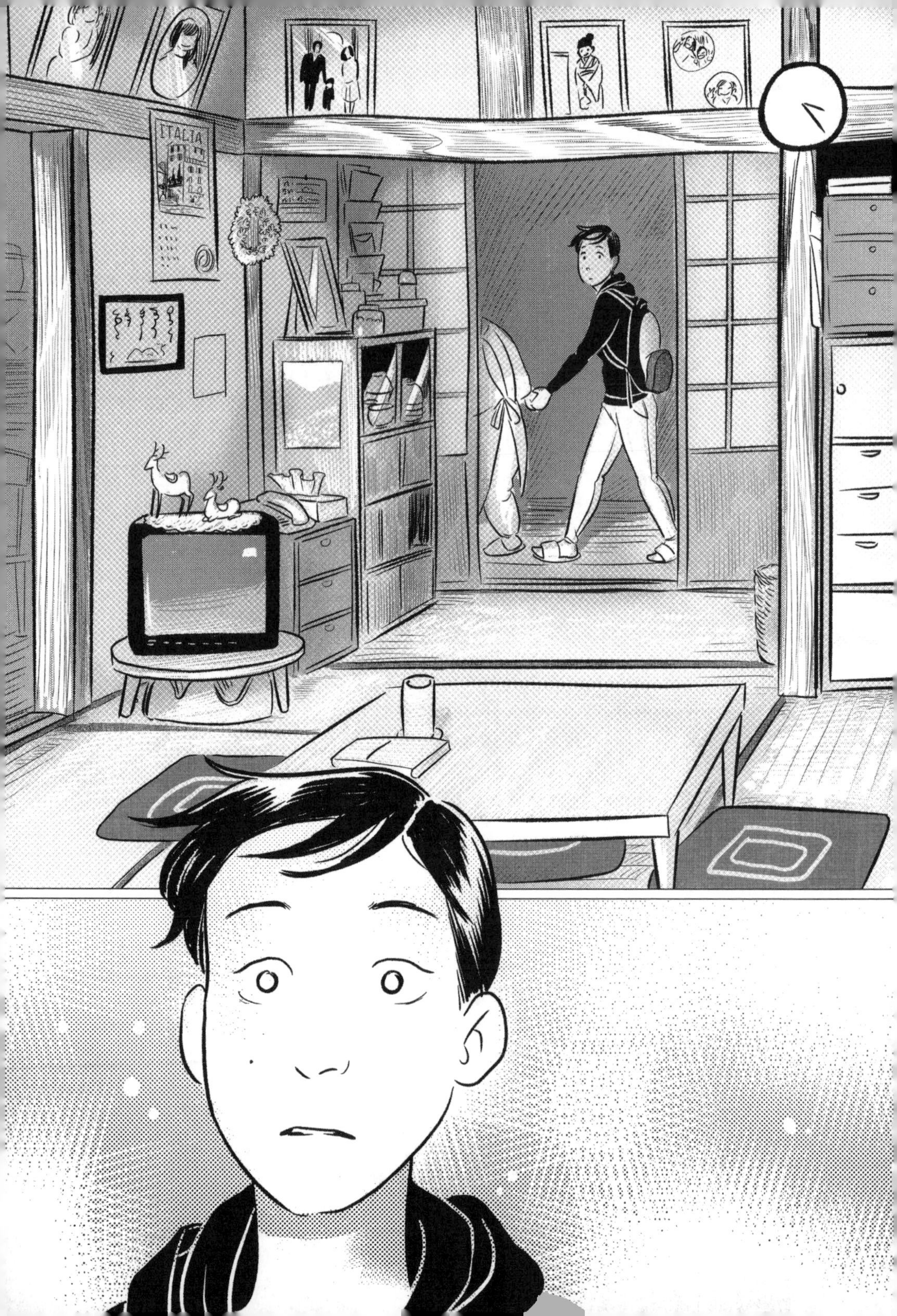
ITALIA

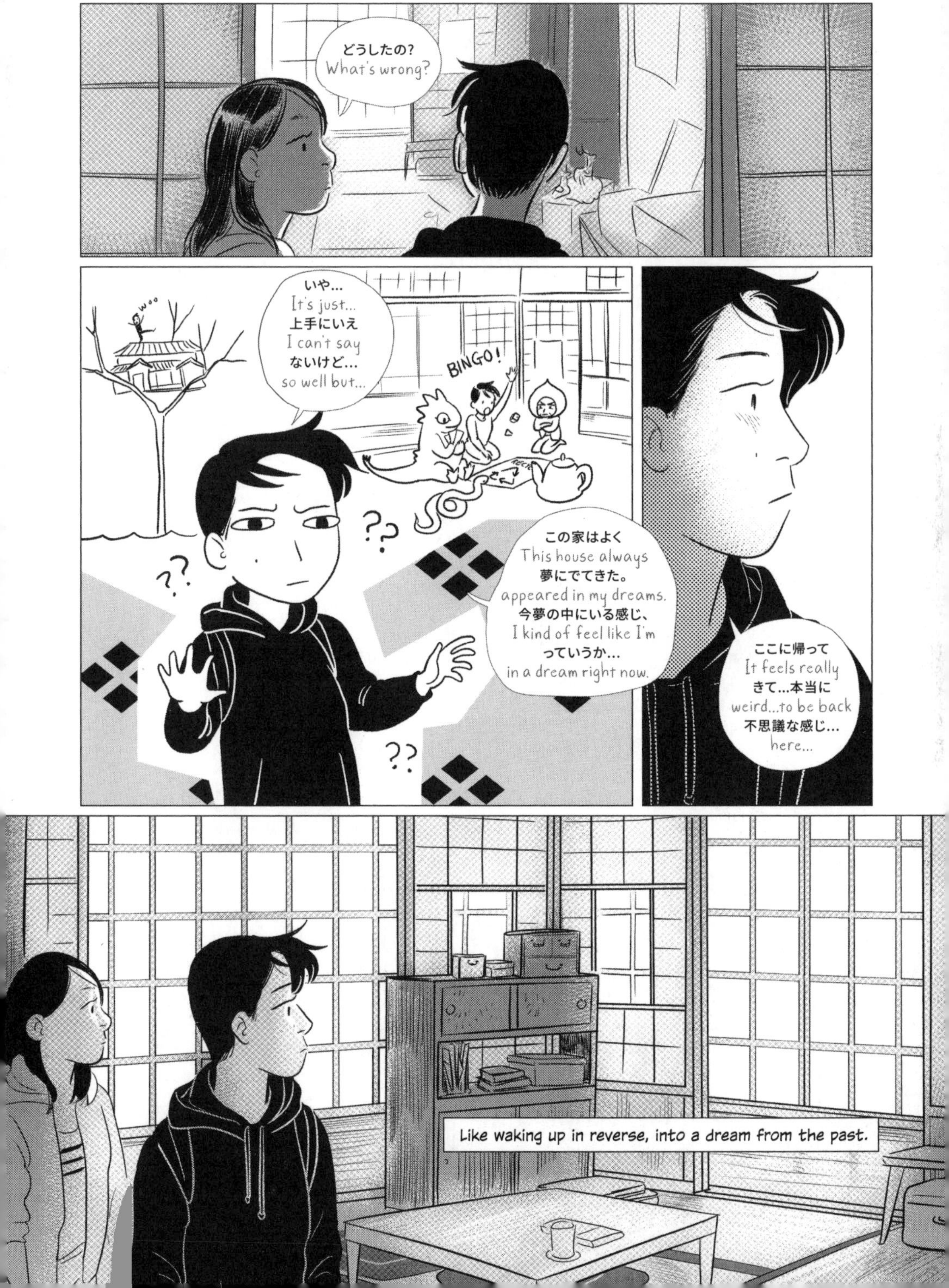

どうしたの?
What's wrong?
いや…
It's just…
上手にいえ
I can't say
ないけど…
so well but…
BINGO!
この家はよく
This house always
夢にでてきた。
appeared in my dreams.
今夢の中にいる感じ、
I kind of feel like I'm
っていうか…
in a dream right now.
ここに帰って
It feels really
きて…本当に
weird…to be back
不思議な感じ…
here…
Like waking up in reverse, into a dream from the past.

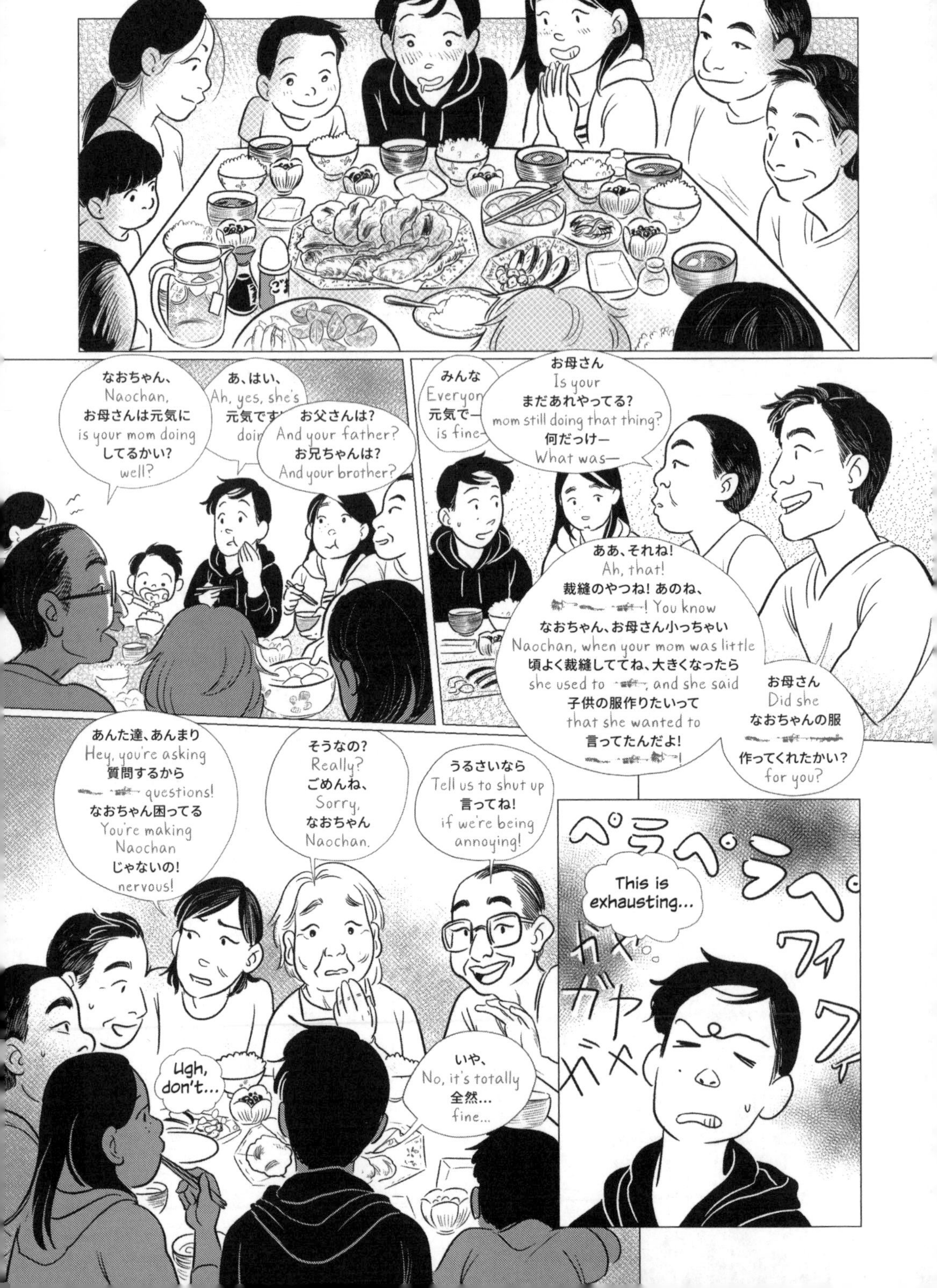

なおちゃん、 Naochan, お母さんは元気に is your mom doing してるかい? well?
あ、はい、 Ah, yes, she's 元気です doin
お父さんは? And your father? お兄ちゃんは? And your brother?
みんな Everyon 元気で— is fine—
お母さん Is your まだあれやってる? mom still doing that thing? 何だっけ— What was—
ああ、それね! Ah, that! 裁縫のやつね! あのね、 ! You know なおちゃん、お母さん小っちゃい Naochan, when your mom was little 頃よく裁縫しててね、大きくなったら she used to , and she said 子供の服作りたいって that she wanted to 言ってたんだよ!
お母さん Did she なおちゃんの服 作ってくれたかい? for you?
あんた達、あんまり Hey, you're asking 質問するから questions! なおちゃん困ってる You're making Naochan じゃないの! nervous!
そうなの? Really? ごめんね、 Sorry, なおちゃん Naochan.
うるさいなら Tell us to shut up 言ってね! if we're being annoying!
Ugh, don't...
いや、 No, it's totally 全然... fine...
This is exhausting...
ペラペラペラ
ワイワイ
ガヤガヤ

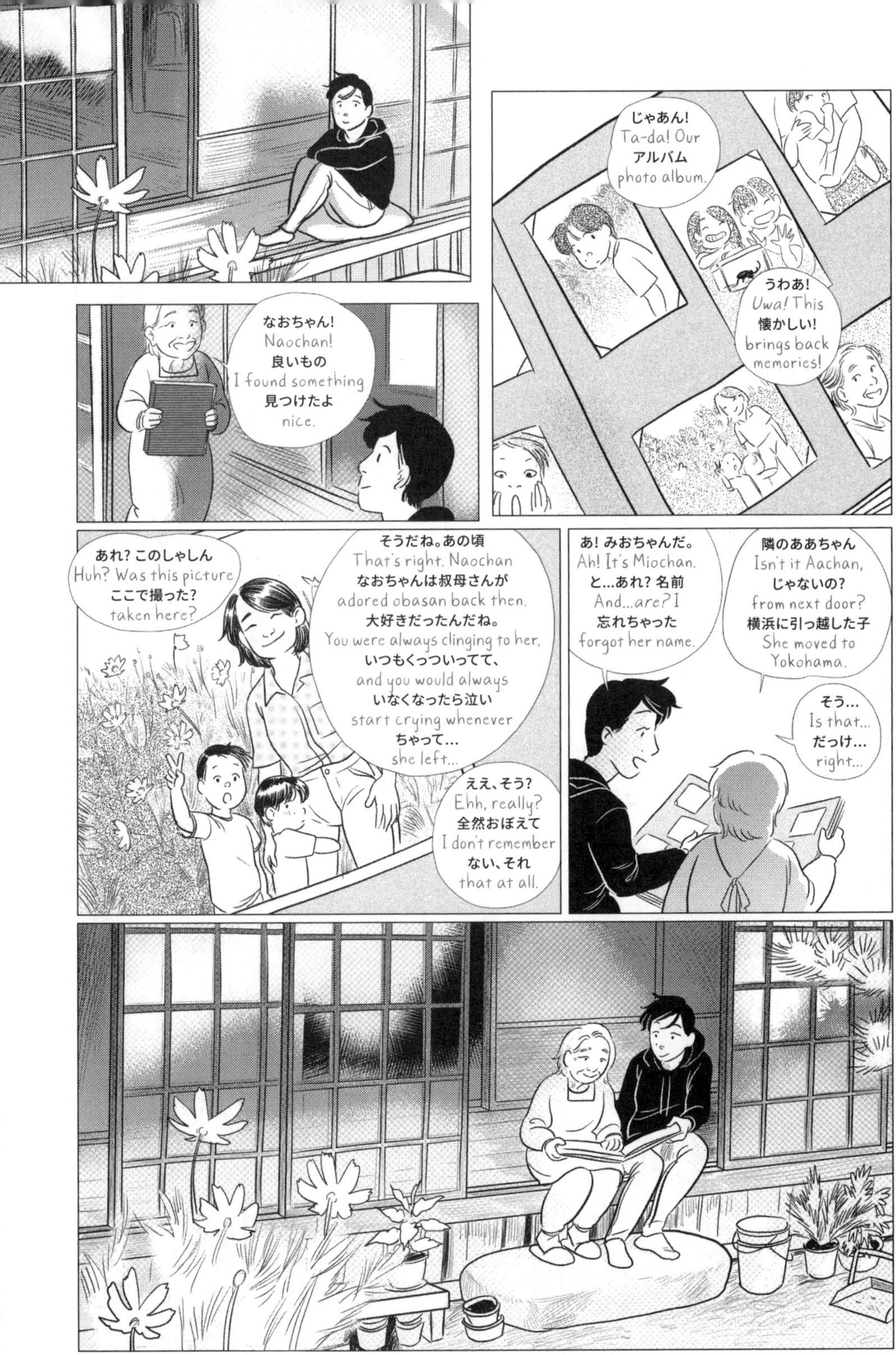

なおちゃん! Naochan! 良いもの I found something 見つけたよ nice.
じゃあん! Ta-da! Our アルバム photo album.
うわあ! Uwa! This 懐かしい! brings back memories!
あれ? このしゃしん Huh? Was this picture ここで撮った? taken here?
そうだね。あの頃 That's right. Naochan なおちゃんは叔母さんが adored obasan back then. 大好きだったんだね。 You were always clinging to her, いつもくっついってて、 and you would always いなくなったら泣い start crying whenever ちゃって… she left…
ええ、そう? Ehh, really? 全然おぼえて I don't remember ない、それ that at all.
あ! みおちゃんだ。 Ah! It's Miochan. と…あれ? 名前 And…are? I 忘れちゃった forgot her name.
隣のああちゃん Isn't it Aachan, じゃないの? from next door? 横浜に引っ越した子 She moved to Yokohama.
そう… Is that… だっけ… right…

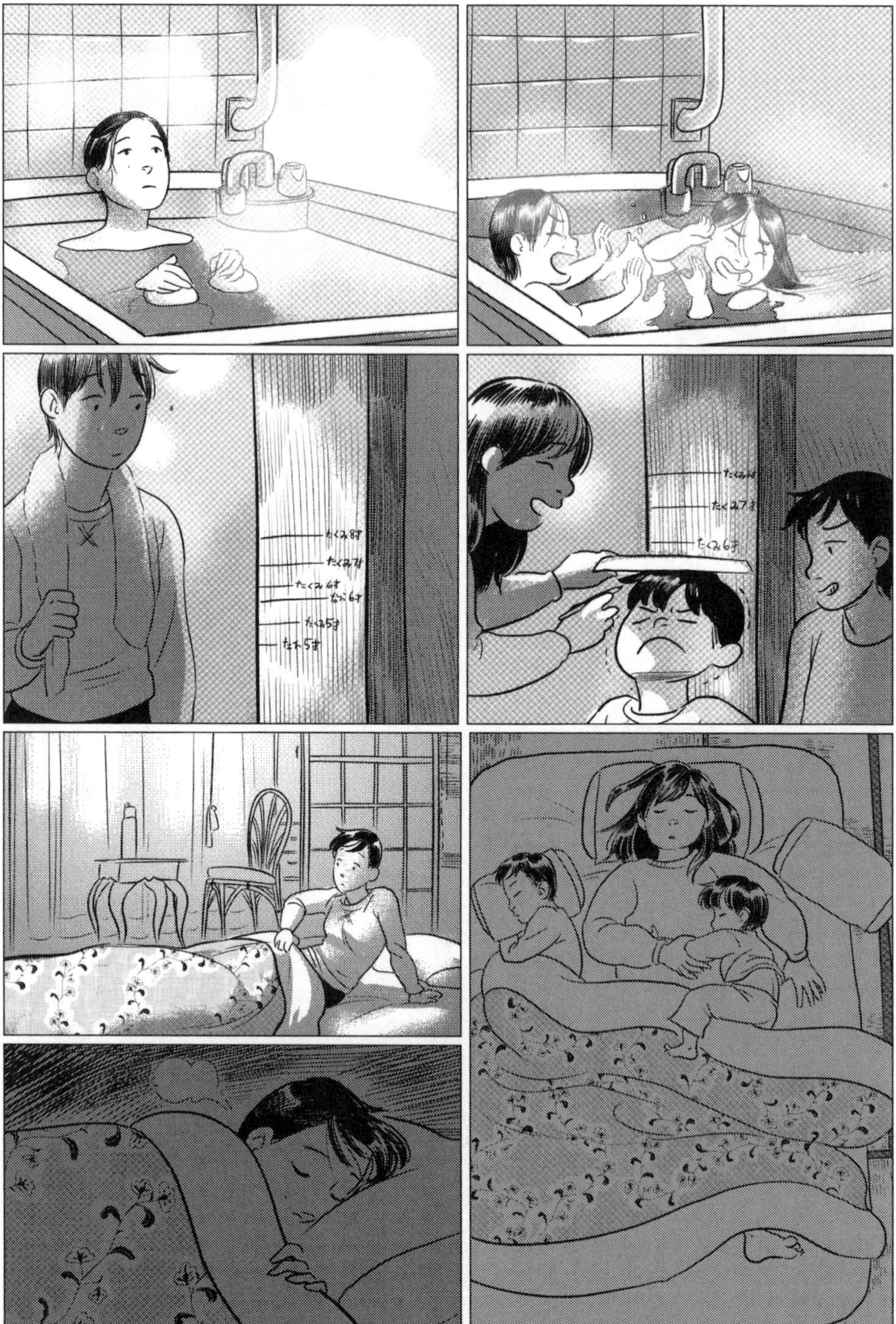
たくみ8才
たくみ7才
たくみ6才
なお6才
たくみ5才
なお5才
たくみ7才
たくみ6才
The futon is so heavy. It feels like being embraced.

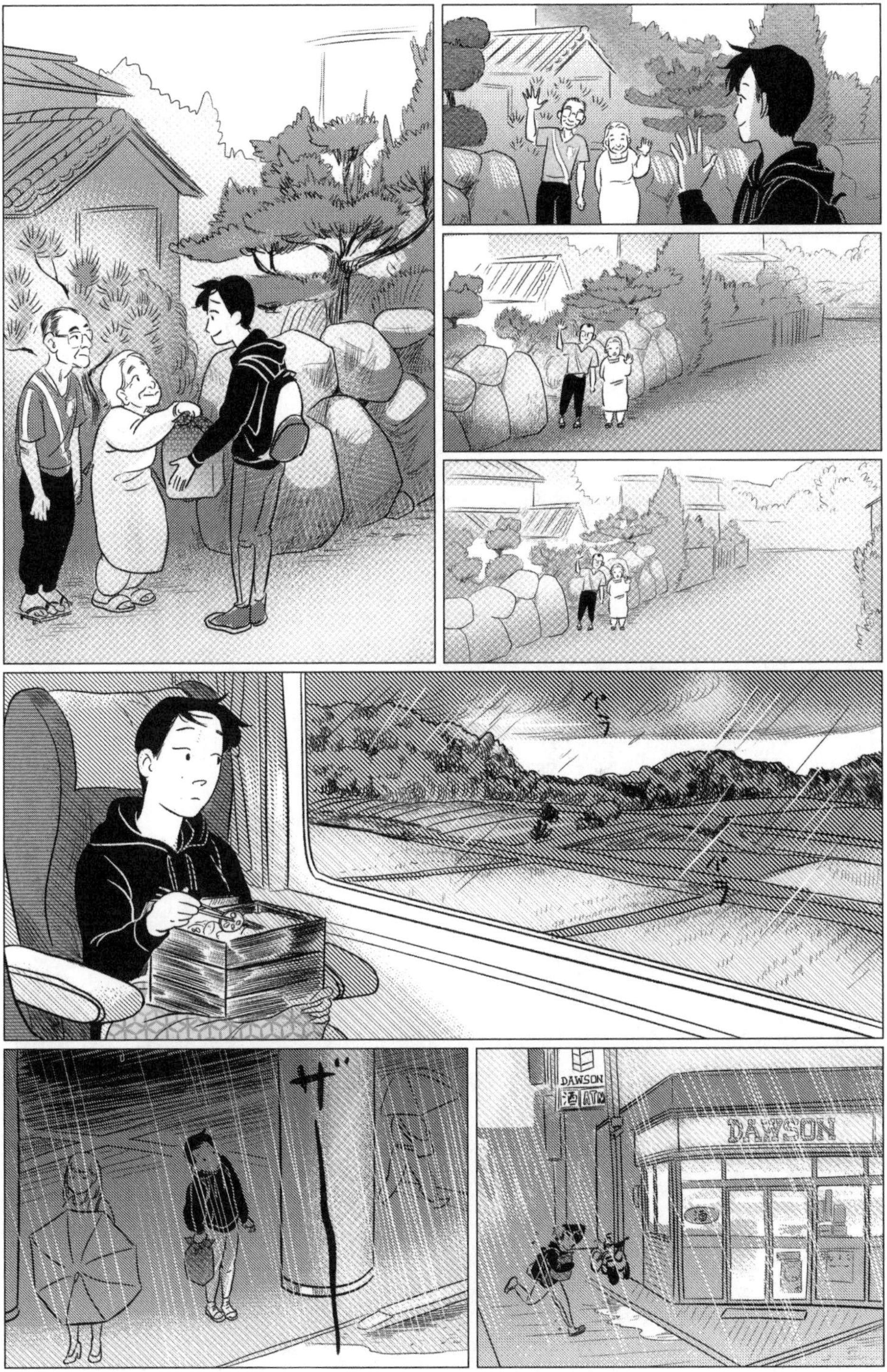
パラ
パラ
ザ
DAWSON
酒 ATM
DAWSON
酒

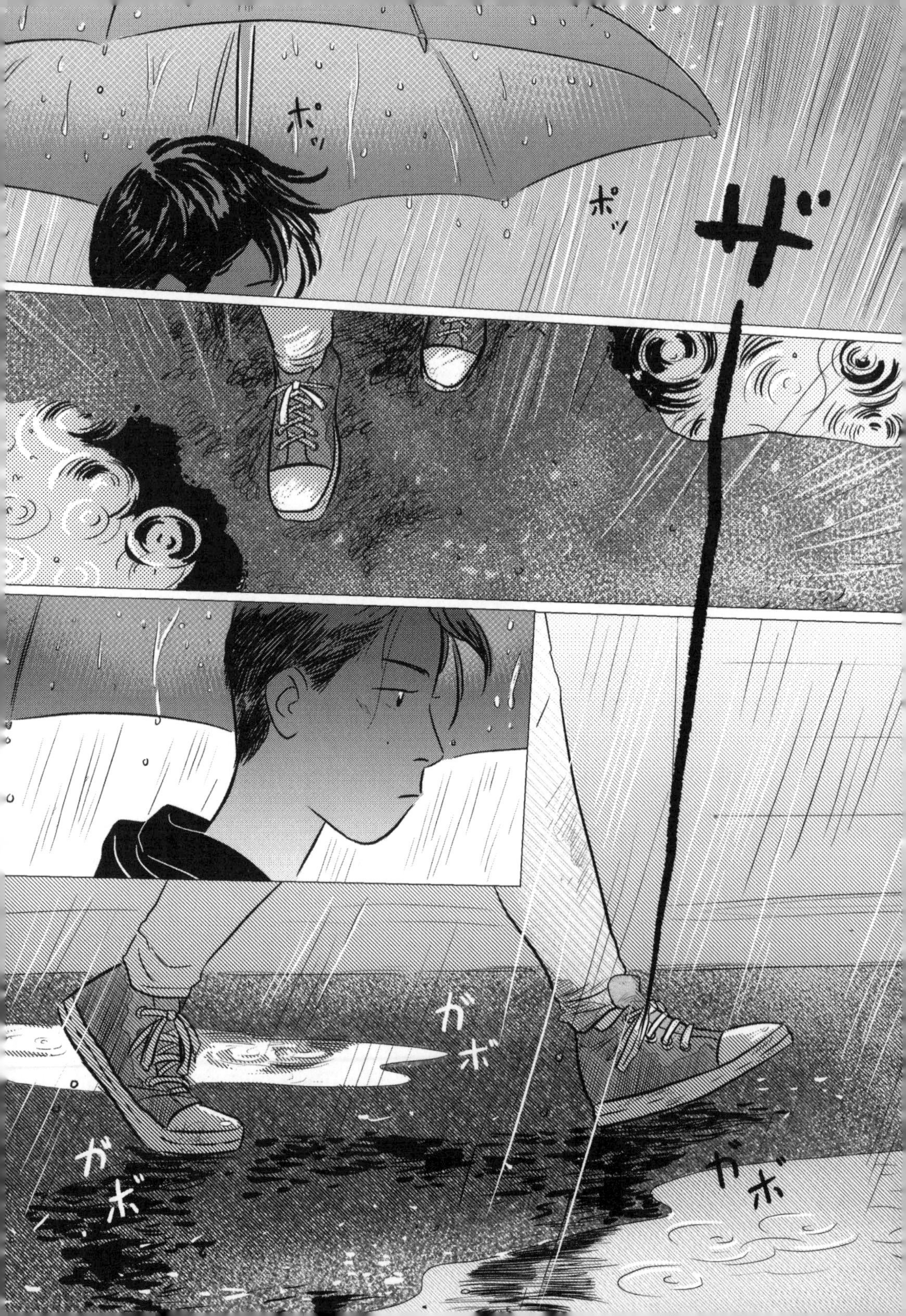
ポッ
ポッ
ザ
ガボ
ガボ
ガボ

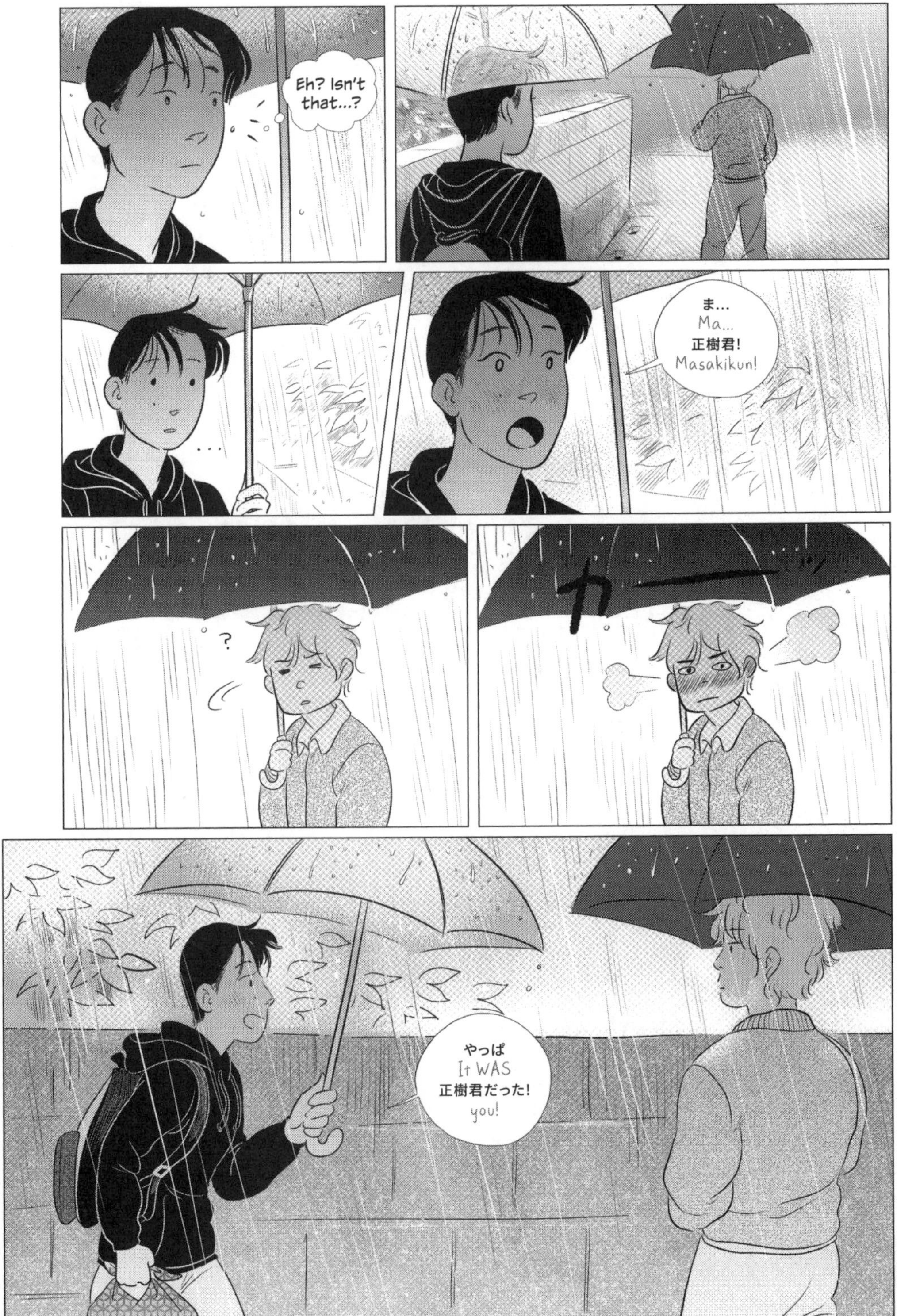

Eh? Isn't that...?
...
ま...
Ma...
正樹君!
Masakikun!
?
カーッ
やっぱ
It WAS
正樹君だった!
you!

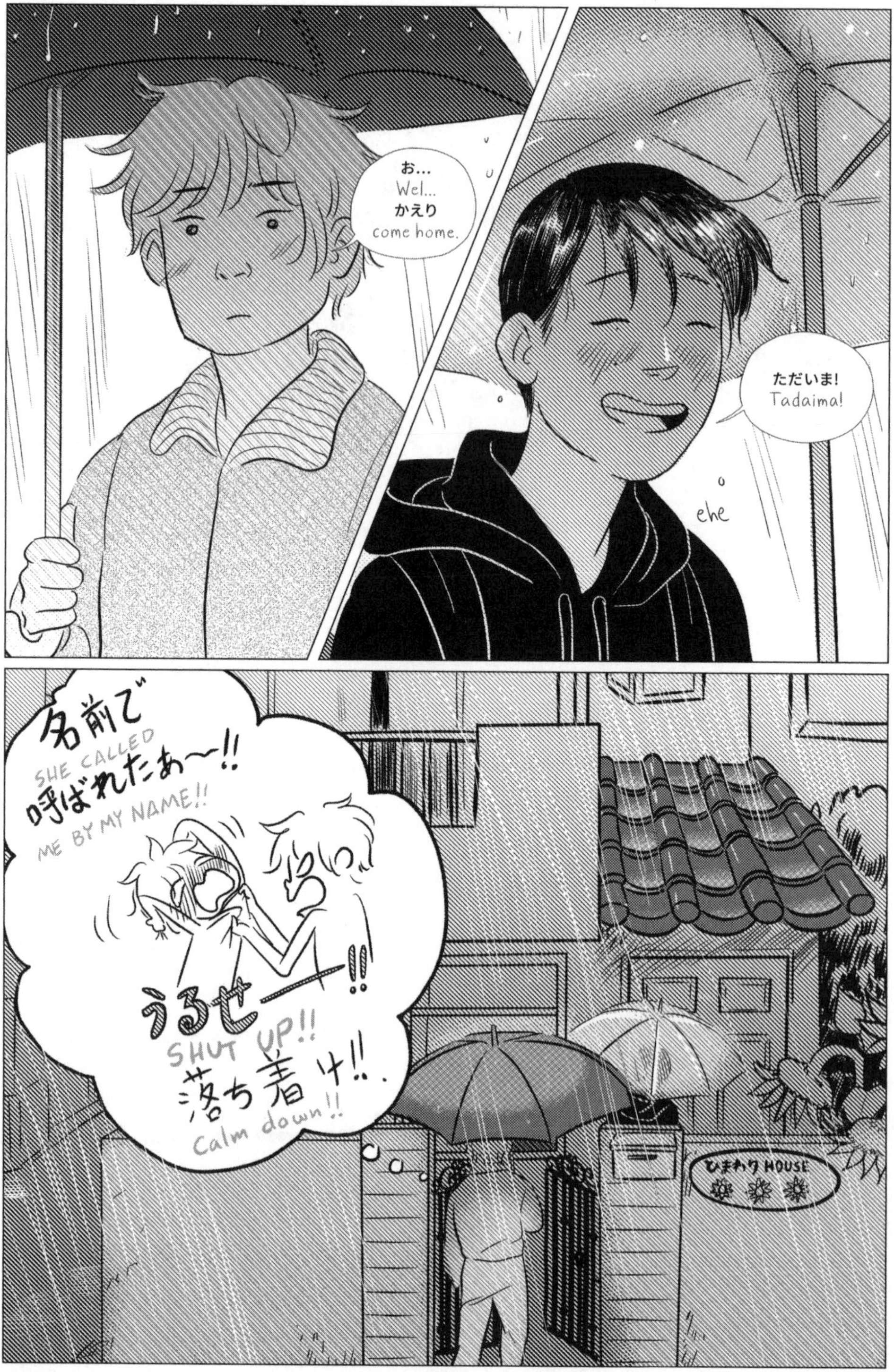
お…
Wel…
かえり
come home.
ただいま!
Tadaima!
ehe
名前で
SHE CALLED
呼ばれたあ〜〜!!
ME BY MY NAME!!
うるせーー!!
SHUT UP!!
落ち着け!!
Calm down!!
ひまわり HOUSE

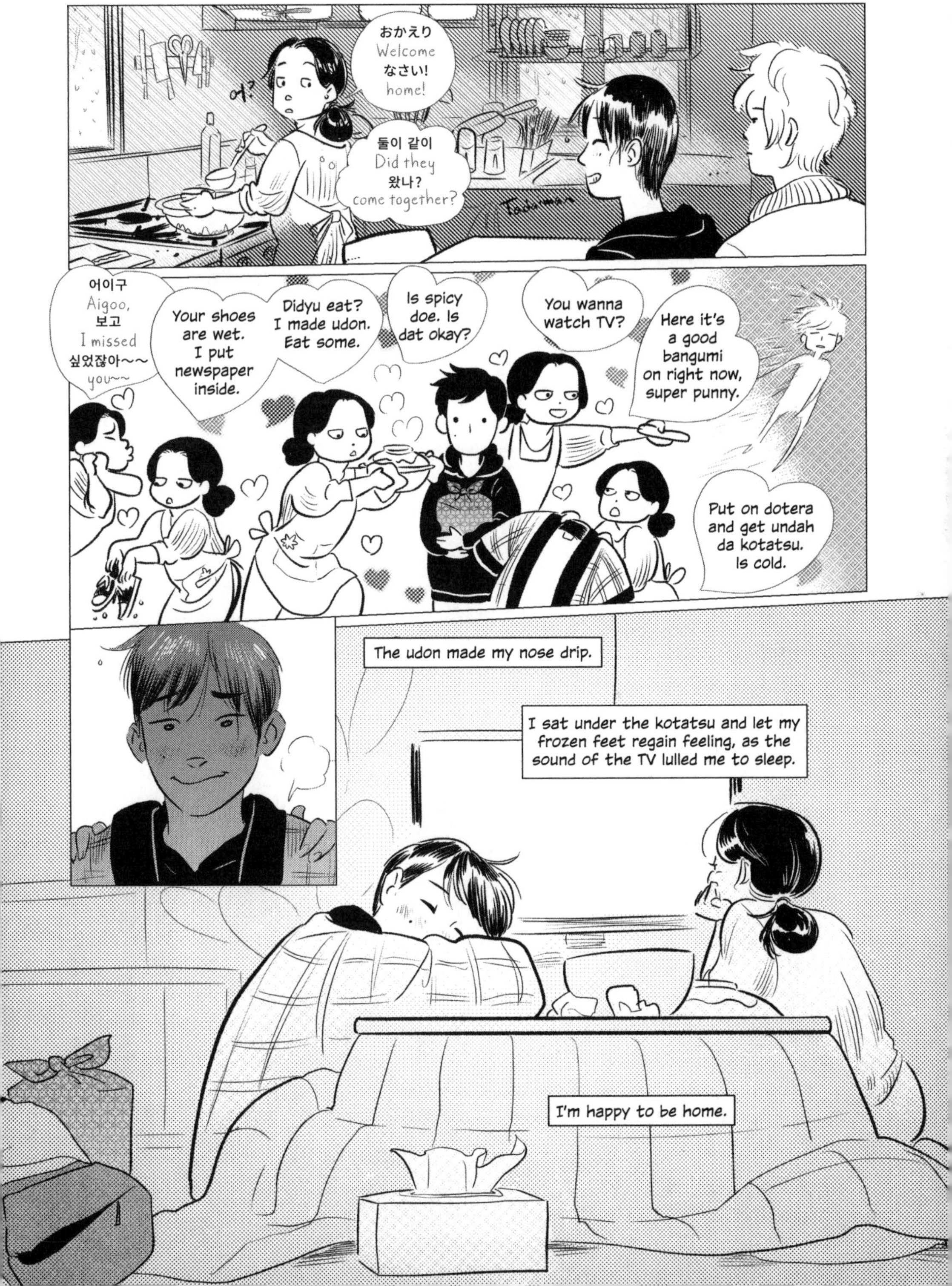
어?
おかえり Welcome なさい! home!
둘이 같이 Did they 왔나? come together?
Tadaima
어이구 Aigoo, 보고 I missed 싶었잖아~~ you~~
Your shoes are wet. I put newspaper inside.
Didyu eat? I made udon. Eat some.
Is spicy doe. Is dat okay?
You wanna watch TV?
Here it's a good bangumi on right now, super punny.
Put on dotera and get undah da kotatsu. Is cold.
The udon made my nose drip.
I sat under the kotatsu and let my frozen feet regain feeling, as the sound of the TV lulled me to sleep.
I'm happy to be home.

Chapter 10

Tetsuya Tachibana

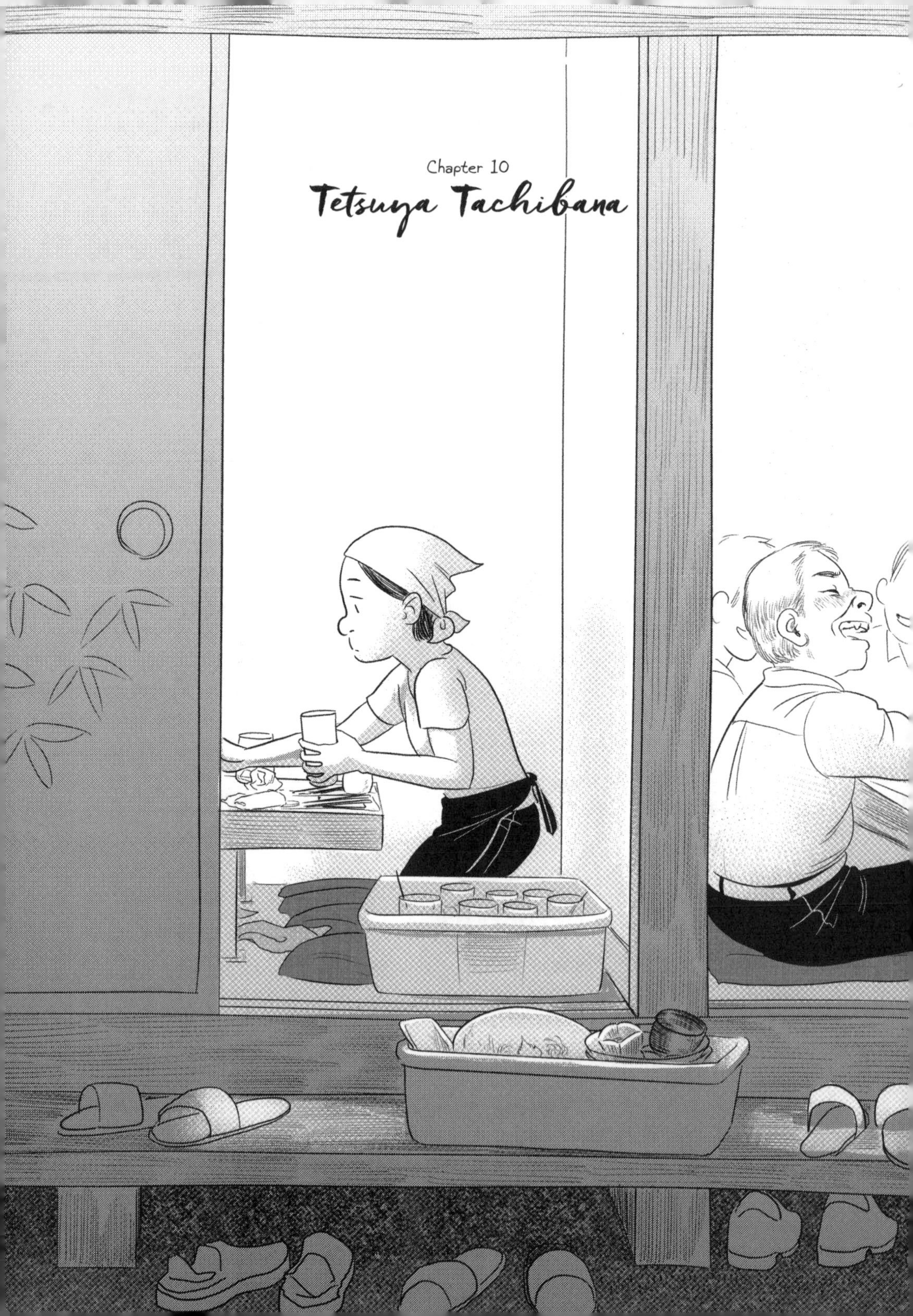

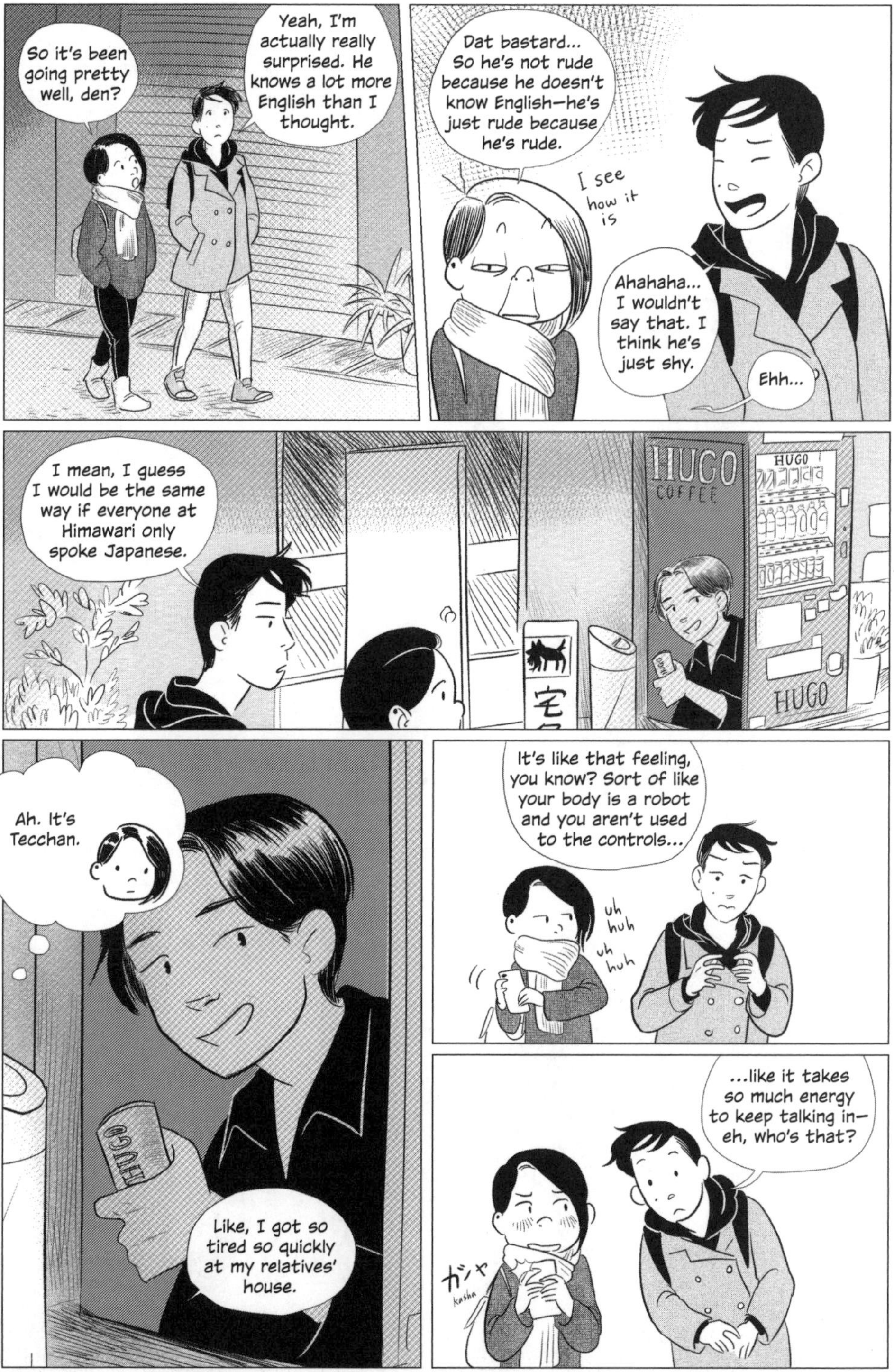
So it's been going pretty well, den?
Yeah, I'm actually really surprised. He knows a lot more English than I thought.
Dat bastard... So he's not rude because he doesn't know English—he's just rude because he's rude.
I see how it is
Ahahaha... I wouldn't say that. I think he's just shy.
Ehh...
I mean, I guess I would be the same way if everyone at Himawari only spoke Japanese.
HUGO
COFFEE
HUGO
HUGO
宅
Ah. It's Tecchan.
Like, I got so tired so quickly at my relatives' house.
It's like that feeling, you know? Sort of like your body is a robot and you aren't used to the controls...
uh huh
uh huh
...like it takes so much energy to keep talking in—eh, who's that?
ガシャ
kasha

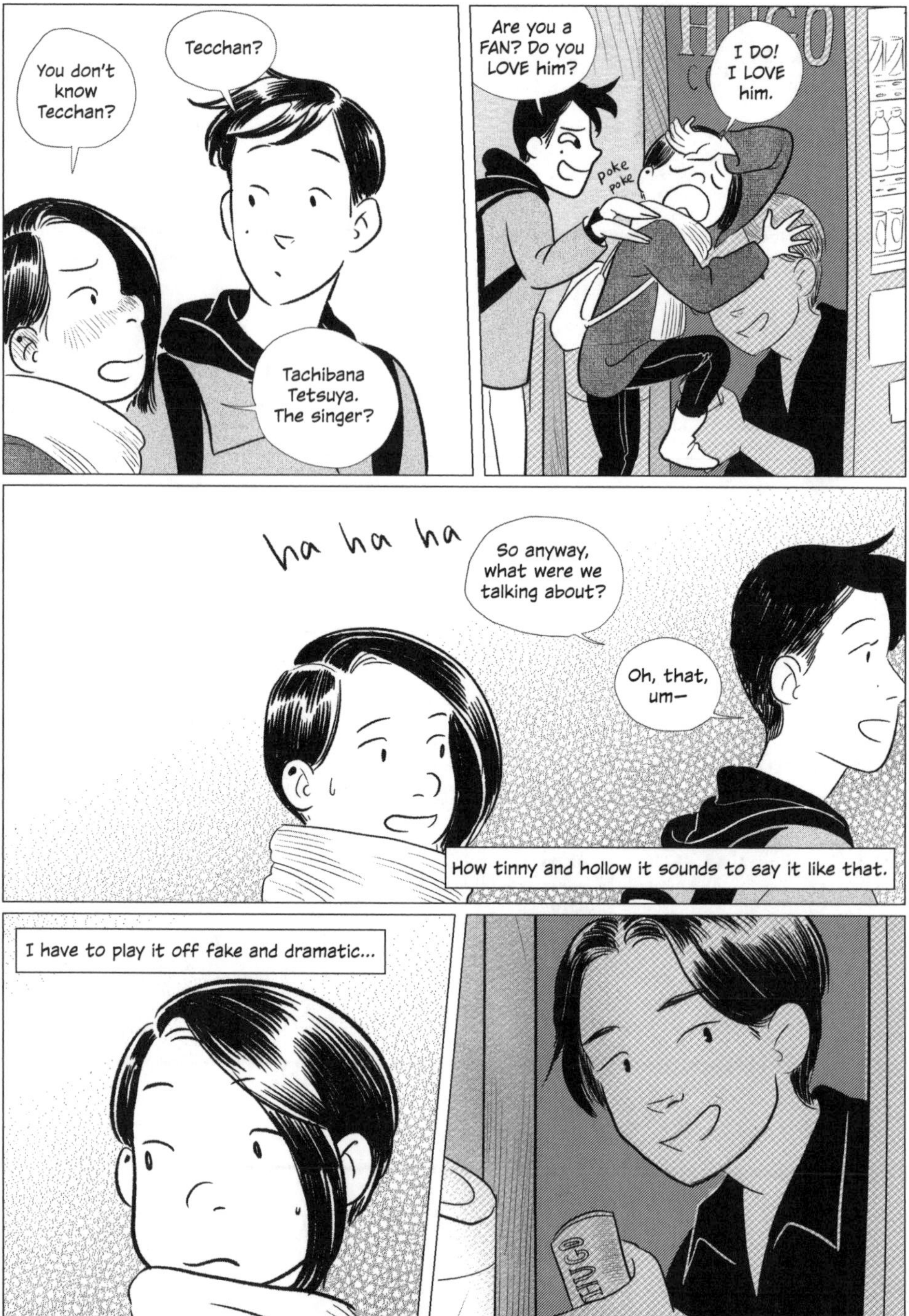
Tecchan?
You don't know Tecchan?
Tachibana Tetsuya. The singer?
Are you a FAN? Do you LOVE him?
I DO! I LOVE him.
poke poke
ha ha ha
So anyway, what were we talking about?
Oh, that, um—
How tinny and hollow it sounds to say it like that.
I have to play it off fake and dramatic...
...because otherwise I feel so transparent I can't stand it.

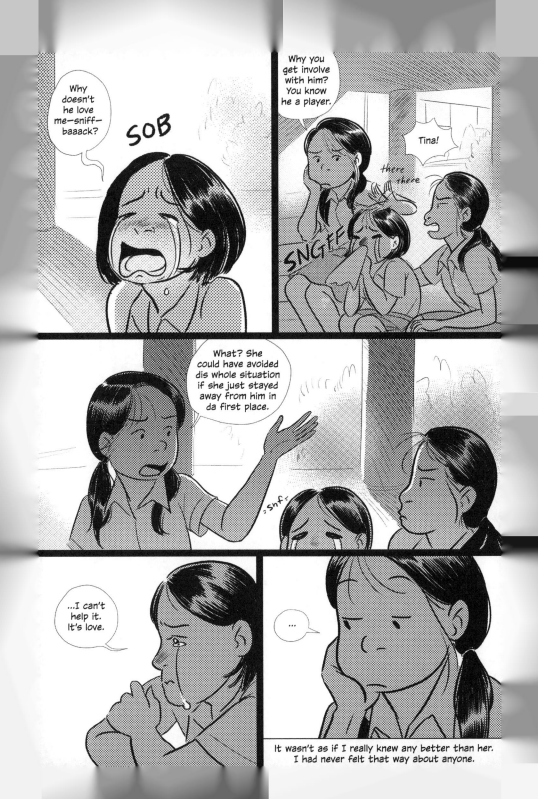

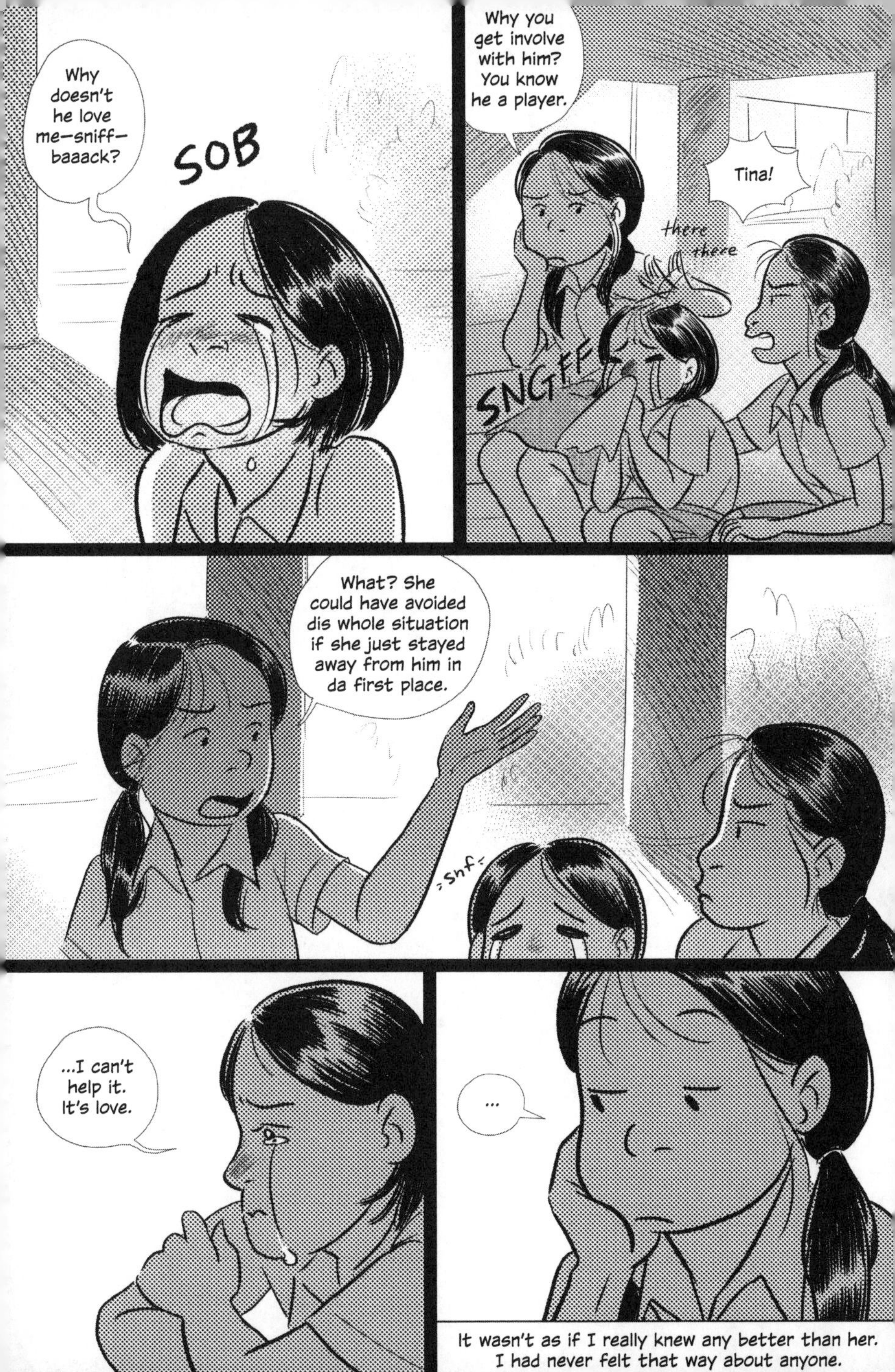
Why doesn't he love me—sniff—baaack?
SOB
Why you get involve with him? You know he a player.
Tina!
there there
SNGFF
What? She could have avoided dis whole situation if she just stayed away from him in da first place.
Shf
...I can't help it. It's love.
...
It wasn't as if I really knew any better than her.
I had never felt that way about anyone.

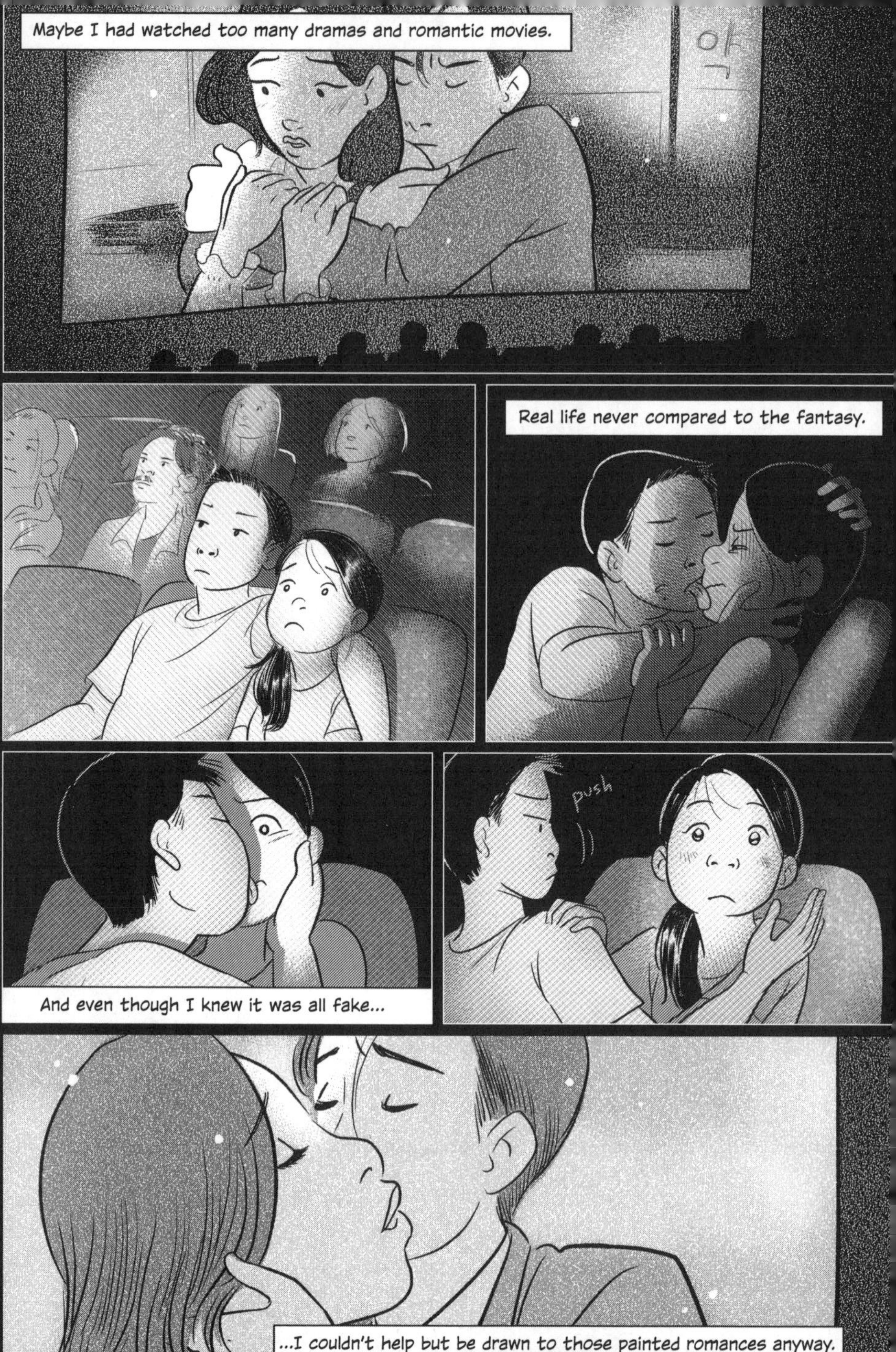
Maybe I had watched too many dramas and romantic movies.
Real life never compared to the fantasy.
And even though I knew it was all fake...
push
...I couldn't help but be drawn to those painted romances anyway.

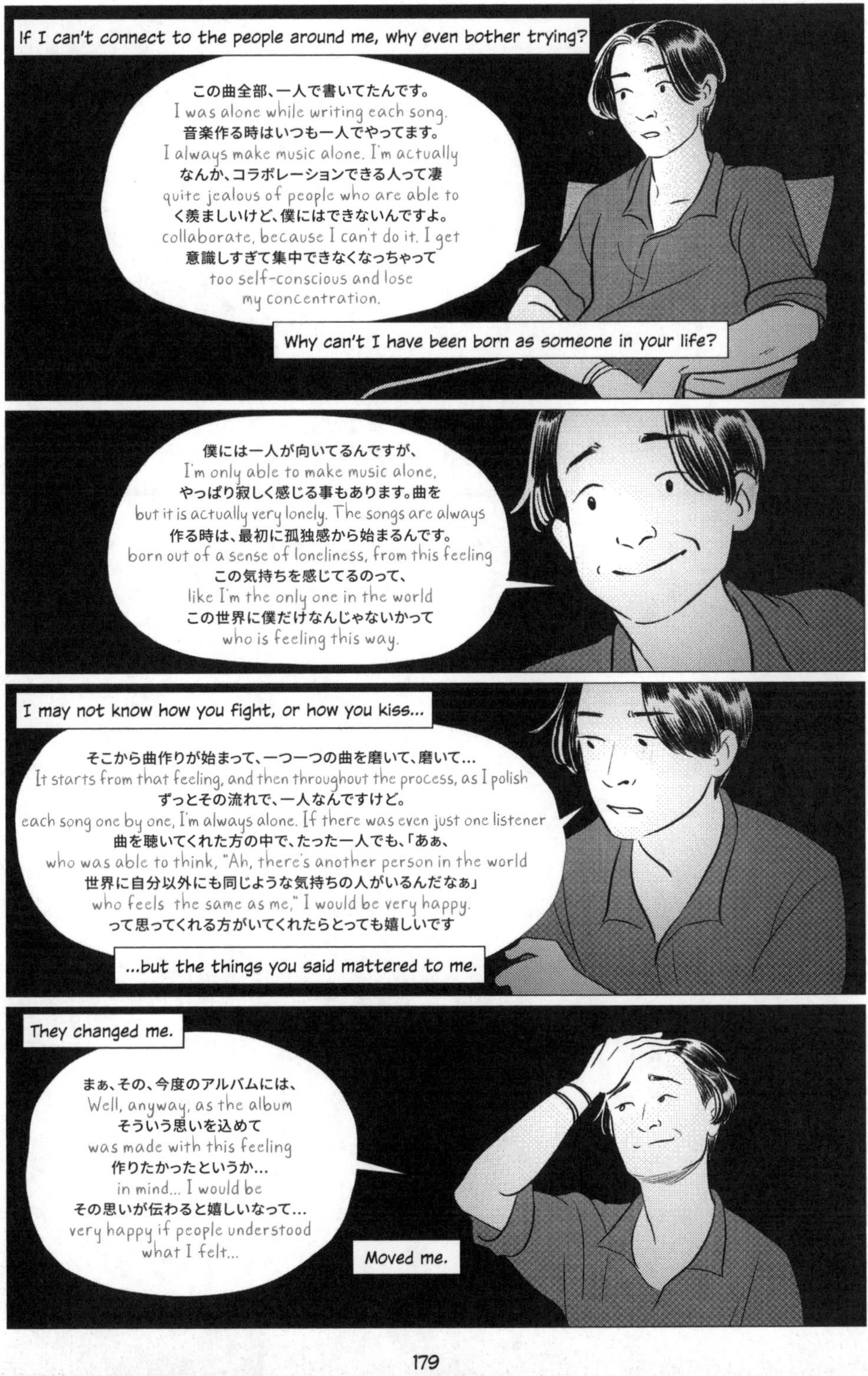
If I can't connect to the people around me, why even bother trying?
この曲全部、一人で書いてたんです。 I was alone while writing each song. 音楽作る時はいつも一人でやってます。 I always make music alone. I'm actually なんか、コラボレーションできる人って凄 quite jealous of people who are able to く羨ましいけど、僕にはできないんですよ。 collaborate, because I can't do it. I get 意識しすぎて集中できなくなっちゃって too self-conscious and lose my concentration.
Why can't I have been born as someone in your life?
僕には一人が向いてるんですが、 I'm only able to make music alone, やっぱり寂しく感じる事もあります。曲を but it is actually very lonely. The songs are always 作る時は、最初に孤独感から始まるんです。 born out of a sense of loneliness, from this feeling この気持ちを感じてるのって、 like I'm the only one in the world この世界に僕だけなんじゃないかって who is feeling this way.
I may not know how you fight, or how you kiss...
そこから曲作りが始まって、一つ一つの曲を磨いて、磨いて… It starts from that feeling, and then throughout the process, as I polish ずっとその流れで、一人なんですけど。 each song one by one, I'm always alone. If there was even just one listener 曲を聴いてくれた方の中で、たった一人でも、「あぁ、 who was able to think, "Ah, there's another person in the world 世界に自分以外にも同じような気持ちの人がいるんだなぁ」 who feels the same as me," I would be very happy. って思ってくれる方がいてくれたらとっても嬉しいです
...but the things you said mattered to me.
They changed me.
まぁ、その、今度のアルバムには、 Well, anyway, as the album そういう思いを込めて was made with this feeling 作りたかったというか… in mind... I would be その思いが伝わると嬉しいなって… very happy if people understood what I felt...
Moved me.

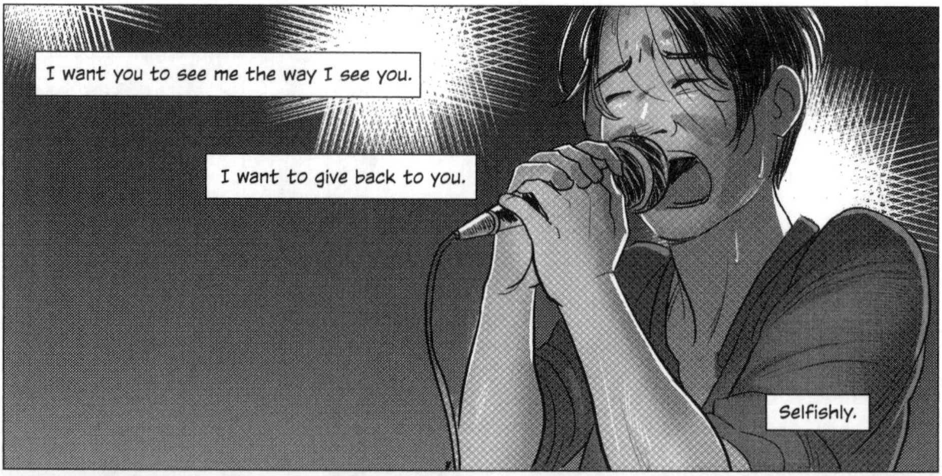
I want you to see me the way I see you.
I want to give back to you.
Selfishly.

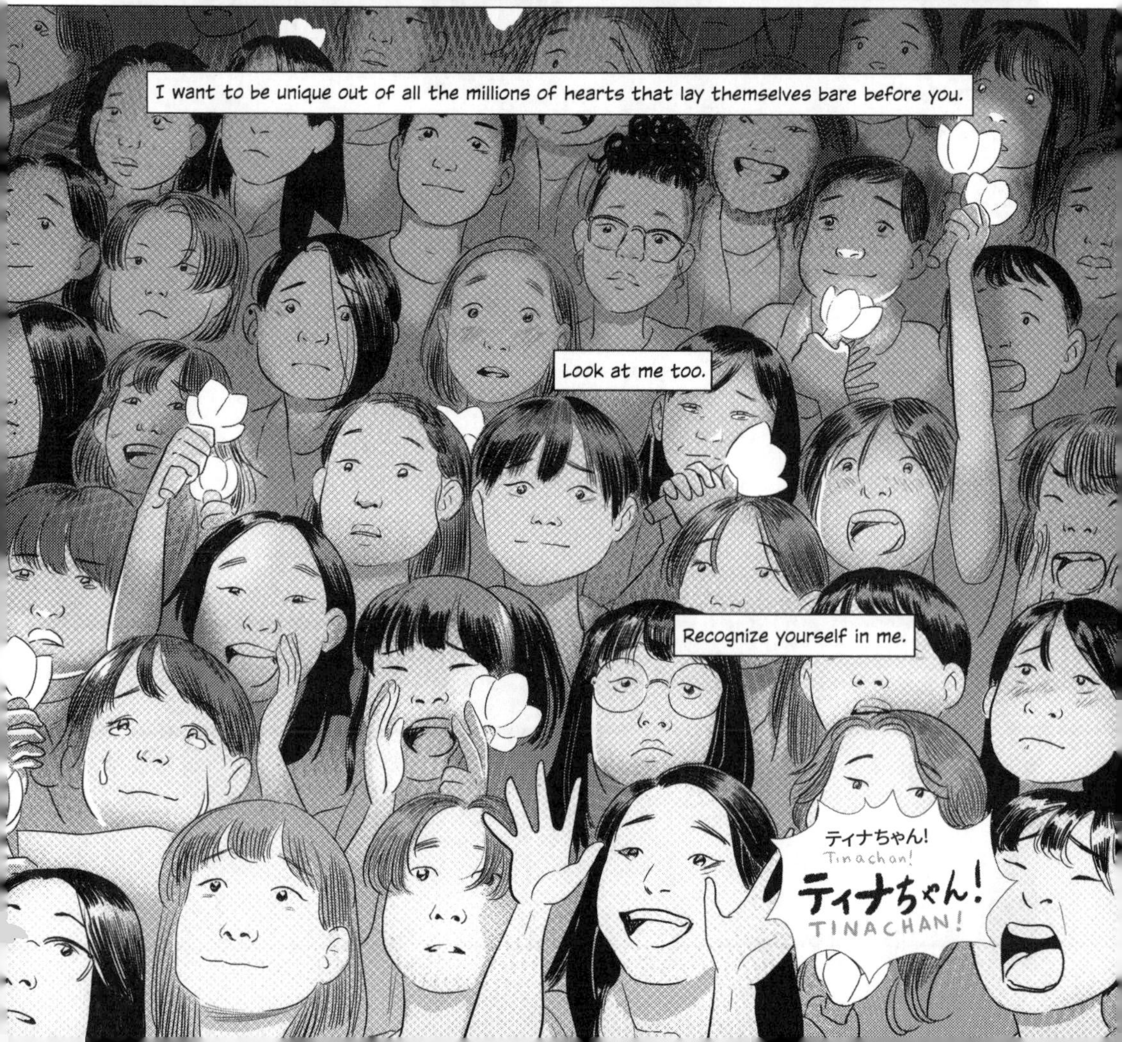
I want to be unique out of all the millions of hearts that lay themselves bare before you.
Look at me too.
Recognize yourself in me.
ティナちゃん!
Tinachan!
ティナちゃん!
TINACHAN!

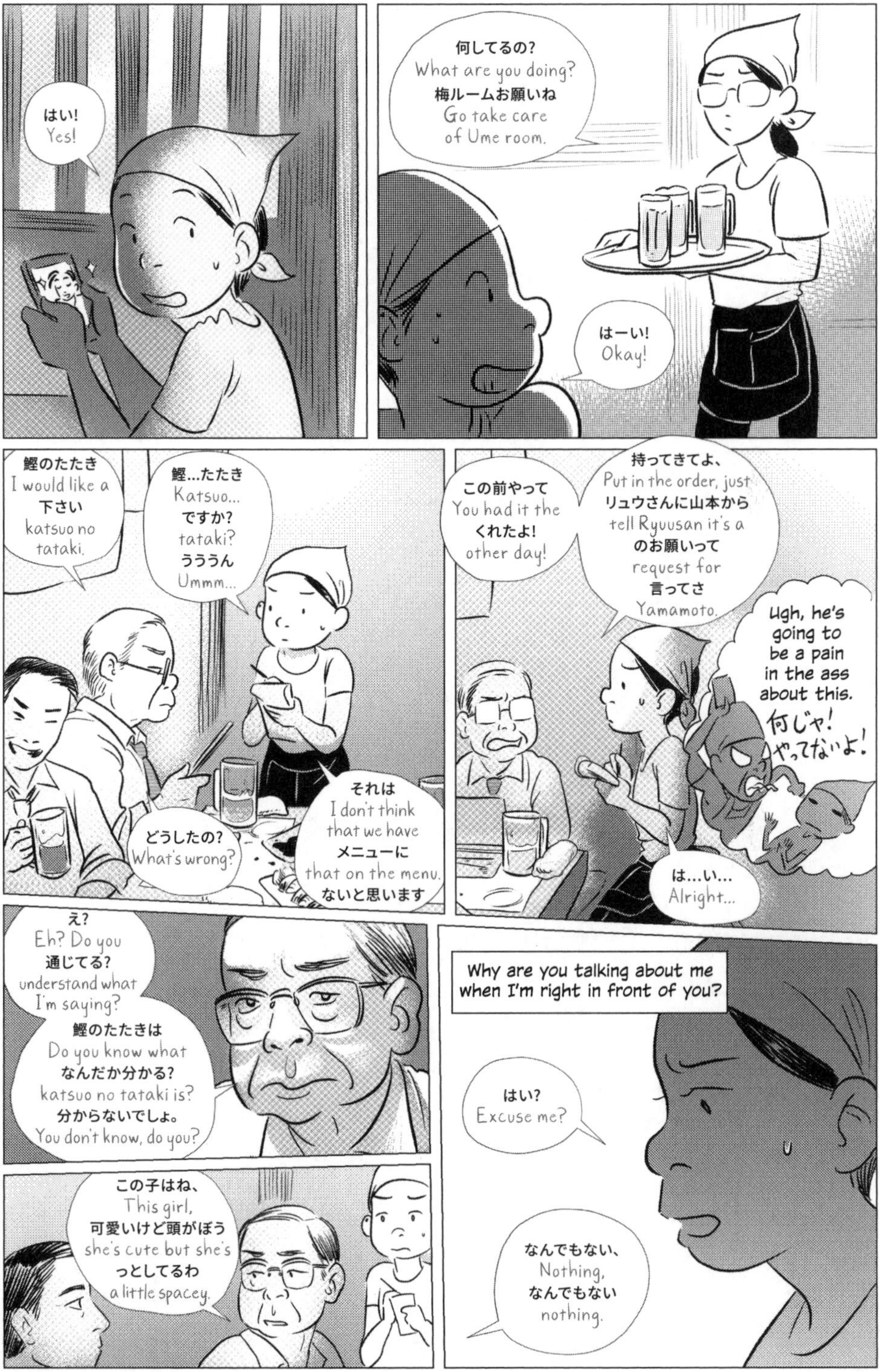
はい!
Yes!
何してるの?
What are you doing?
梅ルームお願いね
Go take care
of Ume room.
はーい!
Okay!
鰹のたたき
I would like a
下さい
katsuo no
tataki.
鰹…たたき
Katsuo…
ですか?
tataki?
うううん
Ummm…
どうしたの?
What's wrong?
それは
I don't think
that we have
メニューに
that on the menu.
ないと思います
この前やって
You had it the
くれたよ!
other day!
持ってきてよ、
Put in the order, just
リュウさんに山本から
tell Ryuusan it's a
のお願いって
request for
言ってさ
Yamamoto.
Ugh, he's going to be a pain in the ass about this.
何じゃ! やってないよ!
は…い…
Alright…
え?
Eh? Do you
通じてる?
understand what
I'm saying?
鰹のたたきは
Do you know what
なんだか分かる?
katsuo no tataki is?
分からないでしょ。
You don't know, do you?
この子はね、
This girl,
可愛いけど頭がぼう
she's cute but she's
っとしてるわ
a little spacey.
Why are you talking about me when I'm right in front of you?
はい?
Excuse me?
なんでもない、
Nothing,
なんでもない
nothing.

What if I did that to you, huh?

Uncle! Milo "O" beng dapao! Then two LoHanGuo mai beng! Also one Teh Tarik beng ah!

Even when I speak in Japanese, it's like it doesn't mean anything.

I get one word wrong and they act like they can talk about me in front of me as if I don't understand.

Ugh, I even feel bad for him in my fantasy. Never mind.

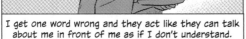

ええ？
Ehh??
鰹のたたき?
Katsuo no tataki??
やってないよ今
It's not on the menu right now.

でも山本さん
But Yamamotosan
からのお願い
told me to tell you it was
だって...
a special request from him...

無理無理
Nope. Can't do it.

Ugh.

確かに
It is true
鰹のたたきは今
that we don't have
やってないです
katsuo no tataki right now.

申し訳
My deepest
ありません
apologies.

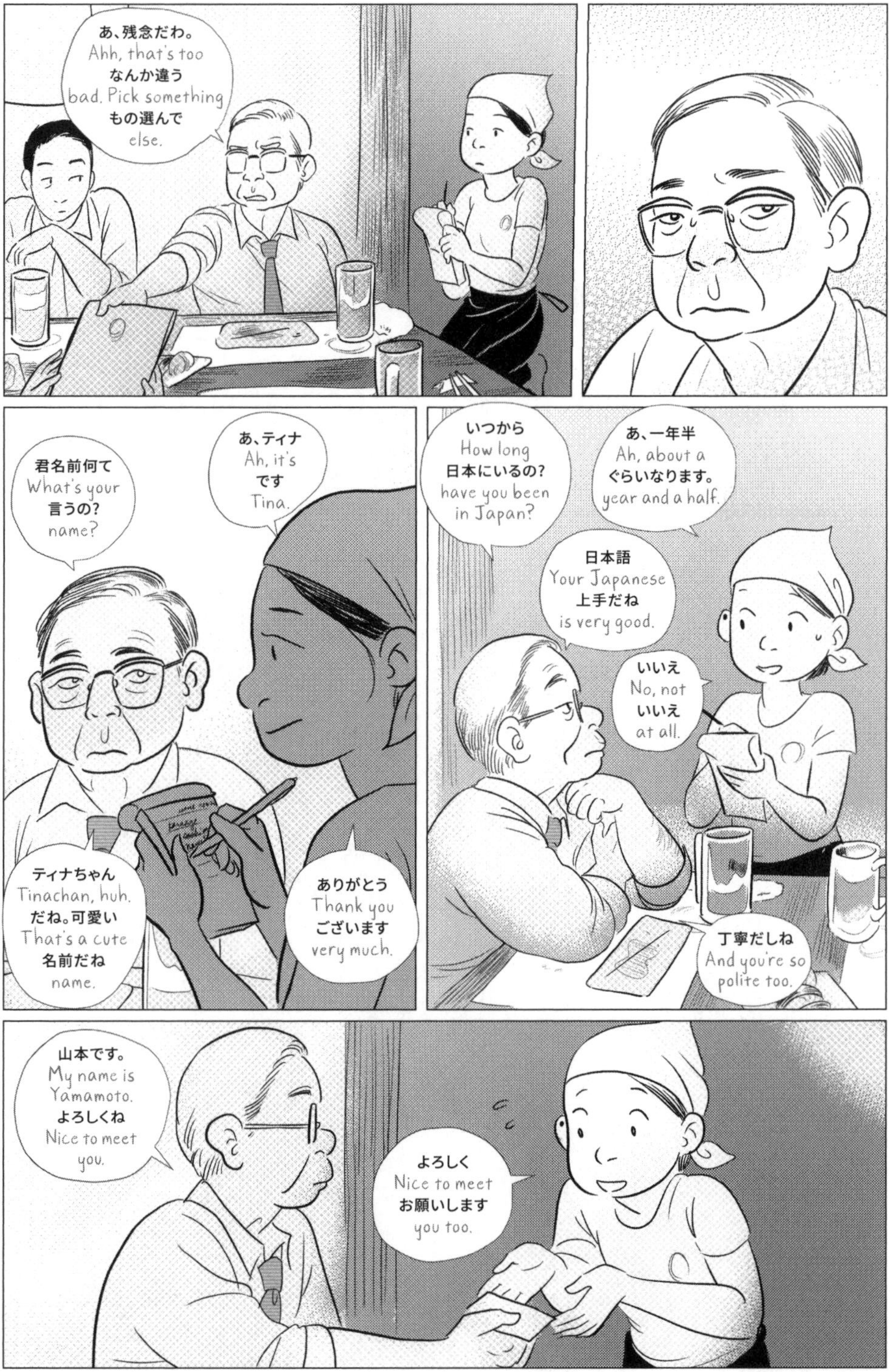

あ、残念だわ。 Ahh, that's too なんか違う bad. Pick something もの選んで else.
君名前何て What's your 言うの? name?
あ、ティナ Ah, it's です Tina.
ティナちゃん Tinachan, huh. だね。可愛い That's a cute 名前だね name.
ありがとう Thank you ございます very much.
いつから How long 日本にいるの? have you been in Japan?
あ、一年半 Ah, about a ぐらいなります。 year and a half.
日本語 Your Japanese 上手だね is very good.
いいえ No, not いいえ at all.
丁寧だしね And you're so polite too.
山本です。 My name is Yamamoto. よろしくね Nice to meet you.
よろしく Nice to meet お願いします you too.

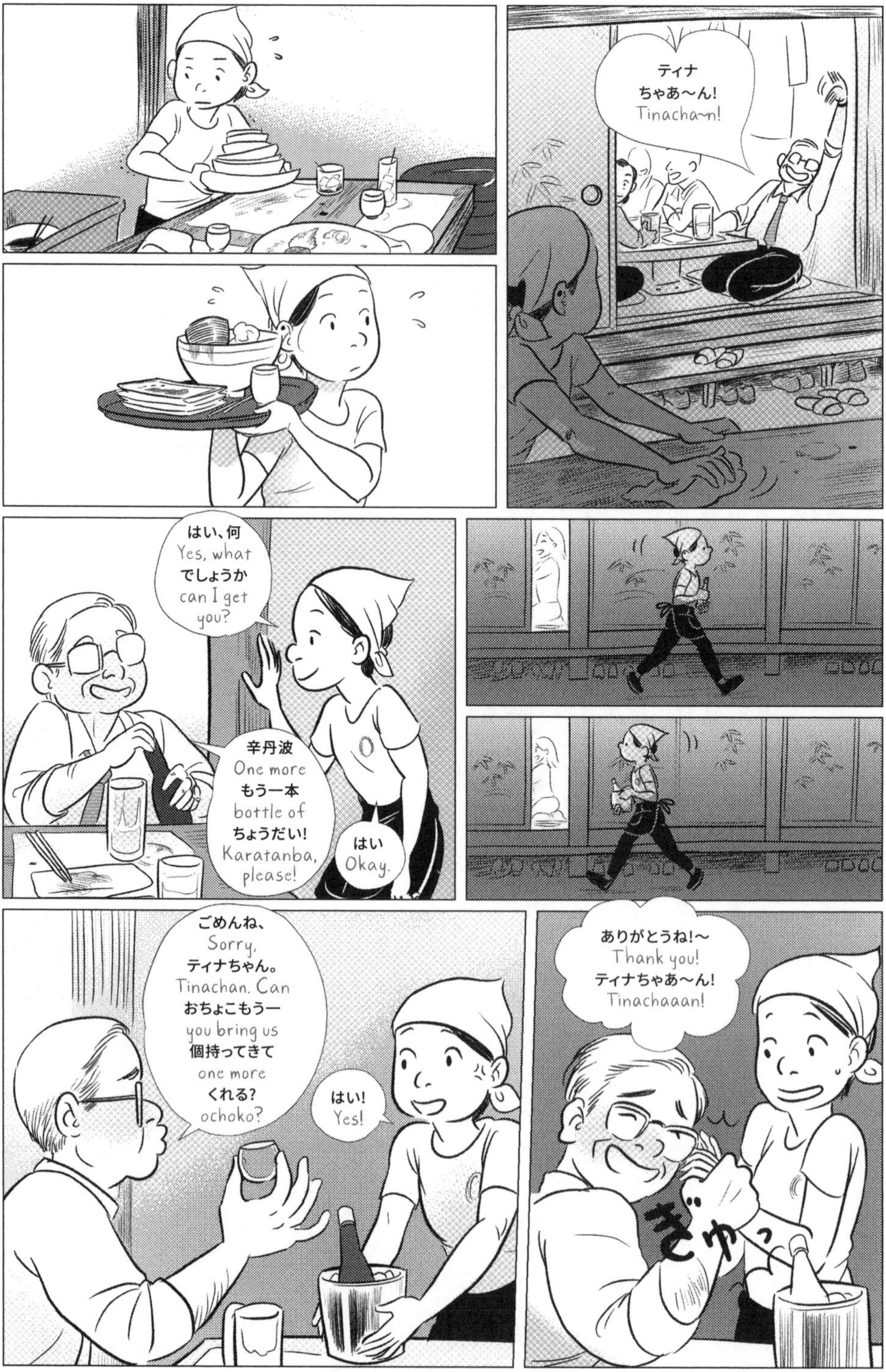
ティナ
ちゃあ~ん!
Tinacha~n!
はい、何
Yes, what
でしょうか
can I get
you?
辛丹波
One more
もう一本
bottle of
ちょうだい!
Karatanba,
please!
はい
Okay.
ごめんね、
Sorry,
ティナちゃん。
Tinachan. Can
おちょこもう一
you bring us
個持ってきて
one more
くれる?
ochoko?
はい!
Yes!
ありがとうね!~
Thank you!
ティナちゃあ~ん!
Tinachaaan!
ぎゅっ

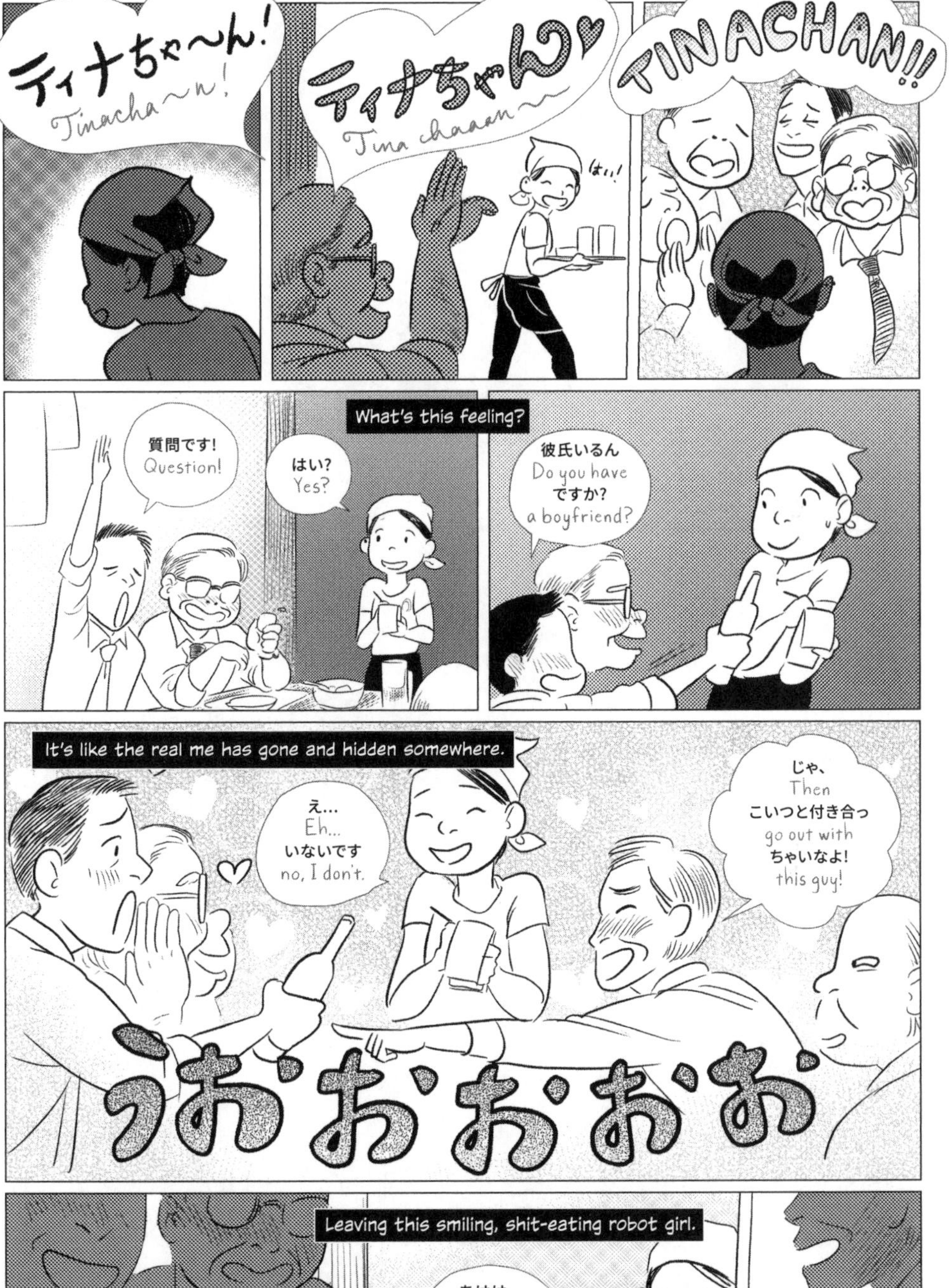
ティナちゃ~ん!
Tinacha~n!
ティナちゃん♡
Tina chaaan~~
はい!
TINACHAN!!
What's this feeling?
質問です!
Question!
はい?
Yes?
彼氏いるんですか?
Do you have a boyfriend?
It's like the real me has gone and hidden somewhere.
え… いないです
Eh... no, I don't.
じゃ、こいつと付き合っちゃいなよ!
Then go out with this guy!
うおおおおお
Leaving this smiling, shit-eating robot girl.
あはは、失礼致します
Ahaha, please excuse me.

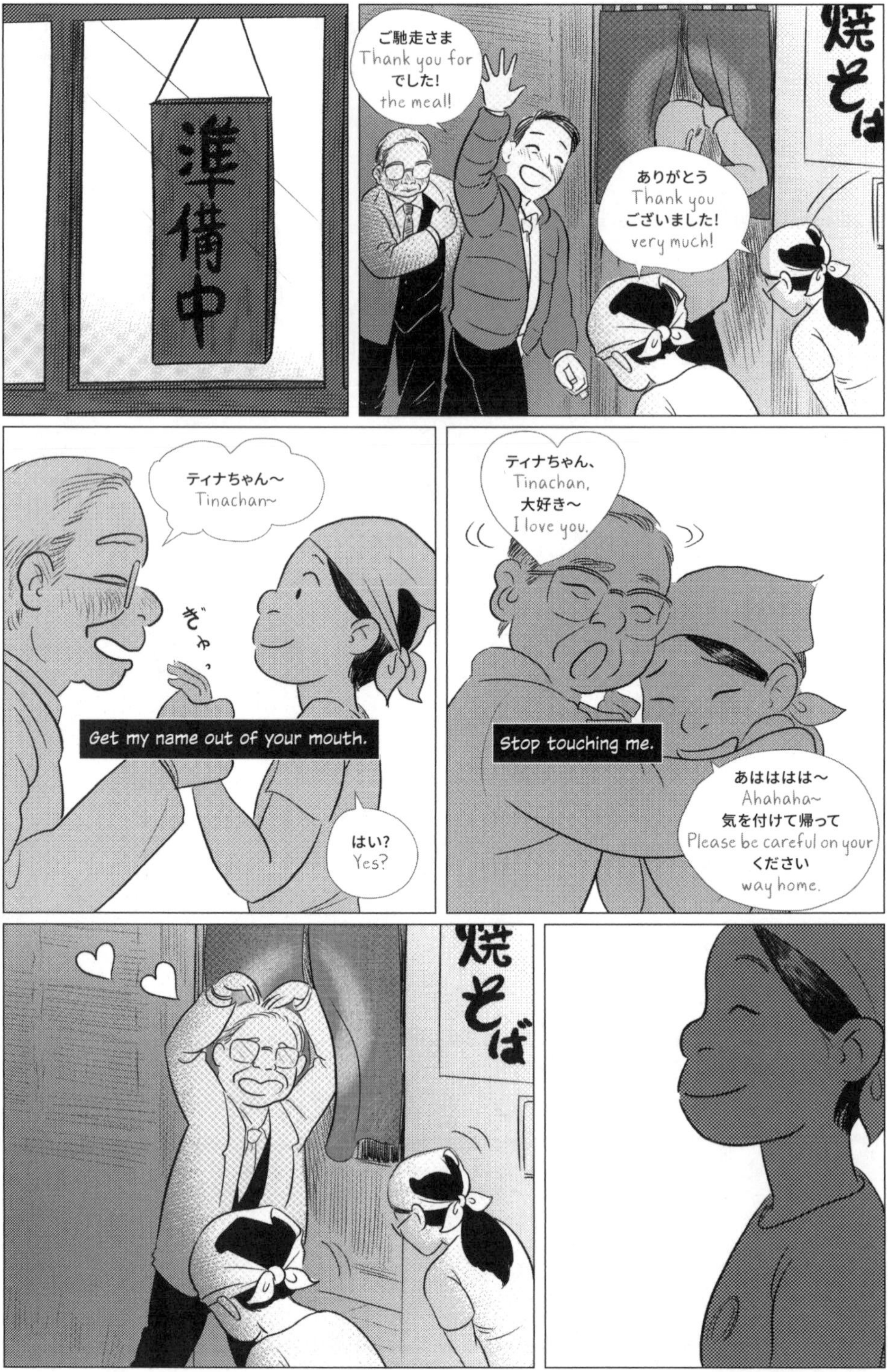
準備中
ご馳走さま Thank you for でした! the meal!
焼そば
ありがとう Thank you ございました! very much!
ティナちゃん〜 Tinachan~
ぎゅっ
Get my name out of your mouth.
はい? Yes?
ティナちゃん、 Tinachan, 大好き〜 I love you.
Stop touching me.
あはははは〜 Ahahaha~ 気を付けて帰って Please be careful on your ください way home.
焼そば

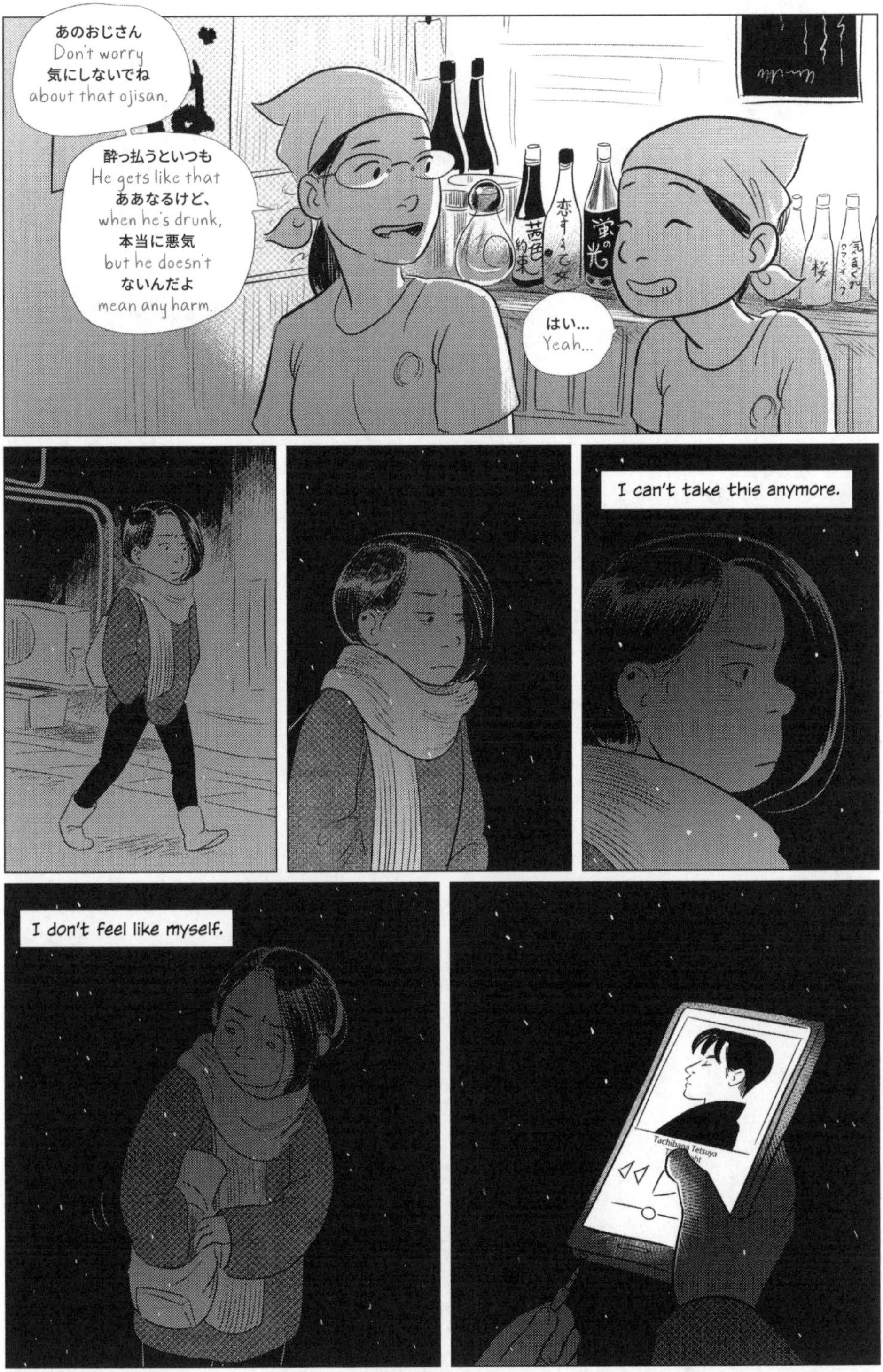
あのおじさん
Don't worry
気にしないでね
about that ojisan.
酔っ払うといつも
He gets like that
ああなるけど、
when he's drunk,
本当に悪気
but he doesn't
ないんだよ
mean any harm.
はい…
Yeah…
I can't take this anymore.
I don't feel like myself.
Tachibana Tetsuya

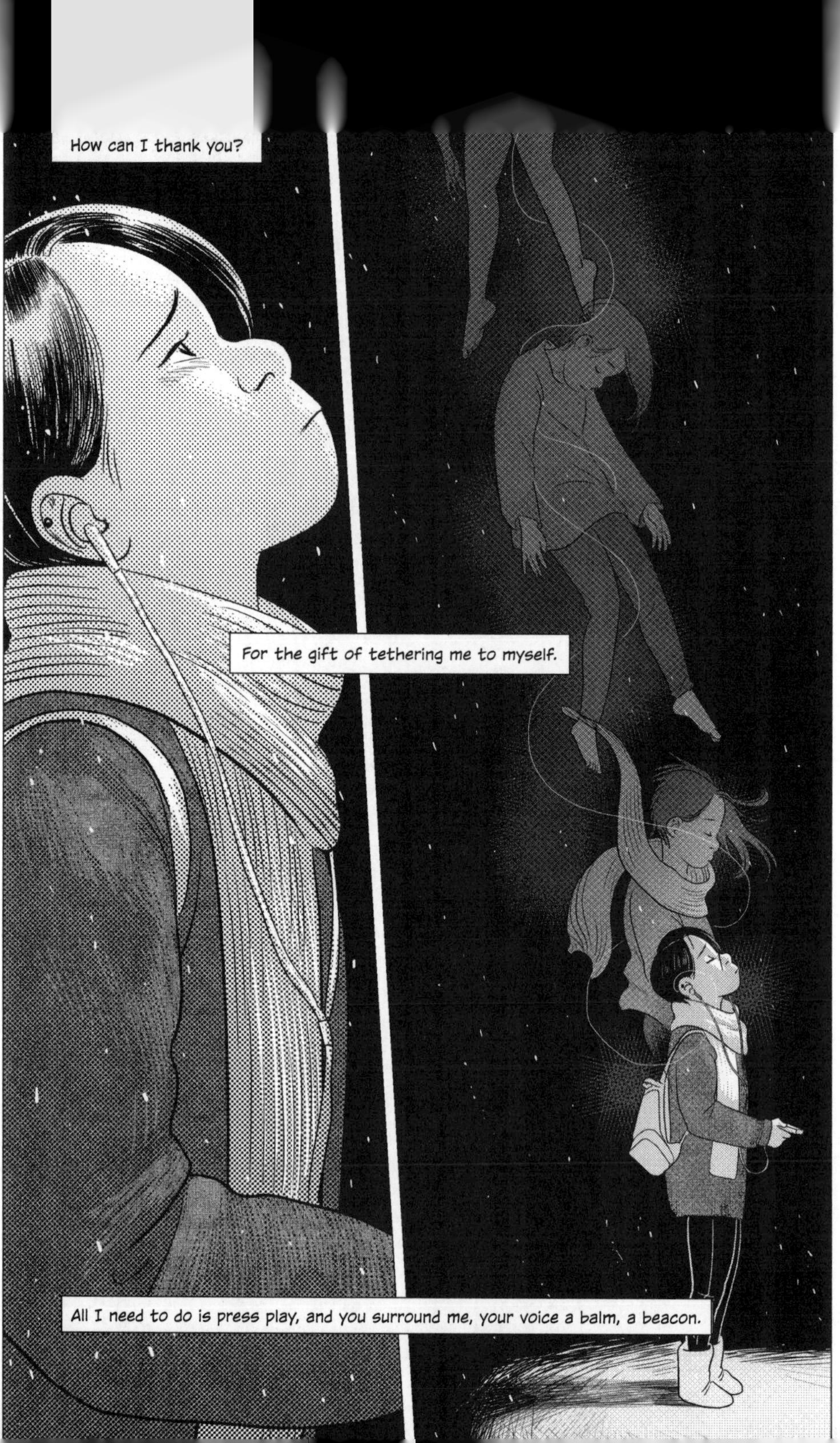
How can I thank you?
For the gift of tethering me to myself.
All I need to do is press play, and you surround me, your voice a balm, a beacon.

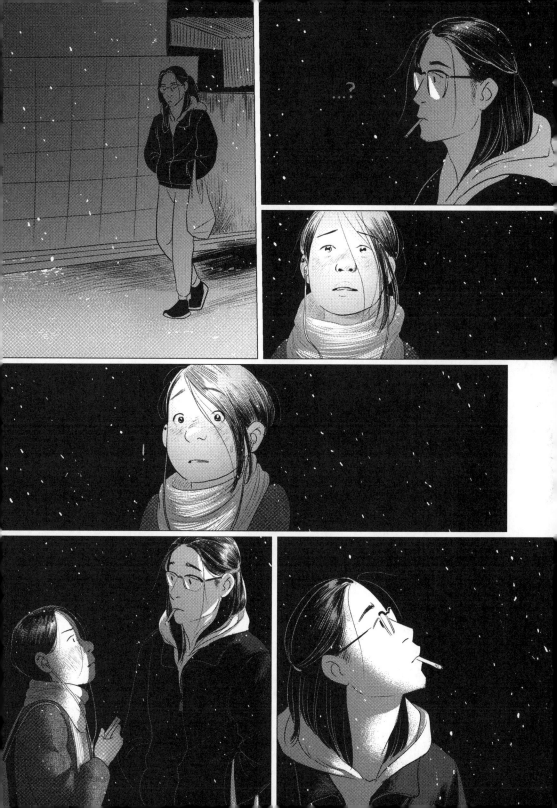

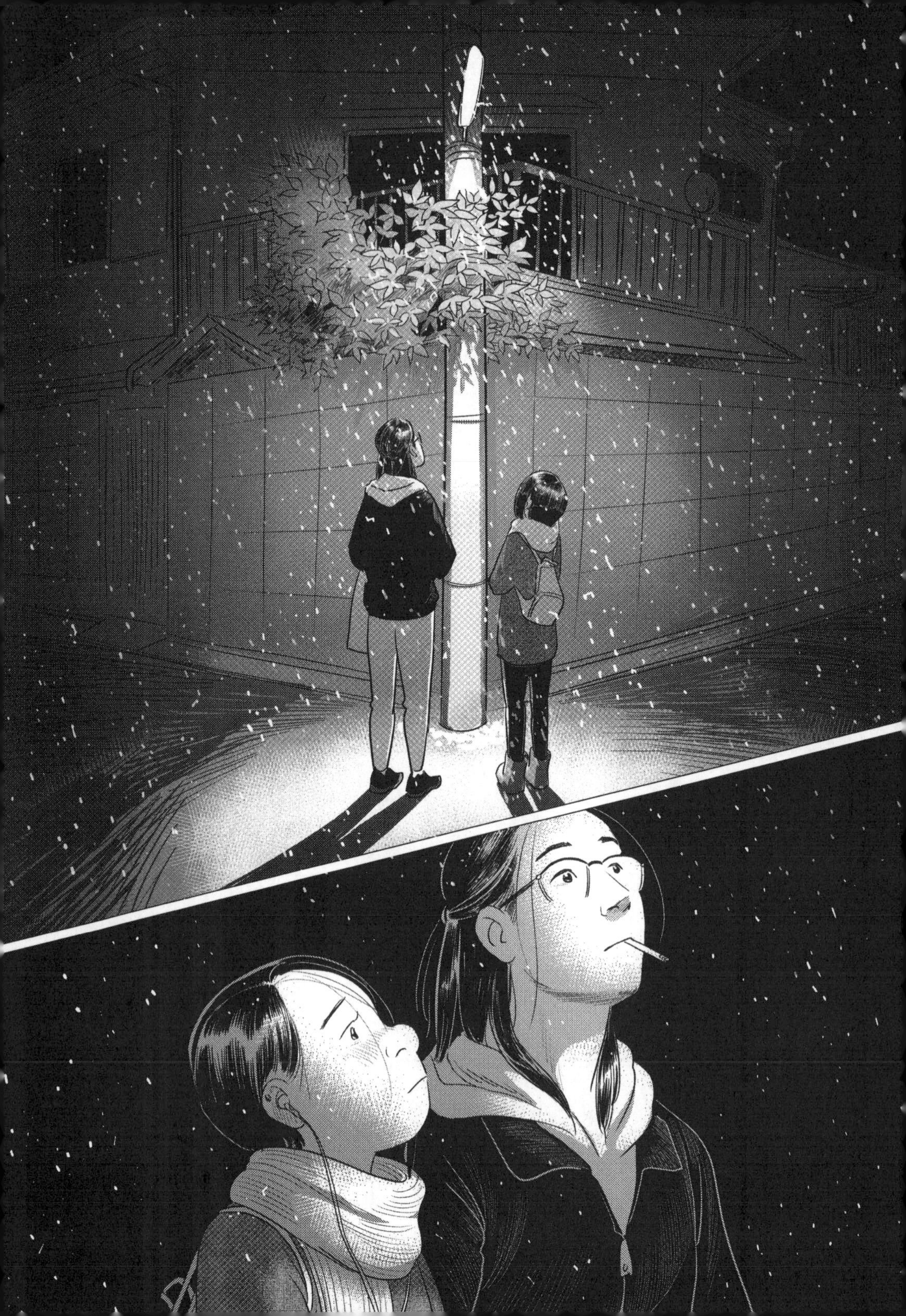

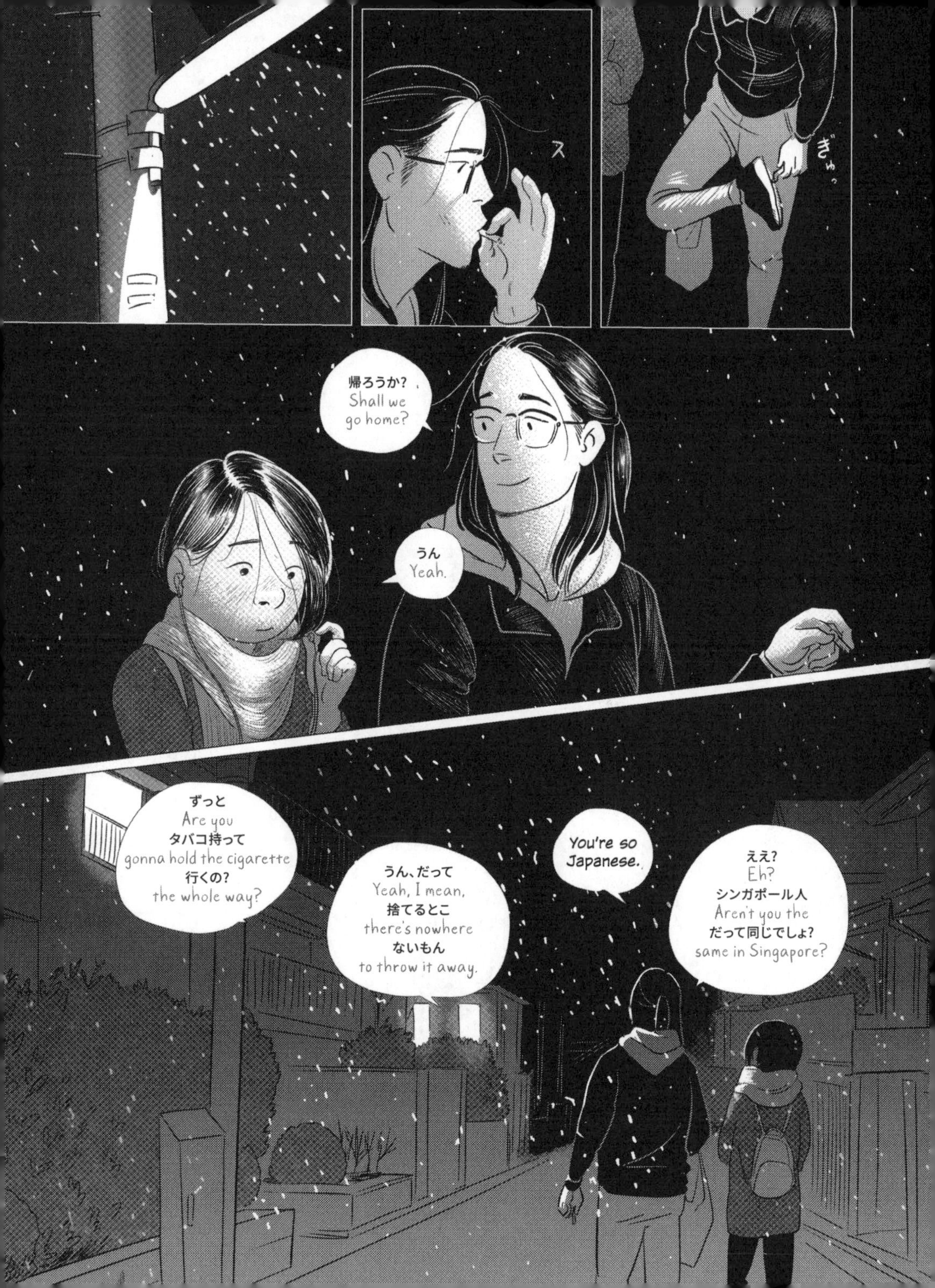

ス
ぎゅっ
帰ろうか? Shall we go home?
うん Yeah.
ずっと Are you タバコ持って gonna hold the cigarette 行くの? the whole way?
うん、だって Yeah, I mean, 捨てるとこ there's nowhere ないもん to throw it away.
You're so Japanese.
ええ? Eh? シンガポール人 Aren't you the だって同じでしょ? same in Singapore?

Chapter 11

Onabe

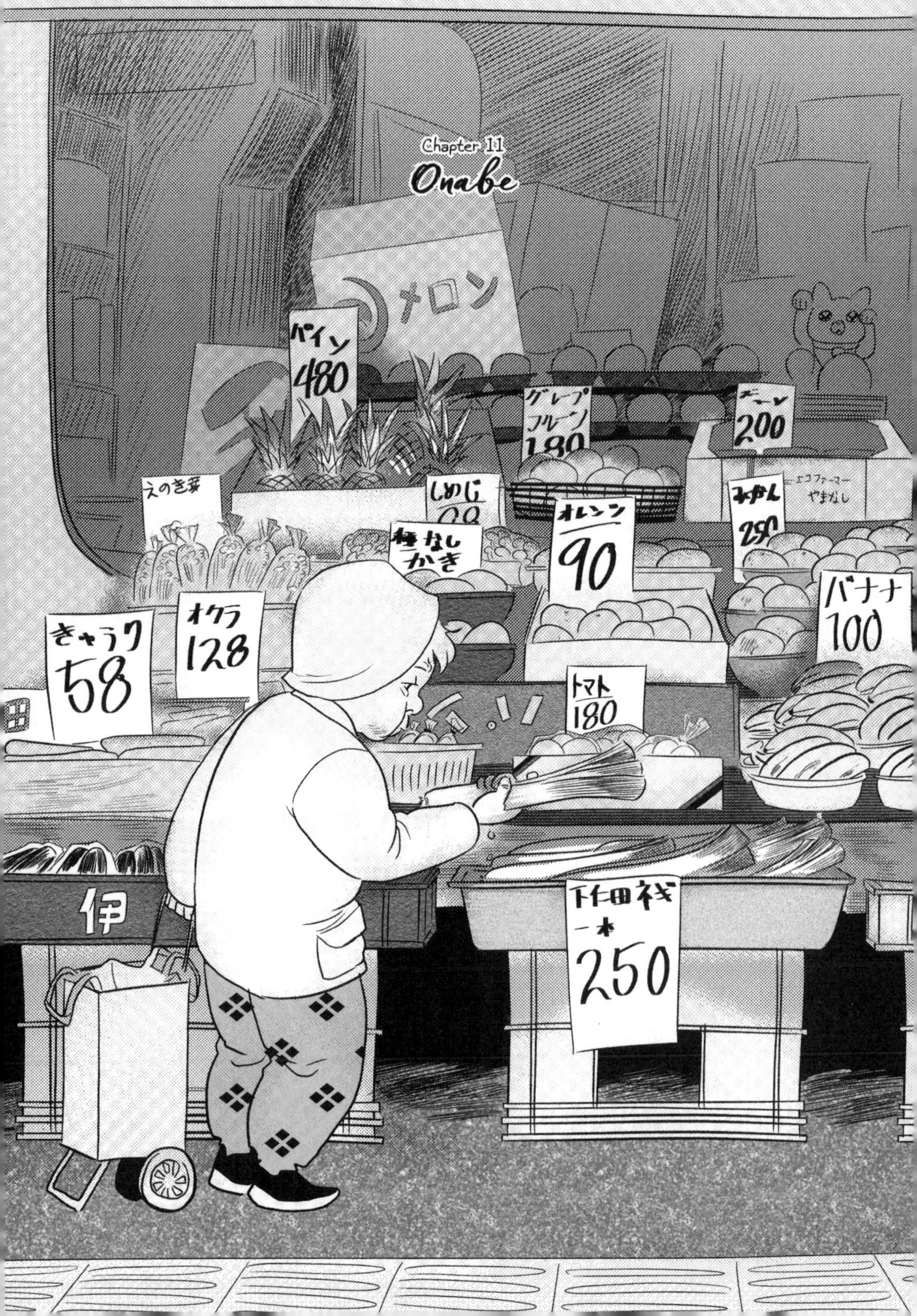
メロン
パイン 480
グレープフルーツ
200
えのき茸
しめじ
エコファーマー やまなし
みかん 250
オレンジ 90
種なしかき
バナナ 100
キャベツ 58
オクラ 128
トマト 180
伊
下仁田ネギ 一本 250

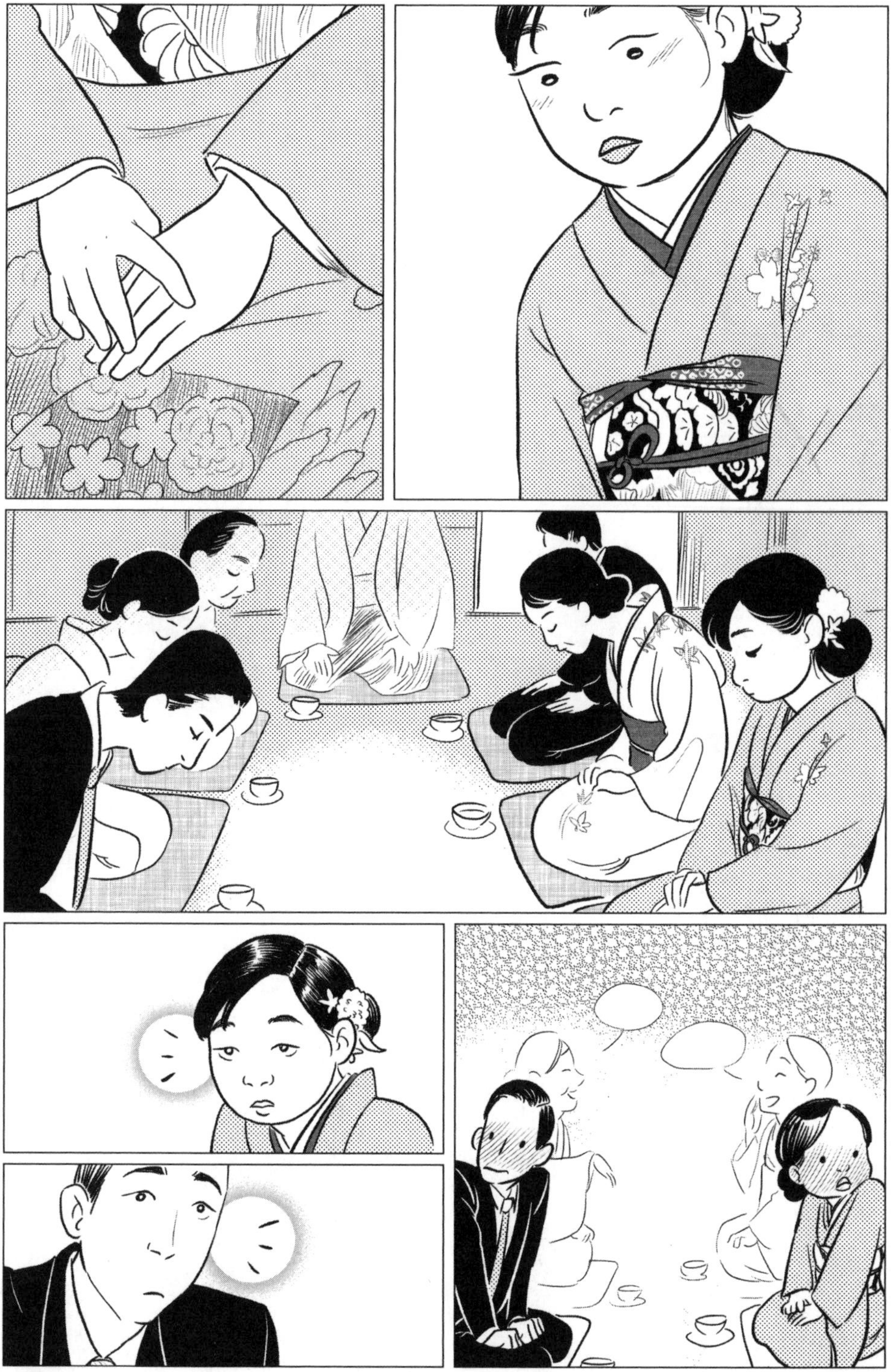

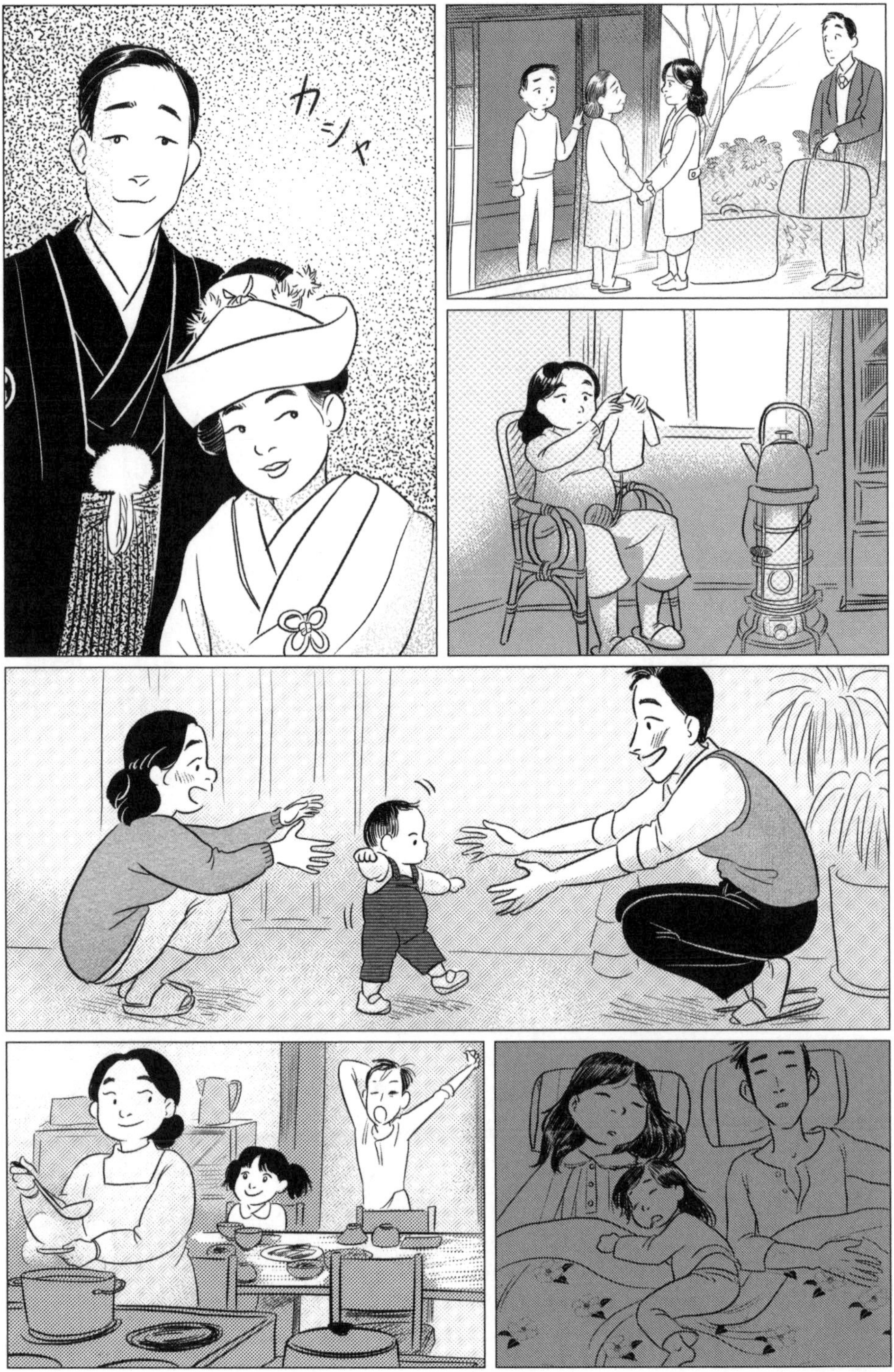
カシャ

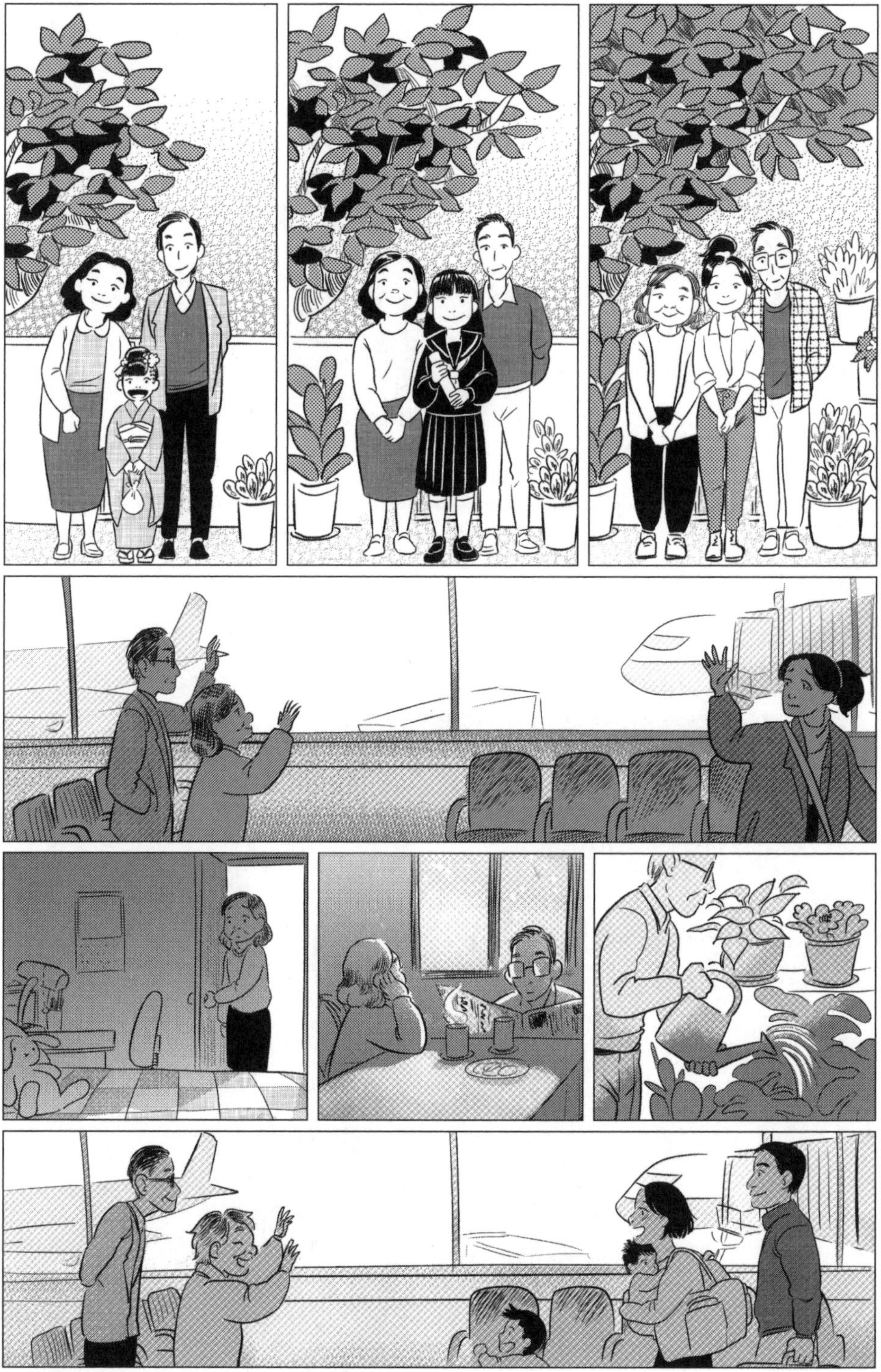

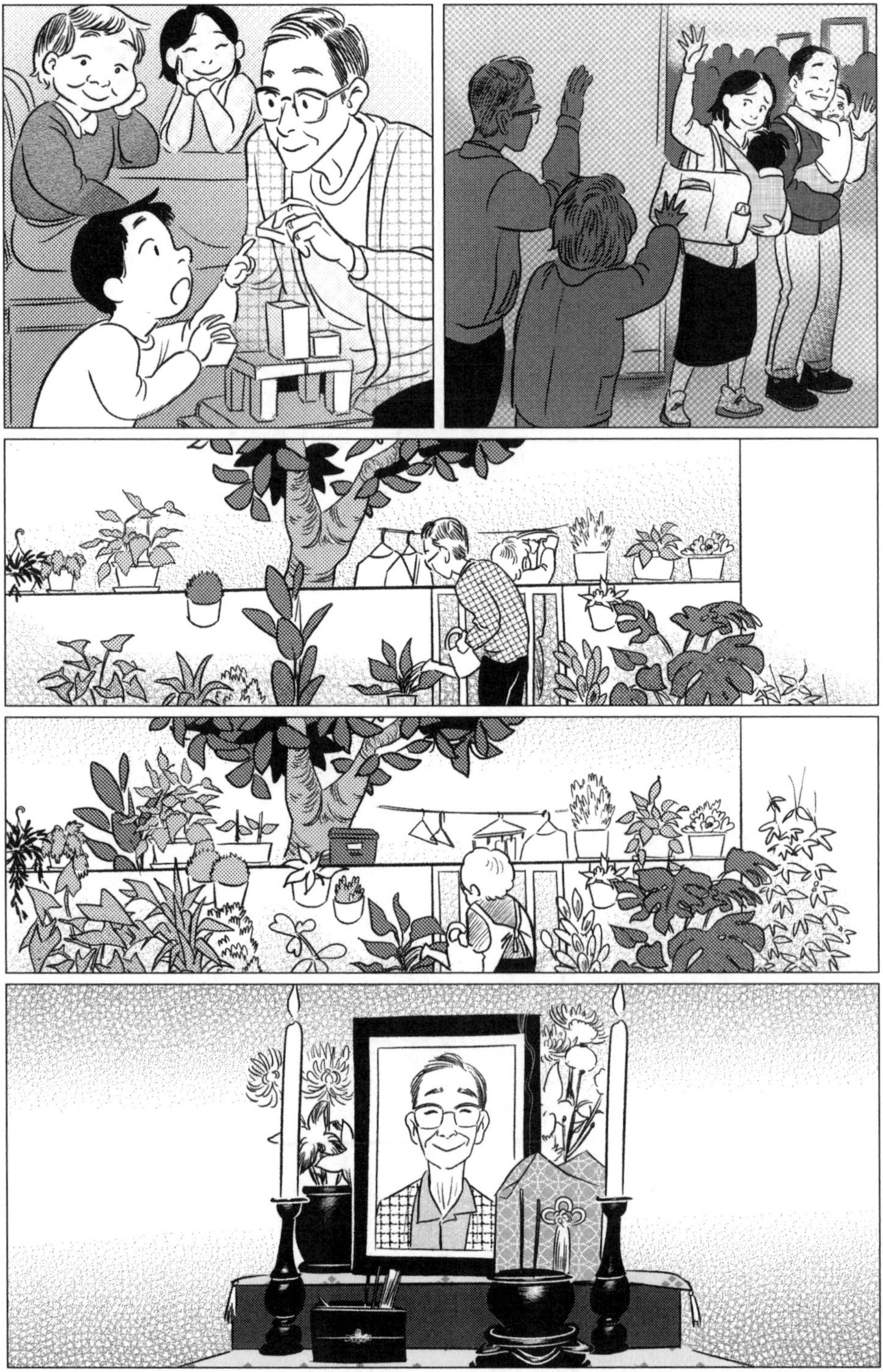

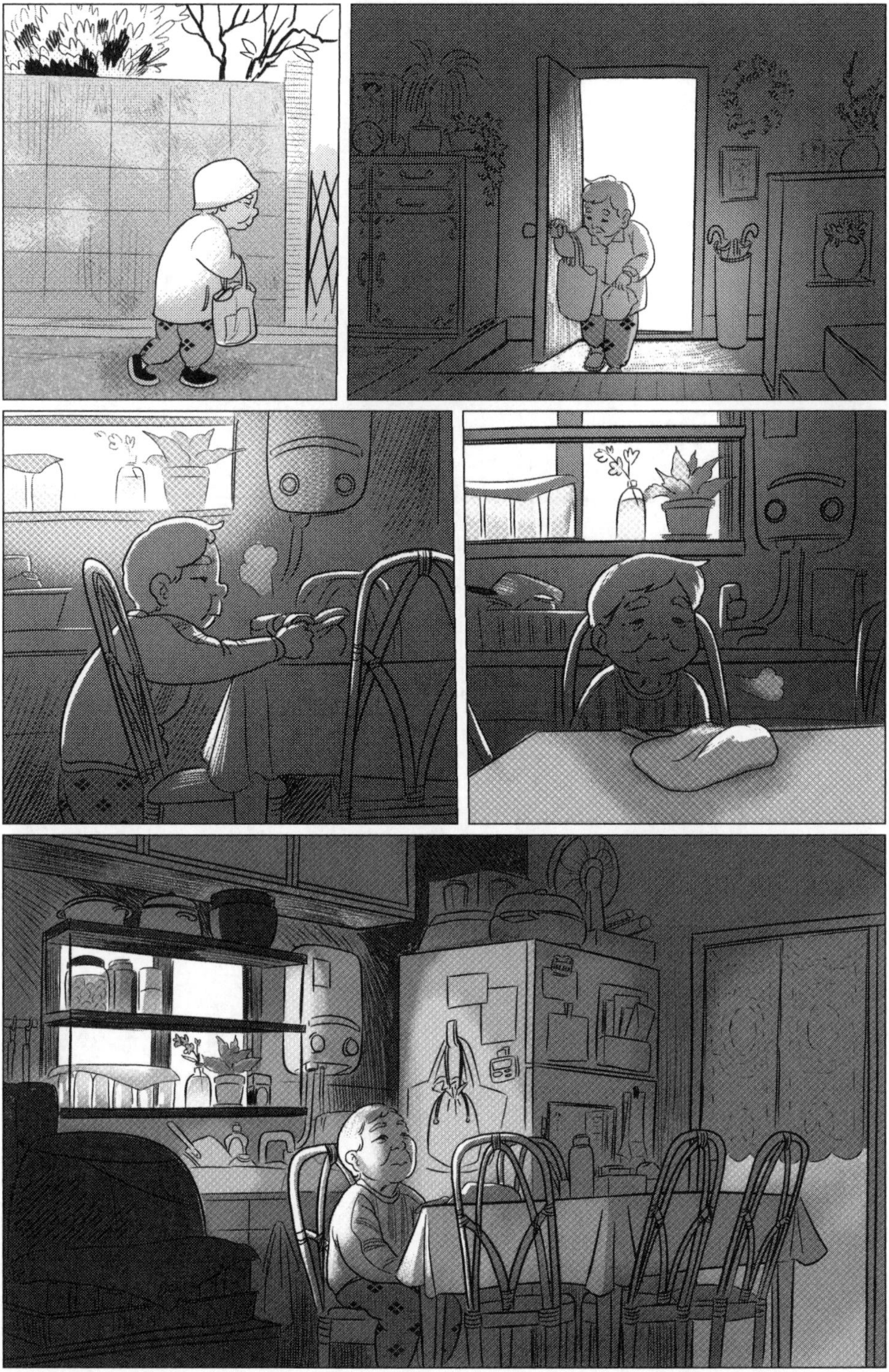

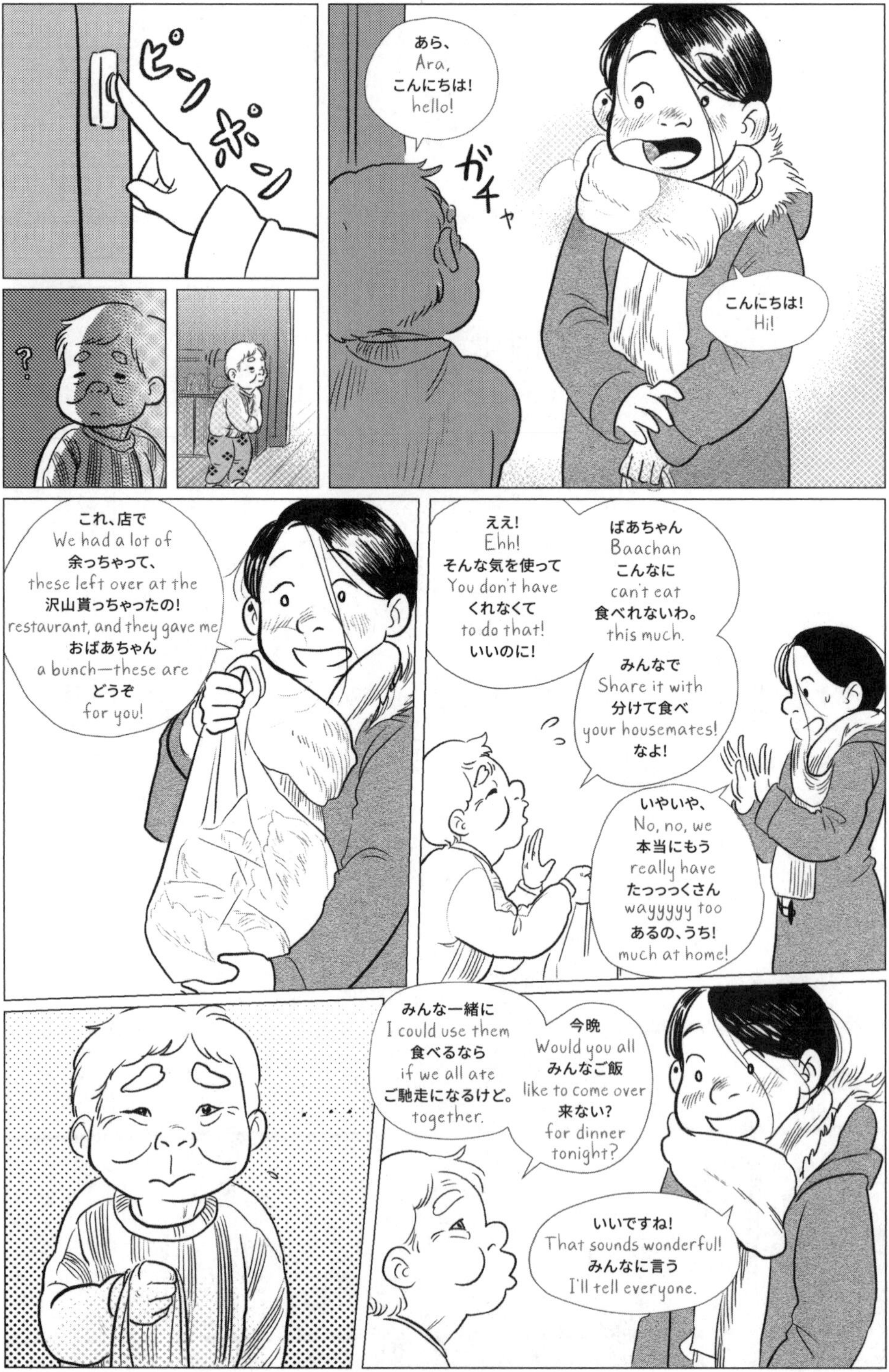
ピーンポーン
あら、 Ara, こんにちは! hello!
ガチャ
こんにちは! Hi!
?
これ、店で We had a lot of 余っちゃって、 these left over at the 沢山貰っちゃったの! restaurant, and they gave me おばあちゃん a bunch—these are どうぞ for you!
ええ! Ehh! そんな気を使って You don't have くれなくて to do that! いいのに!
ばあちゃん Baachan こんなに can't eat 食べれないわ。 this much.
みんなで Share it with 分けて食べ your housemates! なよ!
いやいや、 No, no, we 本当にもう really have たっっっくさん wayyyyy too あるの、うち! much at home!
みんな一緒に I could use them 食べるなら if we all ate ご馳走になるけど。 together.
今晩 Would you all みんなご飯 like to come over 来ない? for dinner tonight?
いいですね! That sounds wonderful! みんなに言う I'll tell everyone.

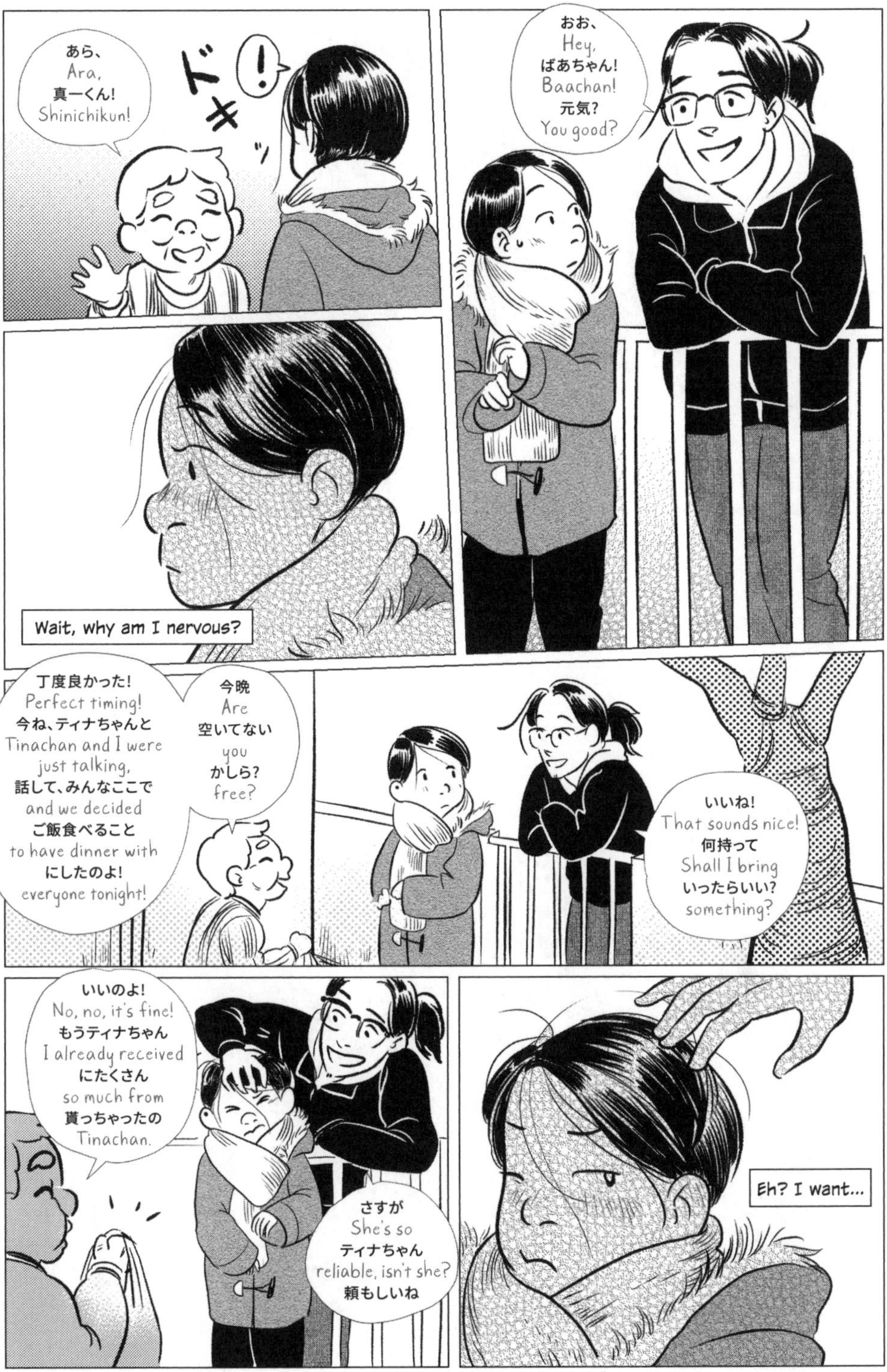

あら、 Ara, 真一くん! Shinichikun!
ドキッ
!
おお、 Hey, ばあちゃん! Baachan! 元気? You good?
Wait, why am I nervous?
丁度良かった! Perfect timing! 今ね、ティナちゃんと Tinachan and I were just talking, 話して、みんなここで and we decided ご飯食べること to have dinner with にしたのよ! everyone tonight!
今晩 Are 空いてない you かしら? free?
いいね! That sounds nice! 何持って Shall I bring いったらいい? something?
いいのよ! No, no, it's fine! もうティナちゃん I already received にたくさん so much from 貰っちゃったの Tinachan.
さすが She's so ティナちゃん reliable, isn't she? 頼もしいね
Eh? I want...

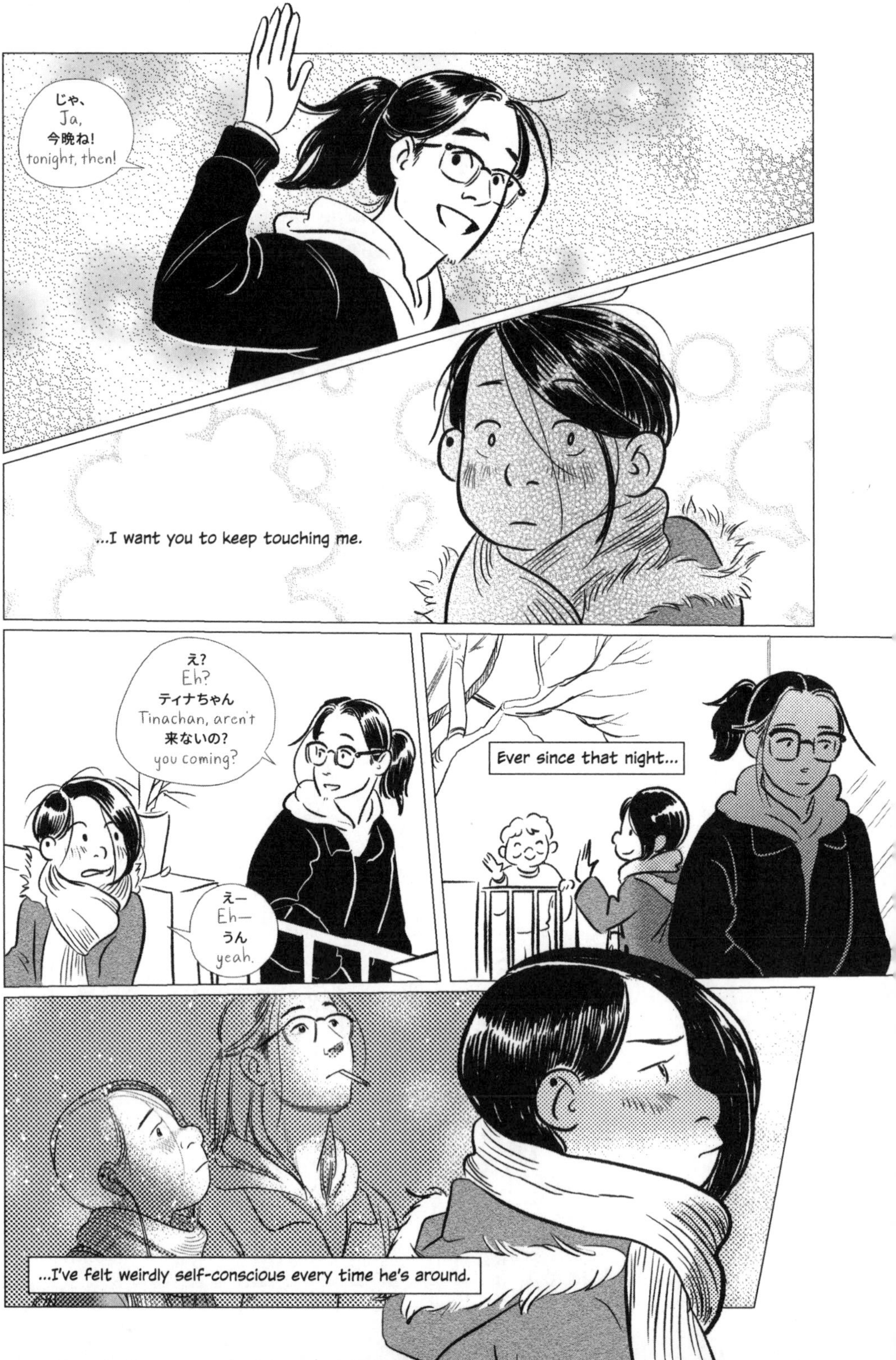
じゃ、
Ja,
今晩ね!
tonight, then!
...I want you to keep touching me.
え?
Eh?
ティナちゃん
Tinachan, aren't
来ないの?
you coming?
えー
Eh—
うん
yeah.
Ever since that night...
...I've felt weirdly self-conscious every time he's around.

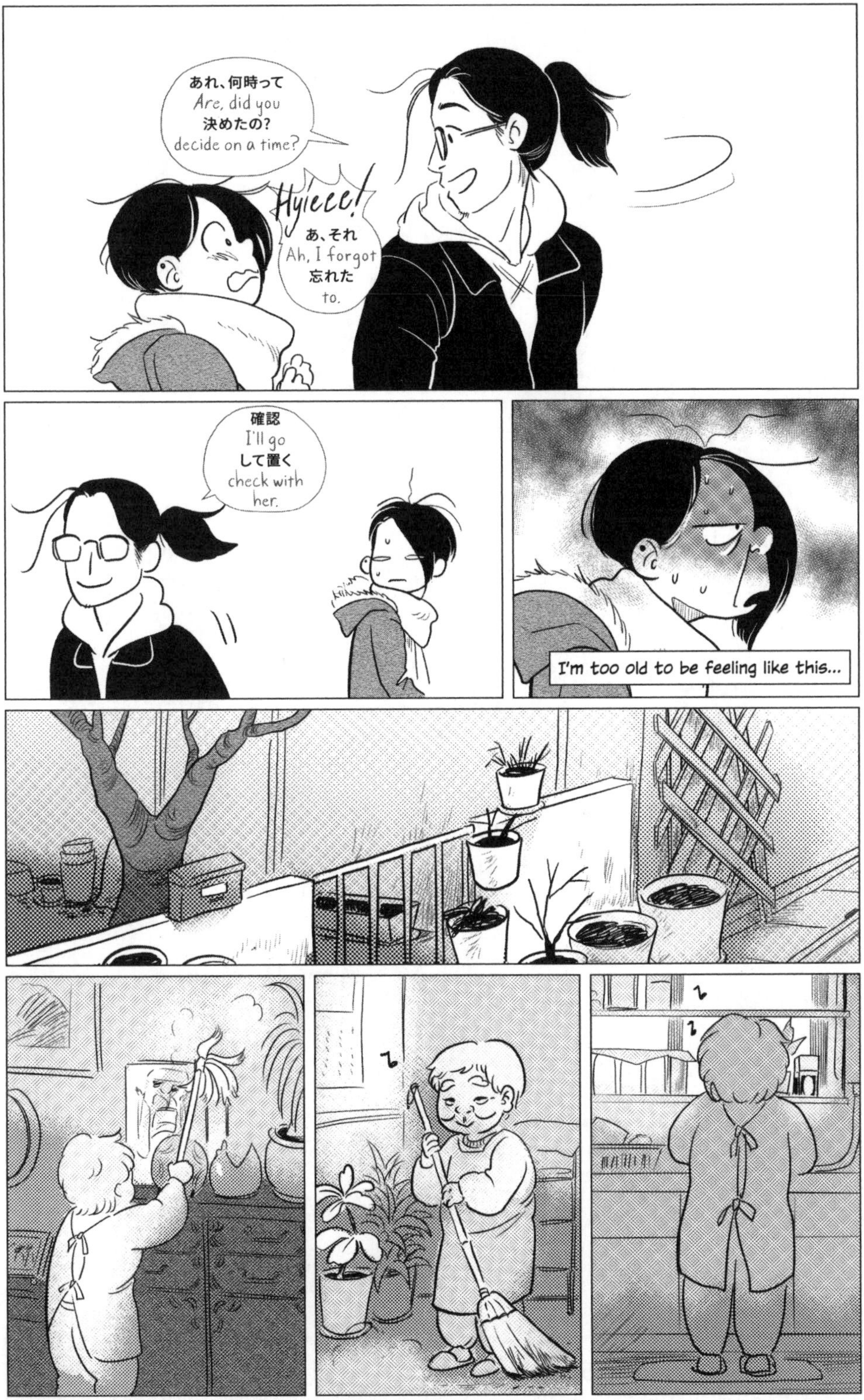
あれ、何時って
Are, did you
決めたの?
decide on a time?
Hyieee!
あ、それ
Ah, I forgot
忘れた
to.
確認
I'll go
して置く
check with
her.
I'm too old to be feeling like this...

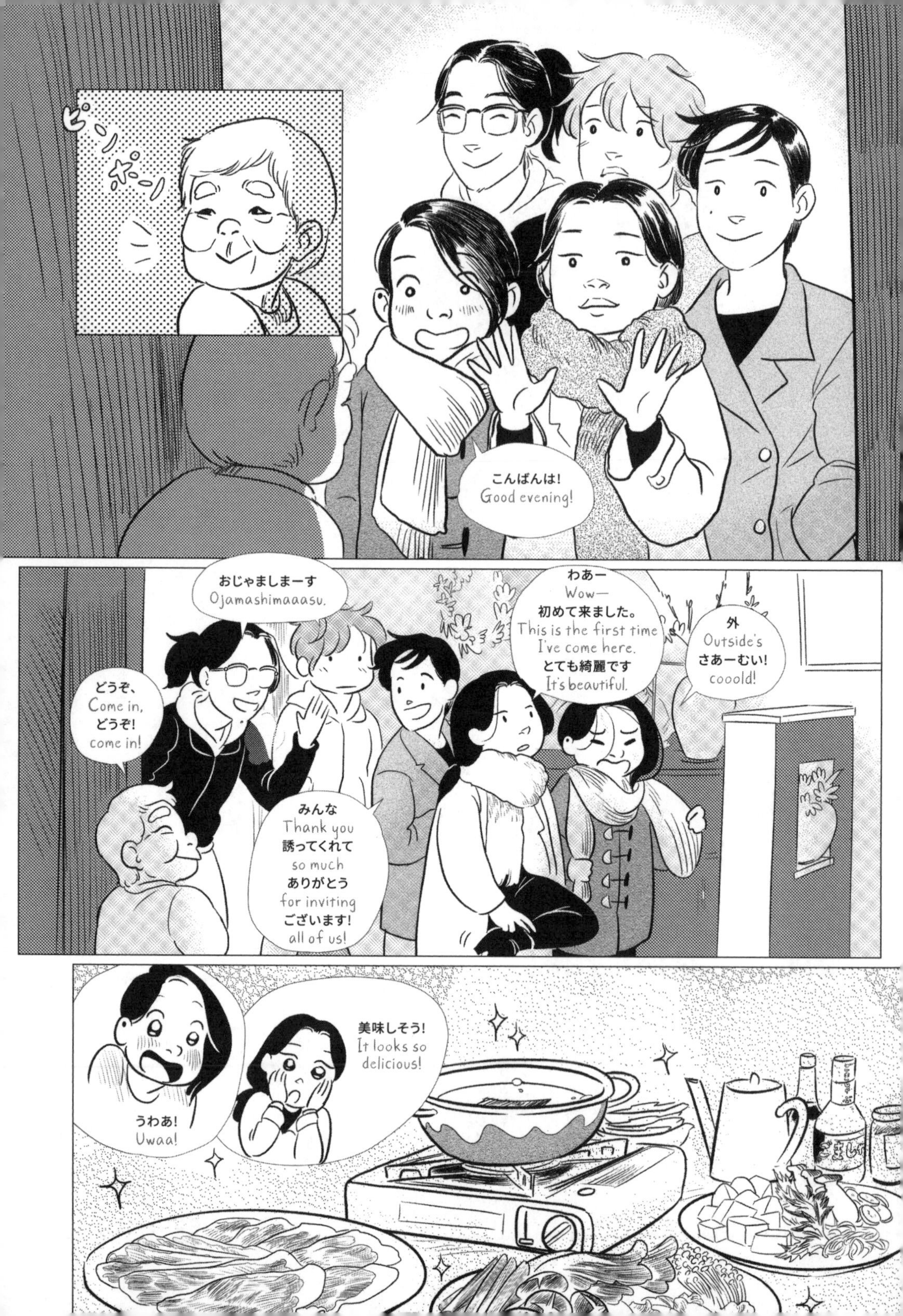

こんばんは!
Good evening!
おじゃましまーす
Ojamashimaaasu.
どうぞ、
Come in,
どうぞ!
come in!
みんな
Thank you
誘ってくれて
so much
ありがとう
for inviting
ございます!
all of us!
わあー
Wow—
初めて来ました。
This is the first time
I've come here.
とても綺麗です
It's beautiful.
外
Outside's
さあーむい!
cooold!
うわあ!
Uwaa!
美味しそう!
It looks so
delicious!

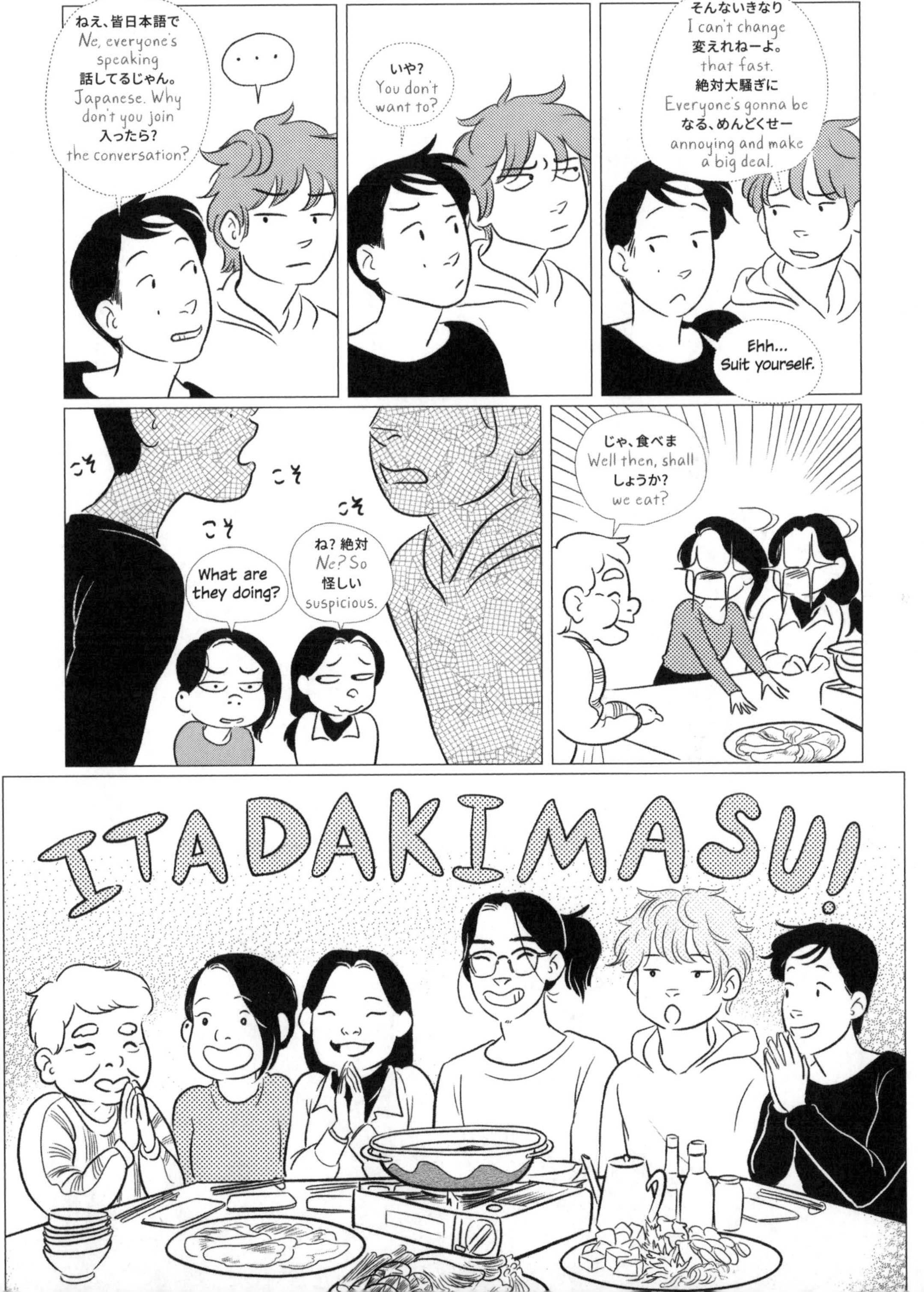

ねえ、皆日本語で Ne, everyone's speaking 話してるじゃん。 Japanese. Why don't you join 入ったら? the conversation?
...
いや? You don't want to?
そんないきなり I can't change 変えれねーよ。 that fast. 絶対大騒ぎに Everyone's gonna be なる、めんどくせー annoying and make a big deal.
Ehh... Suit yourself.
こそ
こそ
こそ
こそ
What are they doing?
ね? 絶対 Ne? So 怪しい suspicious.
じゃ、食べま Well then, shall しょうか? we eat?
ITADAKIMASU!

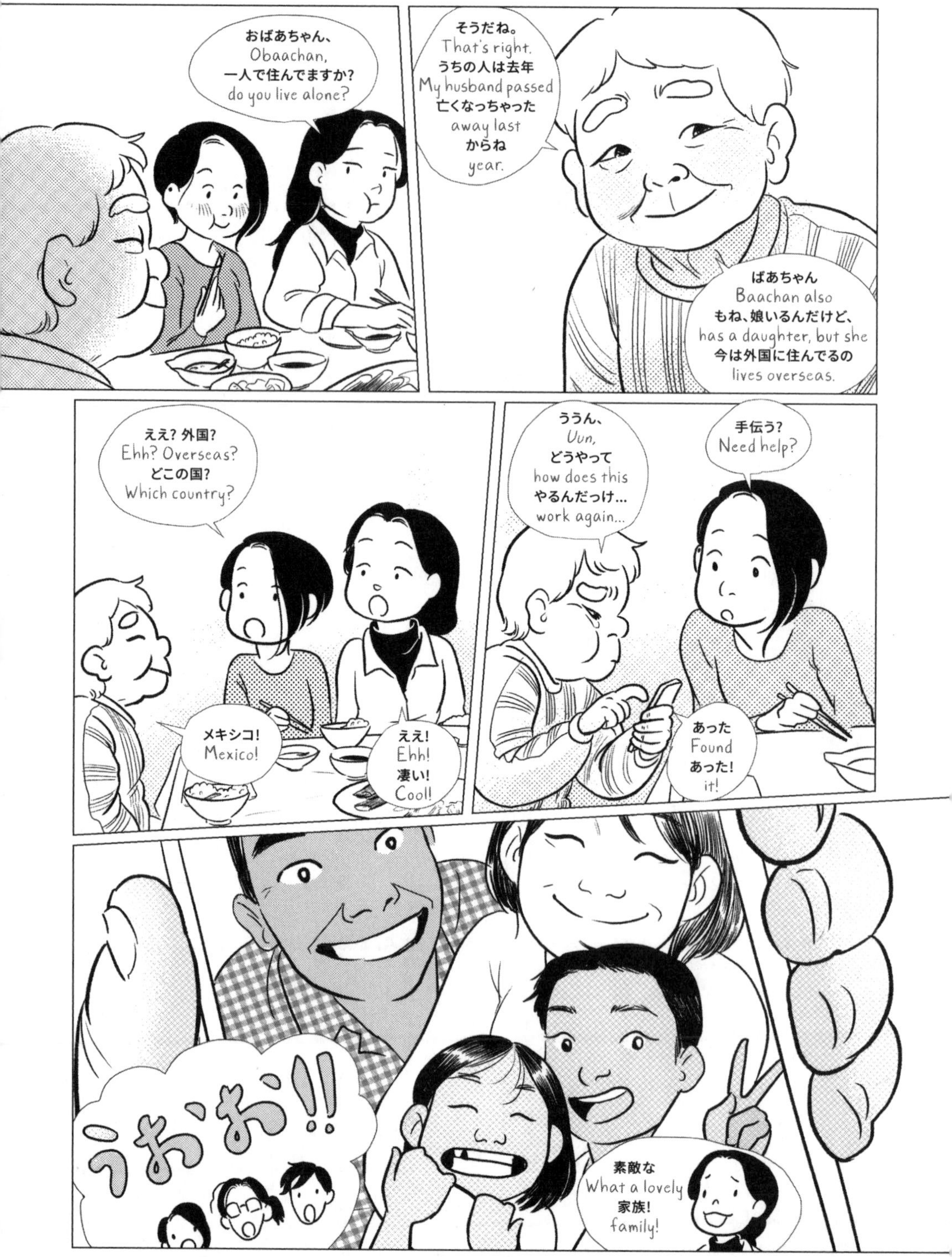

おばあちゃん、 Obaachan, 一人で住んでますか? do you live alone?
そうだね。 That's right. うちの人は去年 My husband passed 亡くなっちゃった away last からね year.
ばあちゃん Baachan also もね、娘いるんだけど、 has a daughter, but she 今は外国に住んでるの lives overseas.
ええ? 外国? Ehh? Overseas? どこの国? Which country?
メキシコ! Mexico!
ええ! Ehh! 凄い! Cool!
ううん、 Uun, どうやって how does this やるんだっけ… work again...
手伝う? Need help?
あった Found あった! it!
うおお!!
素敵な What a lovely 家族! family!

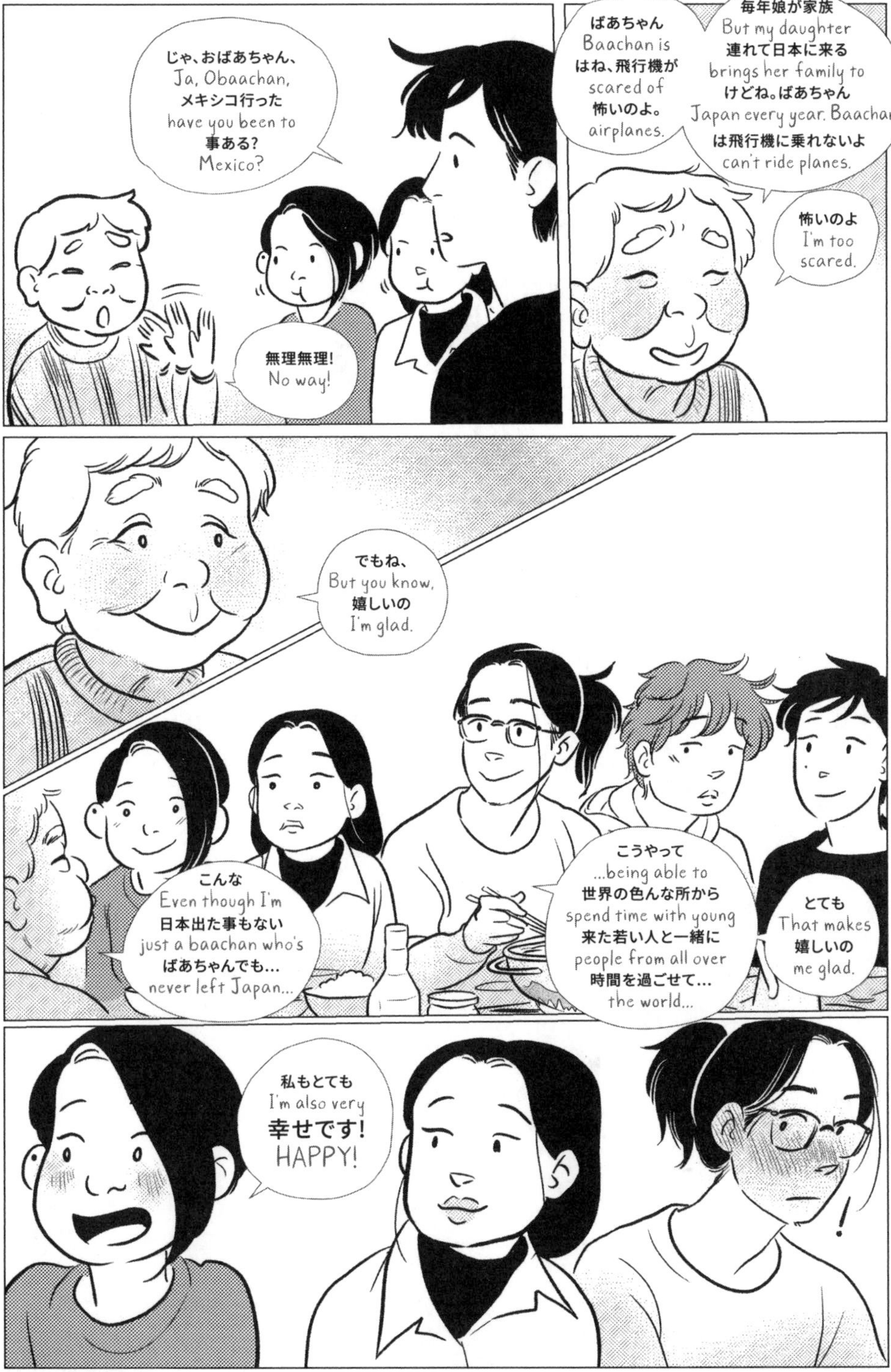
じゃ、おばあちゃん、メキシコ行った事ある?
Ja, Obaachan, have you been to Mexico?
無理無理!
No way!
ばあちゃんはね、飛行機が怖いのよ。
Baachan is scared of airplanes.
毎年娘が家族連れて日本に来るけどね。ばあちゃんは飛行機に乗れないよ
But my daughter brings her family to Japan every year. Baachan can't ride planes.
怖いのよ
I'm too scared.
でもね、嬉しいの
But you know, I'm glad.
こんな日本出た事もないばあちゃんでも…
Even though I'm just a baachan who's never left Japan...
こうやって世界の色んな所から来た若い人と一緒に時間を過ごせて…
...being able to spend time with young people from all over the world...
とても嬉しいの
That makes me glad.
私もとても幸せです!
I'm also very HAPPY!
!

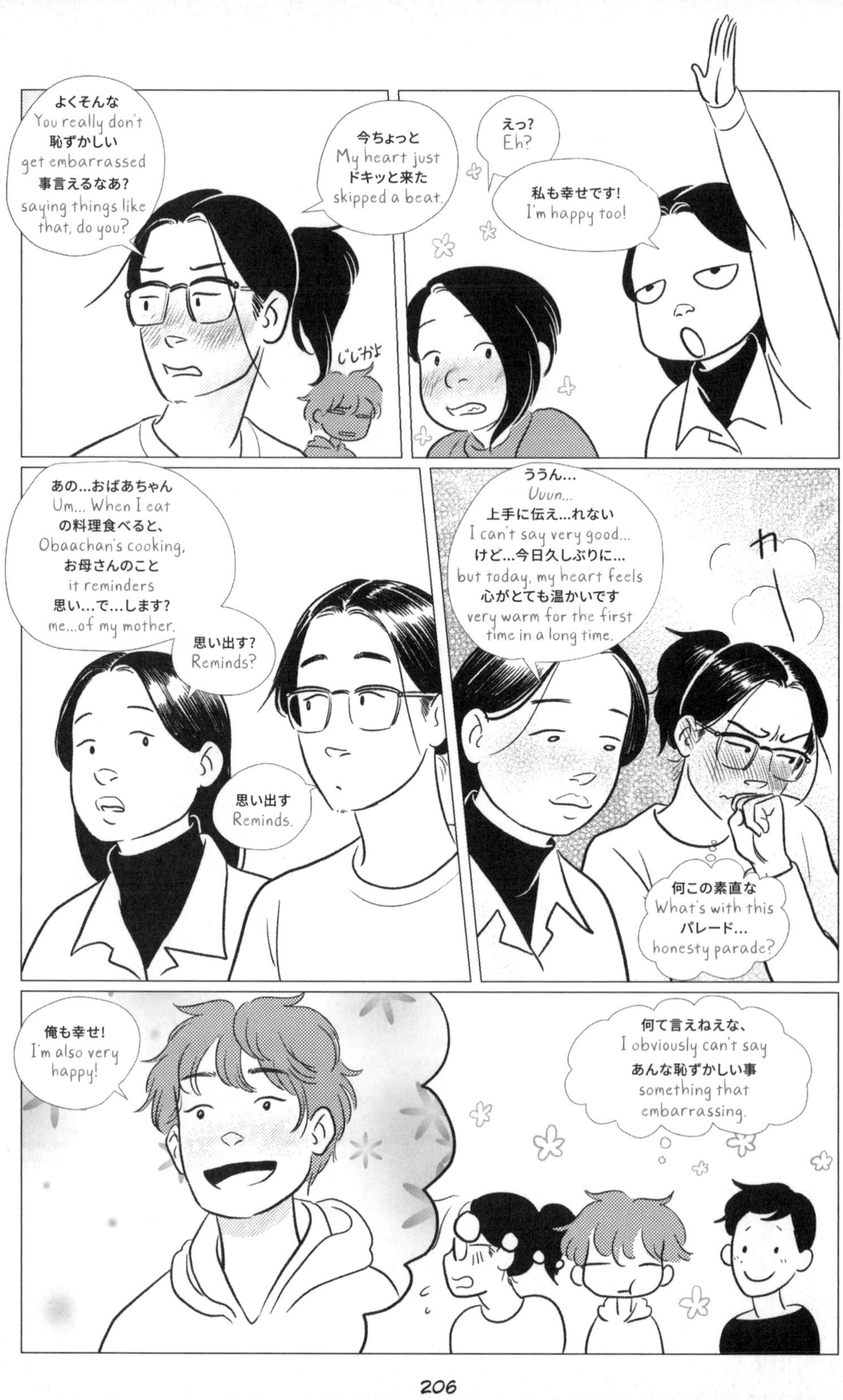
よくそんな
You really don't
恥ずかしい
get embarrassed
事言えるなあ?
saying things like
that, do you?
今ちょっと
My heart just
ドキッと来た
skipped a beat.
えっ?
Eh?
私も幸せです!
I'm happy too!
あの…おばあちゃん
Um... When I eat
の料理食べると、
Obaachan's cooking,
お母さんのこと
it reminders
思い…で…します?
me...of my mother.
思い出す?
Reminds?
思い出す
Reminds.
ううん…
Uuun...
上手に伝え…れない
I can't say very good...
けど…今日久しぶりに…
but today, my heart feels
心がとても温かいです
very warm for the first
time in a long time.
カー
何この素直な
What's with this
パレード…
honesty parade?
俺も幸せ!
I'm also very
happy!
何て言えねえな、
I obviously can't say
あんな恥ずかしい事
something that
embarrassing.

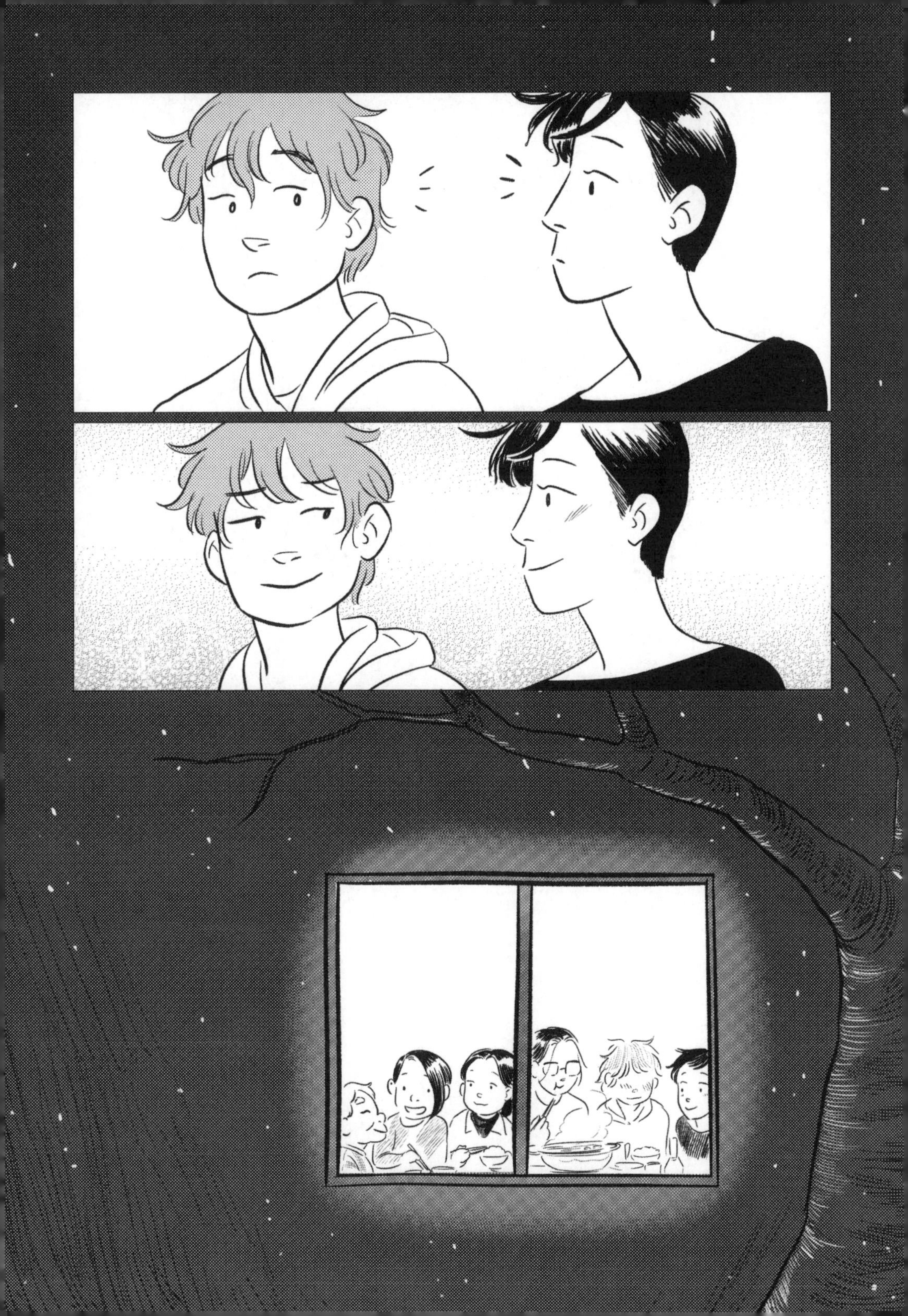

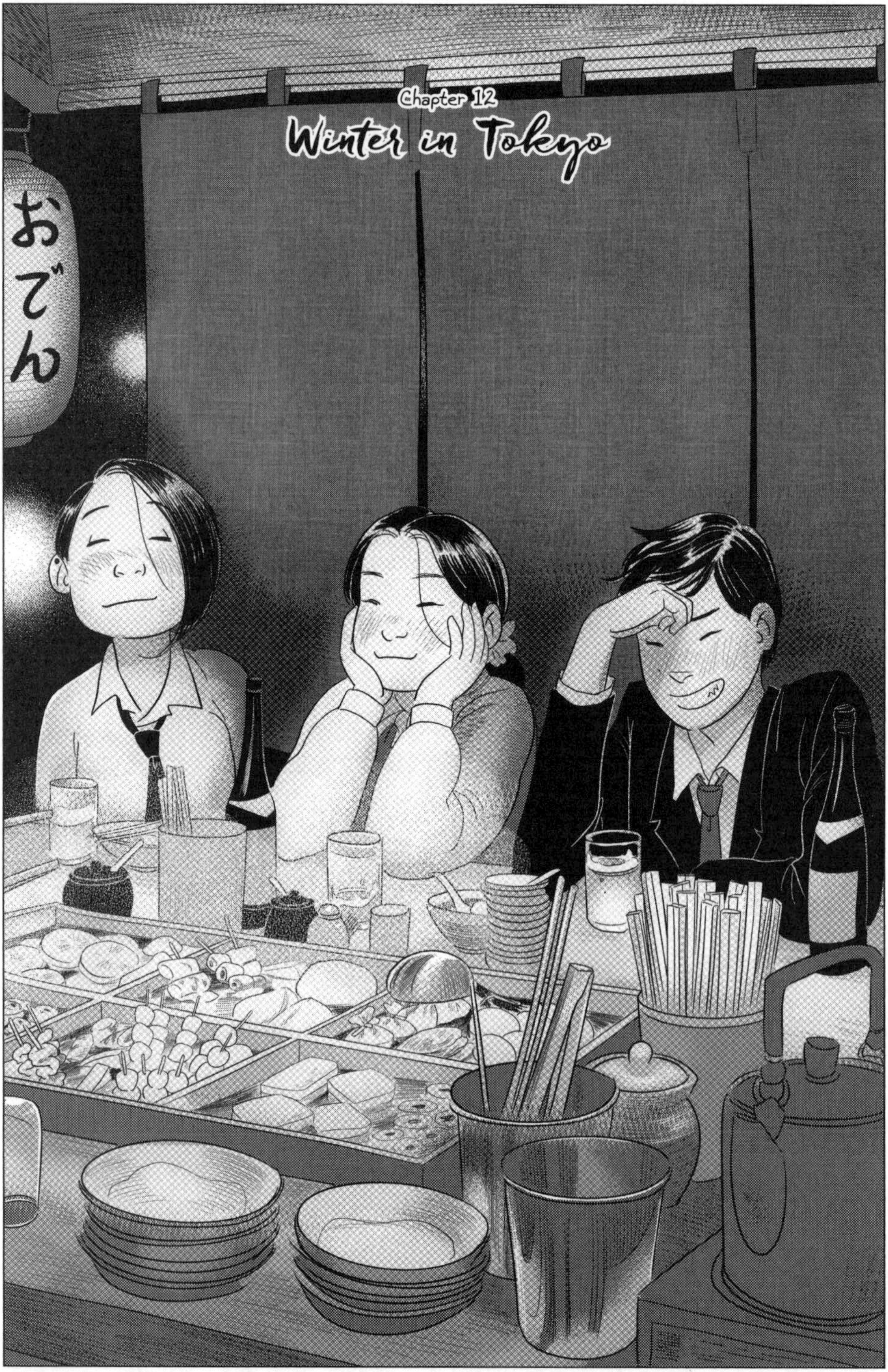
Chapter 12
Winter in Tokyo
おでん

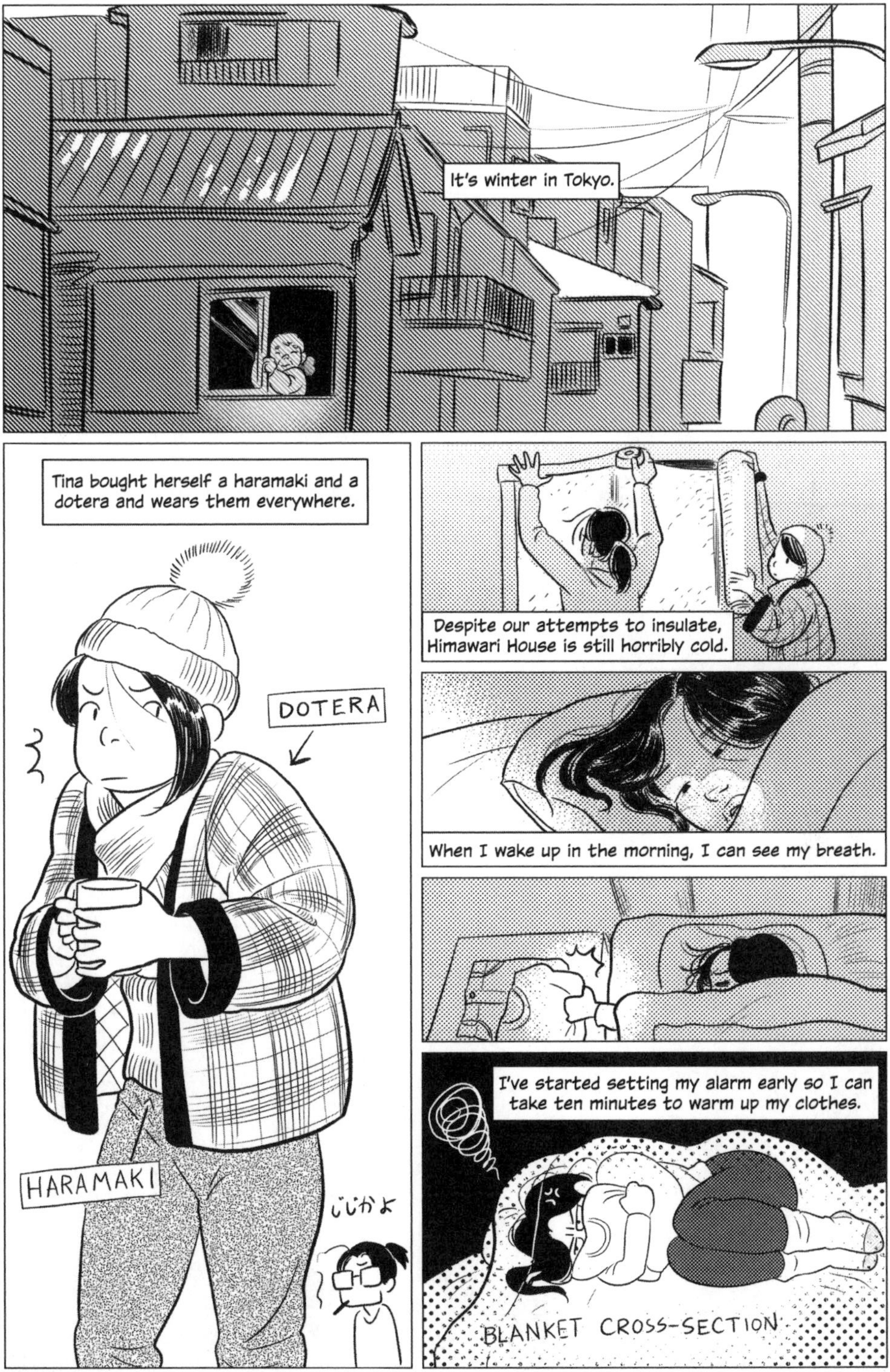
It's winter in Tokyo.
Tina bought herself a haramaki and a dotera and wears them everywhere.
DOTERA
HARAMAKI
じじかよ
Despite our attempts to insulate, Himawari House is still horribly cold.
When I wake up in the morning, I can see my breath.
I've started setting my alarm early so I can take ten minutes to warm up my clothes.
BLANKET CROSS-SECTION

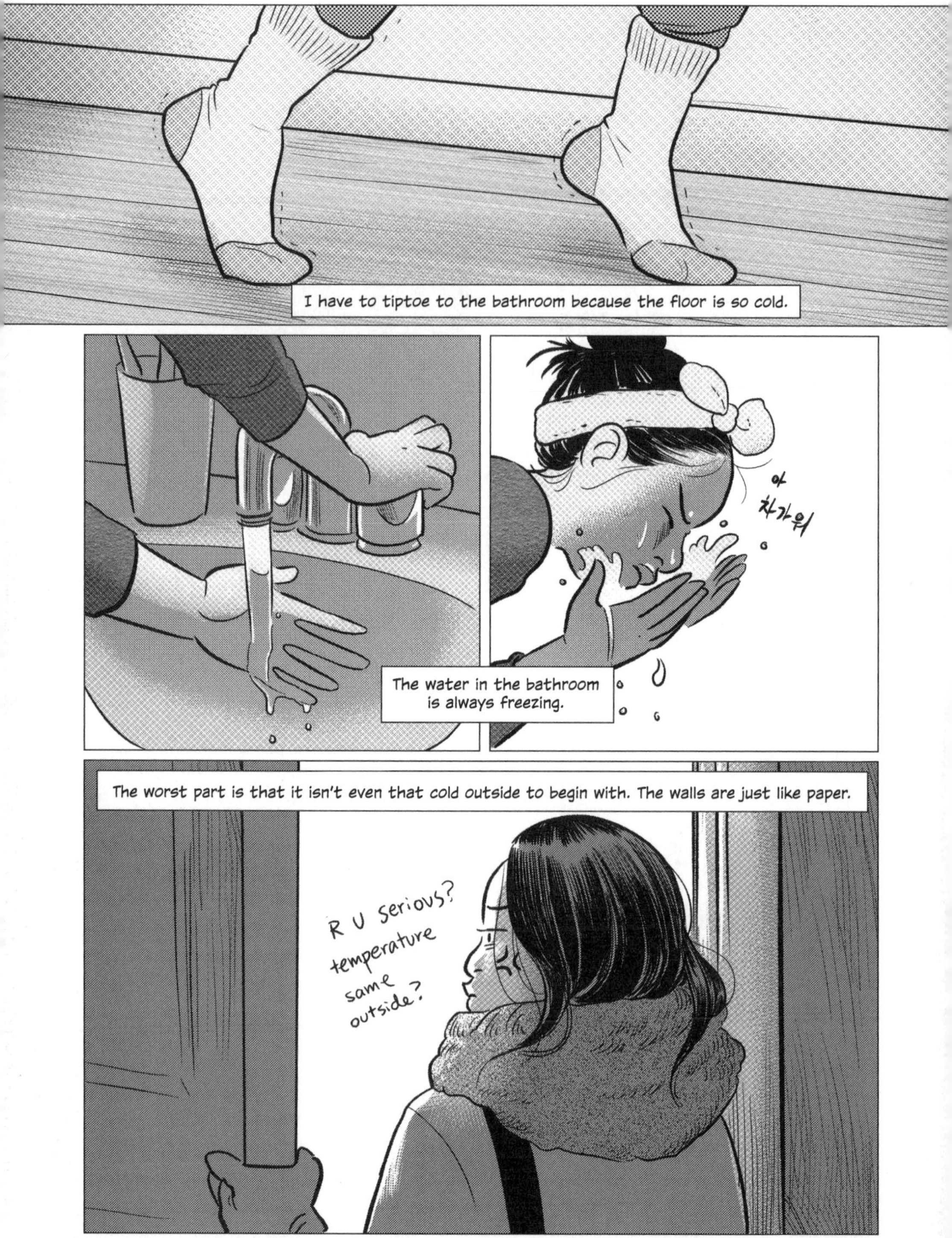
I have to tiptoe to the bathroom because the floor is so cold.
아
차가워
The water in the bathroom is always freezing.
The worst part is that it isn't even that cold outside to begin with. The walls are just like paper.
R U Serious?
temperature same outside?

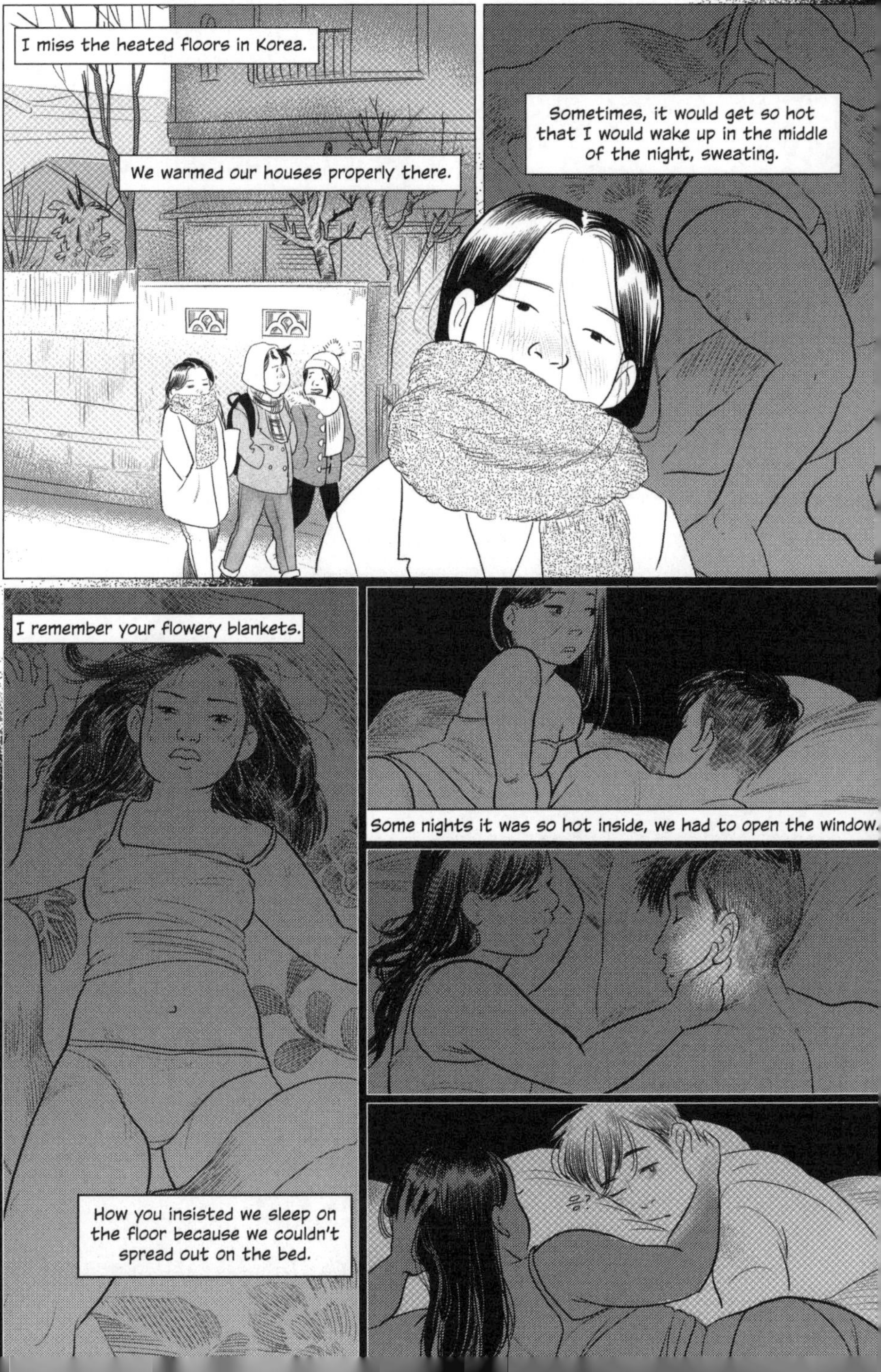
I miss the heated floors in Korea.
We warmed our houses properly there.
Sometimes, it would get so hot that I would wake up in the middle of the night, sweating.
I remember your flowery blankets.
How you insisted we sleep on the floor because we couldn't spread out on the bed.
Some nights it was so hot inside, we had to open the window.
응?

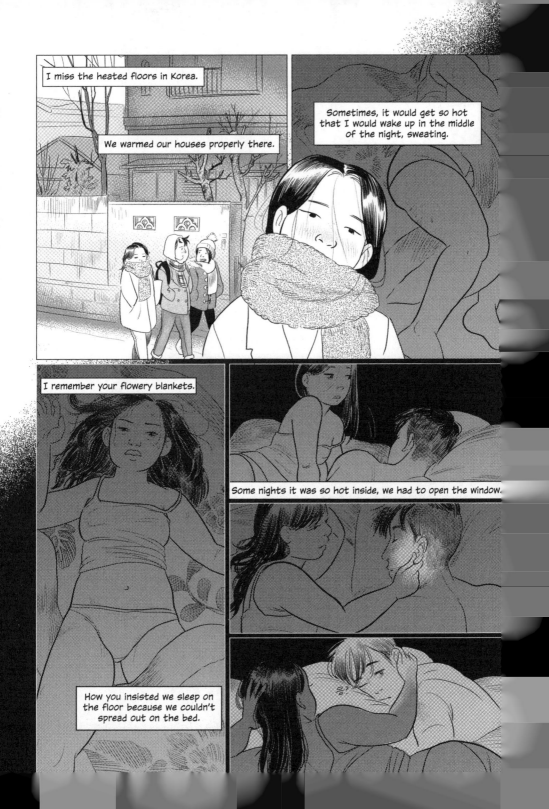

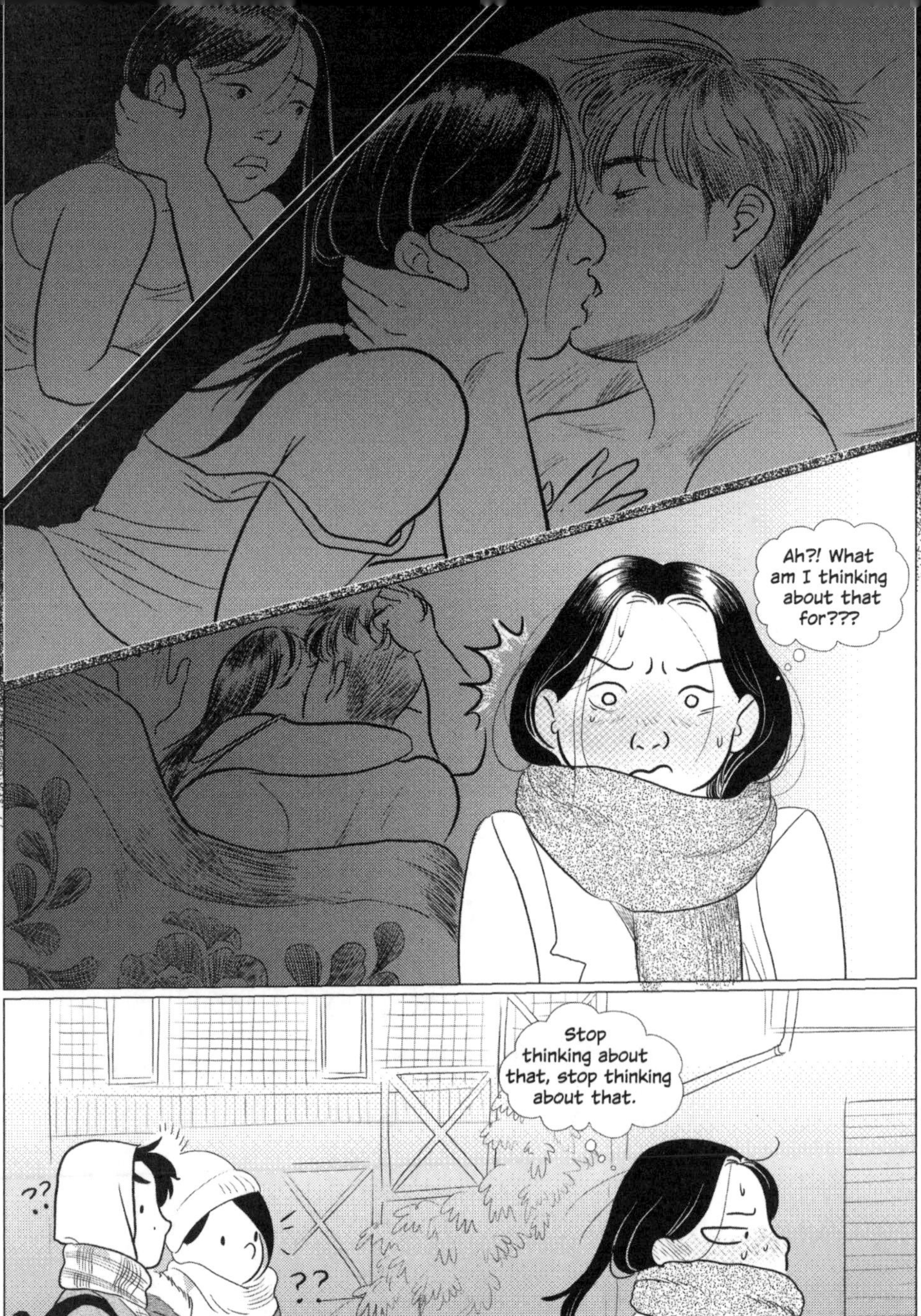
Ah?! What am I thinking about that for???
Stop thinking about that, stop thinking about that.
??
??

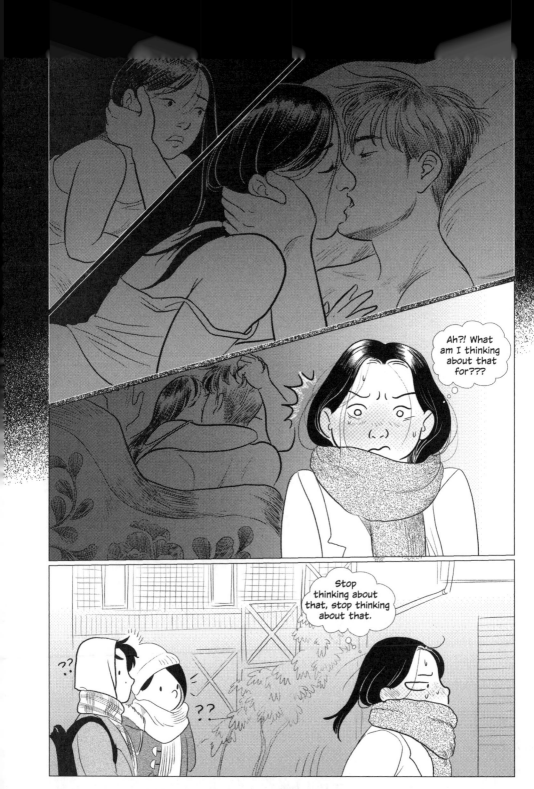

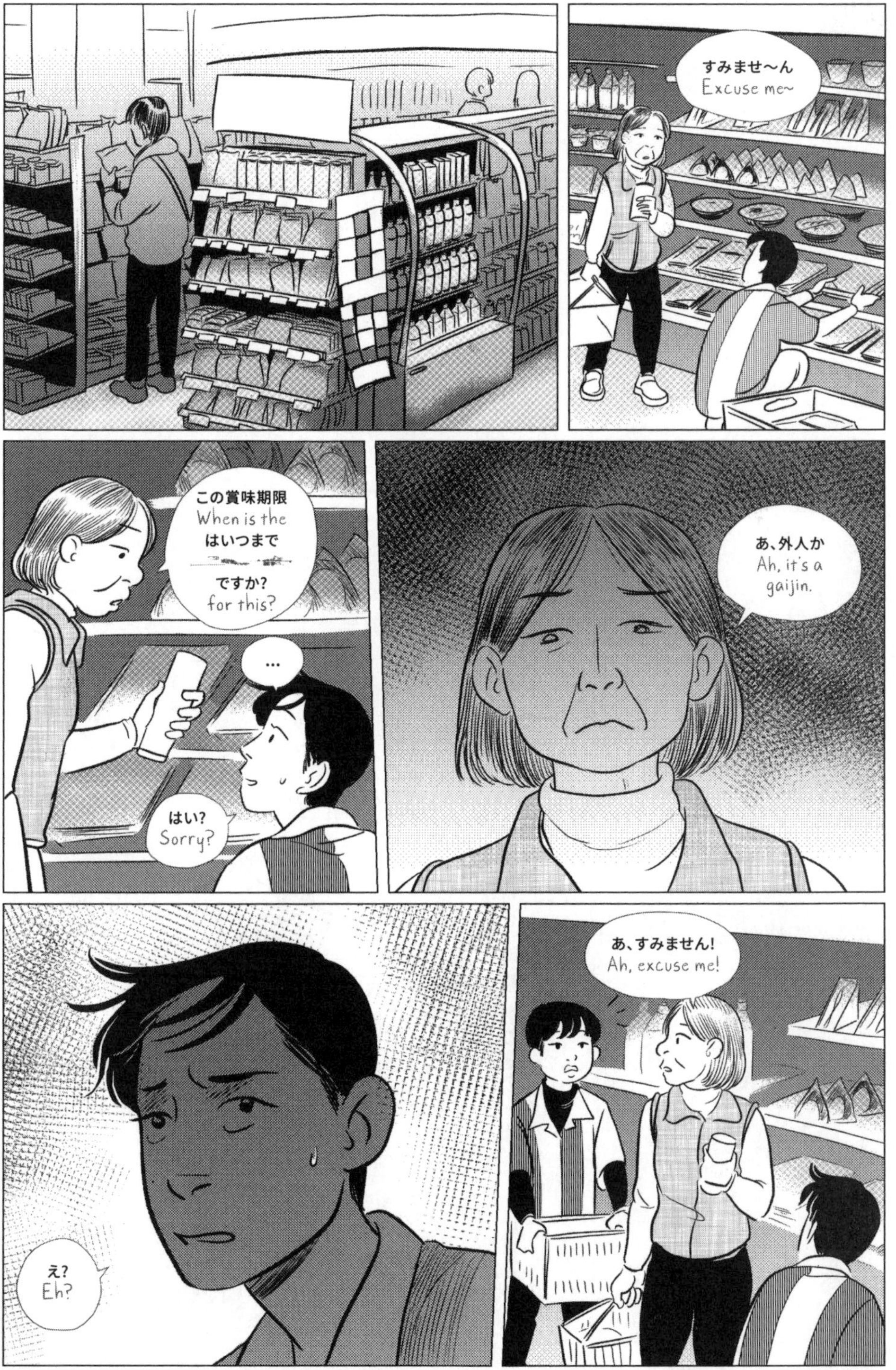
すみませ〜ん
Excuse me~
この賞味期限
When is the
はいつまで
ですか?
for this?
...
はい?
Sorry?
あ、外人か
Ah, it's a gaijin.
え?
Eh?
あ、すみません!
Ah, excuse me!

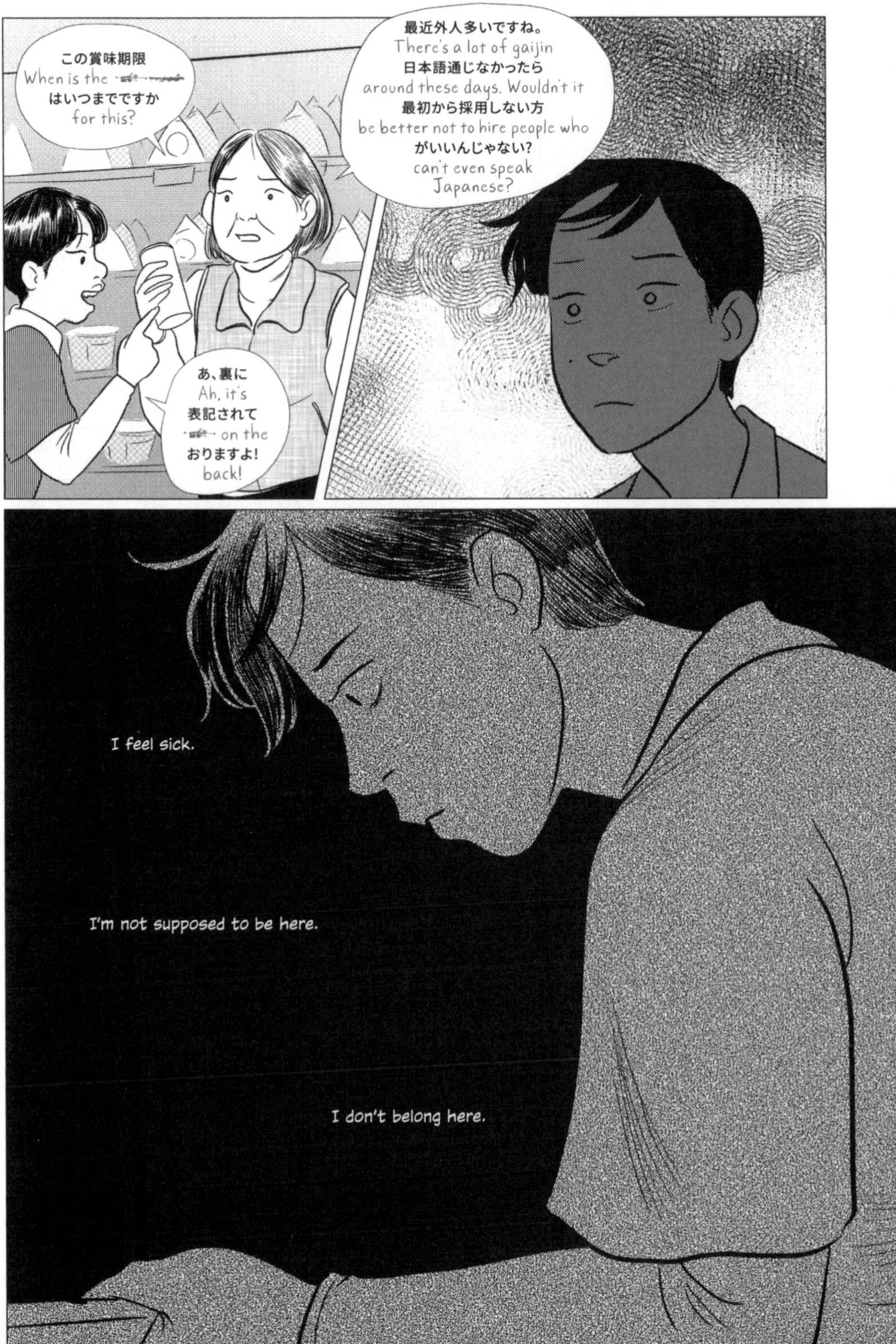

この賞味期限 When is the はいつまでですか for this?
あ、裏に Ah, it's 表記されて on the おりますよ! back!
最近外人多いですね。 There's a lot of gaijin 日本語通じなかったら around these days. Wouldn't it 最初から採用しない方 be better not to hire people who がいいんじゃない? can't even speak Japanese?
I feel sick.
I'm not supposed to be here.
I don't belong here.

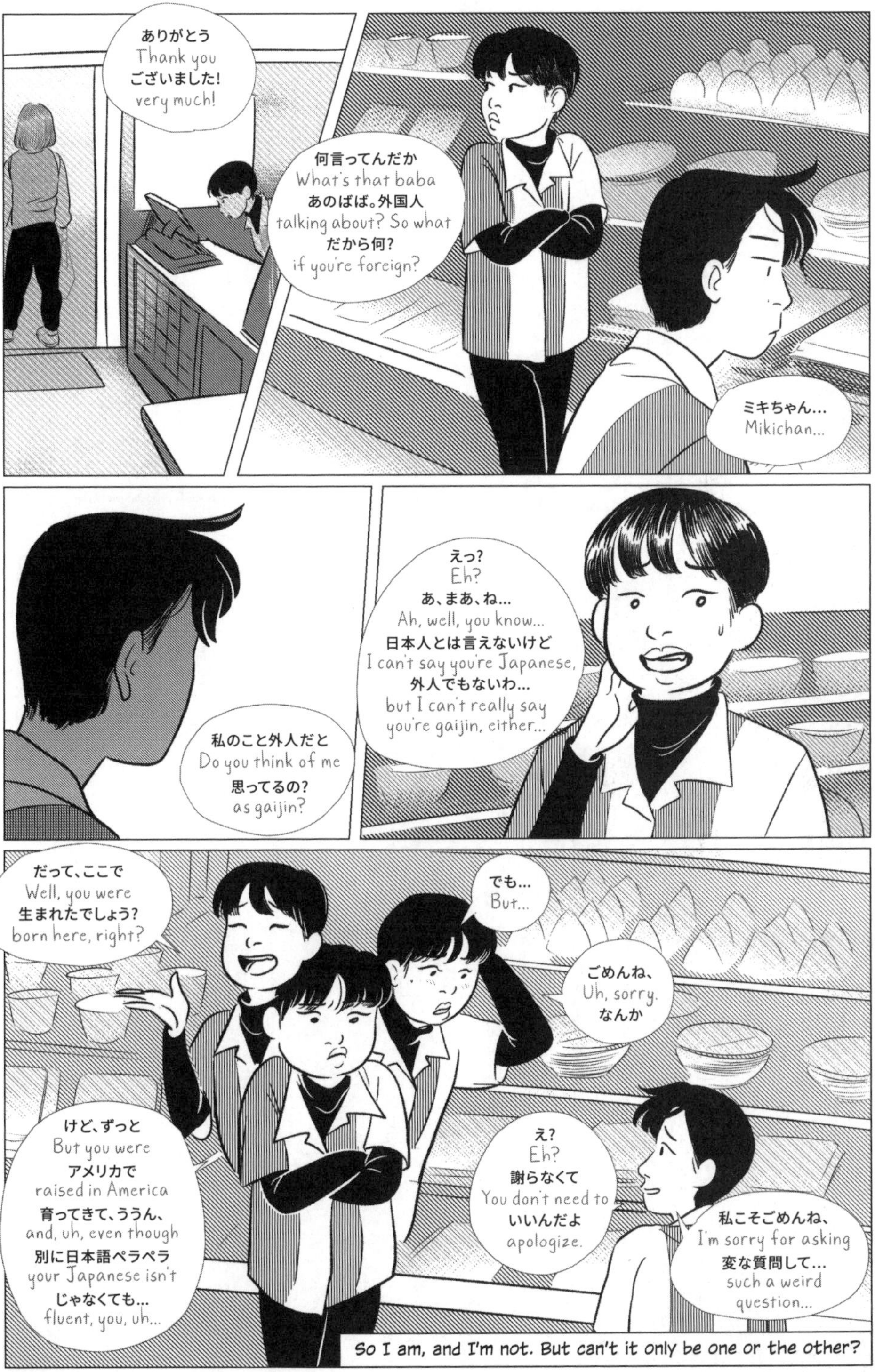
ありがとう
Thank you
ございました!
very much!
何言ってんだか
What's that baba
あのばば。外国人
talking about? So what
だから何?
if you're foreign?
ミキちゃん…
Mikichan...
私のこと外人だと
Do you think of me
思ってるの?
as gaijin?
えっ?
Eh?
あ、まあ、ね…
Ah, well, you know...
日本人とは言えないけど
I can't say you're Japanese,
外人でもないわ…
but I can't really say
you're gaijin, either...
だって、ここで
Well, you were
生まれたでしょう?
born here, right?
でも…
But...
けど、ずっと
But you were
アメリカで
raised in America
育ってきて、ううん、
and, uh, even though
別に日本語ペラペラ
your Japanese isn't
じゃなくても…
fluent, you, uh...
ごめんね、
Uh, sorry.
なんか
え?
Eh?
謝らなくて
You don't need to
いいんだよ
apologize.
私こそごめんね、
I'm sorry for asking
変な質問して…
such a weird
question...
So I am, and I'm not. But can't it only be one or the other?

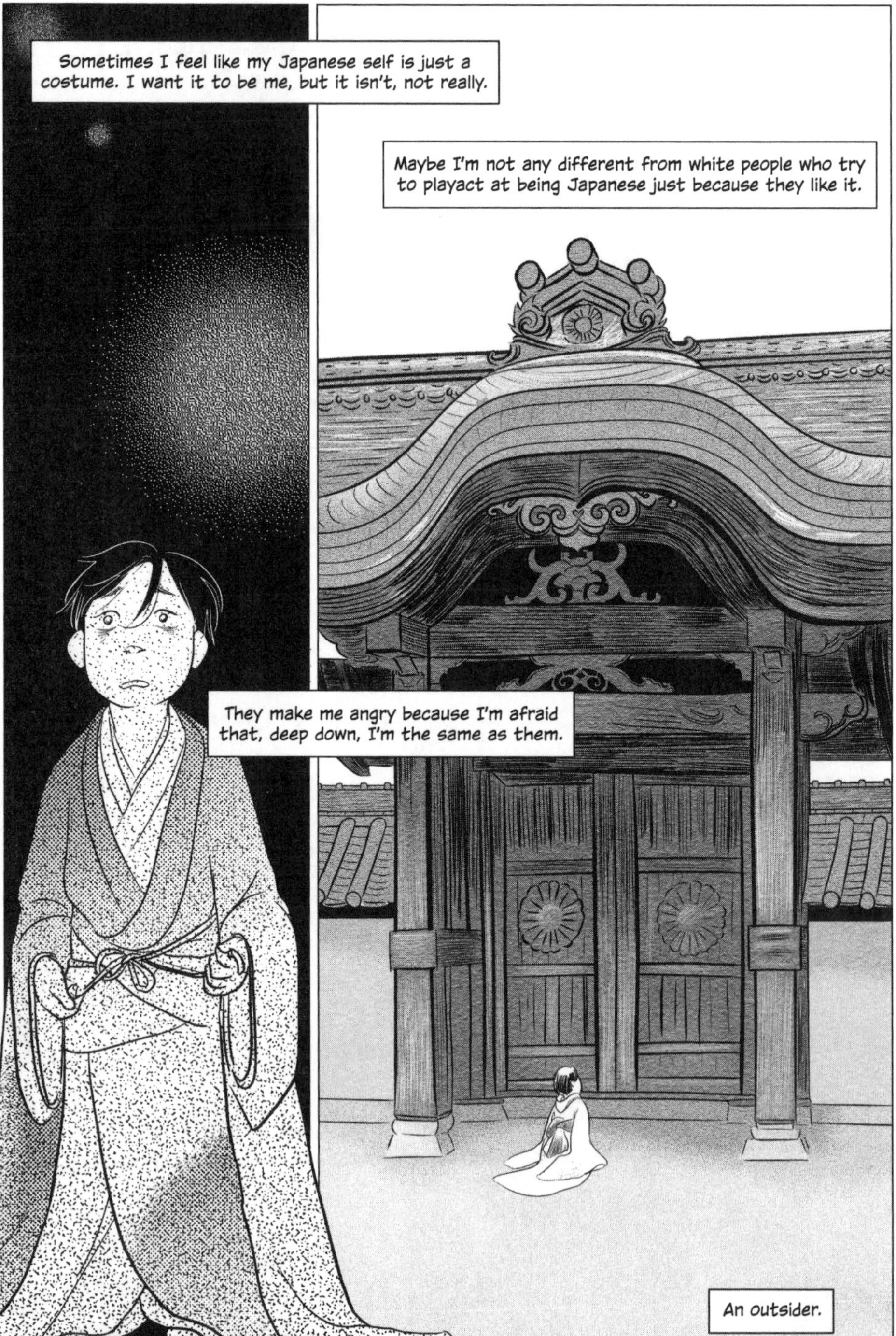
Sometimes I feel like my Japanese self is just a costume. I want it to be me, but it isn't, not really.
Maybe I'm not any different from white people who try to playact at being Japanese just because they like it.
They make me angry because I'm afraid that, deep down, I'm the same as them.
An outsider.

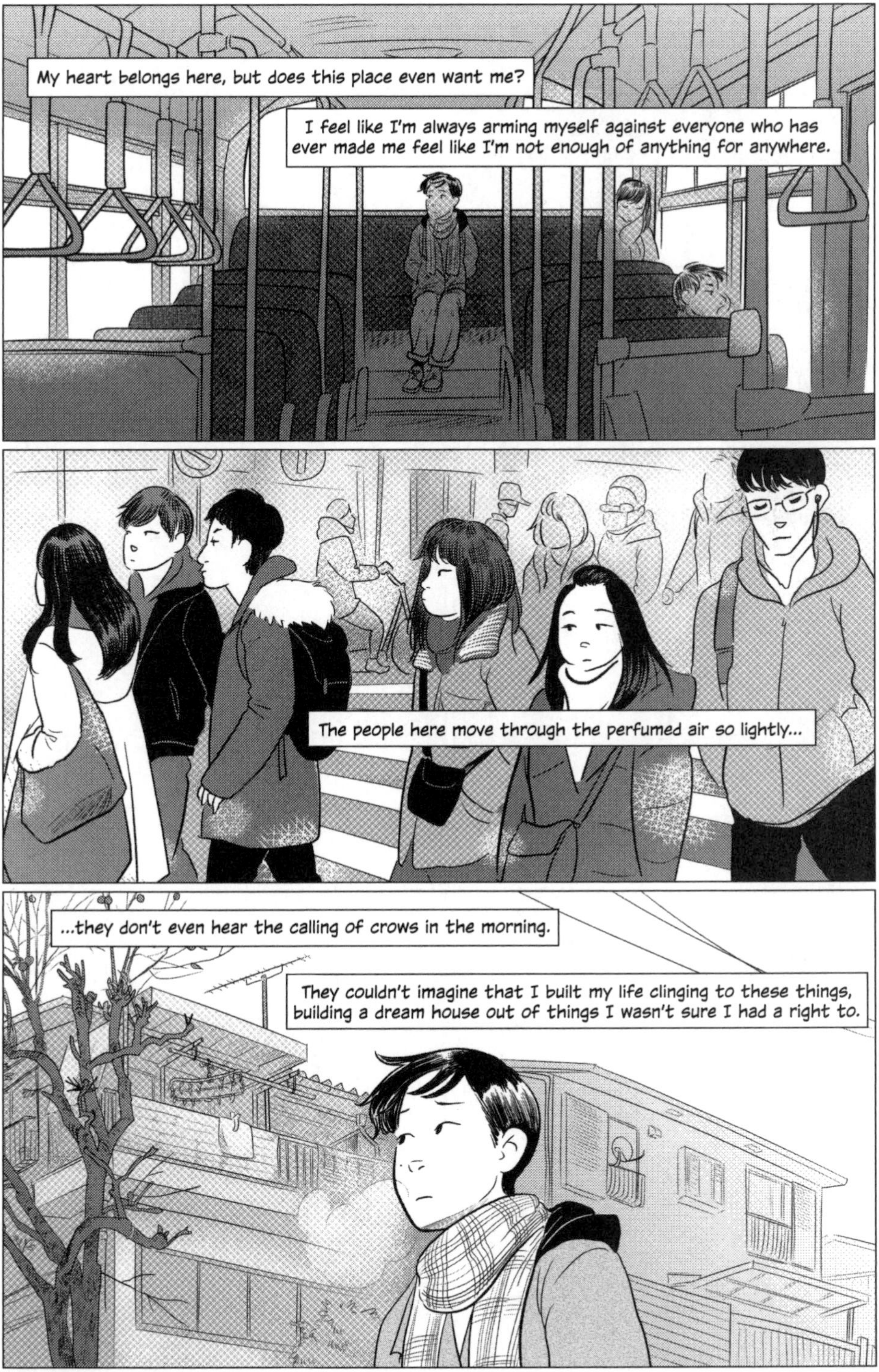
My heart belongs here, but does this place even want me?
I feel like I'm always arming myself against everyone who has ever made me feel like I'm not enough of anything for anywhere.
The people here move through the perfumed air so lightly...
...they don't even hear the calling of crows in the morning.
They couldn't imagine that I built my life clinging to these things, building a dream house out of things I wasn't sure I had a right to.

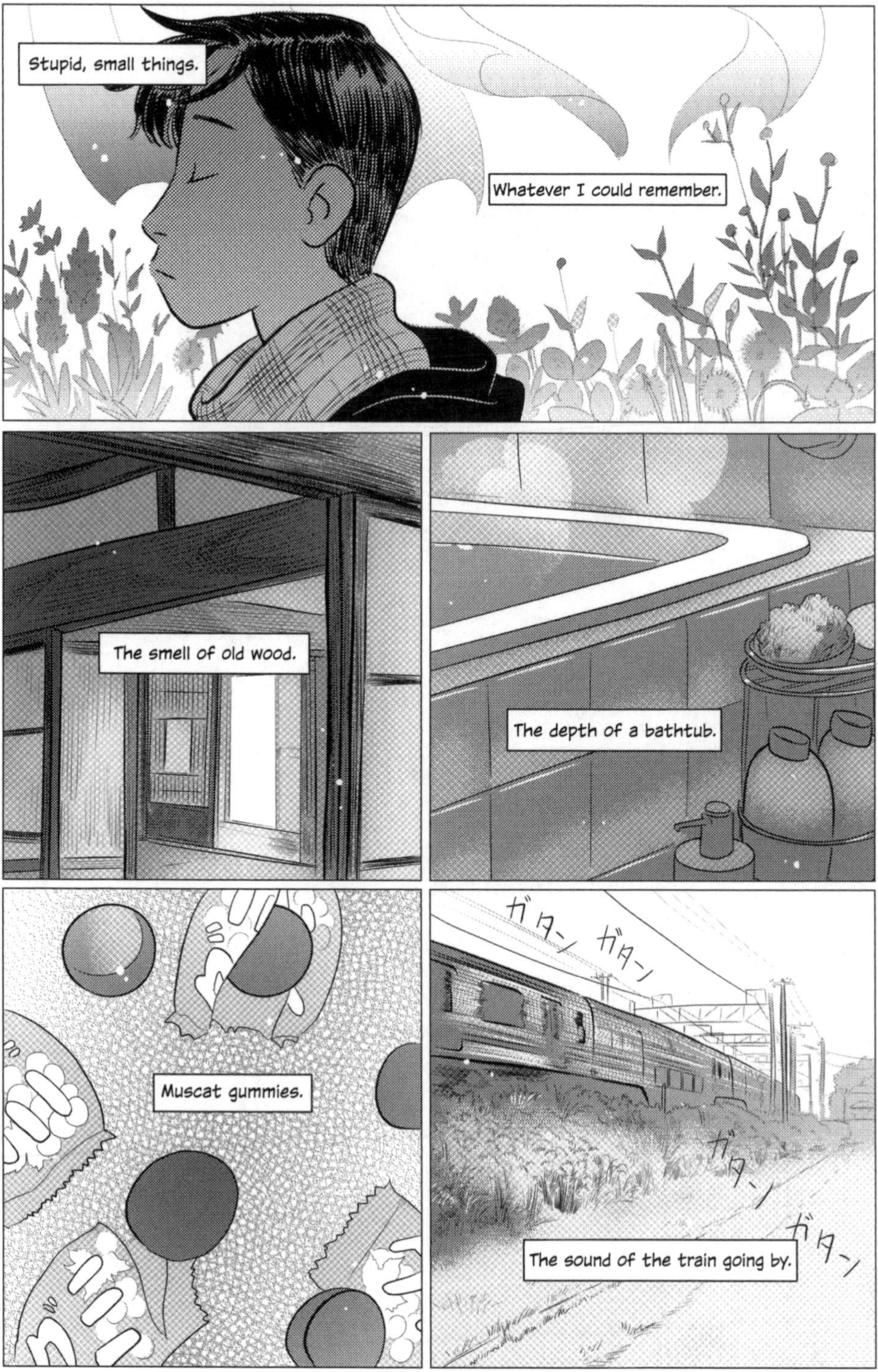
Stupid, small things.
Whatever I could remember.
The smell of old wood.
The depth of a bathtub.
Muscat gummies.
ガターン ガターン
ガターン
ガターン
The sound of the train going by.

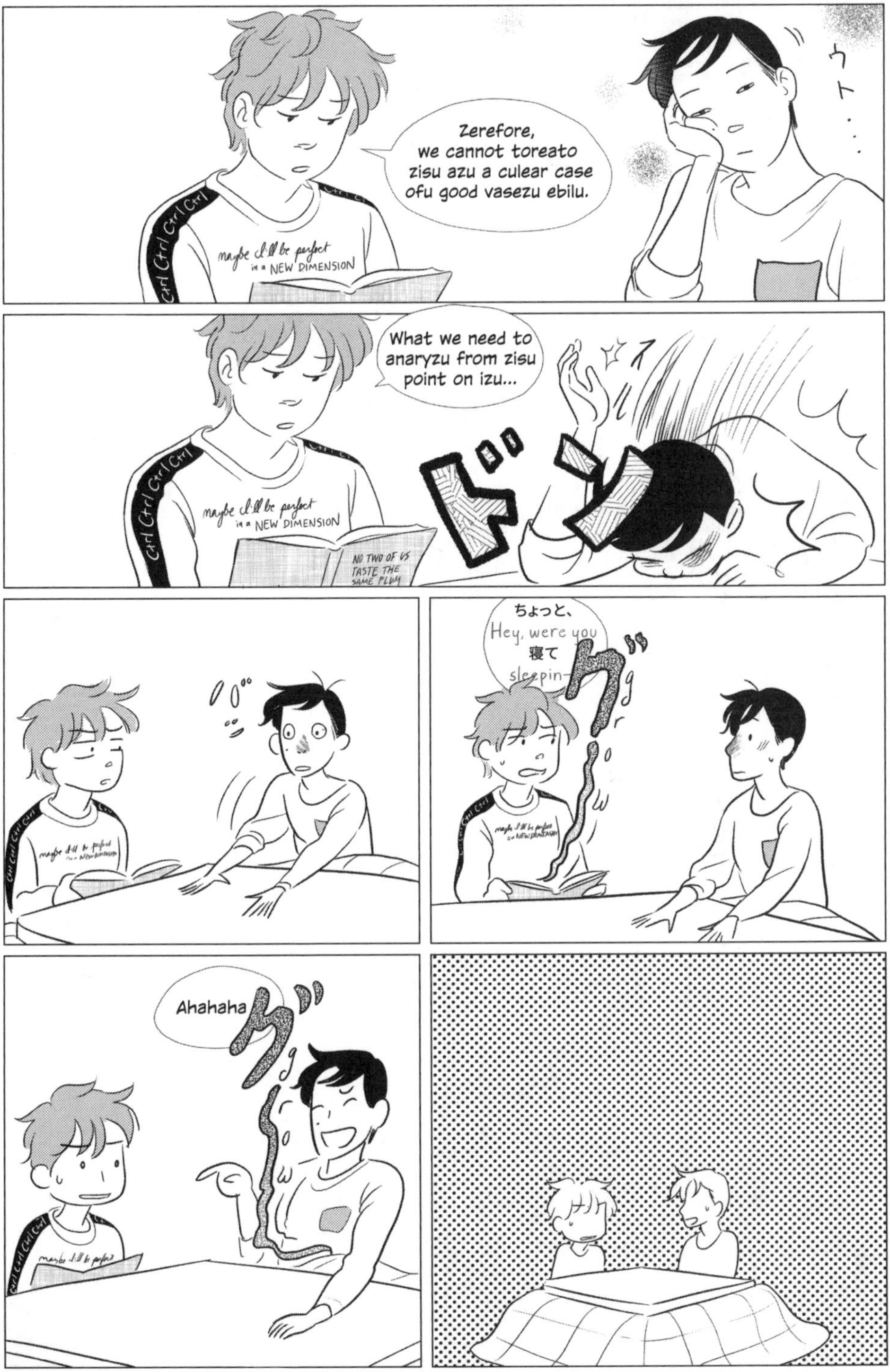
Zerefore, we cannot toreato zisu azu a culear case ofu good vasezu ebilu.
ウト・・・
maybe I'll be perfect in a NEW DIMENSION
What we need to anaryzu from zisu point on izu...
イ
ドン
NO TWO OF US TASTE THE SAME PLUM
ちょっと、
Hey, were you
寝て
sleepin—
Ahahaha

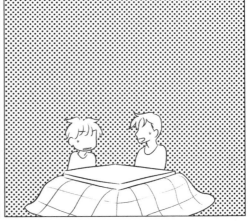

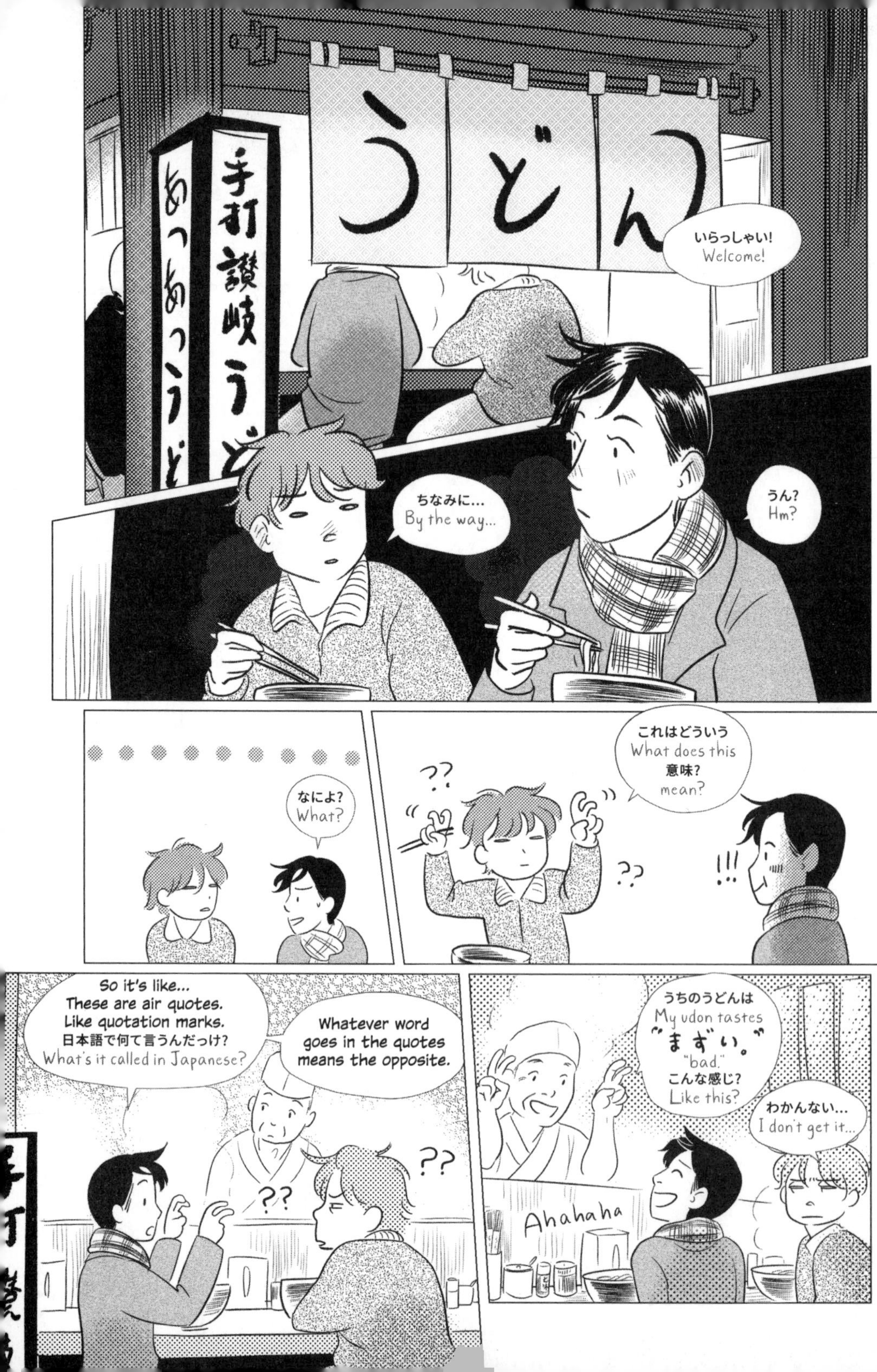
うどん
手打讃岐うど
あつあつうど
いらっしゃい!
Welcome!
ちなみに…
By the way...
うん?
Hm?
なによ?
What?
これはどういう
What does this
意味?
mean?
So it's like...
These are air quotes.
Like quotation marks.
日本語で何て言うんだっけ?
What's it called in Japanese?
Whatever word goes in the quotes means the opposite.
うちのうどんは
My udon tastes
"まずい。"
"bad."
こんな感じ?
Like this?
Ahahaha
わかんない…
I don't get it...

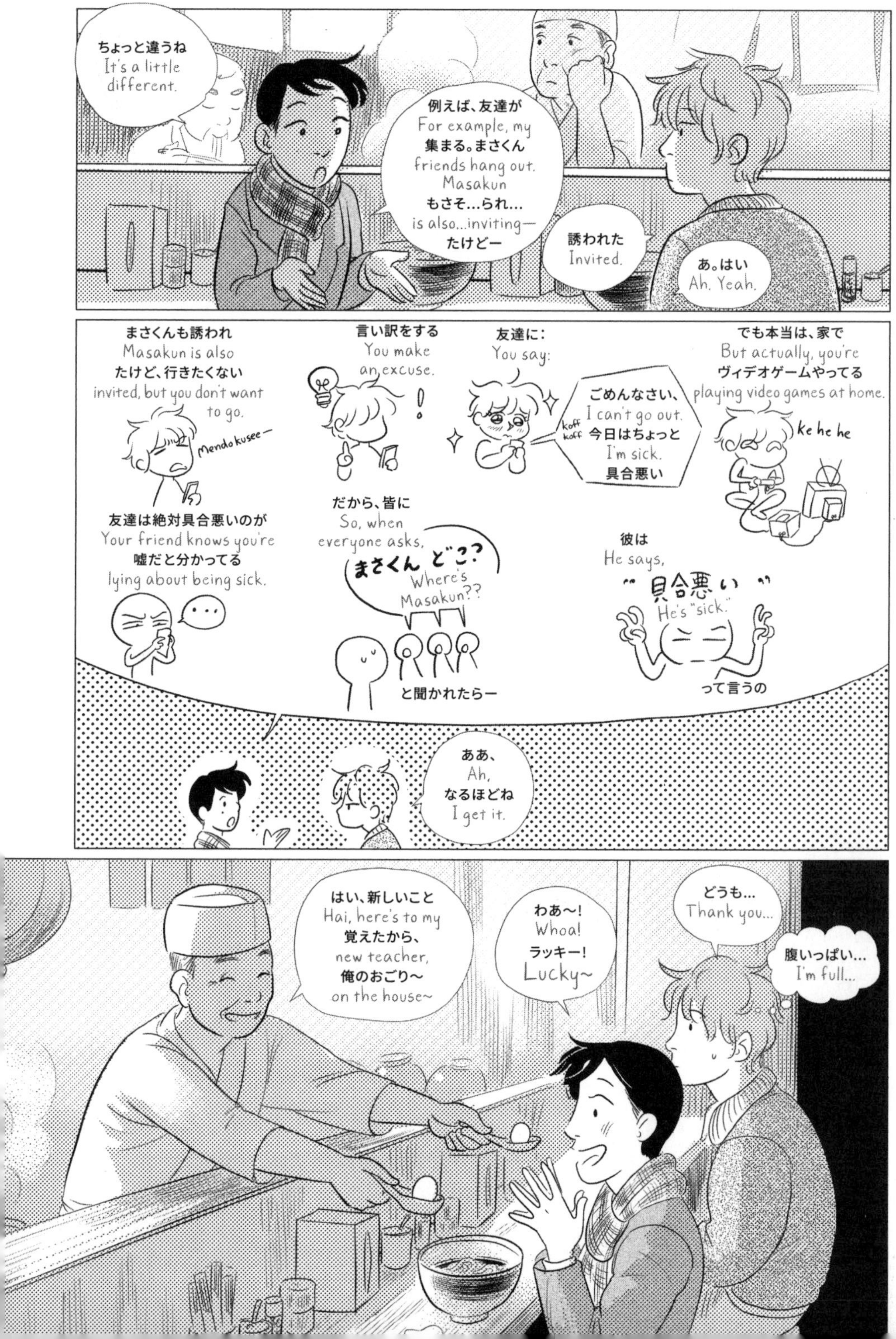
ちょっと違うね
It's a little different.
例えば、友達が
For example, my
集まる。まさくん
friends hang out. Masakun
もさそ…られ…
is also…inviting—
たけどー
誘われた
Invited.
あ。はい
Ah. Yeah.
まさくんも誘われ
Masakun is also
たけど、行きたくない
invited, but you don't want to go.
Mendokusee~
言い訳をする
You make an excuse.
友達に:
You say:
ごめんなさい、
I can't go out.
今日はちょっと
I'm sick.
具合悪い
koff koff
でも本当は、家で
But actually, you're
ヴィデオゲームやってる
playing video games at home.
ke he he
友達は絶対具合悪いのが
Your friend knows you're
嘘だと分かってる
lying about being sick.
…
だから、皆に
So, when everyone asks,
まさくん どこ?
Where's Masakun??
と聞かれたらー
彼は
He says,
"具合悪い"
He's "sick."
って言うの
ああ、
Ah,
なるほどね
I get it.
はい、新しいこと
Hai, here's to my
覚えたから、
new teacher,
俺のおごり~
on the house~
わあ~!
Whoa!
ラッキー!
Lucky~
どうも…
Thank you…
腹いっぱい…
I'm full…

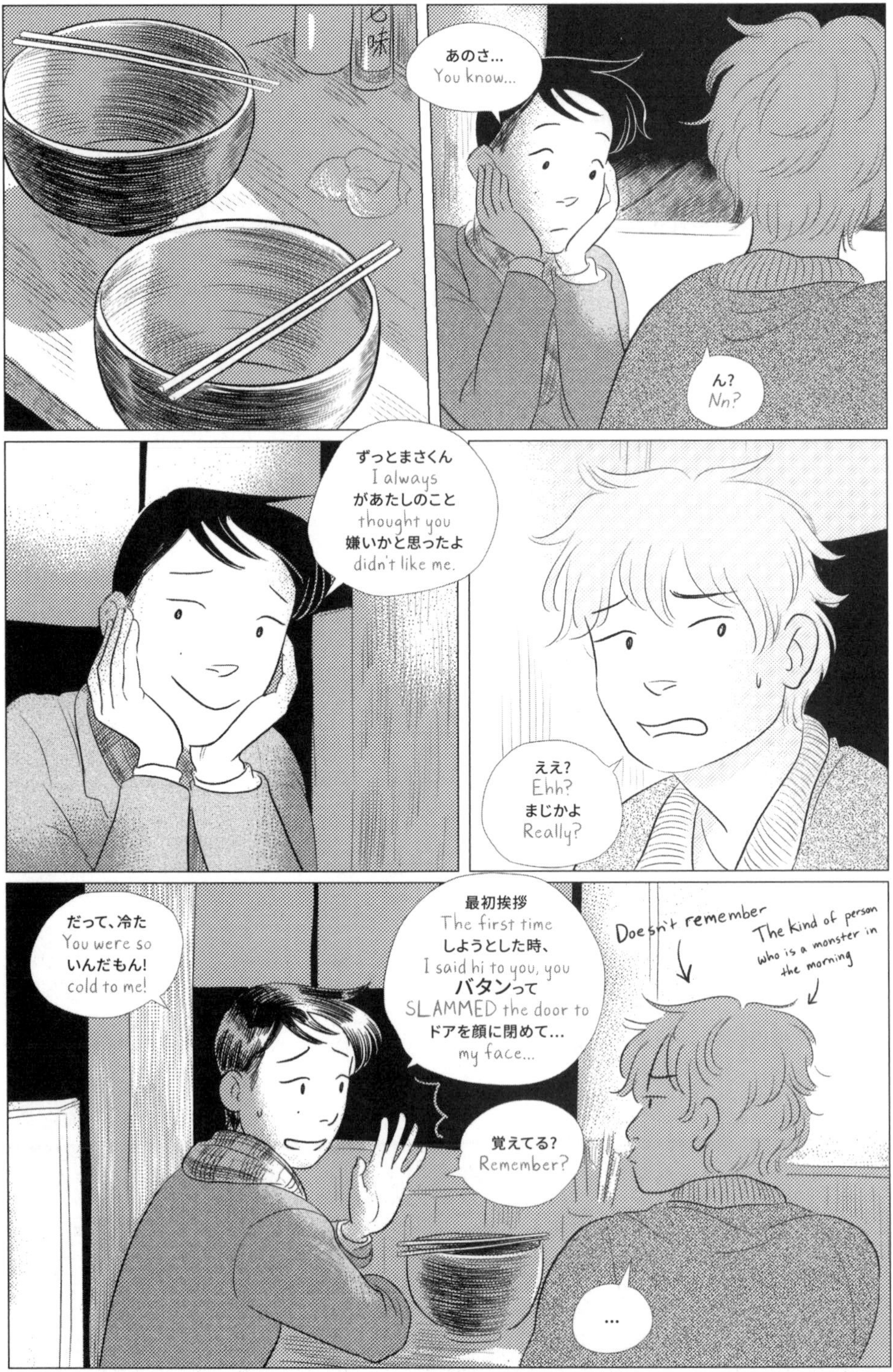
あのさ…
You know...
ん?
Nn?
ずっとまさくんがあたしのこと嫌いかと思ったよ
I always thought you didn't like me.
ええ?
Ehh?
まじかよ
Really?
だって、冷たいんだもん!
You were so cold to me!
最初挨拶しようとした時、バタンってドアを顔に閉めて…
The first time I said hi to you, you SLAMMED the door to my face...
覚えてる?
Remember?
Doesn't remember
The kind of person who is a monster in the morning
…

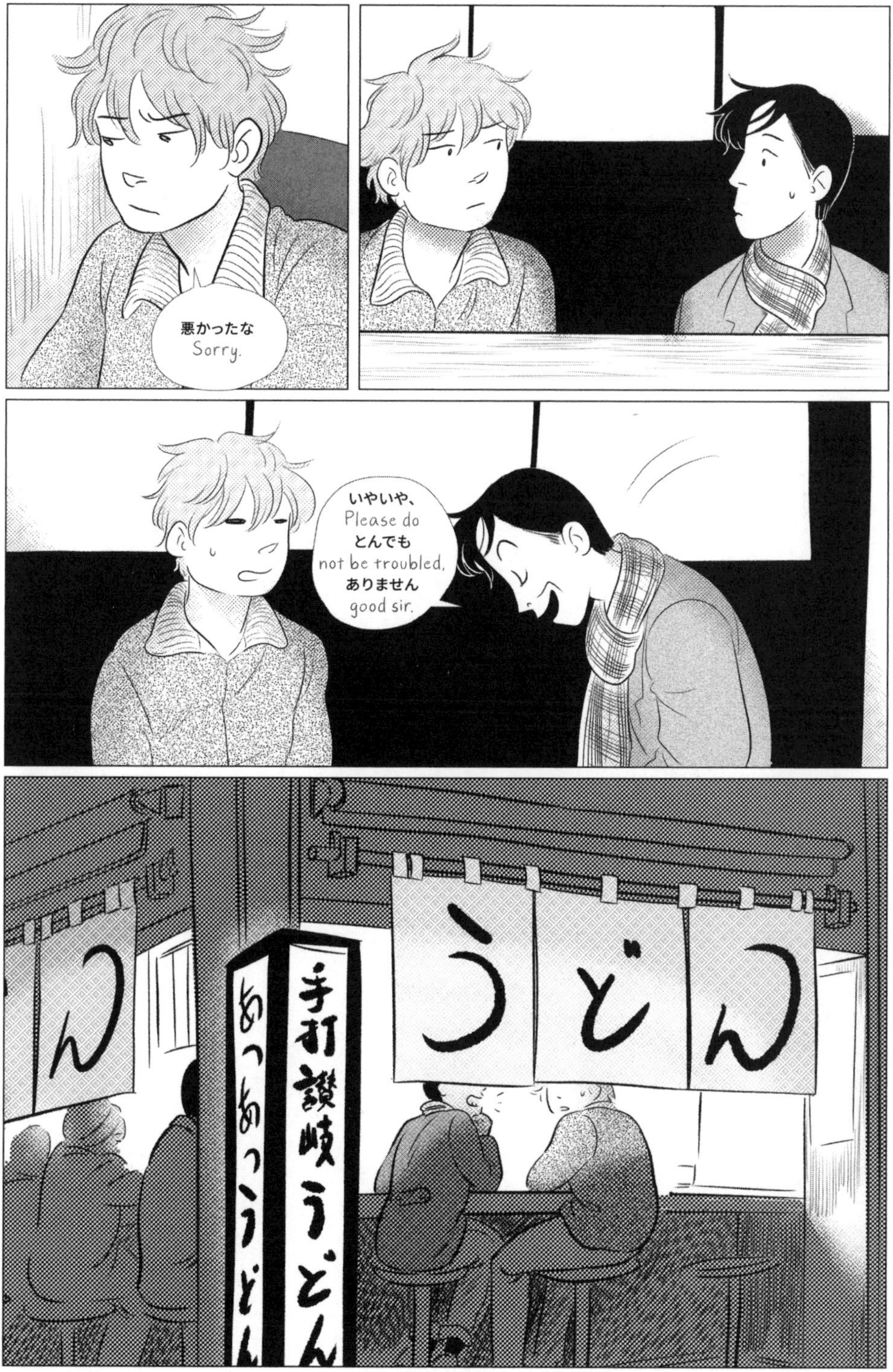

悪かったな
Sorry.
いやいや、
Please do
とんでも
not be troubled,
ありません
good sir.
うどん
手打讃岐うどん
あつあつうどん

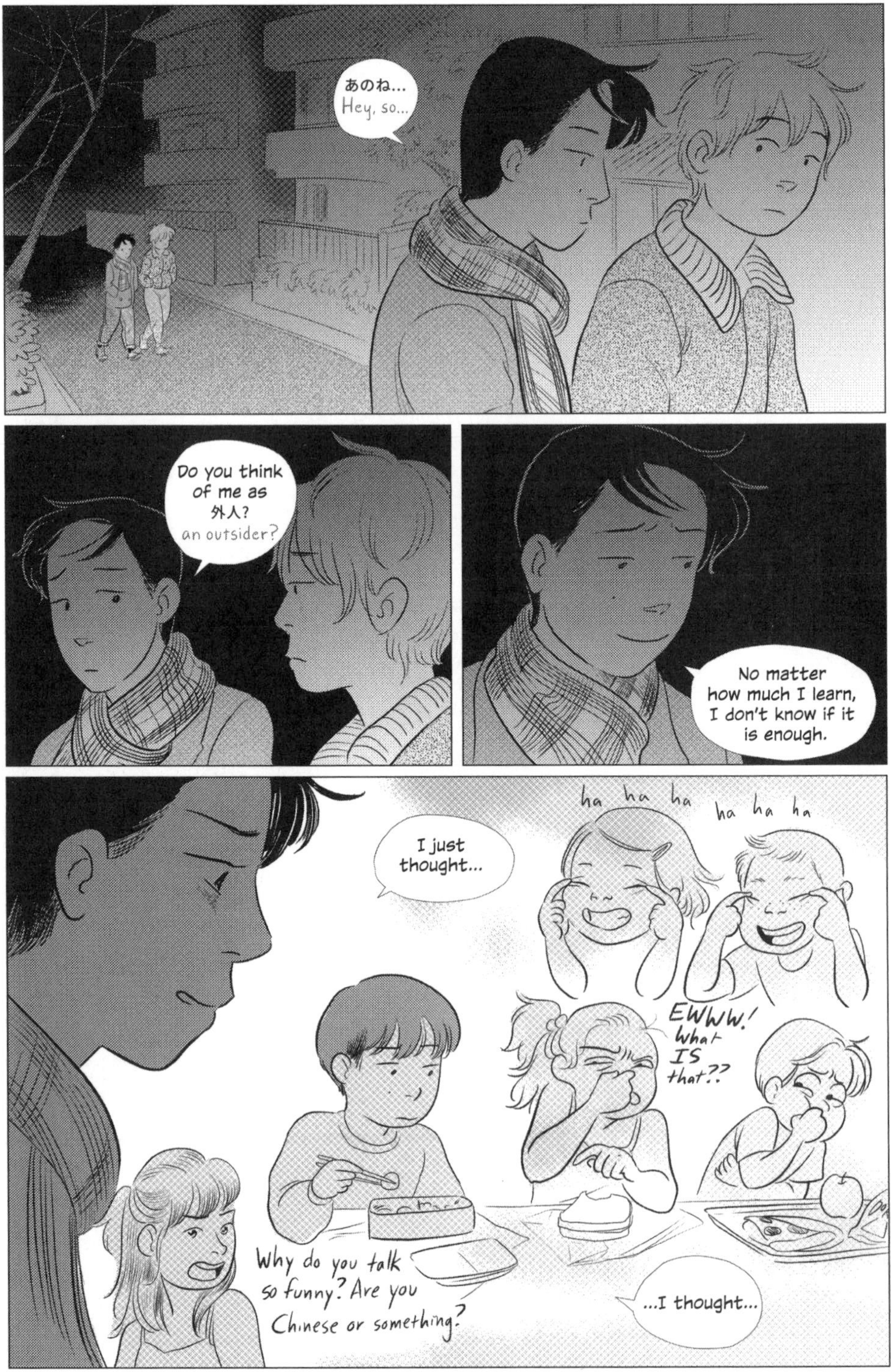
あのね…
Hey, so...
Do you think of me as 外人?
an outsider?
No matter how much I learn, I don't know if it is enough.
I just thought...
ha ha ha
ha ha ha
EWWW! What IS that??
Why do you talk so funny? Are you Chinese or something?
...I thought...

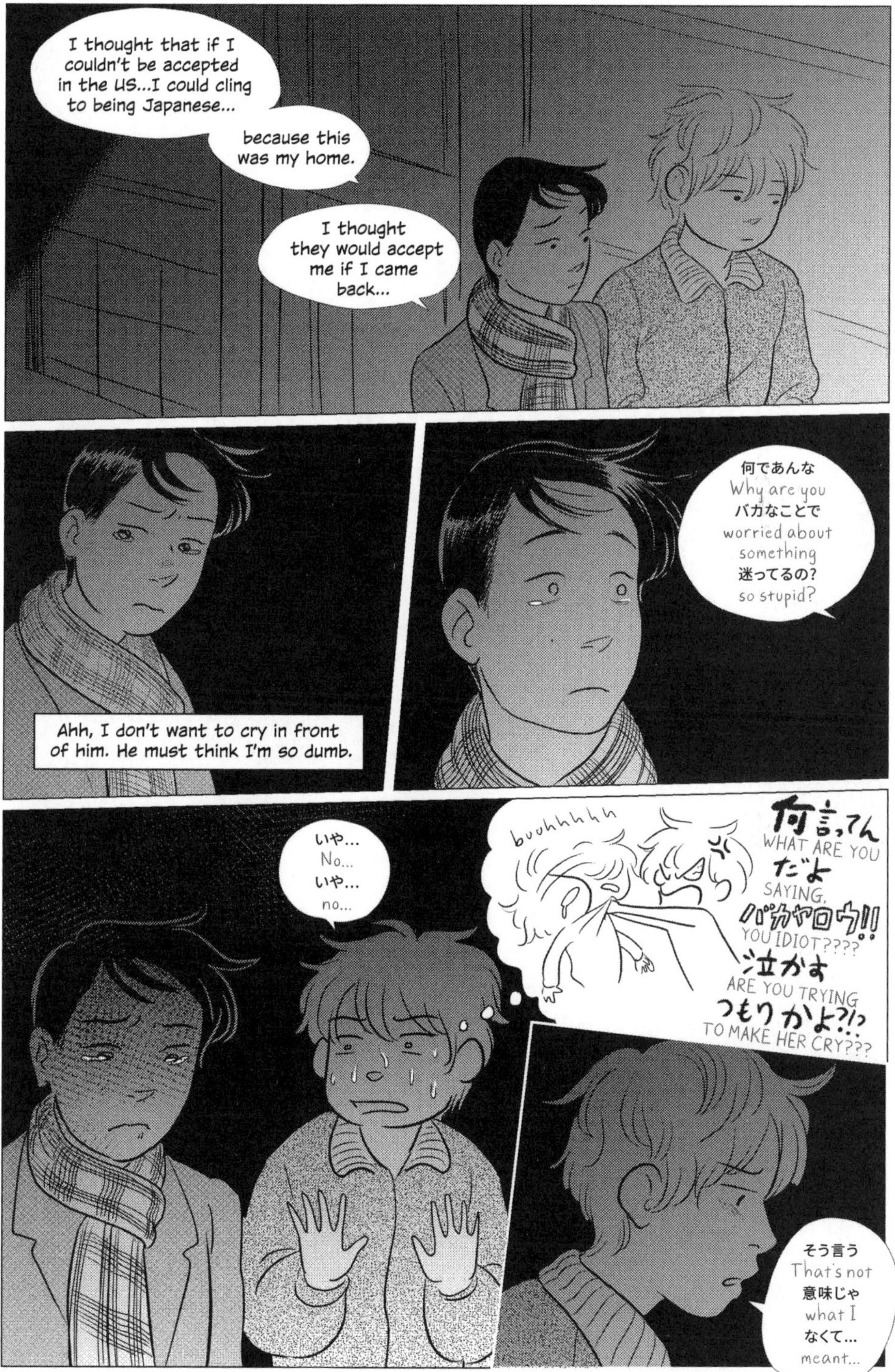

I thought that if I couldn't be accepted in the US...I could cling to being Japanese...
because this was my home.
I thought they would accept me if I came back...
Ahh, I don't want to cry in front of him. He must think I'm so dumb.
何であんな Why are you バカなことで worried about something 迷ってるの? so stupid?
いや... No... いや... no...
buuhhhhh
何言ってん WHAT ARE YOU だよ SAYING, バカヤロウ!! YOU IDIOT???? 泣かす ARE YOU TRYING つもりかよ?!? TO MAKE HER CRY???
そう言う That's not 意味じゃ what I なくて... meant...

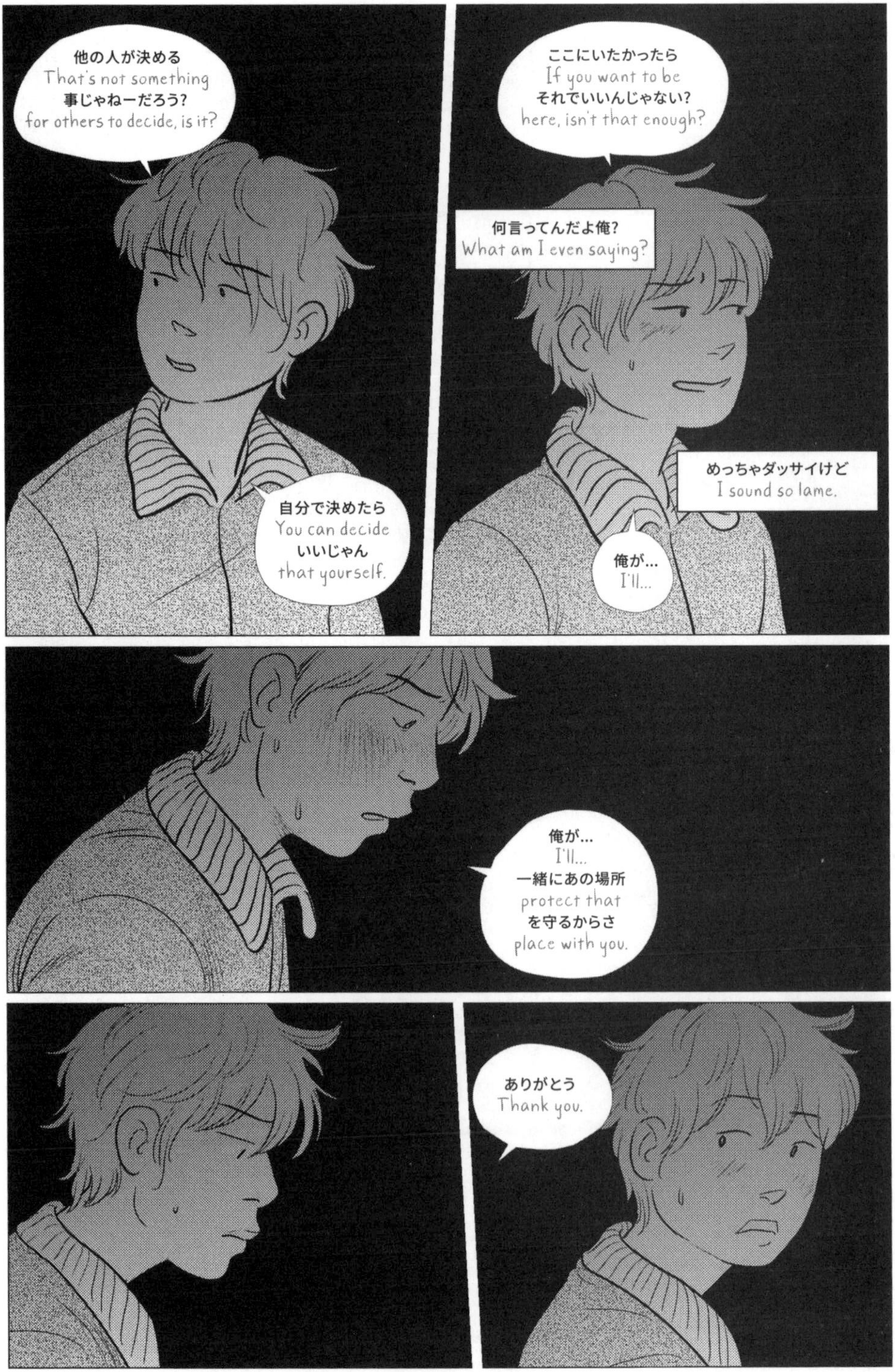

他の人が決める
That's not something
事じゃねーだろう?
for others to decide, is it?
自分で決めたら
You can decide
いいじゃん
that yourself.
ここにいたかったら
If you want to be
それでいいんじゃない?
here, isn't that enough?
何言ってんだよ俺?
What am I even saying?
めっちゃダッサイけど
I sound so lame.
俺が…
I'll…
俺が…
I'll…
一緒にあの場所
protect that
を守るからさ
place with you.
ありがとう
Thank you.

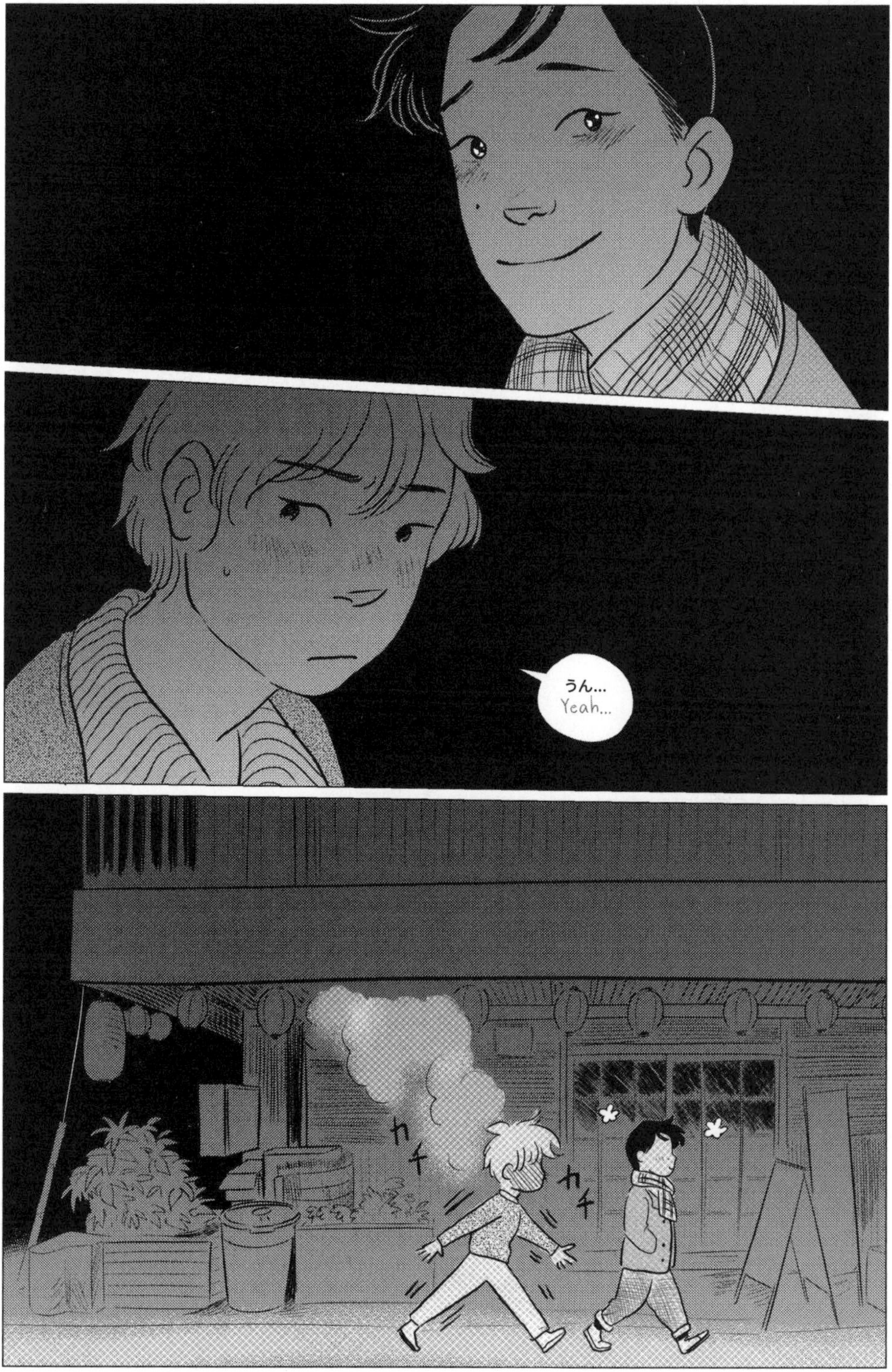
うん…
Yeah…
カチ
カチ

Chapter 13

Hatsumonde

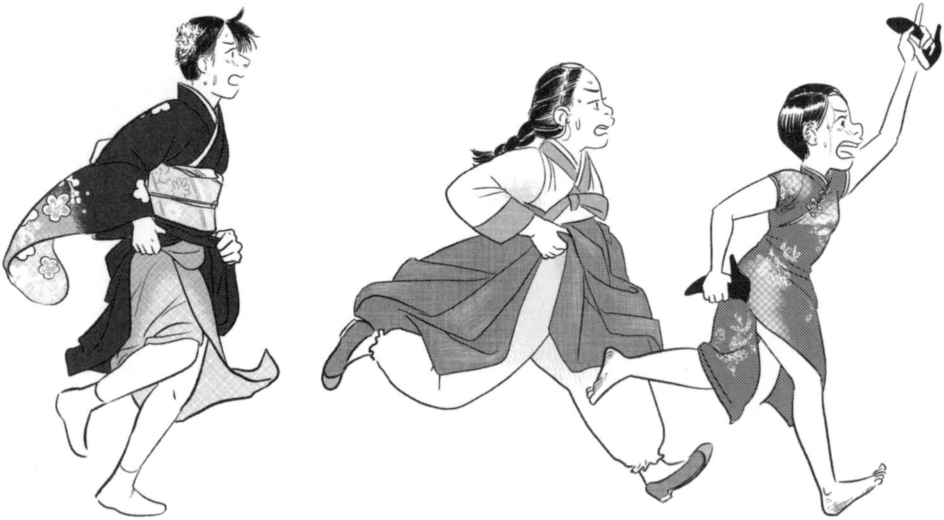

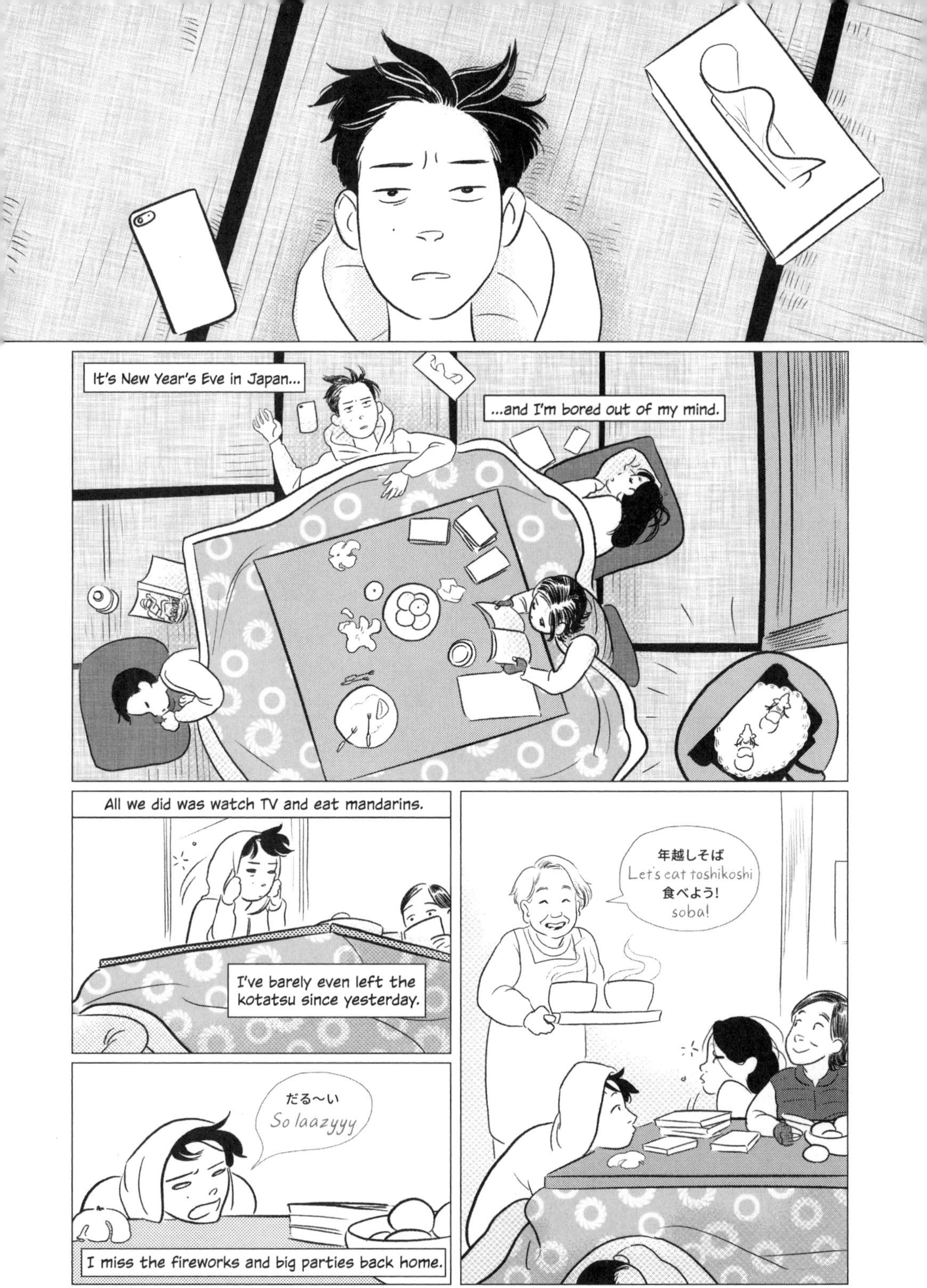
It's New Year's Eve in Japan...
...and I'm bored out of my mind.
All we did was watch TV and eat mandarins.
I've barely even left the kotatsu since yesterday.
だる～い
So laazyyy
I miss the fireworks and big parties back home.
年越しそば 食べよう!
Let's eat toshikoshi soba!

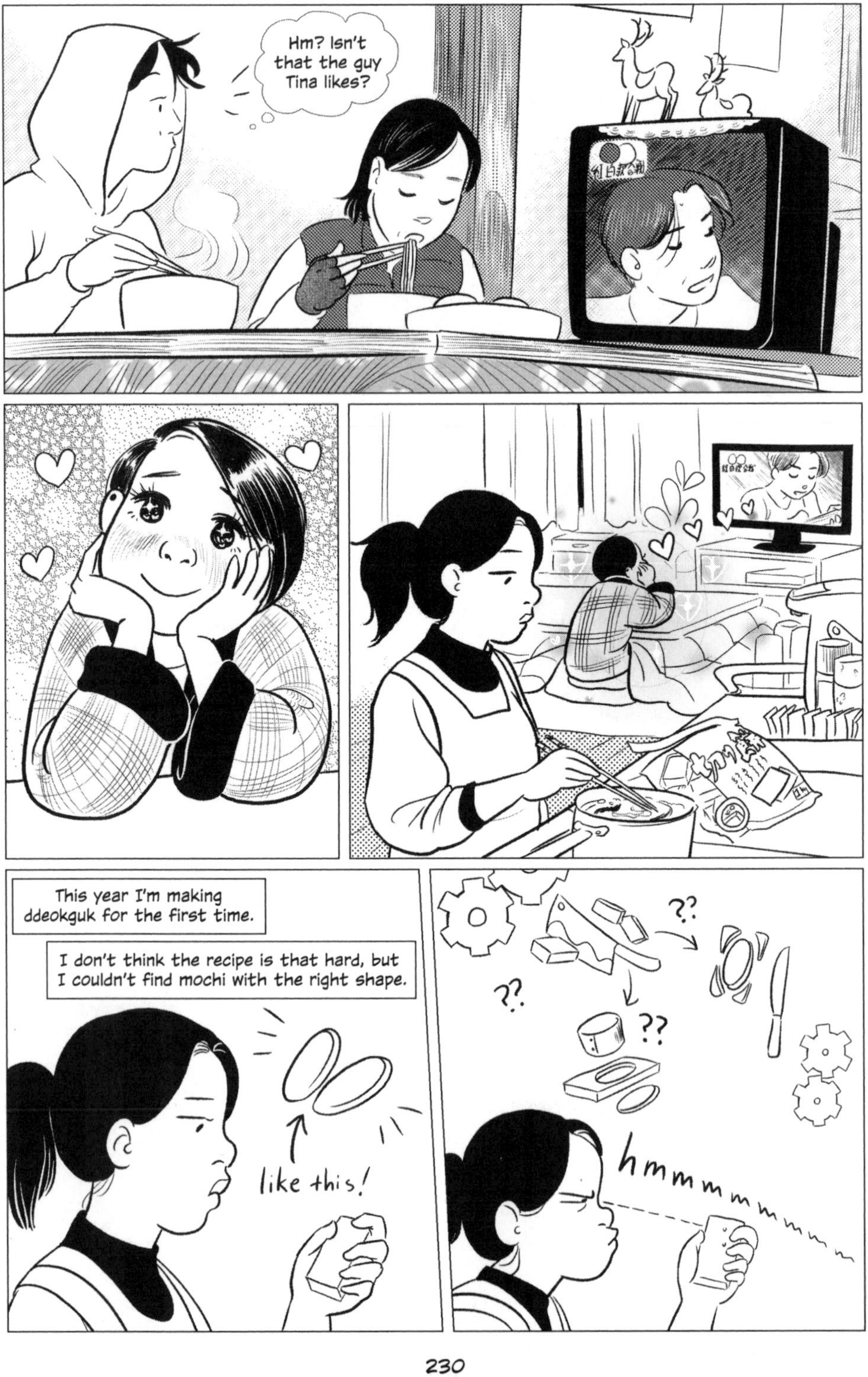
Hm? Isn't that the guy Tina likes?
This year I'm making ddeokguk for the first time.
I don't think the recipe is that hard, but I couldn't find mochi with the right shape.
like this!
??
??
??
hmmmmmmmmmm

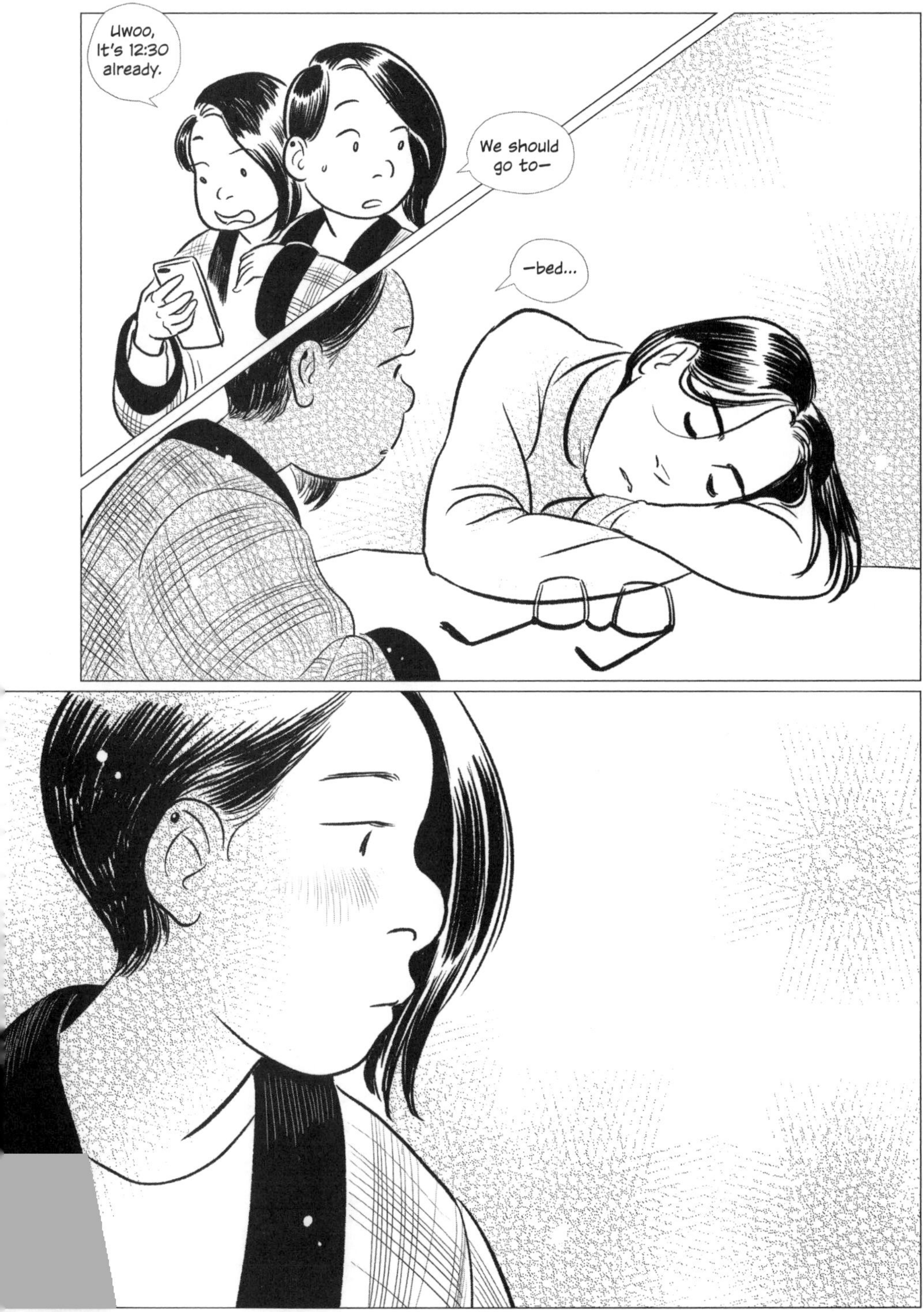
Uwoo,
It's 12:30
already.
We should
go to—
—bed...

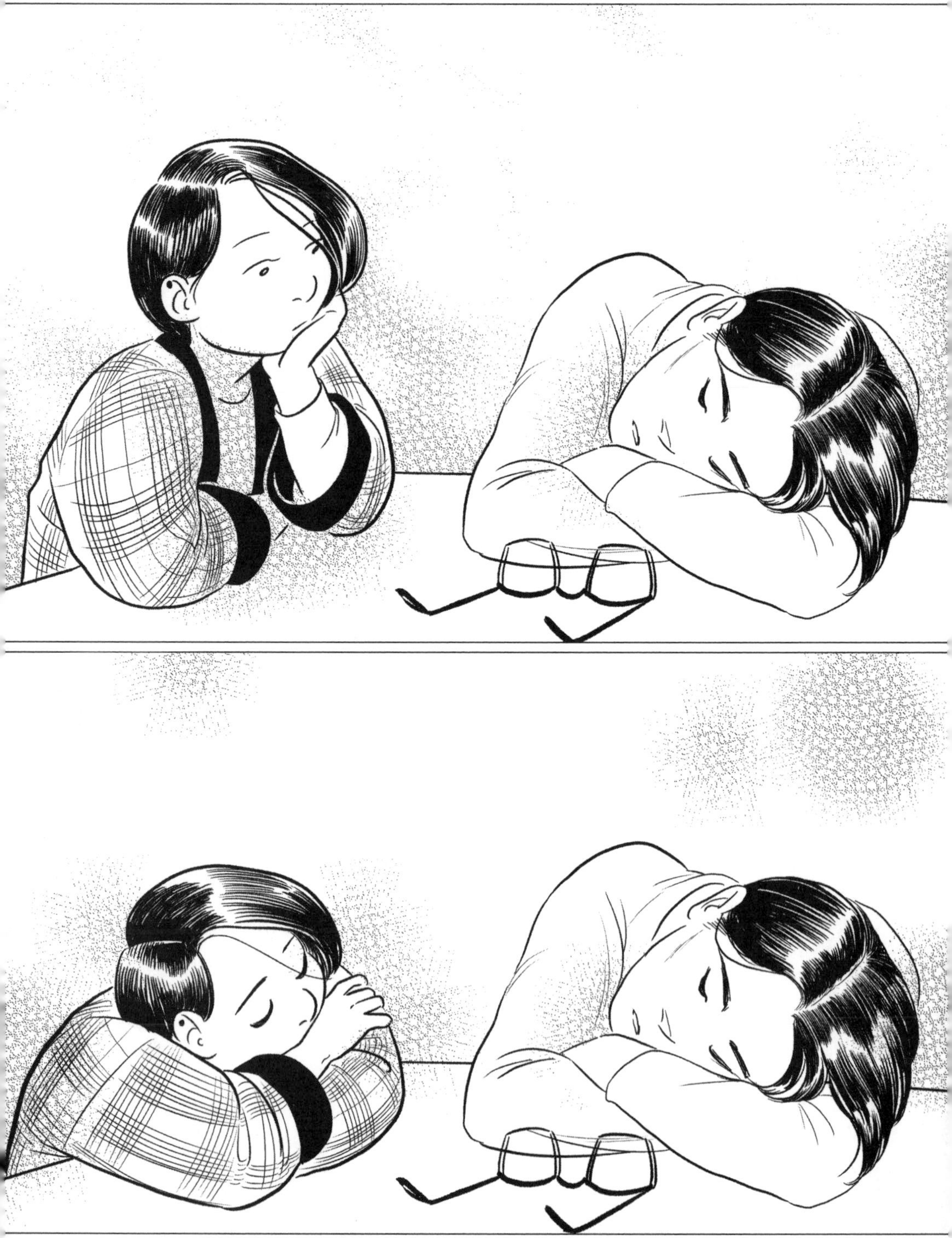

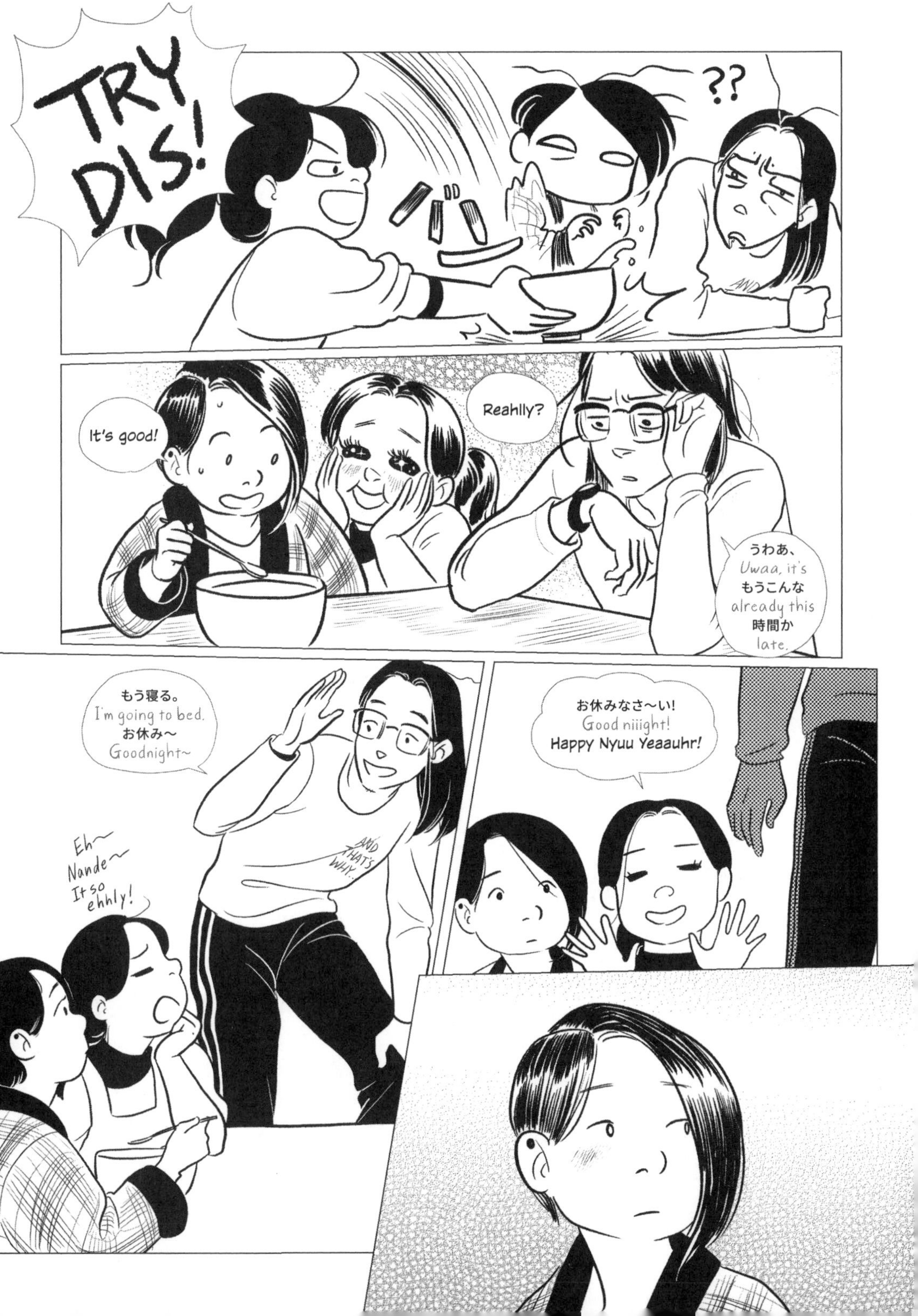

TRY DIS!
??
It's good!
Reahlly?
うわあ、
Uwaa, it's
もうこんな
already this
時間か
late.
もう寝る。
I'm going to bed.
お休み～
Goodnight~
Eh~
Nande~
It's so
ehhly!
お休みなさ～い!
Good niiight!
Happy Nyuu Yeaauhr!

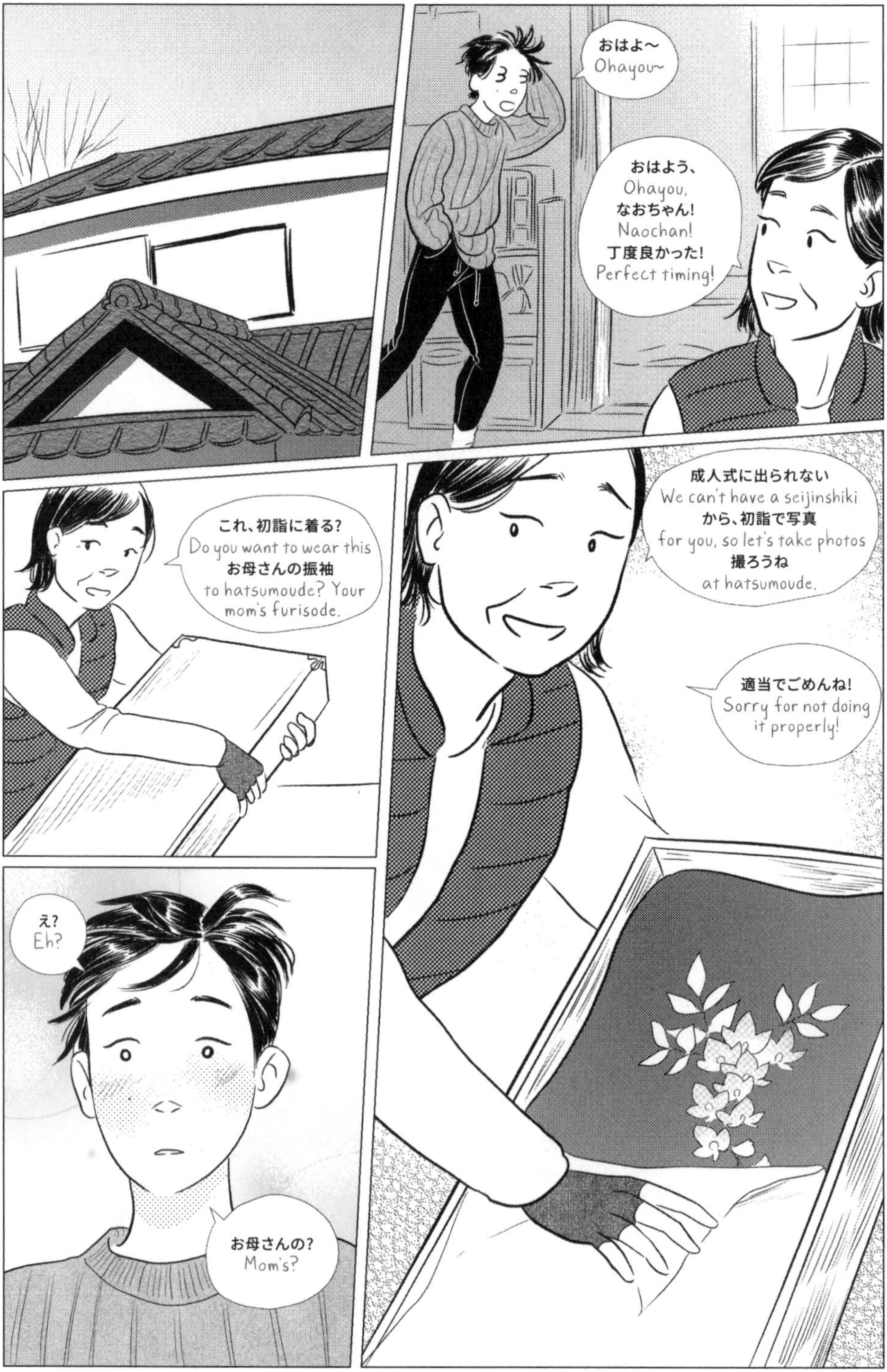
おはよ〜
Ohayou~
おはよう、
Ohayou,
なおちゃん!
Naochan!
丁度良かった!
Perfect timing!
これ、初詣に着る?
Do you want to wear this
お母さんの振袖
to hatsumoude? Your mom's furisode.
成人式に出られない
We can't have a seijinshiki
から、初詣で写真
for you, so let's take photos
撮ろうね
at hatsumoude.
適当でごめんね!
Sorry for not doing it properly!
え?
Eh?
お母さんの?
Mom's?

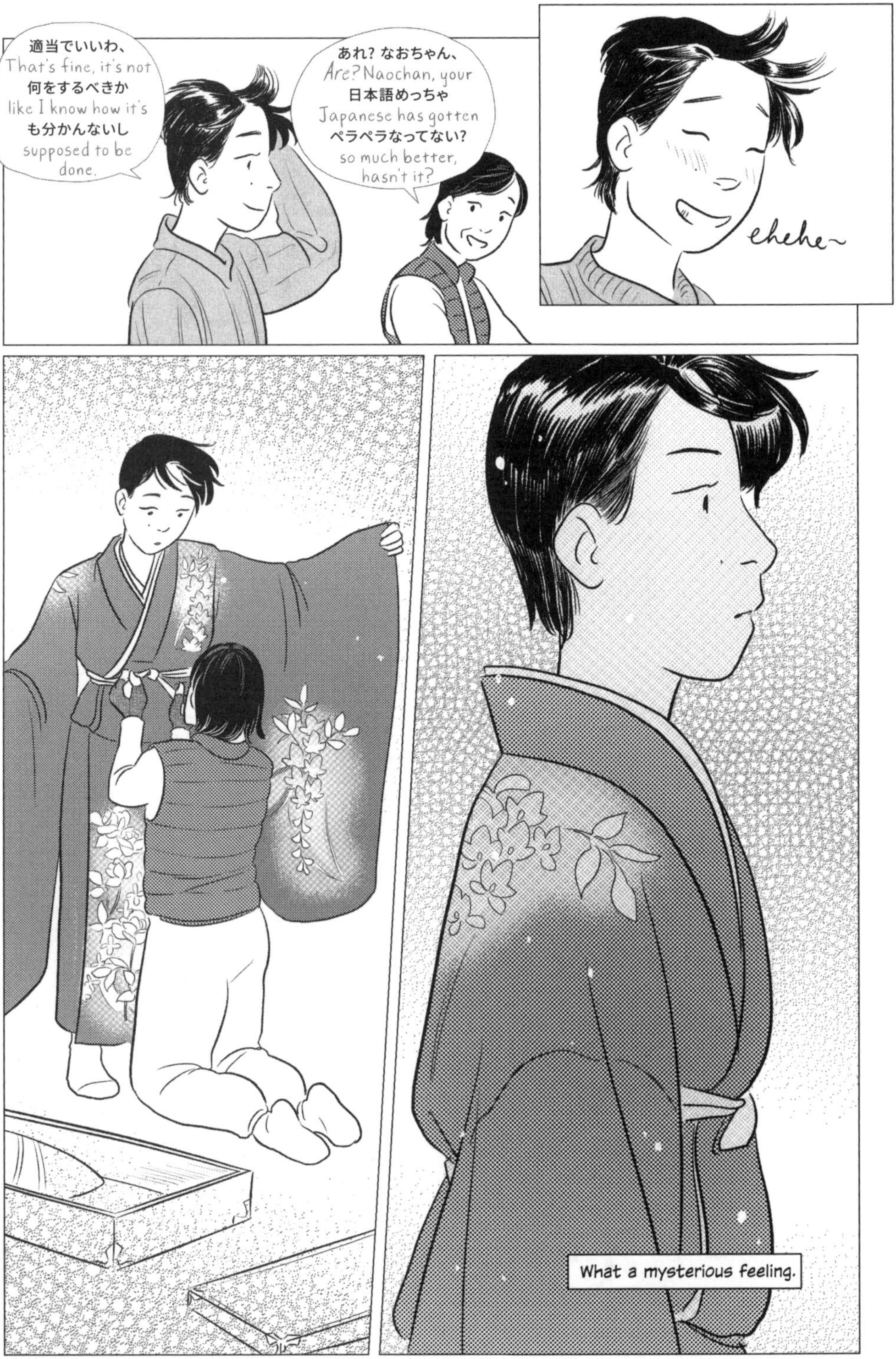

適当でいいわ、
That's fine, it's not
何をするべきか
like I know how it's
も分かんないし
supposed to be done.
あれ? なおちゃん、
Are? Naochan, your
日本語めっちゃ
Japanese has gotten
ペラペラなってない?
so much better, hasn't it?
ehehe~
What a mysterious feeling.

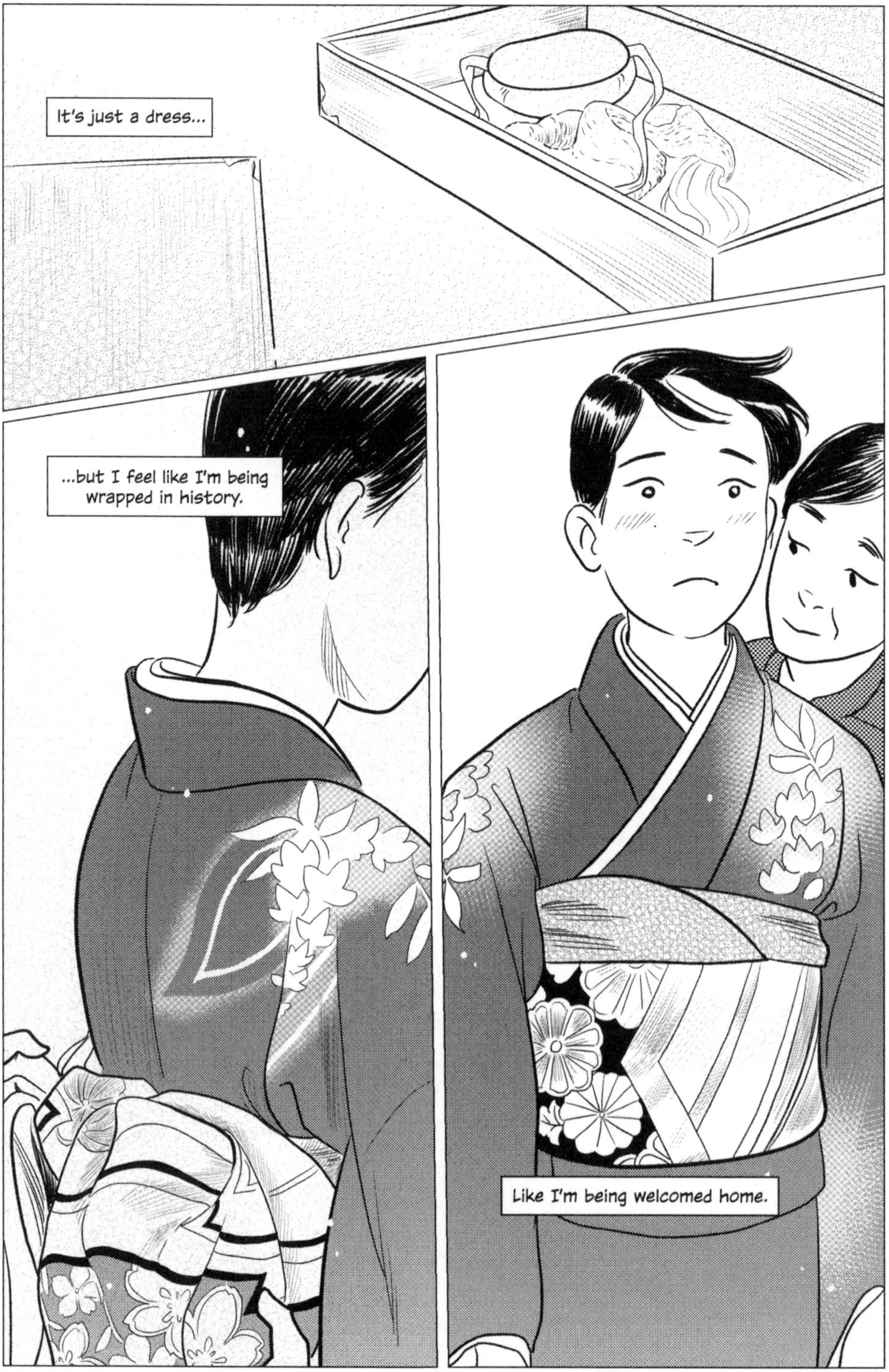
It's just a dress...
...but I feel like I'm being wrapped in history.
Like I'm being welcomed home.

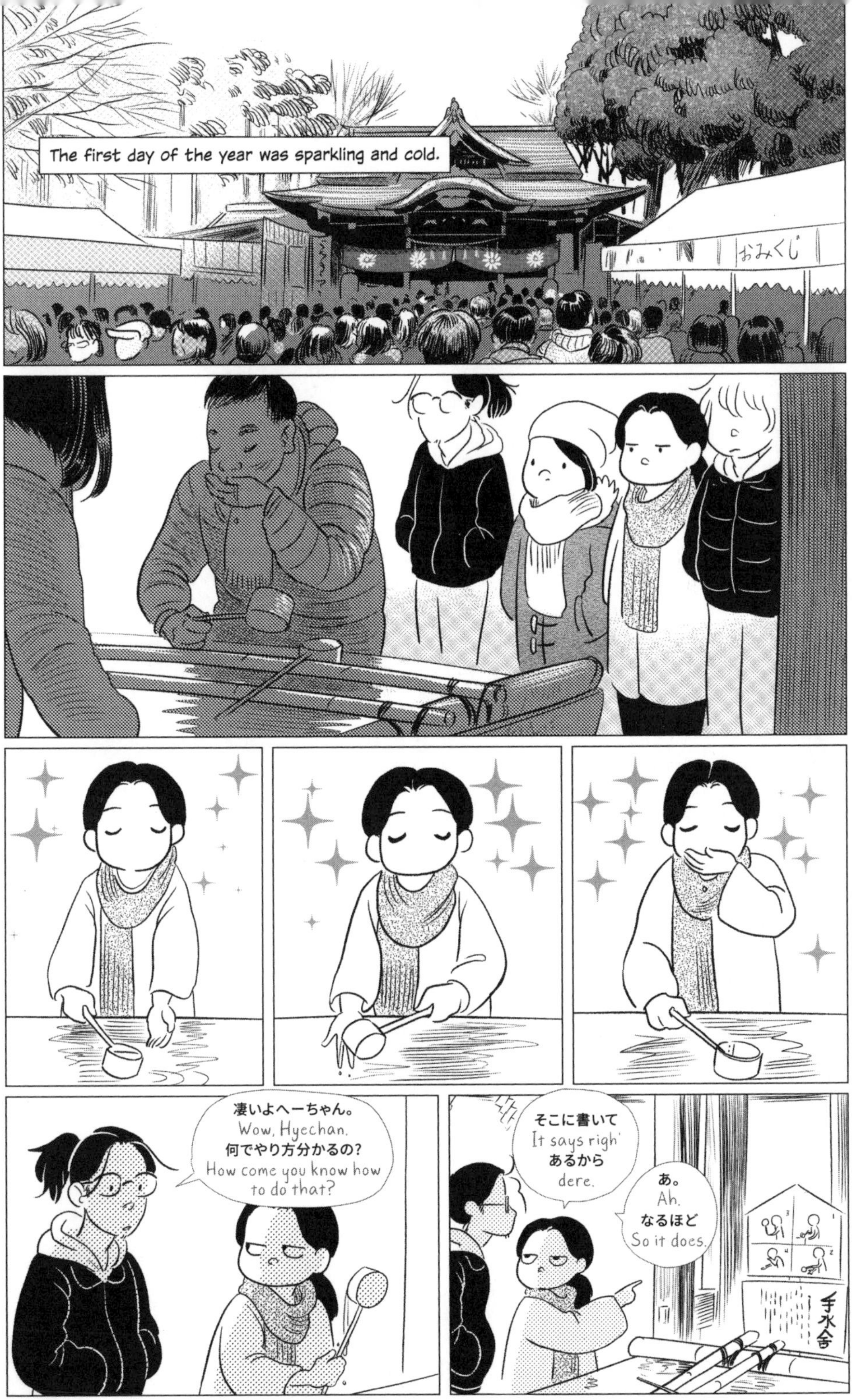
The first day of the year was sparkling and cold.
おみくじ
凄いよへーちゃん。
Wow, Hyechan.
何でやり方分かるの?
How come you know how to do that?
そこに書いて
It says righ'
あるから
dere.
あ。
Ah.
なるほど
So it does.
手水舎

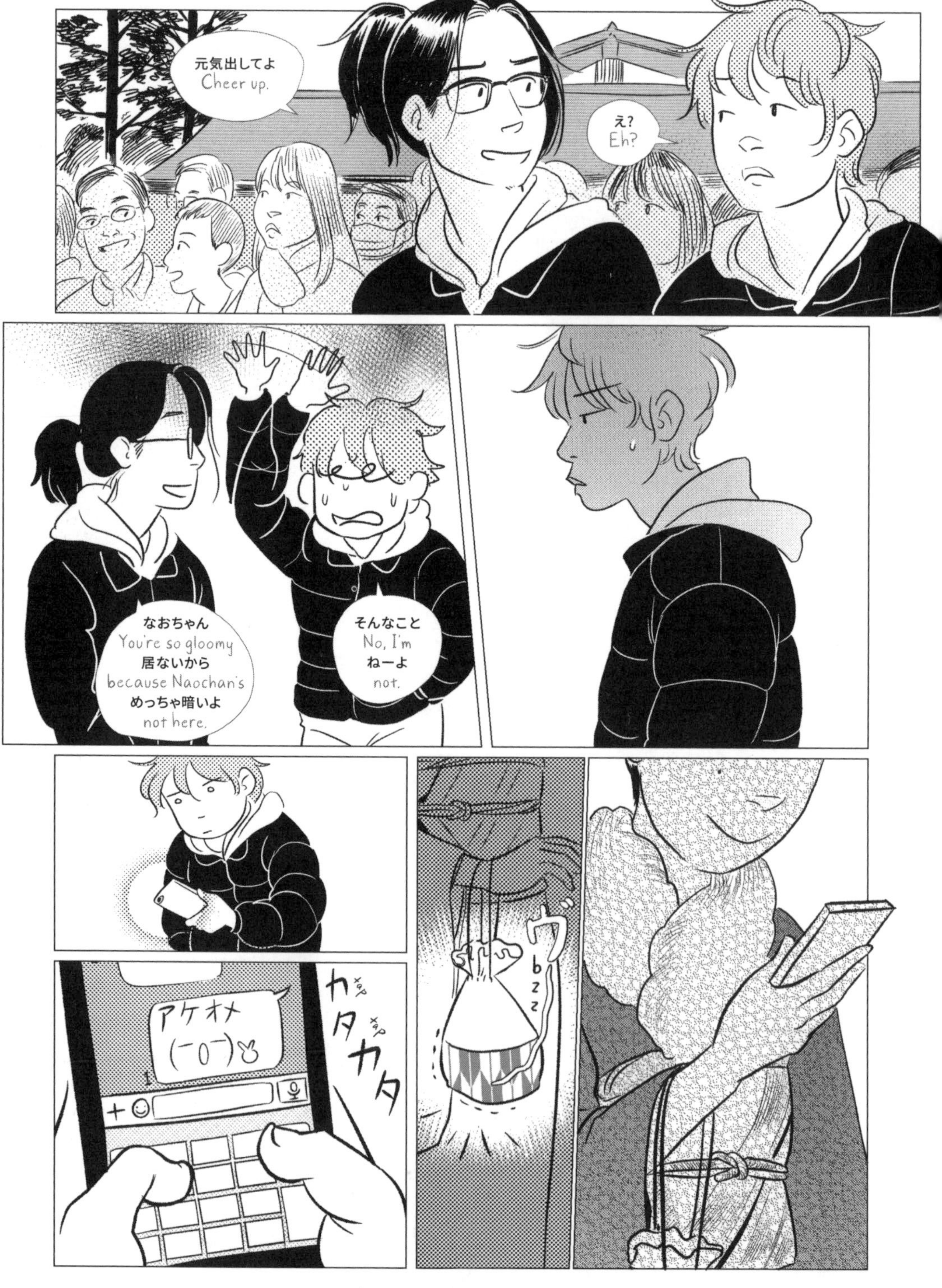
元気出してよ
Cheer up.
え?
Eh?
なおちゃん
You're so gloomy
居ないから
because Naochan's
めっちゃ暗いよ
not here.
そんなこと
No, I'm
ねーよ
not.
アケオメ
(¯▽¯)
カタ カタ カタ
ウ
bzz

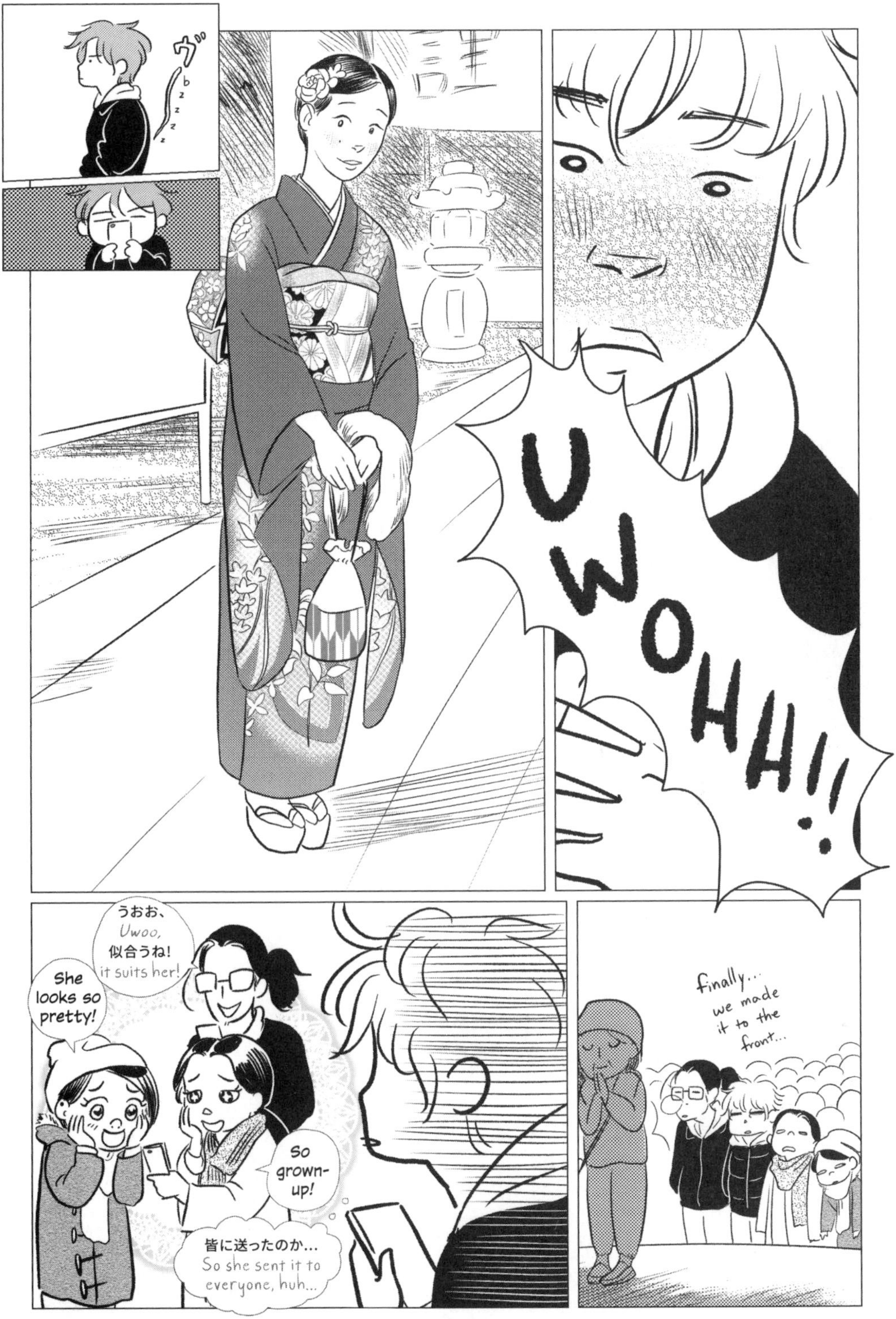
ヴ
bzzzz
UWOHH!!
うおお、
Uwoo,
似合うね!
it suits her!
She looks so pretty!
So grown-up!
皆に送ったのか…
So she sent it to everyone, huh…
finally… we made it to the front…

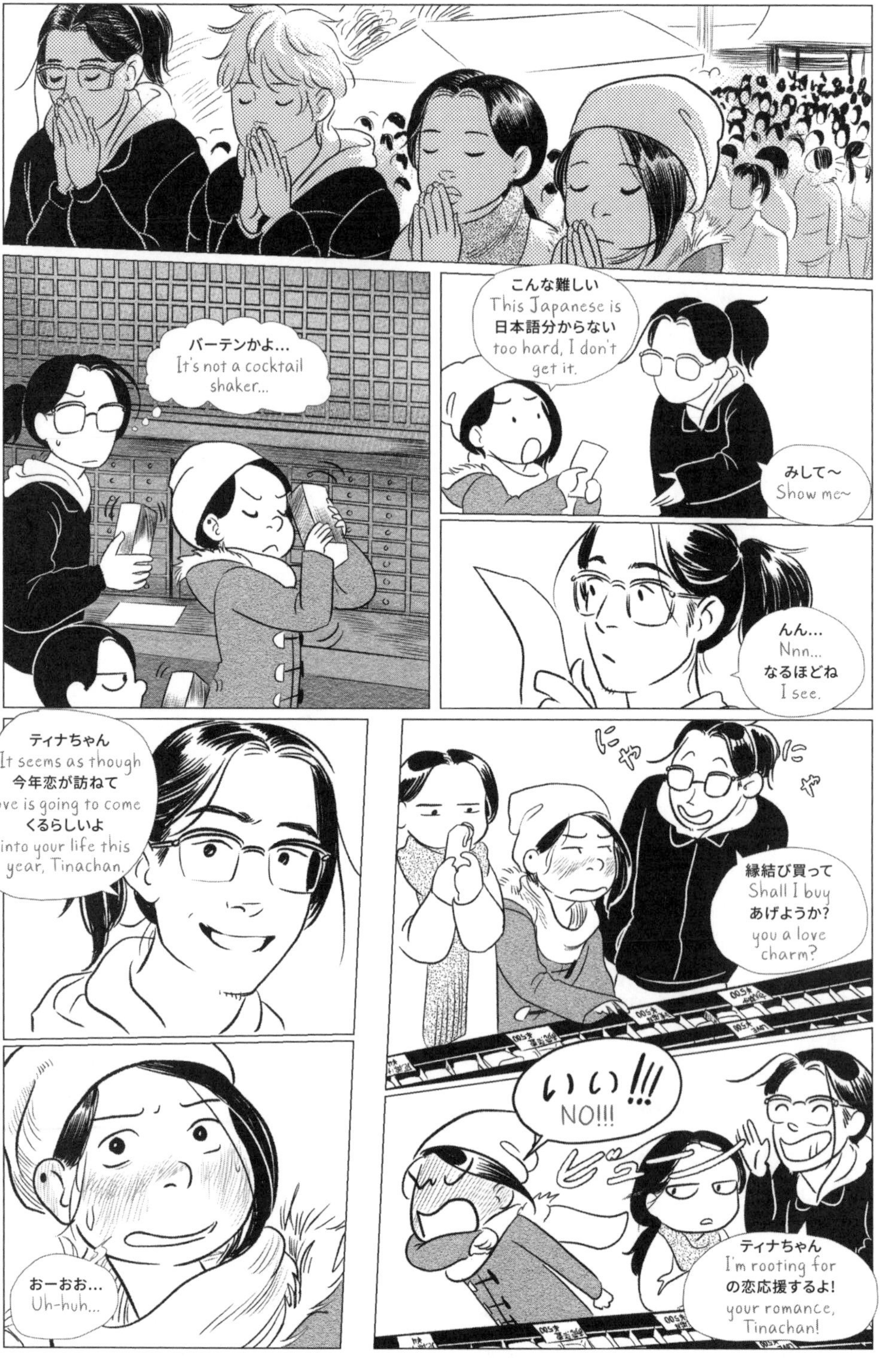

バーテンかよ… It's not a cocktail shaker...
こんな難しい 日本語分からない This Japanese is too hard, I don't get it.
みして~ Show me~
んん… Nnn... なるほどね I see.
ティナちゃん 今年恋が訪ねて くるらしいよ It seems as though love is going to come into your life this year, Tinachan.
縁結び買って あげようか? Shall I buy you a love charm?
おーおお… Uh-huh...
いい!!! NO!!!
ティナちゃん の恋応援するよ! I'm rooting for your romance, Tinachan!

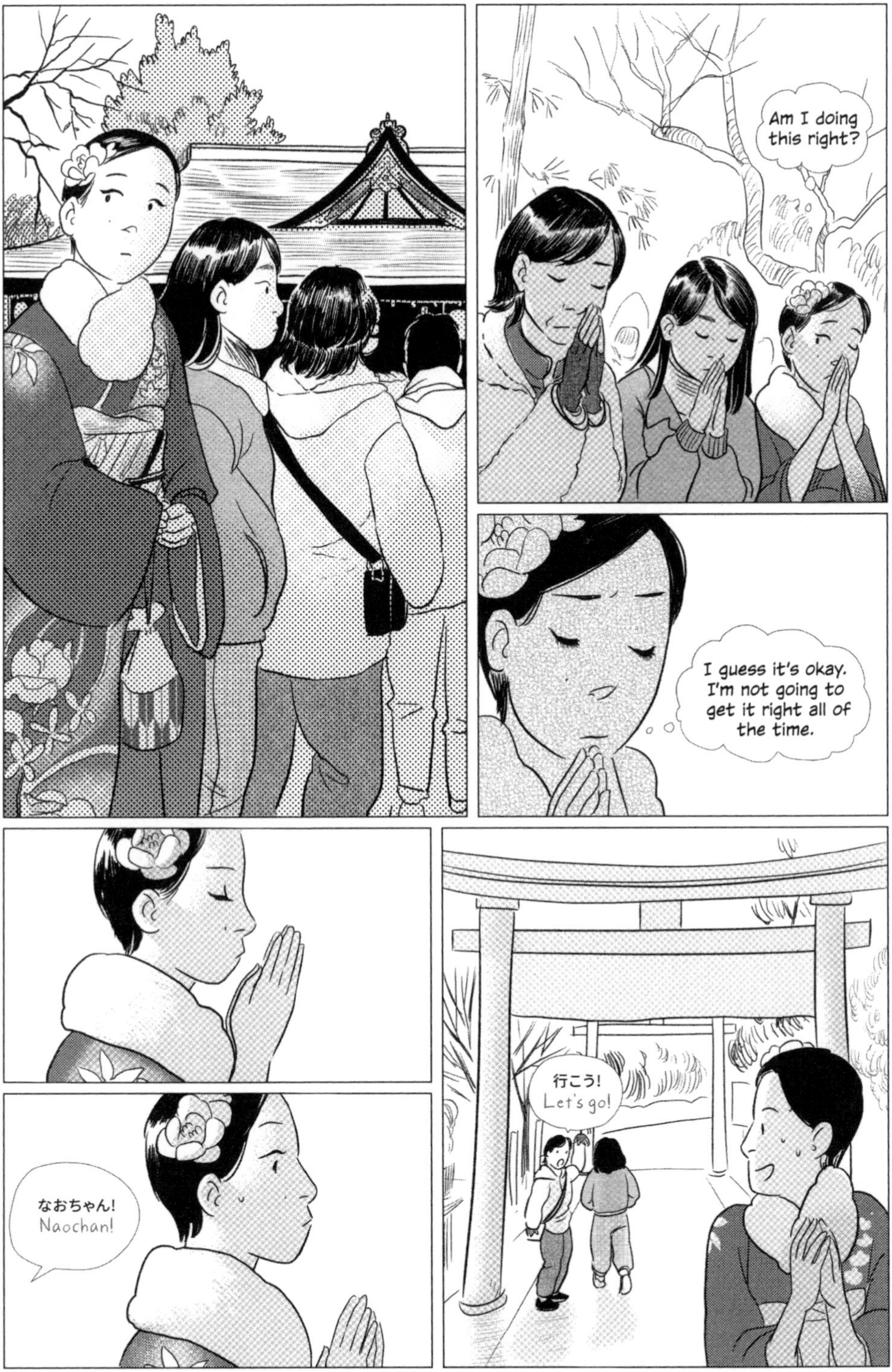
Am I doing this right?
I guess it's okay. I'm not going to get it right all of the time.
なおちゃん! Naochan!
行こう! Let's go!

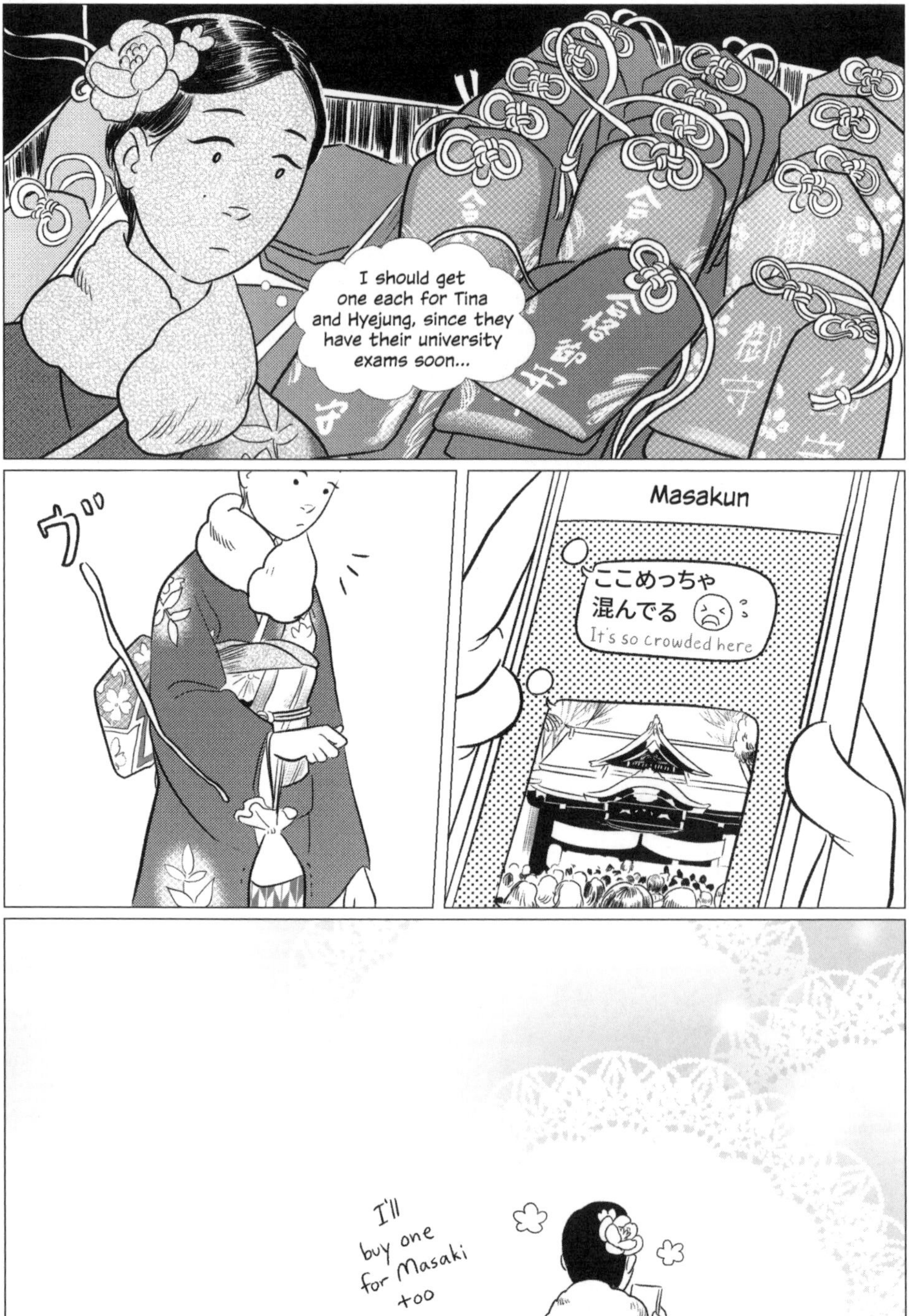
I should get one each for Tina and Hyejung, since they have their university exams soon...
ヴ
Masakun
ここめっちゃ混んでる
It's so crowded here
I'll buy one for Masaki too

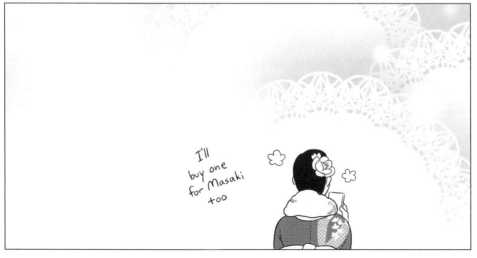

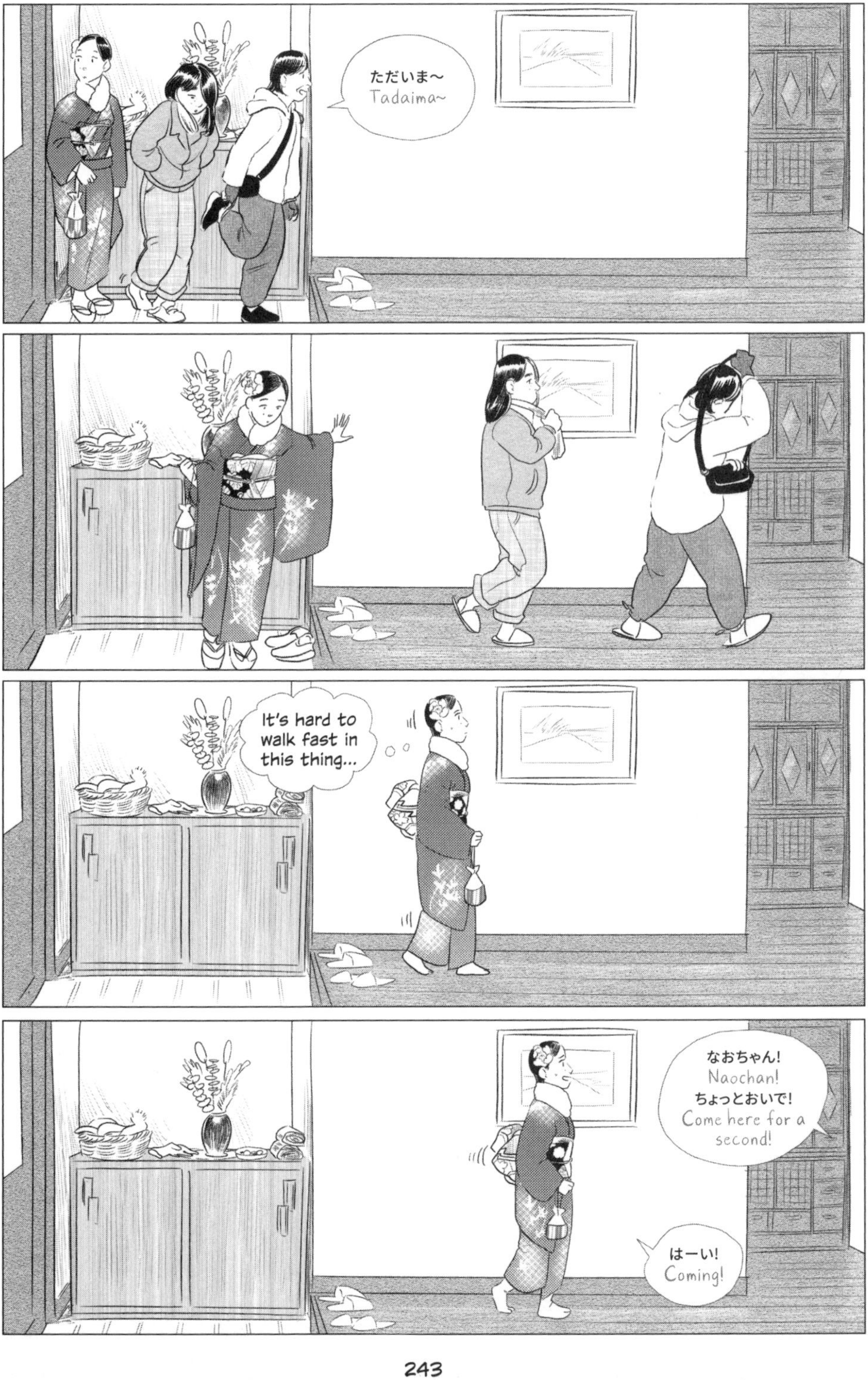
ただいま～
Tadaima~
It's hard to walk fast in this thing...
なおちゃん!
Naochan!
ちょっとおいで!
Come here for a second!
はーい!
Coming!

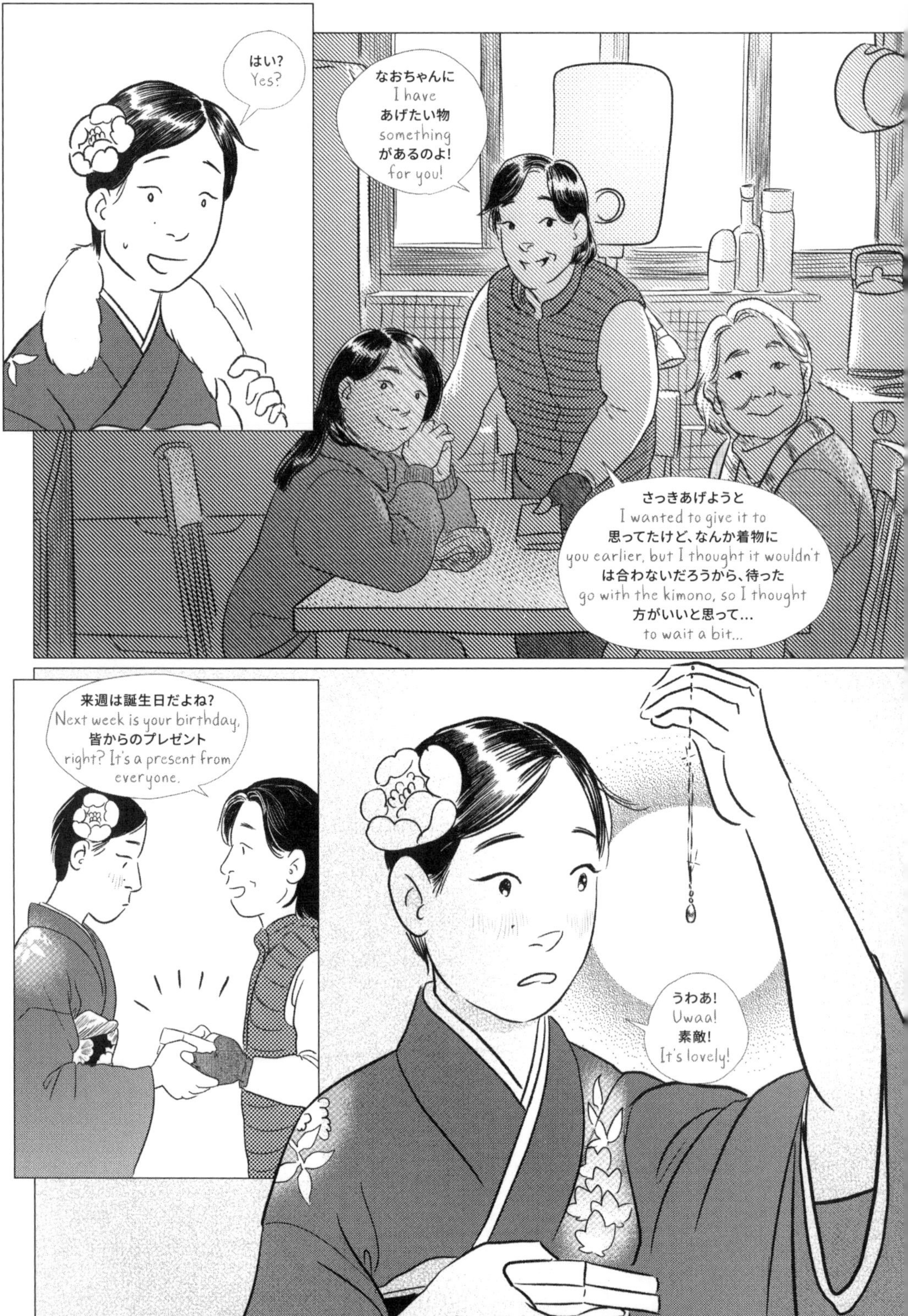
はい?
Yes?
なおちゃんに
I have
あげたい物
something
があるのよ!
for you!
さっきあげようと
I wanted to give it to
思ってたけど、なんか着物に
you earlier, but I thought it wouldn't
は合わないだろうから、待った
go with the kimono, so I thought
方がいいと思って…
to wait a bit...
来週は誕生日だよね?
Next week is your birthday,
皆からのプレゼント
right? It's a present from
everyone.
うわあ!
Uwaa!
素敵!
It's lovely!

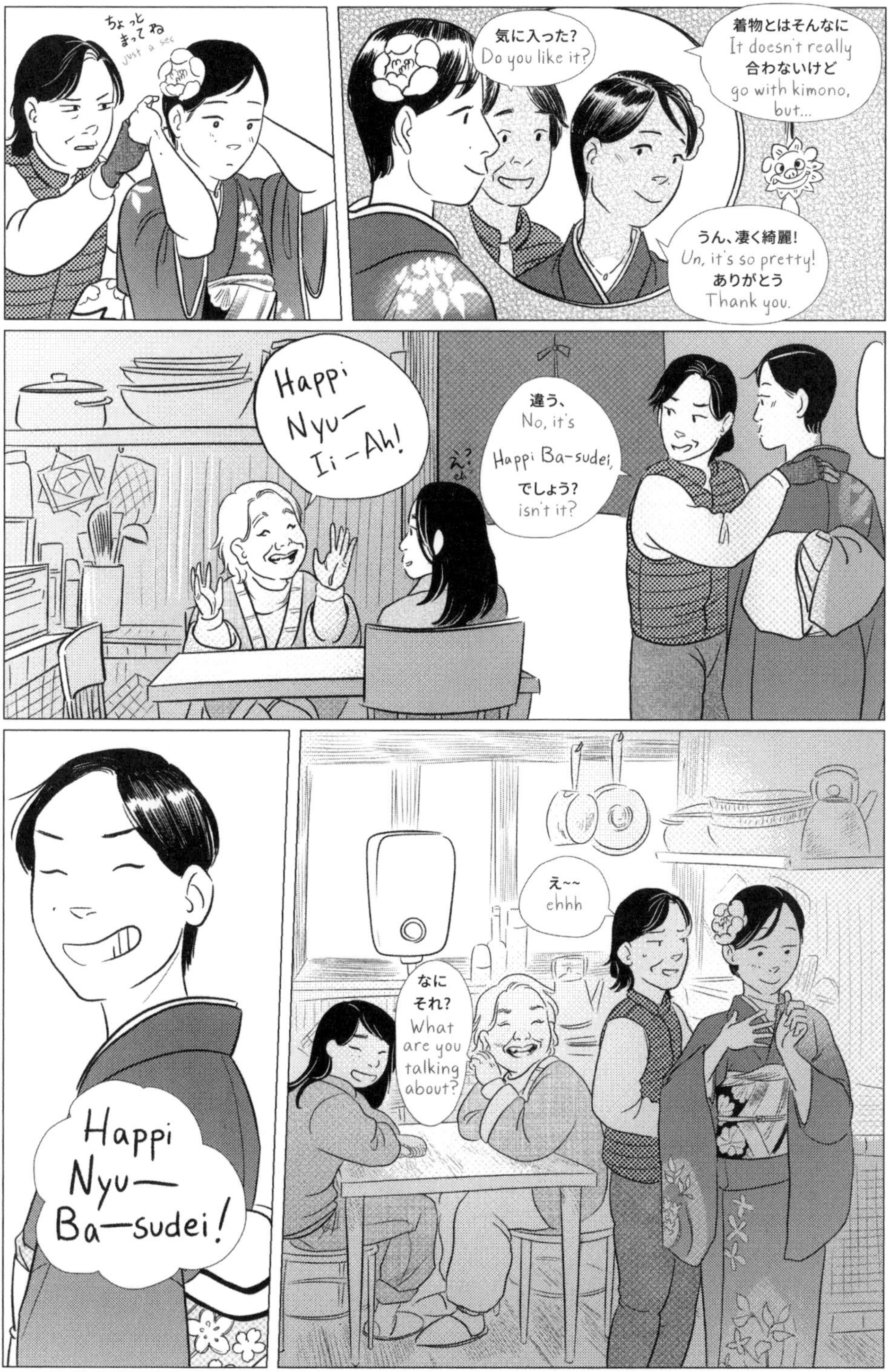
ちょっとまってね
Just a sec
気に入った?
Do you like it?
着物とはそんなに
It doesn't really
合わないけど
go with kimono, but...
うん、凄く綺麗!
Un, it's so pretty!
ありがとう
Thank you.
Happi Nyu— Ii—Ah!
え?
違う、
No, it's
Happi Ba-sudei,
でしょう?
isn't it?
Happi Nyu— Ba—sudei!
え~~
ehhh
なにそれ?
What are you talking about?

Chapter 14
Gong Xi Fa Cai

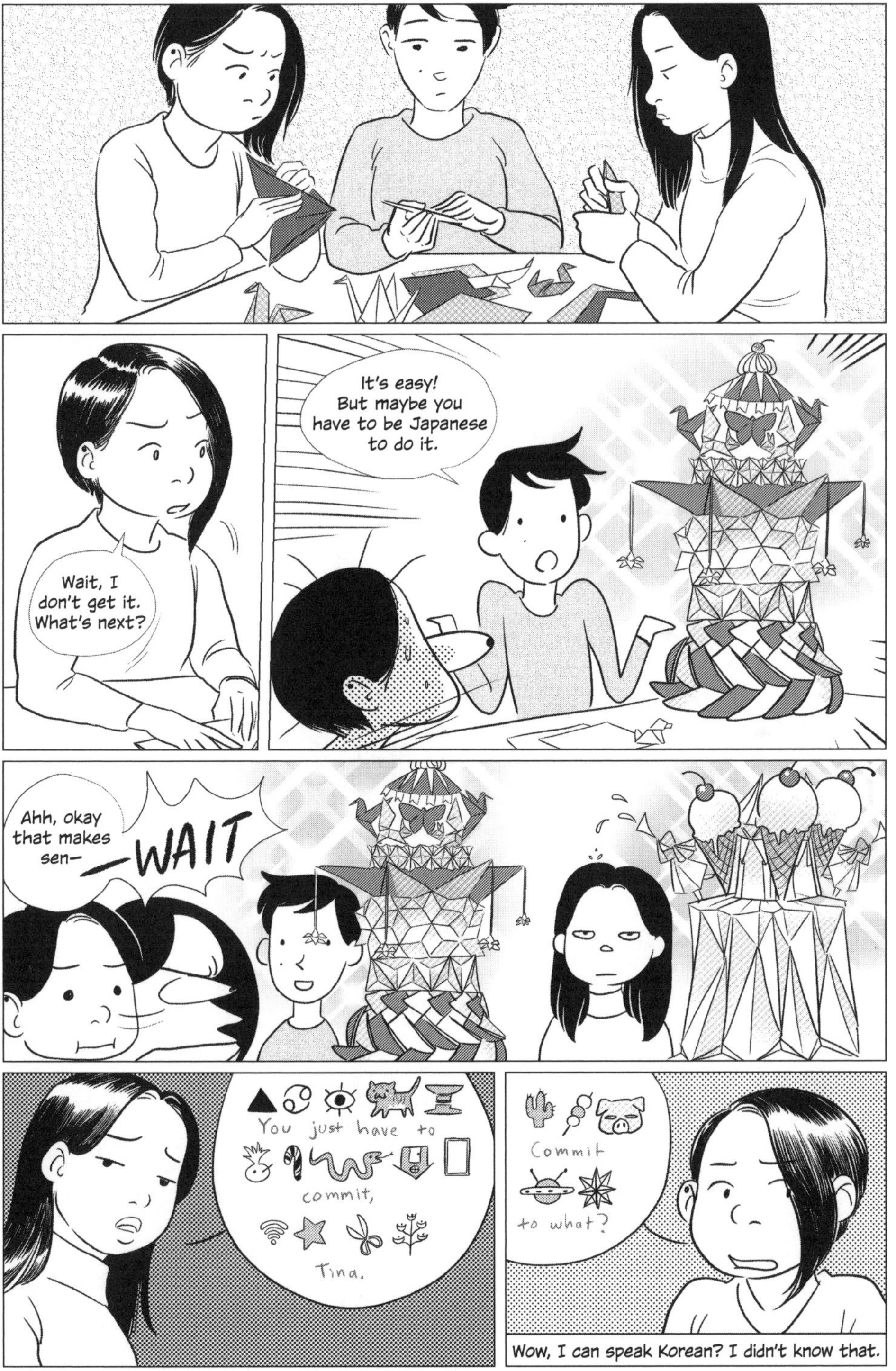
Wait, I don't get it. What's next?
It's easy! But maybe you have to be Japanese to do it.
Ahh, okay that makes sen—
—WAIT
You just have to commit, Tina.
Commit to what?
Wow, I can speak Korean? I didn't know that.

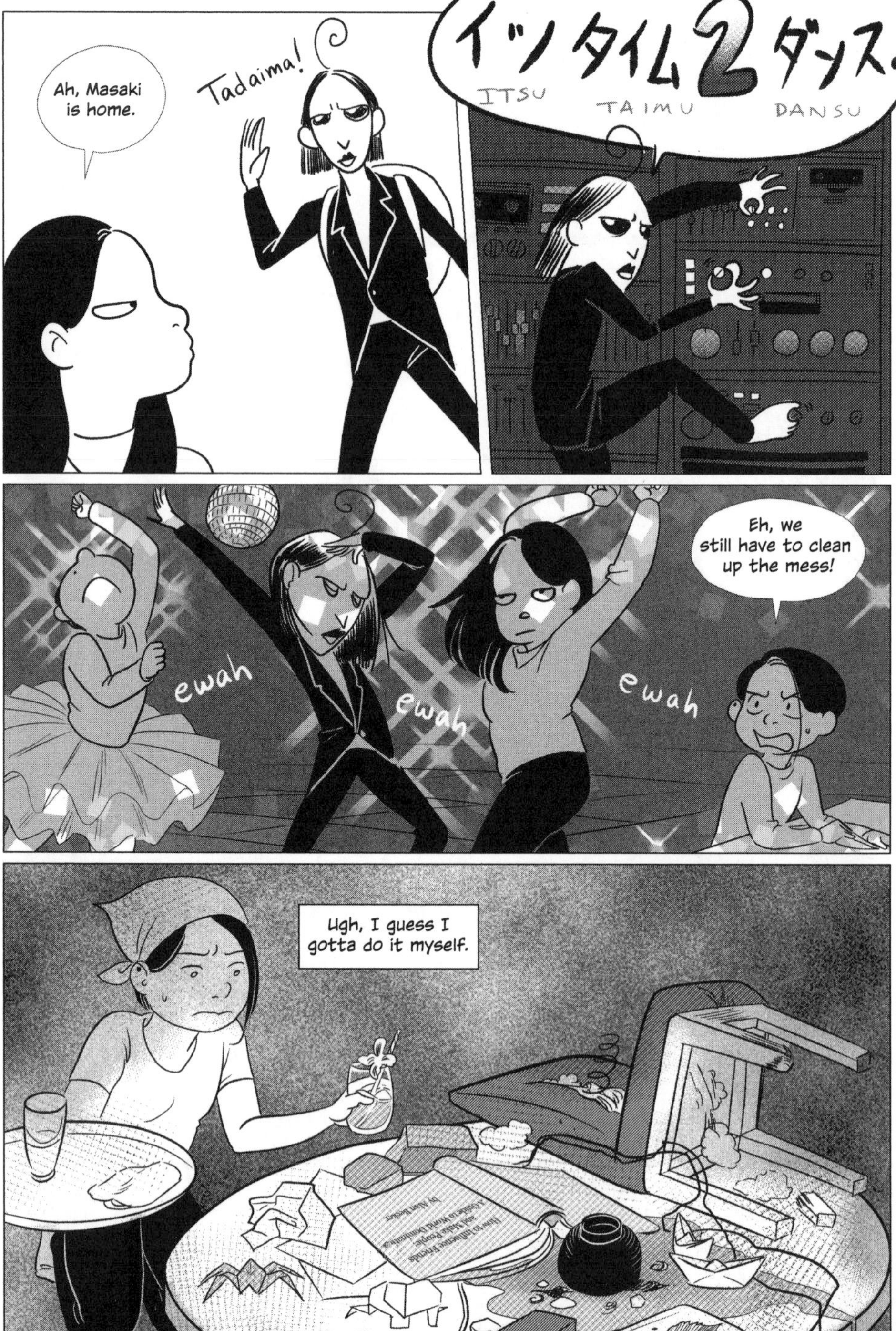
Ah, Masaki is home.
Tadaima!
イッタイム2ダンス。
ITSU TAIMU DANSU
ewah
ewah
ewah
Eh, we still have to clean up the mess!
Ugh, I guess I gotta do it myself.

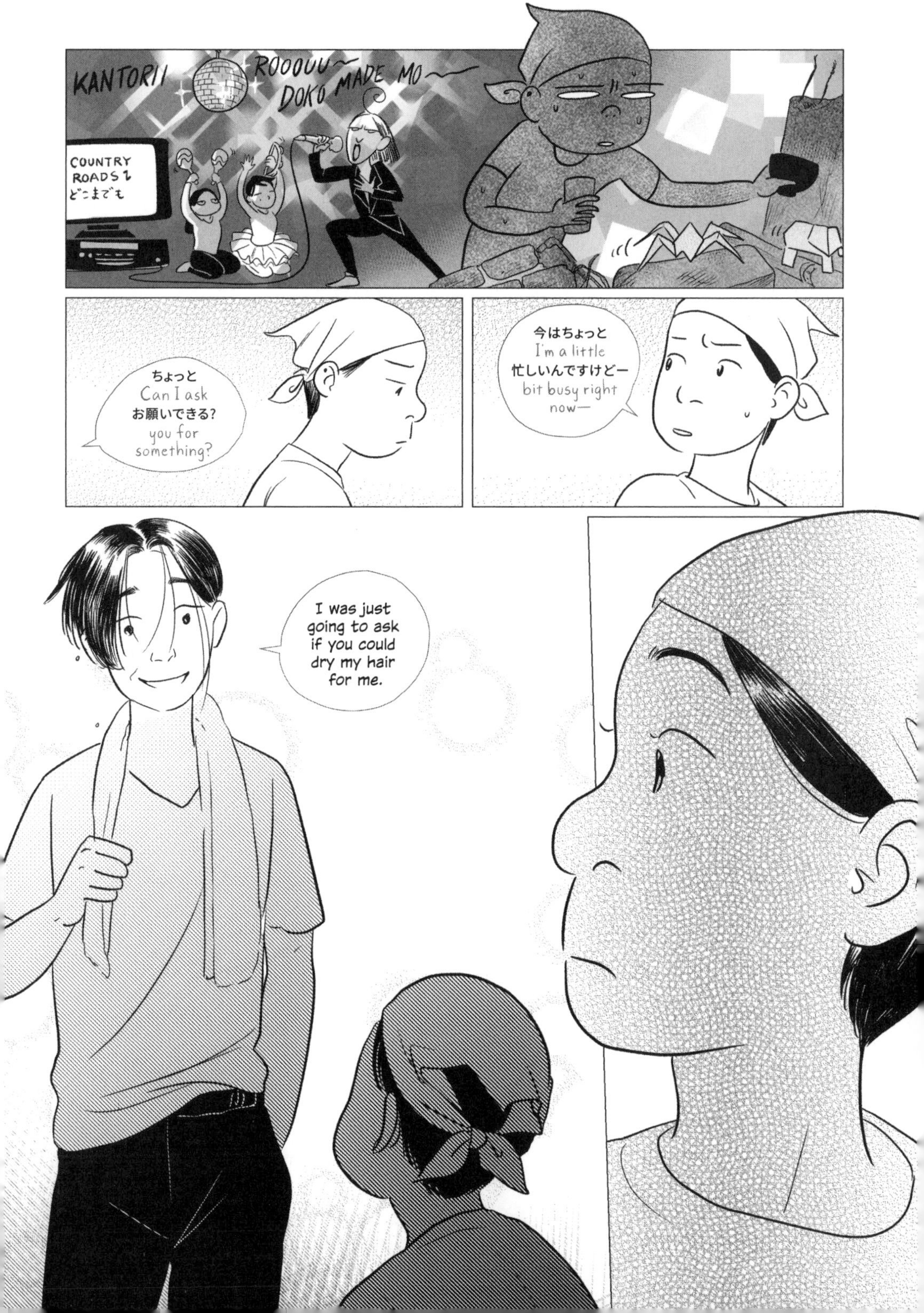
KANTORII ROOOUU~ DOKO MADE MO~~
COUNTRY ROADS
どこまでも
ちょっと
Can I ask
お願いできる?
you for something?
今はちょっと
I'm a little
忙しいんですけどー
bit busy right now—
I was just going to ask if you could dry my hair for me.

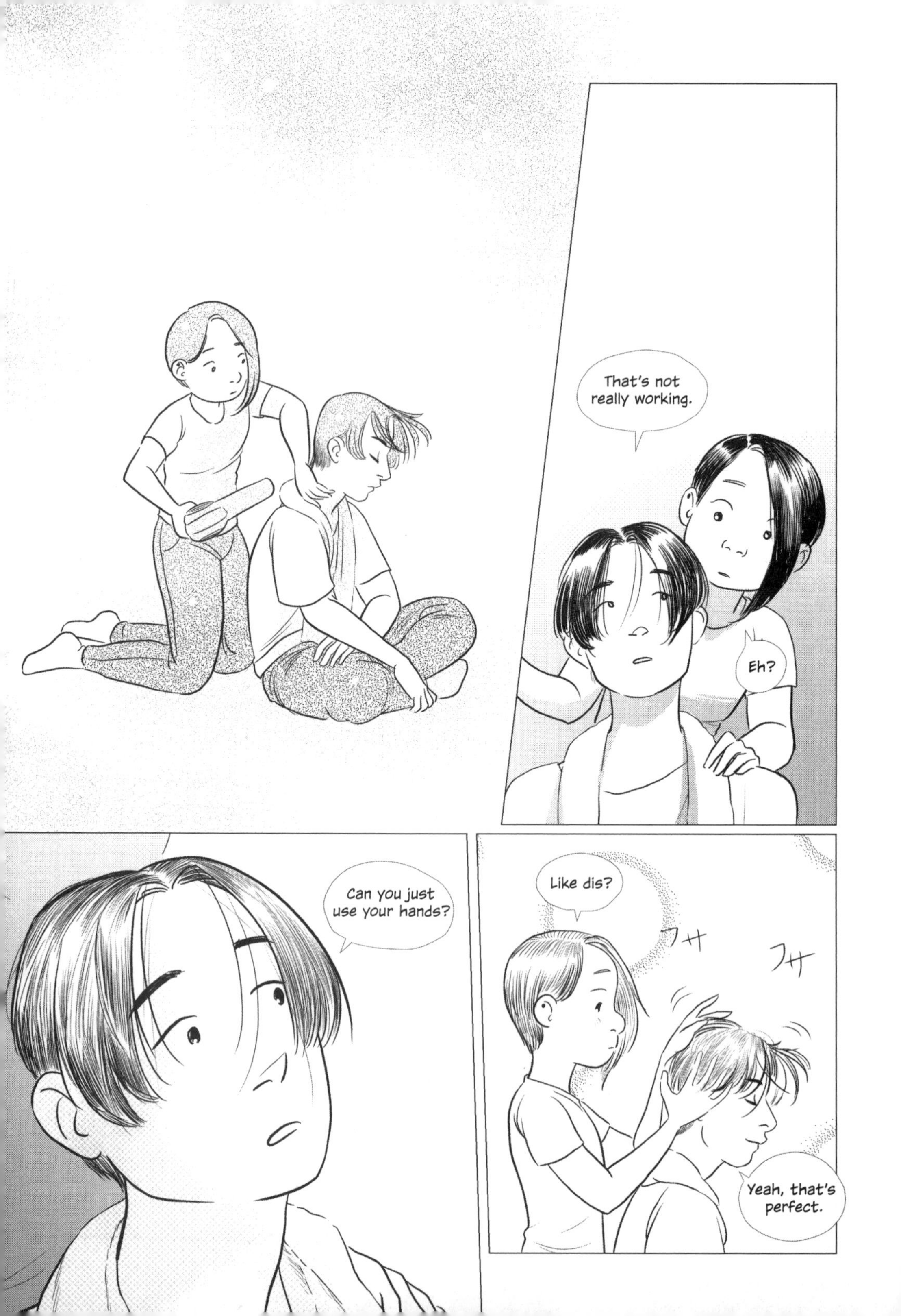
That's not really working.
Eh?
Can you just use your hands?
Like dis?
フサ
フサ
Yeah, that's perfect.

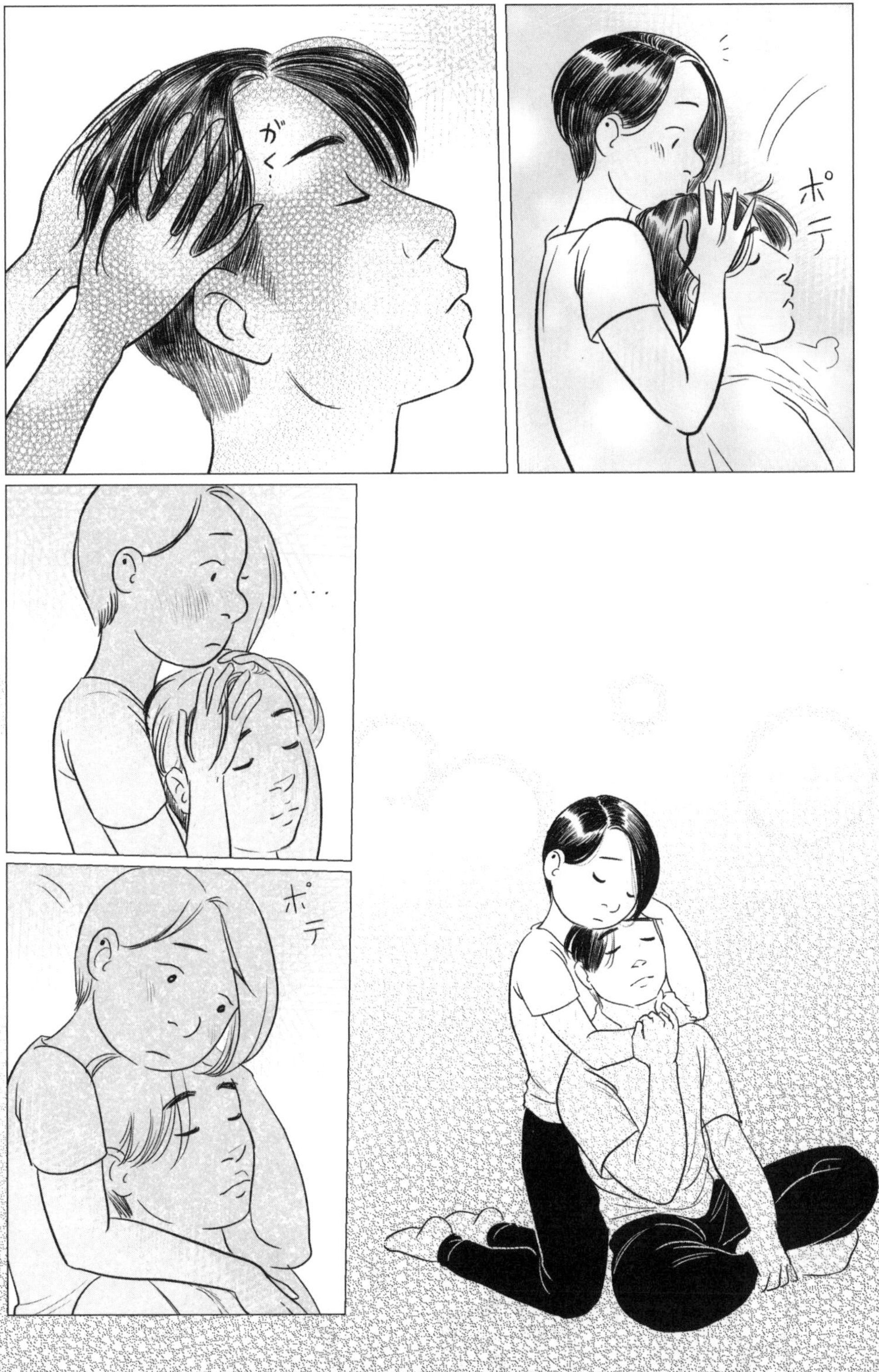
がく…
ポテ
・・・
ポテ

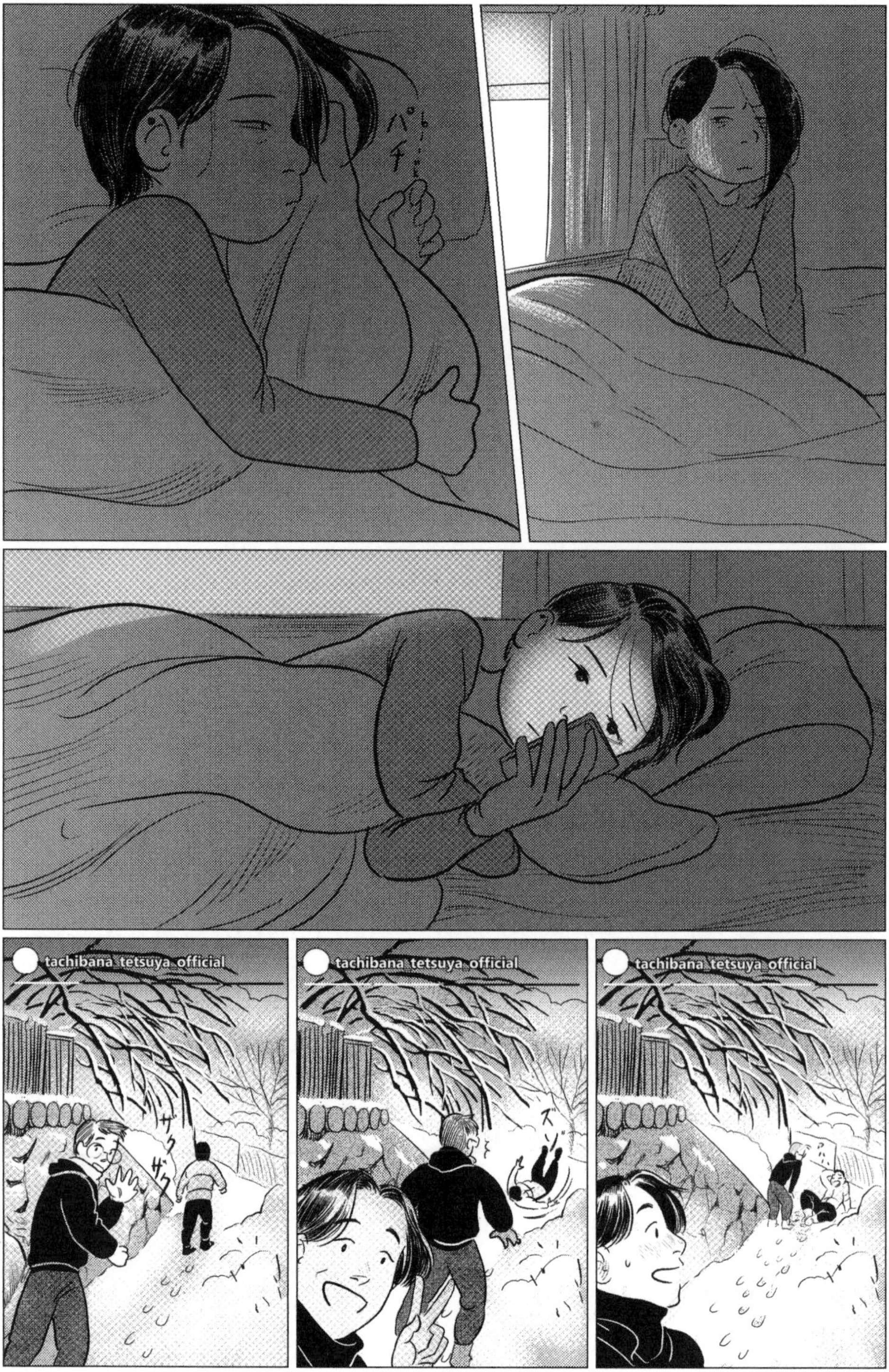
パチ
ト…
tachibana_tetsuya_official
ザク
ザク
tachibana_tetsuya_official
ズザ
tachibana_tetsuya_official
アハハ

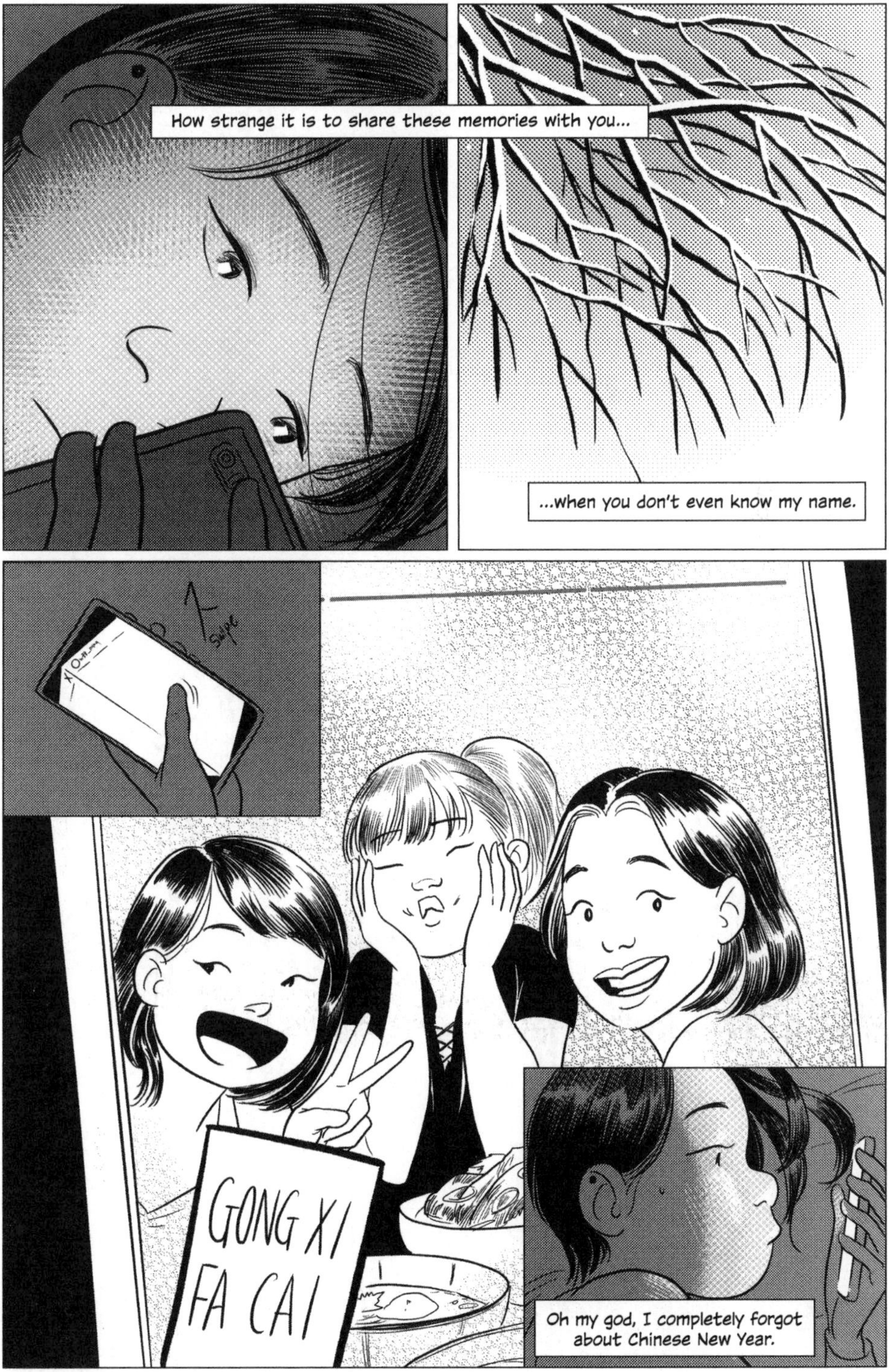
How strange it is to share these memories with you...
...when you don't even know my name.
swipe
GONG XI FA CAI
Oh my god, I completely forgot about Chinese New Year.

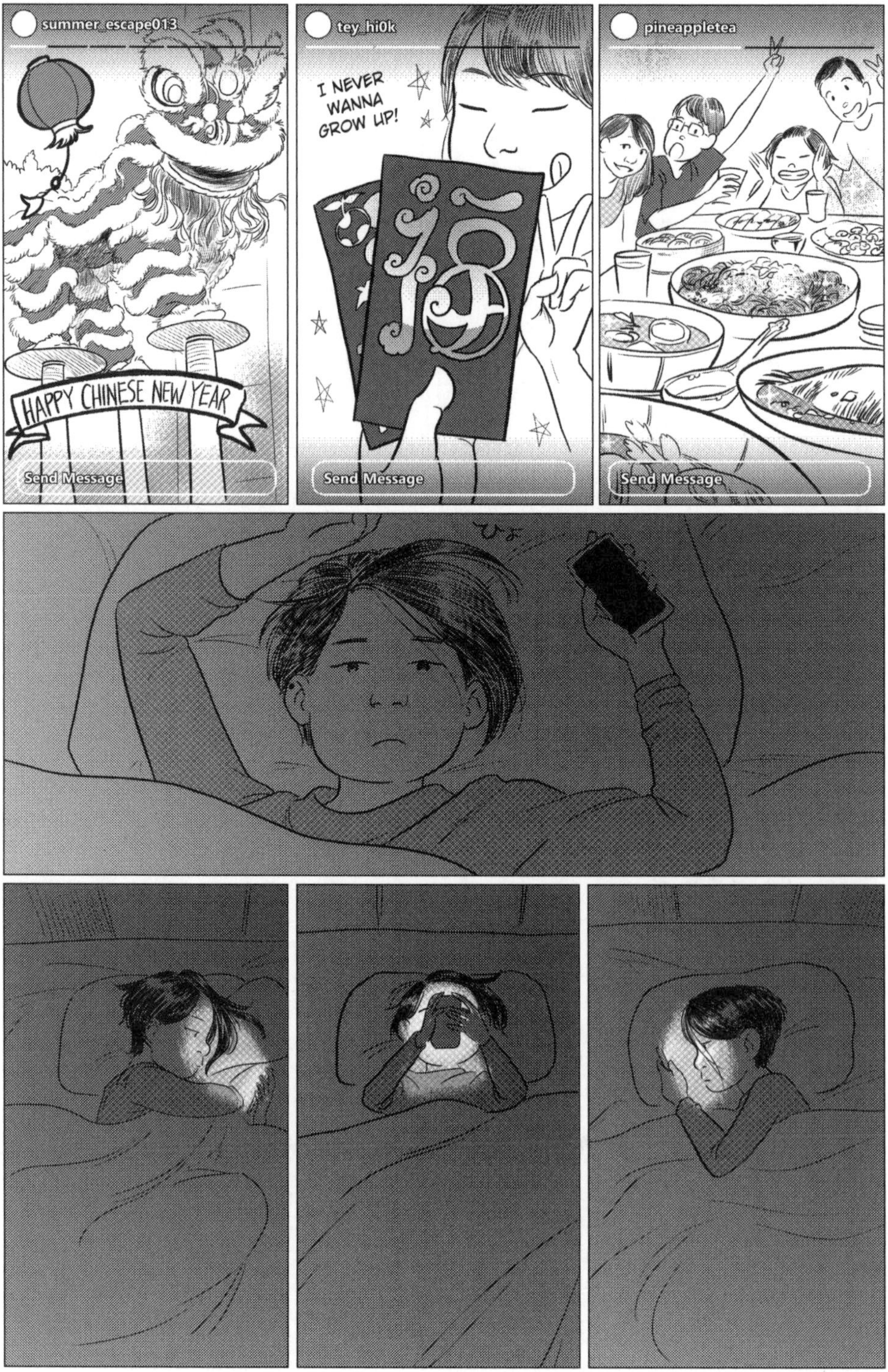
summer_escape013
HAPPY CHINESE NEW YEAR
Send Message
tey_hi0k
I NEVER WANNA GROW UP!
Send Message
pineappletea
Send Message

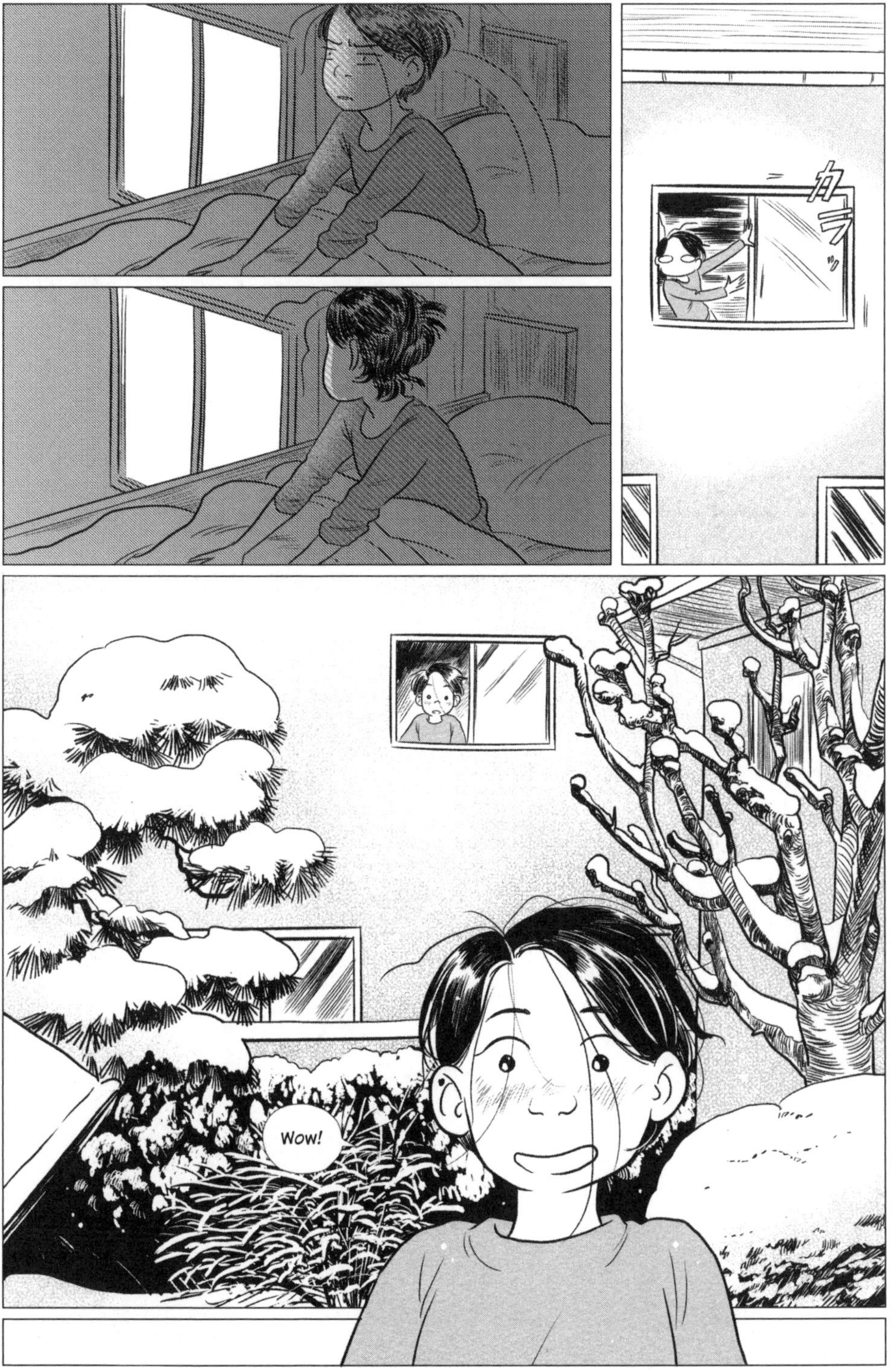

カラッ
Wow!

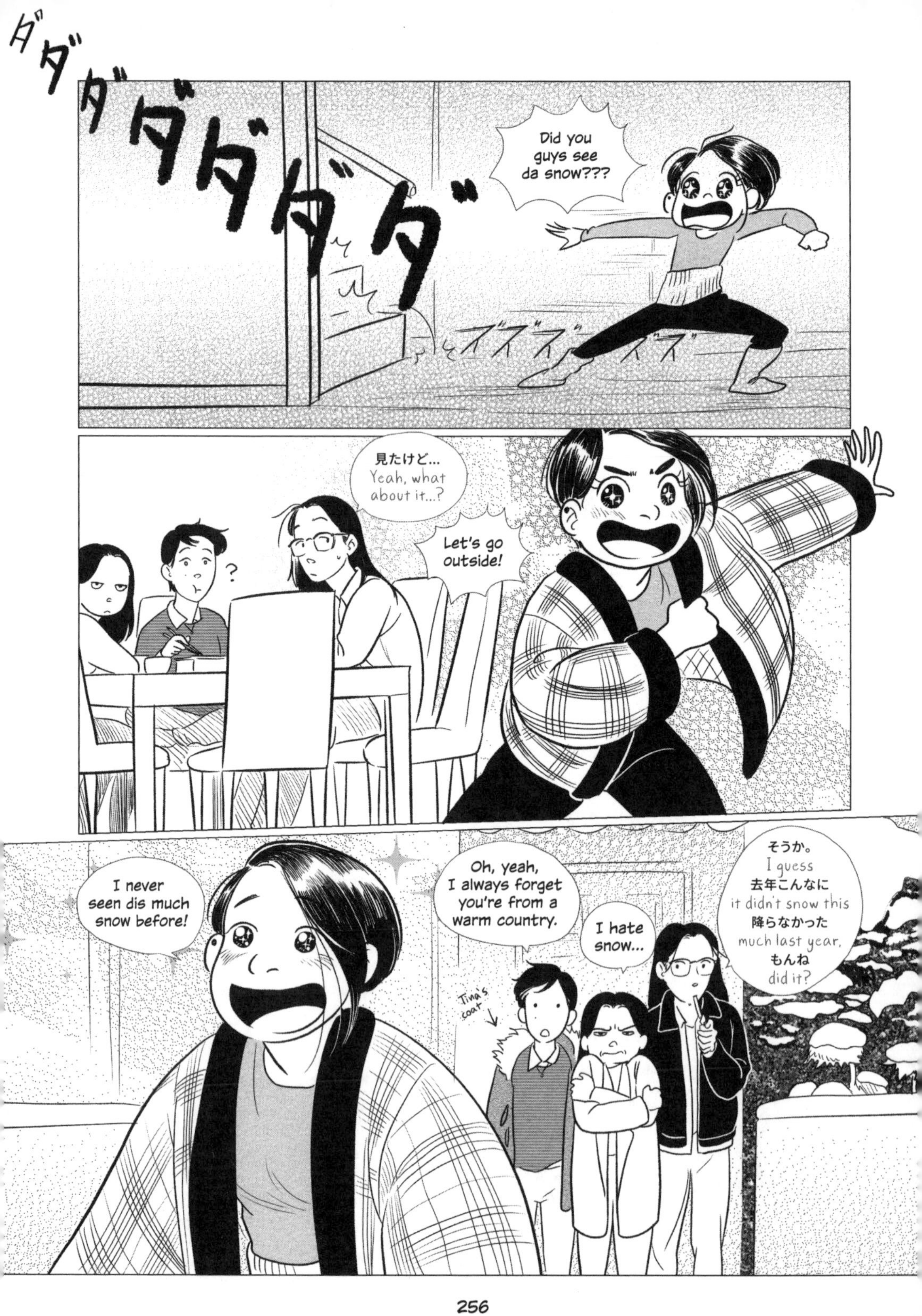
Did you guys see da snow???
見たけど… Yeah, what about it…?
Let's go outside!
I never seen dis much snow before!
Oh, yeah, I always forget you're from a warm country.
I hate snow…
そうか。 I guess 去年こんなに it didn't snow this 降らなかった much last year, もんね did it?
Tina's coat

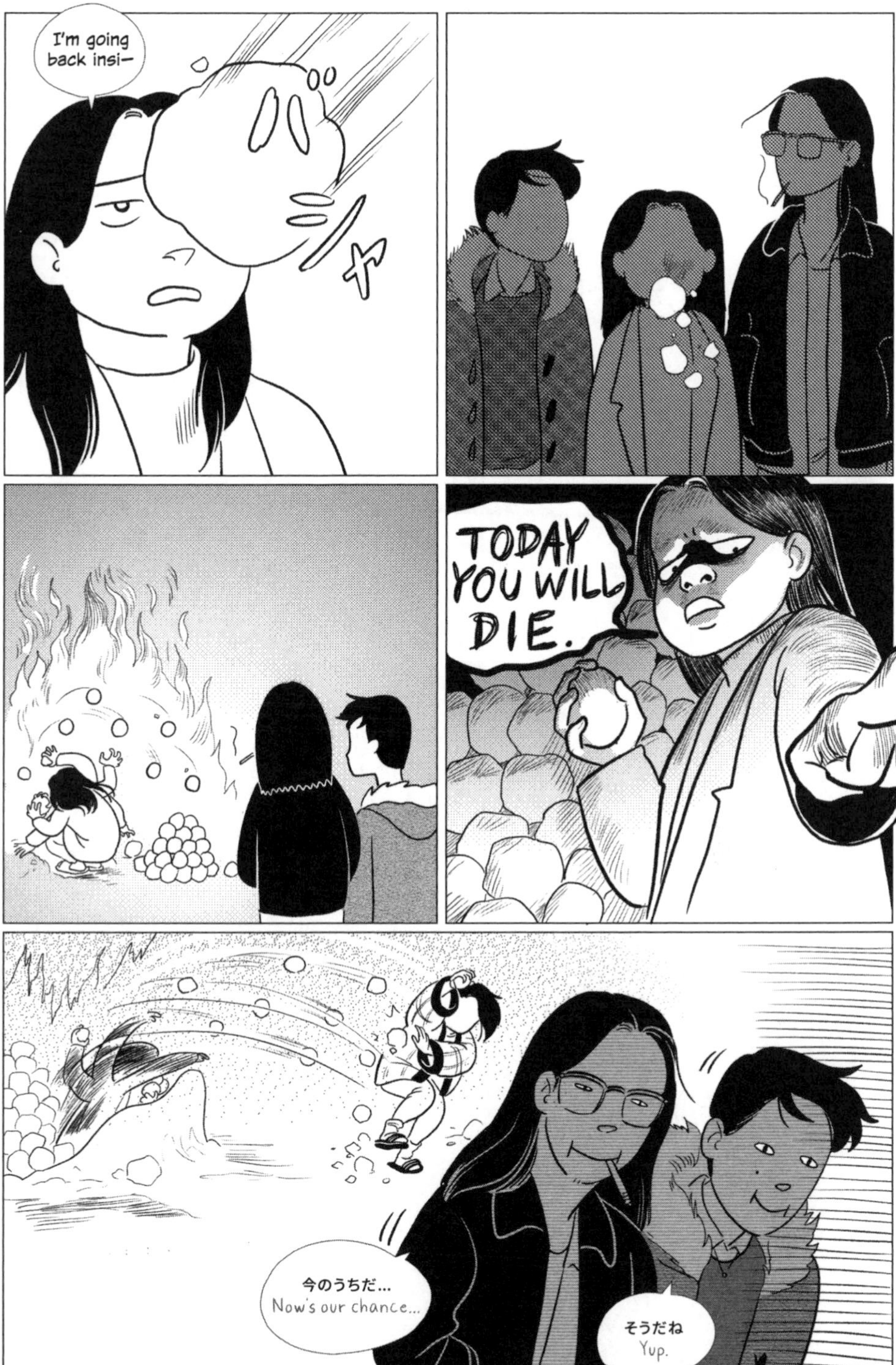
I'm going back insi—
TODAY YOU WILL DIE.
今のうちだ...
Now's our chance...
そうだね
Yup.

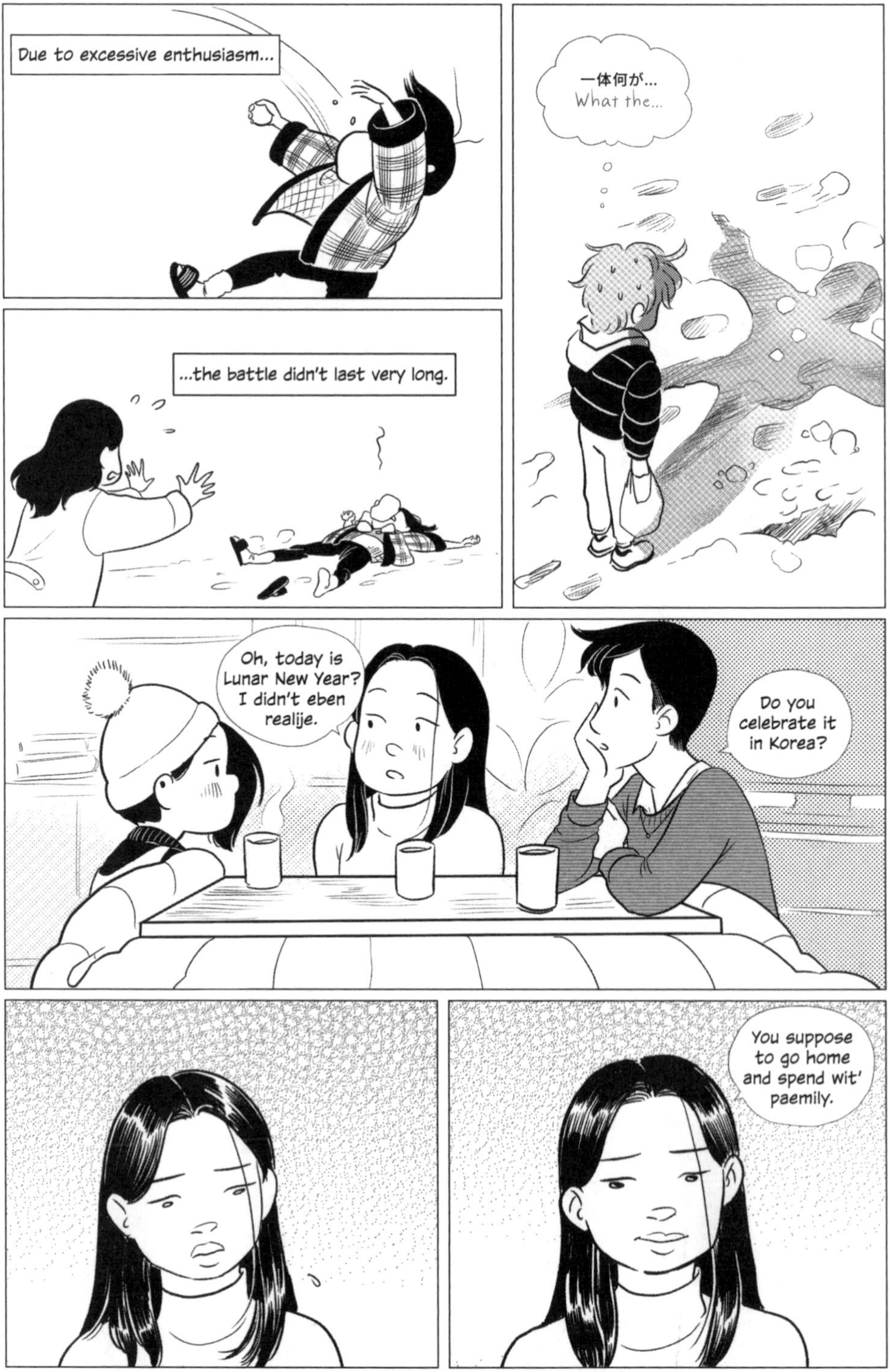
Due to excessive enthusiasm...
一体何が...
What the...
...the battle didn't last very long.
Oh, today is Lunar New Year? I didn't eben realije.
Do you celebrate it in Korea?
You suppose to go home and spend wit' paemily.

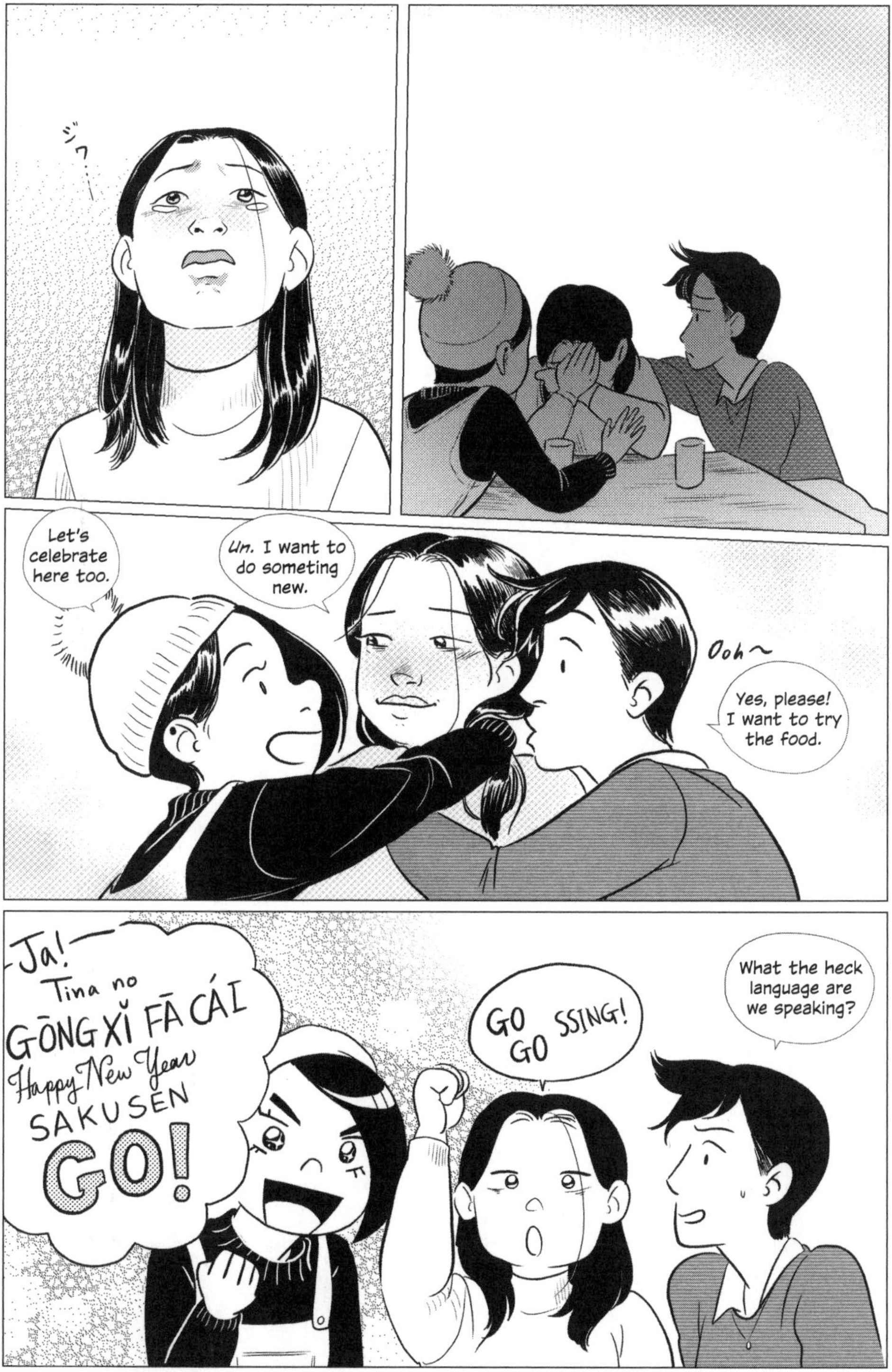
ジワ…
Let's celebrate here too.
Un. I want to do someting new.
Ooh~
Yes, please! I want to try the food.
Ja! Tina no GŌNG XǏ FĀ CÁI Happy New Year SAKUSEN GO!
GO GO SSING!
What the heck language are we speaking?

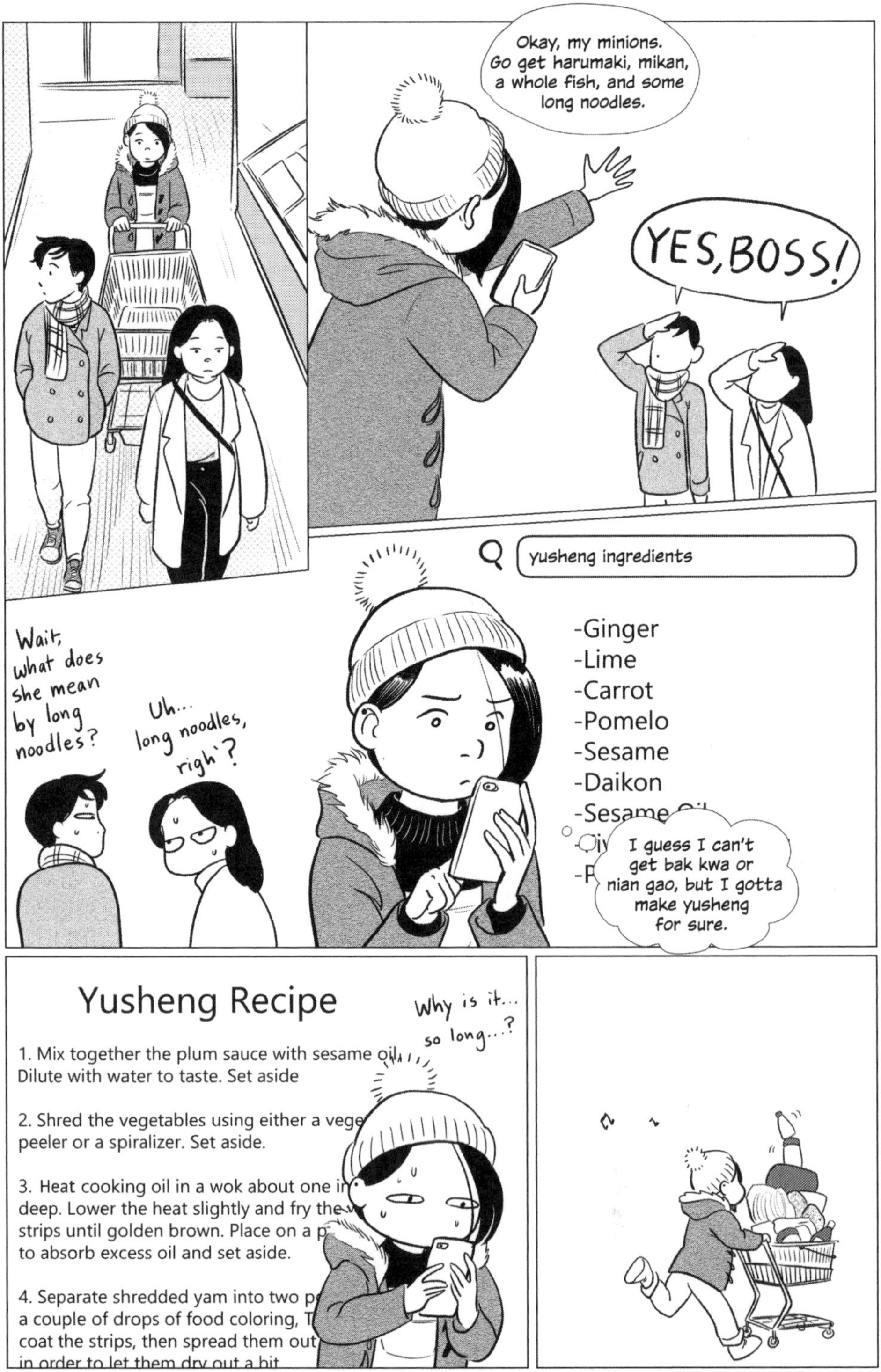
Okay, my minions. Go get harumaki, mikan, a whole fish, and some long noodles.
YES, BOSS!
yusheng ingredients
-Ginger
-Lime
-Carrot
-Pomelo
-Sesame
-Daikon
Wait, what does she mean by long noodles?
Uh... long noodles, righ`?
I guess I can't get bak kwa or nian gao, but I gotta make yusheng for sure.
Yusheng Recipe
1. Mix together the plum sauce with sesame oi
Dilute with water to taste. Set aside
2. Shred the vegetables using either a vege
peeler or a spiralizer. Set aside.
3. Heat cooking oil in a wok about one i
deep. Lower the heat slightly and fry the
strips until golden brown. Place on a p
to absorb excess oil and set aside.
4. Separate shredded yam into two p
a couple of drops of food coloring, T
coat the strips, then spread them out
Why is it... so long...?

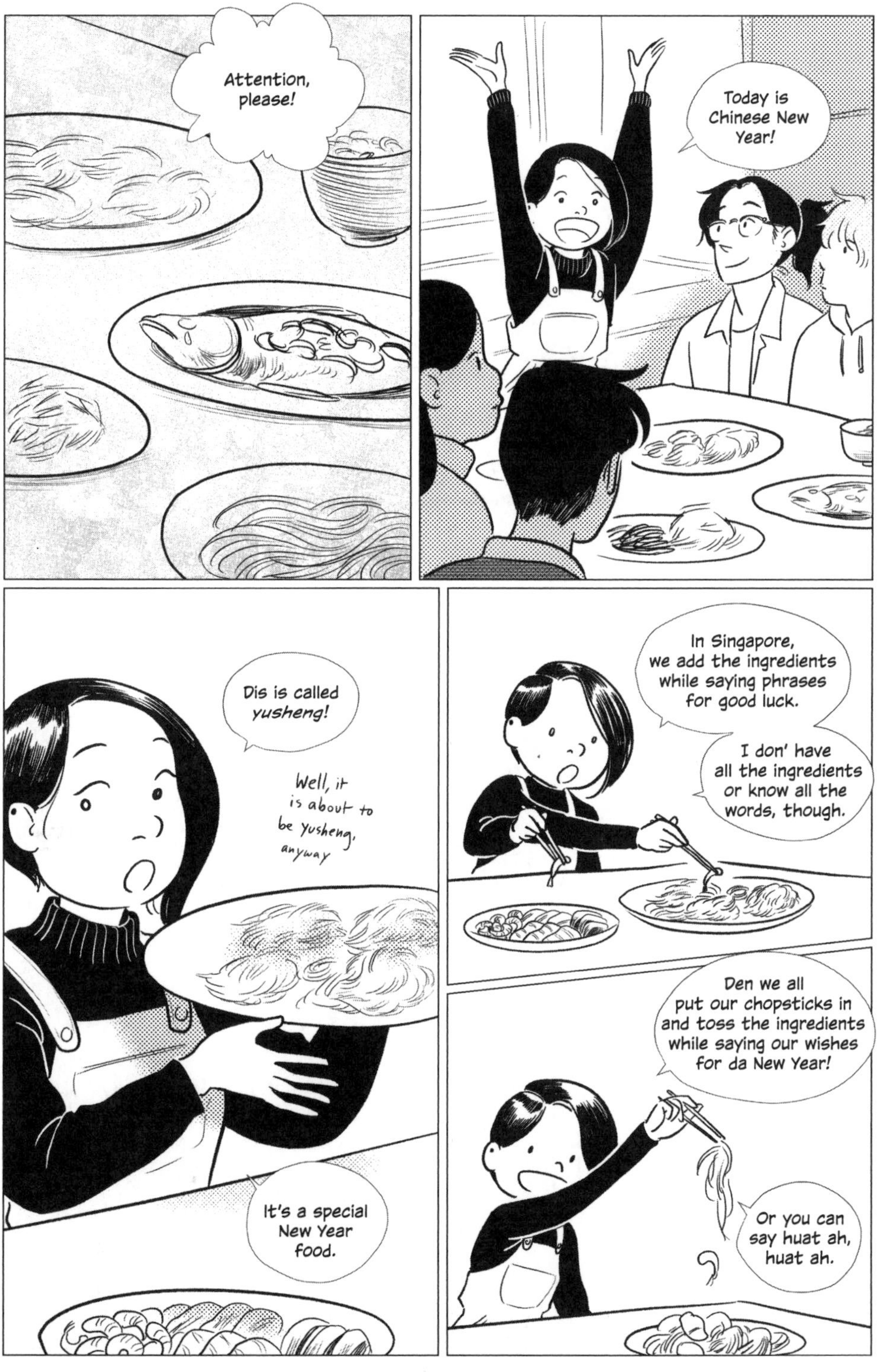

Attention, please!
Today is Chinese New Year!
Dis is called *yusheng*!
Well, it is about to be yusheng, anyway
It's a special New Year food.
In Singapore, we add the ingredients while saying phrases for good luck.
I don' have all the ingredients or know all the words, though.
Den we all put our chopsticks in and toss the ingredients while saying our wishes for da New Year!
Or you can say huat ah, huat ah.

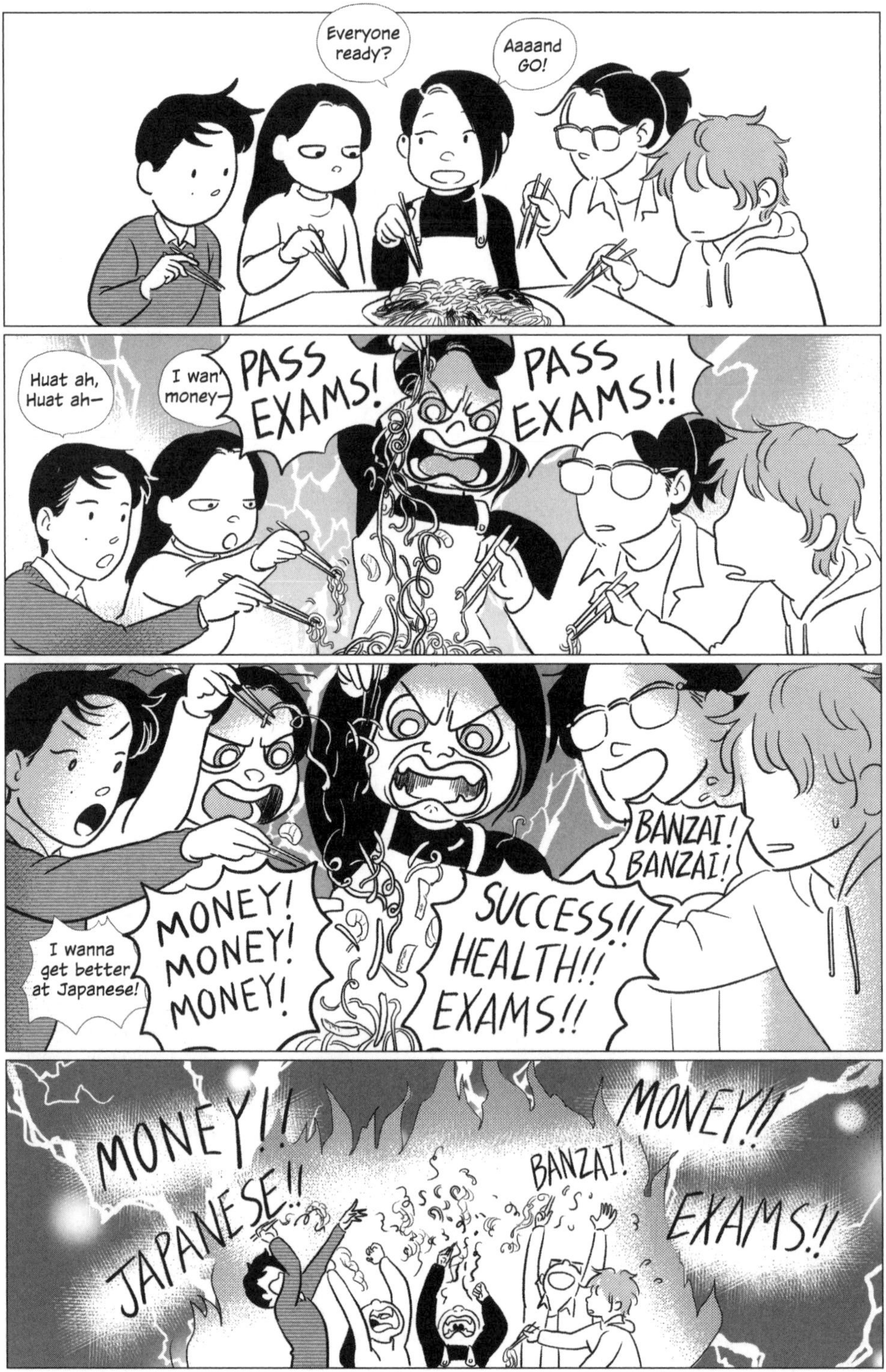

Everyone ready?
Aaaand GO!
Huat ah, Huat ah—
I wan' money—
PASS EXAMS!
PASS EXAMS!!
BANZAI! BANZAI!
I wanna get better at Japanese!
MONEY! MONEY! MONEY!
SUCCESS!! HEALTH!! EXAMS!!
MONEY!!
JAPANESE!!
BANZAI!
MONEY!!
EXAMS!!

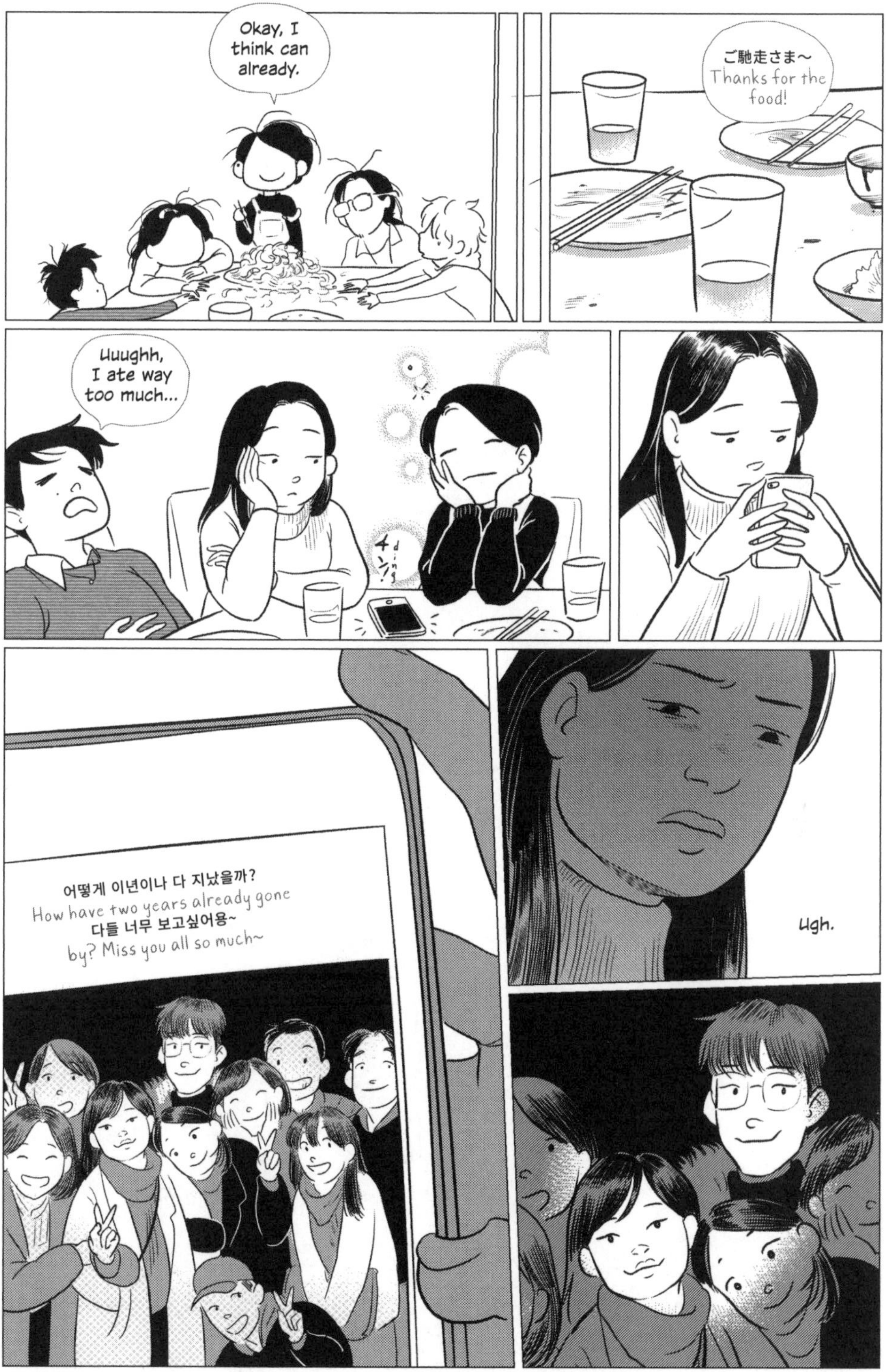
Okay, I think can already.
ご馳走さま～
Thanks for the food!
Uuughh, I ate way too much...
어떻게 이년이나 다 지났을까?
How have two years already gone
다들 너무 보고싶어용~
by? Miss you all so much~
Ugh.

Chapter 15
Yoojoon

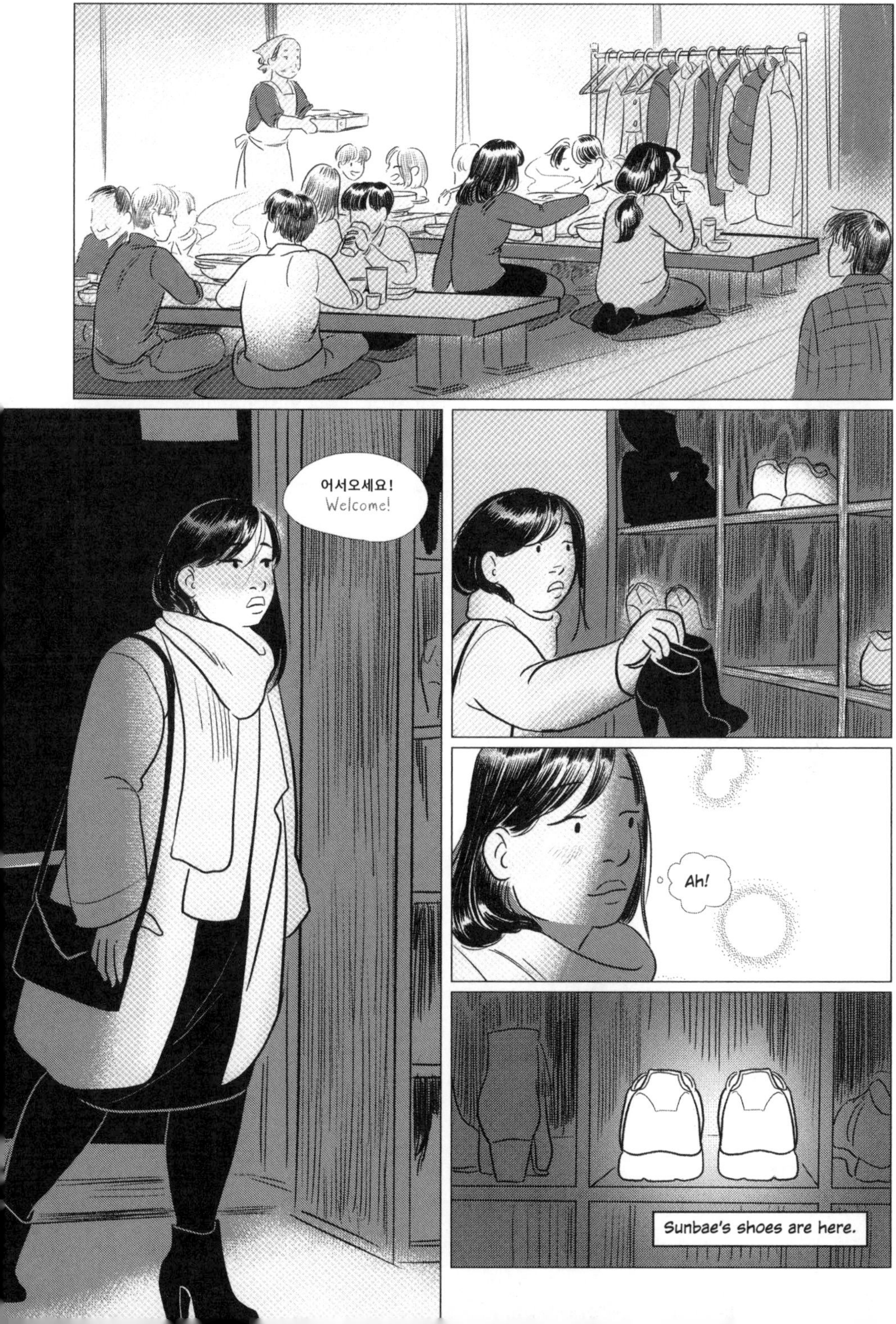

어서오세요!
Welcome!
Ah!
Sunbae's shoes are here.

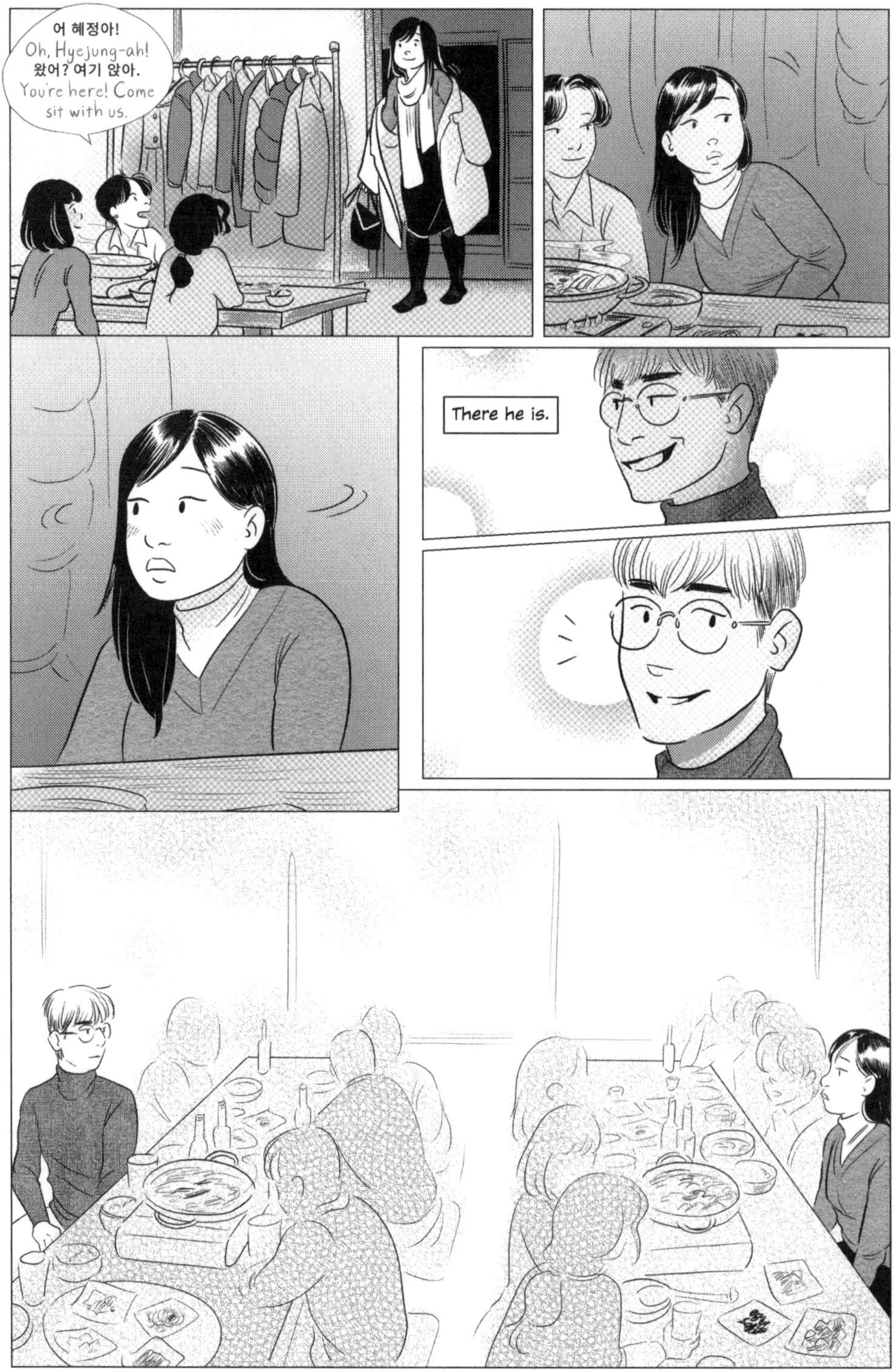
어 혜정아!
Oh, Hyejung-ah!
왔어? 여기 앉아.
You're here! Come sit with us.
There he is.

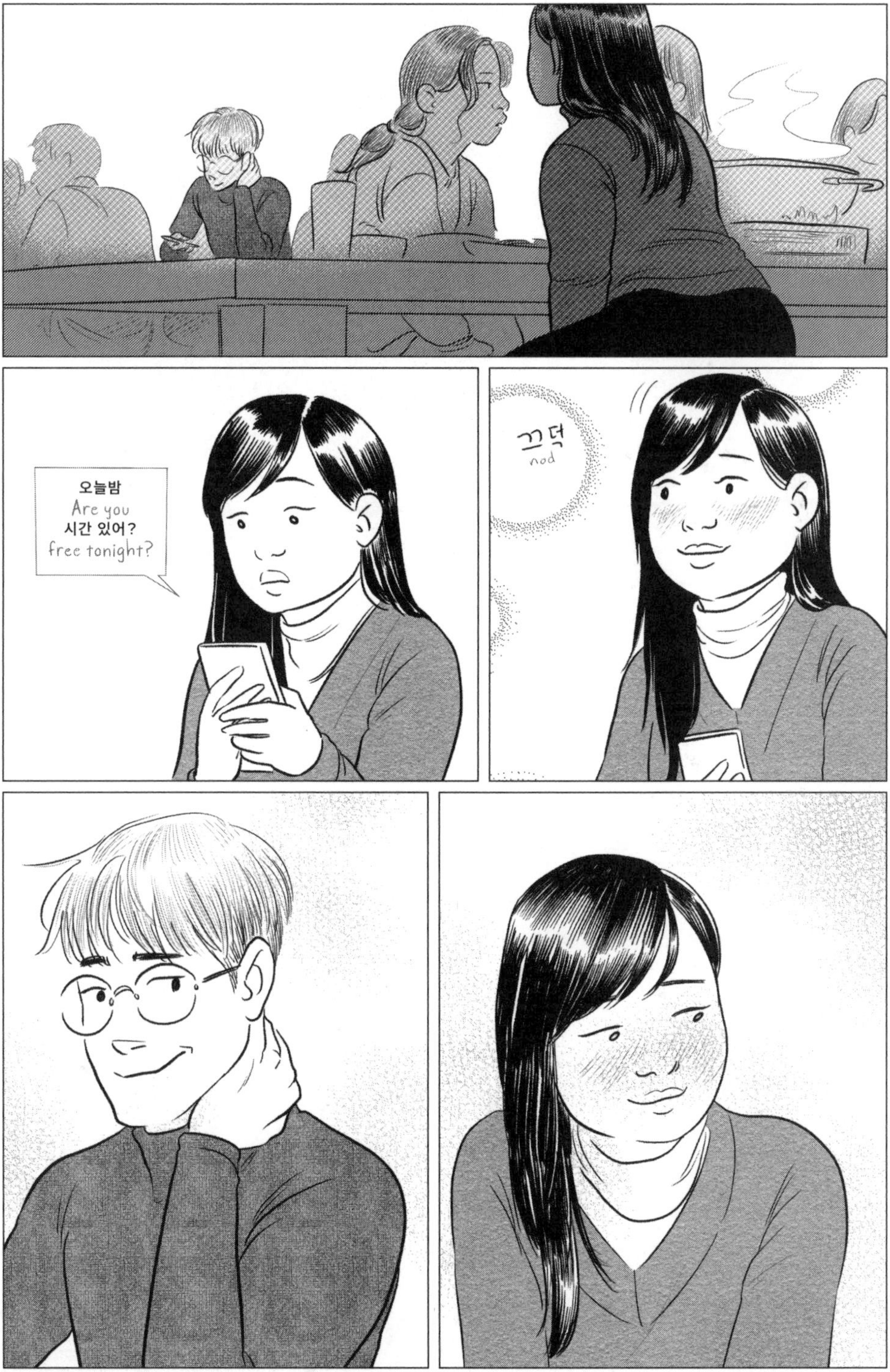

오늘밤
Are you
시간 있어?
free tonight?
끄덕
nod

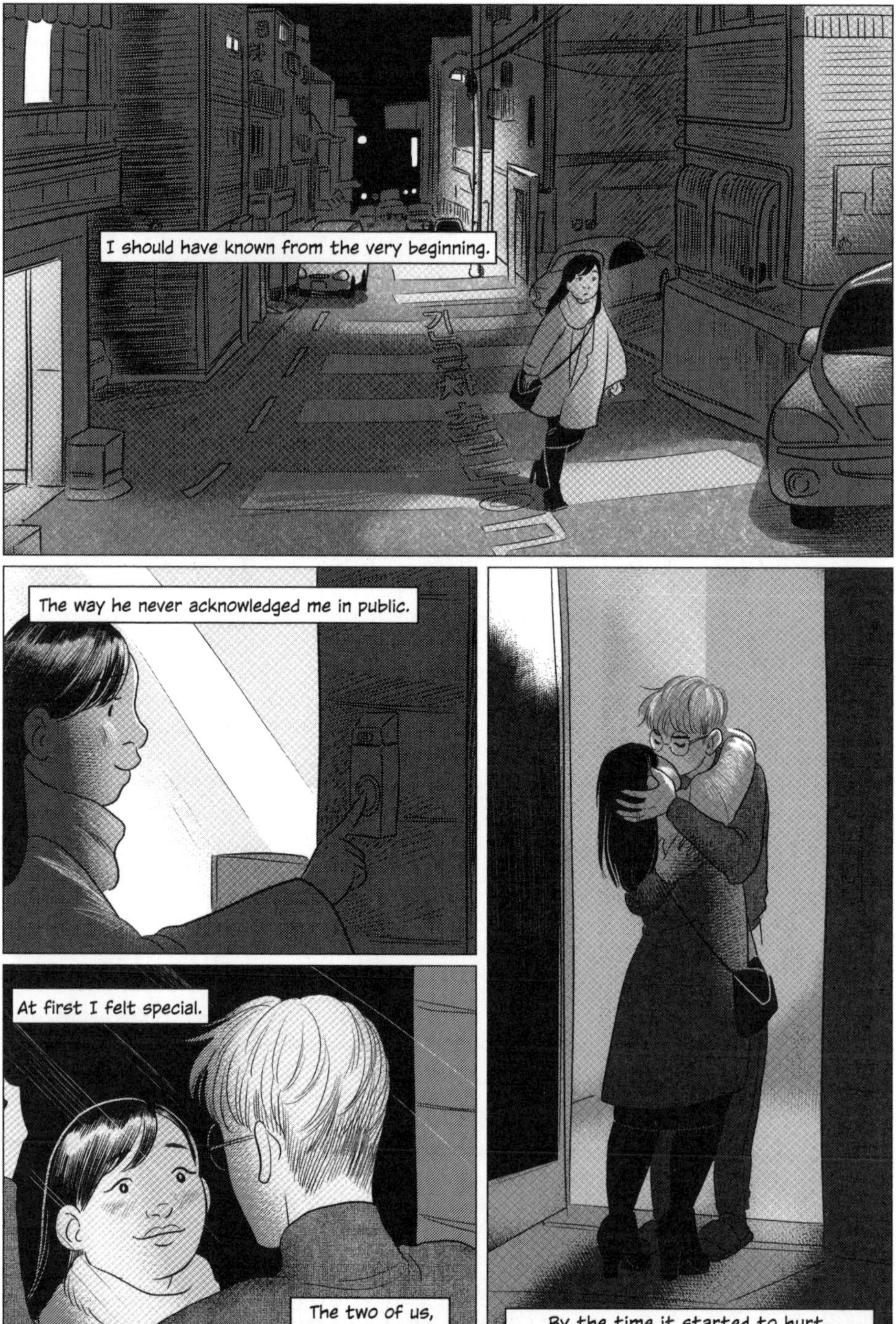
I should have known from the very beginning.
The way he never acknowledged me in public.
At first I felt special.
The two of us, sharing a secret.
By the time it started to hurt, it was too late.

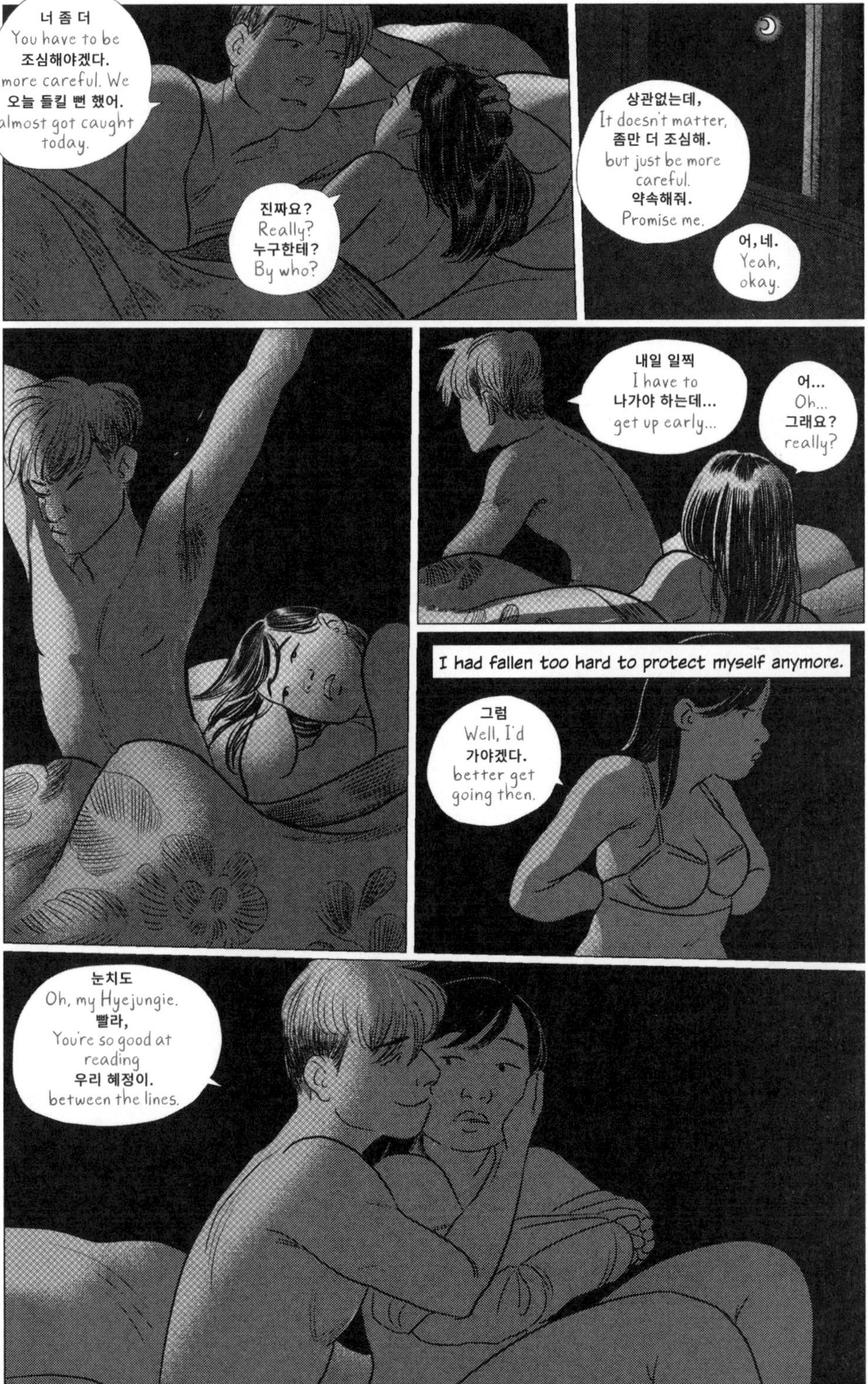
너 좀 더 You have to be 조심해야겠다. more careful. We 오늘 들킬 뻔 했어. almost got caught today.
진짜요? Really? 누구한테? By who?
상관없는데, It doesn't matter, 좀만 더 조심해. but just be more careful. 약속해줘. Promise me.
어, 네. Yeah, okay.
내일 일찍 I have to 나가야 하는데... get up early...
어... Oh... 그래요? really?
I had fallen too hard to protect myself anymore.
그럼 Well, I'd 가야겠다. better get going then.
눈치도 Oh, my Hyejungie. 빨라, You're so good at reading 우리 혜정이. between the lines.

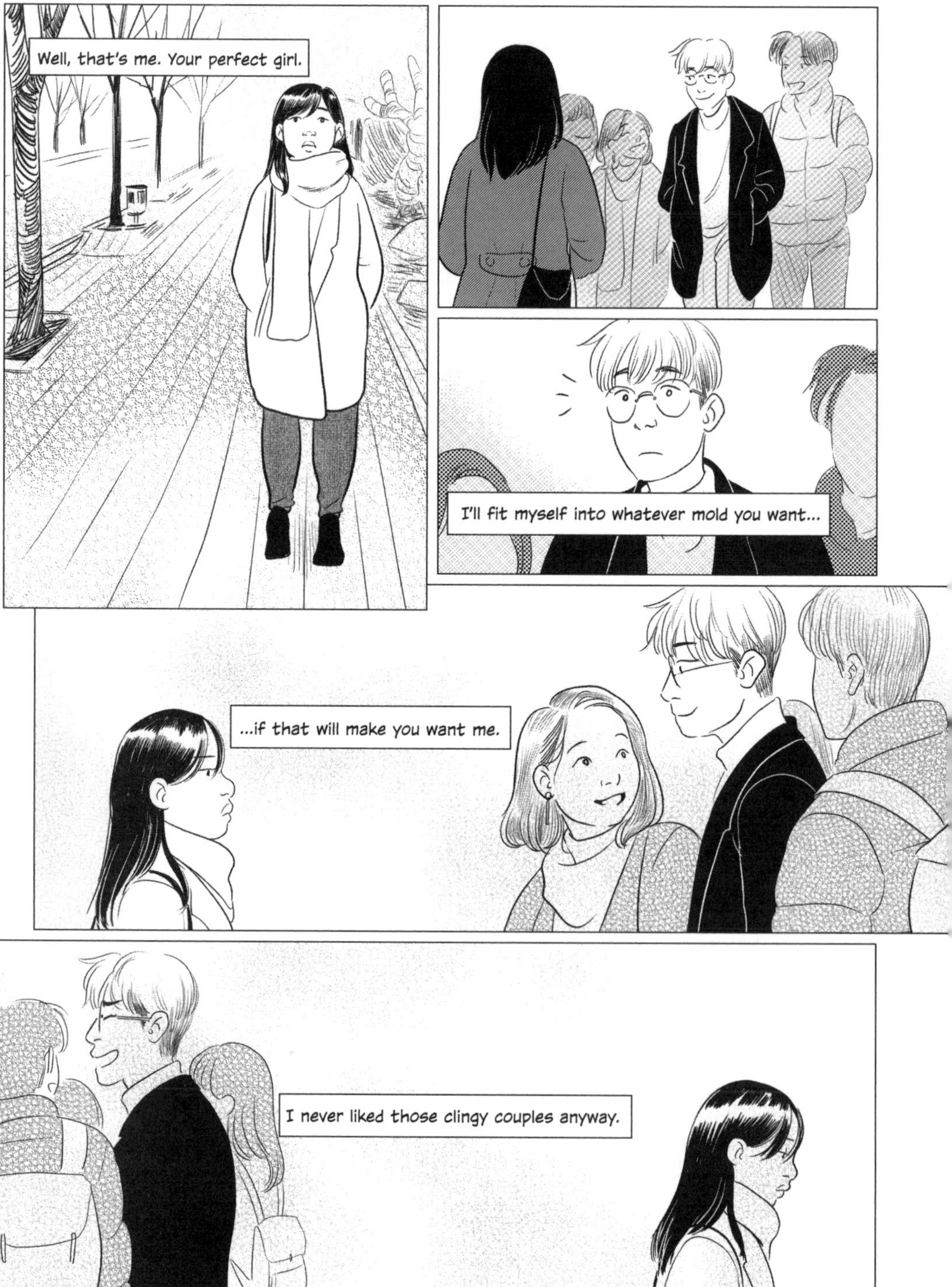
Well, that's me. Your perfect girl.
I'll fit myself into whatever mold you want...
...if that will make you want me.
I never liked those clingy couples anyway.

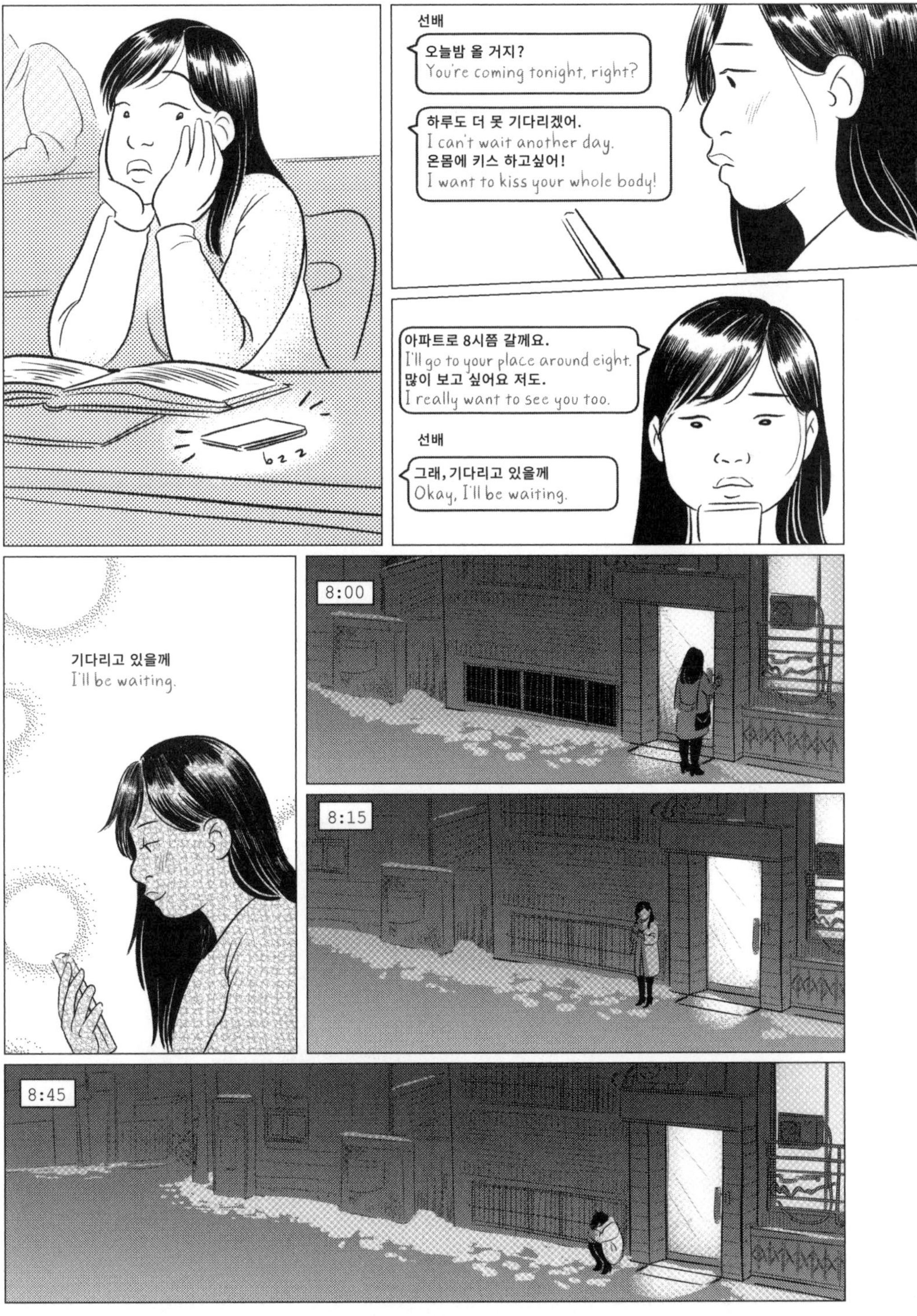
bzz
선배
오늘밤 올 거지?
You're coming tonight, right?
하루도 더 못 기다리겠어.
I can't wait another day.
온몸에 키스 하고싶어!
I want to kiss your whole body!
아파트로 8시쯤 갈께요.
I'll go to your place around eight.
많이 보고 싶어요 저도.
I really want to see you too.
선배
그래, 기다리고 있을께
Okay, I'll be waiting.
기다리고 있을께
I'll be waiting.
8:00
8:15
8:45

내일 보자!
그럼 내일 봐요 Tomorrow!

바이!
bye!

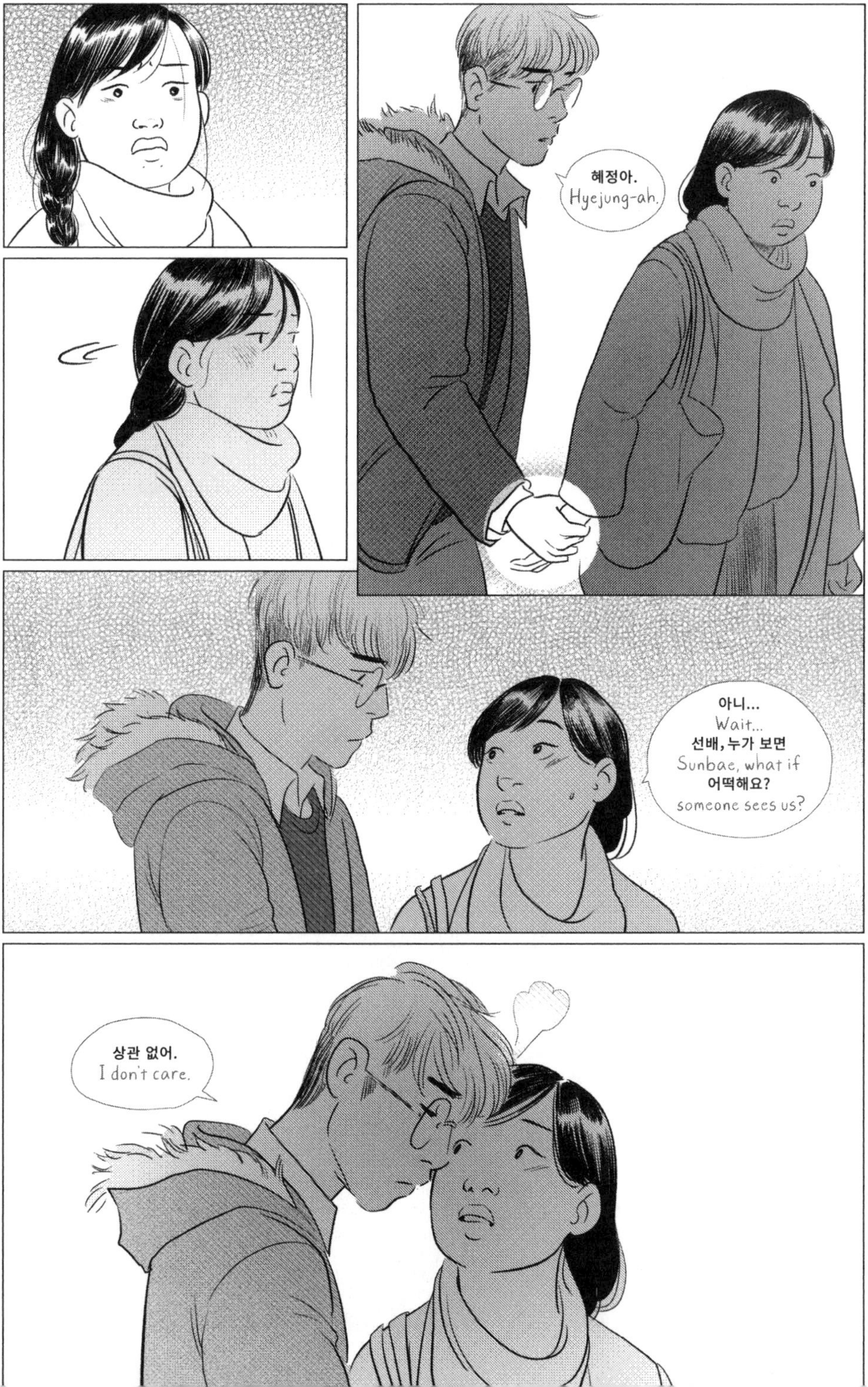
혜정아.
Hyejung-ah.
아니...
Wait...
선배, 누가 보면
Sunbae, what if
어떡해요?
someone sees us?
상관 없어.
I don't care.

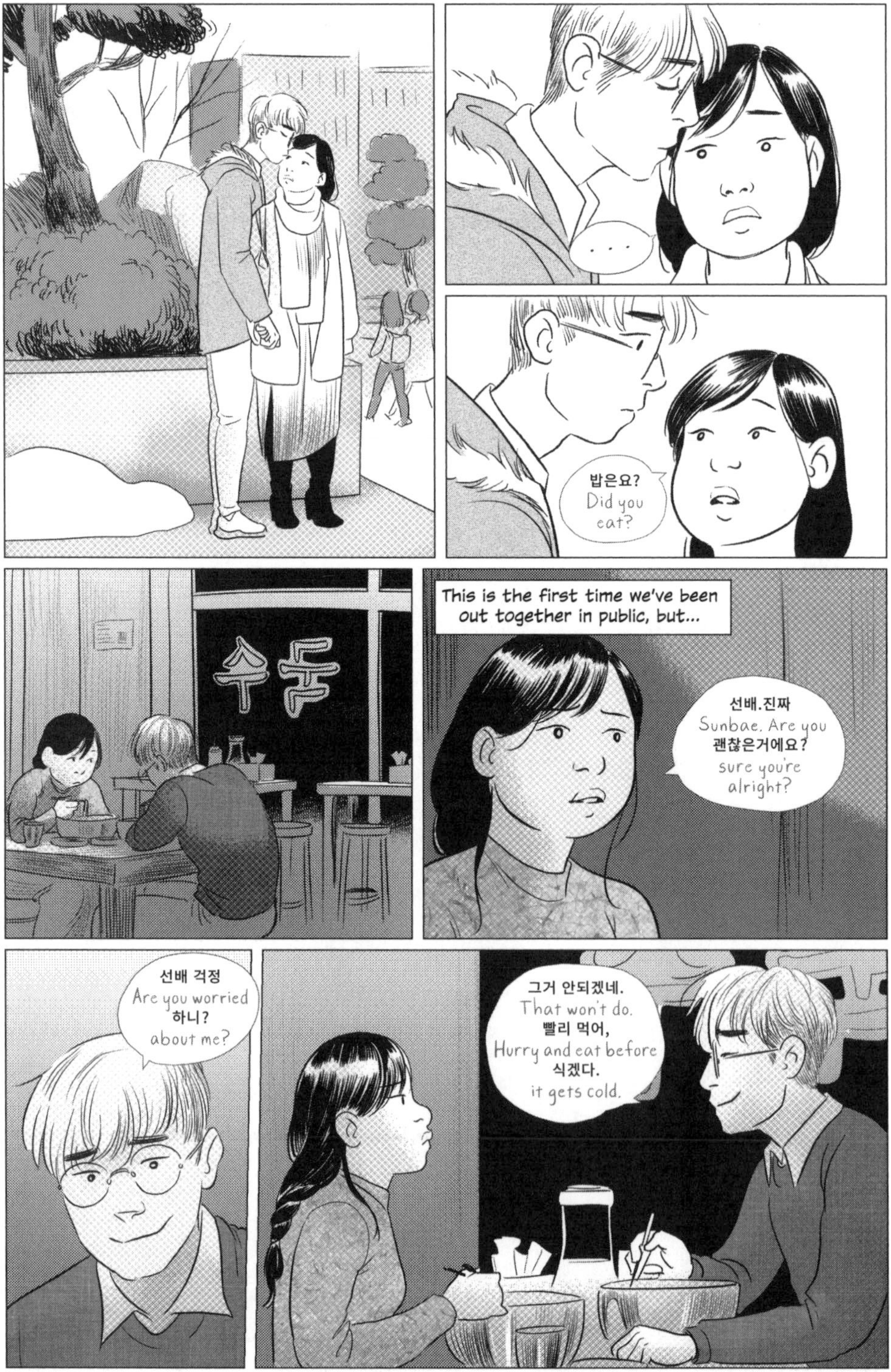
...
밥은요? Did you eat?
This is the first time we've been out together in public, but...
선배.진짜 Sunbae. Are you 괜찮은거에요? sure you're alright?
선배 걱정 Are you worried 하니? about me?
그거 안되겠네. That won't do. 빨리 먹어, Hurry and eat before 식겠다. it gets cold.

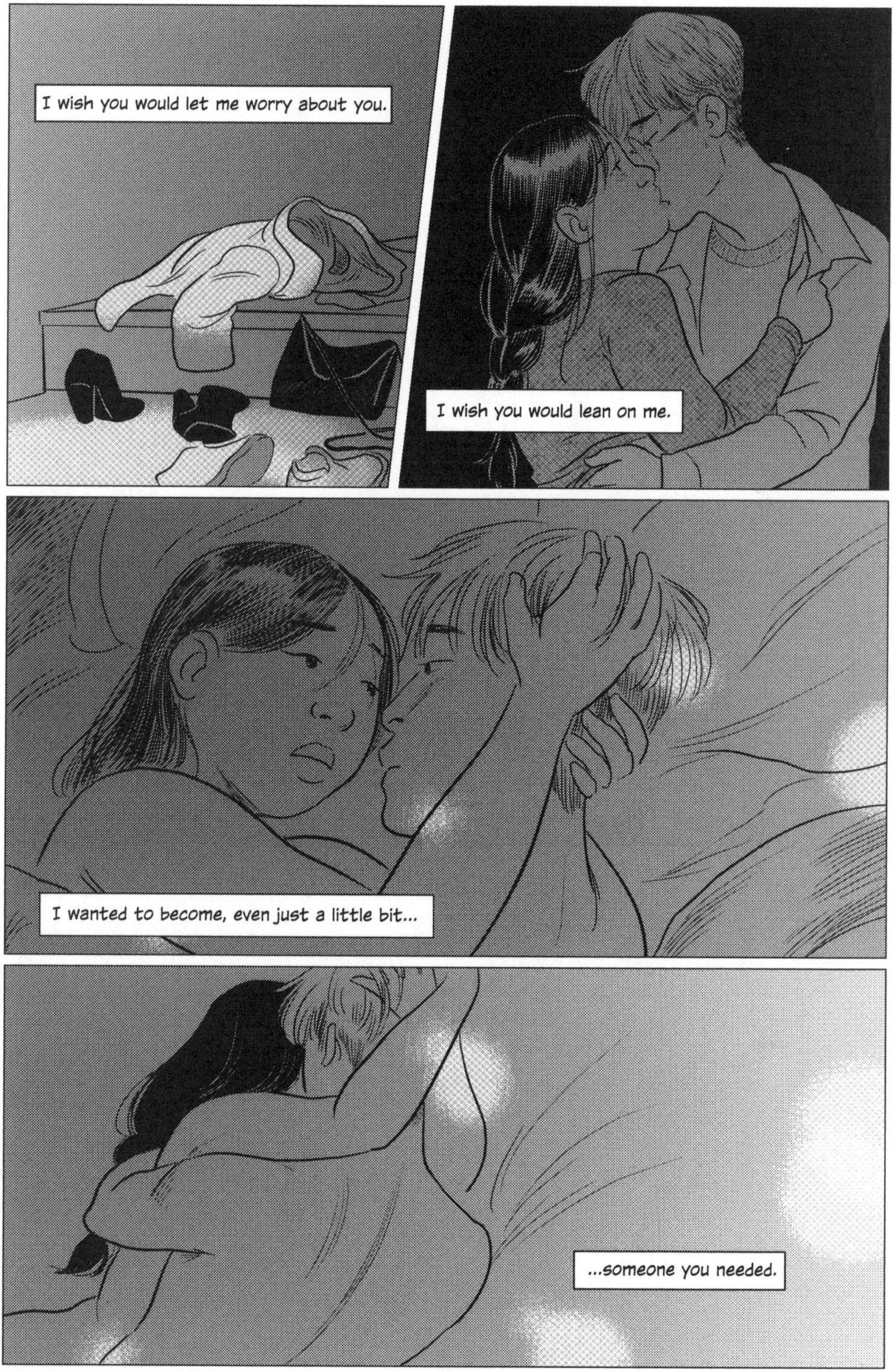
I wish you would let me worry about you.
I wish you would lean on me.
I wanted to become, even just a little bit...
...someone you needed.

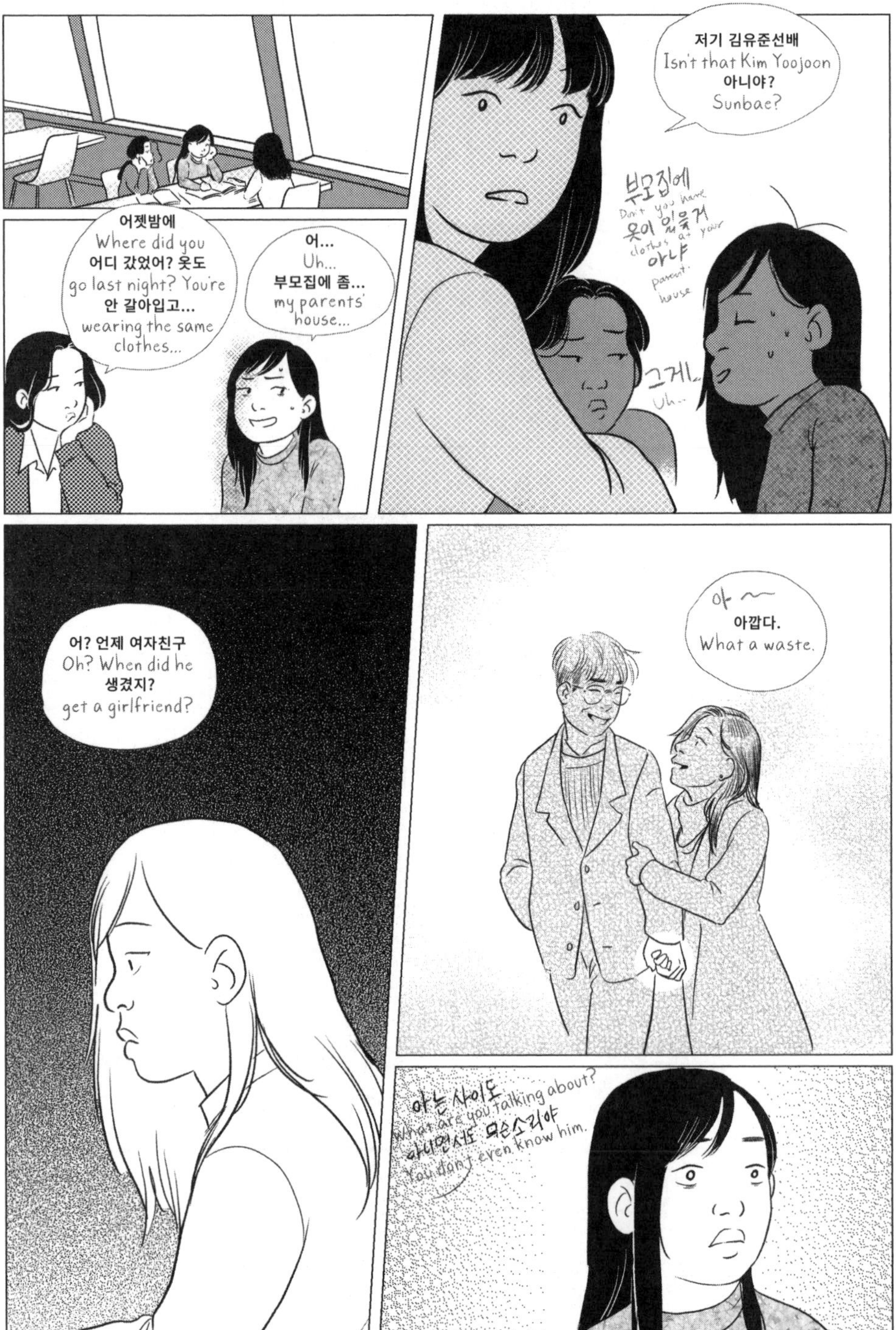
어젯밤에
Where did you
어디 갔었어? 옷도
go last night? You're
안 갈아입고…
wearing the same
clothes…
어…
Uh…
부모집에 좀…
my parents'
house…
저기 김유준선배
Isn't that Kim Yoojoon
아니야?
Sunbae?
부모집에
Don't you have
옷이 있을거
clothes at your
아냐
parent.
house
그게…
Uh…
어? 언제 여자친구
Oh? When did he
생겼지?
get a girlfriend?
아 ~
아깝다.
What a waste.
아는 사이도
What are you talking about?
아니면서도 무슨소리야
You don't even know him.
I never talked to him again after that.

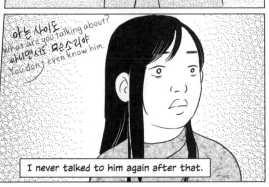

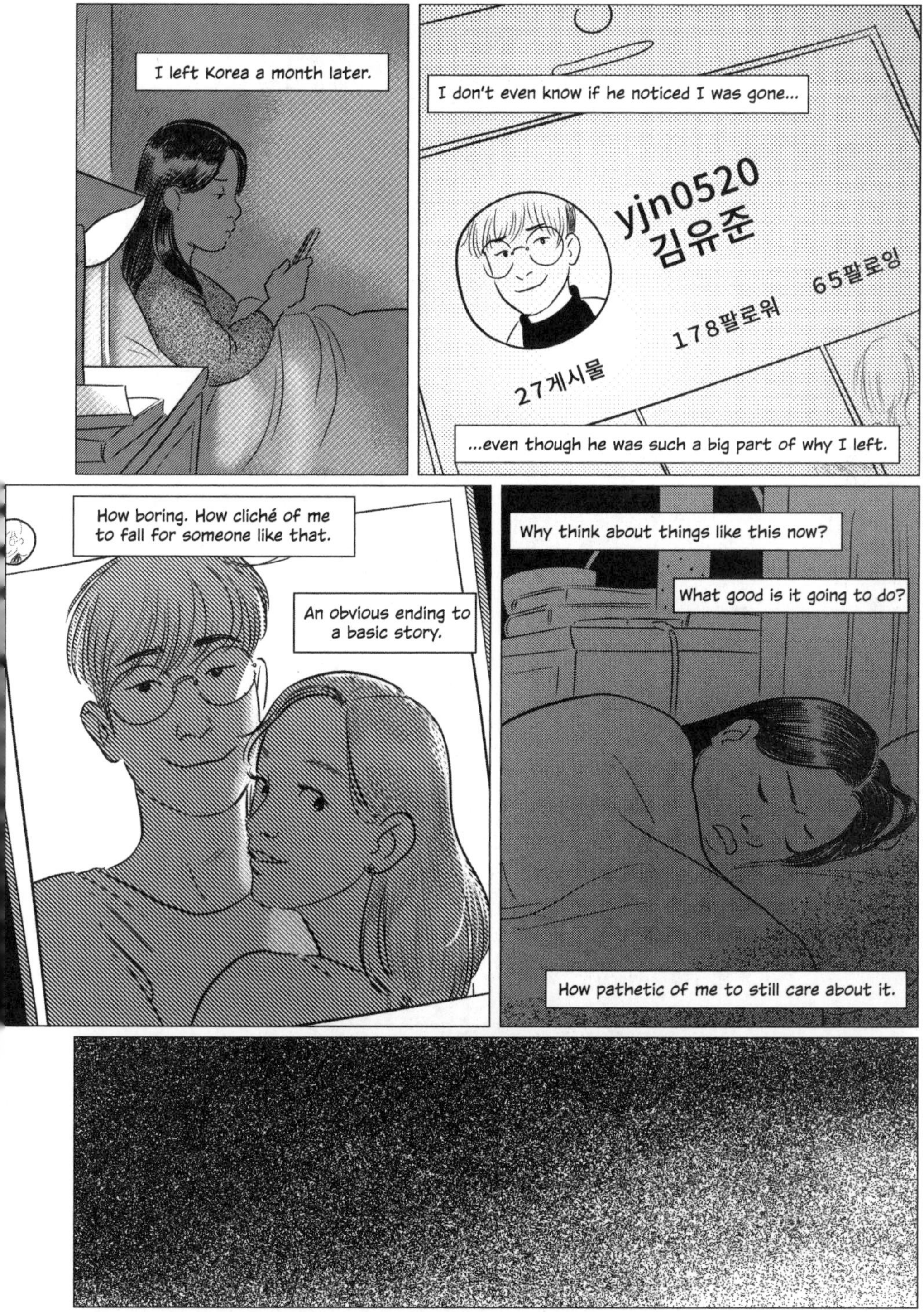
I left Korea a month later.
I don't even know if he noticed I was gone...
yjn0520
김유준
65팔로잉
178팔로워
27게시물
...even though he was such a big part of why I left.
How boring. How cliché of me to fall for someone like that.
An obvious ending to a basic story.
Why think about things like this now?
What good is it going to do?
How pathetic of me to still care about it.

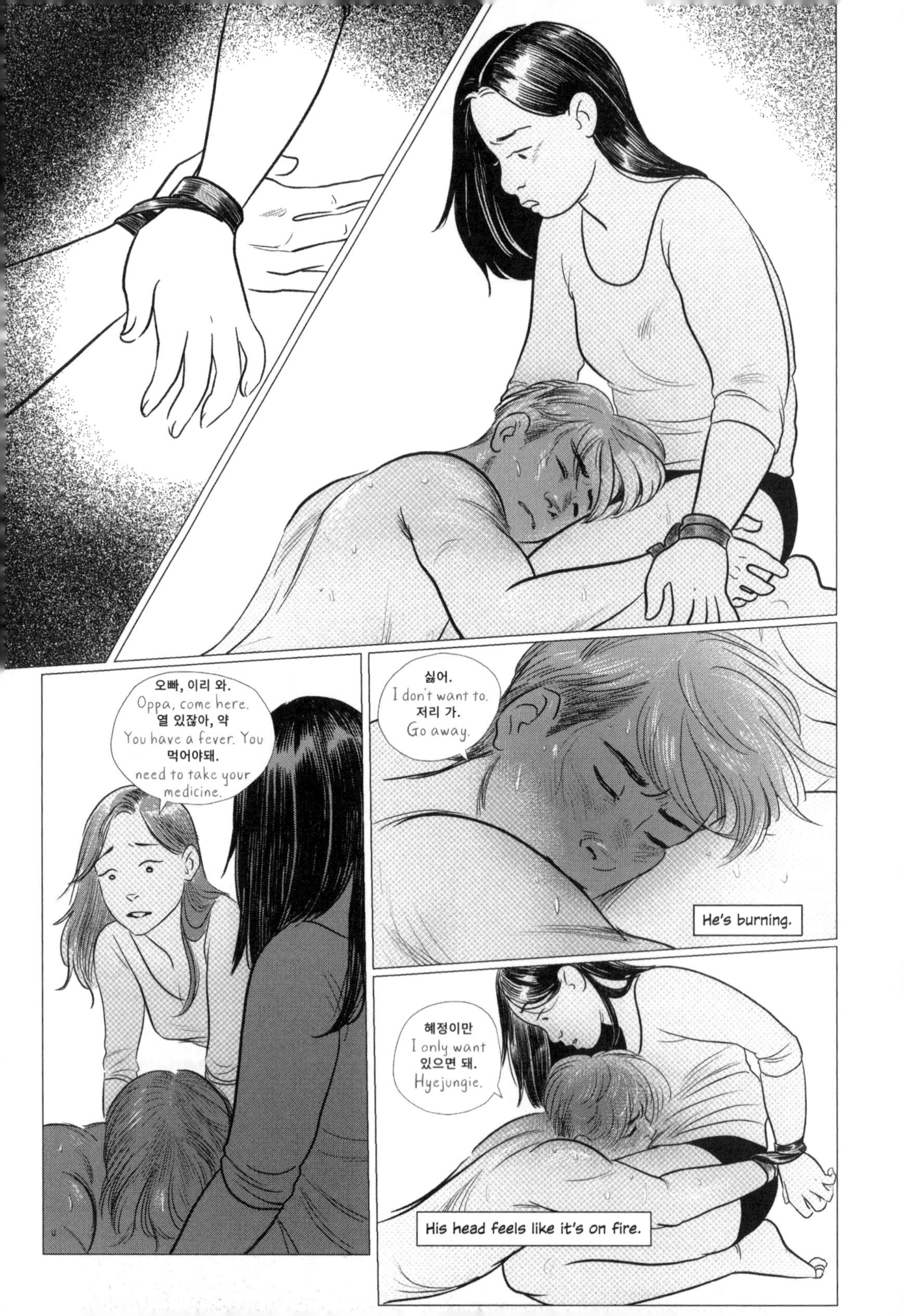

오빠, 이리 와.
Oppa, come here.
열 있잖아, 약
You have a fever. You
먹어야돼.
need to take your
medicine.
싫어.
I don't want to.
저리 가.
Go away.
He's burning.
혜정이만
I only want
있으면 돼.
Hyejungie.
His head feels like it's on fire.

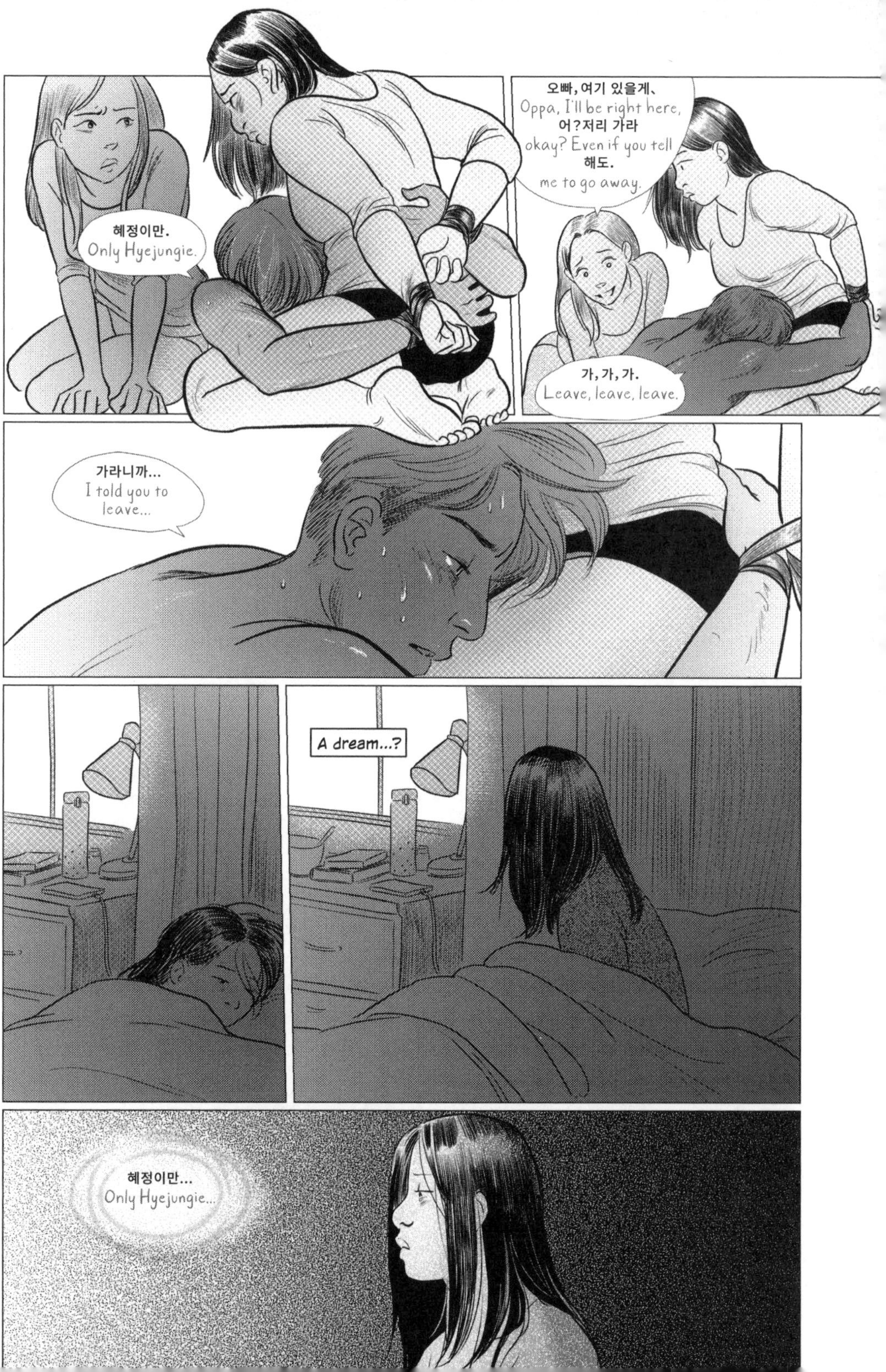
혜정이만.
Only Hyejungie.
오빠, 여기 있을게, 어?저리 가라 해도.
Oppa, I'll be right here, okay? Even if you tell me to go away.
가, 가, 가.
Leave, leave, leave.
가라니까...
I told you to leave...
A dream...?
혜정이만...
Only Hyejungie...

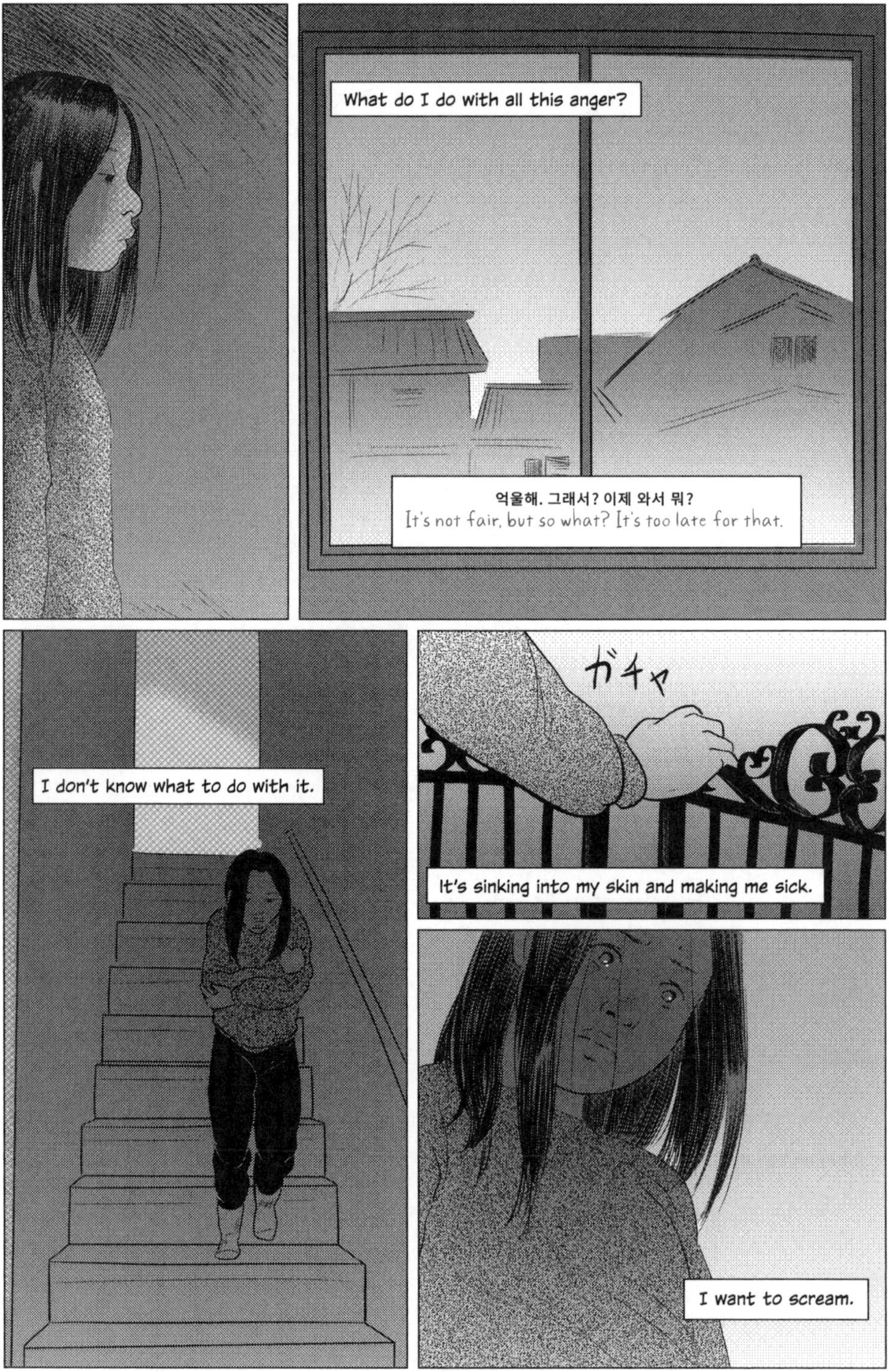
What do I do with all this anger?
억울해. 그래서? 이제 와서 뭐?
It's not fair, but so what? It's too late for that.
I don't know what to do with it.
ガチャ
It's sinking into my skin and making me sick.
I want to scream.

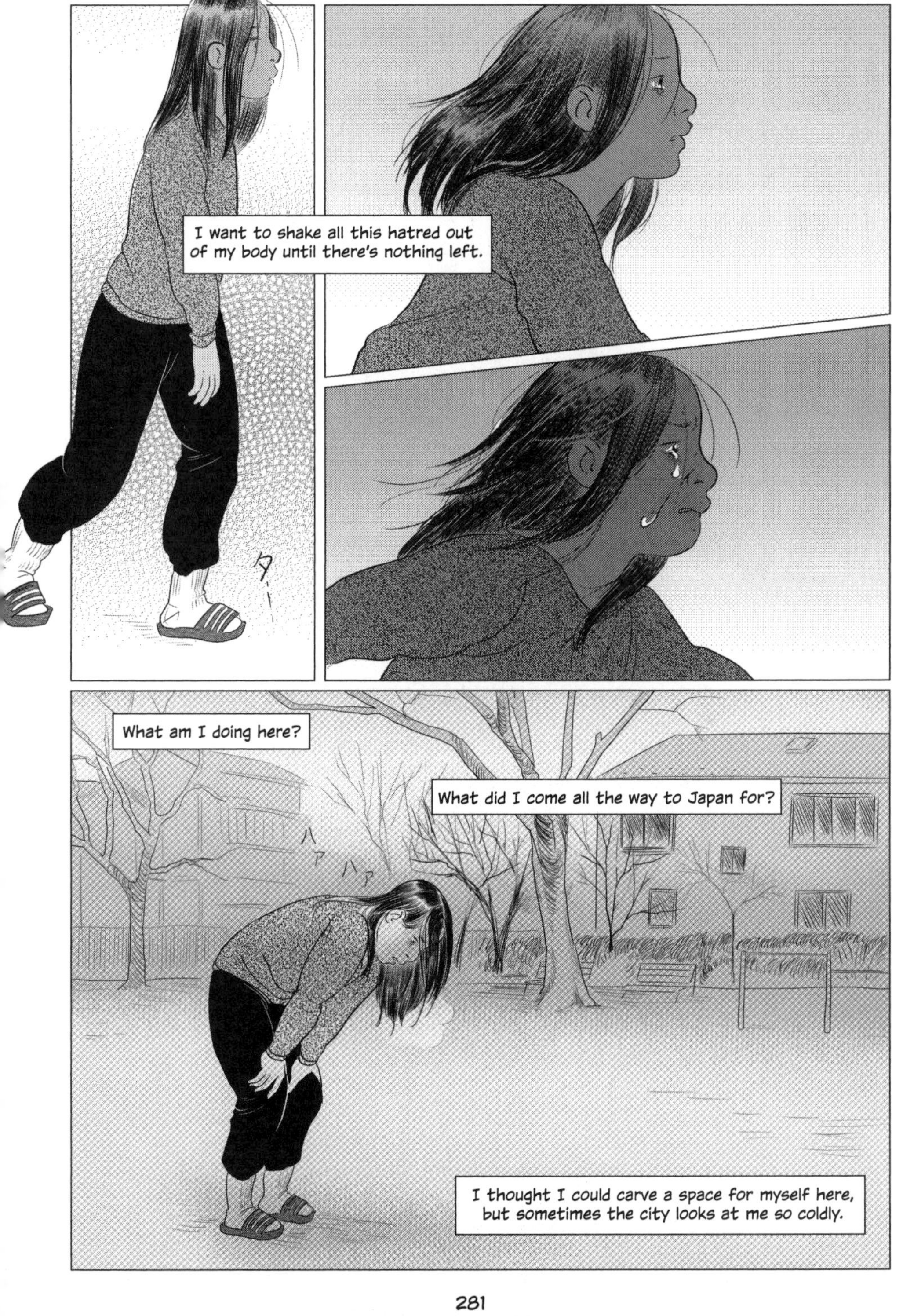
I want to shake all this hatred out of my body until there's nothing left.
What am I doing here?
What did I come all the way to Japan for?
I thought I could carve a space for myself here, but sometimes the city looks at me so coldly.

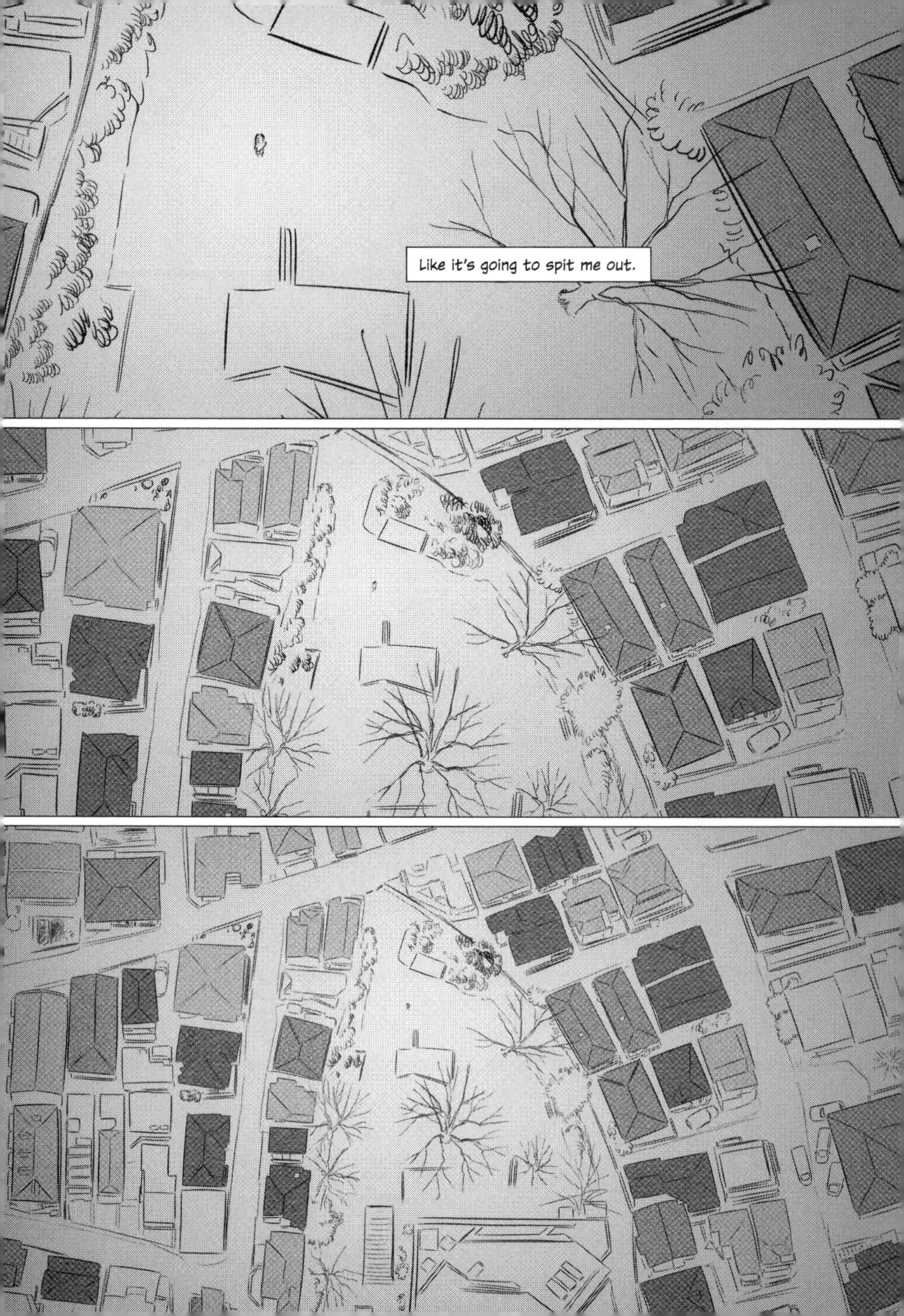
Like it's going to spit me out.

Chapter 16
Rakudai

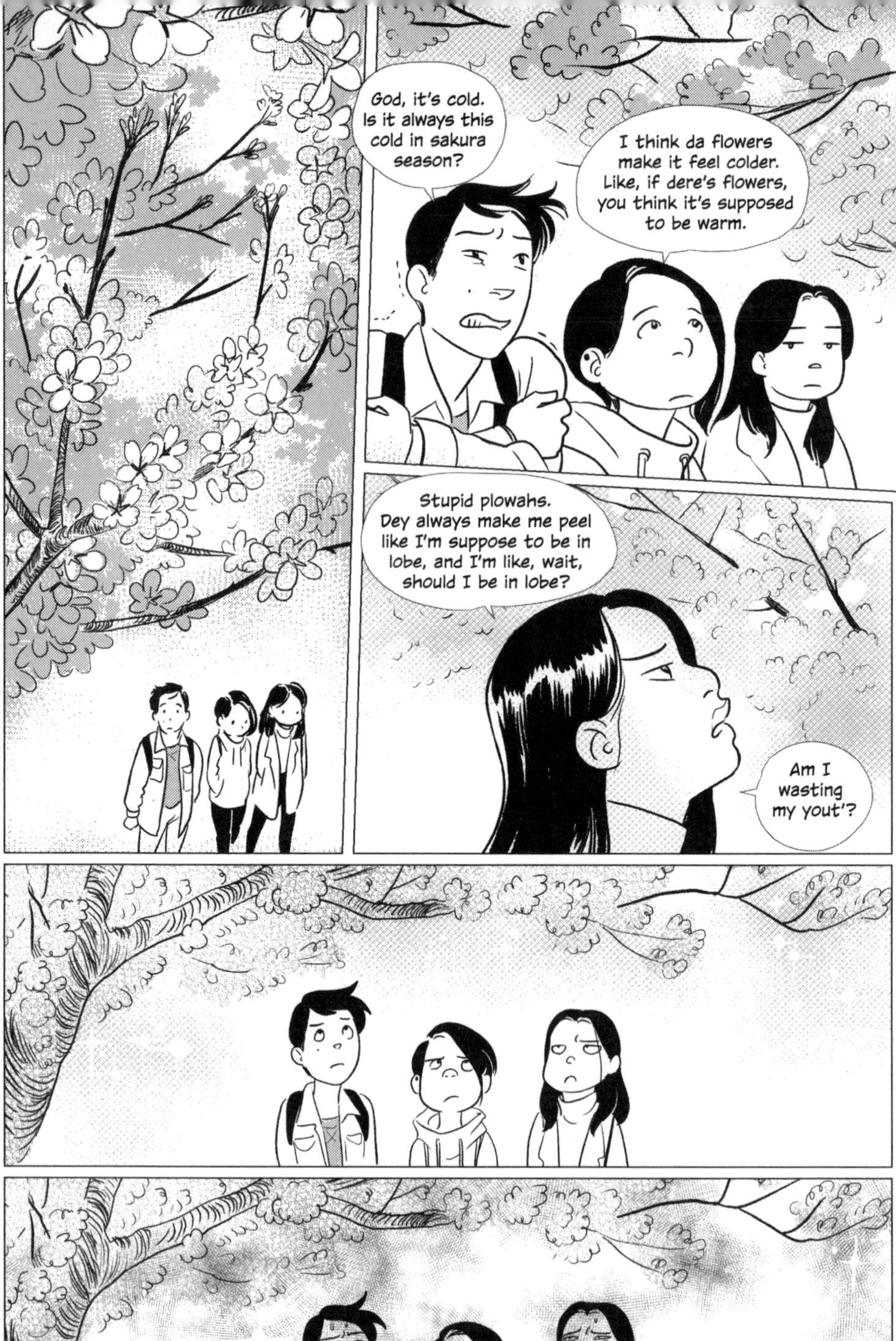
God, it's cold. Is it always this cold in sakura season?
I think da flowers make it feel colder. Like, if dere's flowers, you think it's supposed to be warm.
Stupid plowahs. Dey always make me peel like I'm suppose to be in lobe, and I'm like, wait, should I be in lobe?
Am I wasting my yout'?

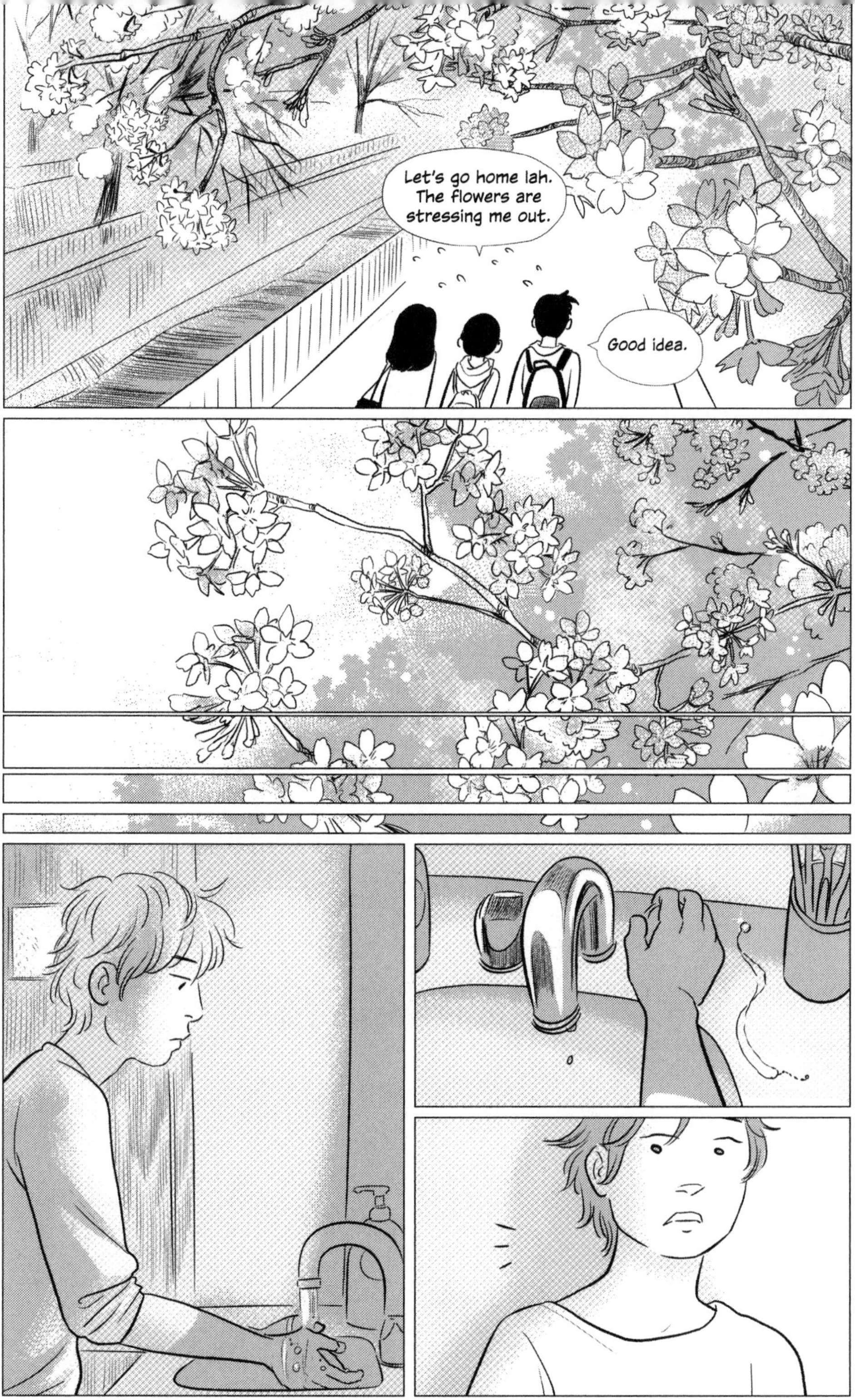
Let's go home lah. The flowers are stressing me out.
Good idea.

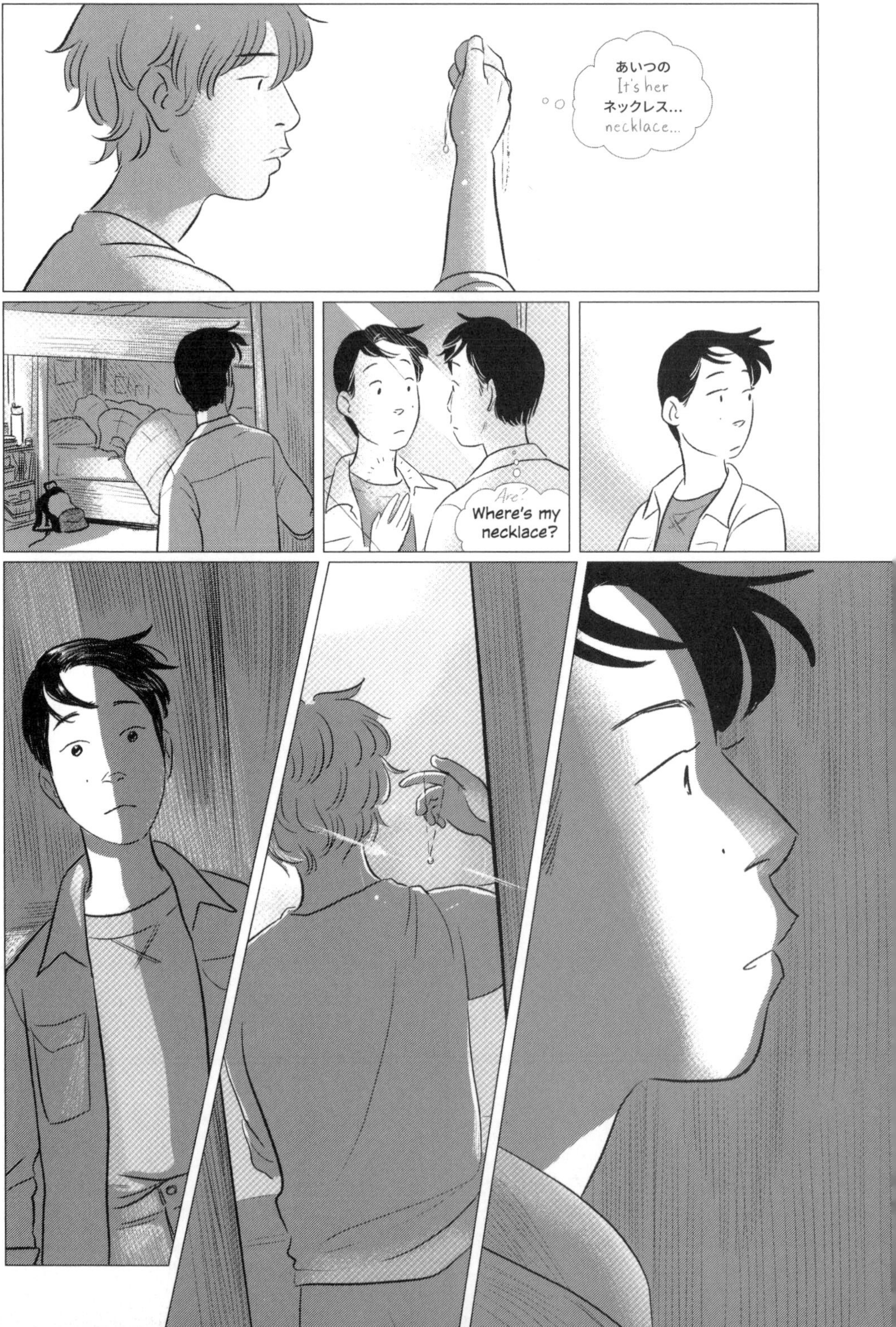
あいつの
It's her
ネックレス…
necklace...
Are?
Where's my necklace?

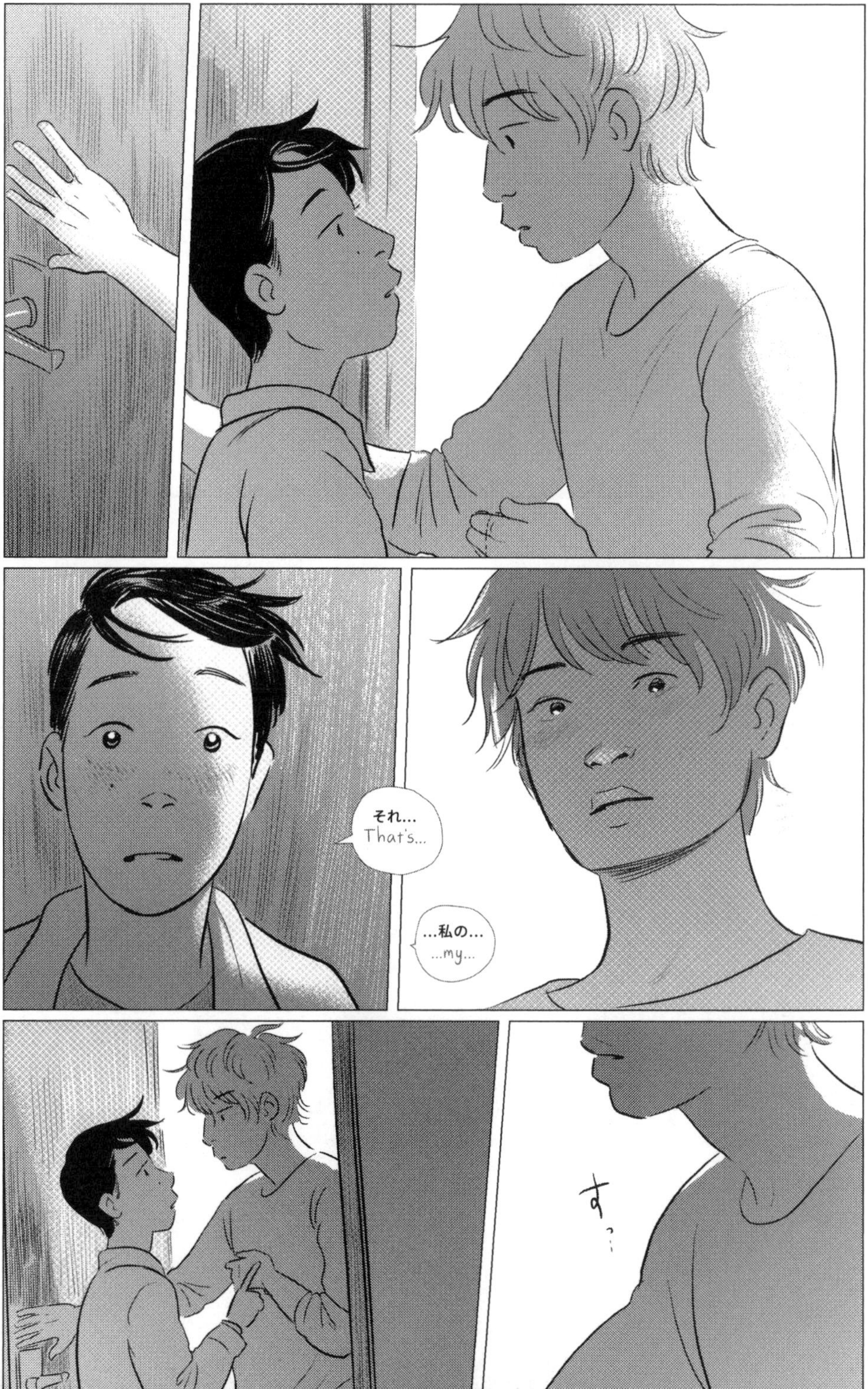
それ…
That's…
…私の…
…my…
すっ…

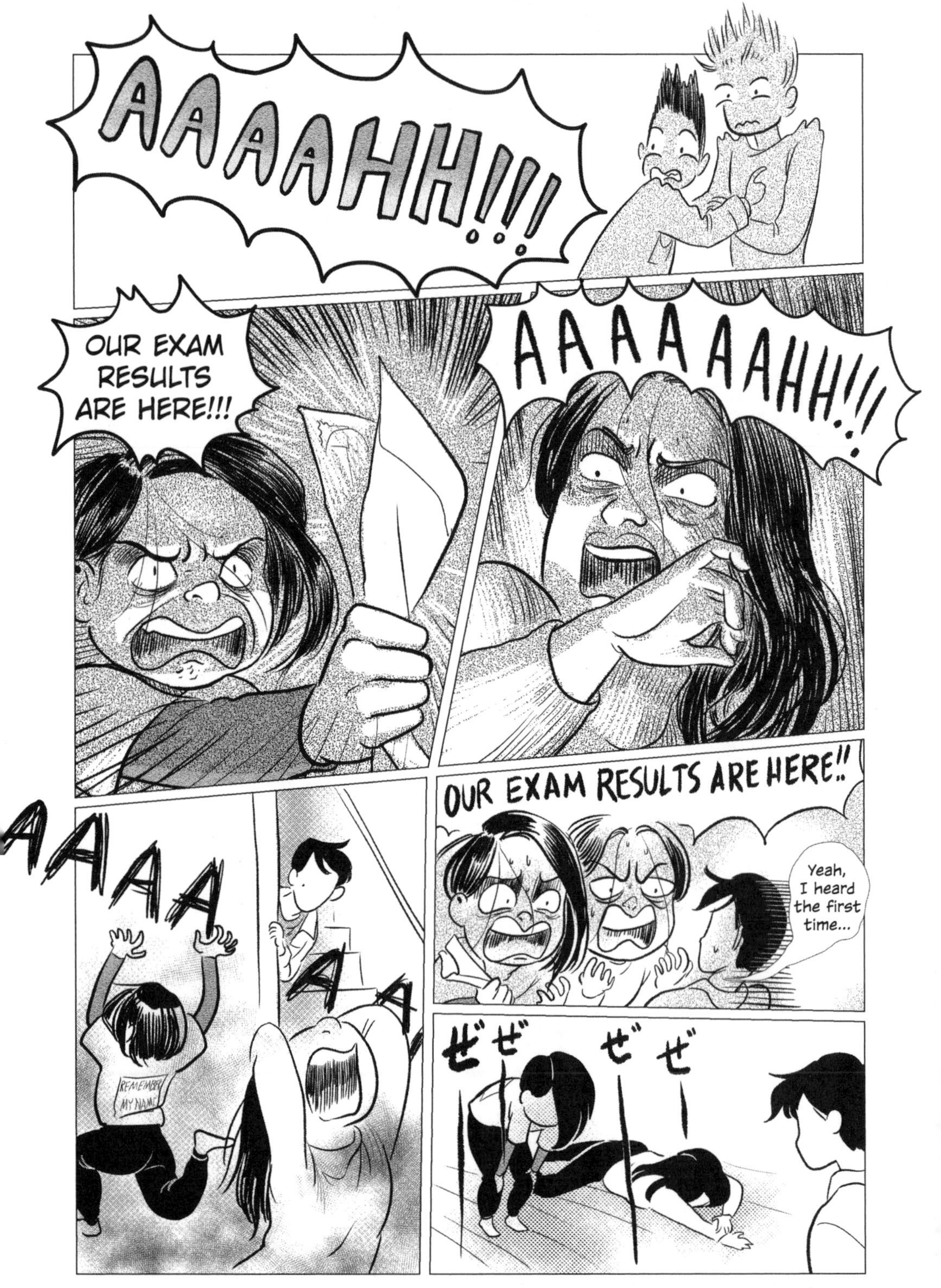
AAAAHH!!!
OUR EXAM RESULTS ARE HERE!!!
AAAAAAHH!!!
AAAAA
AA
OUR EXAM RESULTS ARE HERE!!
Yeah, I heard the first time...
REMEMBER MY NAME
ぜぜ
ぜぜ

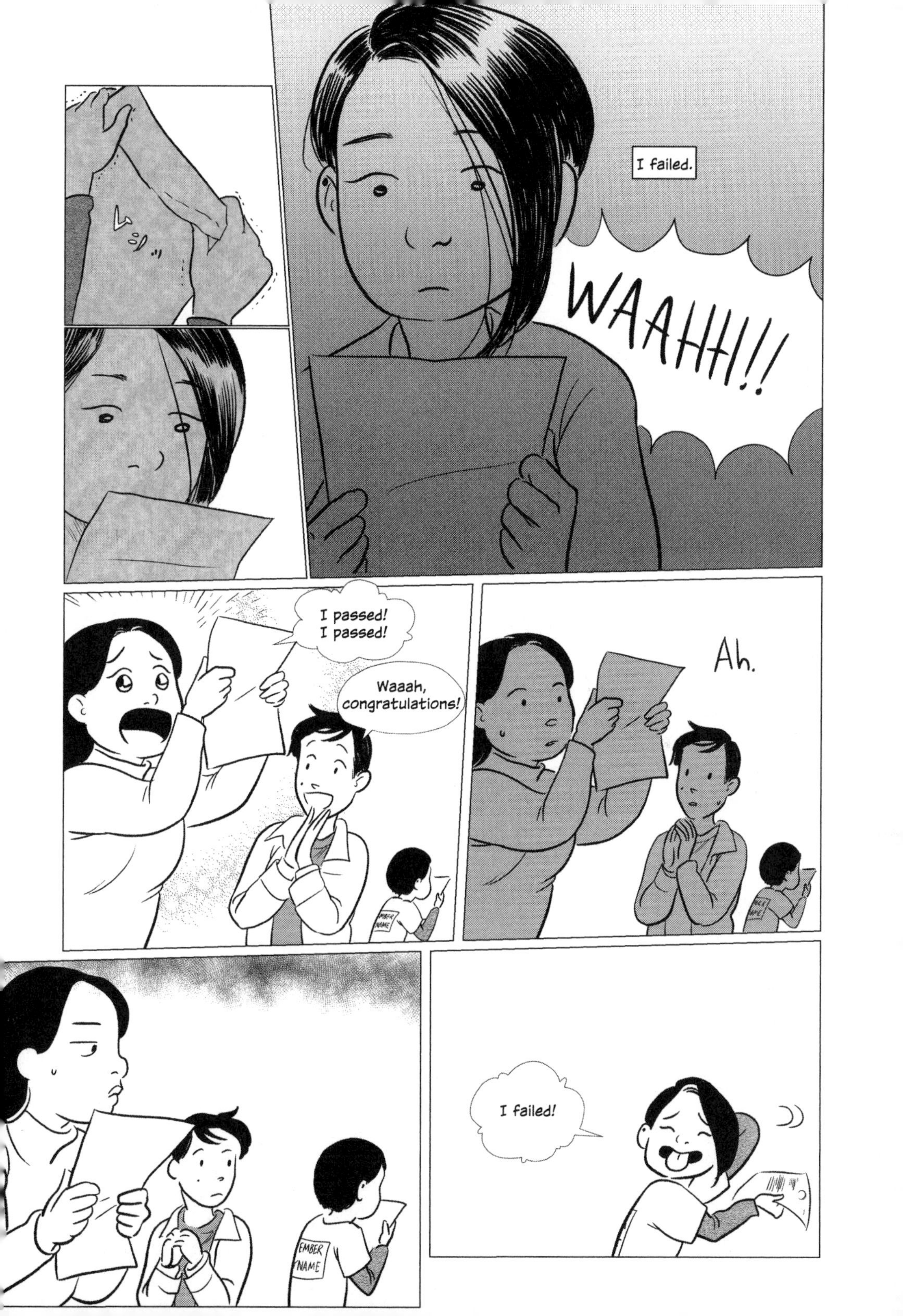
I failed.
WAAHH!!!
I passed! I passed!
Waaah, congratulations!
EMBER NAME
Ah.
EMBER NAME
I failed!

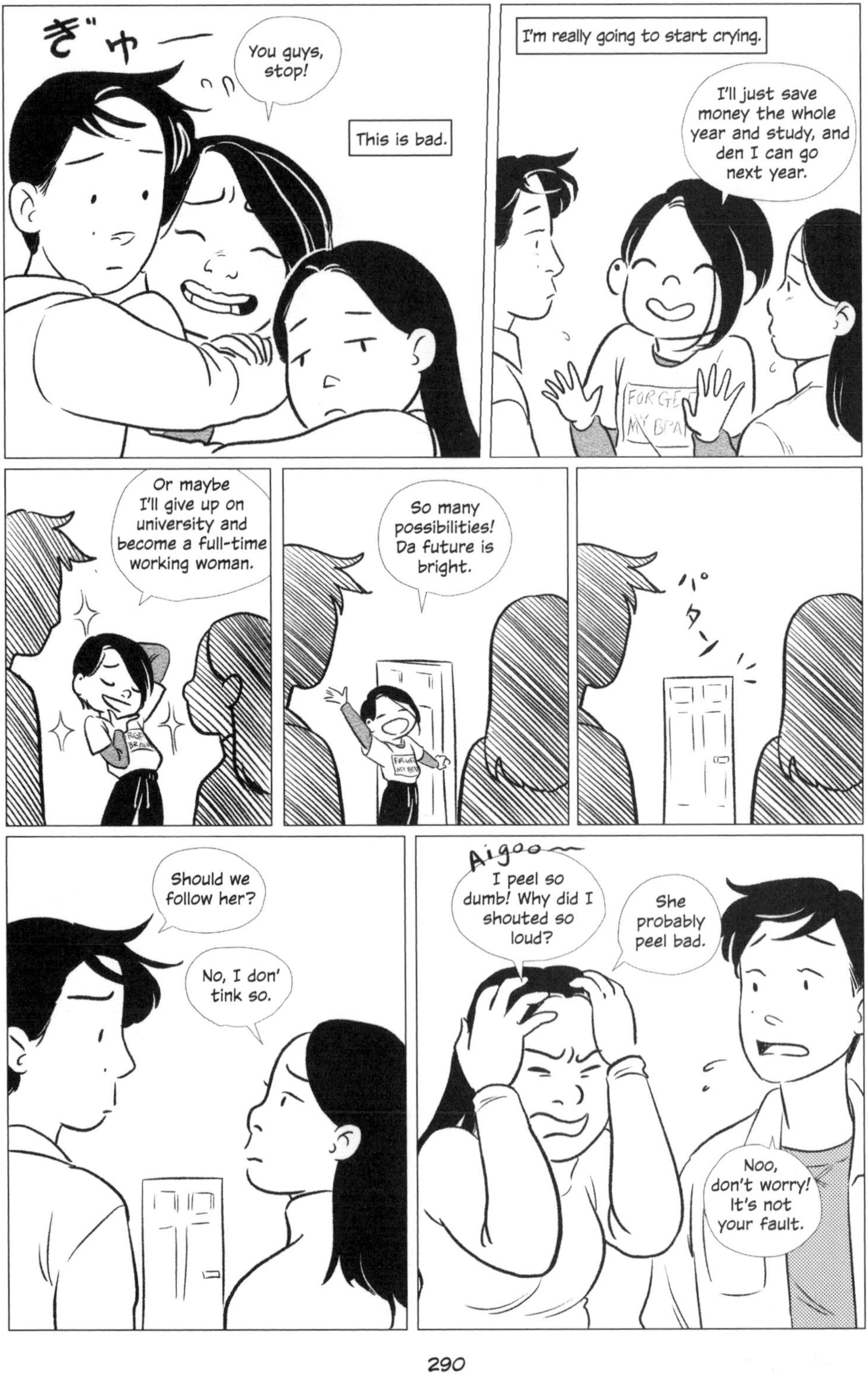
ぎゅー
You guys, stop!
This is bad.
I'm really going to start crying.
I'll just save money the whole year and study, and den I can go next year.
FORGET MY BRA
Or maybe I'll give up on university and become a full-time working woman.
So many possibilities! Da future is bright.
パターン
Should we follow her?
No, I don' tink so.
Aigoo~
I peel so dumb! Why did I shouted so loud?
She probably peel bad.
Noo, don't worry! It's not your fault.

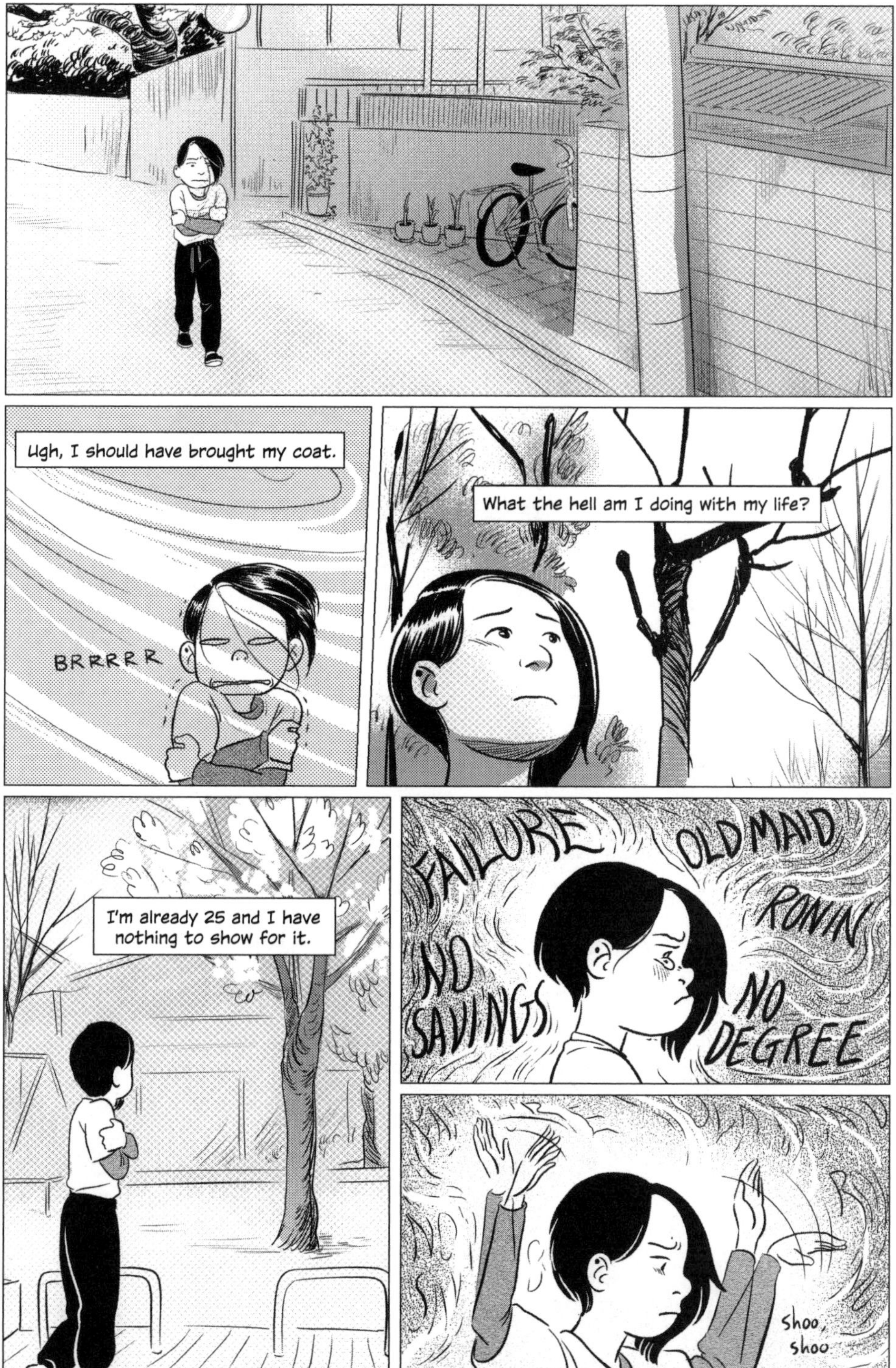

Ugh, I should have brought my coat.
BRRRRR
What the hell am I doing with my life?
I'm already 25 and I have nothing to show for it.
FAILURE
OLD MAID
RONIN
NO SAVINGS
NO DEGREE
Shoo, shoo

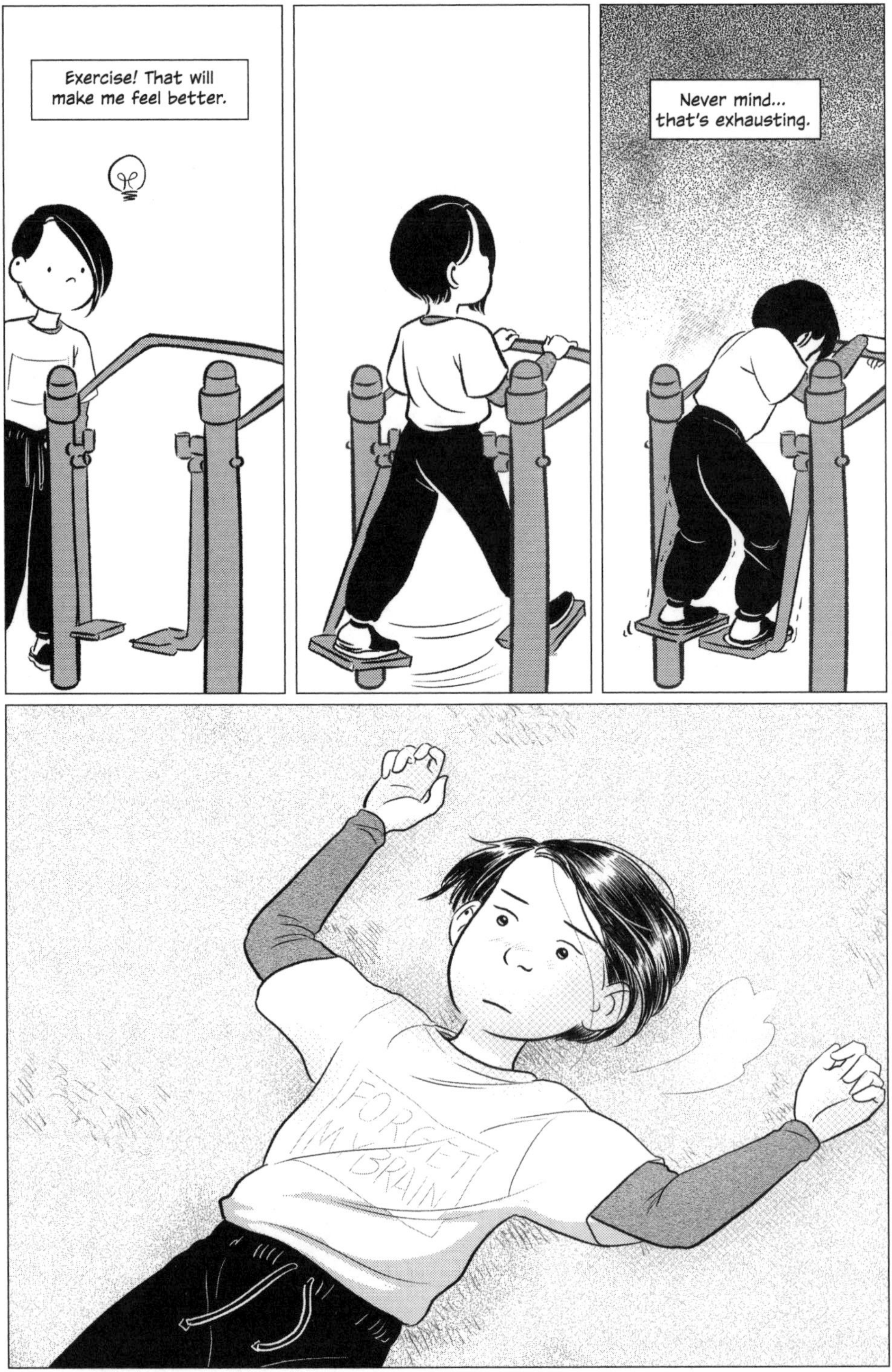
Exercise! That will make me feel better.
Never mind... that's exhausting.
FORGET MY BRAIN

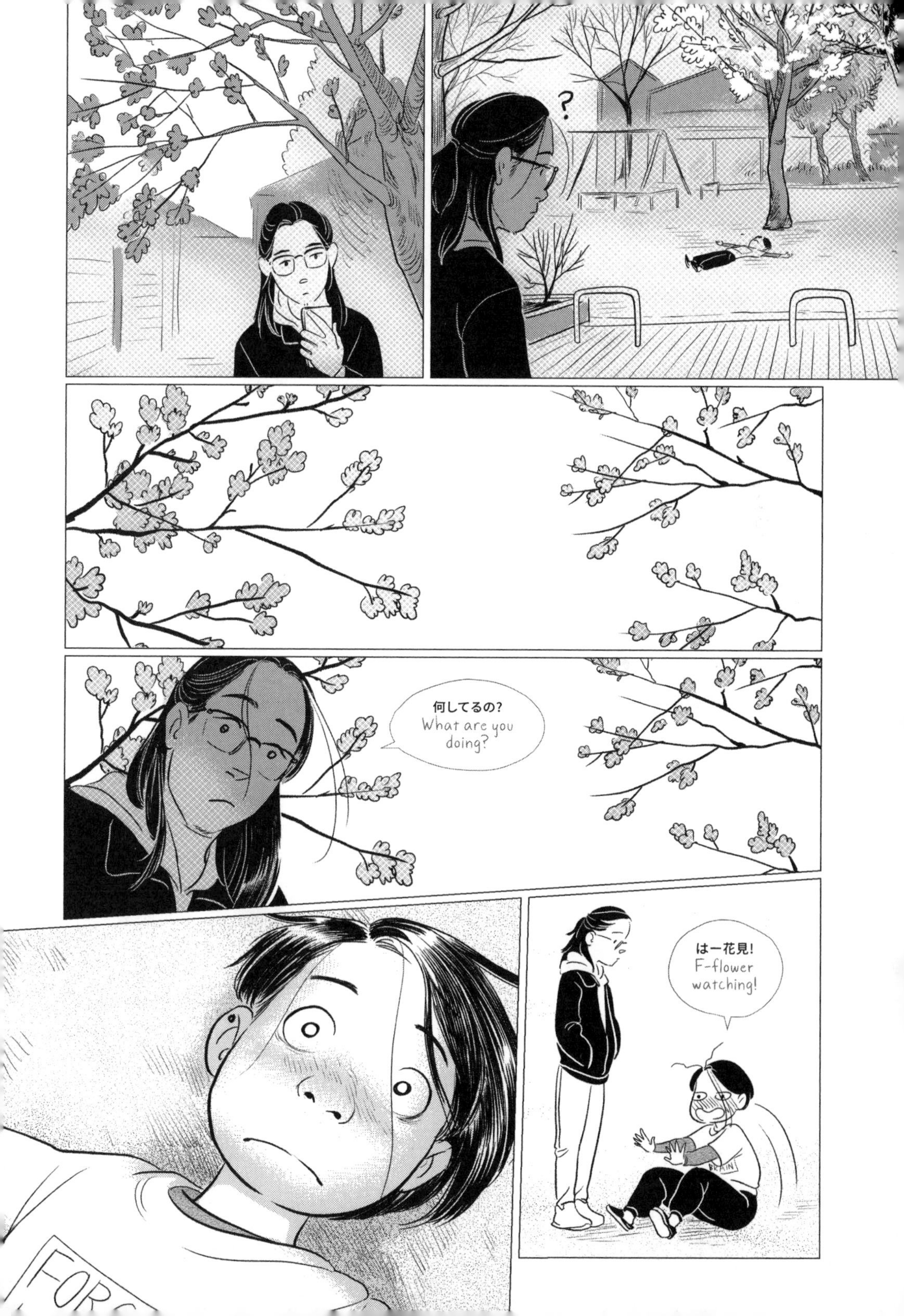
?
何してるの? What are you doing?
はー花見! F-flower watching!

ん？まだ
Nn? There's
ちょっとしか
barely any blooming
咲いてないけど
yet, though.

っていうか、
What's
どうしたの？
wrong?

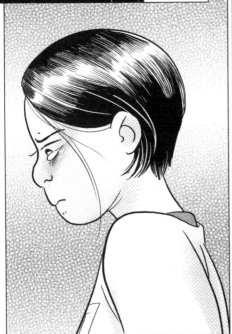

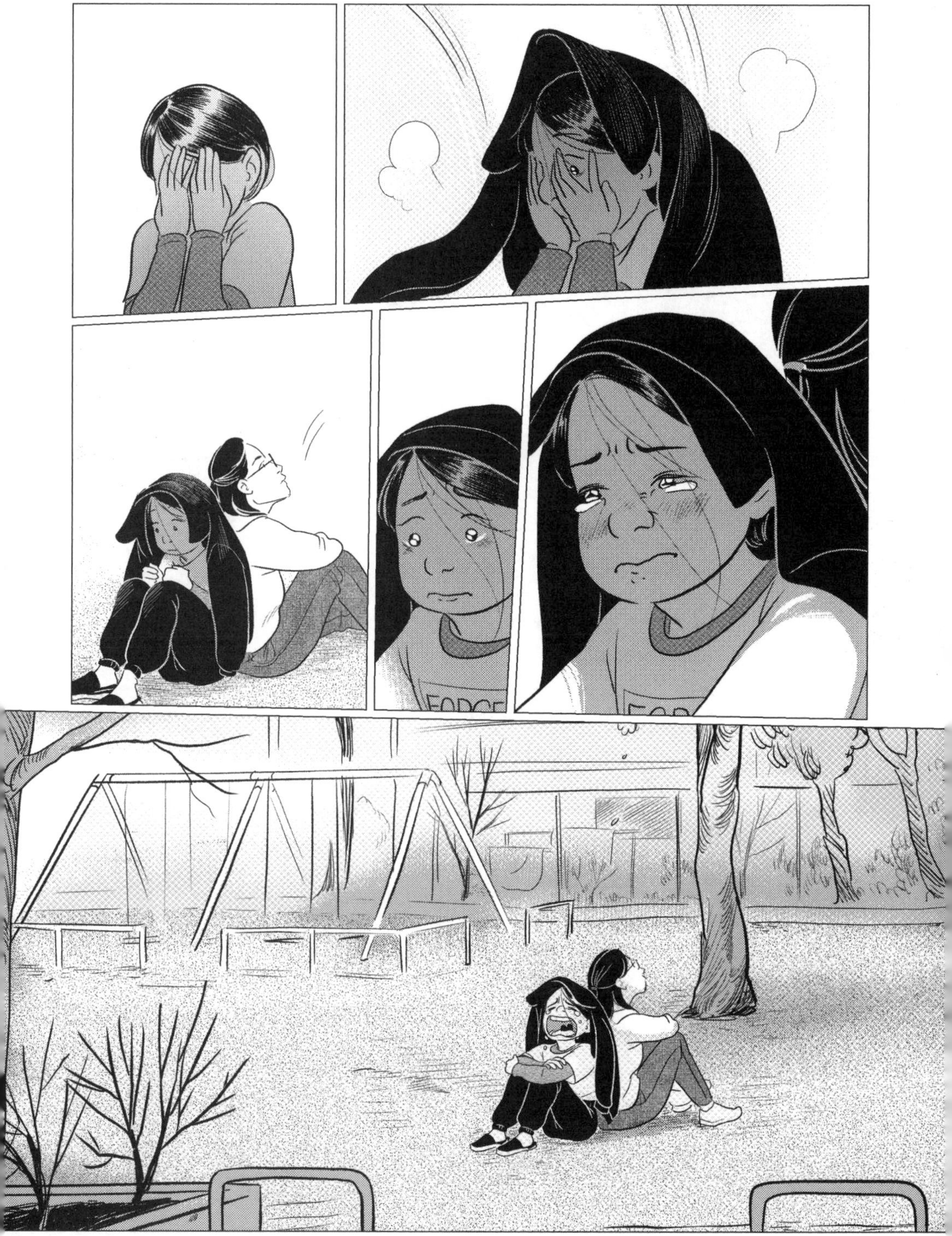

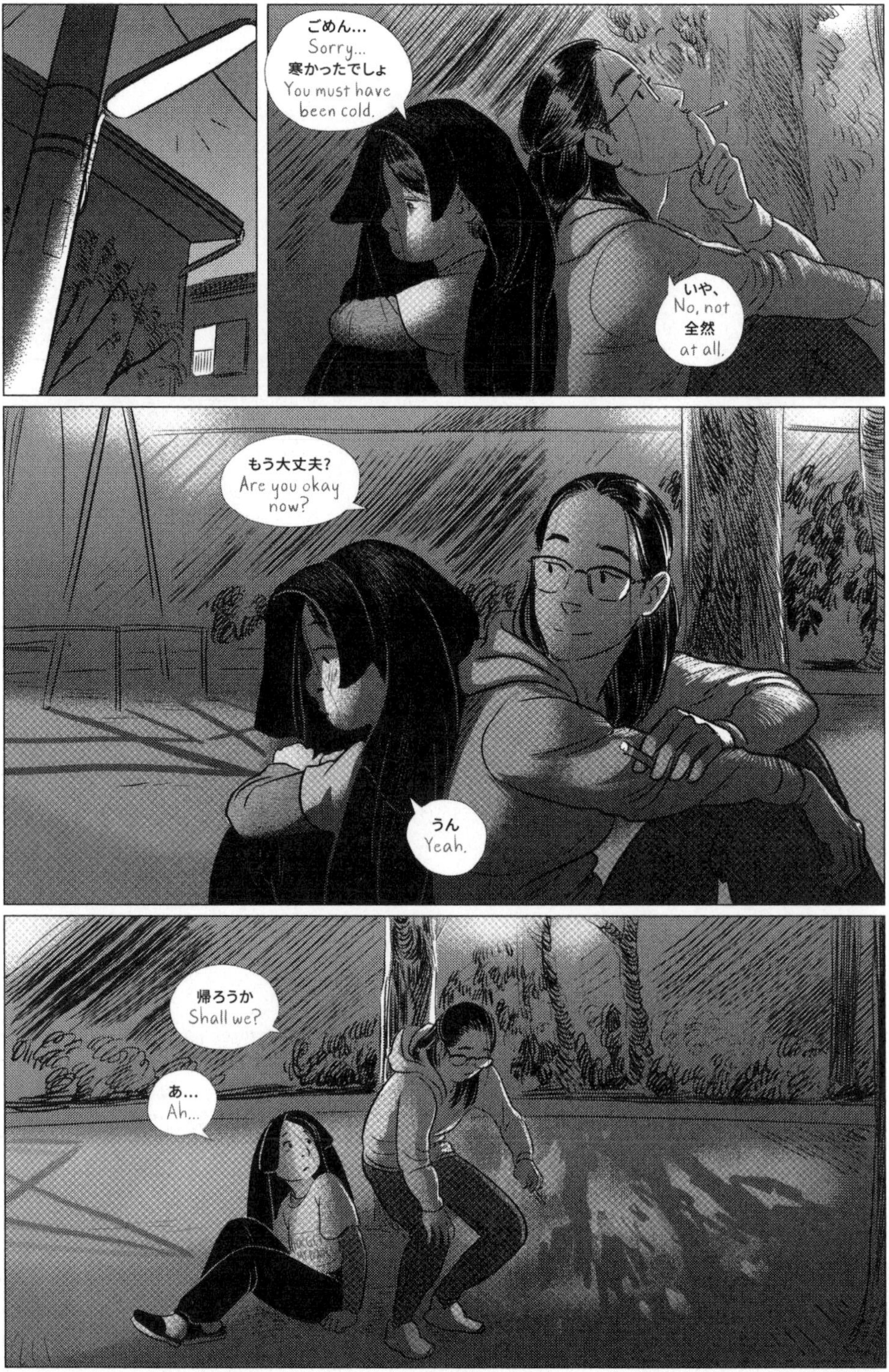
ごめん… Sorry… 寒かったでしょ You must have been cold.
いや、No, not 全然 at all.
もう大丈夫? Are you okay now?
うん Yeah.
帰ろうか Shall we?
あ… Ah…

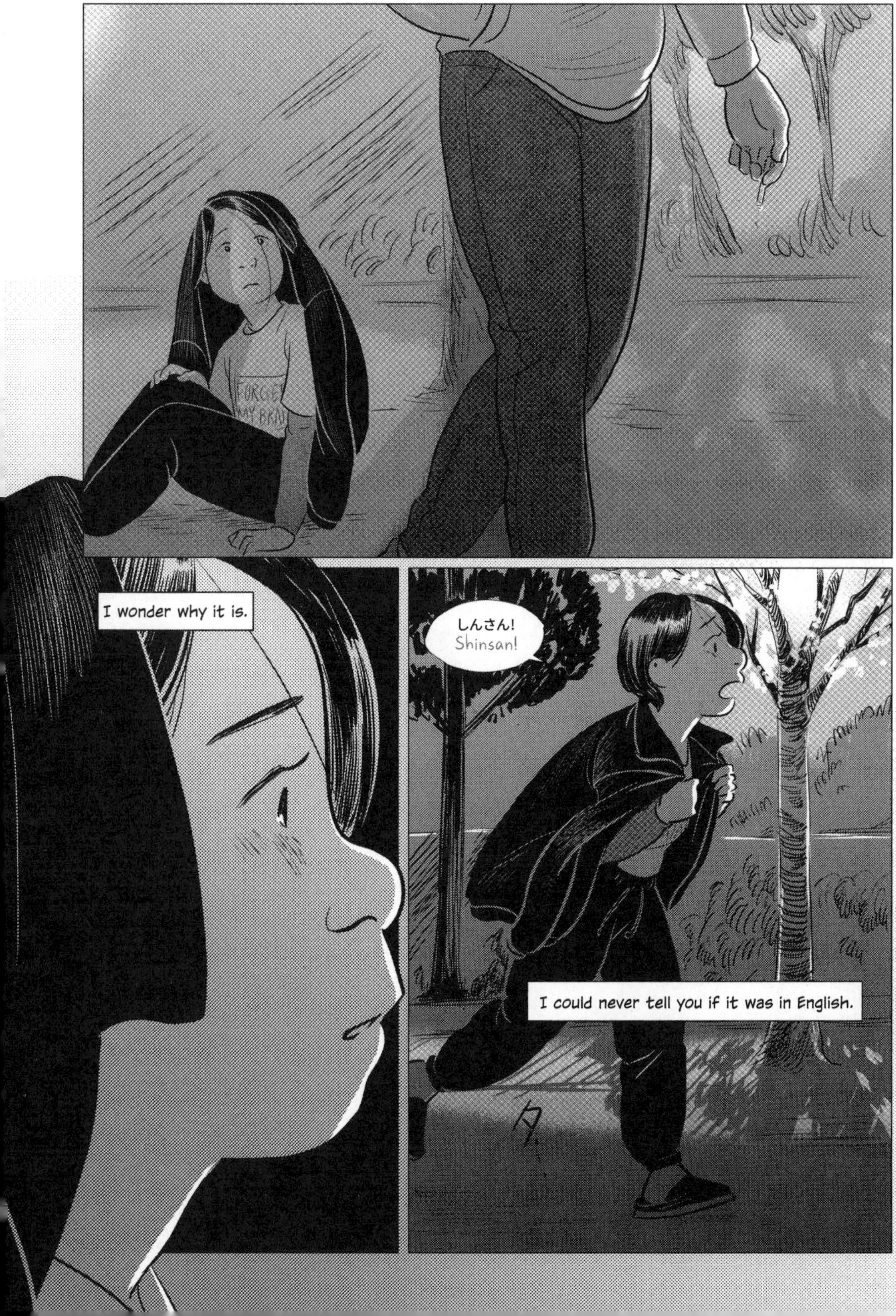
I wonder why it is.
しんさん!
Shinsan!
I could never tell you if it was in English.

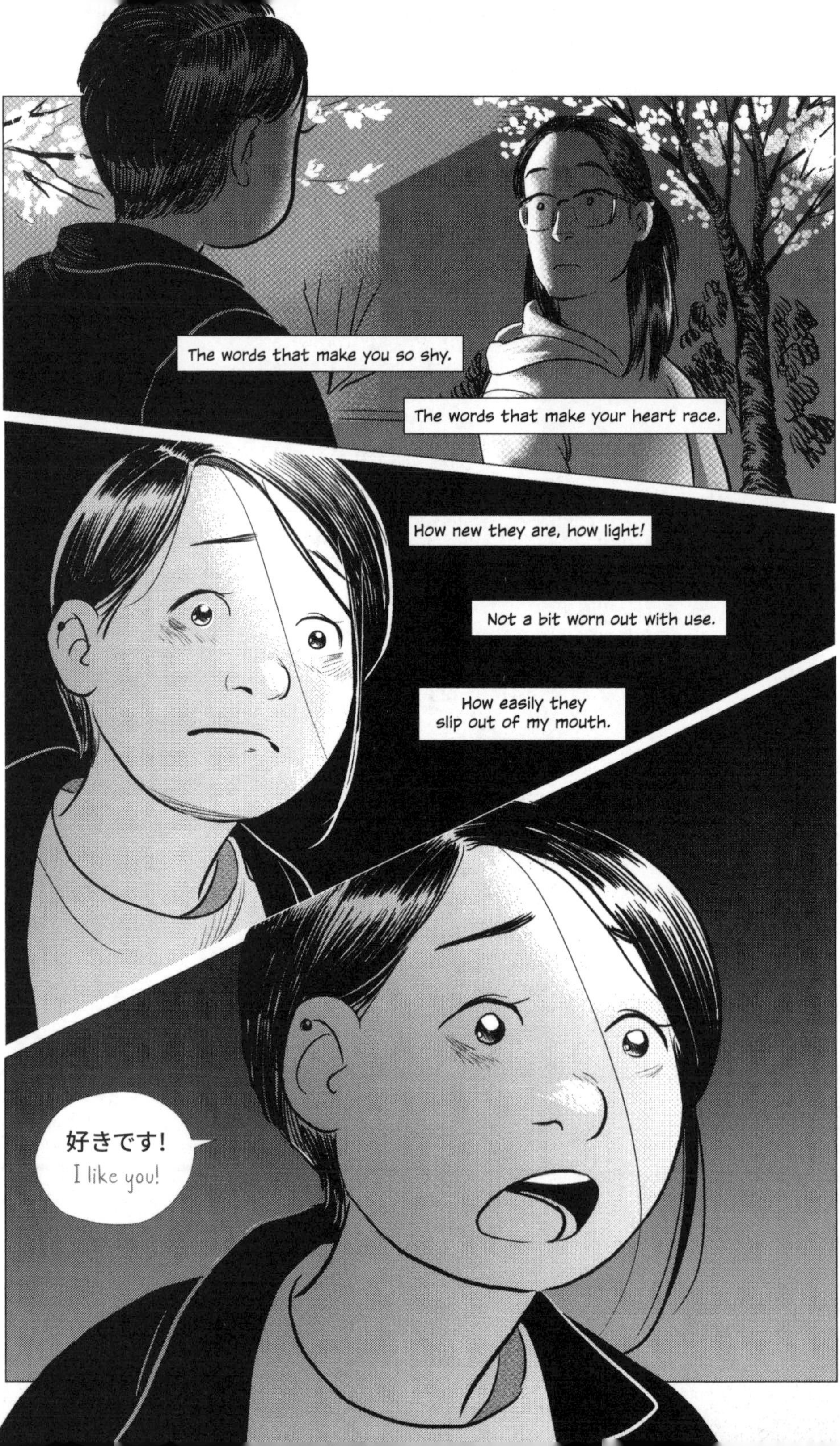
The words that make you so shy.
The words that make your heart race.
How new they are, how light!
Not a bit worn out with use.
How easily they slip out of my mouth.
好きです!
I like you!

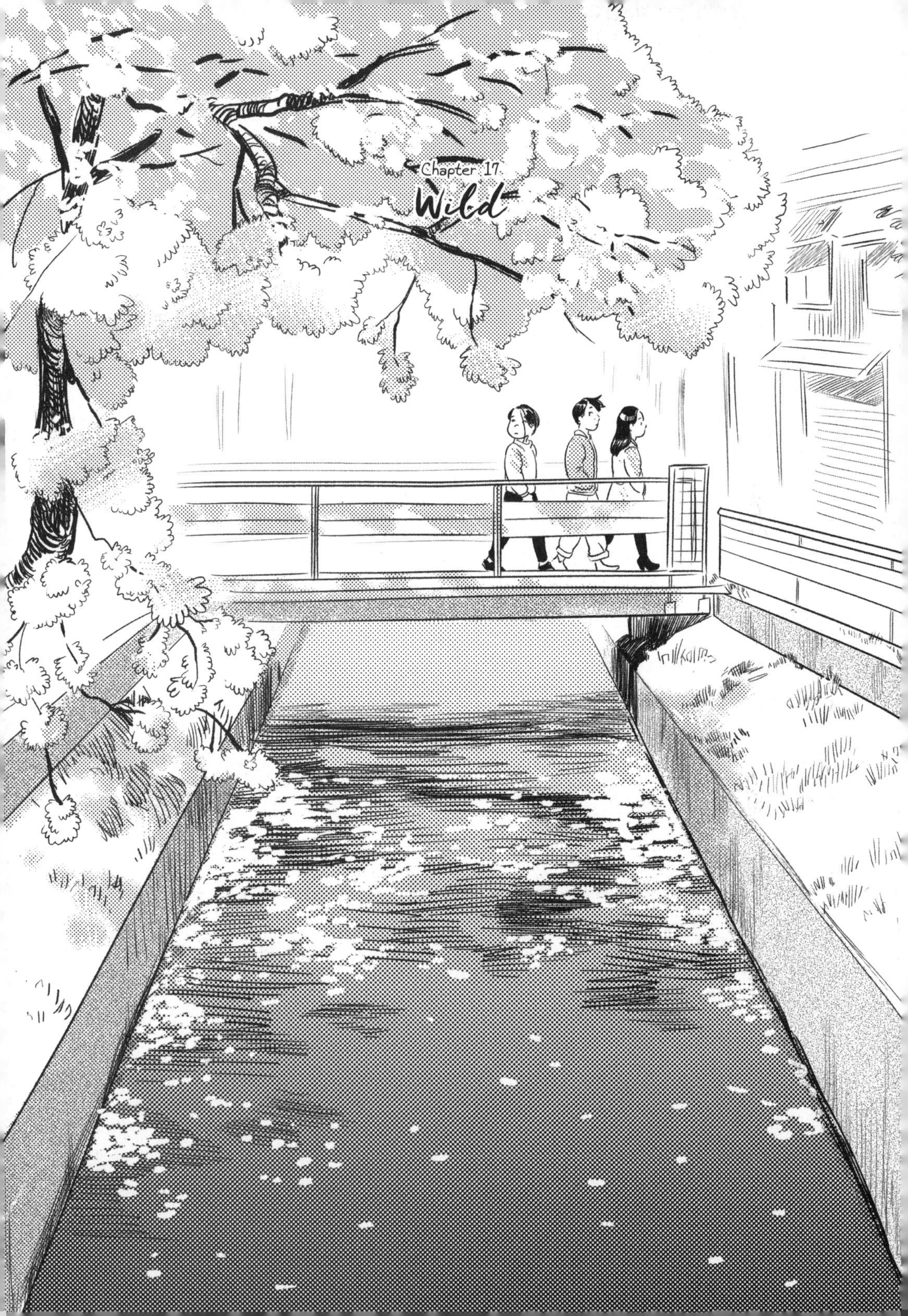
Chapter 17
Wild

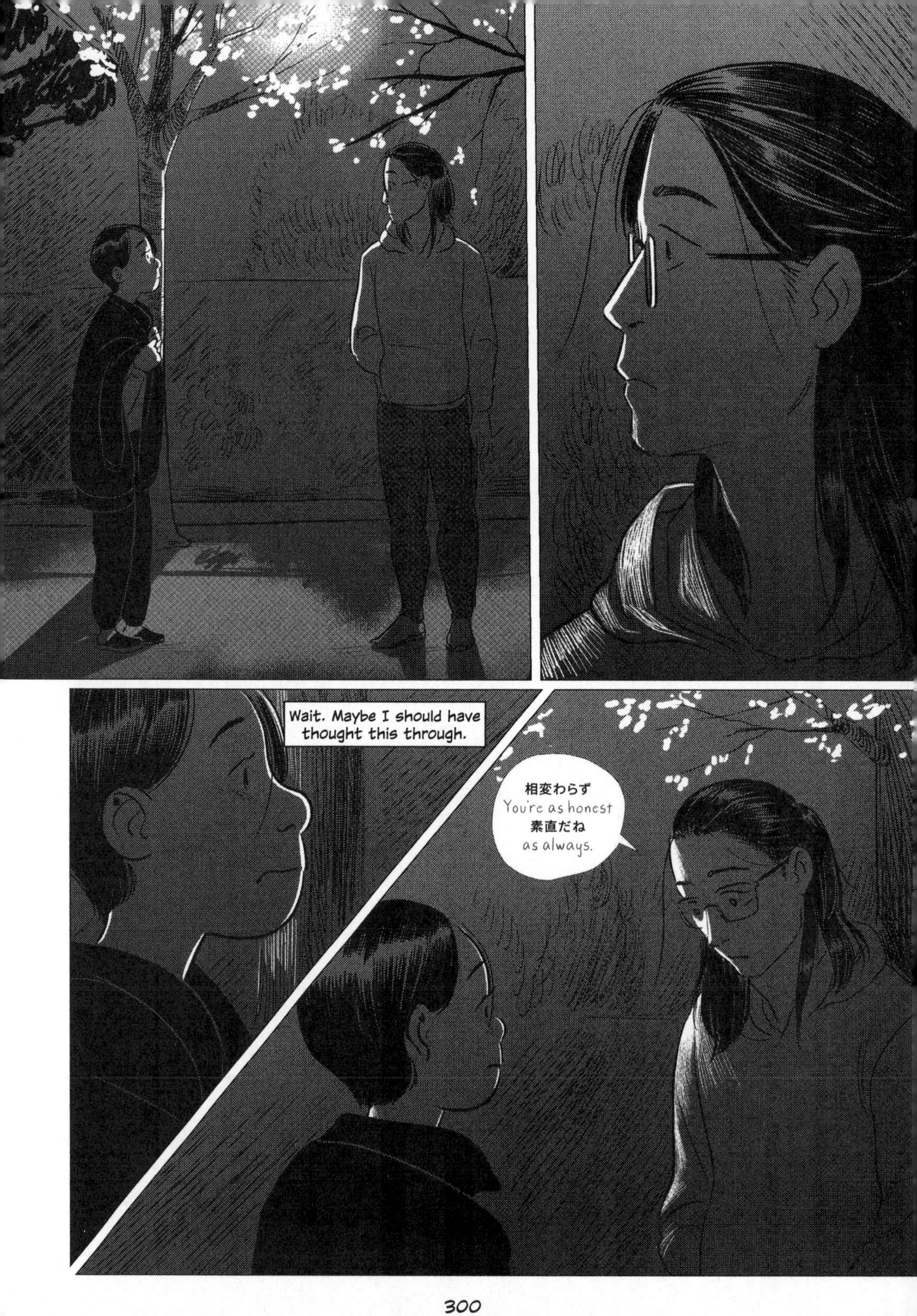
Wait. Maybe I should have thought this through.
相変わらず
You're as honest
素直だね
as always.

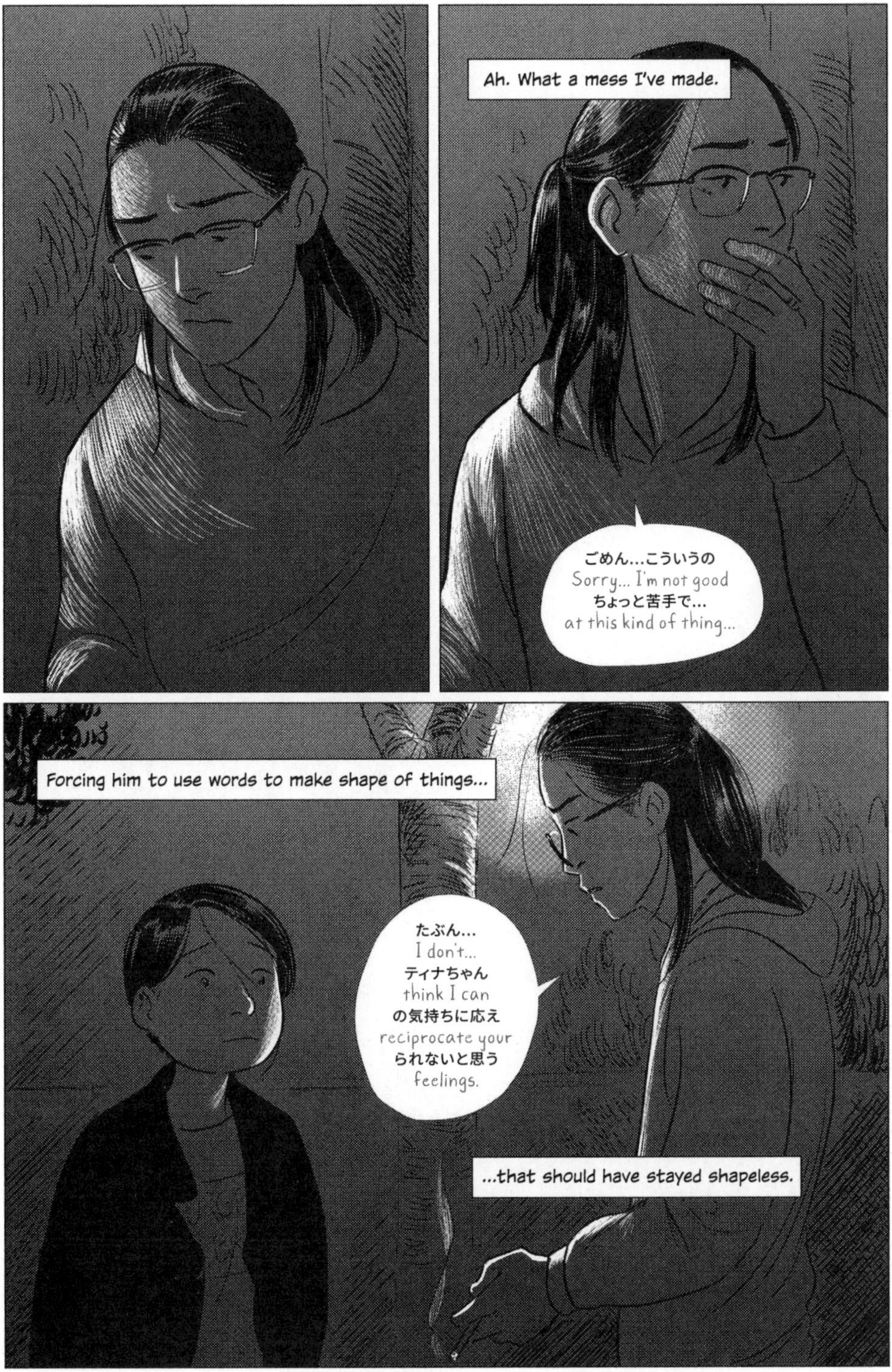
Ah. What a mess I've made.
ごめん…こういうの
Sorry... I'm not good
ちょっと苦手で…
at this kind of thing...
Forcing him to use words to make shape of things...
たぶん…
I don't...
ティナちゃん
think I can
の気持ちに応え
reciprocate your
られないと思う
feelings.
...that should have stayed shapeless.

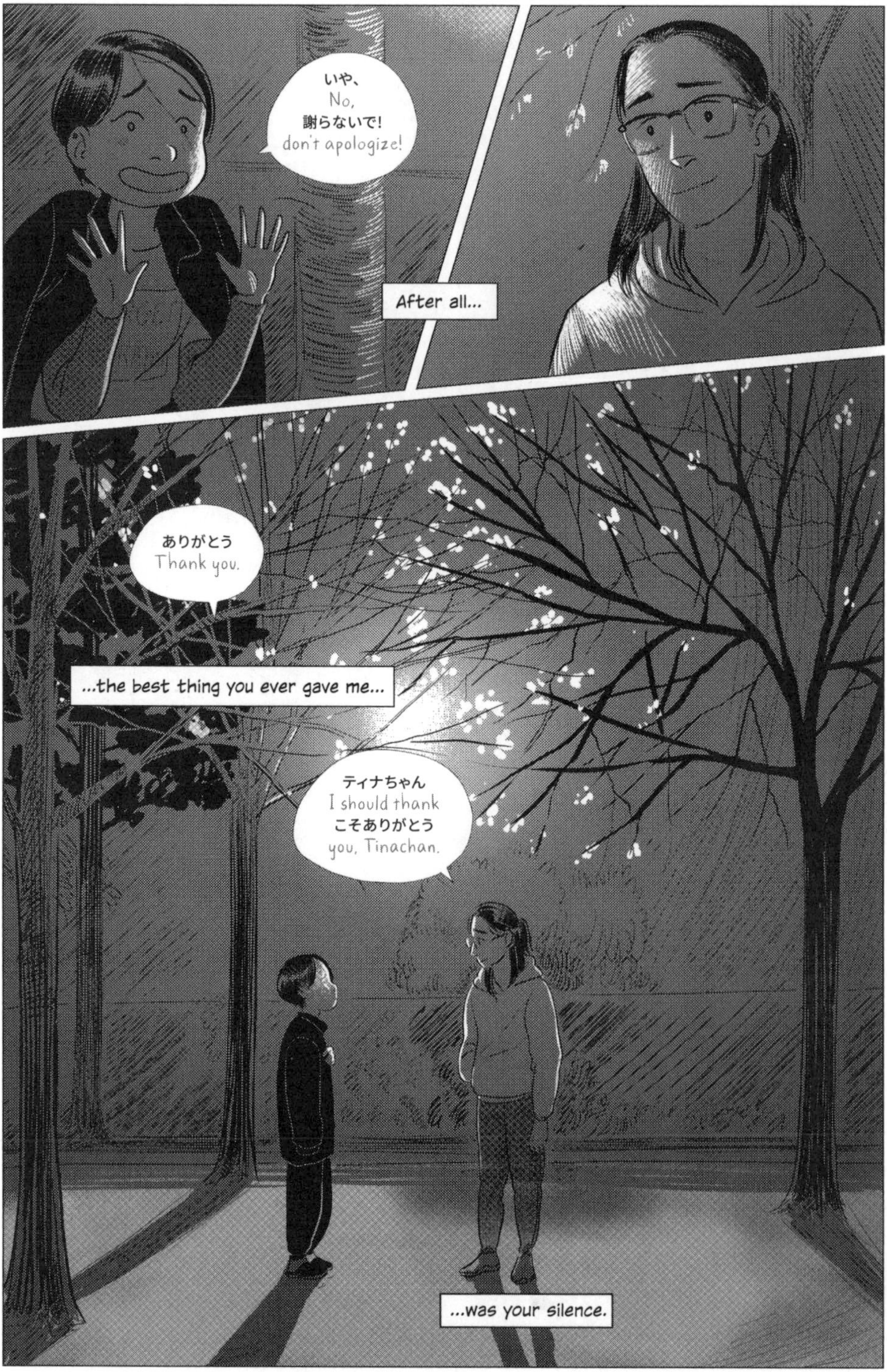
いや、
No,
謝らないで!
don't apologize!
After all...
ありがとう
Thank you.
...the best thing you ever gave me...
ティナちゃん
I should thank
こそありがとう
you, Tinachan.
...was your silence.

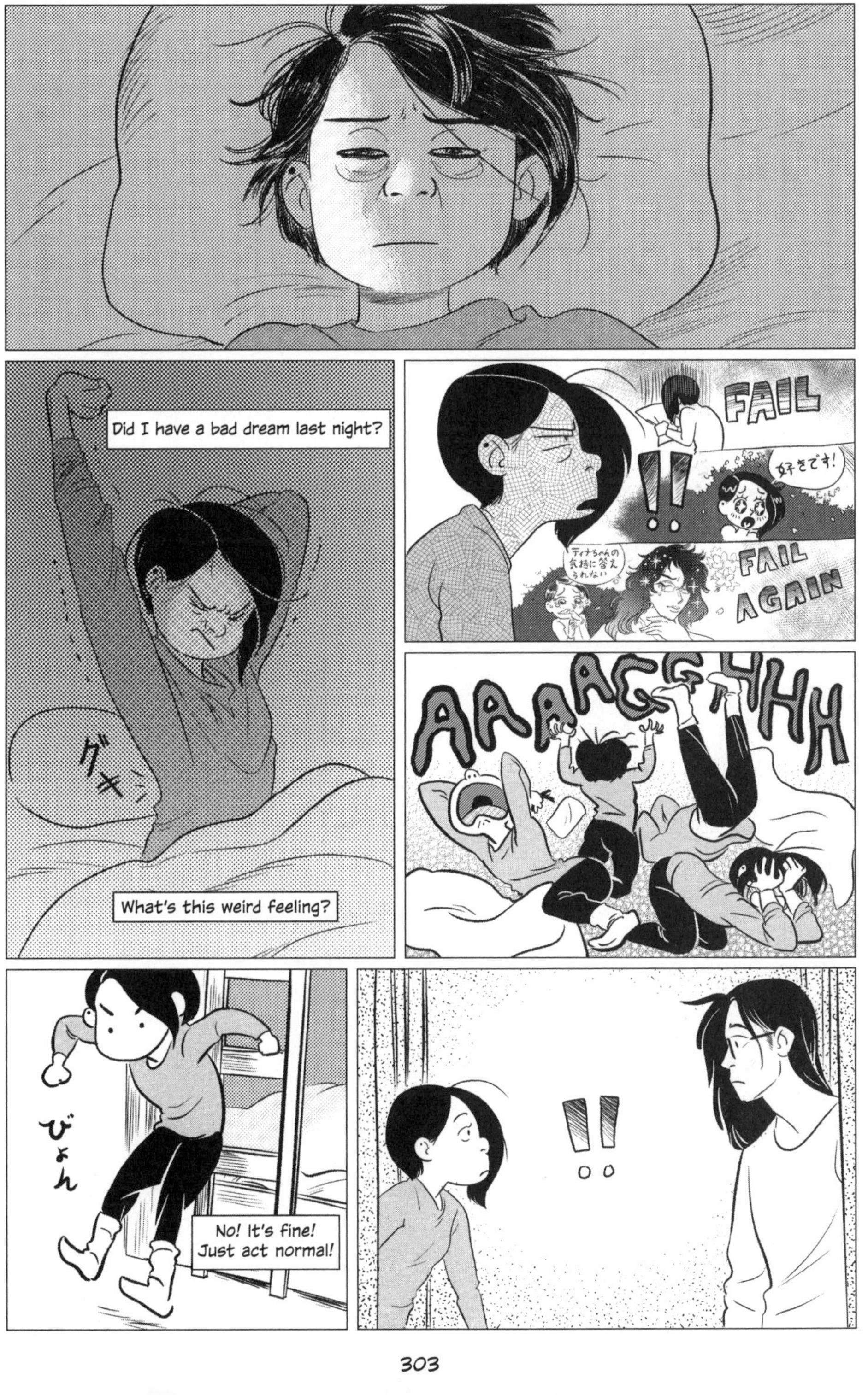
Did I have a bad dream last night?
グキッ
What's this weird feeling?
FAIL
!!
好きです!
ティナちゃんの気持に答えられない
FAIL AGAIN
AAAAGGHHH
ぴょん
No! It's fine! Just act normal!
!!

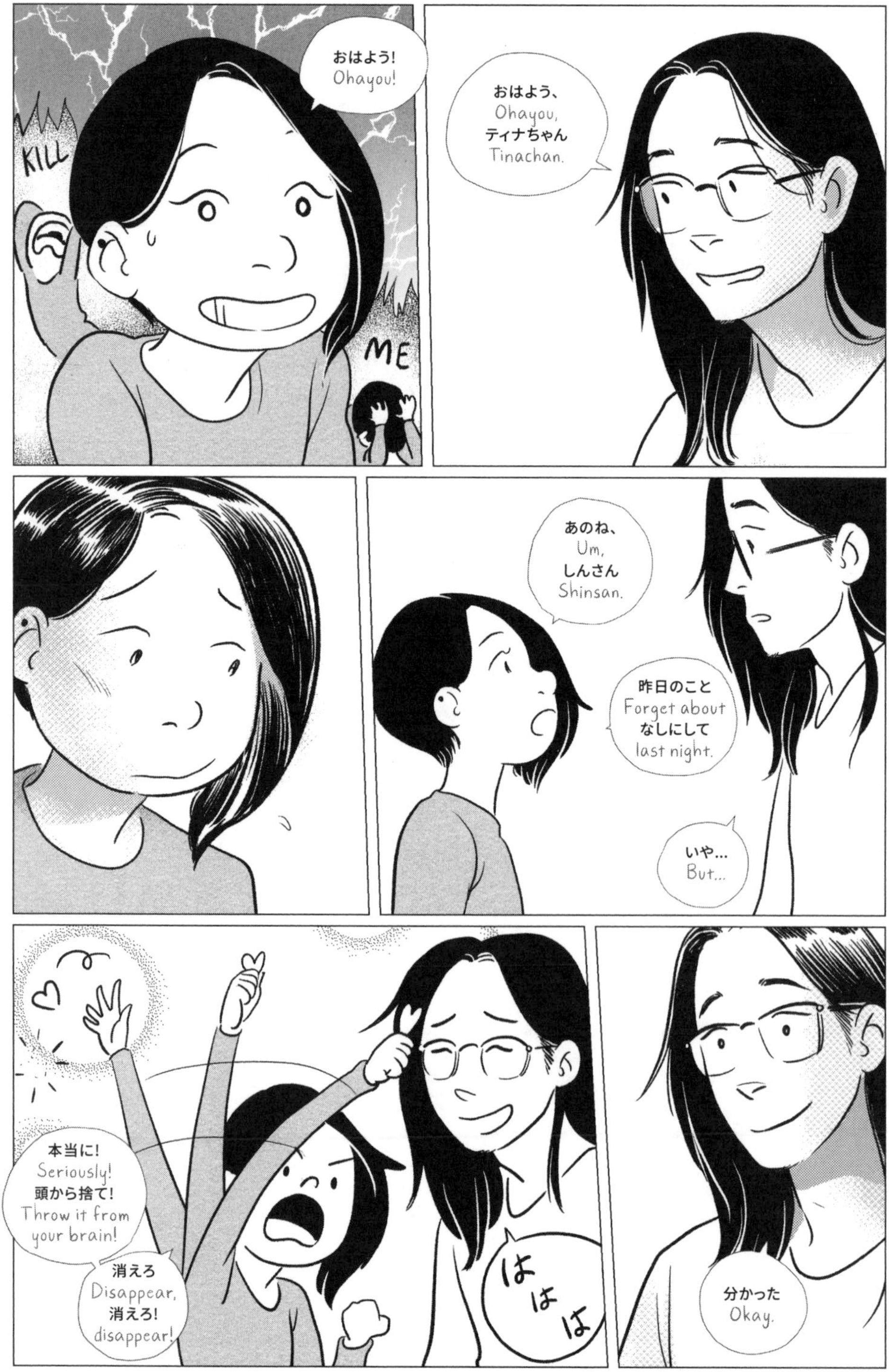
おはよう!
Ohayou!
KILL
ME
おはよう、
Ohayou,
ティナちゃん
Tinachan.
あのね、
Um,
しんさん
Shinsan.
昨日のこと
Forget about
なしにして
last night.
いや…
But…
本当に!
Seriously!
頭から捨て!
Throw it from your brain!
消えろ
Disappear,
消えろ!
disappear!
ははは
分かった
Okay.

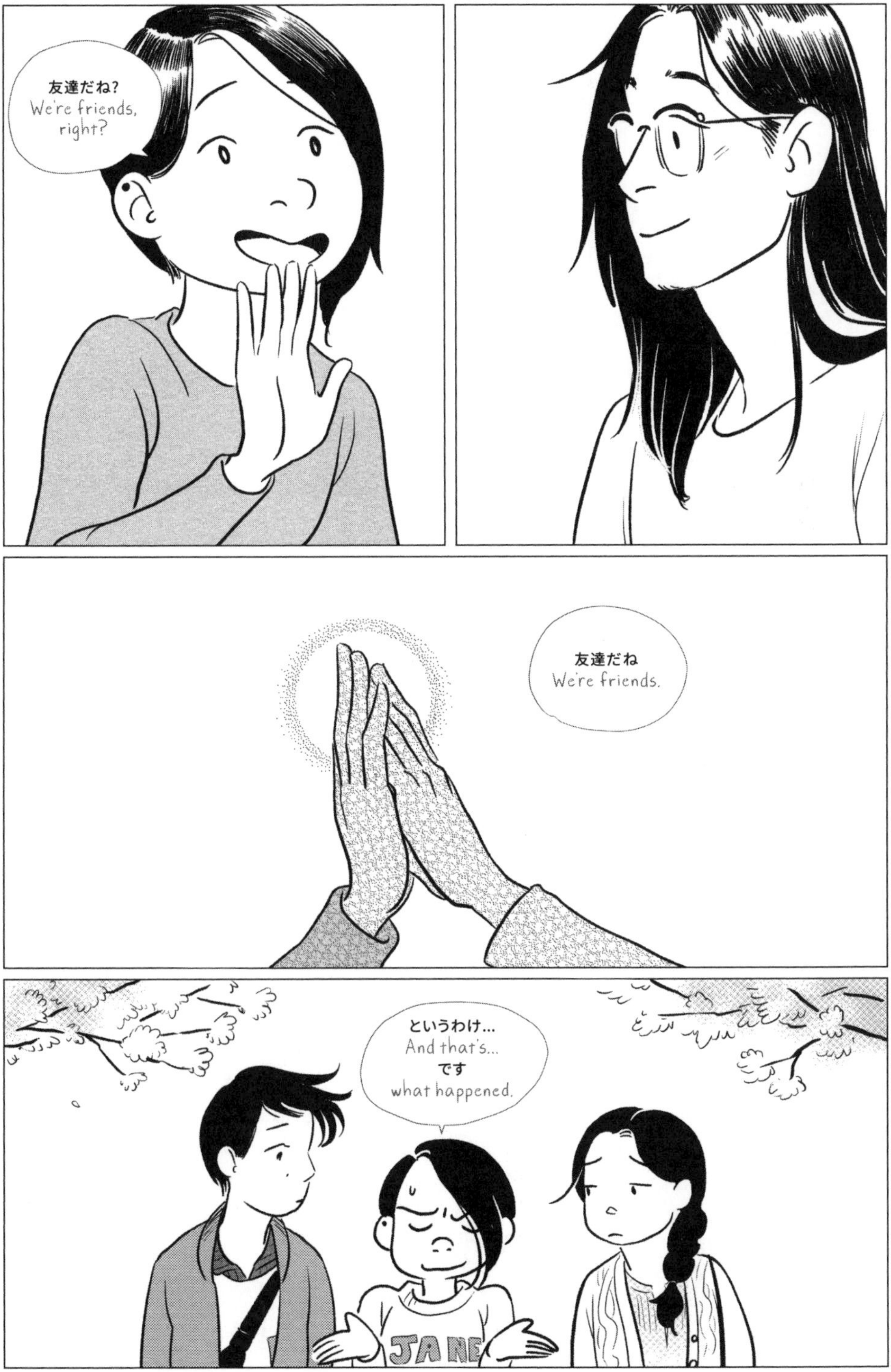

友達だね?
We're friends, right?
友達だね
We're friends.
というわけ...
And that's...
です
what happened.
JANE

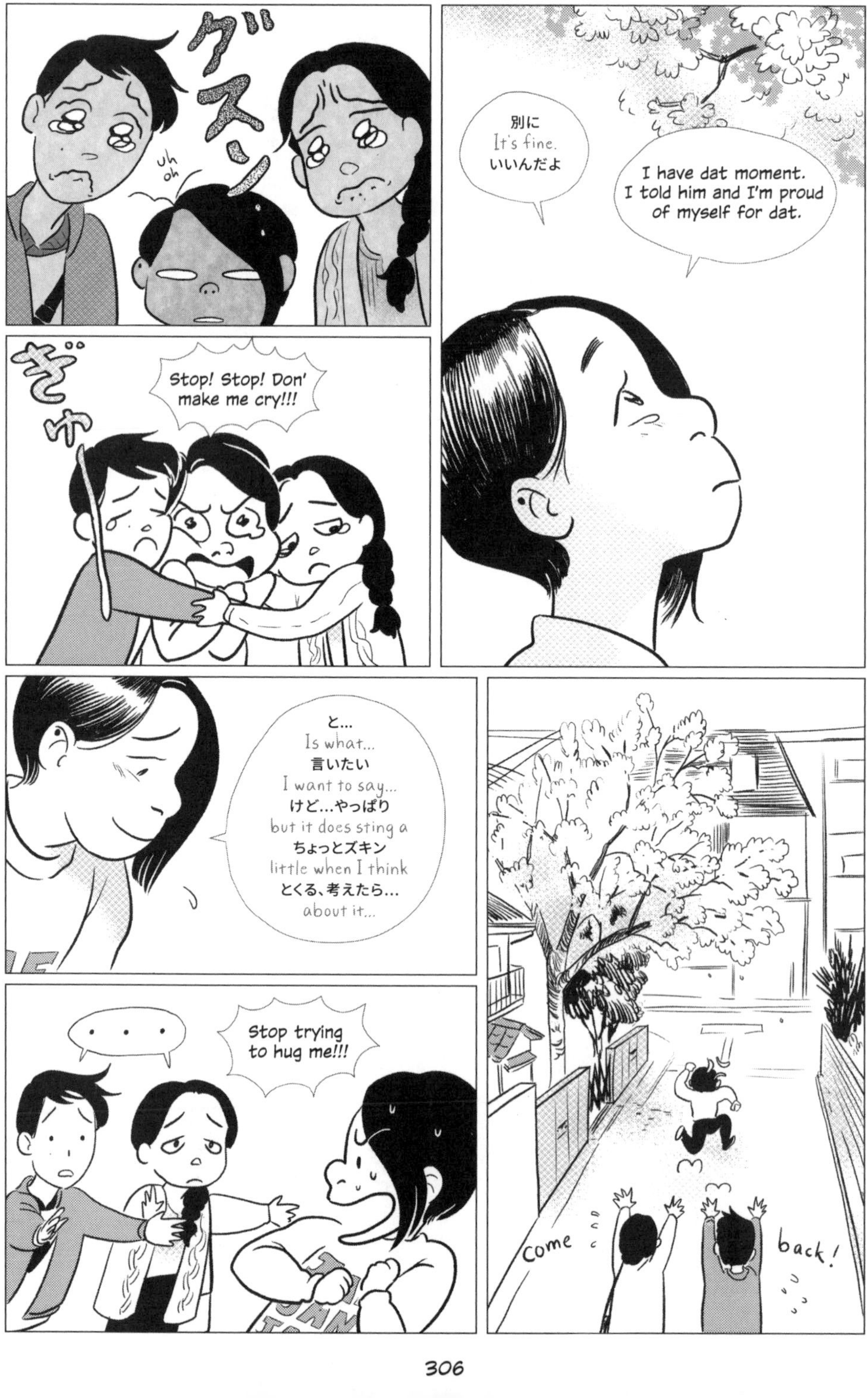
グスン
uh oh
別に
It's fine.
いいんだよ
I have dat moment. I told him and I'm proud of myself for dat.
ぎゅ
Stop! Stop! Don' make me cry!!!
と…
Is what…
言いたい
I want to say…
けど…やっぱり
but it does sting a
ちょっとズキン
little when I think
とくる、考えたら…
about it…
. . .
Stop trying to hug me!!!
Come back!

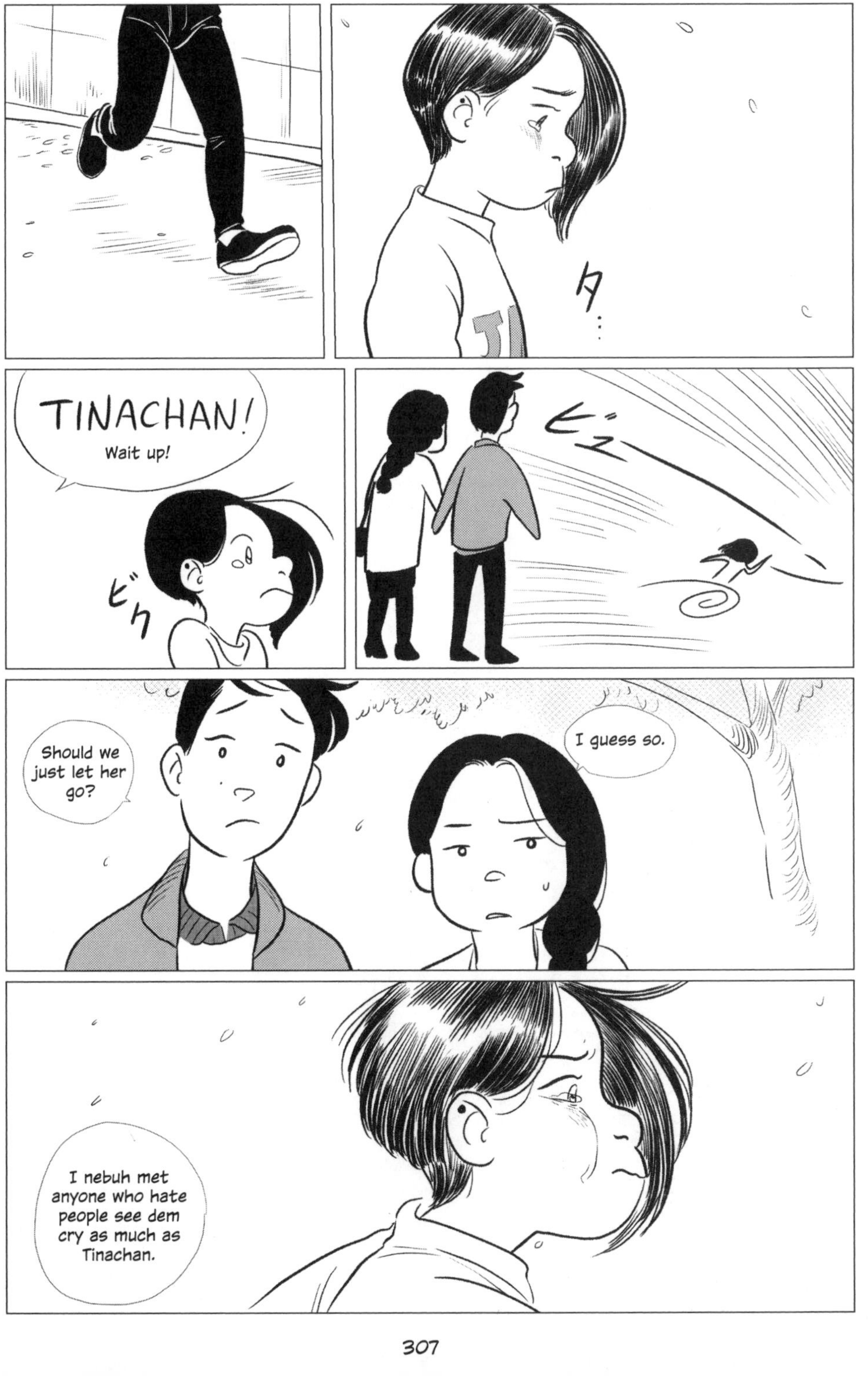
タ…
TINACHAN!
Wait up!
ビク
ビュ
Should we just let her go?
I guess so.
I nebuh met anyone who hate people see dem cry as much as Tinachan.

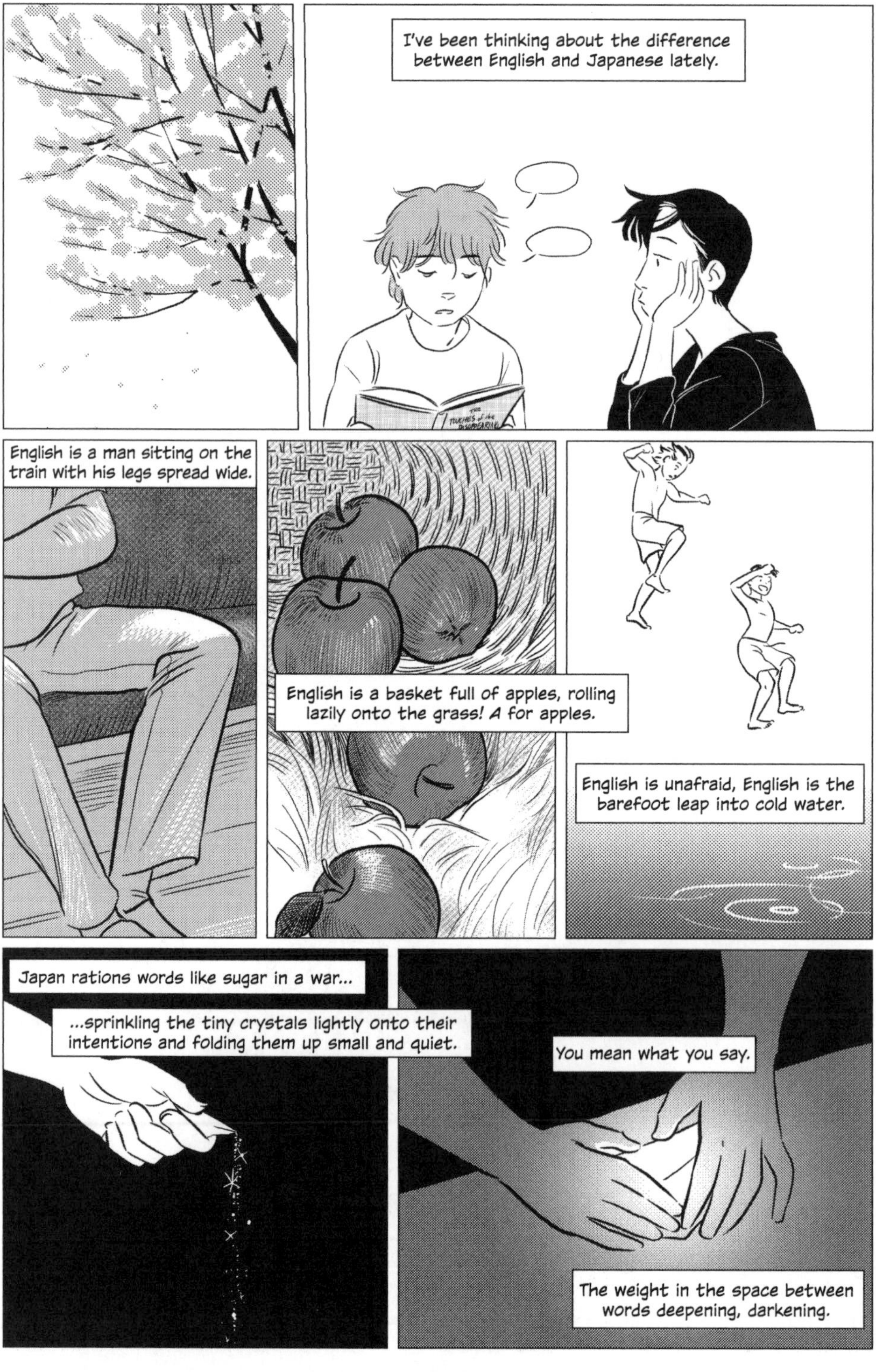
I've been thinking about the difference between English and Japanese lately.
English is a man sitting on the train with his legs spread wide.
English is a basket full of apples, rolling lazily onto the grass! A for apples.
English is unafraid, English is the barefoot leap into cold water.
Japan rations words like sugar in a war...
...sprinkling the tiny crystals lightly onto their intentions and folding them up small and quiet.
You mean what you say.
The weight in the space between words deepening, darkening.

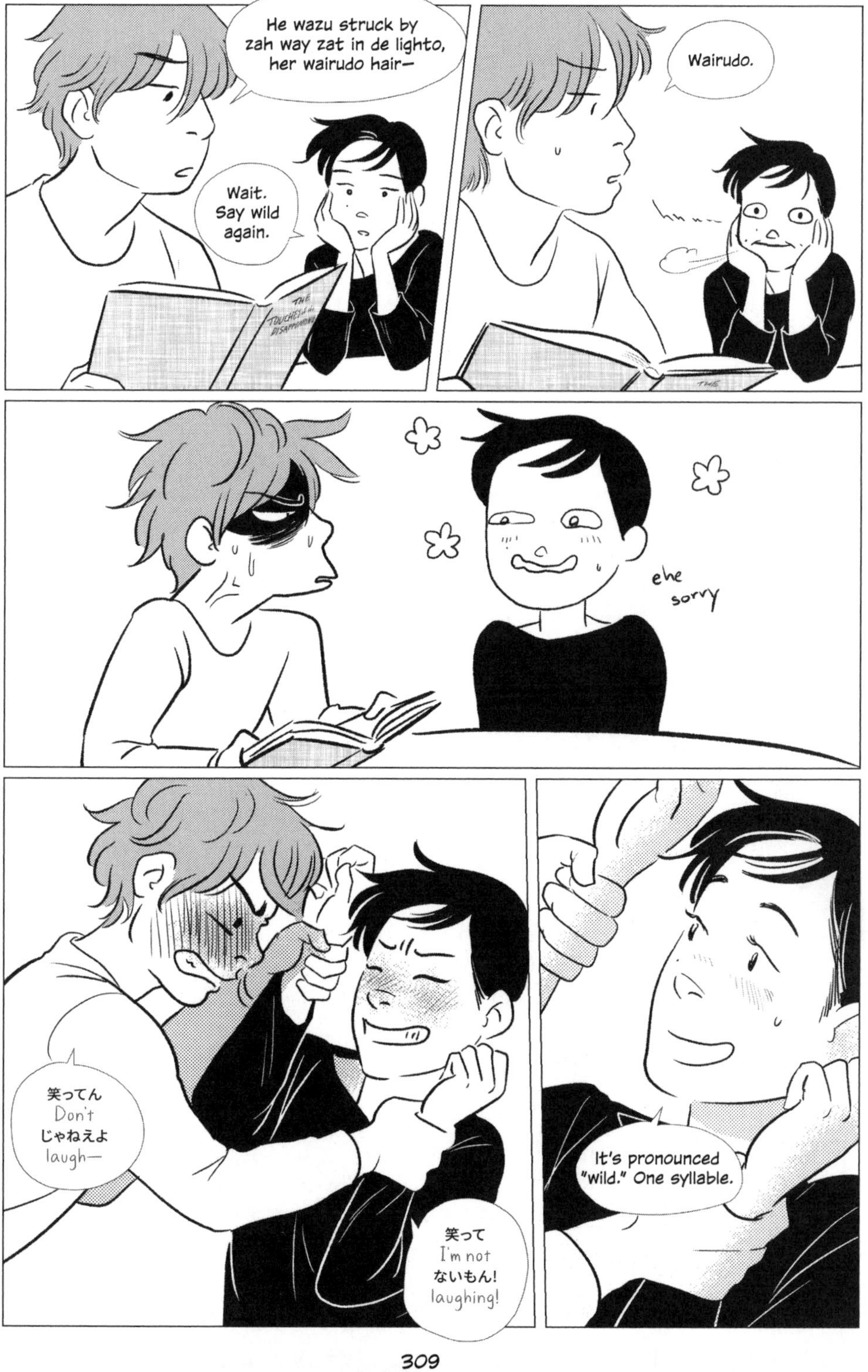
He wazu struck by zah way zat in de lighto, her wairudo hair—
Wait. Say wild again.
Wairudo.
hn n—
ehe sorry
笑ってん Don't じゃねえよ laugh—
笑って I'm not ないもん! laughing!
It's pronounced "wild." One syllable.

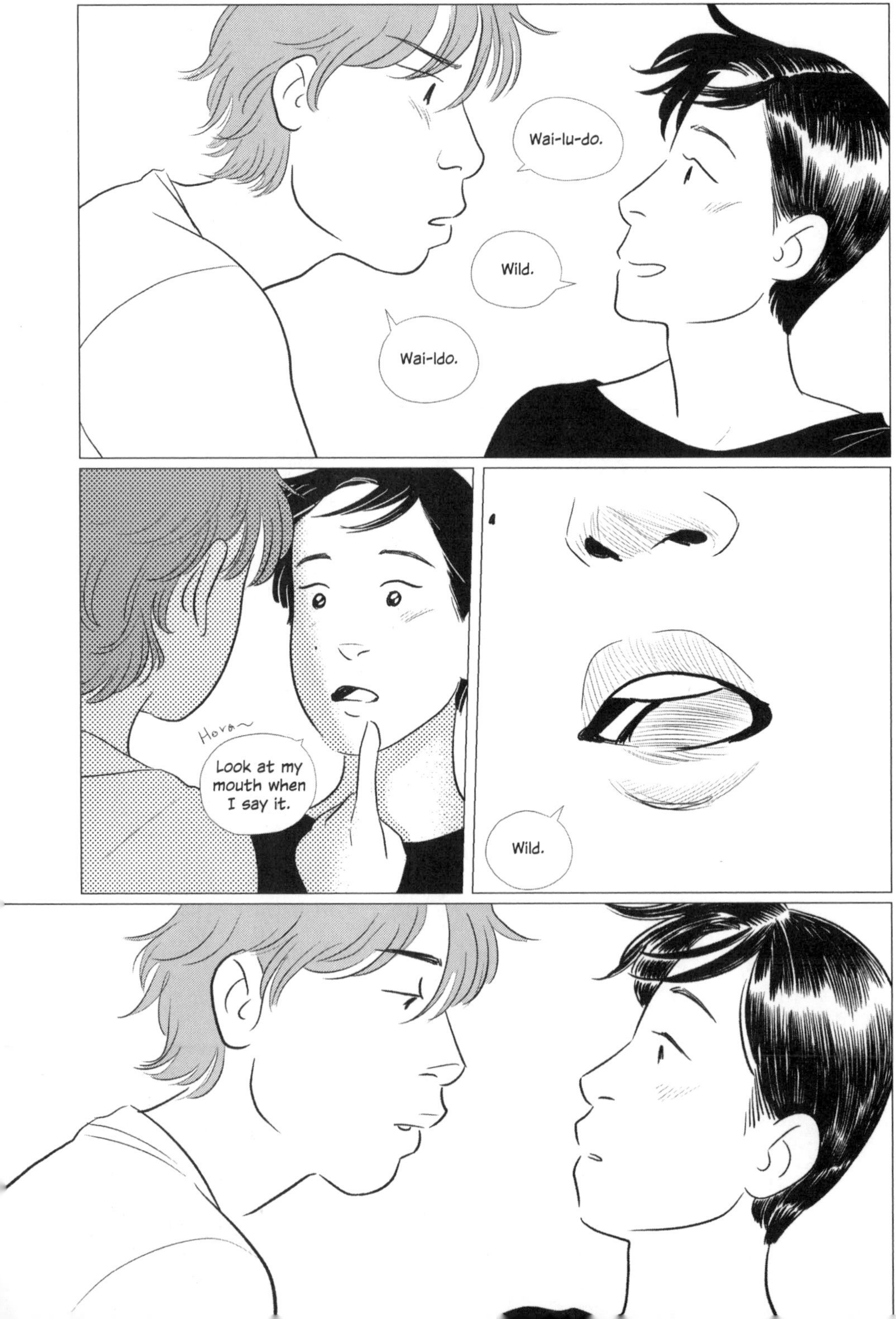
Wai-lu-do.
Wild.
Wai-ldo.
Hora~
Look at my mouth when I say it.
Wild.

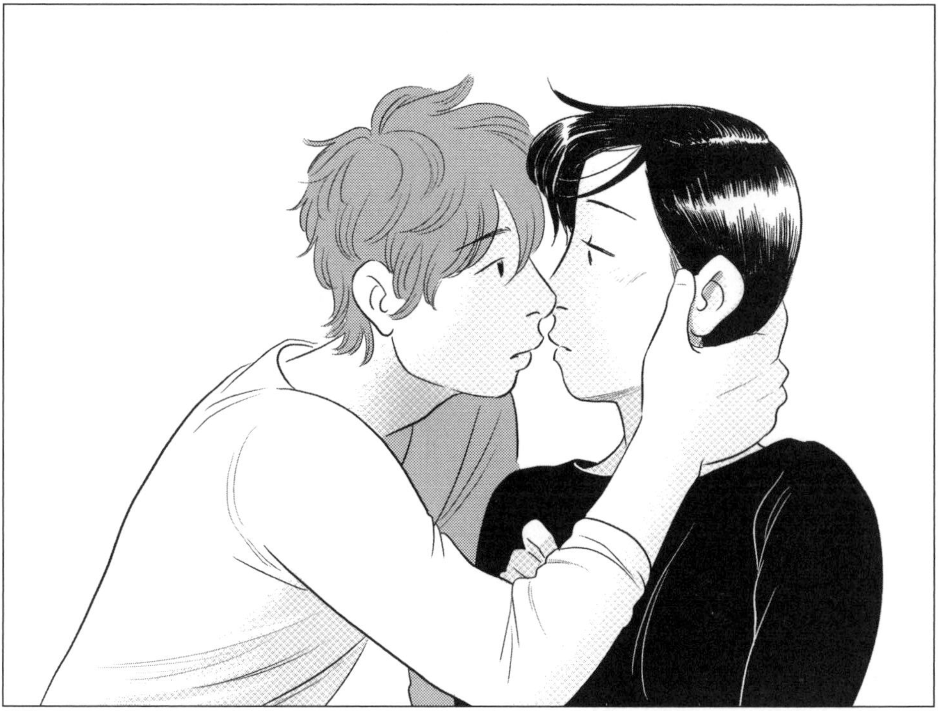
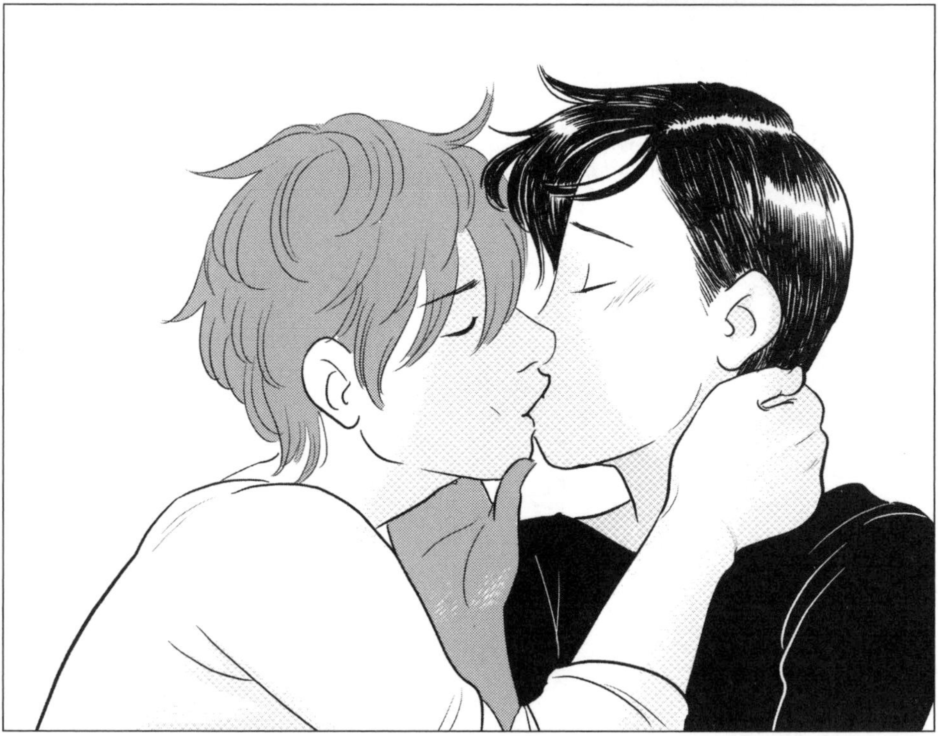

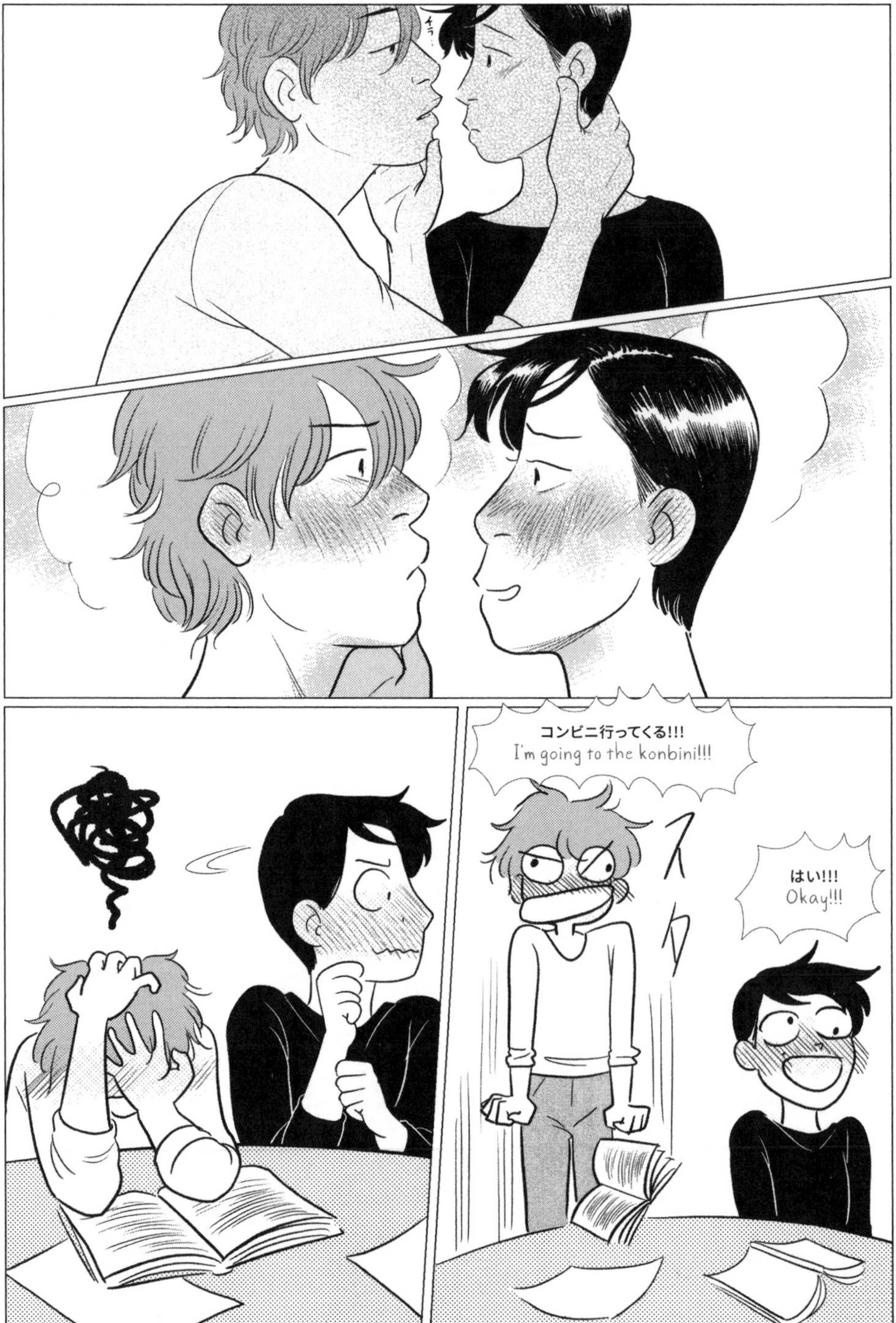
コンビニ行ってくる!!!
I'm going to the konbini!!!
はい!!!
Okay!!!

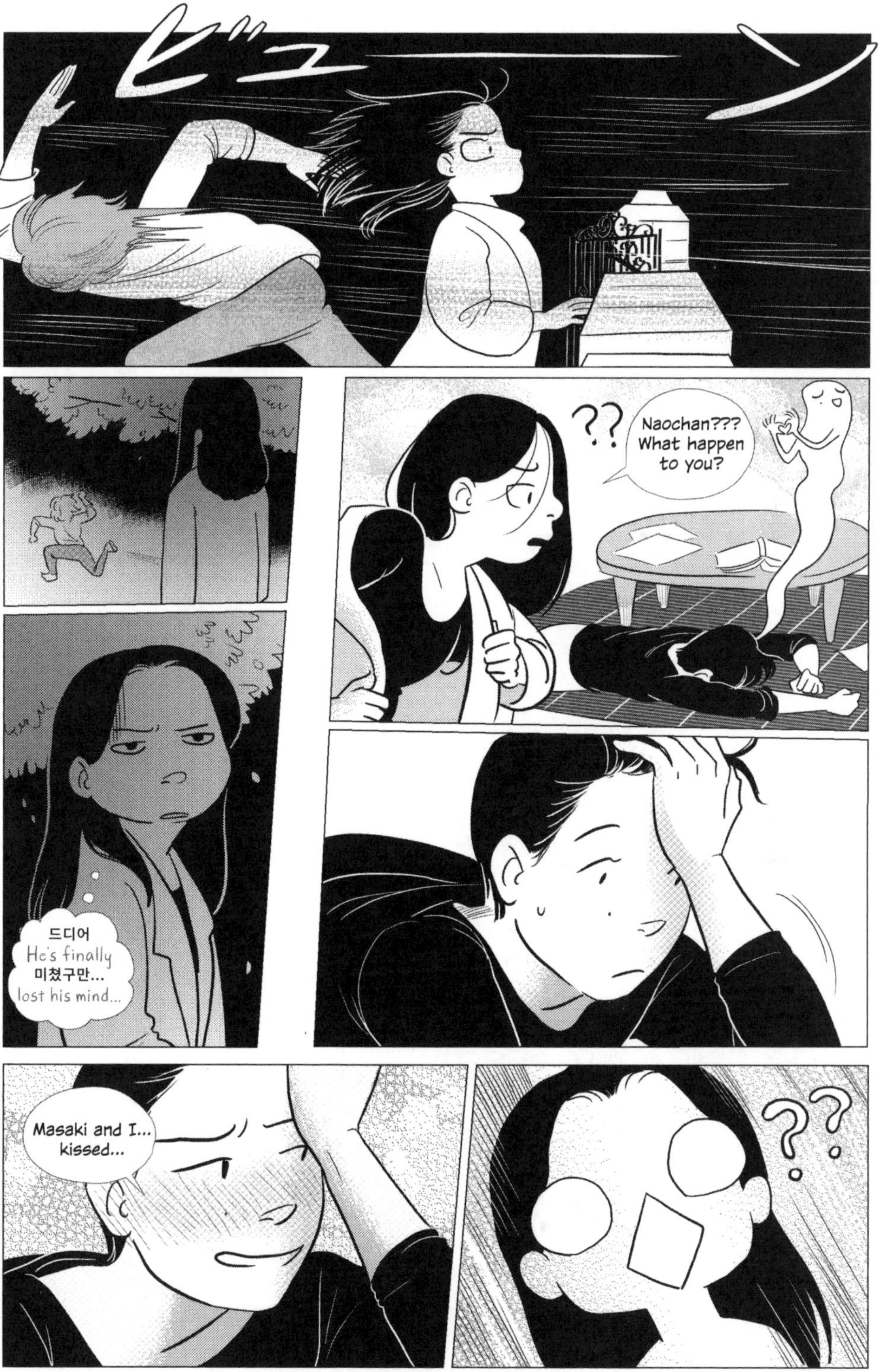
ビュ———ン
드디어
He's finally
미쳤구만...
lost his mind...
??
Naochan??? What happen to you?
Masaki and I... kissed...
??

Chapter 18

Hanami

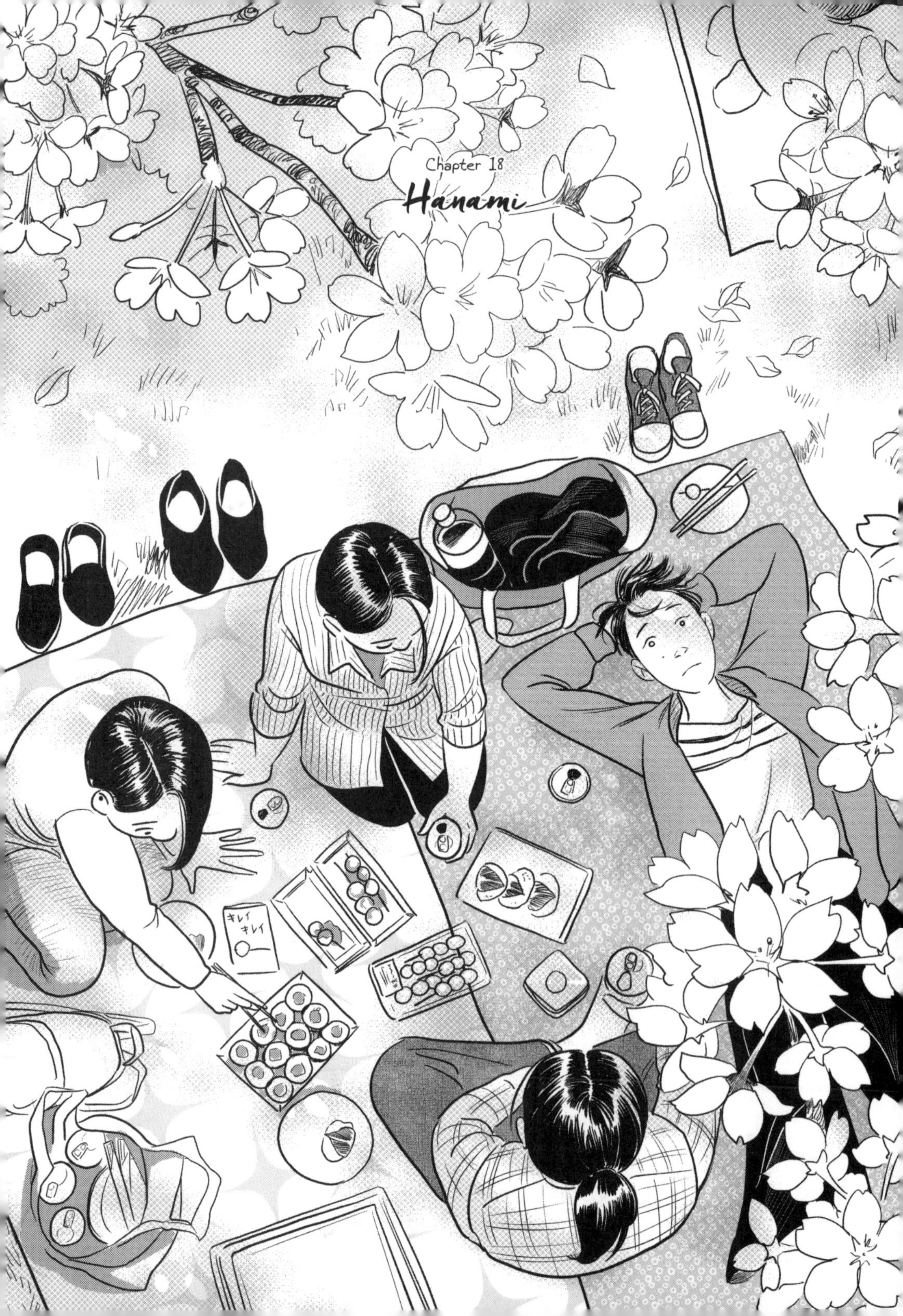

キレイ
キレイ

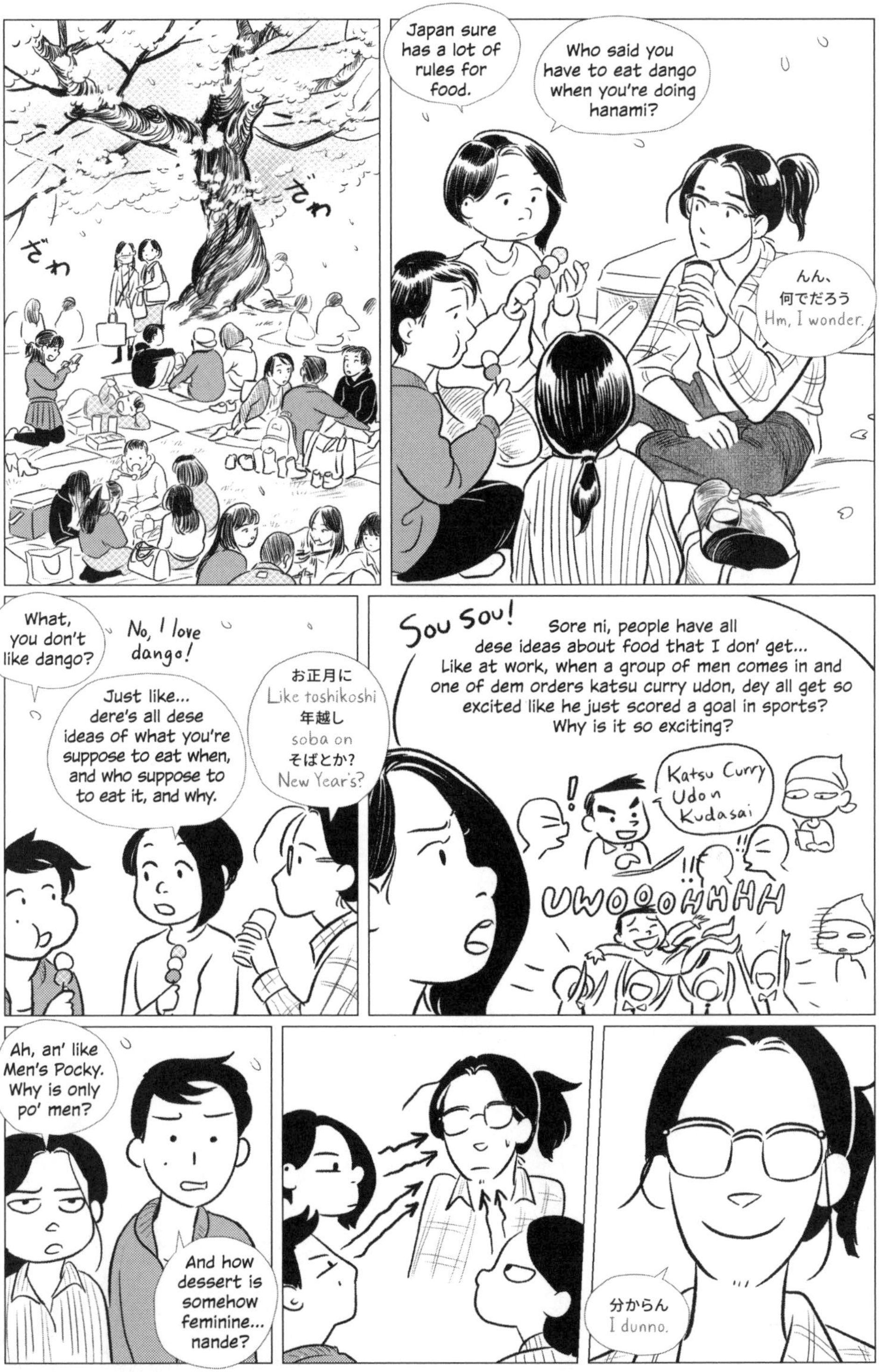
ざわ
ざわ
Japan sure has a lot of rules for food.
Who said you have to eat dango when you're doing hanami?
んん、何でだろう
Hm, I wonder.
What, you don't like dango?
No, I love dango!
Just like... dere's all dese ideas of what you're suppose to eat when, and who suppose to to eat it, and why.
お正月に
Like toshikoshi
年越し
soba on
そばとか?
New Year's?
Sou Sou!
Sore ni, people have all dese ideas about food that I don' get... Like at work, when a group of men comes in and one of dem orders katsu curry udon, dey all get so excited like he just scored a goal in sports? Why is it so exciting?
Katsu Curry Udon Kudasai
UWOOOOHHHH
Ah, an' like Men's Pocky. Why is only po' men?
And how dessert is somehow feminine... nande?
分からん
I dunno.

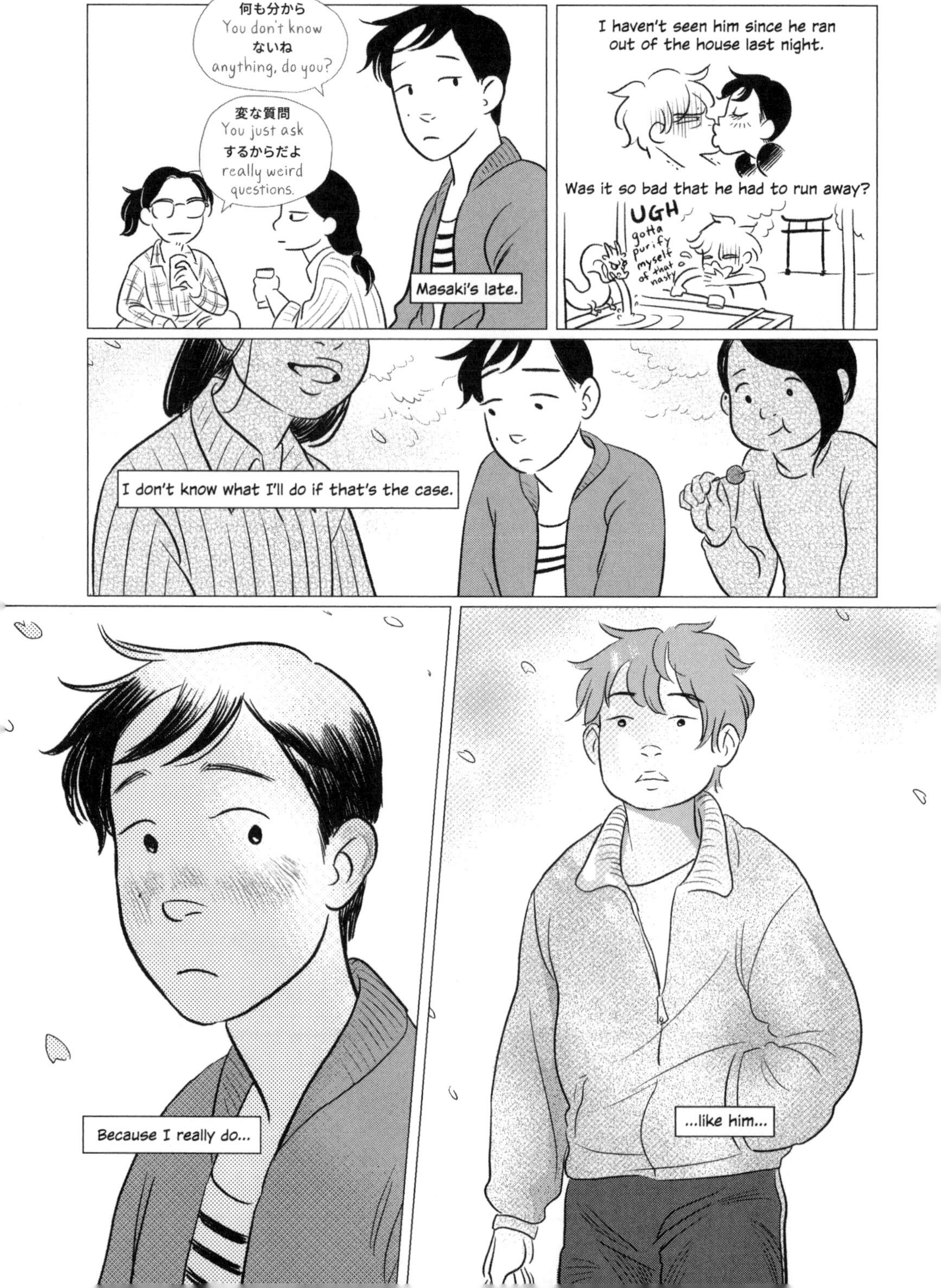

何も分から
You don't know
ないね
anything, do you?
変な質問
You just ask
するからだよ
really weird
questions.
Masaki's late.
I haven't seen him since he ran out of the house last night.
Was it so bad that he had to run away?
UGH
gotta purify myself of that nasty
I don't know what I'll do if that's the case.
Because I really do...
...like him...

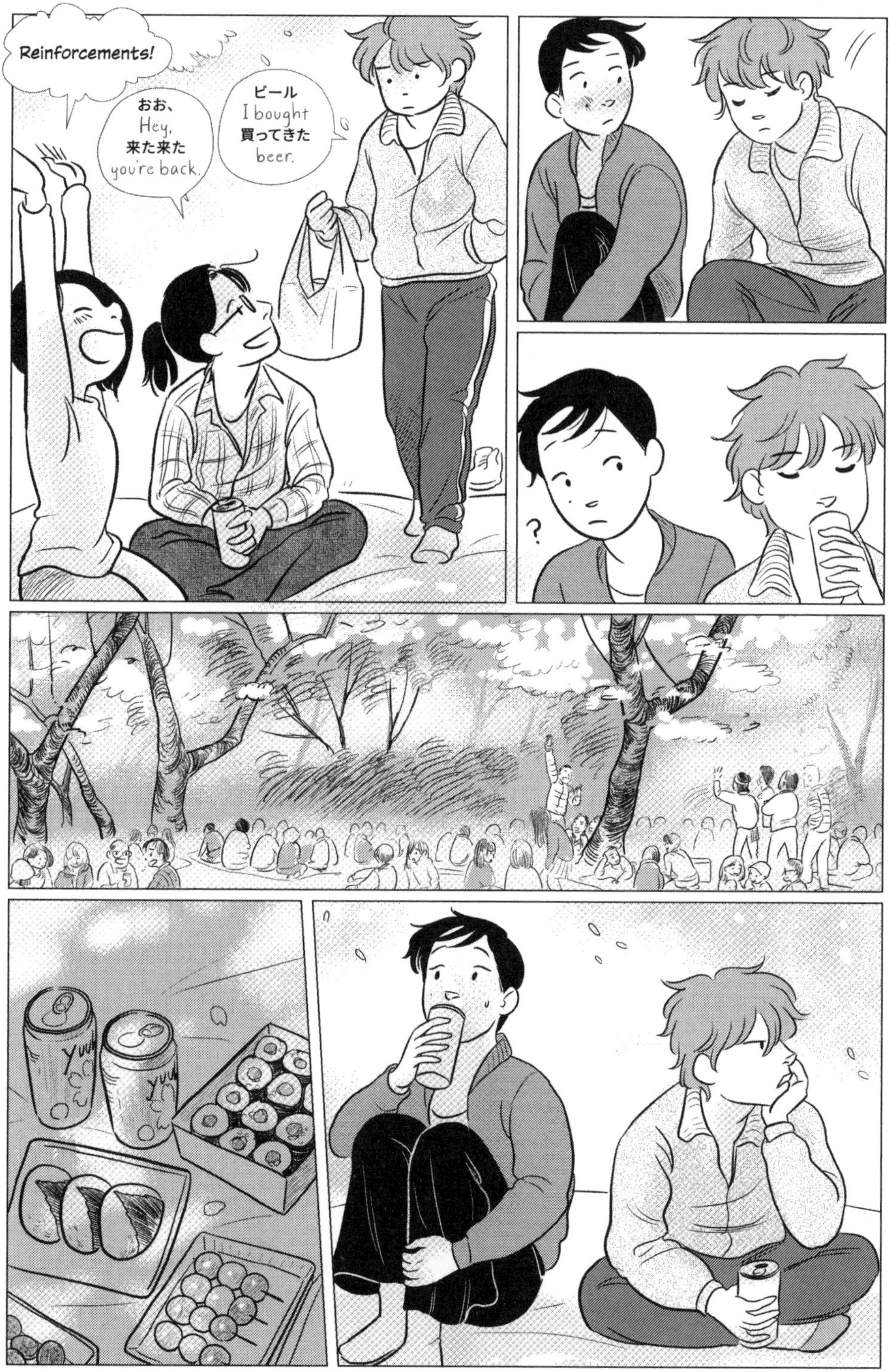
Reinforcements!
おお、Hey, 来た来た you're back.
ビール I bought 買ってきた beer.
?

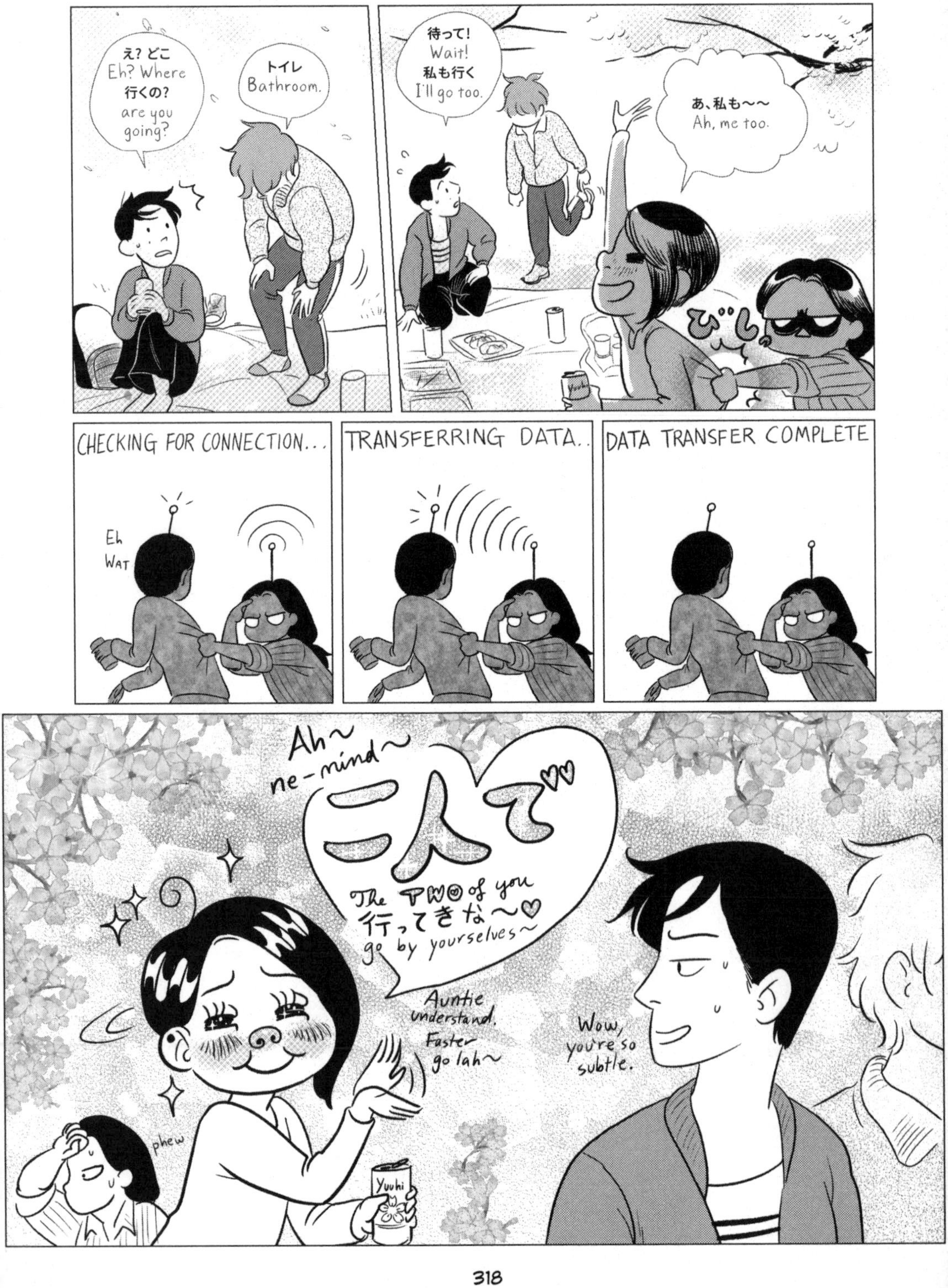

え? どこ
Eh? Where
行くの?
are you going?
トイレ
Bathroom.
待って!
Wait!
私も行く
I'll go too.
あ、私も～～
Ah, me too.
びし
CHECKING FOR CONNECTION...
Eh
WAT
TRANSFERRING DATA..
DATA TRANSFER COMPLETE
Ah~
ne-mind~
二人で
The TWO of you
行ってきな～
go by yourselves~
Auntie understand.
Faster go lah~
Wow, you're so subtle.
phew
Yuuhi

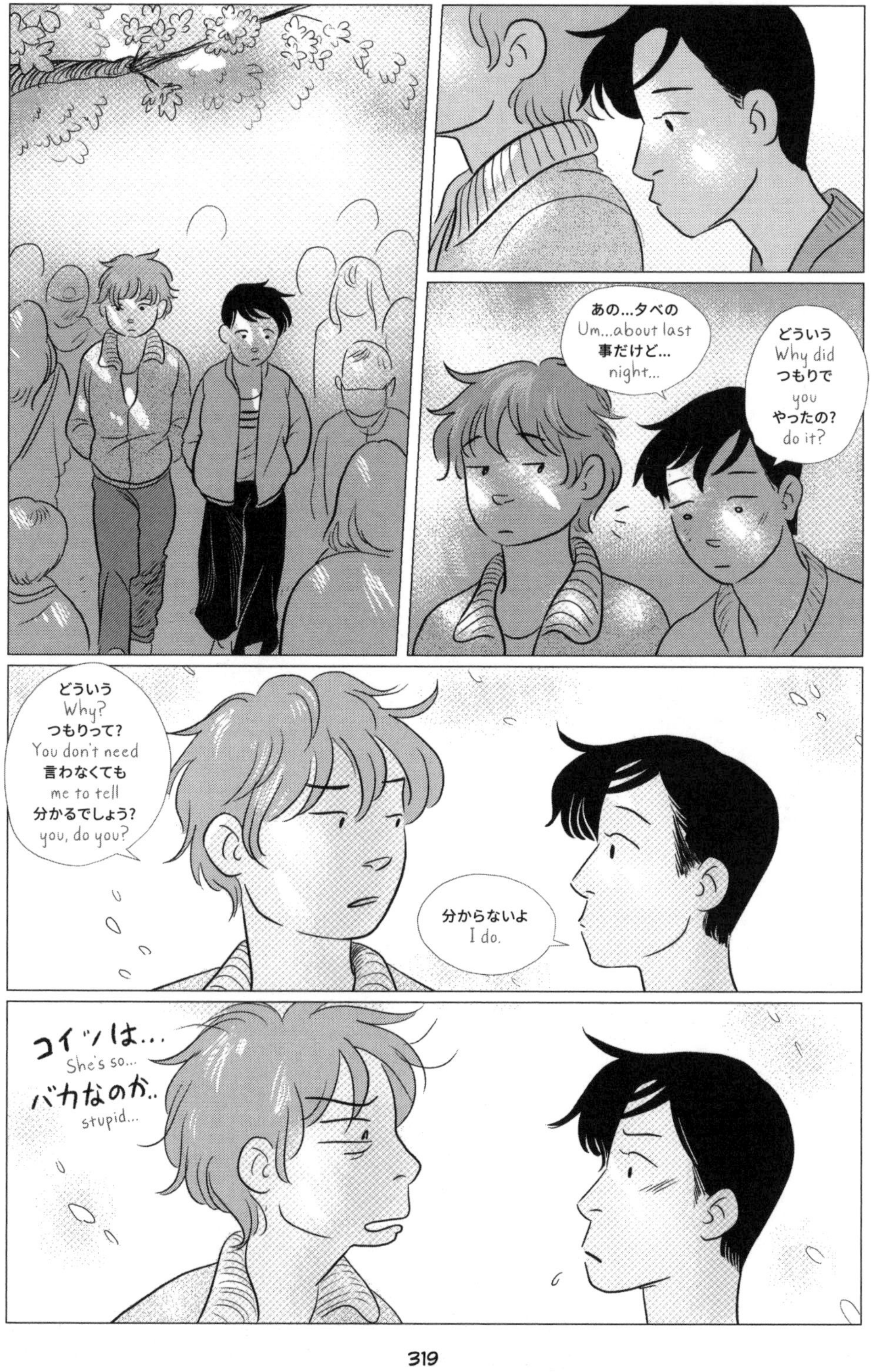
あの…夕べの Um...about last 事だけど… night...
どういう Why did つもりで you やったの? do it?
どういう Why? つもりって? You don't need 言わなくても me to tell 分かるでしょう? you, do you?
分からないよ I do.
コイツは… She's so... バカなのか.. stupid...

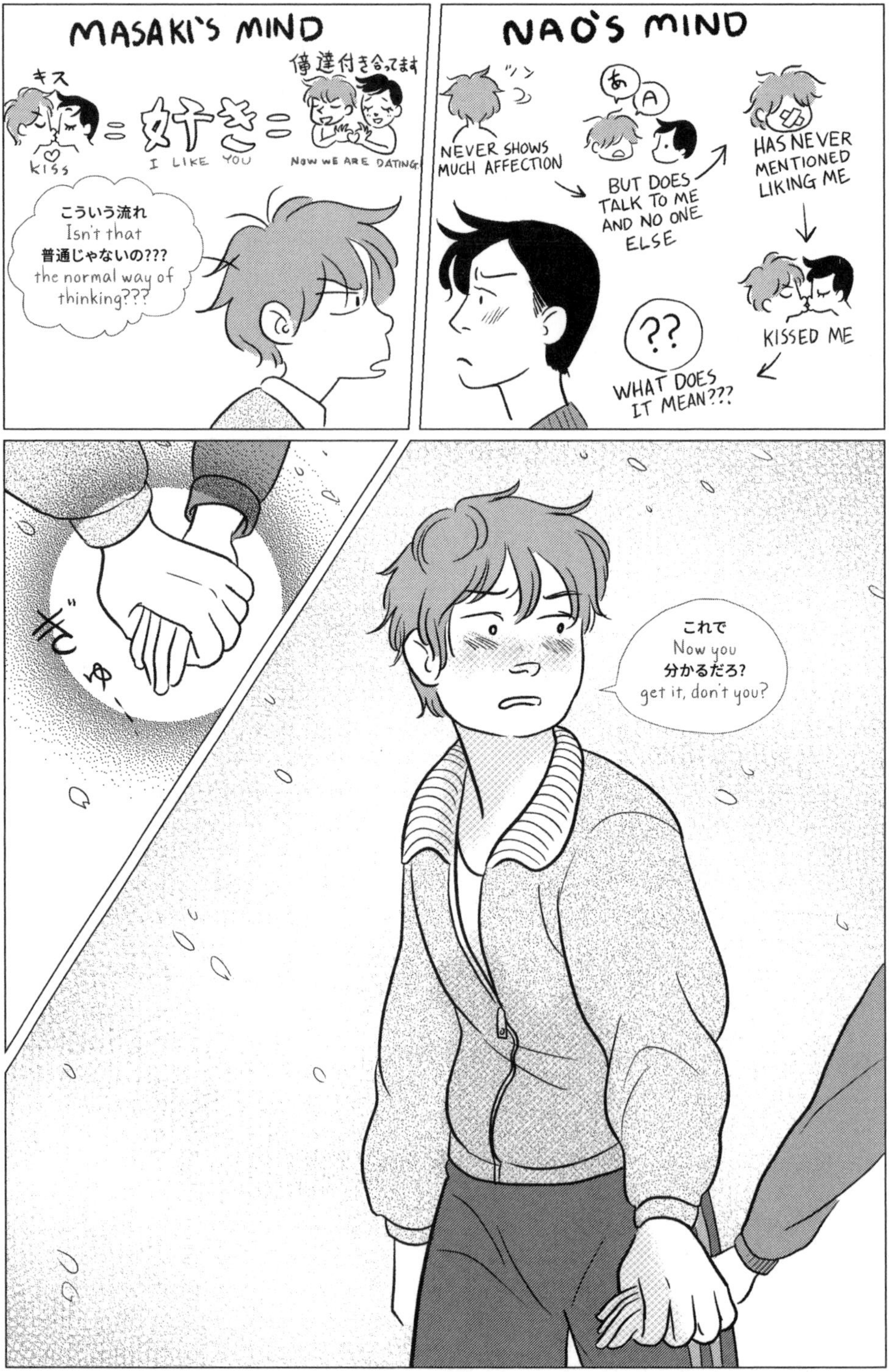
MASAKI'S MIND
キス
KISS
好き
I LIKE YOU
俺達付き合ってます
NOW WE ARE DATING!
こういう流れ
Isn't that
普通じゃないの???
the normal way of thinking???
NAO'S MIND
ツン
NEVER SHOWS MUCH AFFECTION
あ
A
BUT DOES TALK TO ME AND NO ONE ELSE
HAS NEVER MENTIONED LIKING ME
KISSED ME
??
WHAT DOES IT MEAN???
ぎゅ
これで
Now you
分かるだろ?
get it, don't you?

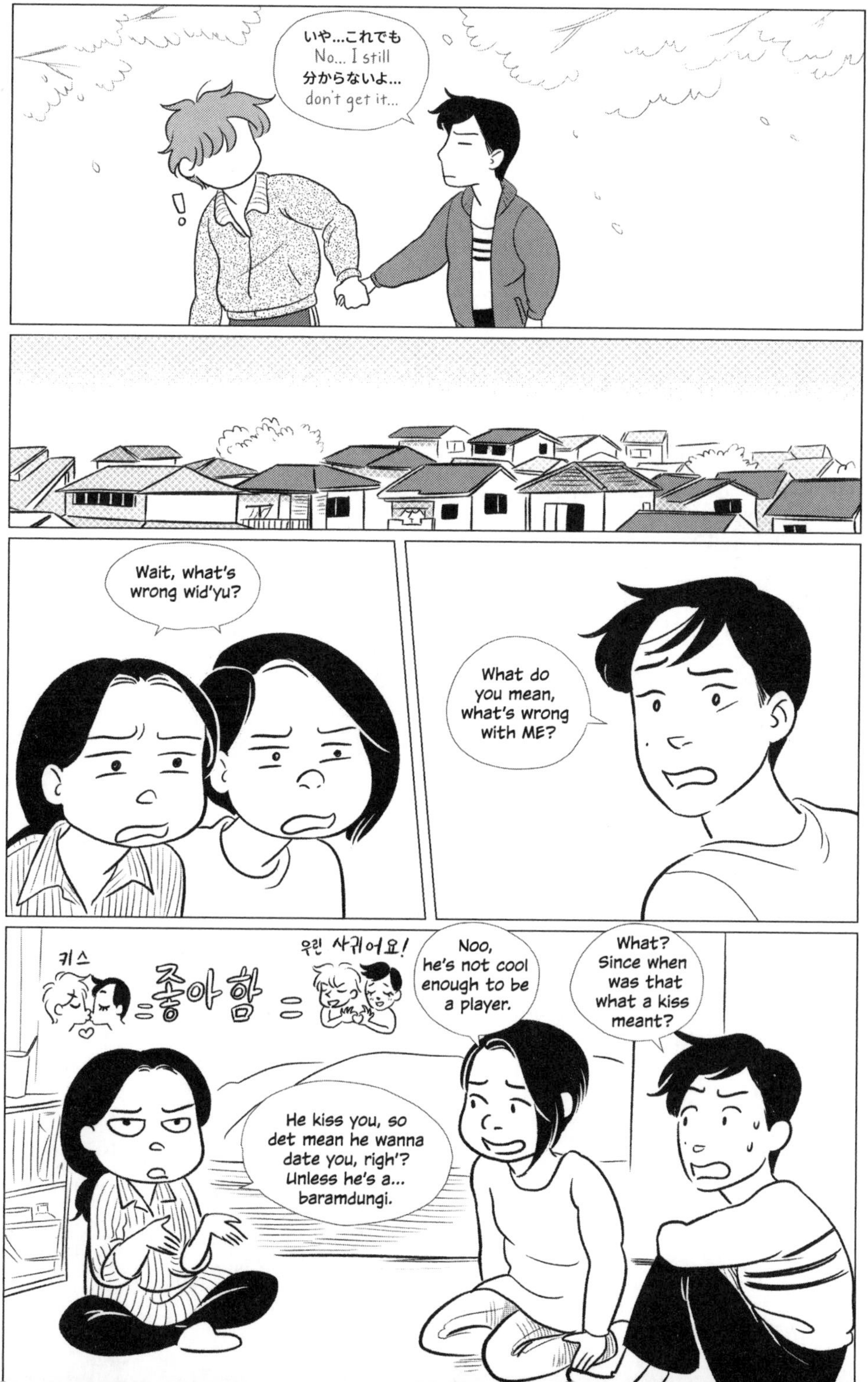
いや…これでも
No… I still
分からないよ…
don't get it…
Wait, what's wrong wid'yu?
What do you mean, what's wrong with ME?
키스
좋아함
우린 사귀어요!
Noo, he's not cool enough to be a player.
What? Since when was that what a kiss meant?
He kiss you, so det mean he wanna date you, righ'? Unless he's a… baramdungi.

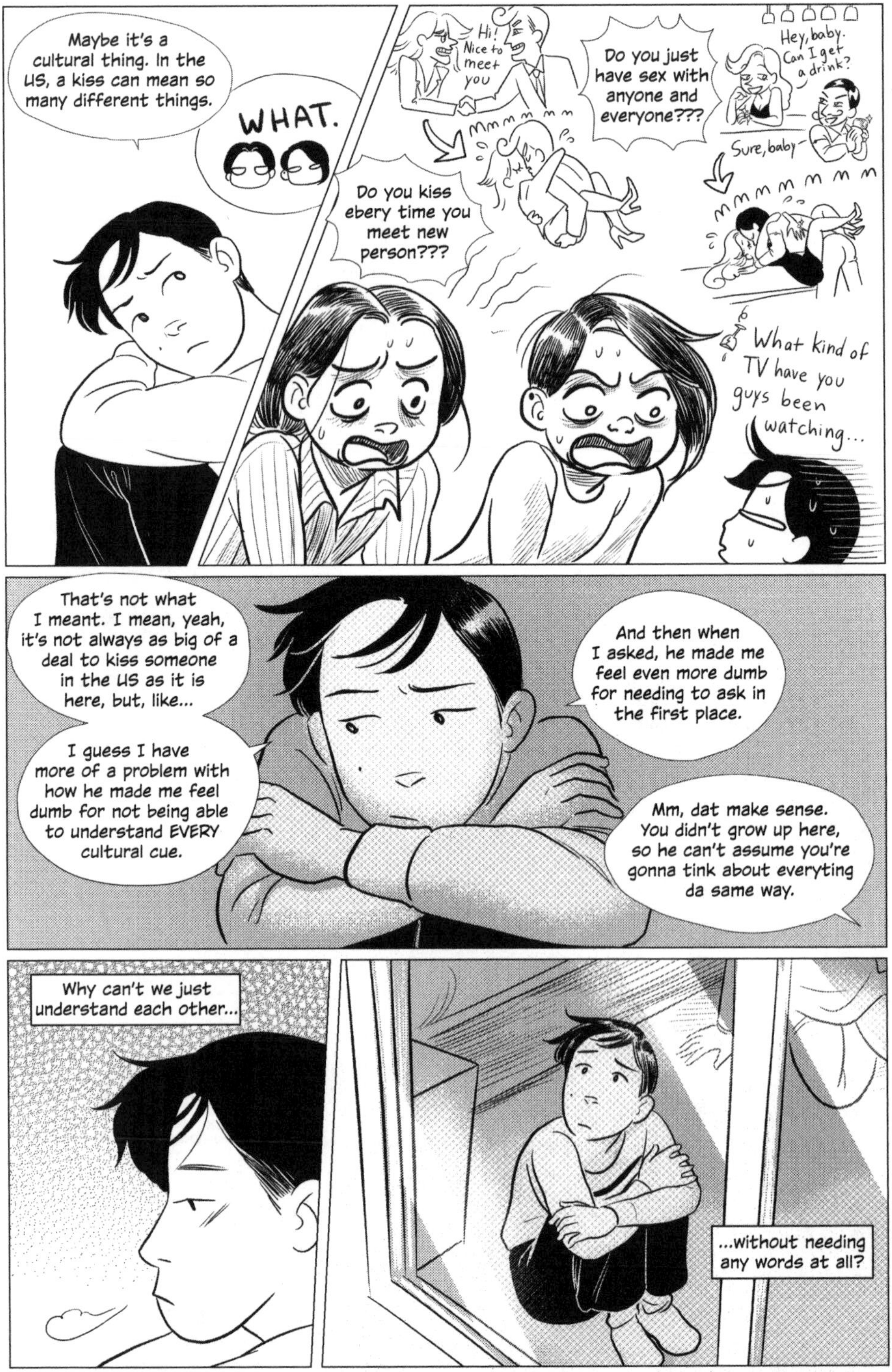

Maybe it's a cultural thing. In the US, a kiss can mean so many different things.
WHAT.
Hi! Nice to meet you
Do you just have sex with anyone and everyone???
Hey, baby. Can I get a drink?
Sure, baby
Do you kiss ebery time you meet new person???
What kind of TV have you guys been watching...
That's not what I meant. I mean, yeah, it's not always as big of a deal to kiss someone in the US as it is here, but, like...
I guess I have more of a problem with how he made me feel dumb for not being able to understand EVERY cultural cue.
And then when I asked, he made me feel even more dumb for needing to ask in the first place.
Mm, dat make sense. You didn't grow up here, so he can't assume you're gonna tink about everyting da same way.
Why can't we just understand each other...
...without needing any words at all?

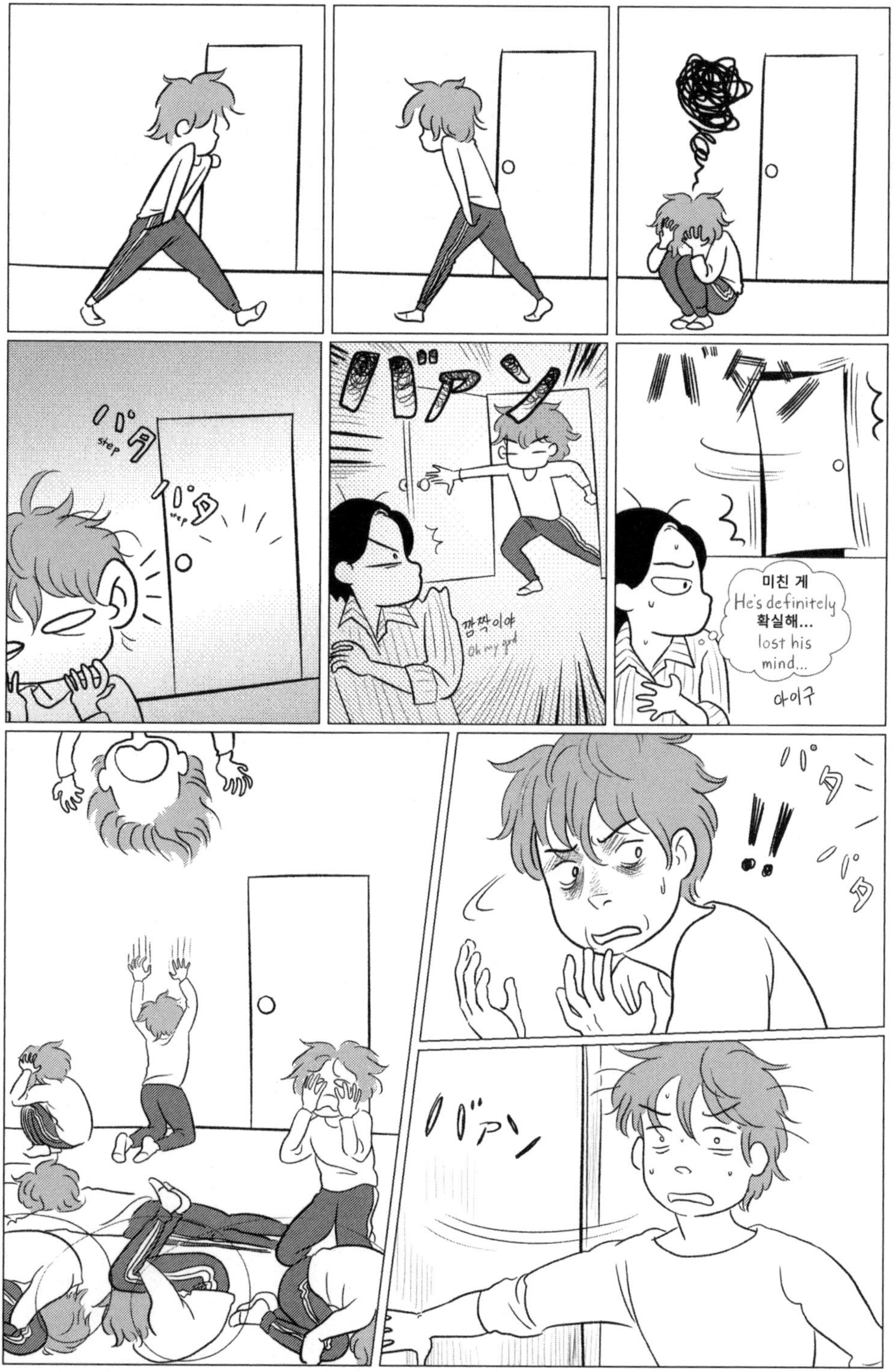
パタ
step
パタ
step
バアン
깜짝이야
Oh my god
バタン
미친 게
He's definitely
확실해...
lost his
mind...
아이구
パタ
パタ
!!
バアン

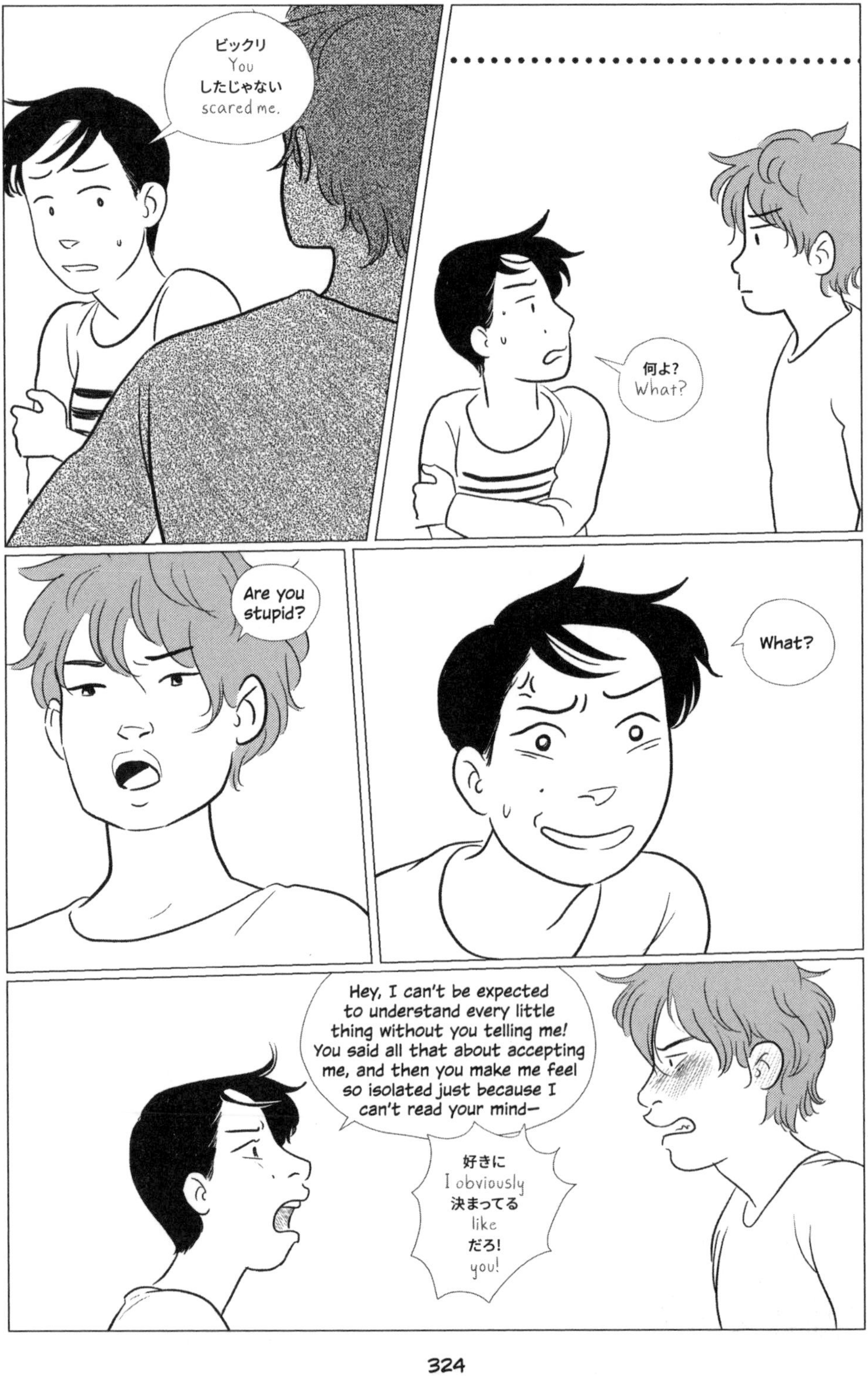
ビックリ You したじゃない scared me.
What?
何よ? What?
Are you stupid?
What?
Hey, I can't be expected to understand every little thing without you telling me! You said all that about accepting me, and then you make me feel so isolated just because I can't read your mind—
好きに I obviously 決まってる like だろ! you!

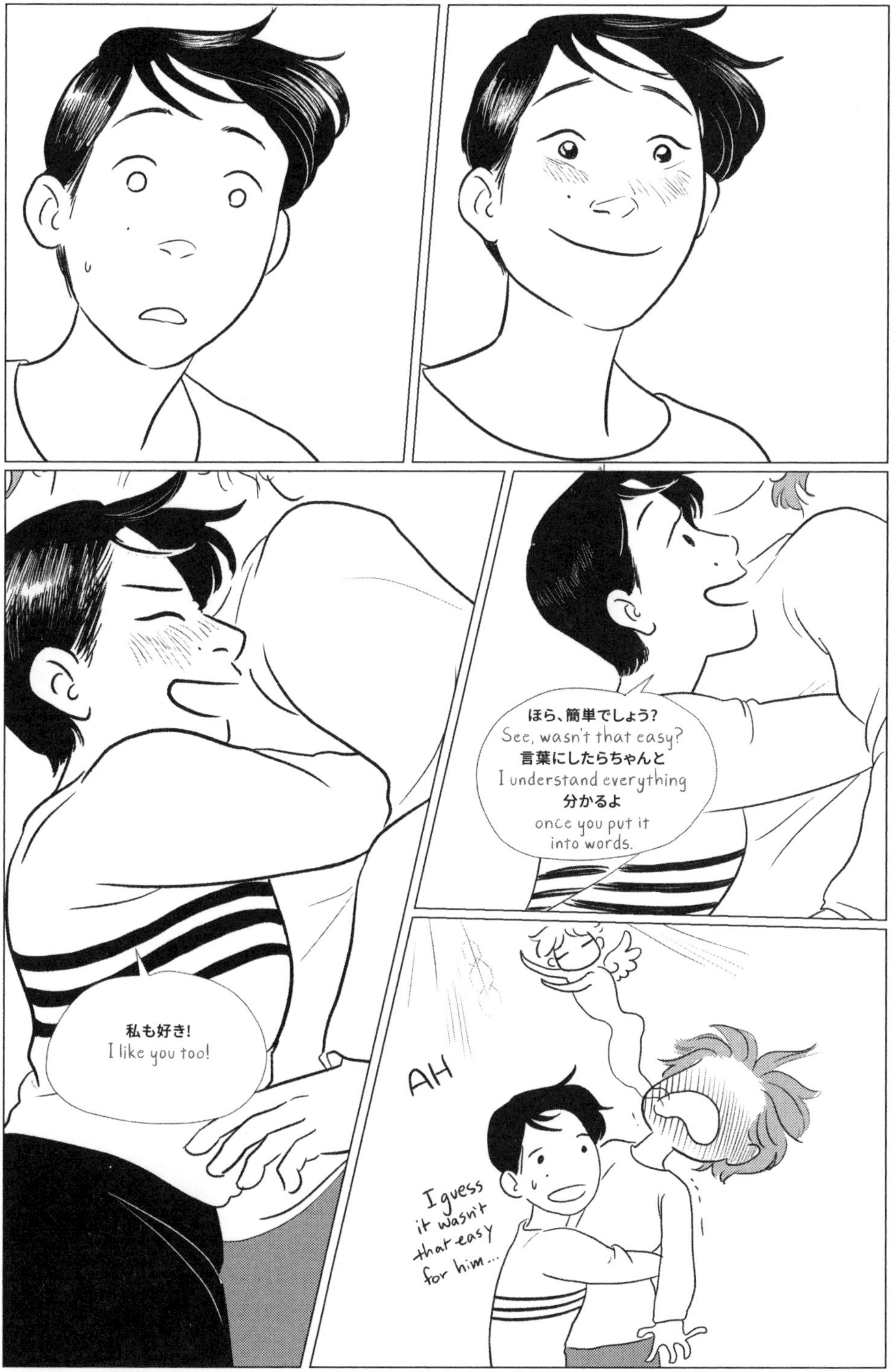
ほら、簡単でしょう?
See, wasn't that easy?
言葉にしたらちゃんと
I understand everything
分かるよ
once you put it into words.
私も好き!
I like you too!
AH
I guess it wasn't that easy for him...

Chapter 19

Omma

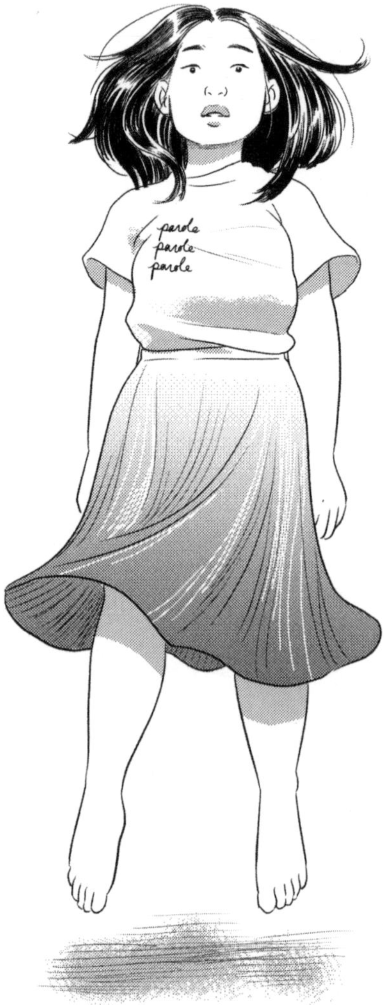
parole
parole
parole

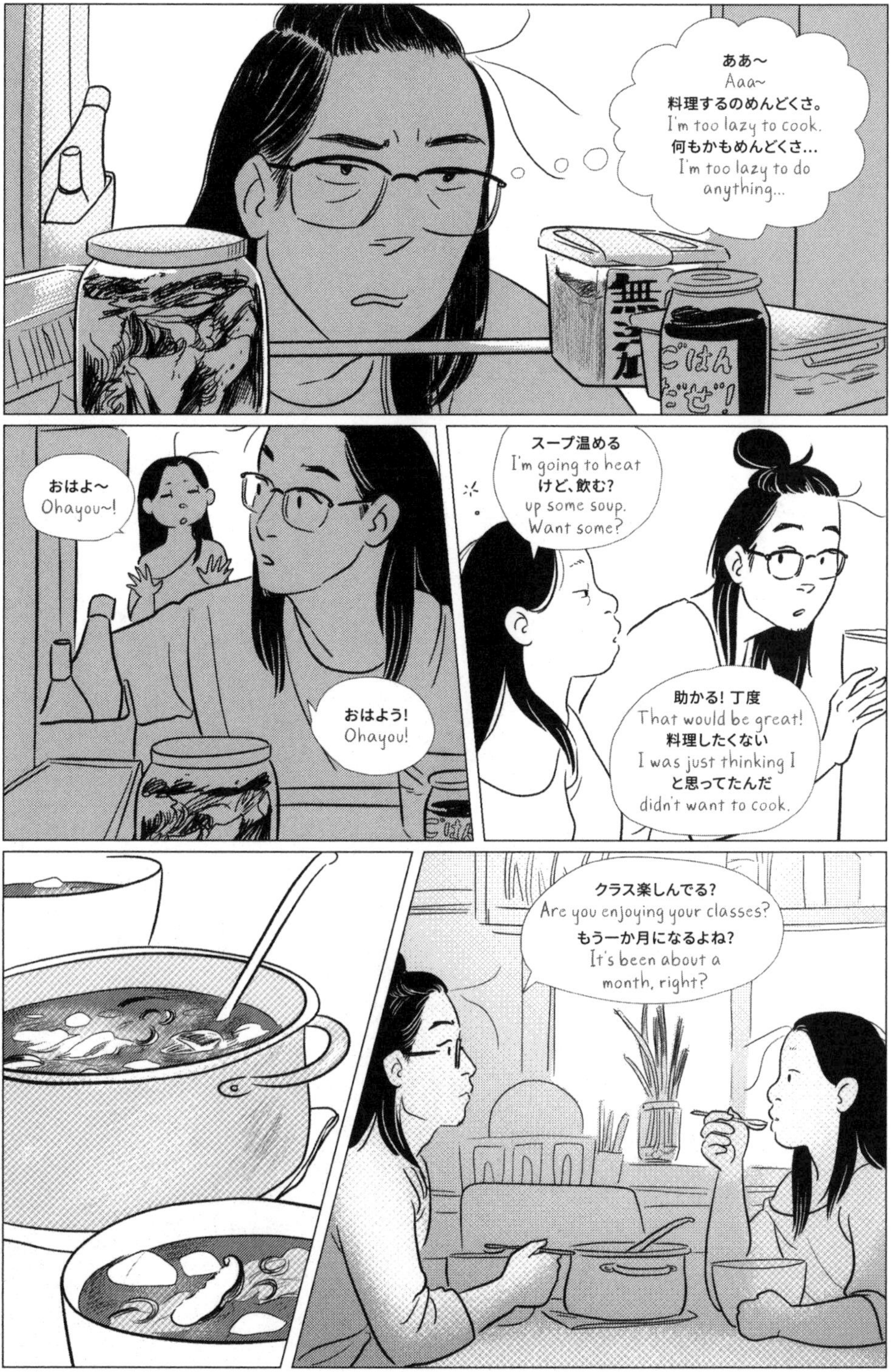

ああ～
Aaa~
料理するのめんどくさ。
I'm too lazy to cook.
何もかもめんどくさ…
I'm too lazy to do anything...
おはよ～
Ohayou~!
おはよう!
Ohayou!
スープ温める
I'm going to heat
けど、飲む?
up some soup. Want some?
助かる! 丁度
That would be great!
料理したくない
I was just thinking I
と思ってたんだ
didn't want to cook.
クラス楽しんでる?
Are you enjoying your classes?
もう一か月になるよね?
It's been about a month, right?

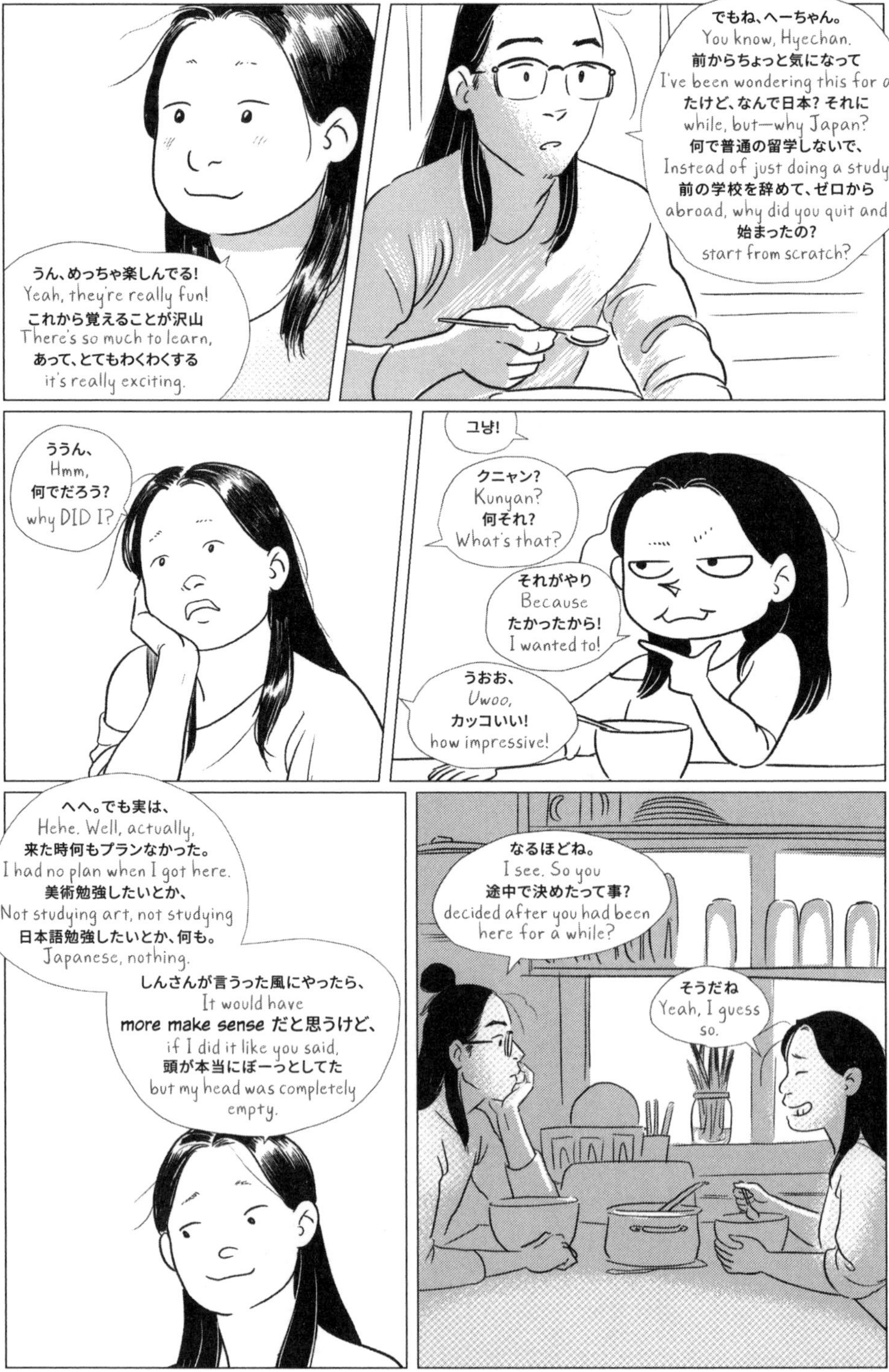
うん、めっちゃ楽しんでる!
Yeah, they're really fun!
これから覚えることが沢山
There's so much to learn,
あって、とてもわくわくする
it's really exciting.
でもね、へーちゃん。
You know, Hyechan.
前からちょっと気になって
I've been wondering this for a
たけど、なんで日本? それに
while, but—why Japan?
何で普通の留学しないで、
Instead of just doing a study
前の学校を辞めて、ゼロから
abroad, why did you quit and
始まったの?
start from scratch?
ううん、
Hmm,
何でだろう?
why DID I?
그냥!
クニャン?
Kunyan?
何それ?
What's that?
それがやり
Because
たかったから!
I wanted to!
うおお、
Uwoo,
カッコいい!
how impressive!
へへ。でも実は、
Hehe. Well, actually,
来た時何もプランなかった。
I had no plan when I got here.
美術勉強したいとか、
Not studying art, not studying
日本語勉強したいとか、何も。
Japanese, nothing.
しんさんが言うった風にやったら、
It would have
more make sense だと思うけど、
if I did it like you said,
頭が本当にぼーっとしてた
but my head was completely
empty.
なるほどね。
I see. So you
途中で決めたって事?
decided after you had been
here for a while?
そうだね
Yeah, I guess
so.

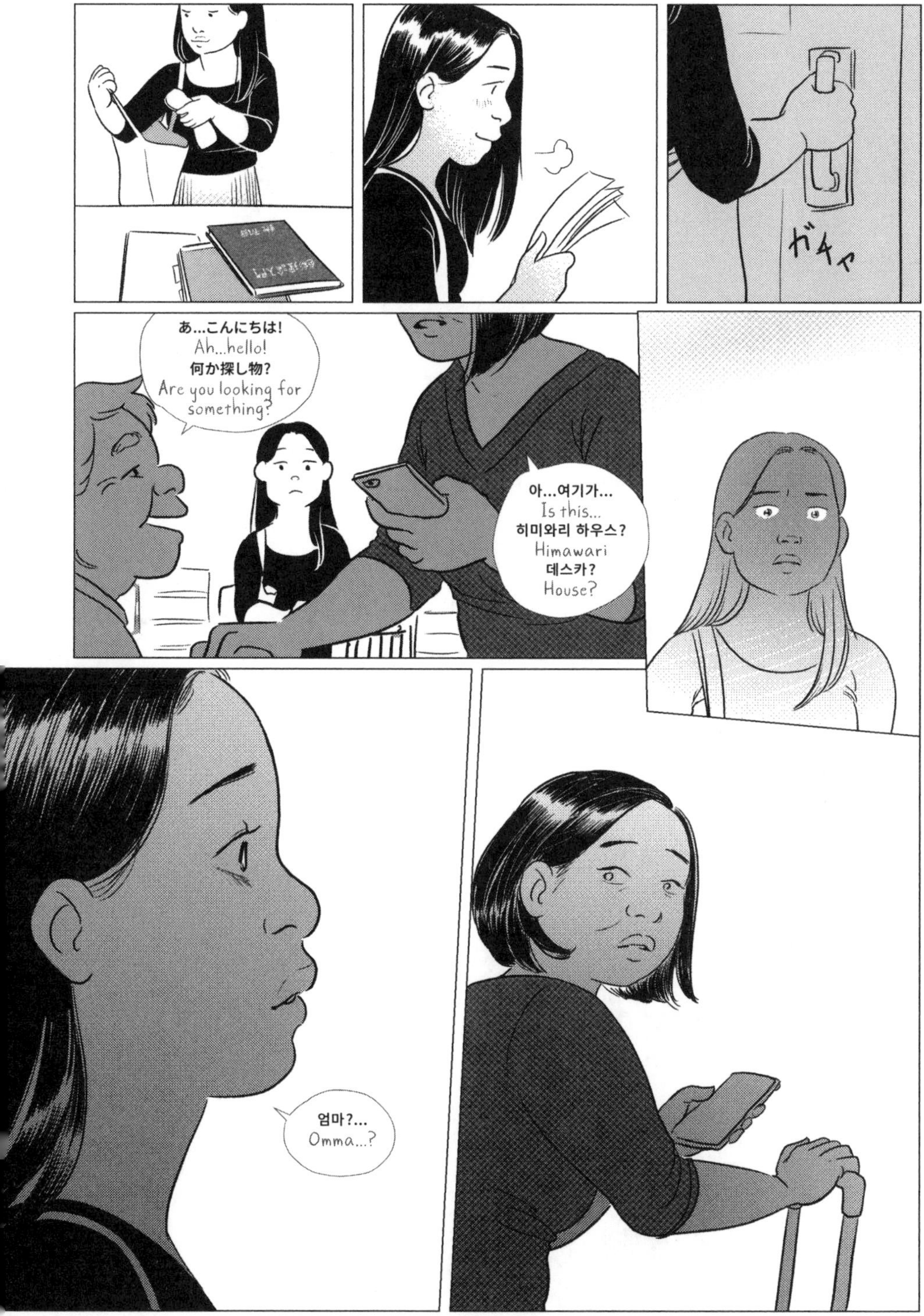
ガチャ
あ…こんにちは!
Ah…hello!
何か探し物?
Are you looking for something?
아…여기가…
Is this…
히미와리 하우스?
Himawari
데스카?
House?
엄마?…
Omma…?

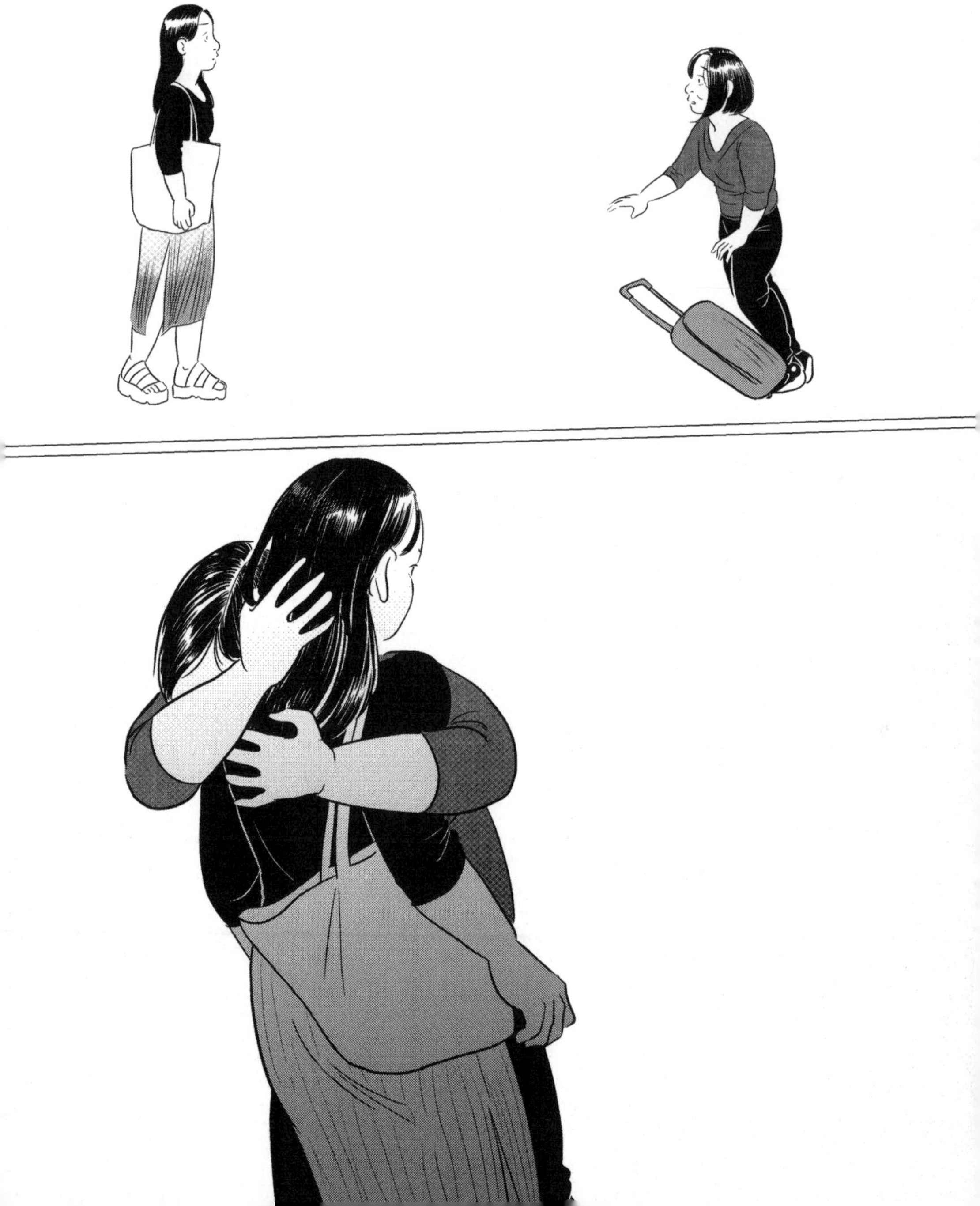

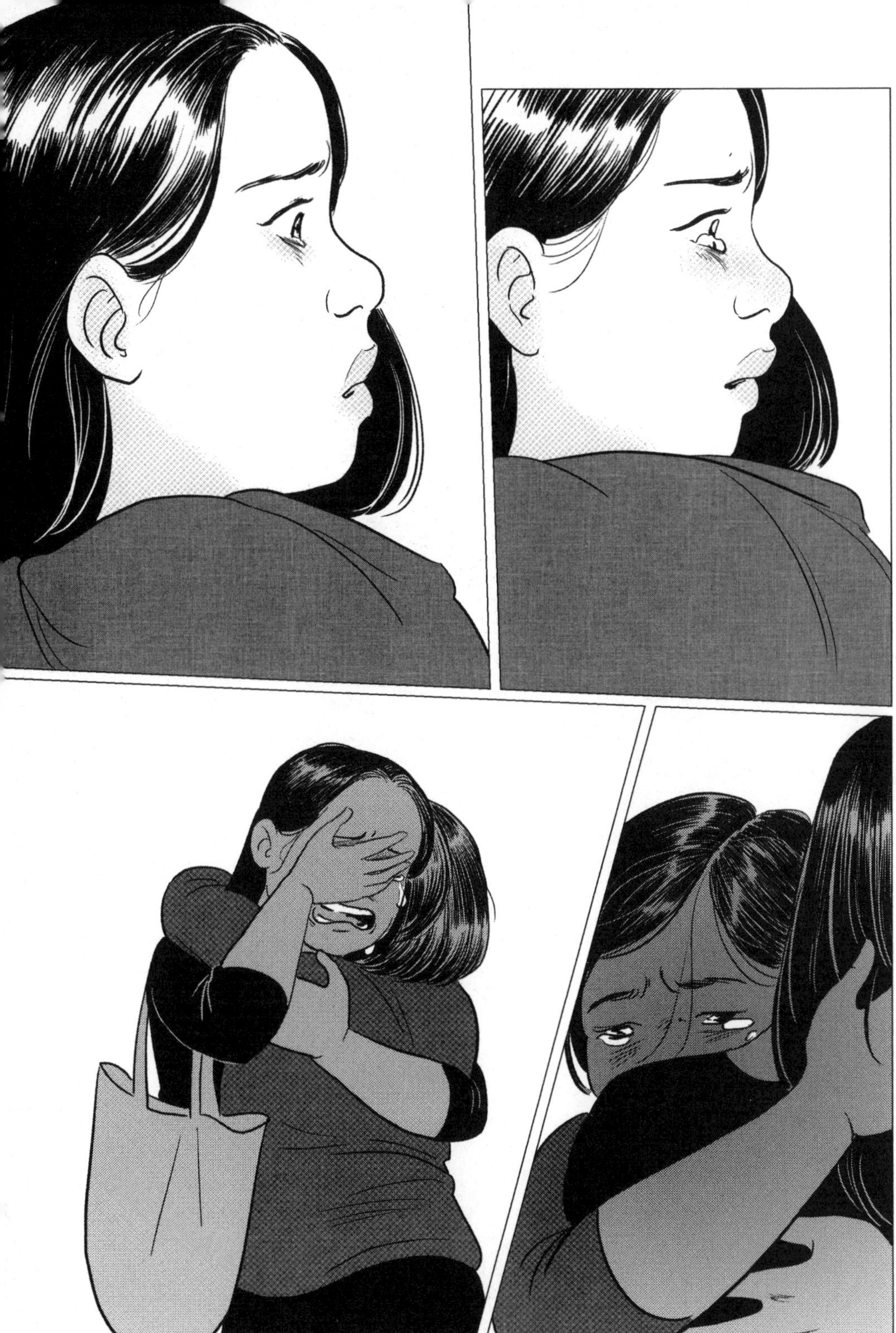

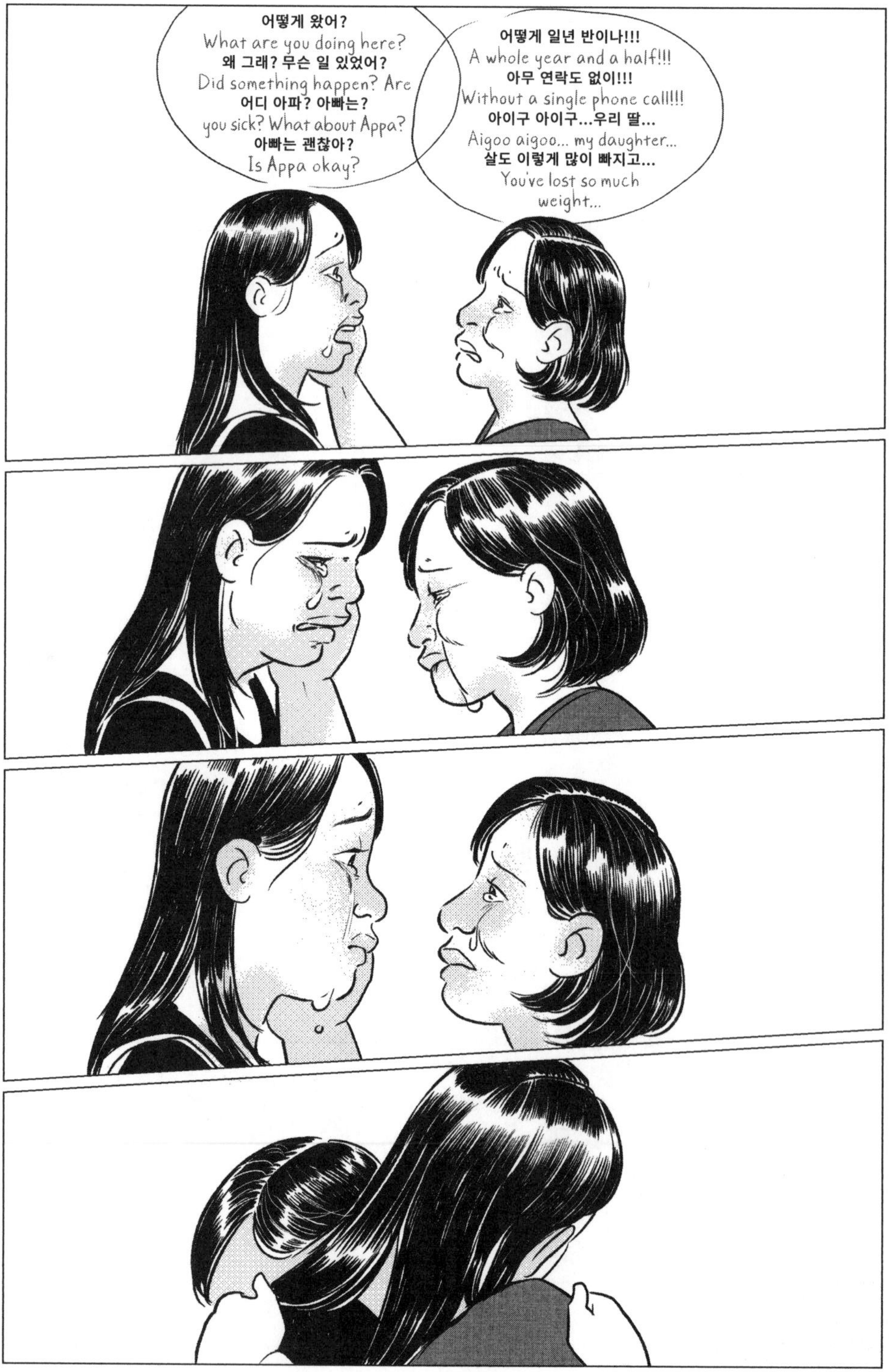
어떻게 왔어?
What are you doing here?
왜 그래? 무슨 일 있었어?
Did something happen? Are
어디 아파? 아빠는?
you sick? What about Appa?
아빠는 괜찮아?
Is Appa okay?
어떻게 일년 반이나!!!
A whole year and a half!!!
아무 연락도 없이!!!
Without a single phone call!!!
아이구 아이구...우리 딸...
Aigoo aigoo... my daughter...
살도 이렇게 많이 빠지고...
You've lost so much
weight...

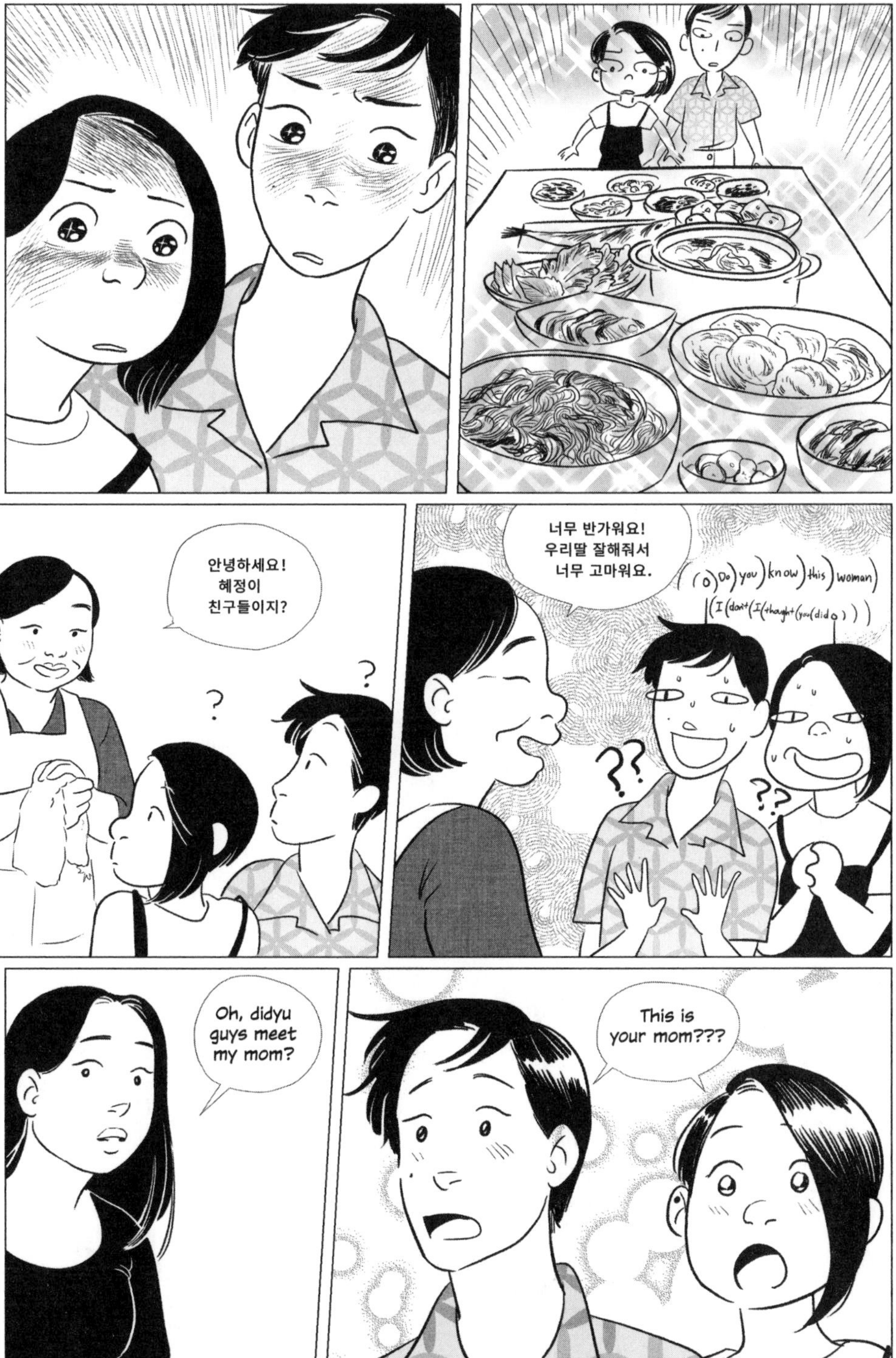

안녕하세요!
혜정이
친구들이지?
?
?
너무 반가워요!
우리딸 잘해줘서
너무 고마워요.
Do you know this woman
I don't I thought you did
??
??
Oh, didyu
guys meet
my mom?
This is
your mom???

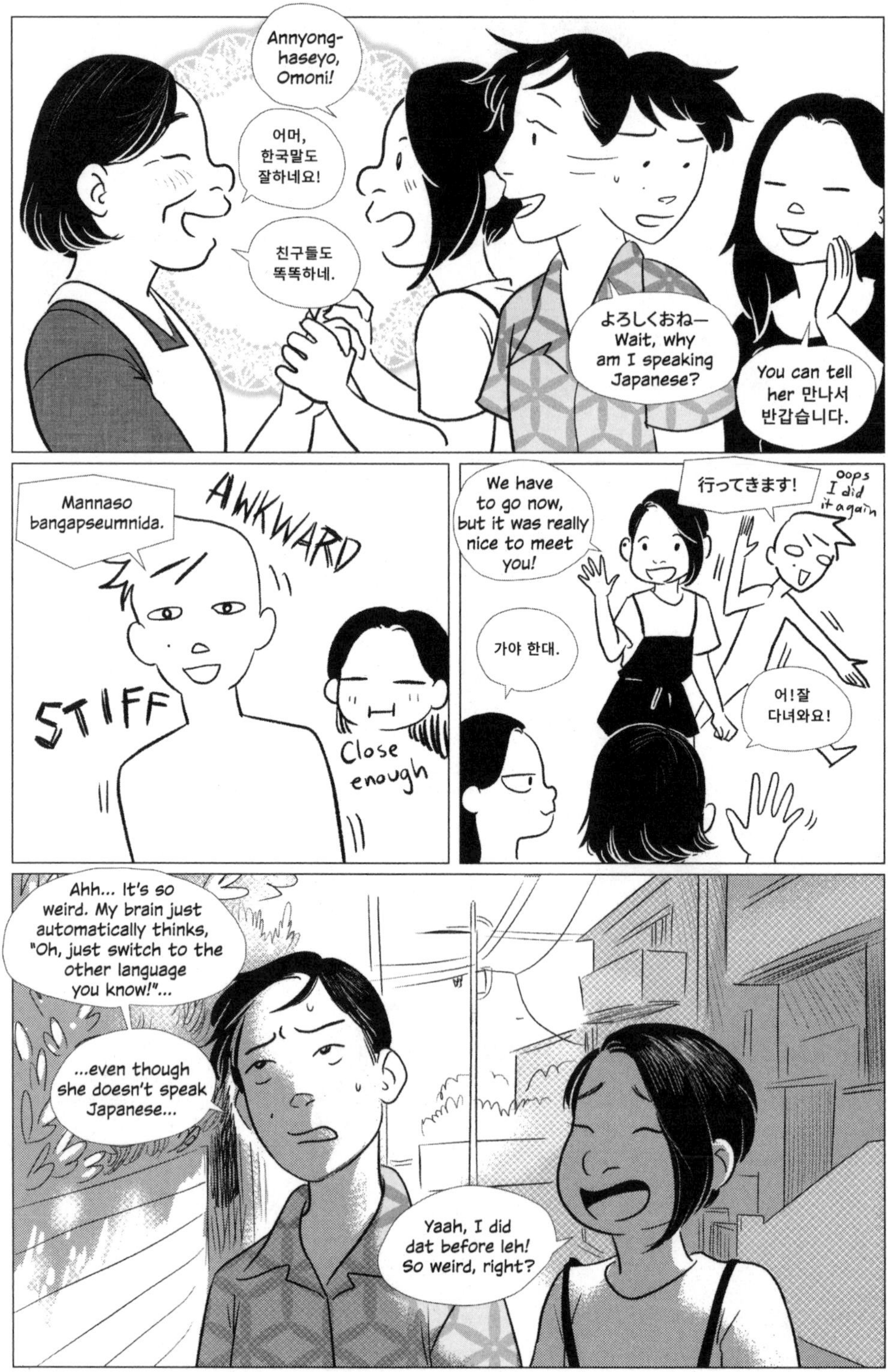
Annyong-haseyo, Omoni!
어머, 한국말도 잘하네요!
친구들도 똑똑하네.
よろしくおねー Wait, why am I speaking Japanese?
You can tell her 만나서 반갑습니다.
Mannaso bangapseumnida.
AWKWARD
STIFF
Close enough
We have to go now, but it was really nice to meet you!
가야 한대.
行ってきます!
oops I did it again
어!잘 다녀와요!
Ahh... It's so weird. My brain just automatically thinks, "Oh, just switch to the other language you know!"...
...even though she doesn't speak Japanese...
Yaah, I did dat before leh! So weird, right?

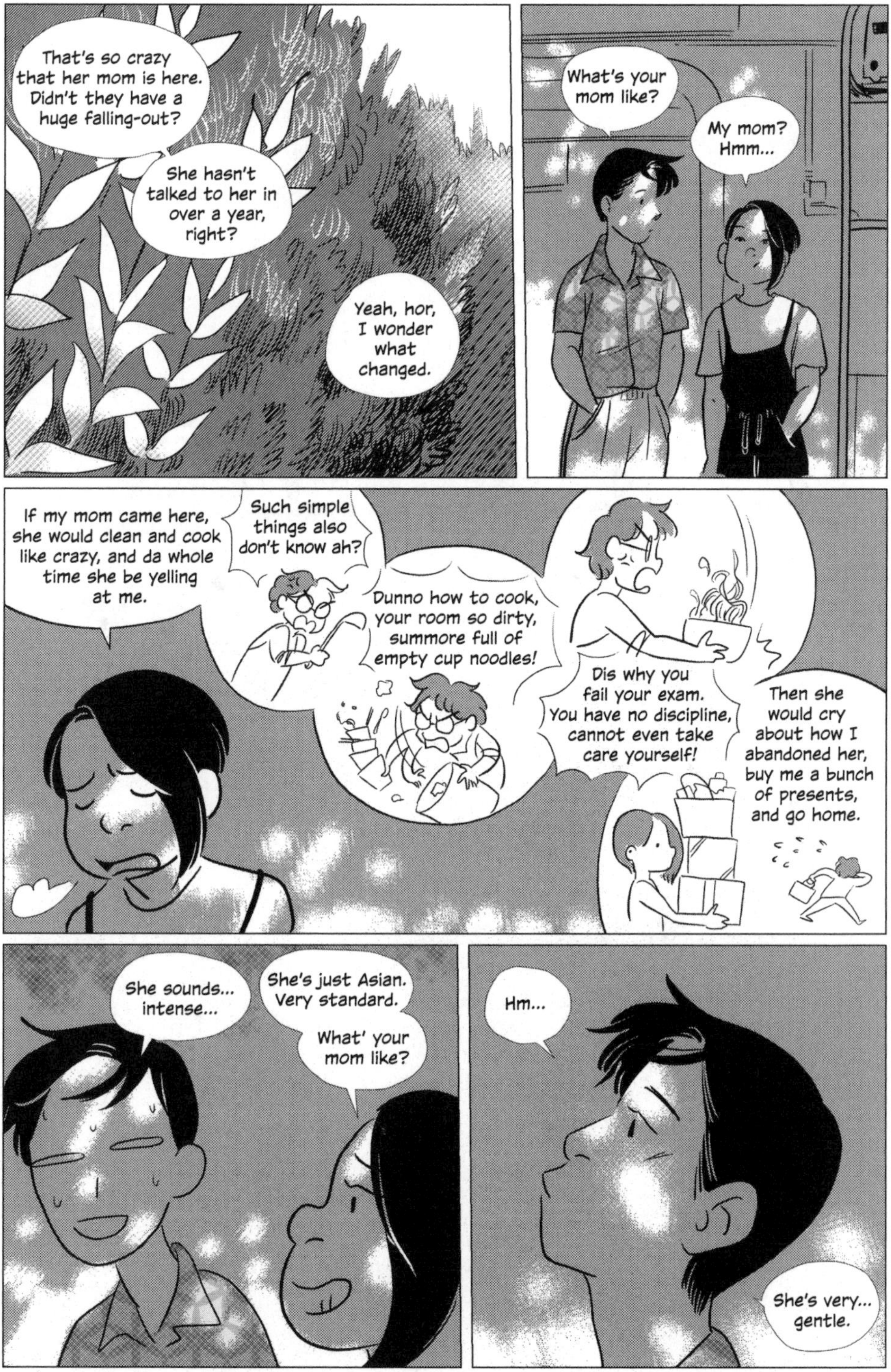
That's so crazy that her mom is here. Didn't they have a huge falling-out?
She hasn't talked to her in over a year, right?
Yeah, hor, I wonder what changed.
What's your mom like?
My mom? Hmm...
If my mom came here, she would clean and cook like crazy, and da whole time she be yelling at me.
Such simple things also don't know ah?
Dunno how to cook, your room so dirty, summore full of empty cup noodles!
Dis why you fail your exam. You have no discipline, cannot even take care yourself!
Then she would cry about how I abandoned her, buy me a bunch of presents, and go home.
She sounds... intense...
She's just Asian. Very standard.
What' your mom like?
Hm...
She's very... gentle.

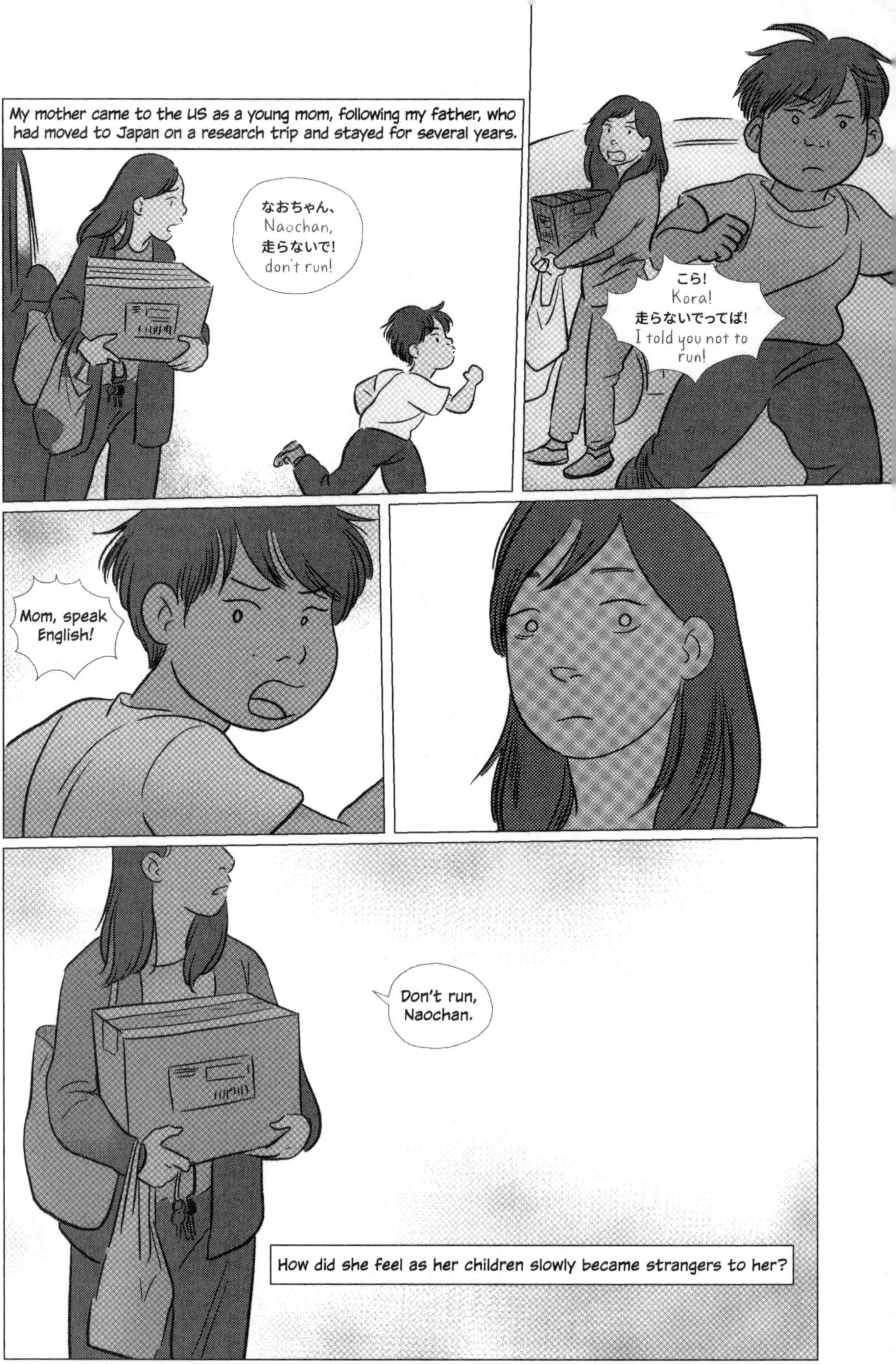
My mother came to the US as a young mom, following my father, who had moved to Japan on a research trip and stayed for several years.
なおちゃん、 Naochan, 走らないで! don't run!
こら! Kora! 走らないでってば! I told you not to run!
Mom, speak English!
Don't run, Naochan.
How did she feel as her children slowly became strangers to her?

Doushitano? What happen?

I don't want bento anymore! Everyone said it was smelly and made fun of me!

Rejecting her words, her food, her culture.

How many times did she have to swallow her own tongue?

Why can't you just make sandwiches like everyone else?

My mother, who could weave complex tapestries, rich with nuance and humor, in Japanese...

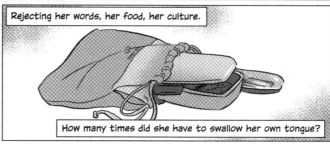

...reduced to stringing simple words together like flimsy plastic beads on a necklace.

How could she stand it when there was always so much to say?

337

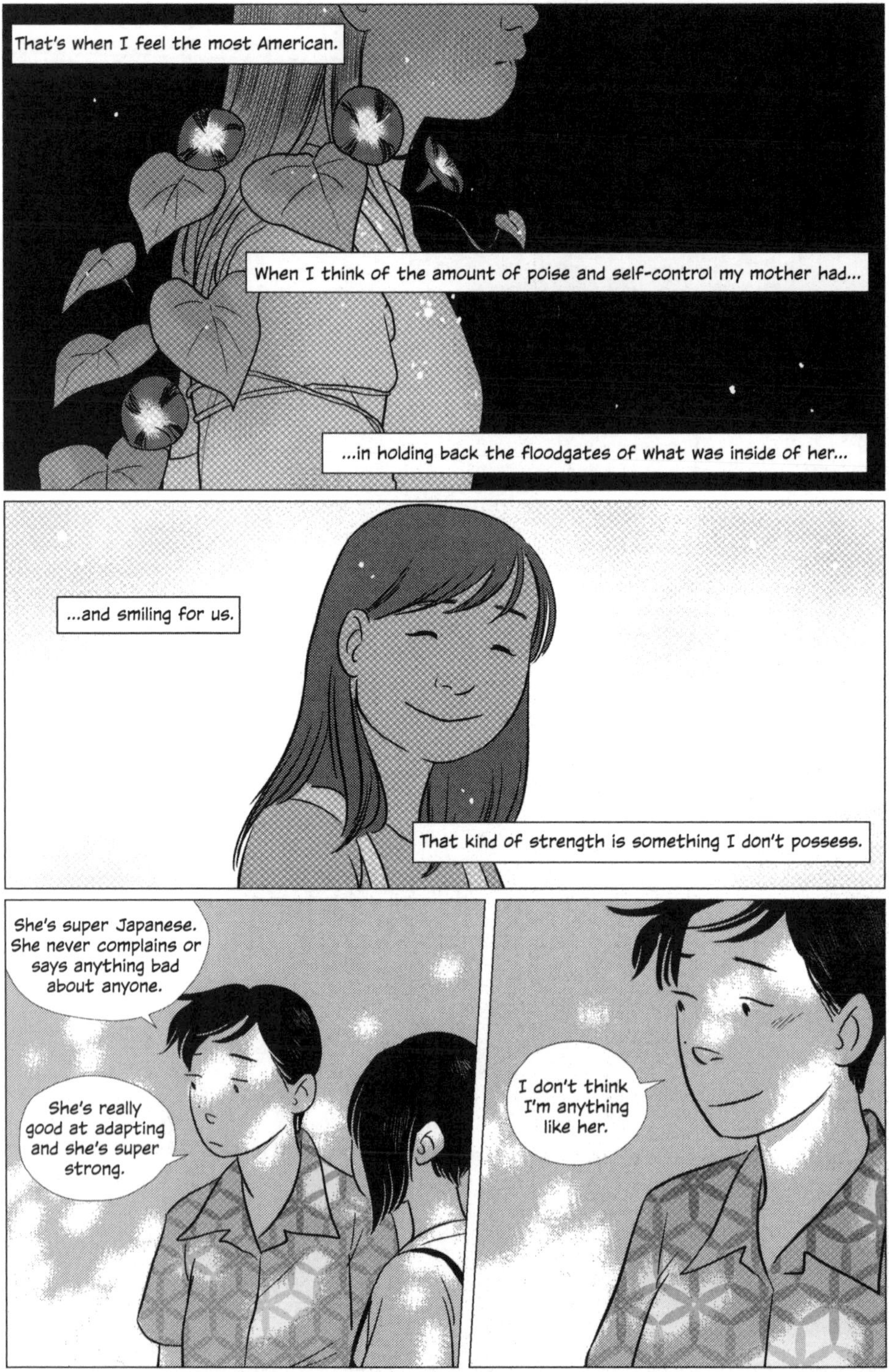
That's when I feel the most American.
When I think of the amount of poise and self-control my mother had...
...in holding back the floodgates of what was inside of her...
...and smiling for us.
That kind of strength is something I don't possess.
She's super Japanese. She never complains or says anything bad about anyone.
She's really good at adapting and she's super strong.
I don't think I'm anything like her.

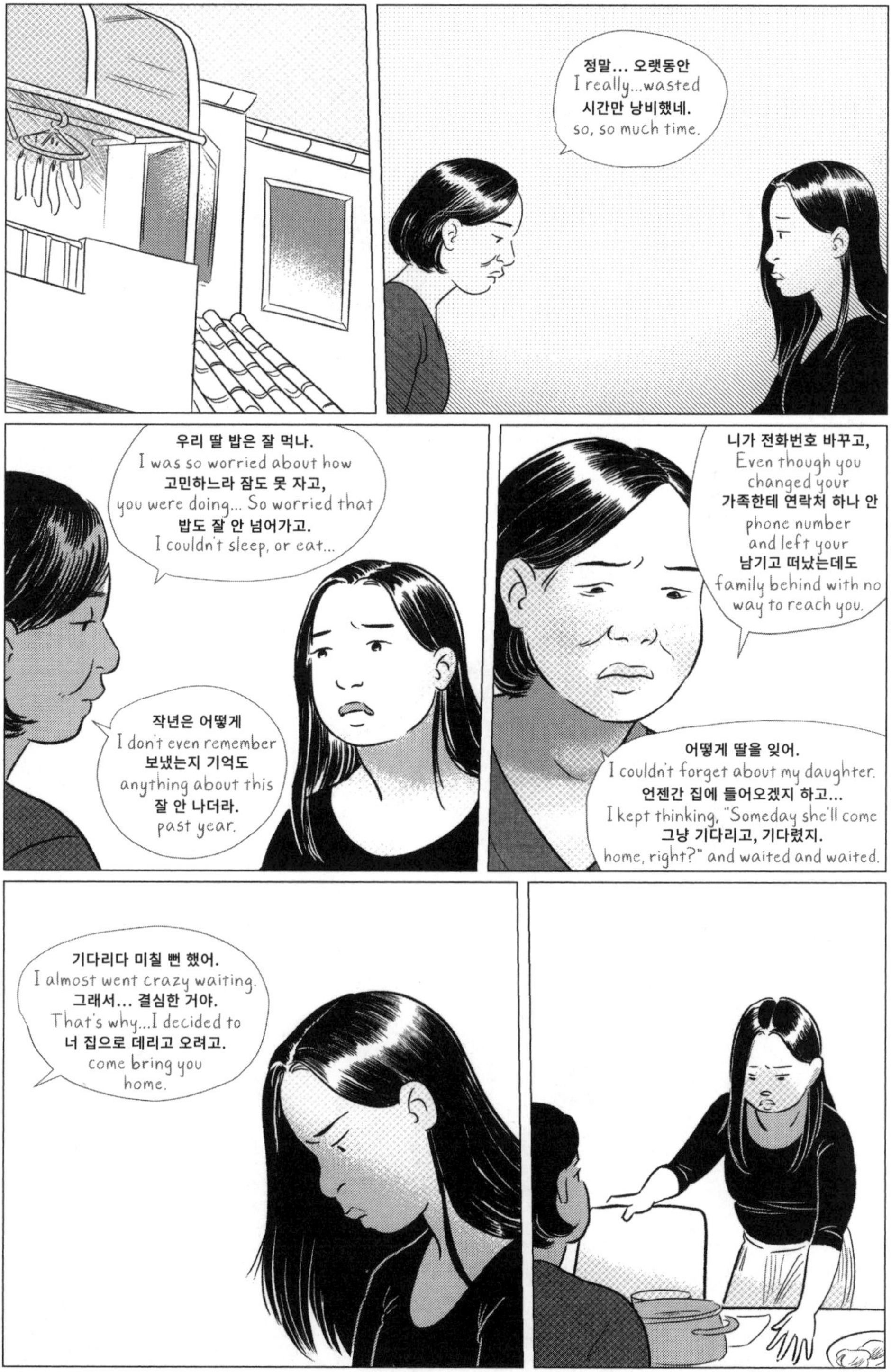

정말... 오랫동안
I really...wasted
시간만 낭비했네.
so, so much time.
우리 딸 밥은 잘 먹나.
I was so worried about how
고민하느라 잠도 못 자고,
you were doing... So worried that
밥도 잘 안 넘어가고.
I couldn't sleep, or eat...
작년은 어떻게
I don't even remember
보냈는지 기억도
anything about this
잘 안 나더라.
past year.
니가 전화번호 바꾸고,
Even though you
changed your
가족한테 연락처 하나 안
phone number
and left your
남기고 떠났는데도
family behind with no
way to reach you.
어떻게 딸을 잊어.
I couldn't forget about my daughter.
언젠간 집에 들어오겠지 하고...
I kept thinking, "Someday she'll come
그냥 기다리고, 기다렸지.
home, right?" and waited and waited.
기다리다 미칠 뻔 했어.
I almost went crazy waiting.
그래서... 결심한 거야.
That's why...I decided to
너 집으로 데리고 오려고.
come bring you
home.

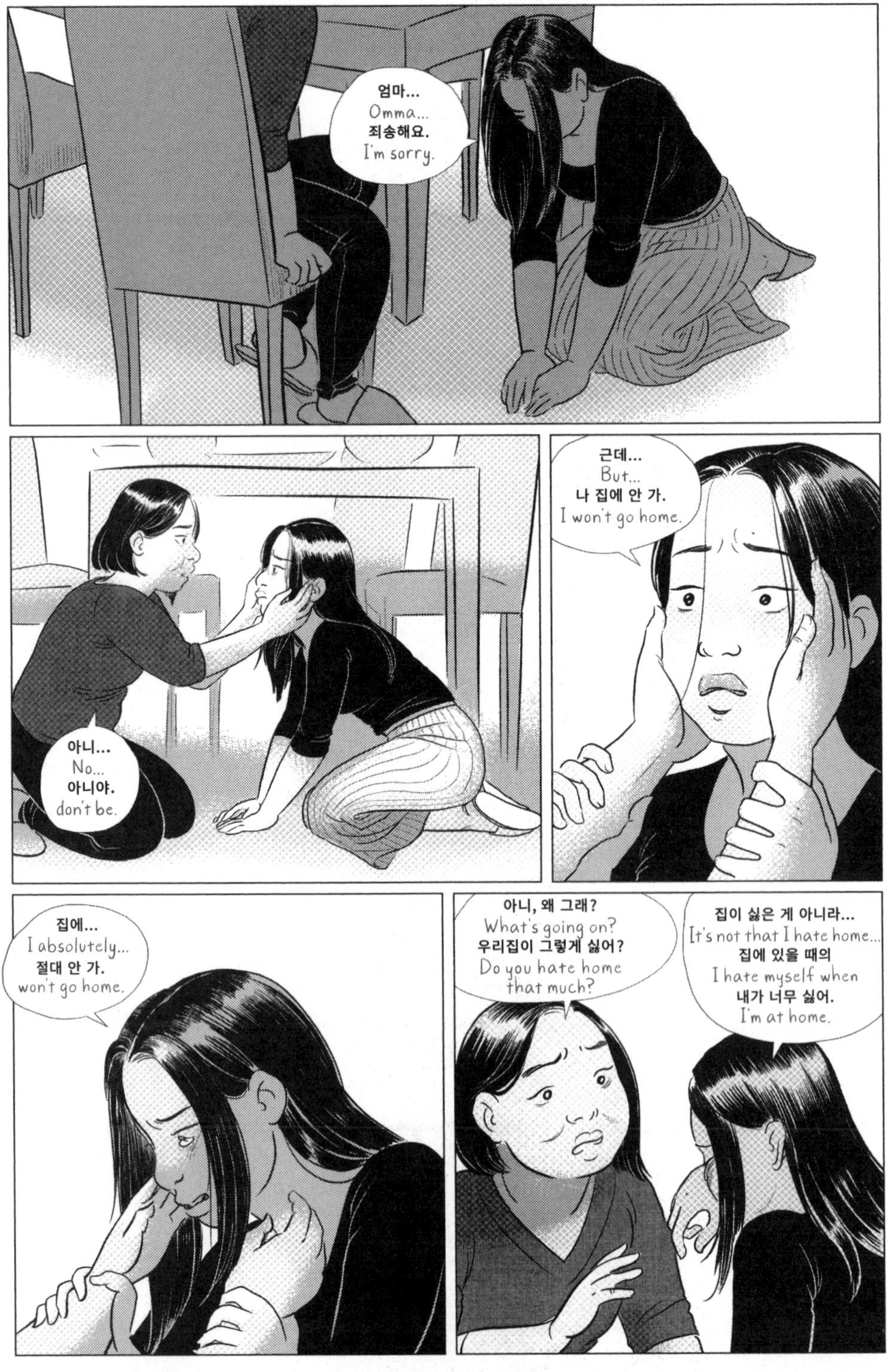
엄마...
Omma...
죄송해요.
I'm sorry.
아니...
No...
아니야.
don't be.
근데...
But...
나 집에 안 가.
I won't go home.
집에...
I absolutely...
절대 안 가.
won't go home.
아니, 왜 그래?
What's going on?
우리집이 그렇게 싫어?
Do you hate home that much?
집이 싫은 게 아니라...
It's not that I hate home...
집에 있을 때의
I hate myself when
내가 너무 싫어.
I'm at home.

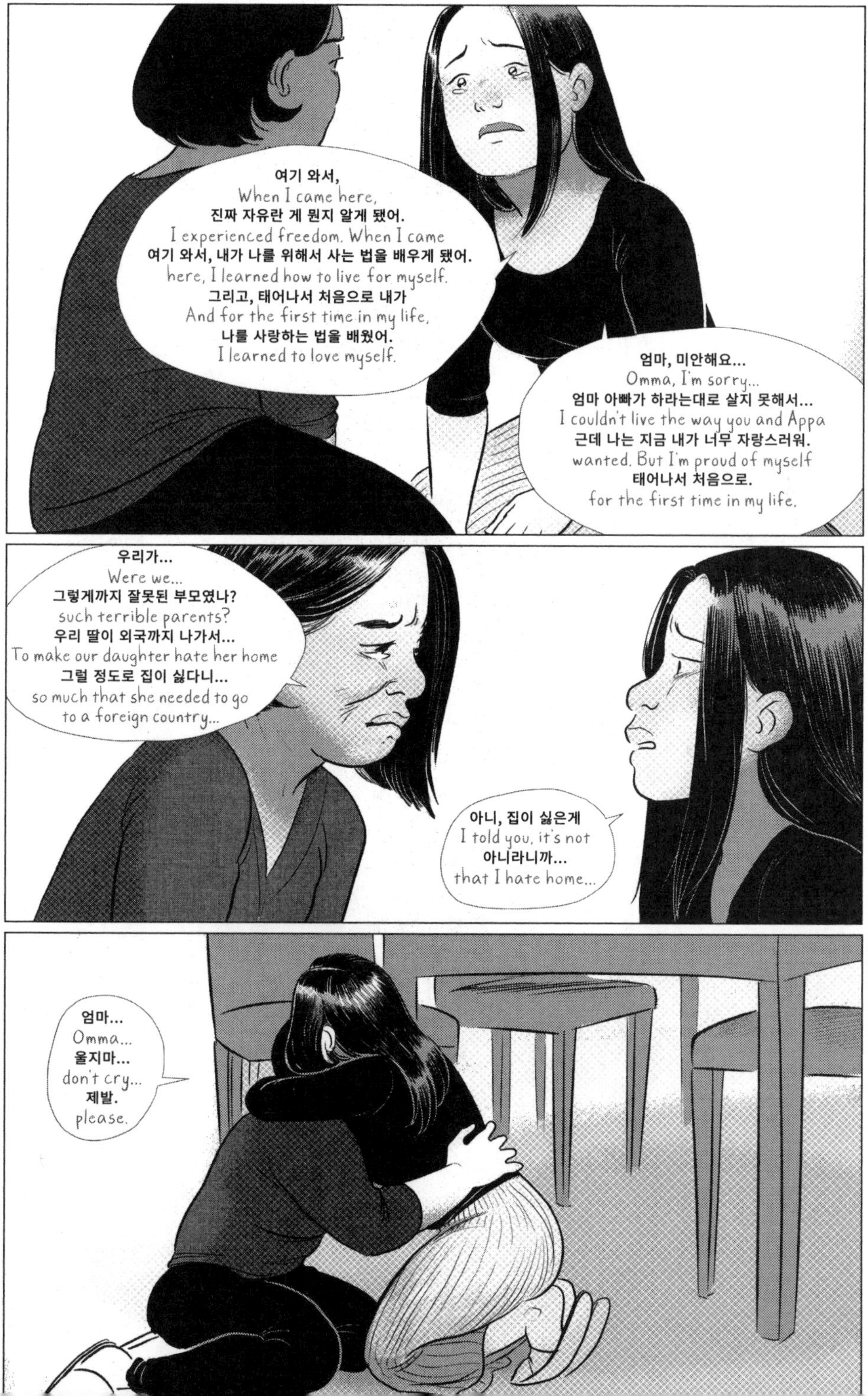
여기 와서,
When I came here,
진짜 자유란 게 뭔지 알게 됐어.
I experienced freedom. When I came
여기 와서, 내가 나를 위해서 사는 법을 배우게 됐어.
here, I learned how to live for myself.
그리고, 태어나서 처음으로 내가
And for the first time in my life,
나를 사랑하는 법을 배웠어.
I learned to love myself.
엄마, 미안해요...
Omma, I'm sorry...
엄마 아빠가 하라는대로 살지 못해서...
I couldn't live the way you and Appa
근데 나는 지금 내가 너무 자랑스러워.
wanted. But I'm proud of myself
태어나서 처음으로.
for the first time in my life.
우리가...
Were we...
그렇게까지 잘못된 부모였나?
such terrible parents?
우리 딸이 외국까지 나가서...
To make our daughter hate her home
그럴 정도로 집이 싫다니...
so much that she needed to go
to a foreign country...
아니, 집이 싫은게
I told you, it's not
아니라니까...
that I hate home...
엄마...
Omma...
울지마...
don't cry...
제발.
please.

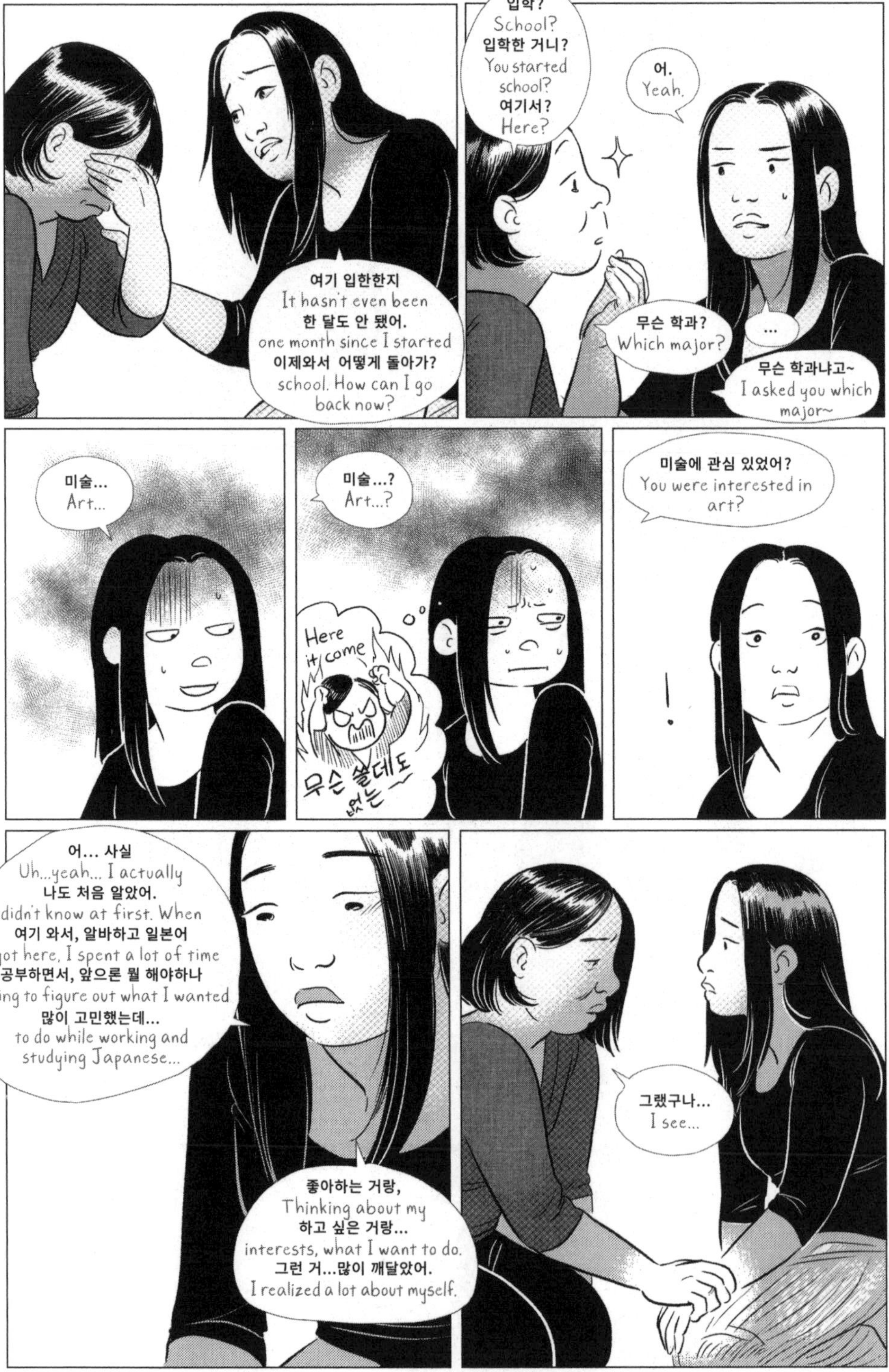
여기 입한한지
It hasn't even been
한 달도 안 됐어.
one month since I started
이제와서 어떻게 돌아가?
school. How can I go back now?
입학?
School?
입학한 거니?
You started school?
여기서?
Here?
어.
Yeah.
무슨 학과?
Which major?
...
무슨 학과냐고~
I asked you which major~
미술...
Art...
미술...?
Art...?
Here it come
무슨 쓸데도 없는~
미술에 관심 있었어?
You were interested in art?
!
어... 사실
Uh...yeah... I actually
나도 처음 알았어.
didn't know at first. When
여기 와서, 알바하고 일본어
I got here, I spent a lot of time
공부하면서, 앞으론 뭘 해야하나
trying to figure out what I wanted
많이 고민했는데...
to do while working and studying Japanese...
좋아하는 거랑,
Thinking about my
하고 싶은 거랑...
interests, what I want to do.
그런 거...많이 깨달았어.
I realized a lot about myself.
그랬구나...
I see...

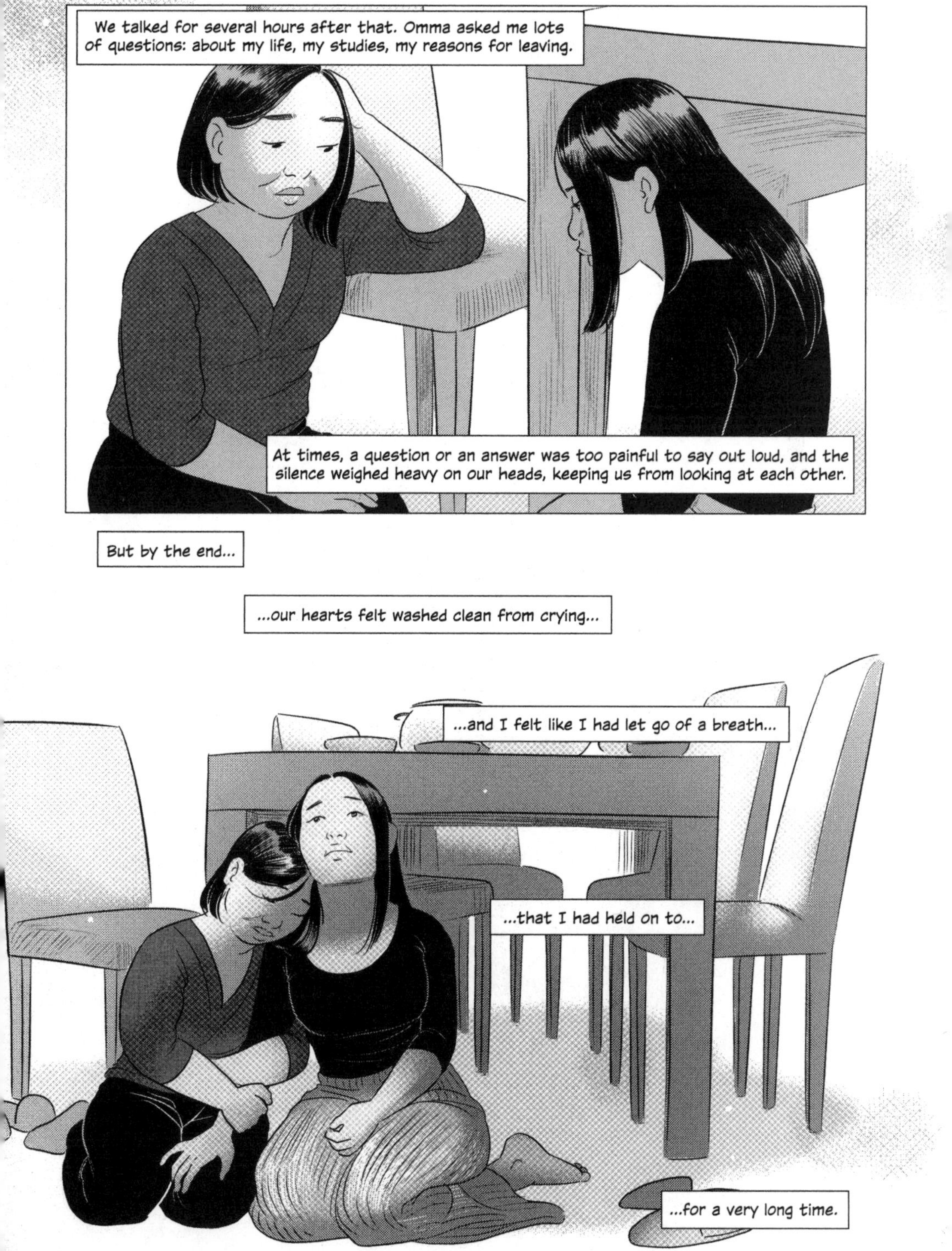
We talked for several hours after that. Omma asked me lots of questions: about my life, my studies, my reasons for leaving.
At times, a question or an answer was too painful to say out loud, and the silence weighed heavy on our heads, keeping us from looking at each other.
But by the end...
...our hearts felt washed clean from crying...
...and I felt like I had let go of a breath...
...that I had held on to...
...for a very long time.

Chapter 20

Forward

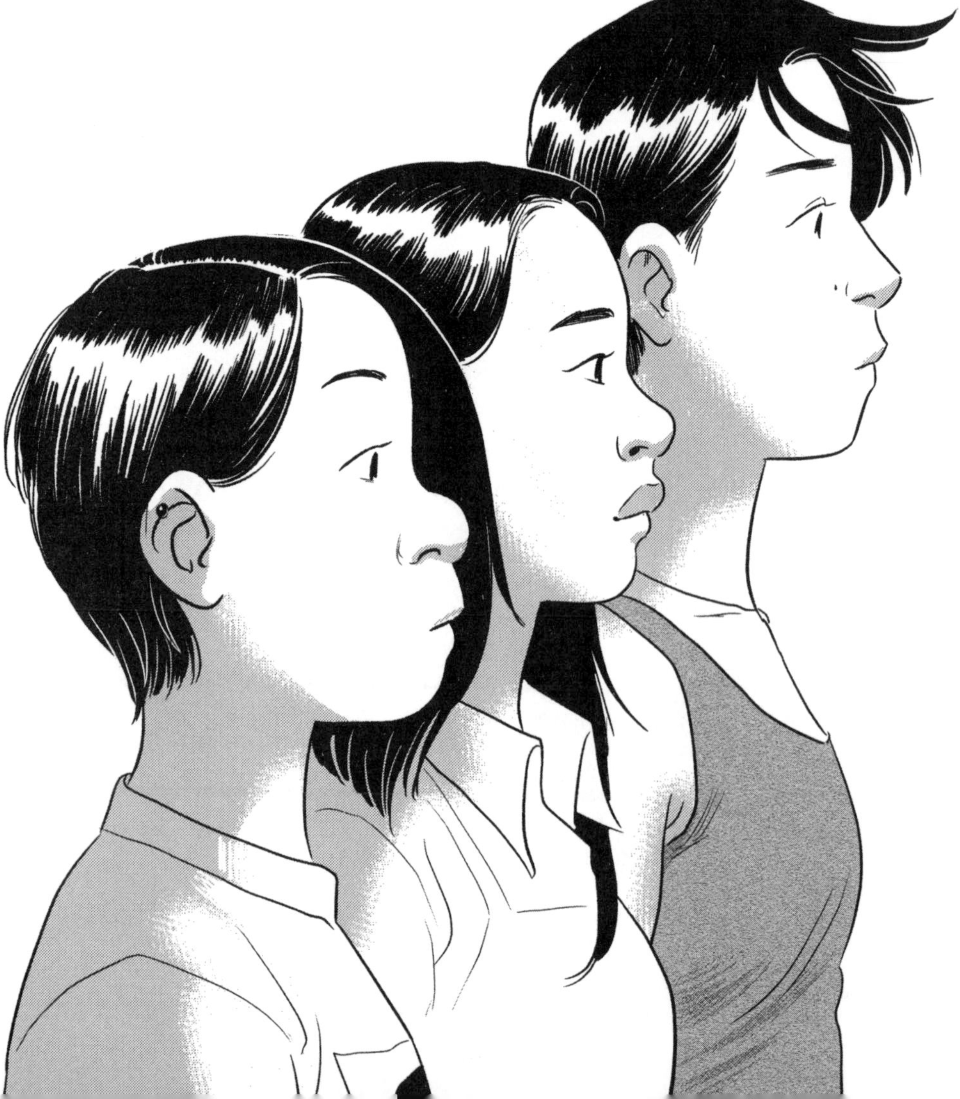

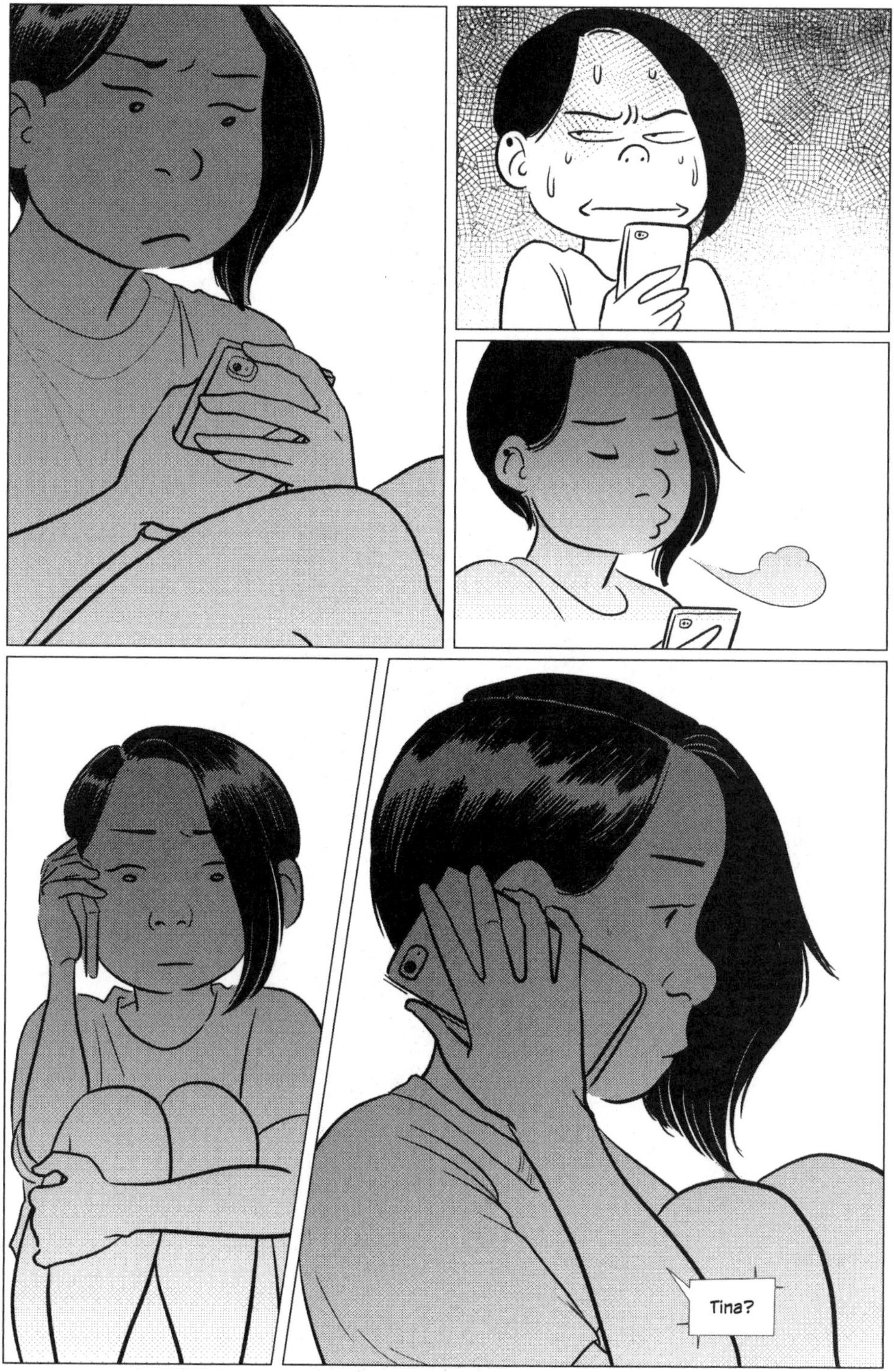
Tina?

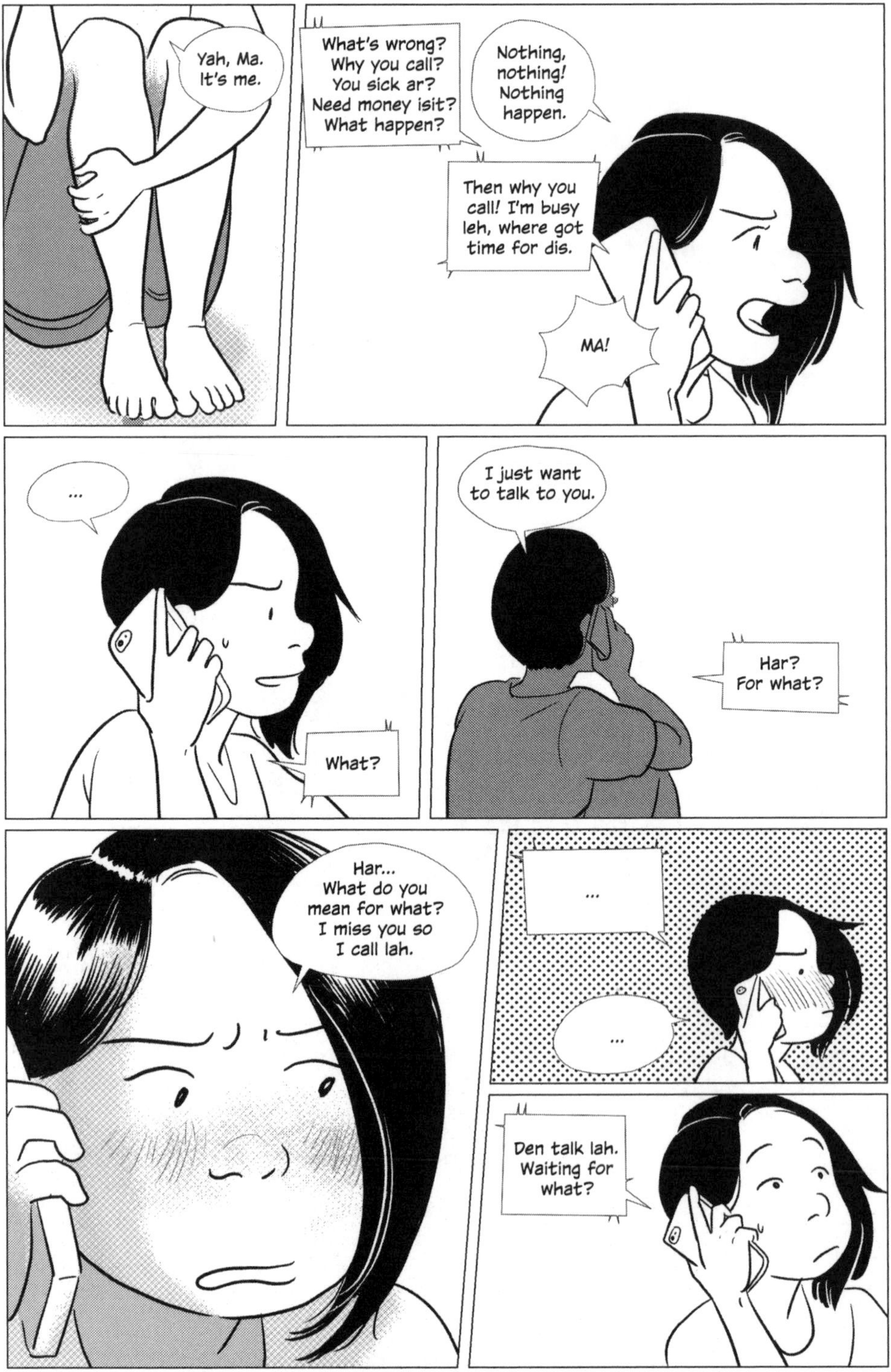
Yah, Ma. It's me.
What's wrong? Why you call? You sick ar? Need money isit? What happen?
Nothing, nothing! Nothing happen.
Then why you call! I'm busy leh, where got time for dis.
MA!
...
What?
I just want to talk to you.
Har? For what?
Har... What do you mean for what? I miss you so I call lah.
...
...
Den talk lah. Waiting for what?

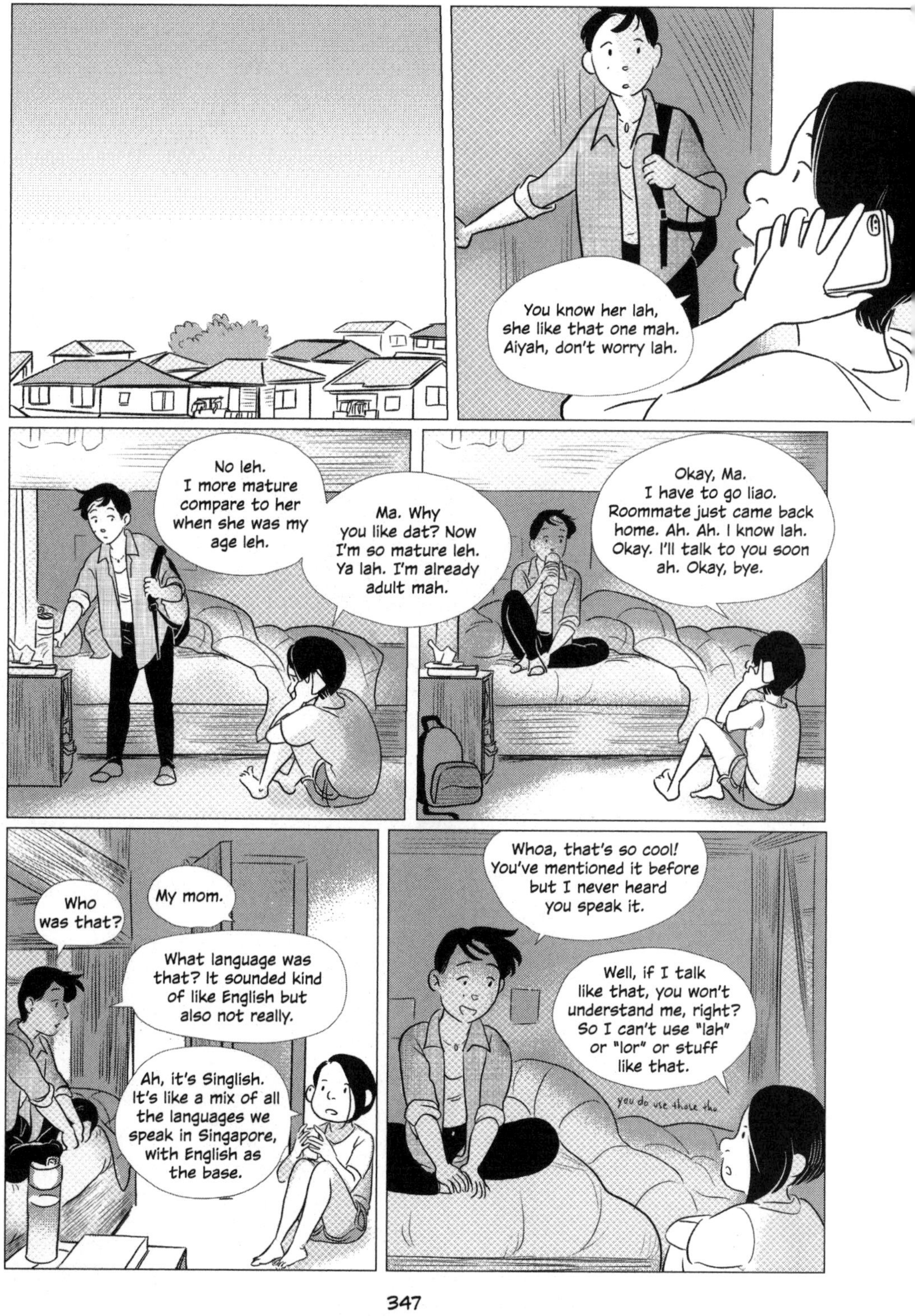
You know her lah, she like that one mah. Aiyah, don't worry lah.
No leh. I more mature compare to her when she was my age leh.
Ma. Why you like dat? Now I'm so mature leh. Ya lah. I'm already adult mah.
Okay, Ma. I have to go liao. Roommate just came back home. Ah. Ah. I know lah. Okay. I'll talk to you soon ah. Okay, bye.
Who was that?
My mom.
What language was that? It sounded kind of like English but also not really.
Ah, it's Singlish. It's like a mix of all the languages we speak in Singapore, with English as the base.
Whoa, that's so cool! You've mentioned it before but I never heard you speak it.
Well, if I talk like that, you won't understand me, right? So I can't use "lah" or "lor" or stuff like that.
you do use those tho

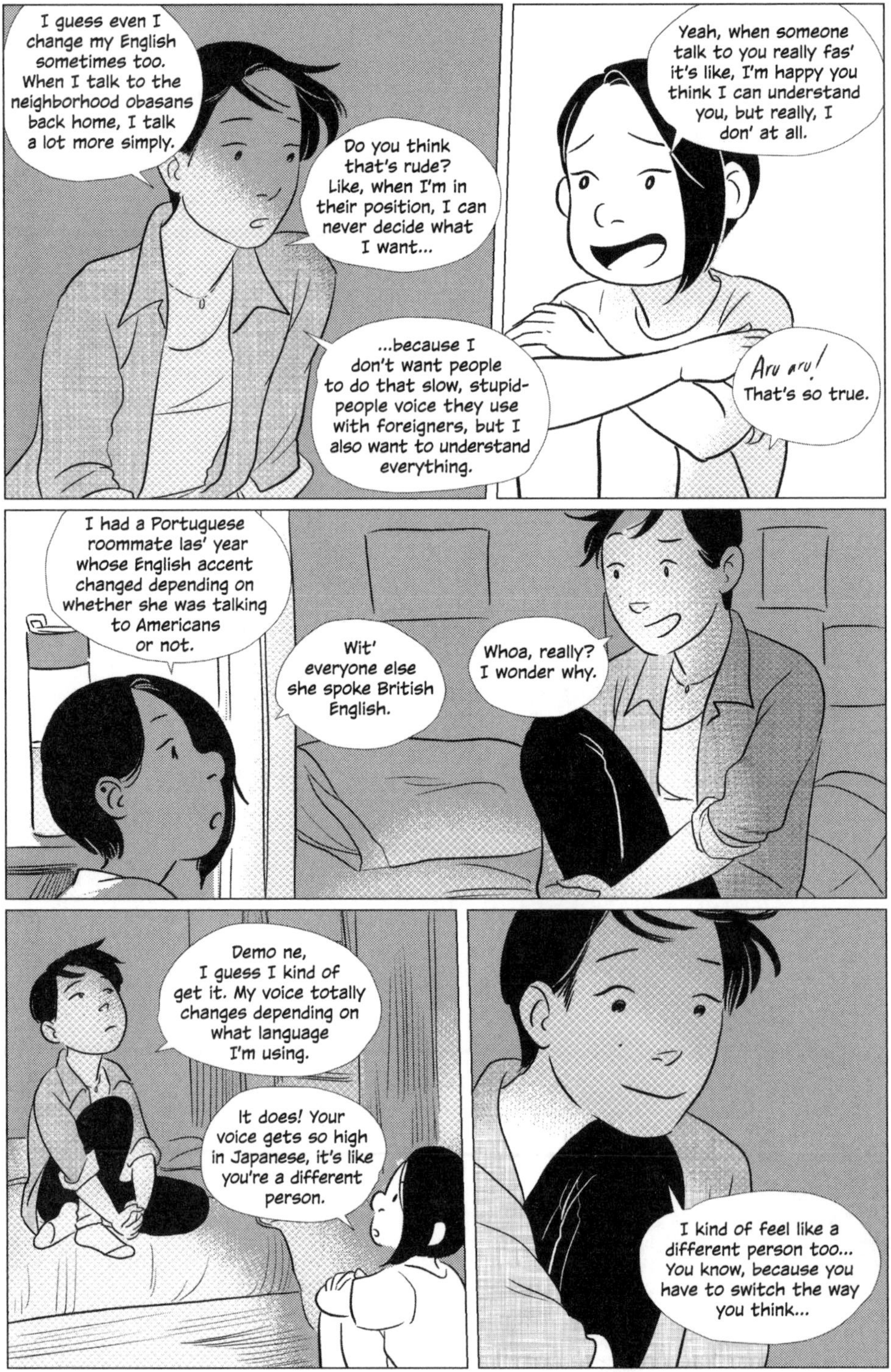
I guess even I change my English sometimes too. When I talk to the neighborhood obasans back home, I talk a lot more simply.
Do you think that's rude? Like, when I'm in their position, I can never decide what I want...
...because I don't want people to do that slow, stupid-people voice they use with foreigners, but I also want to understand everything.
Yeah, when someone talk to you really fas' it's like, I'm happy you think I can understand you, but really, I don' at all.
Aru aru! That's so true.
I had a Portuguese roommate las' year whose English accent changed depending on whether she was talking to Americans or not.
Wit' everyone else she spoke British English.
Whoa, really? I wonder why.
Demo ne, I guess I kind of get it. My voice totally changes depending on what language I'm using.
It does! Your voice gets so high in Japanese, it's like you're a different person.
I kind of feel like a different person too... You know, because you have to switch the way you think...

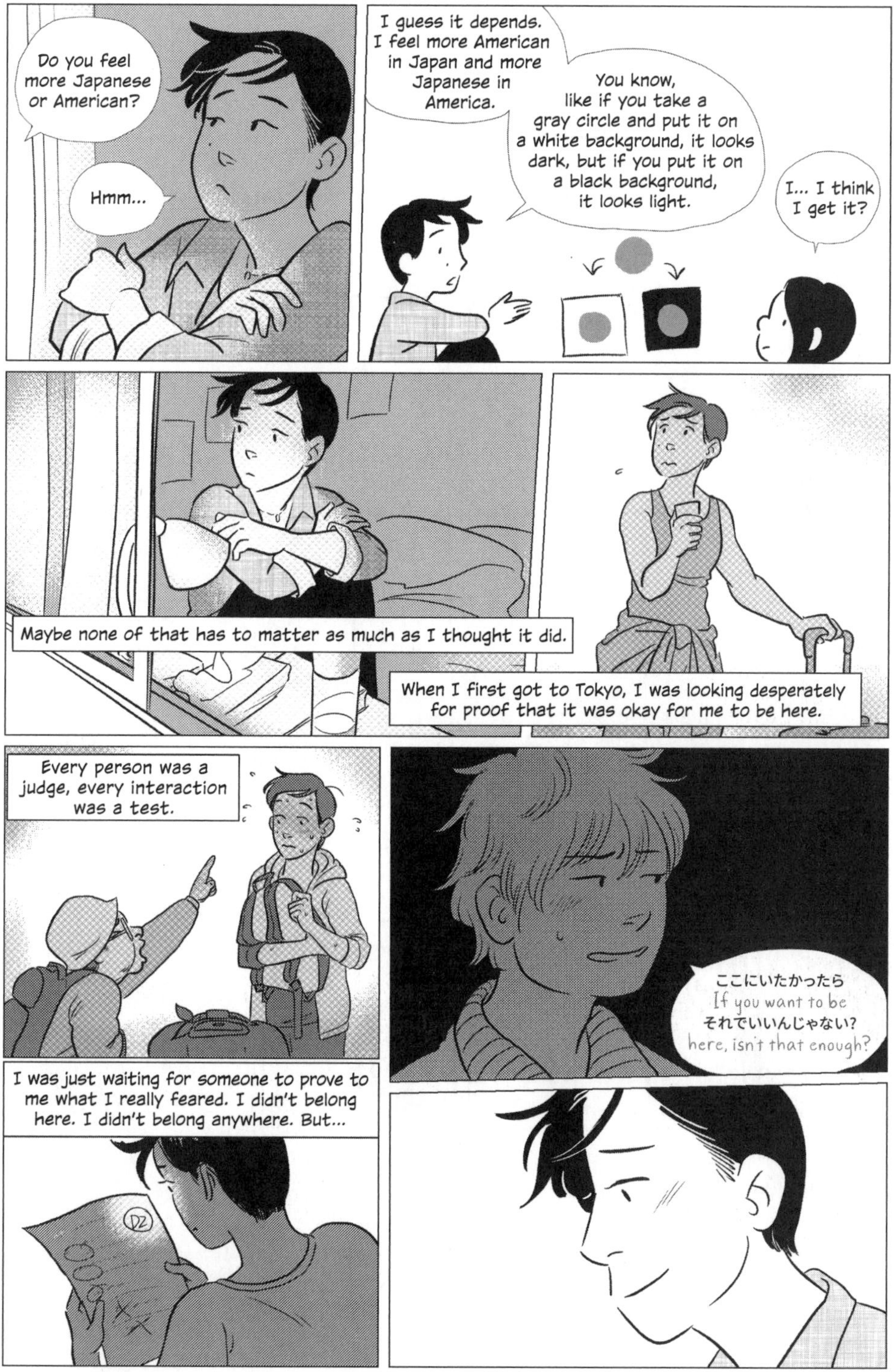

Do you feel more Japanese or American?
Hmm...
I guess it depends. I feel more American in Japan and more Japanese in America.
You know, like if you take a gray circle and put it on a white background, it looks dark, but if you put it on a black background, it looks light.
I... I think I get it?
Maybe none of that has to matter as much as I thought it did.
When I first got to Tokyo, I was looking desperately for proof that it was okay for me to be here.
Every person was a judge, every interaction was a test.
ここにいたかったら
If you want to be
それでいいんじゃない?
here, isn't that enough?
I was just waiting for someone to prove to me what I really feared. I didn't belong here. I didn't belong anywhere. But...

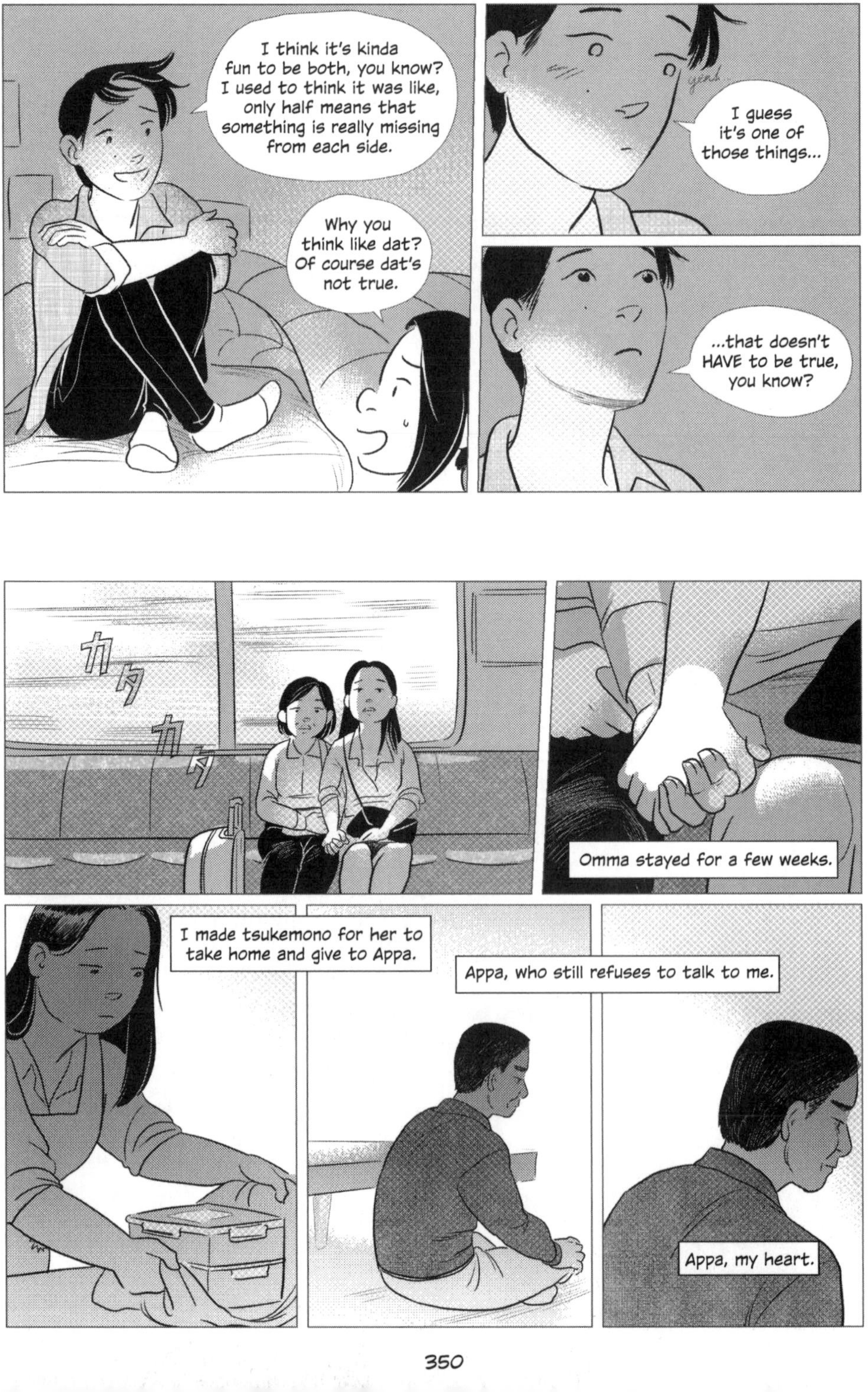

I think it's kinda fun to be both, you know? I used to think it was like, only half means that something is really missing from each side.
Why you think like dat? Of course dat's not true.
I guess it's one of those things...
...that doesn't HAVE to be true, you know?
カタ
カタ
Omma stayed for a few weeks.
I made tsukemono for her to take home and give to Appa.
Appa, who still refuses to talk to me.
Appa, my heart.

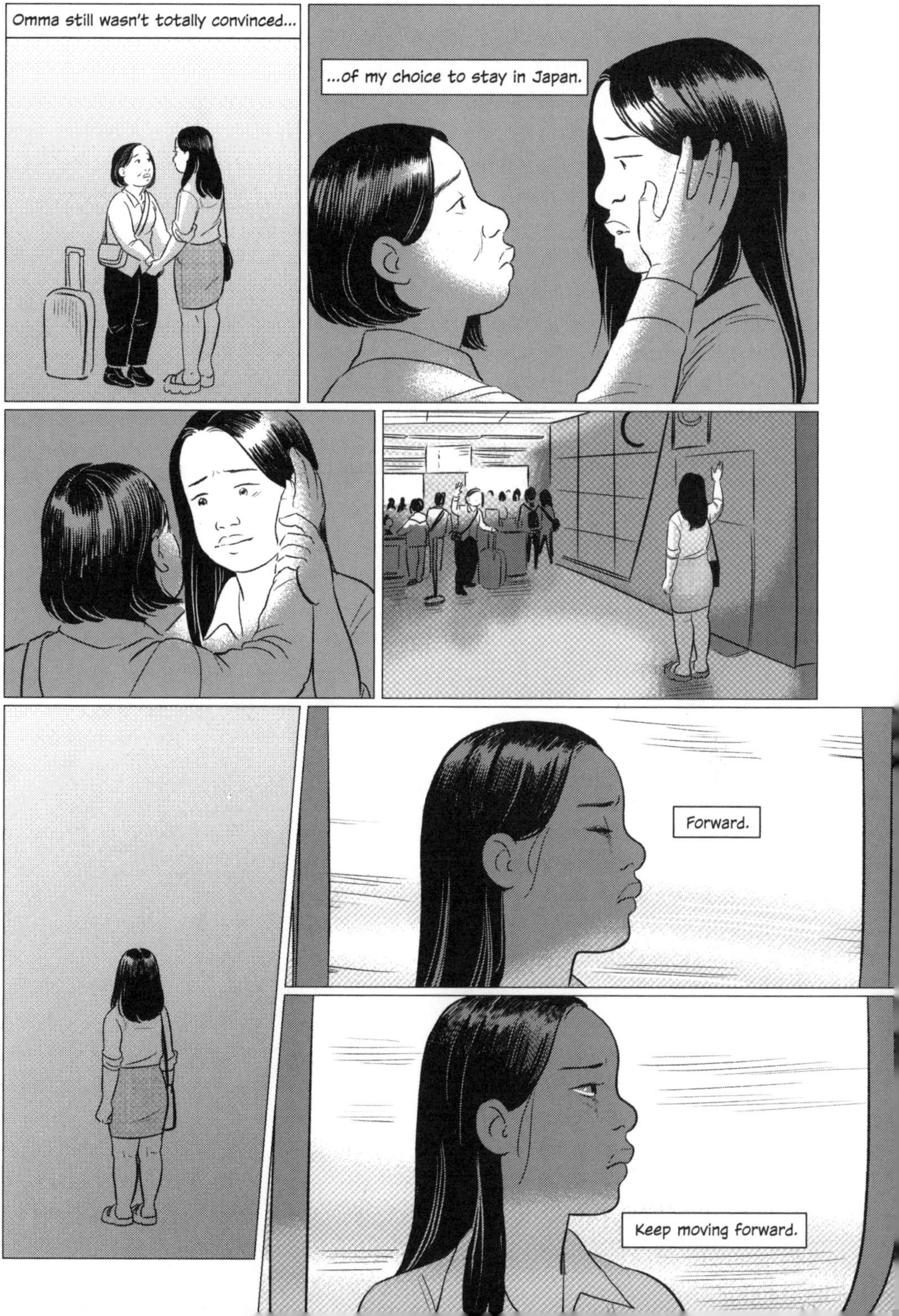
Omma still wasn't totally convinced...
...of my choice to stay in Japan.
Forward.
Keep moving forward.

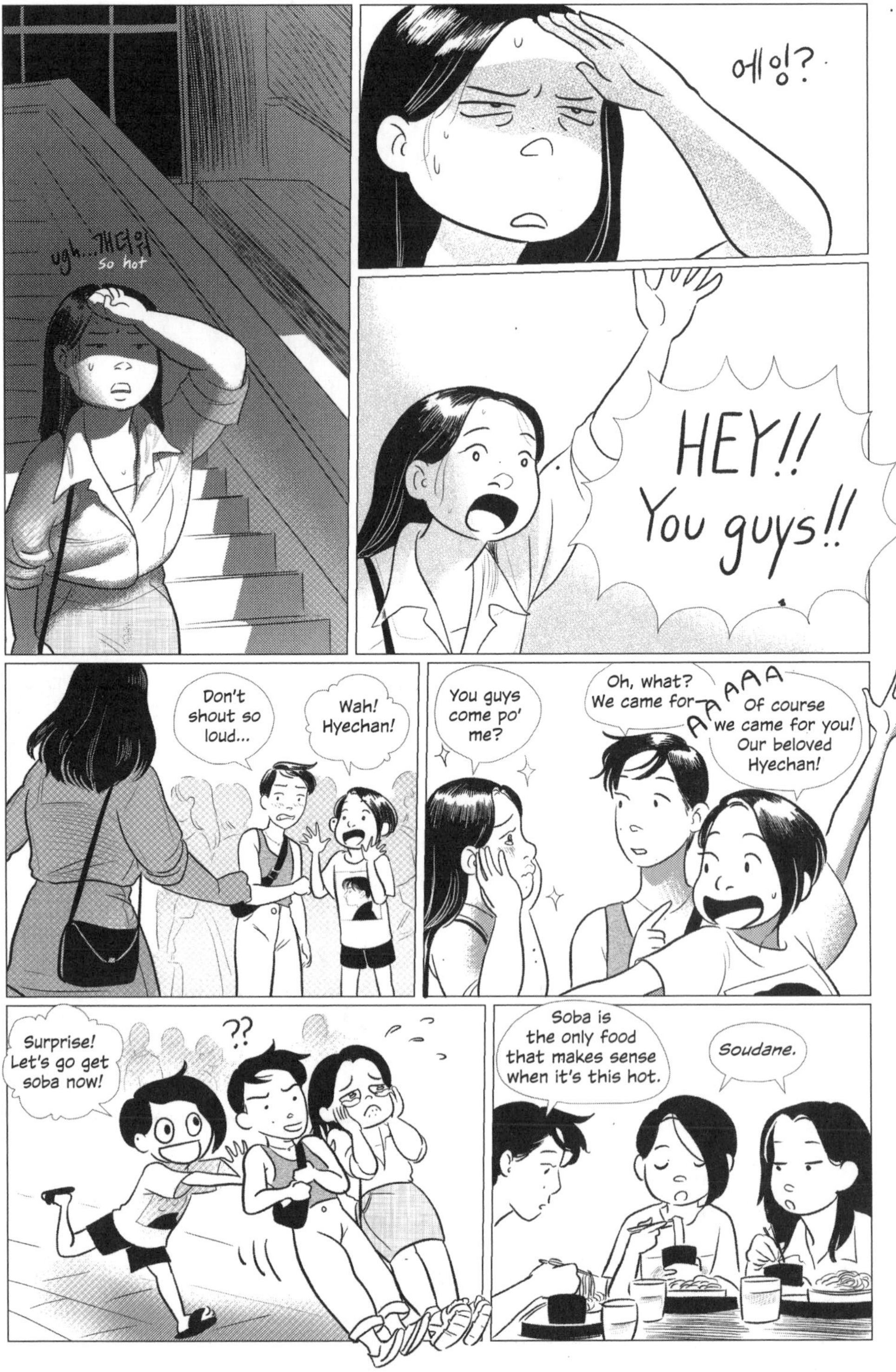
ugh... 개더워
so hot
에잉?
HEY!! You guys!!
Don't shout so loud...
Wah! Hyechan!
You guys come po' me?
Oh, what? We came for—
AAAAA
Of course we came for you! Our beloved Hyechan!
Surprise! Let's go get soba now!
??
Soba is the only food that makes sense when it's this hot.
Soudane.

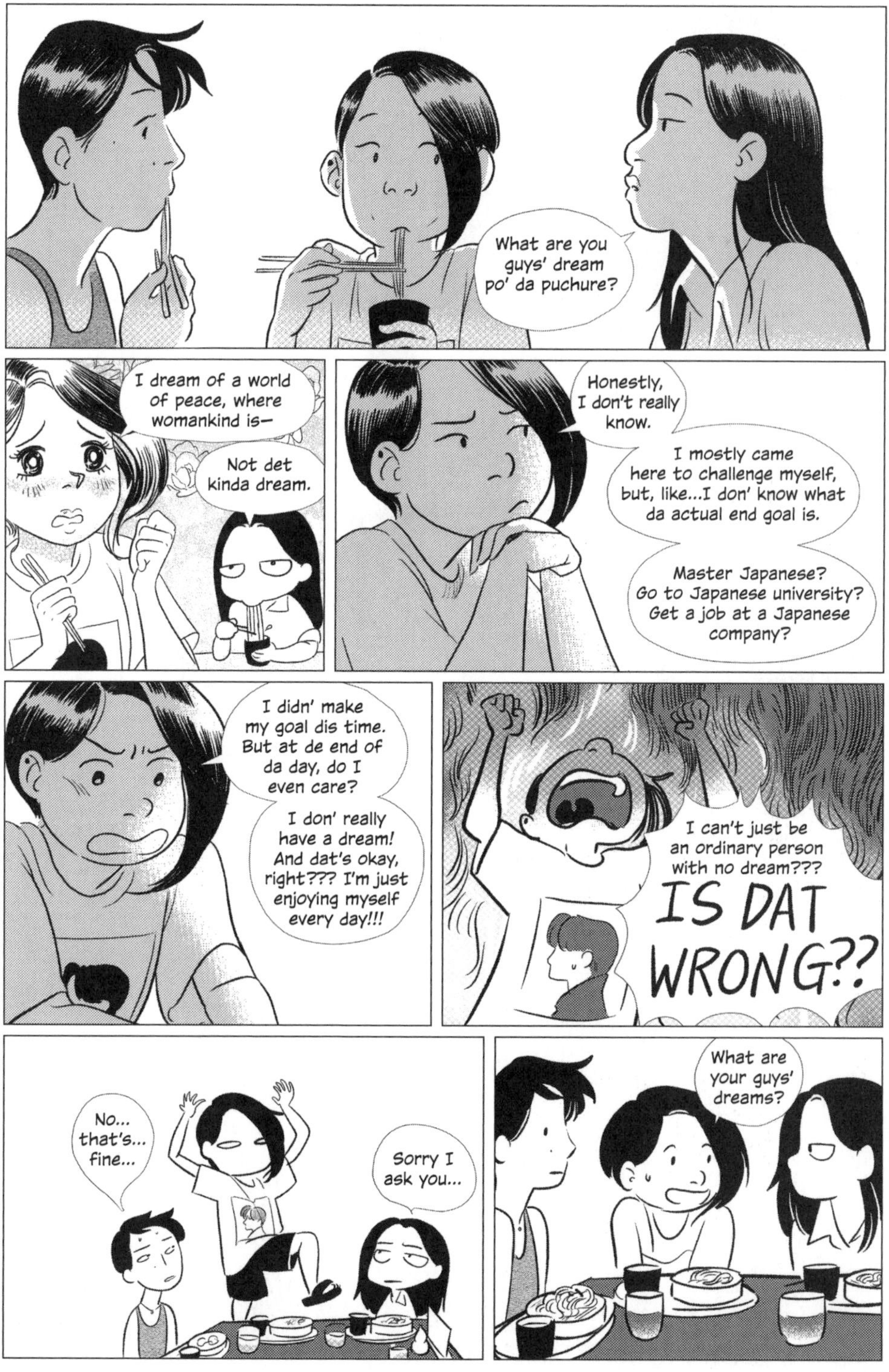
What are you guys' dream po' da puchure?
I dream of a world of peace, where womankind is—
Not det kinda dream.
Honestly, I don't really know.
I mostly came here to challenge myself, but, like...I don' know what da actual end goal is.
Master Japanese? Go to Japanese university? Get a job at a Japanese company?
I didn' make my goal dis time. But at de end of da day, do I even care?
I don' really have a dream! And dat's okay, right??? I'm just enjoying myself every day!!!
I can't just be an ordinary person with no dream???
IS DAT WRONG??
No... that's... fine...
Sorry I ask you...
What are your guys' dreams?

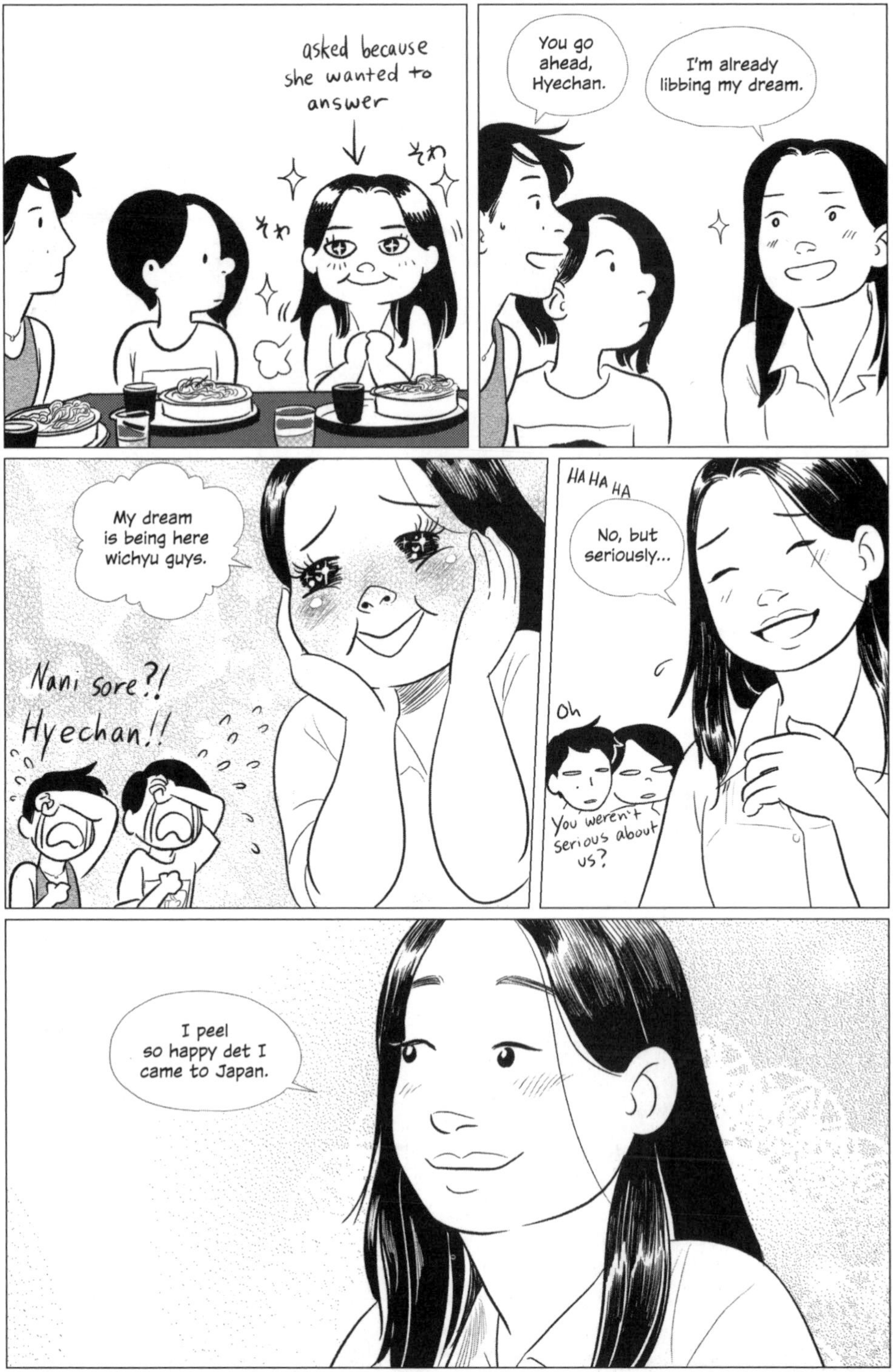
asked because she wanted to answer
そわ
そわ
You go ahead, Hyechan.
I'm already libbing my dream.
My dream is being here wichyu guys.
Nani sore?! Hyechan!!
HA HA HA
No, but seriously...
Oh
You weren't serious about us?
I peel so happy det I came to Japan.

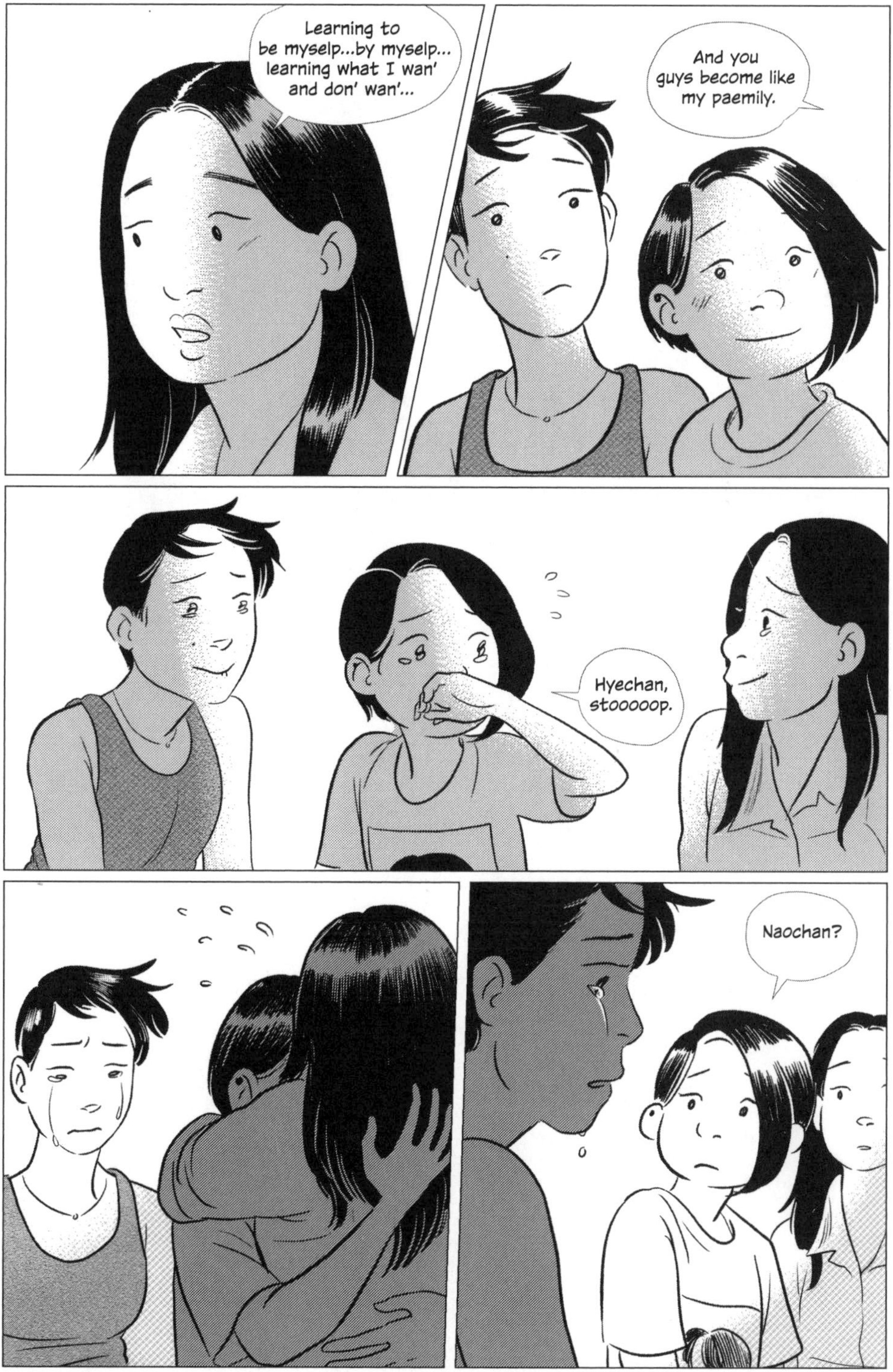
Learning to be myselp...by myselp... learning what I wan' and don' wan'...
And you guys become like my paemily.
Hyechan, stoooooop.
Naochan?

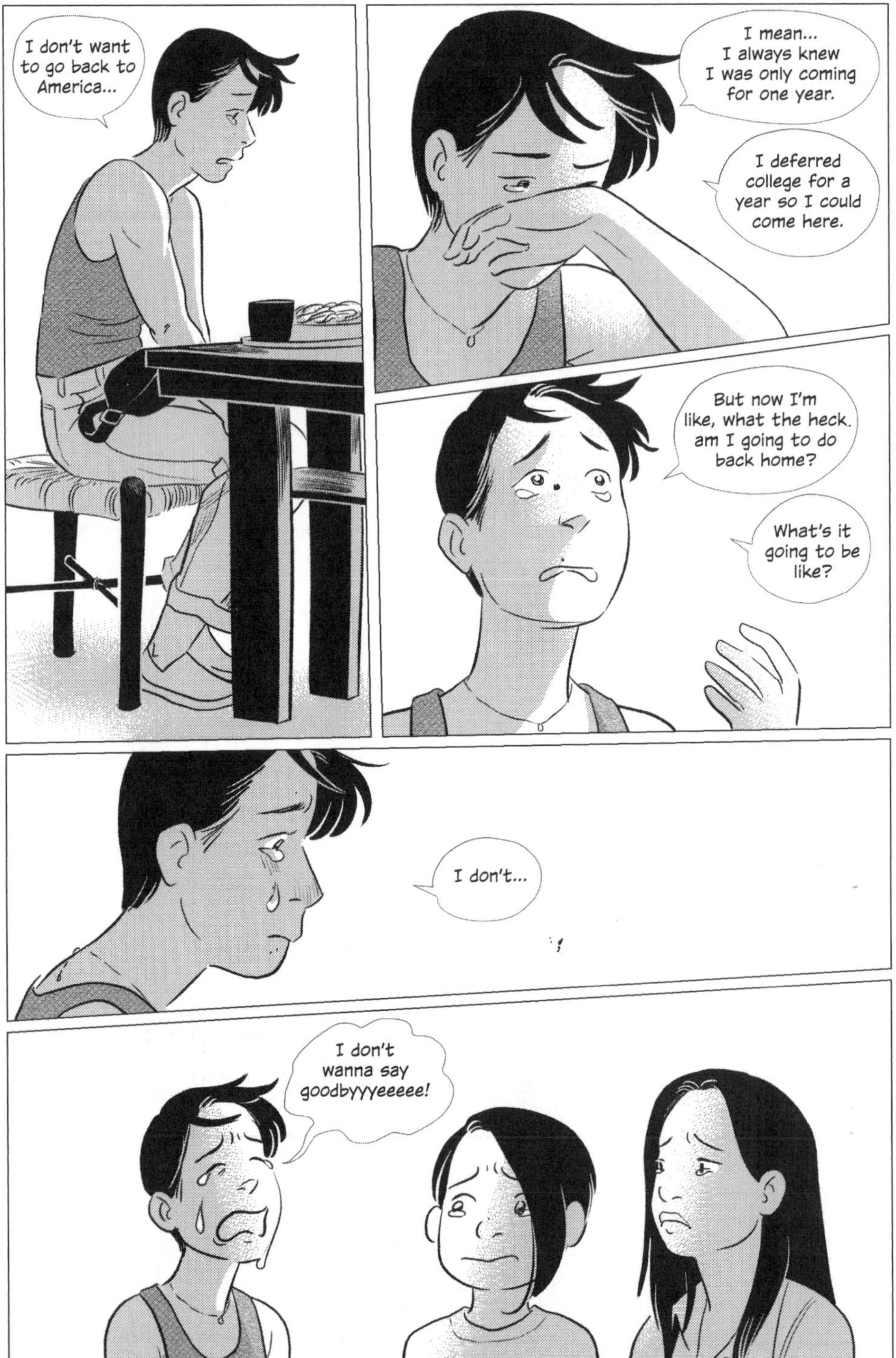
I don't want to go back to America...
I mean... I always knew I was only coming for one year.
I deferred college for a year so I could come here.
But now I'm like, what the heck. am I going to do back home?
What's it going to be like?
I don't...
I don't wanna say goodbyyyeeeee!

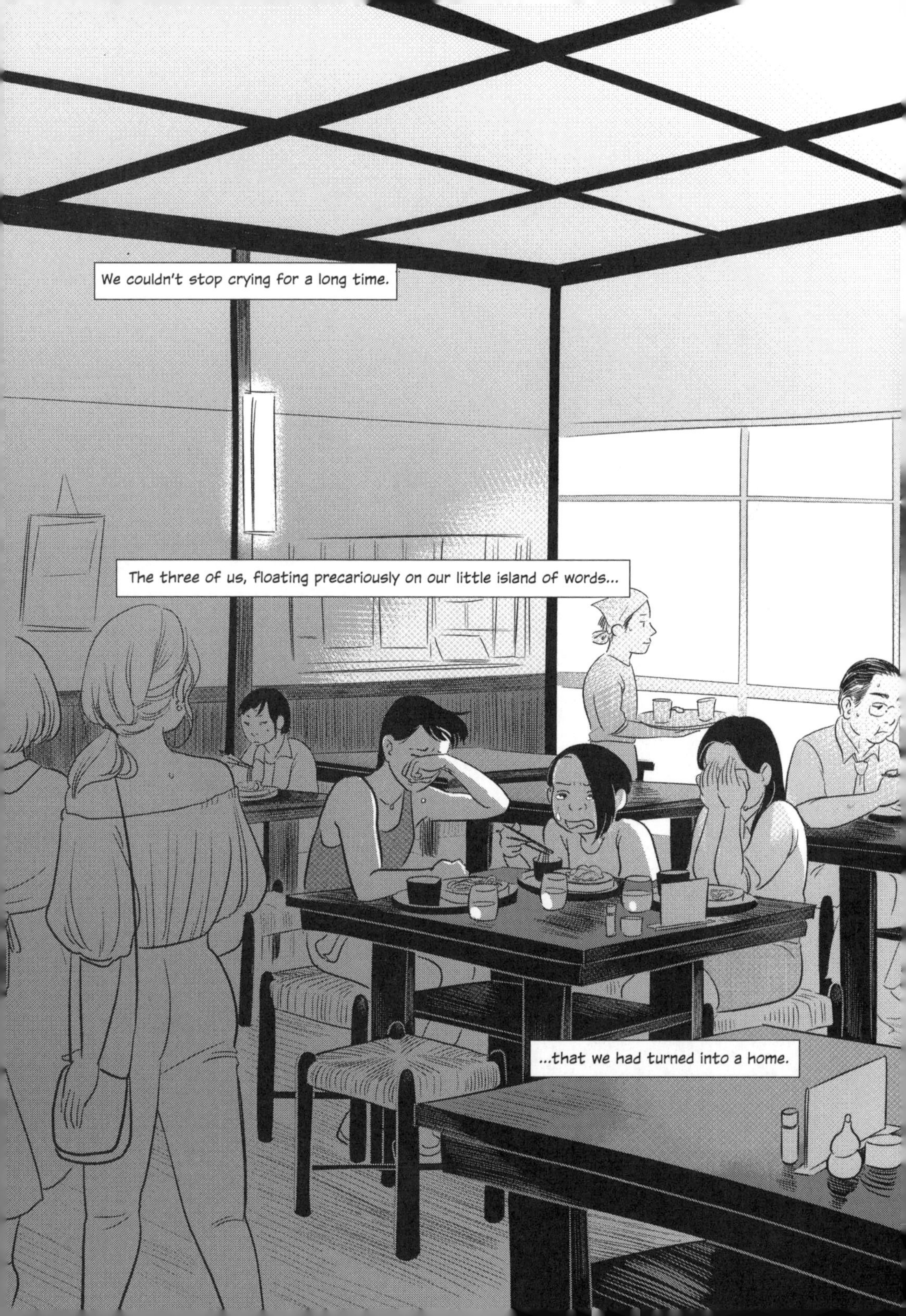
We couldn't stop crying for a long time.
The three of us, floating precariously on our little island of words...
...that we had turned into a home.

Chapter 21

Mata ne

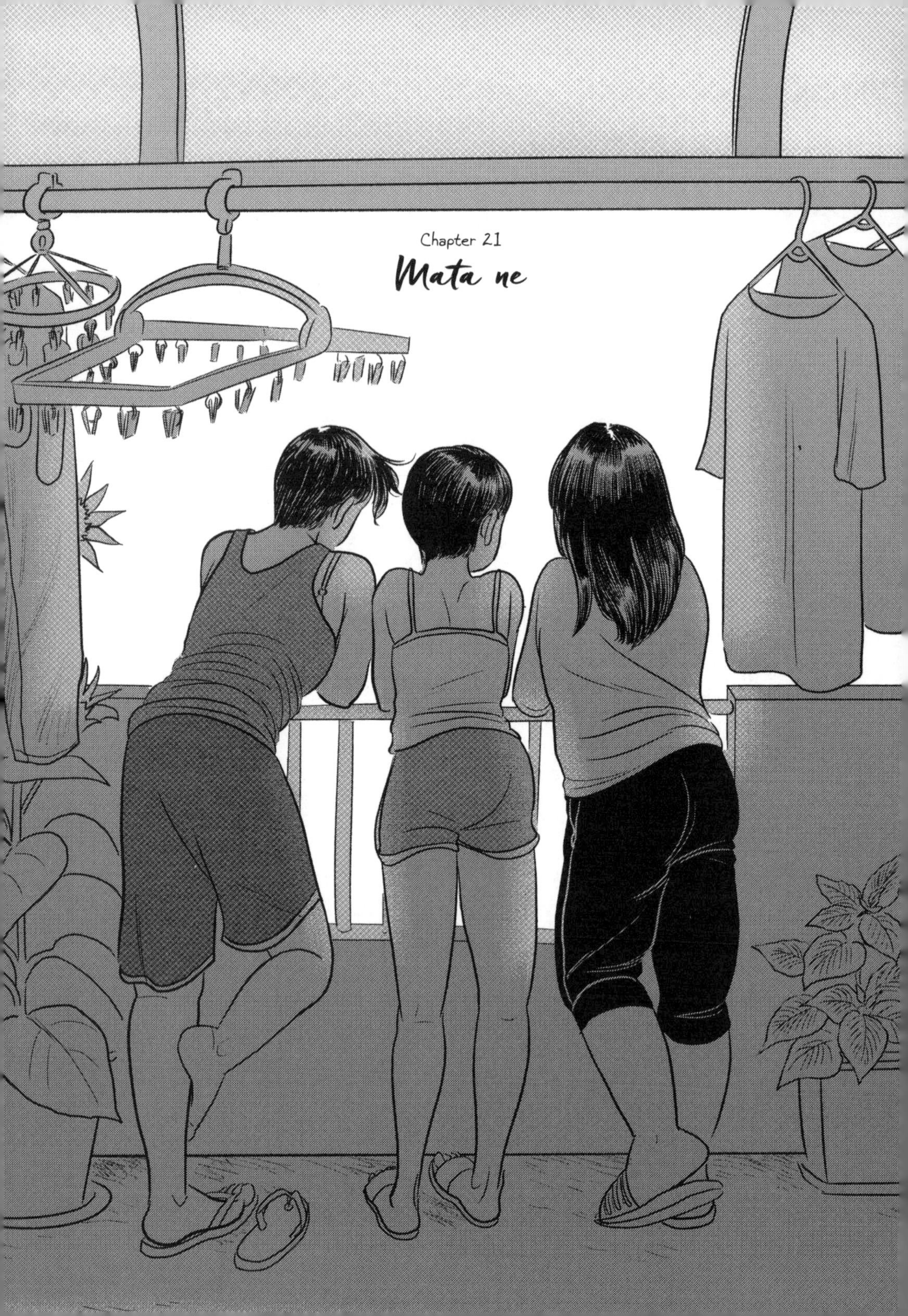

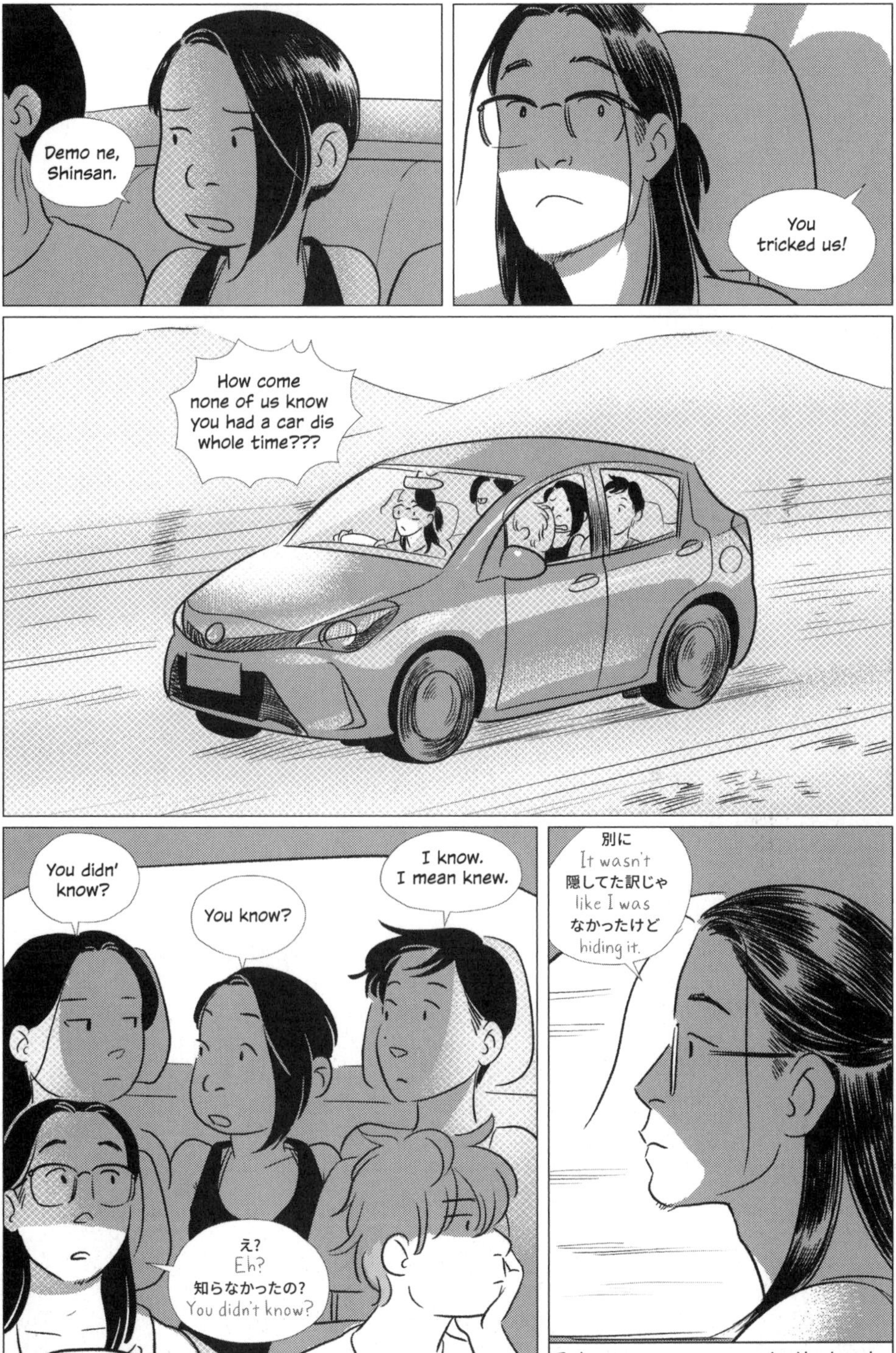

Demo ne, Shinsan.
You tricked us!
How come none of us know you had a car dis whole time???
You didn' know?
You know?
I know. I mean knew.
え? Eh? 知らなかったの? You didn't know?
別に It wasn't 隠してた訳じゃ like I was なかったけど hiding it.
Today we are on our way to the beach.

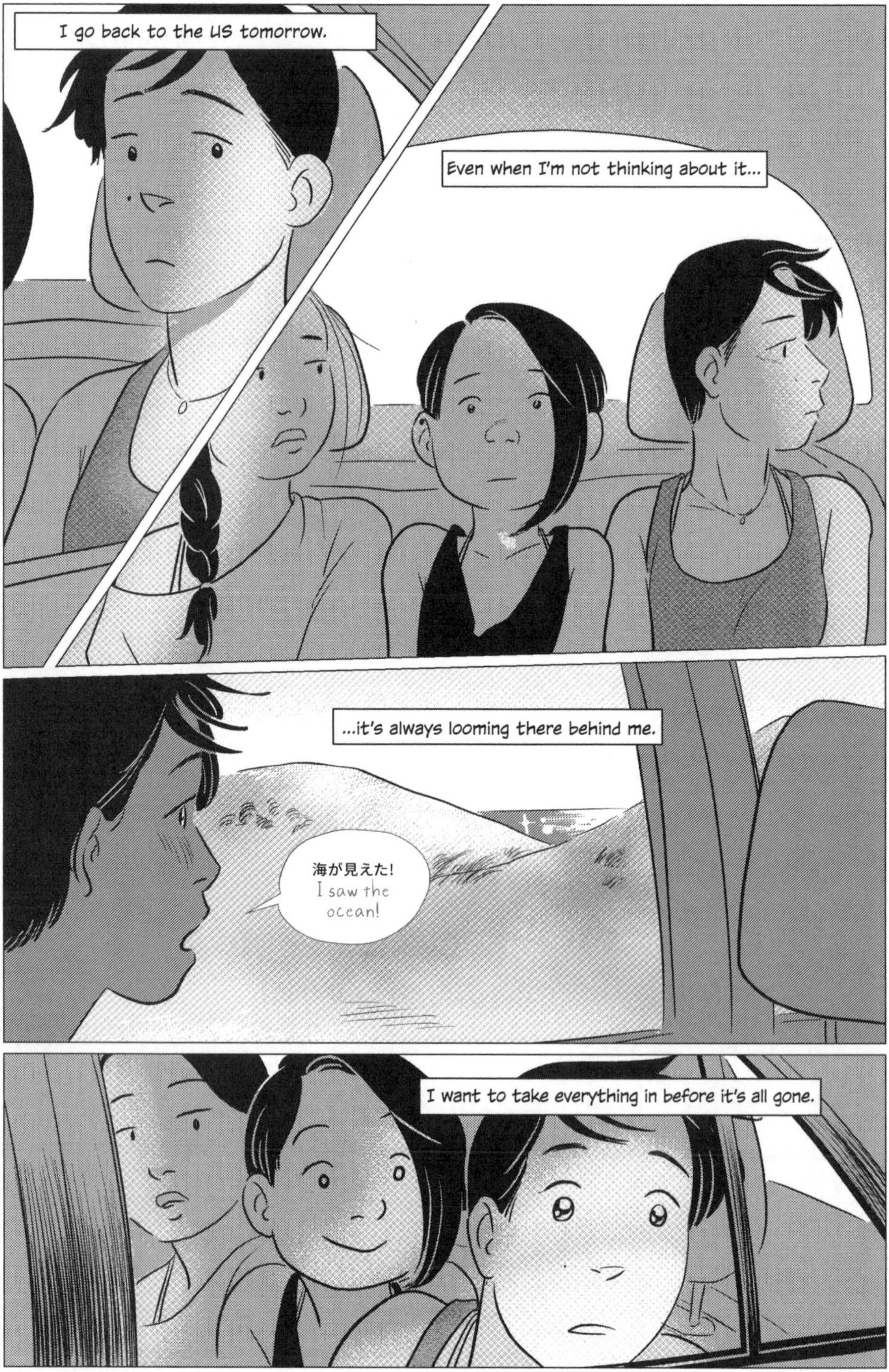
I go back to the US tomorrow.
Even when I'm not thinking about it...
...it's always looming there behind me.
海が見えた! I saw the ocean!
I want to take everything in before it's all gone.

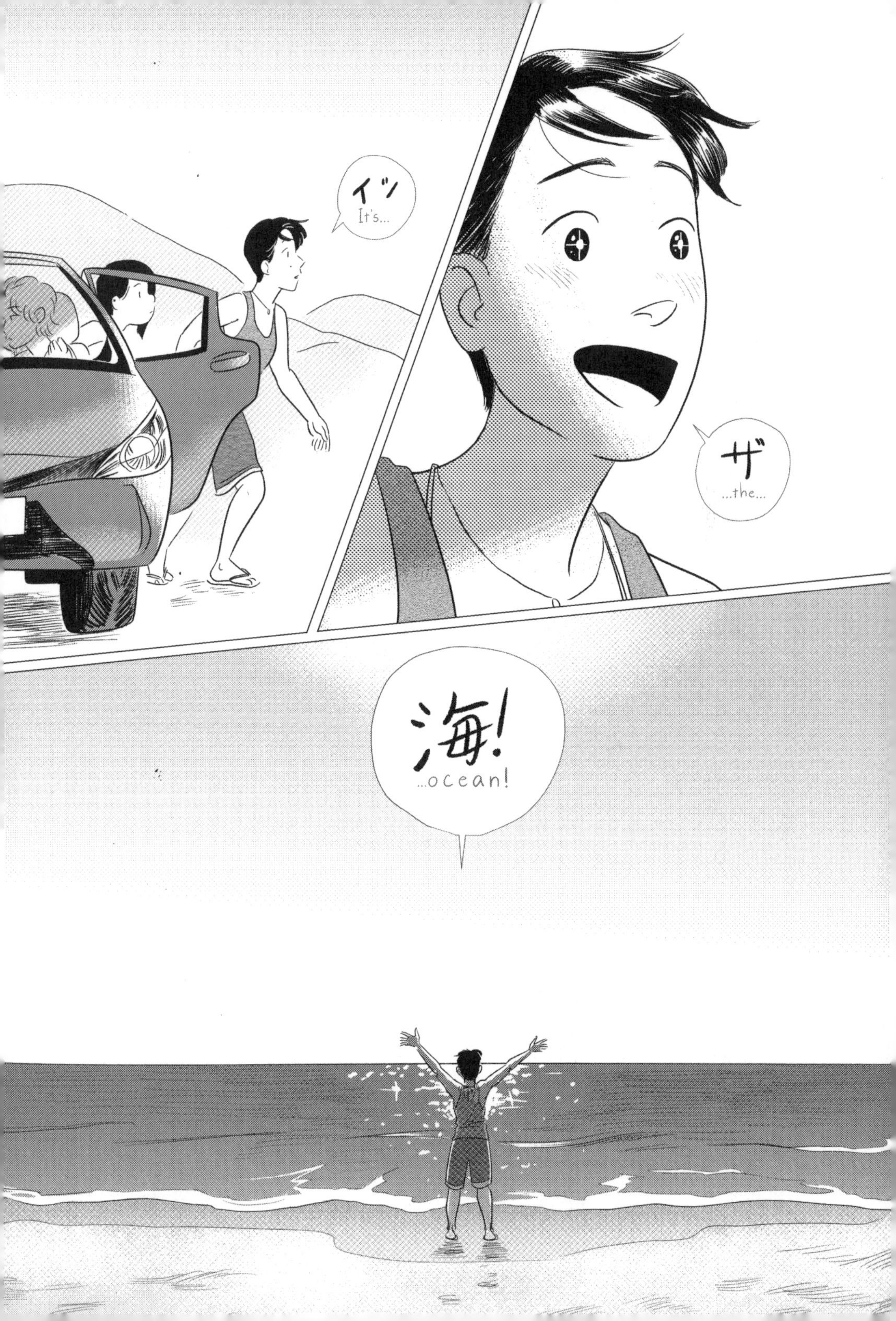
イツ
It's...
ザ
...the...
海!
...ocean!

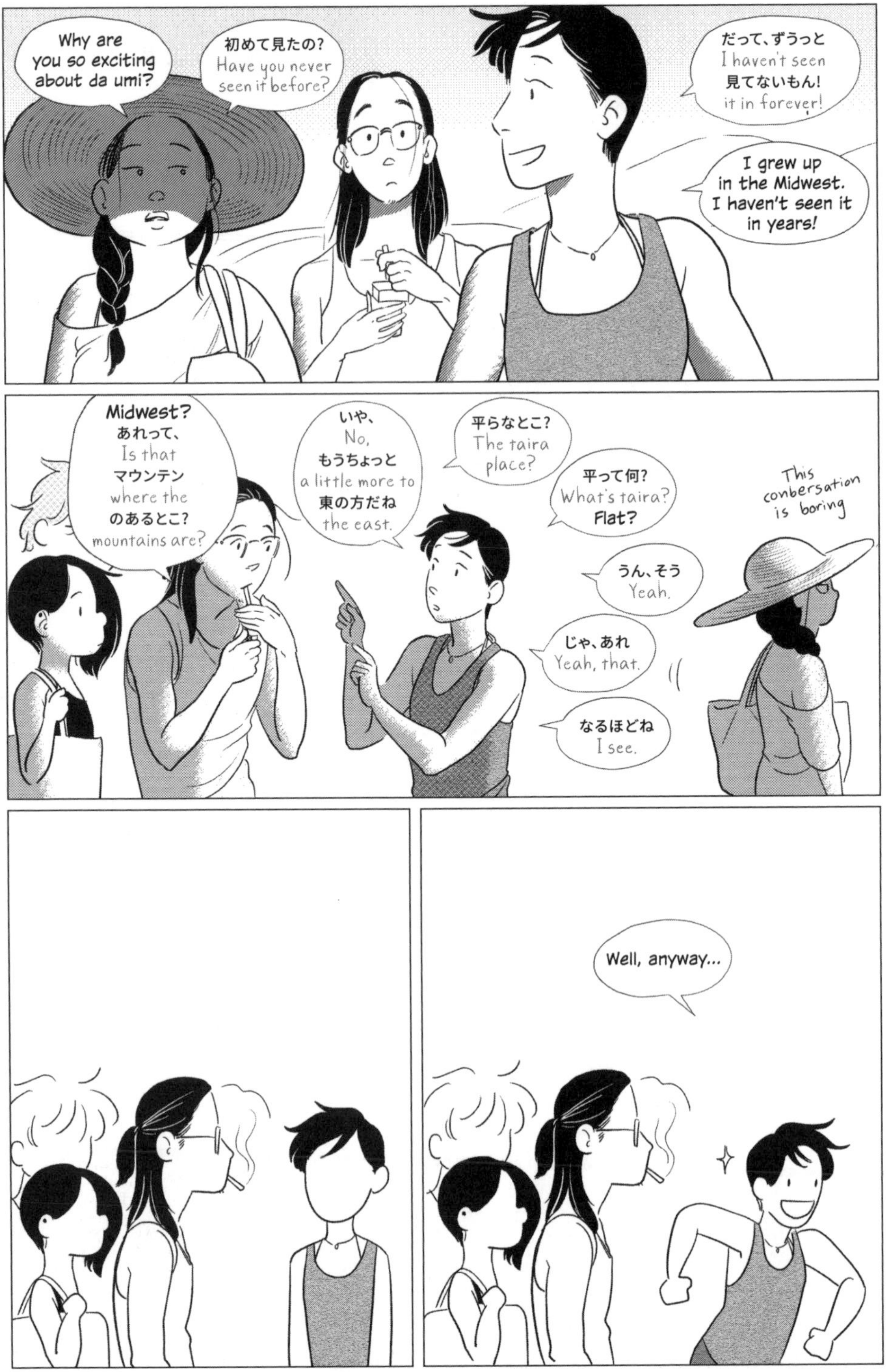
Why are you so exciting about da umi?
初めて見たの? Have you never seen it before?
だって、ずうっと I haven't seen 見てないもん! it in forever!
I grew up in the Midwest. I haven't seen it in years!
Midwest? あれって、 Is that マウンテン where the のあるとこ? mountains are?
いや、 No, もうちょっと a little more to 東の方だね the east.
平らなとこ? The taira place?
平って何? What's taira? Flat?
This conbersation is boring
うん、そう Yeah.
じゃ、あれ Yeah, that.
なるほどね I see.
Well, anyway...

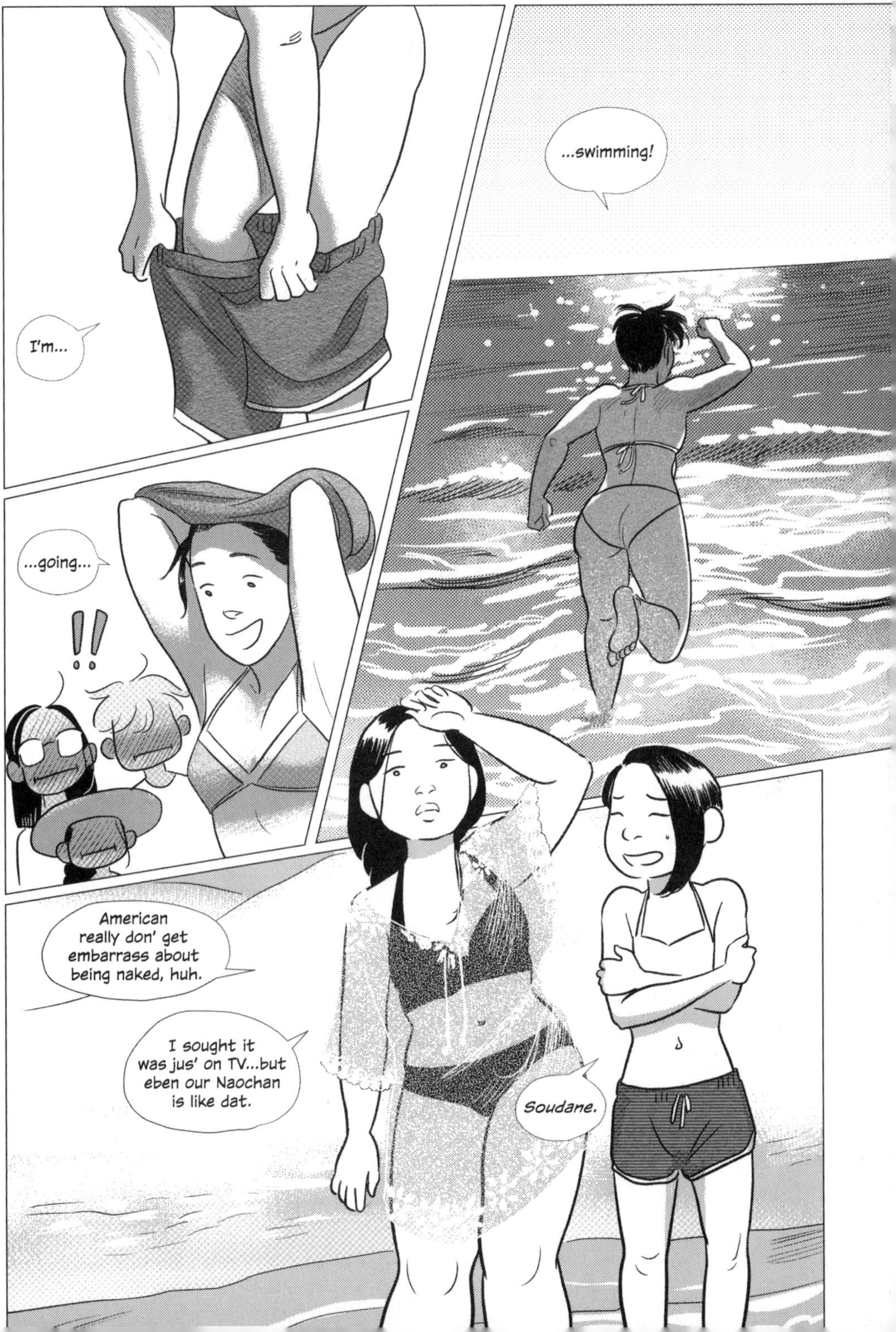
I'm...
...going...
...swimming!
American really don' get embarrass about being naked, huh.
I sought it was jus' on TV...but eben our Naochan is like dat.
Soudane.

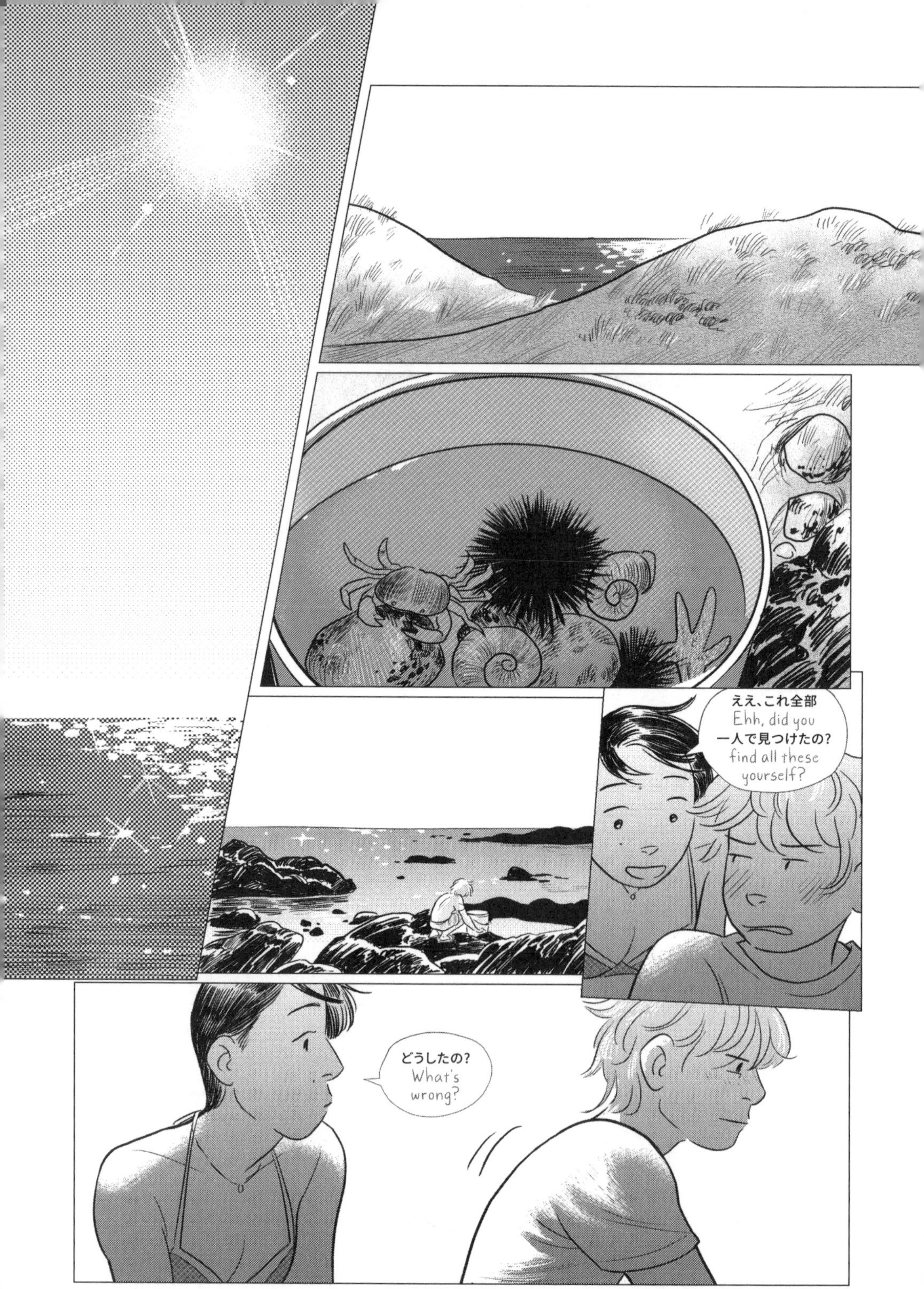
ええ、これ全部
Ehh, did you
一人で見つけたの?
find all these
yourself?
どうしたの?
What's
wrong?

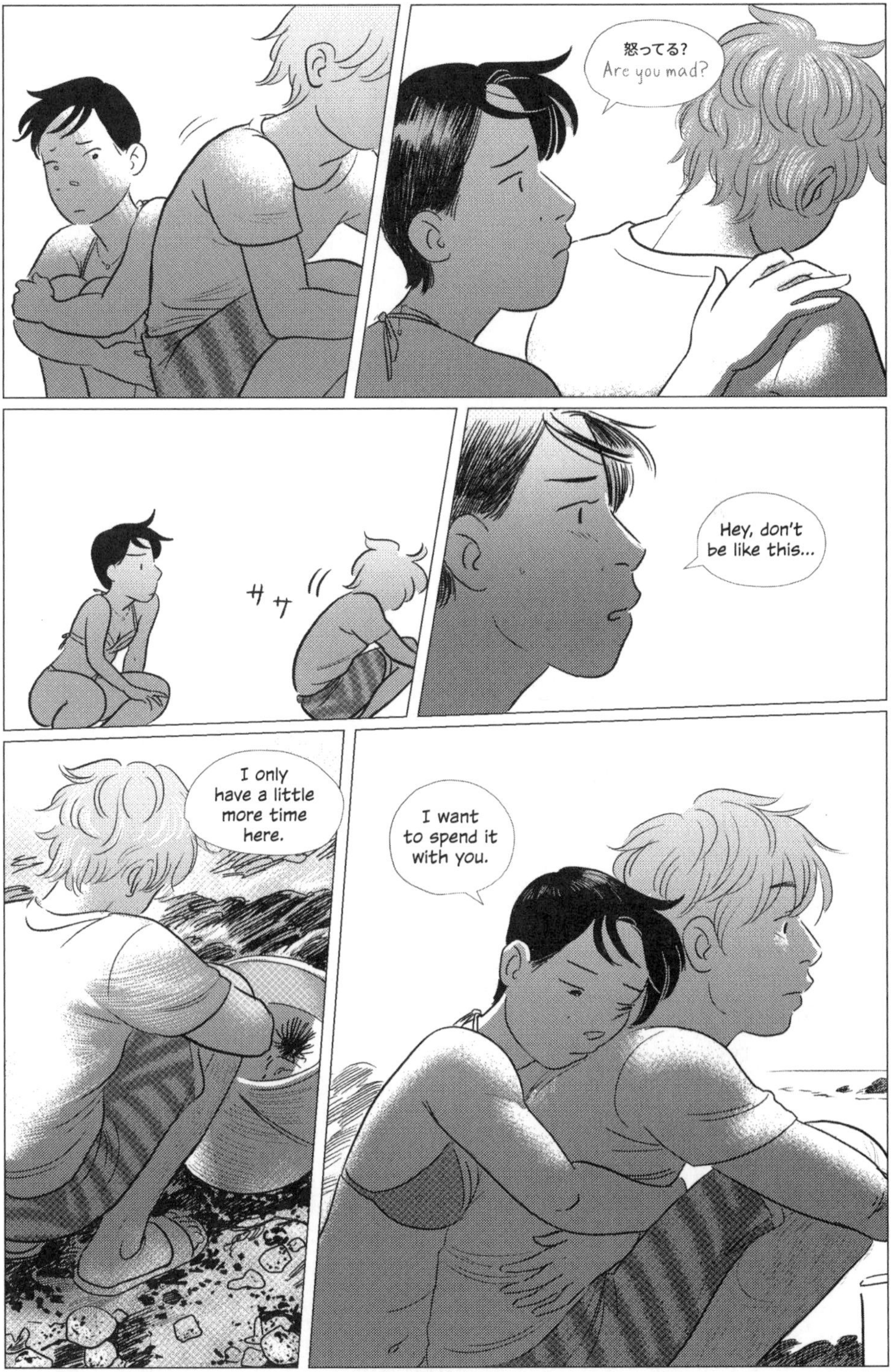
怒ってる?
Are you mad?
サ サ
Hey, don't be like this...
I only have a little more time here.
I want to spend it with you.

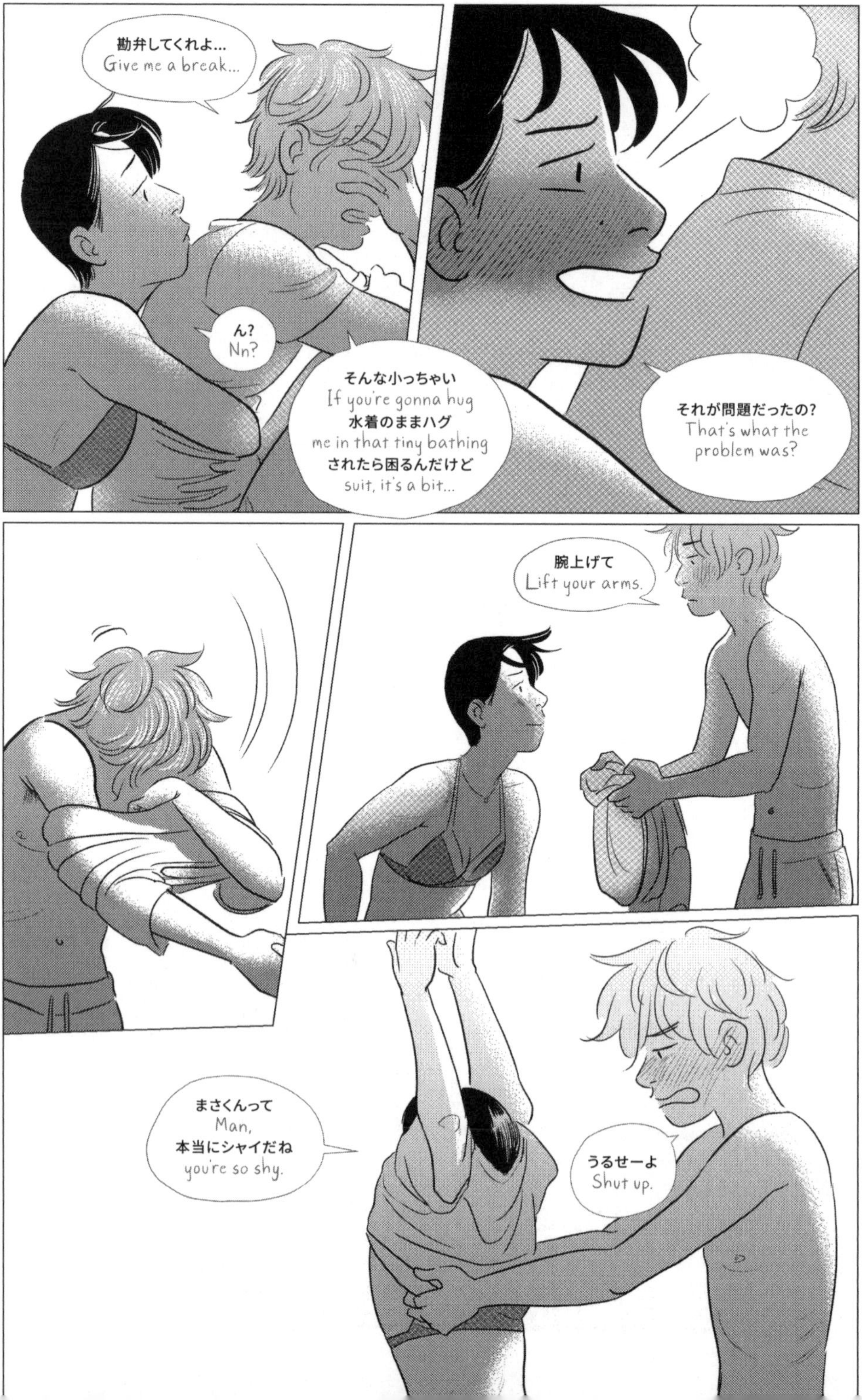

勘弁してくれよ…
Give me a break...
ん?
Nn?
そんな小っちゃい
If you're gonna hug
水着のままハグ
me in that tiny bathing
されたら困るんだけど
suit, it's a bit...
それが問題だったの?
That's what the
problem was?
腕上げて
Lift your arms.
まさくんって
Man,
本当にシャイだね
you're so shy.
うるせーよ
Shut up.

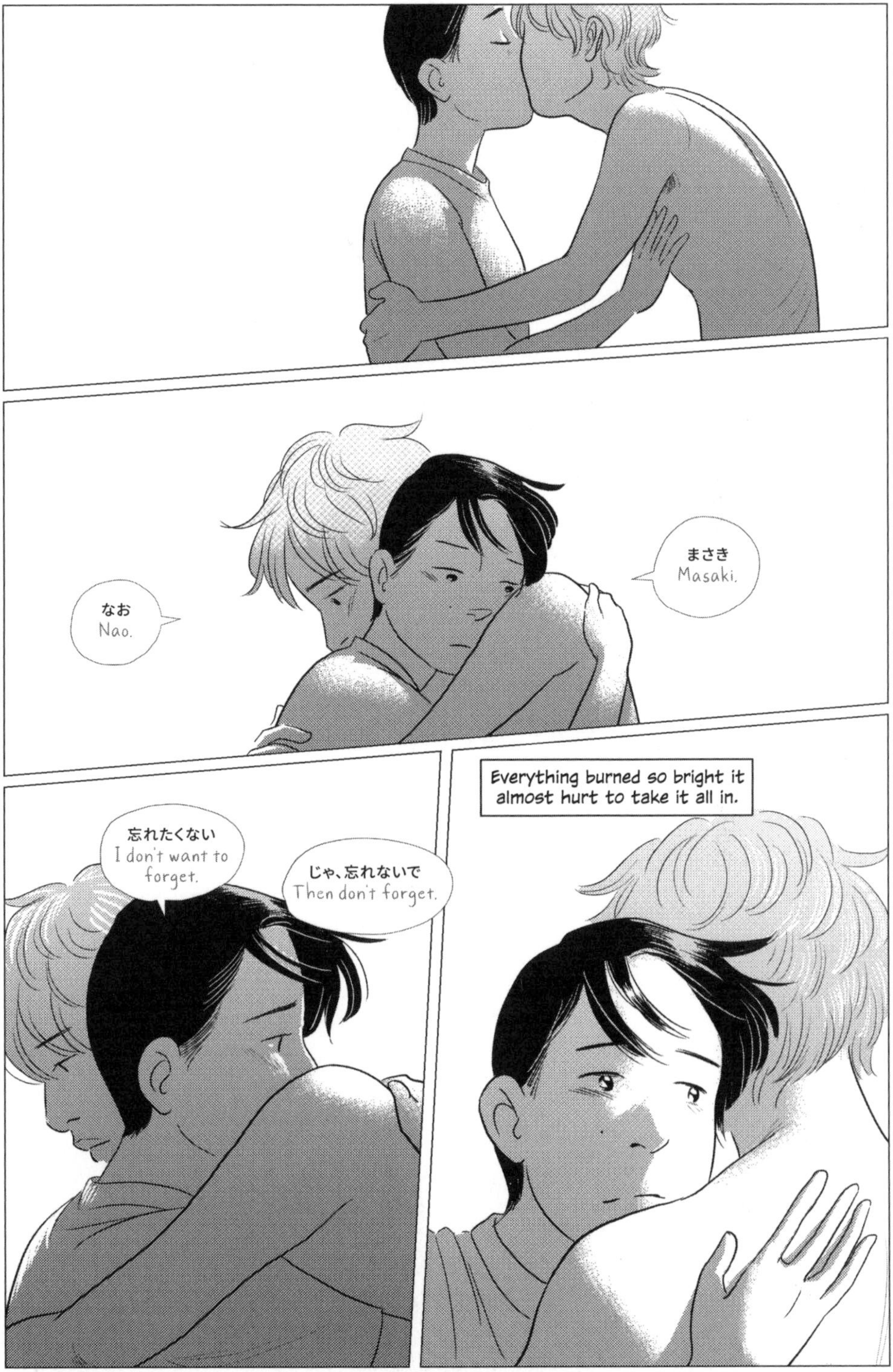
まさき
Masaki.
なお
Nao.
Everything burned so bright it almost hurt to take it all in.
忘れたくない
I don't want to forget.
じゃ、忘れないで
Then don't forget.

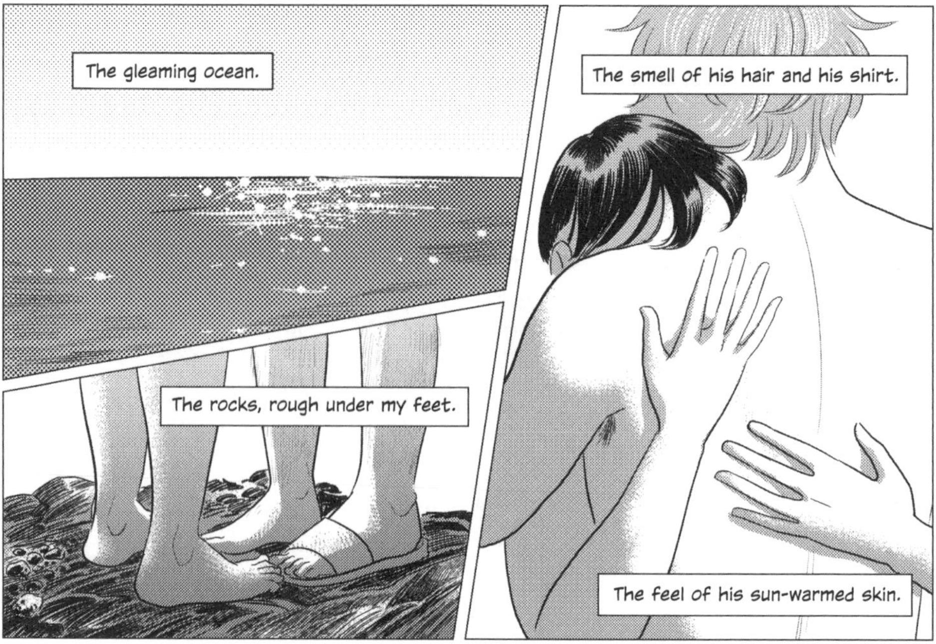
The gleaming ocean.
The rocks, rough under my feet.
The smell of his hair and his shirt.
The feel of his sun-warmed skin.

My heart felt so full I thought it would burst.

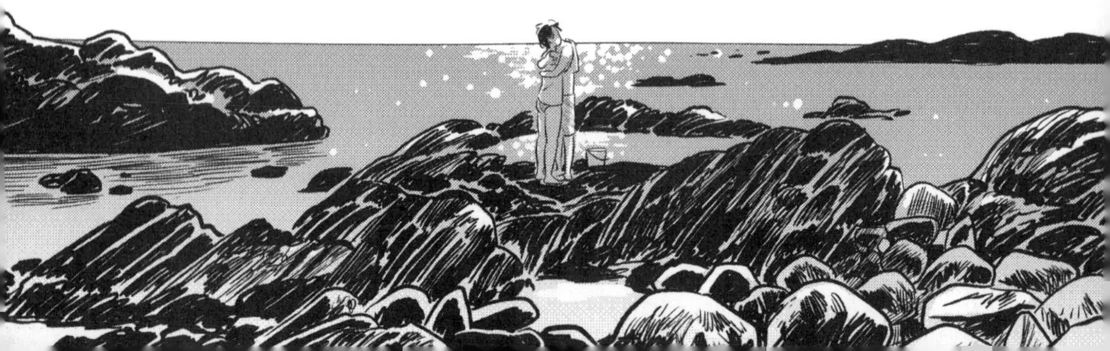

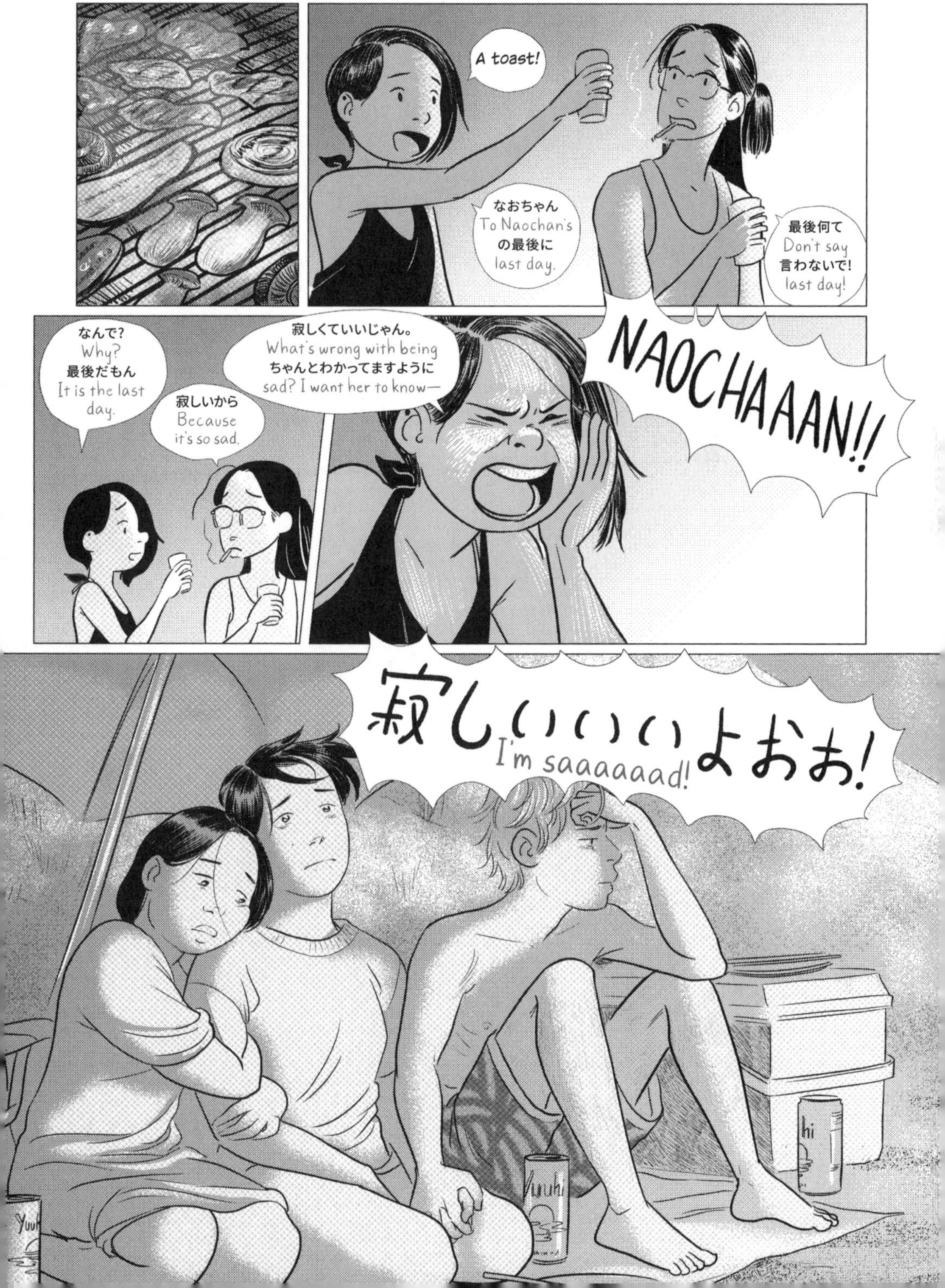

A toast!
なおちゃん
To Naochan's
の最後に
last day.
最後何て
Don't say
言わないで!
last day!
なんで?
Why?
最後だもん
It is the last day.
寂しいから
Because it's so sad.
寂しくていいじゃん。
What's wrong with being
ちゃんとわかってますように
sad? I want her to know—
NAOCHAAAN!!
寂しいいいよおぉ!
I'm saaaaaad!
Yuuhi

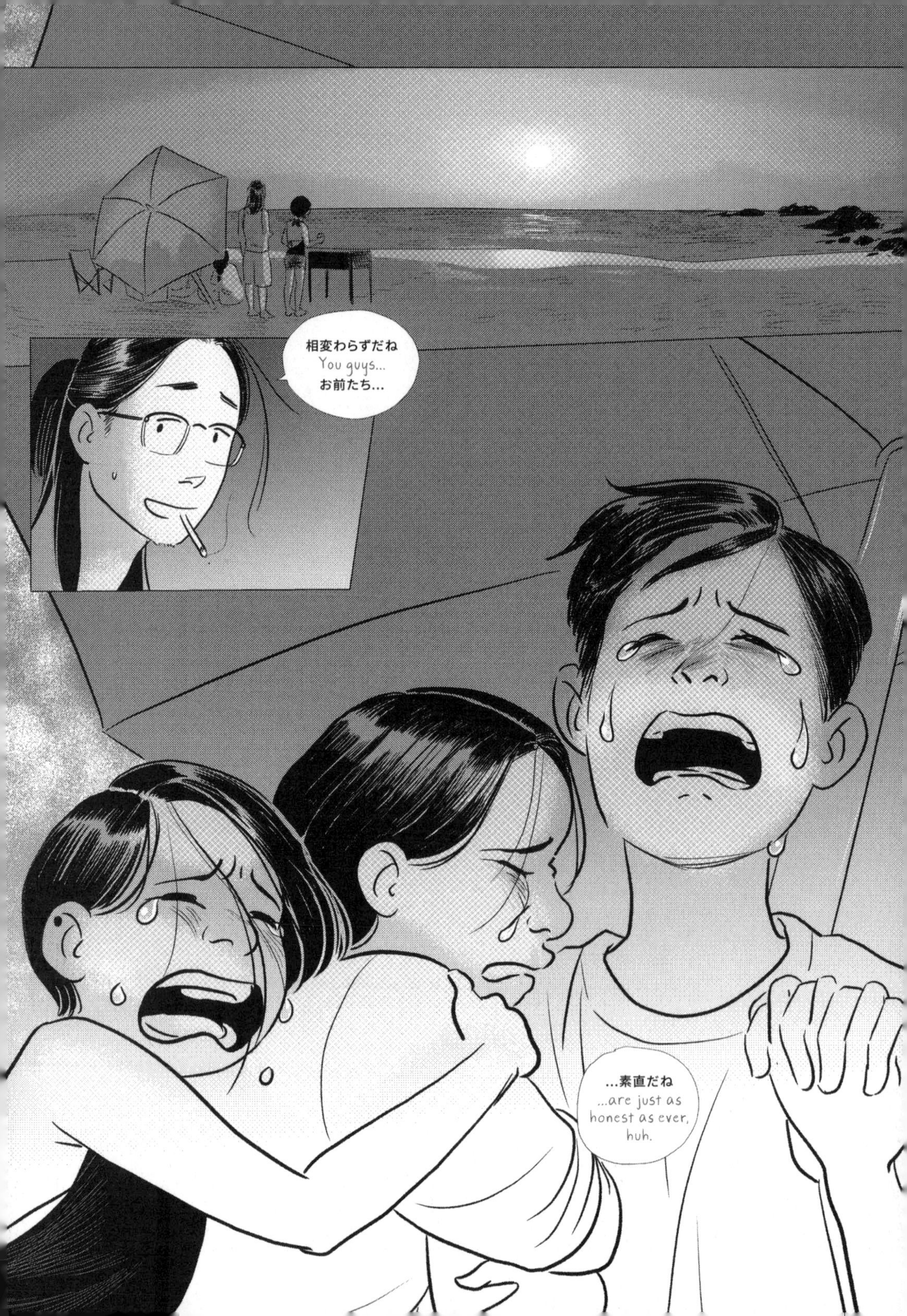
相変わらずだね
You guys...
お前たち...
...素直だね
...are just as honest as ever, huh.

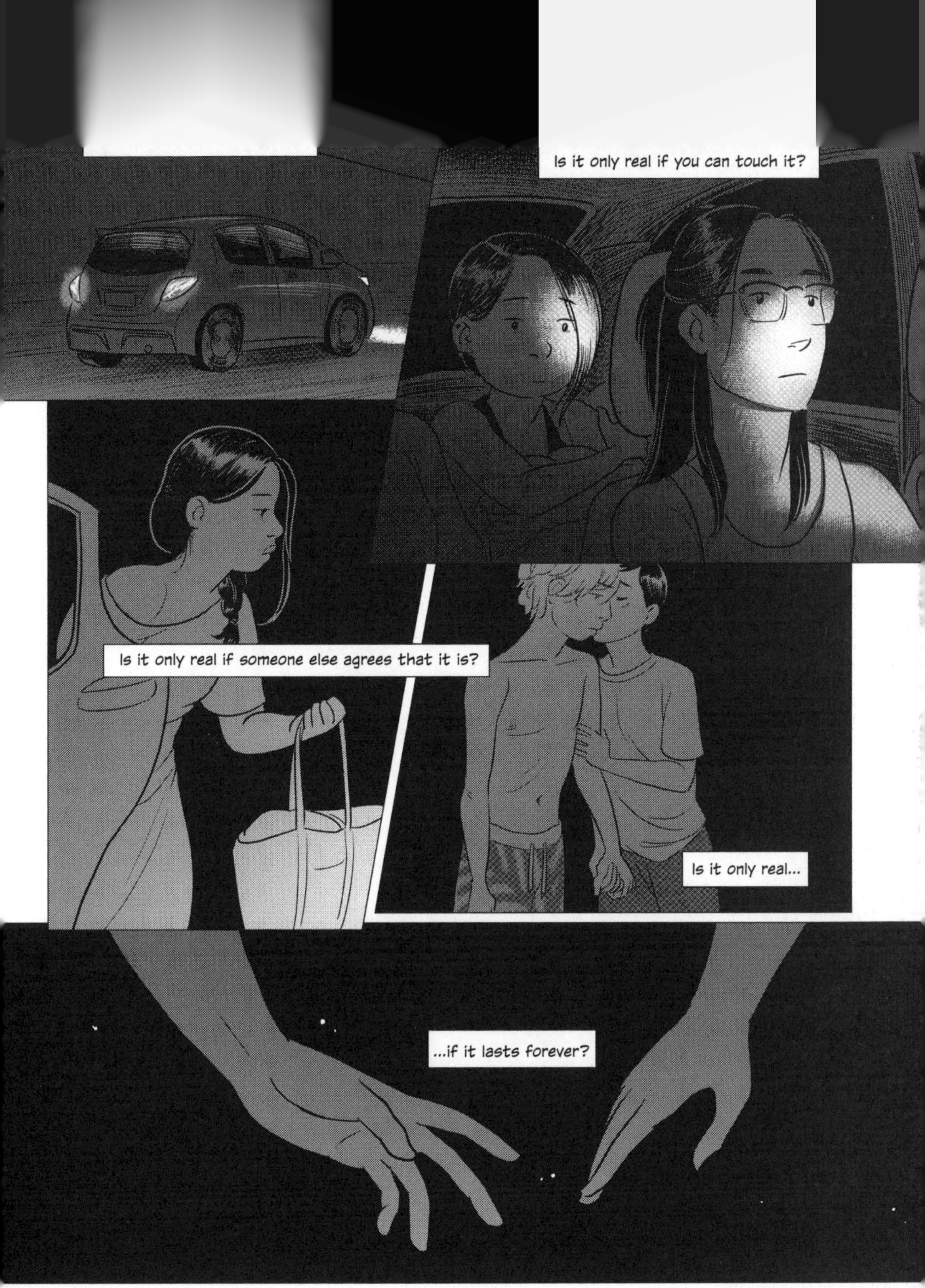
Is it only real if you can touch it?
Is it only real if someone else agrees that it is?
Is it only real...
...if it lasts forever?

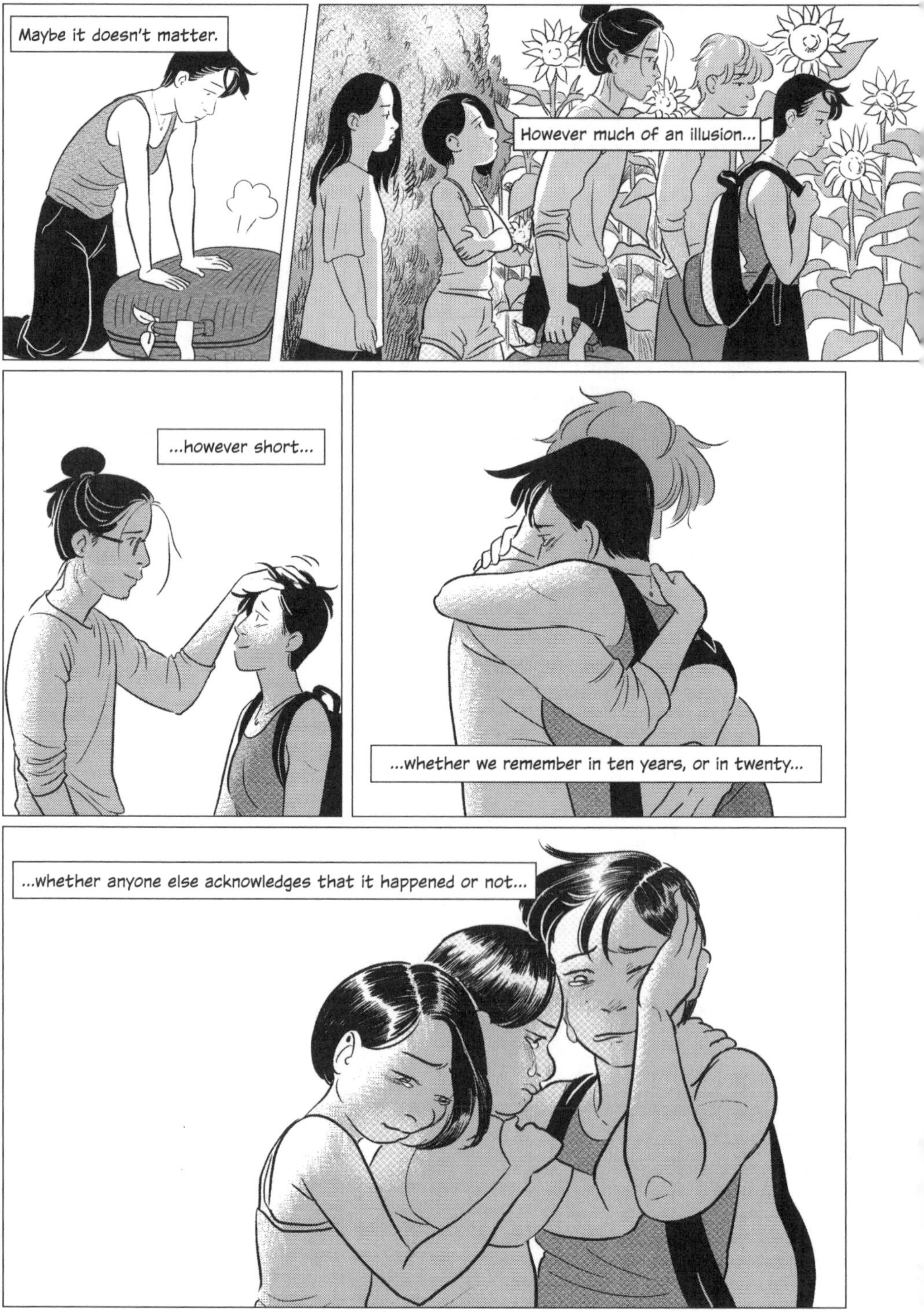
Maybe it doesn't matter.
However much of an illusion...
...however short...
...whether we remember in ten years, or in twenty...
...whether anyone else acknowledges that it happened or not...

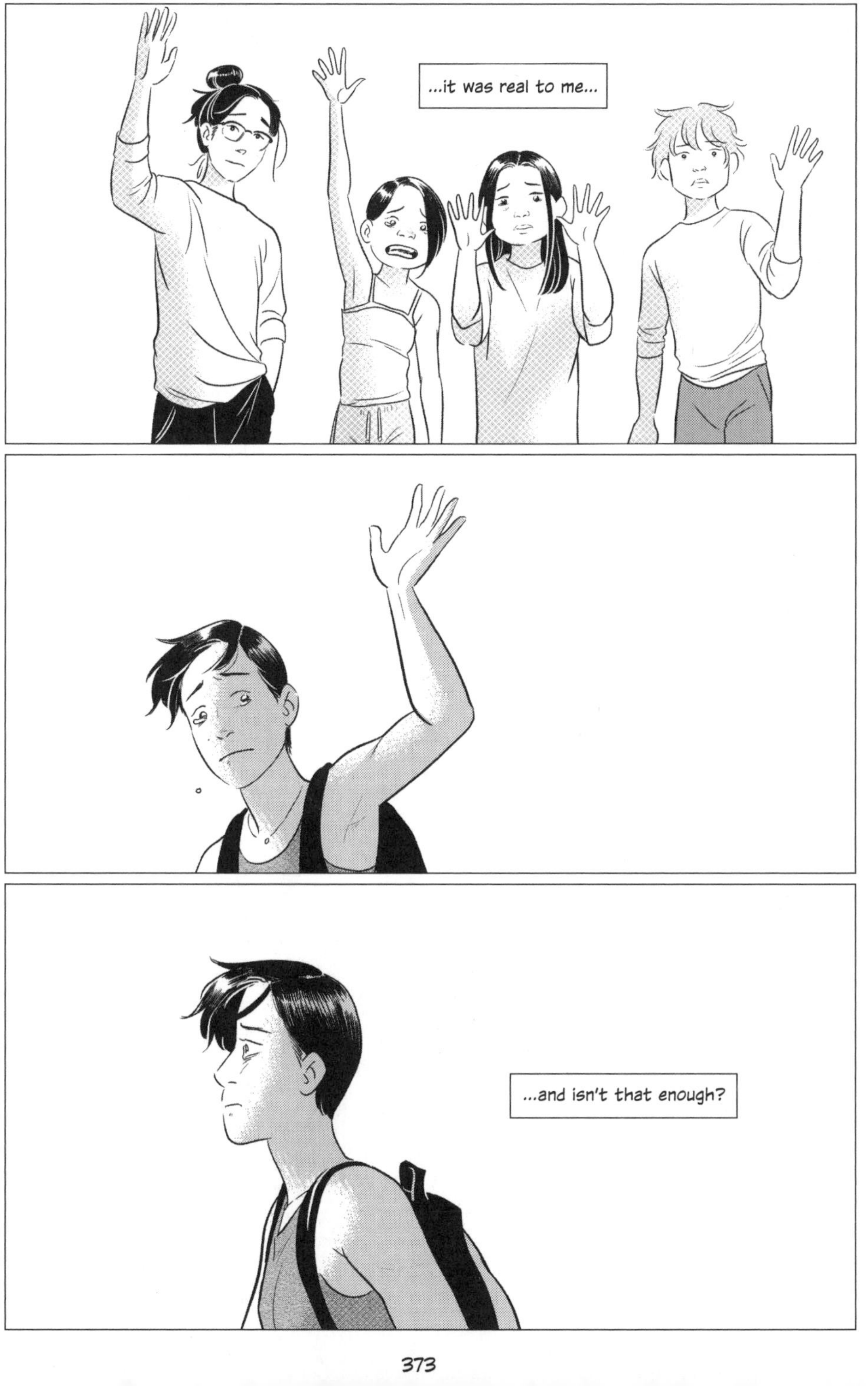
...it was real to me...
...and isn't that enough?

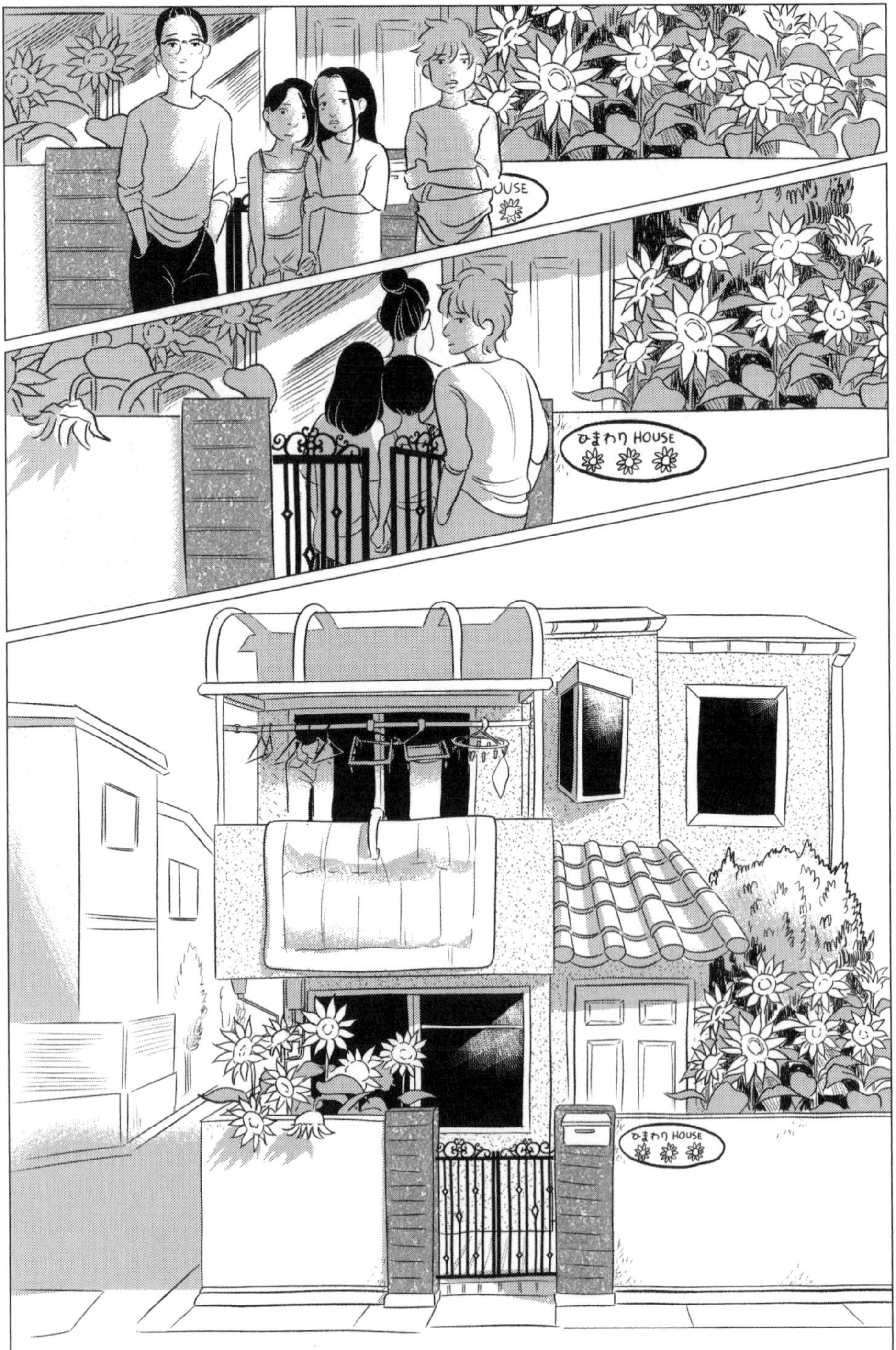

USE
ひまわり HOUSE
ひまわり HOUSE

ON THE USE OF ACCENTS IN THIS BOOK

Western media has a long history of portraying Asian people in offensive, one-dimensional ways. So often characters are written with thick foreign accents for comic or exotic effect. I was surprised that even in movies celebrated for their good Asian representation, the only characters who had Asian accents were written as comic relief. This legacy has cemented the idea that to have an accent is to be laughable, to be stupid, to be "other."

I grew up listening to accented English in my home and community, and I have lived in several countries where I struggled with my own broken Japanese, Korean, and Spanish. My intent with *Himawari House* was to allow characters who spoke with accents, who occasionally stumbled over their grammar, to be fully actualized, three-dimensional people. I love accents, I think that they add depth and character to one's speech—a sense of place. I hope that this book can be a contribution to a different kind of legacy for Asian characters, one in which our accents are not a point of shame but a point of pride, because after all, what is an accent but proof of the ability to speak more than one language?

ACKNOWLEDGMENTS

I would like to thank Gracie, my first-ever reader, and the rest of my family, Mom, Dad, Alan, and Kaori. Thank you for your weirdness, your creativity, your love, and your warmth.

For their work as cultural and language consultants on this book, I want to thank Naoyuki Kuroda, Janelle Wong, Jonghee Choe, Heihachiro Shigematsu, and Yudori. I'd be lost without you!

I want to thank my editor, Kiara Valdez, my agent, DongWon Song, and all the wonderful staff at First Second for their hard work on making this book a reality.

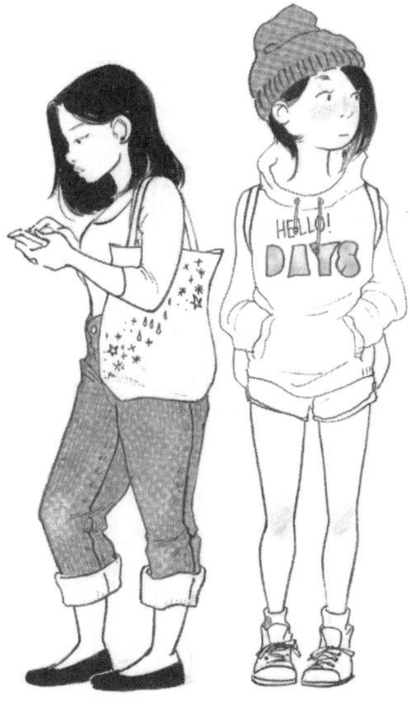
HELLO!
DAYS

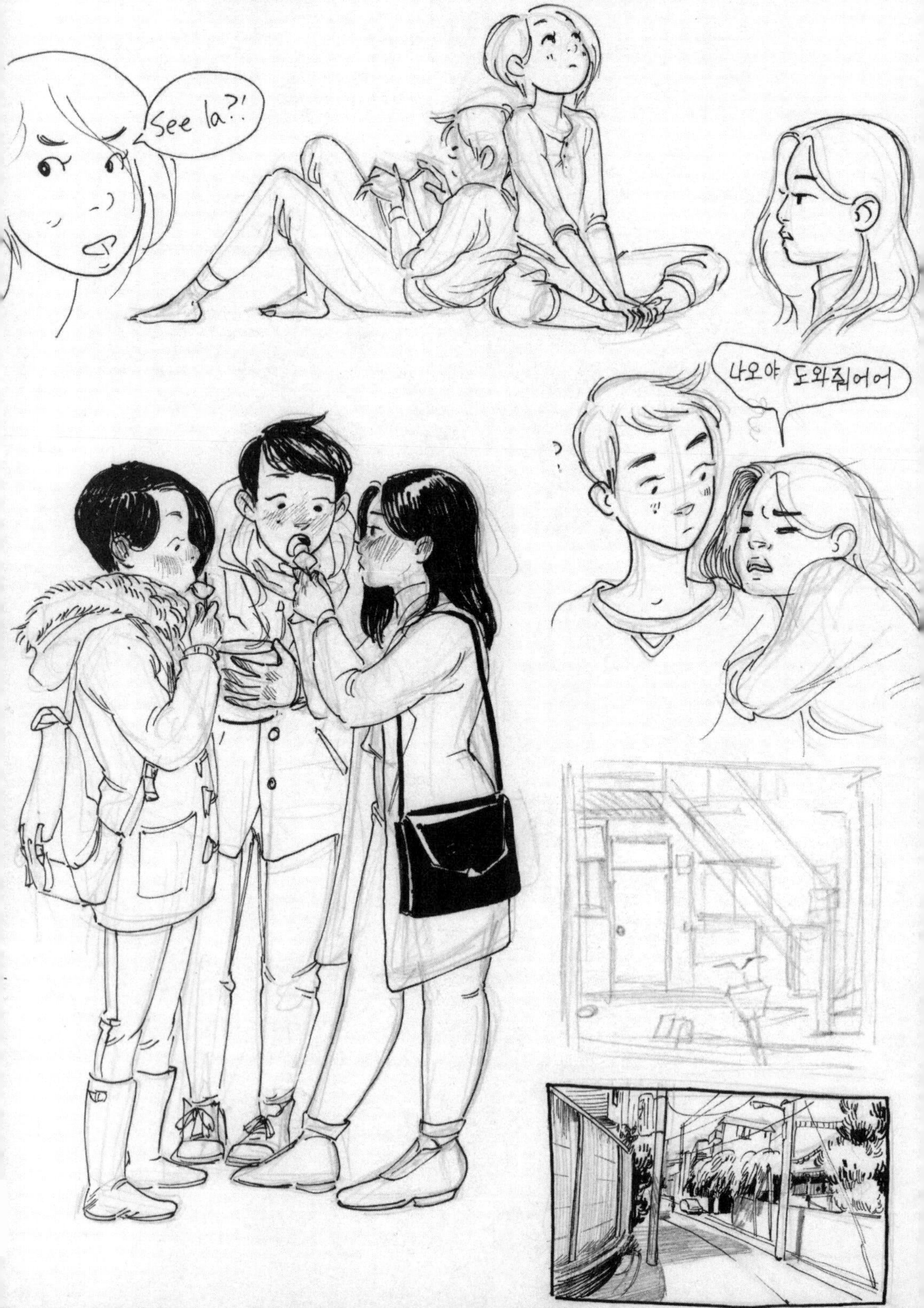
See la?!
나오야 도와줘어어

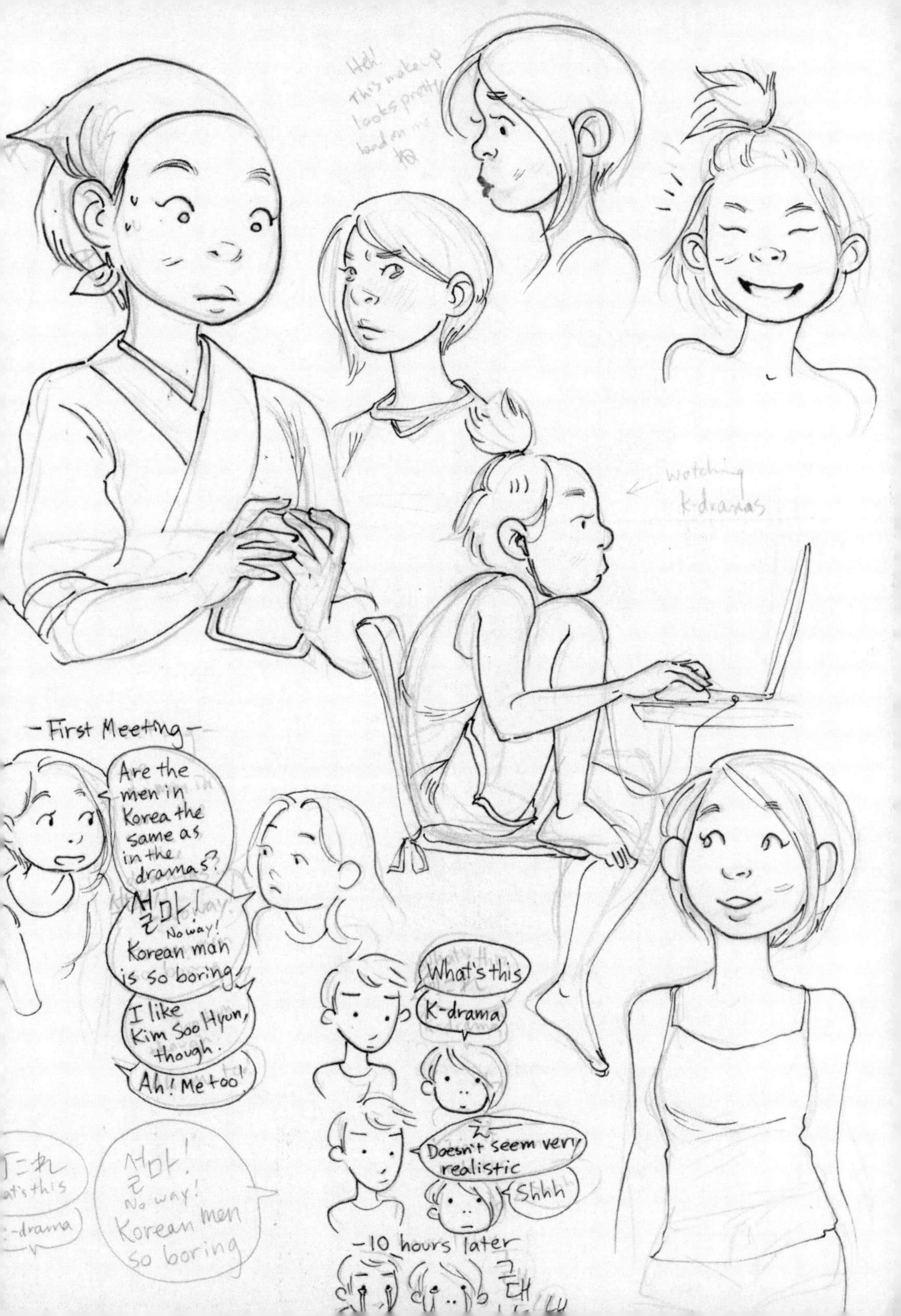
Heh! This makeup looks pretty bad on me
watching K-dramas
-First Meeting-
Are the men in Korea the same as in the dramas?
설마! No way! Korean man is so boring.
I like Kim Soo Hyun, though.
Ah! Me too!
What's this
K-drama
Doesn't seem very realistic
Shhh
-10 hours later
설마! No way! Korean men so boring

First Second

Published by First Second
First Second is an imprint of Roaring Brook Press,
a division of Holtzbrinck Publishing Holdings Limited Partnership
120 Broadway, New York, NY 10271
firstsecondbooks.com

Library of Congress Control Number: 2021906598

Our books may be purchased in bulk for promotional, educational, or business use.
Please contact your local bookseller or the Macmillan Corporate and Premium Sales Department
at (800) 221-7945 ext. 5442 or by email at MacmillanSpecialMarkets@macmillan.com.

First edition, 2021
Edited by Kiara Valdez
Cover design by Sunny Lee
Authenticity readers: Yudori and Anna Lee

Penciled, inked, and toned in Clip Studio Paint.

Printed in the United States of America

ISBN 978-1-250-23557-2 (paperback)
1 3 5 7 9 10 8 6 4 2

ISBN 978-1-250-23556-5 (hardcover)
1 3 5 7 9 10 8 6 4 2

Don't miss your next favorite book from First Second!
For the latest updates go to firstsecondnewsletter.com and sign up for our enewsletter.